THREE COMPLETE NOVELS

THOMAS McGUANE

THREE COMPLETE NOVELS

THOMAS McGUANE

KEEP THE CHANGE

NOBODY'S ANGEL

THE BUSHWHACKED PIANO

WINGS BOOKS
New York · Avenel, New Jersey

This omnibus was originally published in separate volumes under the titles:

Keep the Change, copyright © 1989 by Thomas McGuane.
Nobody's Angel, copyright © 1979, 1980, 1981 by Thomas McGuane.
The Bushwhacked Piano, copyright © 1971 by Thomas McGuane.

This edition contains the complete and unabridged texts of the original editions. They have been completely reset for this volume.

Grateful acknowledgment is made to the following for permission to reprint previously published material in *Nobody's Angel*:
Warner Bros. Music: Two lines of lyric from "Jack Daniels If You Please" by David Allen Coe. © 1978 by Warner-Tamerlane Publishing Corp. All rights reserved. Used by permission.

This 1994 edition is published by Wings Books, distributed by Outlet Book Company, Inc., a Random House Company, 40 Engelhard Avenue, Avenel, New Jersey 07001, by arrangement with Houghton Mifflin Company/Seymour Lawrence, Inc. for *Keep the Change,* copyright © 1989 by Thomas McGuane; Random House for *Nobody's Angel,* copyright © 1979, 1980, 1981 by Thomas McGuane; the author for *The Bushwhacked Piano,* copyright © 1971 by Thomas McGuane.

Random House
New York · Toronto · London · Sydney · Auckland

Printed and bound in the United States of America

Library of Congress Cataloging-in-Publication Data

McGuane, Thomas.
   [Novels. Selections]
   Three complete novels : Keep the change, Nobody's angel, The bushwhacked piano / Thomas McGuane.
     p. cm.
   ISBN 0-517-10019-3
   1. Men—Montana—Fiction.   2. Humorous stories, American.
3. Western stories. I. Title. II. Title: 3 complete novels.
PS3563.A3114A6 1993
813'.54—dc20
                                       93-34511
                                         CIP

8 7 6 5 4 3 2 1

CONTENTS

Keep The Change

1

Nobody's Angel

209

The Bushwhacked Piano

439

KEEP THE CHANGE

For Laurie

I photographed you with my Rolleiflex.
It showed your enormous ingratitude.

—ANTONIO CARLOS JOBIM

1

When Joe Starling was ten years old, his father's bank foreclosed on a fieldstone mansion which was by then a depressing ruin standing by itself in the middle of a fourteen-section cattle pasture. It had been built during the silver rush to house the man who found the vein of ore, but now its mortared walls sheltered cattle against the prevailing west wind. Twenty years later, Joe could not remember much of the house beyond its size and age, and its air of having seen things. Once or twice while he was growing up, he drove over from his family's ranch. He recalled rumors of two old sisters who once lived there, nieces of the Silver King, whose poverty did not prevent them from seeming to have come from a higher caste than other people in the county. The sisters had not been long dead when Joe and his father first visited the house to view a painting that hung over the cavernous fireplace. It was a picture of a range of white hills. At first glance, it had looked like an unblemished canvas until the perplexity of shadows across its surface was seen to be part of the painting.

The picture had been made in the cold part of the year. It was supposed to have been painted long ago on the upper Missouri River. Joe believed that it was a picture of the hills by someone who feared he would never get out of them. But when he looked at the picture with his father, craning his neck to see up into the shadows, his father said, "It must have faded. There's nothing left."

"It's still a beautiful picture," said Joe.

His father turned and smiled down at him. "Yes, it is," his father said.

Joe had come to believe that he understood what the painter had intended and that it was still right there, perfectly clear. That it had faded only enlarged the force of its mystery. The two old sisters were buried in the yard in graves deep below the frost where coyotes could never reach them, and his father was now in a grave of his own on the edge of a suburban golf course in Minnesota where coyotes never ventured. Cattle had seized the mansion altogether for the purpose of escaping storms and drifting snow. It seemed even more important that a painting unseen by anything but bats hanging in the pine-smoked shadows of the big room disclose its meaning once and for all. When his own picture *Chain-Smoking Blind Man* had become known, only he was aware that its variegated white surface served against the canvas with a number-five putty knife was nothing more than his memory of the faded white hills on walls belonging to the long-dead Silver King and his spinster nieces. The feeling that he had invented nothing and that his career had begun with an undiscovered plagiary was disturbing. It was even more disturbing before he quit painting. Now that Joe was living little better than hand to mouth, the story of the plagiarism seemed part of a stranger's biography.

Not long after the visit to the deserted house, Joe's father had been transferred from his job as agricultural vice president of their local bank to a bigger job at the bank headquarters in Minneapolis. And it was there Joe's folks lived forevermore or until they died, neither more nor less happy, but, it had to be admitted, closer to if not their dream, then their view of things. The ranch had been leased to the neighbors, the Overstreets, but the house was available to Joe and so was a summer job of cowboying under the neighbor's foreman, Otis Rosewell, a tight-mouthed Baptist cowboy from Circle. This arrangement prevailed more or less successfully for a few years until Joe came home from his last year in military school in Kentucky, that is, came back to the ranch.

The lessees had but one obligation above and beyond an annual payment adjusted to the fall shipment of cattle, and that was to house up to four English pointers, the health and condition of which were guaranteed in writing by penalty clauses in the lease agreement. Retaining a sporting connection to the property enabled Joe's father to make his annual inspection tours from the gentlemanly stance he now required. The dogs, kenneled for the banker's occasional appearances, generally ran wild, their noses polished off to pink by running in the brush year round and their legs black from excursions through the swamps. But Joe's father was a superior dog handler and within a day or two of hunting in the fall, he usually had them "hitched up" once again, popping along, brightly under control, in search of prairie chickens. Joe remembered this wonderful string of dogs as his father's great pride, especially Neuritis and Neuralgia, the liver and white Elhew males his father raised and broke. And he remembered the three family saddle horses, all geldings, whom Joe's mother called Hart, Schaffner, and Marx because they lurked behind the shelter belt with an air of being in business together.

Joe's father accompanied him on his trip back to the ranch. He wore his gray suit buttoned over his still muscular old cowboy's physique and changed in the bunkhouse when they got there. Otis Rosewell accompanied them on their rounds. They started with the dogs and immediately Joe's father found something to complain about. Otis tilted back on his undershot heels and took it in. "When you see one drag its butt on the ground like that, it needs wormed, Otis. They don't do that as a party gag. You with me?"

"It's just having the time," said Otis in a cool voice and managing to tilt his head so that his hat brim threw a shadow across his already hard-to-read face.

They saddled some horses and started out across the irrigated ground. "I presume your boss means to prove up like he ought to on this lease and that means maintaining the condition of my ranch," Joe's father said. "You can't have spurge and knapweed go on undisturbed like that if you mean to be on this place a long time"—Joe's father stopped his horse and was pointing an incriminating arm at the edges of an undulating hay meadow—"and one place your irrigator has leached all the nutrition out of the alfalfa leaving his water too long in one spot and another it's burning up. Somebody ought to whip his ass."

"I'm the irrigator," said Otis Rosewell from under the brim.

"Who's supposed to watch you?"

"Nobody don't."

Joe's father jogged his horse right over next to Otis. "If I was your boss, I'd make it clear you were to bust your hump."

"I'm sure that's how you feel, Mr. Starling. But it was in poor shape when you had it to yourself."

Joe's father didn't appear to hear him. In fact, he halfway seemed to be talking to himself, muttering away as they rode. ". . . but sometimes a man needs to be afoot to keep from going broke, get down and go to his tasks, instead of posing on the horse no matter how bad off and shameful the farmground is." He turned to Joe. "This ranch is a monument to all I've had to take and I'm not letting anyone run it down."

Joe was startled at how well his father could speak bad English. He knew him best in his guise as a bank executive who, as a self-educated man, took pride in correct speech. In fact, as an agricultural executive, up from loan officer, he was able to create a useful gap between himself and his clients through the improved manner of his speaking. As Joe got older, he was able to read the disciplinary atmosphere by the type of language being directed at him. Buried in his father's life was his original manner, identical to that of the farmers and ranchers who came to him with their hats in their hands. What they didn't know, he often said, couldn't hurt them. He was a cold-blooded Westerner at heart.

When the three of them reached the end of the irri-

gated ground, Joe's father excused Otis Rosewell; he literally said, "You may be excused," and Rosewell started
back. Joe and his father made their way up the hill toward
the sprawling pastures that lay beyond the rims. They
didn't speak for the first and toughest part of the climb.
Joe rode along behind his father, who let his horse work
his way up through the shale and tough footing on a loose
rein. The older man sat straight as a string in his saddle,
feet loose in his stirrups with floating grace. The two
horses had their noses close to the steep ground in front
of them while the big muscles in their rumps jumped and
contracted with the struggle. When Joe and his father got
over the top, they stopped to let the horses blow. The
pastures stretched out in a folding world of grassy hills
until they disappeared into the bluing of faraway sky.

"If you ever wind up with the place," said his father,
"don't have your horses over here in the spring because
it's heck for locoweed. And larkspur too. So don't be putting cattle in here before the grass is really up. In 1959 I
took a whole truckful of saddle horses to the canners that
got locoed right in this exact spot. But whatever you do,
even if you graze it flat and the knapweed and spurge
cover it up and the wind blows the topsoil to Kansas,
don't let that old sonofabitch Overstreet get it. He tried
to break me when I came into this country and he darn
near got it done. We get along okay now but his dream is
to make his ranch a perfect square and this is a big bite
out of his southeast corner." He stopped and thought a
moment, staring persistently in front of himself. "And if
the worst should happen and I am gone and he gets it
from you and makes it square, don't let him get the mineral rights. I can see something like this happening with
the land, but if he gets what's underneath he's cut off
your nuts and it's the Pope's choir for you, kiddo."

Joe loved the place but he didn't expect or really want
to end up on it altogether. If Joe was satisfied by the land
in which the ranch was situated, and he loved it pretty
much wherever his eyes fell, he never quite understood
what that had to do with ownership. Right now it was
enough to feel his father's passion for the place and try to

speculate about how he went on owning something with such deep satisfaction when it was so far from his home on that golf course in Minneapolis. Joe puzzled over the passion with which his father had made a new life there. His father golfed with enthusiasm in his Bermuda shorts, pounding the ball around the fairways with hostile force, the terror of caddies, shaping the land with his clubs, playing through lethargic foursomes with menace and accumulating large numbers of strokes through his enraged putting. They called him "cowboy" in a way that genially suggested that his skills were not suited to civilized life.

As Joe followed his father down the mile-long slope to the main spring he tried to absorb the plain fact that his father meant that this would one day be his. This was not precisely a soaring thought. He really wondered how he would put his heritage in play. He found the future eerie and he already wanted to paint.

The spring lay at the base of the long slope, in a grove of small black cottonwoods and wild currant bushes. It came out of an iron pipe and poured into the end of an old railroad tank car whose thick steel plating and massive rivets made an indestructible water hole that couldn't be trampled into muck the way an undeveloped spring could by cows who stayed thirsty and wouldn't travel to feed, beating the grass down where they lay in diminished vigor. Joe's father explained all this to him and made it clear that it was he who had hauled this great railroad tank up the mountain and developed the spring, wheelbarrowing gravel to the trench and laying the collector pipe one blistering summer in the 1940s.

"But it was worth it," he said, "because every cow who ever came here since then got herself a good long drink of cold water." This made the home on the golf course seem even sadder to Joe, the dawn cries of the foursomes on Sunday even more depressing than he had remembered. The hillsides around Joe and his father were speckled with contented-looking Hereford cattle and their spry calves. His father's satisfaction was a simple one, complicated only by the distance his success had produced.

The horses were lathered when at the end of the day they were turned out once again, white lines of sweat gathered at the outlines of the saddles. The horses ran back into their pasture, stretched to shake from end to end, celebrated liberty by rolling in the dust, jumping back up to shake and stretch again. Then they jogged over the hill and out of sight. Joe's father changed in the bunkhouse, and when he came back, carrying a brown briefcase, he was a banker again in an olive green summer suit, a striped tie, and a dapper straw hat.

2

Joe rode with his father in a rental car to visit his Uncle Smitty and Aunt Lureen. They were his father's brother and sister. It was late afternoon and Lureen would be home from her teaching job. Smitty could always be found at home.

"This is what you call a social obligation," said his father.

"Oh, I like them, Dad."

"They're all yours, son, at least for the summer. I like Lureen and I suppose I should like Smitty better than I do. He's my brother, after all."

The house was three narrow stories tall, with sagging porches on the two upper floors; it was clapboard and painted a pale green that stood out against sky and telephone wires. The scudding spring clouds moved overhead rapidly. When Joe looked at the house, its cheap simplicity reminded him of his modest family origins of city park employees, Democratic party flunkies, mill workers, railroad brakemen, mechanics, grocers, ranch hands. It forever fascinated him that such unassuming people could have been so mad with greed and desire for fame or love. Joe's father was the first and only member of the family to take on the notion of landholding. One uncle had written passionate letters to aborigine women in care of the *National Geographic*. A cousin had lost his dryland farm in a pyramid scheme. A locket his grandmother had worn all her life contained the photograph of a man not known to the family.

Smitty and Lureen were in the doorway, Lureen in a brown suit she had taught in, and Smitty in the checked shirt and beltless slacks that seemed to suggest well-earned leisure. He looked like a commuter.

They got out of the car and Joe's father stormed up the short flight of steps with insincere enthusiasm. He hugged Lureen fiercely and pumped Smitty's thin arm with comradely fervor. Joe stood back smiling until it was his turn for the hugs and handshakes. It was well known that Smitty had great reservations about Joe's father but they didn't show until he greeted Joe with a suspicious squint and wary twitching of his eyebrows.

The visit was a raucous parade behind Joe's father, who thundered through the rooms, refusing Smitty's suggestion of a drink and Lureen's of tea. He borrowed the telephone for a quick call to the bank in Minnesota, then hung up the phone conclusively as though his conversation with the bank had been the end of his conversation with Lureen and Smitty.

"Junior's got to go to work," he said, gesturing at Joe with his straw hat. He bobbed down to kiss Lureen good-bye, then shot his hand out and let Smitty walk over and shake it. "We'll call you Christmastime!" he thundered and got around behind Joe, pushing at his shoulder blades until the two of them were out on the street and a very strained Smitty and Lureen were waving at them. "You can't have a drink with Smitty without having to go his bail that night."

As they drove, his father said, "Can you imagine a grown man living off his spinster sister like that?"

"I thought Smitty had some problem from the war," Joe said.

"Oh, he did, he did. But I was in the same goddamn war. Listen to me, I want to make a long story short. Don't ever take your eyes off Smitty. He's dumb like a fox. Cut Smitty a little slack and he'll take her all."

They drove back out toward the ranch. "I wish I could have found a way of staying in this country," said his father. "But any fool can see it's going nowhere. Still, you look at it and it just makes you think, What if? You know what I mean?" Joe was so startled by what for them was a rare intimacy that he looked straight down the road and waited for his stop. He thought he knew exactly what his father meant. What if.

Joe's father dropped him at the Overstreet headquarters, next to the tin-roofed granary and saddle shed and bunkhouse where Joe would live for the summer. He leaned over and gave Joe a hug. Joe felt his great body heat and smelled the strong and heartening aftershave lotion.

"Well, son," he said, "it's time to whistle up the dogs and piss on the fire. Have a good summer, and keep an eye on things. You make a hand and they'll have to use you. Then you can watch. Think of it as being yours someday and you'll watch fairly closely."

"Tell Mom hi for me."

"In particular," said his father, "the hay ground. If they aren't changing water three times a day they're lying to both of us."

All of Joe's father's quirks, including this one of not listening to him closely, only made Joe love him more. He loved the motion of his father, the bustle, the clear goals he, Joe, could not always understand. After all, he was the only father Joe would have and Joe seemed to know that.

3

Joe was over at the headquarters of the Caywood Fork the next day to get his orders. It was first light and the big riverine cottonwoods that hung over the somber headquarters buildings seemed to hold the last of night in their dense foliage. He had no car for the summer and he'd had to walk. The dogs barked at his arrival and Otis Rosewell came around from behind the saddle shed leading a horse. Joe walked over to him and stopped. Rosewell gazed at him. Finally, a small smile played over his lips.

"Must be tough around your camp," he said.

"What do you mean?"

"Your old man."

"Yes, he is," Joe conceded, wondering in dismay if he was failing some test of loyalty. But he thought Rosewell had extended a small gesture of amiability and he didn't want it to slip away. It could be a long summer.

"Do you know how to run a swather or a bale wagon?"

"No, I don't."

"Can you fence?"

"Sure. And I can run a backpack sprayer, you know, for malathion or whatever."

"Well, most of the fence on your old man's place is falling down because he never took care of it and because it was fenced poorly in the first place. But I imagine he thinks it's perfect and I want you to make his dreams come true because my yearlings are pouring through the sonofabitch like water. Get yourself a pocket notebook and start walking that fence. Pull it up when you can and rebuild it where you have to. Knock out that old crooked cedar and put in some steel. You can get a sledge, stretcher, pliers, post pounder, and staples in the shop and you can use the old Ford to haul it around."

"I'll get started today."

"That's right. And you'll never finish. Now let me tell you something else. You was sent to us. If you don't care to put in an honest day's work, that's your business. I ain't going to hang over you. I work for Mr. Overstreet."

Joe built fence for twenty-one days before he took his first break. He went down all the boundary fence and had five strands of barbed wire on stays sparkling from staple to staple. Where the rotten cedar had given out there were new green-and-white steel T-posts and the soldierly order they gave to the rise and fall of boundaries helped Joe see how his heritage lay on the benign face of the county.

About halfway through his fencing assignment, Joe reached a high divide between two drainages, Crow Creek and Nester Creek. A thousand years of wind had blown all the topsoil to Wyoming and it was just bare rock on top of the world where old barbed wire sang like an Aeolian harp. Otis came up and helped him with this stretch of fence. They started to build jack fence, then changed their minds and dynamited post holes for half a mile until the line pitched down into the woods and was easy again and beyond the eerie sound of the steel strings above them. There was pleasure in working the ratchet on the fence stretcher, watching the wire rise, tighten, and sparkle in the light through the trees, sing in the wind, turn at the corner posts, or drop out of sight over the crown of a hill. Joe was going all round what would one day be his.

On the twenty-first day, he was fencing the bottom of a narrow defile. Cattle had grown accustomed to escaping here by lifting the poles that were meant to hold the bottom wire low. Joe was sewing the fence to the earth along the floor of this cut with a post every ten feet when he was visited by the daughter of the owner, Ellen Overstreet. He had watched her covertly ever since he first got there, mostly when she was riding out through the ranch in the front of a flatbed truck with Billy Kelton, a neighbor Joe hadn't spoken to since a boyhood fistfight almost ten years before. Without any thought of Ellen herself, Joe would have loved to take her away from Billy, who looked so complacent in the truck, lariat hanging in the rear window and his blue-eyed gaze remote under a tall-crown straw hat. It was a grudge.

Joe's first thought was that her timing was perfect. He was dark from the long exposure to sun and the muscles of his arms were hard and defined from driving posts and stretching wire. Ellen was a rangy brunette with startling gray eyes.

"What's the point of this when my dad is going to own it all anyway?" she said with a bright smile.

"I'm getting paid. And I'm here to tell you your dad will never get our place."

"You're getting paid. Otis says you can work or not work, it's no nevermind to him."

"Well, it is to me," said Joe, letting the red post pounder tip over and drop with a clang.

"One way or another, Otis says. He doesn't care."

"You can't go by Otis," said Joe. "If he knew anything he wouldn't be here."

"Otis has been with Daddy since we ranched at Exeter Switch."

"It's not Otis's fault he isn't smart."

Ellen sat down in the deep bluestem and began pulling up the russet pink flowers of prairie smoke, making a bouquet in her left hand and blowing ants off the blossoms.

"Daddy says you're in military school in Kentucky and you're that little bit from graduating and going to Vietnam."

"Only I'm not going to Vietnam. I'm going to college in the East. I'm studying art. Is that for me?"

He reached out for the bouquet of prairie smoke blossoms and she handed them over with a shrug.

"Why aren't we going to Vietnam?"

"Because we aren't supposed to be there in the first place. Everybody knows that."

"Not everybody knows that. A lot of my friends can't wait to get there."

"Well, you've got the wrong friends."

"You better not let them hear your Vietnam theory. I know one or two will fix your little red wagon. We believe in freedom. Y'know Billy Kelton?"

"Yeah, I know Billy."

"Well, he plans to go quick as he can get shut of school."

"That'd be about right for Billy."

"Did you know he was top five saddlebronc rider in the Northern Rodeo Association two years in a row?"

"Nope."

"He's about as pretty a hand with rough stock ever come out of these parts."

"That should just chill the Vietcong," said Joe.

Joe wasn't really paying close attention. Almost the only thing he and Ellen had in common was that they were both being dunned by the Columbia Record Club. He was trying to see what she had in the way of breasts. If she hadn't wanted that noticed, she could have bought the right shirt size.

"Otis said you really know how to work."

"He did?" Joe practically sang.

"That seems to mean quite a little to you."

"Not really."

She scrutinized him. He was at a loss for words. The very sound of air seemed to increase. She took a deep breath. "What bands do you like?" she asked.

"The Stones. What about you?"

"The Byrds." On the word "Byrds" he sensed his opportunity and reached to take her hand. It felt small to him, though it was hard to notice anything more than the nervous energy pouring back and forth between them. He would have liked to announce that he was going to kiss her or that he was attracted to her, which he was. But anything which contained much meaning would have subjected him to overexposure. Nevertheless, for things to continue, it was necessary that he express something about the moment. He said, "Oh, wow." To his immense relief, "Oh, wow" was very acceptable. Ellen Overstreet seemed to melt very slightly at these less than eloquent words. "I mean it," Joe added and took the other hand.

"What are you taking?" she breathed, her face angled down at the ground between them.

"Algebra, History, Spanish, English. What about you?"

"Soc. Home Ec. Comm Skills. Phys Ed." Joe wasn't thinking so much about her courses. He could tell that she was looking to him for leadership. That he knew next to nothing, probably no more than she, didn't matter because he had arrived from out of state and his real background was lost behind this ripped T-shirt, these new muscles, and this tan. He drew Ellen to him and kissed her. Feeling the hard line of her clamped lips, he realized that Ellen was ready to be kissed but didn't know much more than to lean face forward. It might take all summer to get those lips open.

They went on kissing. A couple of times, she had "thoughts" as she called them that made laughter burst through her nose. Joe waited grimly for these "thoughts" to pass and went back to the awkward business of kissing and hugging. He had numb spots from the rough ground, and any attempt to get "more comfortable" as he explained it, that is, to lever Ellen into a reclining posture, failed miserably. Finally, she detached herself and got up.

"Well, it's nice to meet you, Joe. We'll have to do something one of these days."

"That'd be great," he said, quite certain he knew what she meant by "something."

"Like maybe we could ride on Saturday."

"Oh, wow."

When she started to leave, he gave her the peace sign. His best friend back at school, Ivan Slater, said day in and day out you could get familiar with strange girls faster by using the peace sign as a greeting than any other way.

But Ellen, seeing his raised fingers, said, "Two what?" Joe just shook his head.

"The two of us?" she said. "Oh, you're sweet!"

4

Joe and Otis crossed paths as two professionals, and Otis had taken to questioning Joe about little things he was noticing, the levels of springs, the appearance of yearlings that had had diphtheria, pink eye, cancer eye, bag problems, warbles. Joe renewed the fly rubs up in the pasture and ran the chute when Rosewell had cattle in to doctor. He had gotten so he knew all the levers of the headcatch, the catch itself, the gate, the squeeze. He knew which bars to flip out on the cattle they had missed branding so that they could get old man Overstreet's 9-Bar on the left hip. At first, it disturbed Joe to watch the irons smoke into flesh, and the tongue-slung bawling of the cattle as pain drove manure down their back legs. In the end, he turned the irons over in the fire himself to get the right pitch of heat, to make sure the brands went on bright and clean. He quit noticing when the burning smell drifted on the summer air. And to make up for it, he doctored the ones that had eye ulcers from burdocks in the hay they had been eating.

Not long after Joe and Ellen had started to see each other, he was asked up to the Overstreet house. It was an old two-story ranch house with a dirt path beaten from the driveway to the entry. With ill-concealed distaste, small, fat Mrs. Overstreet led Joe to her husband's office, a room off the bedroom where water rights filings, escrow

receipts, bills, brand inspections, road permits, cattle re-
gistries, breeding and veterinary records, defunct phone
books, memorandum pads, and calendars were heaped up
on a rolltop desk. Mr. Overstreet sat on a kind of spring-
loaded stool that permitted him to swivel around, tilt
back, and regard Joe all in one movement. He was nearly
as small as his wife and in every gesture he radiated a
lifetime of sharp trading. Like many old-time ranchers,
there was nothing "Western" about him. A topographical
map on the wall illustrated the boundaries of the ranch.
He went to it and pointed to the large missing piece on
the south side. "See that?" His eyes burned at Joe. They
seemed to consume the papery little face that curved up
under a halo of thin iron-gray hair.

"Yes, sir."

"That belongs," said Overstreet, "to you people."

"Yes, sir."

"It spoils the shape of this other, don't you think?"

Joe said nothing.

"Besides that, I'd like to hear how you're getting
along. In your own words."

"I'm getting along fine."

"Your salary comes out of my lease arrangement with
your daddy. So I'm not out there wringing the last penny
from your hide. I do that mainly with Otis. But he says
we're getting our money's worth." He removed his
glasses and worked his thumb and forefinger into his eye
sockets as he spoke. He turned his gaze to the map of the
ranch and restored his glasses.

"Joe," he said, "you come from the big wide wonderful world out there. Ellen comes from right here on this
little bitty patch of ground. Now no more than I'd try to
sell you a pasture without water, don't you sell Ellen
something she really isn't in a big way of needing. You
catch my meaning?"

"I guess I do."

"You do, Joe. Take it from me. You catch my meaning.
Now go on out and keep doing the good job you've been
doing. Your dad will be proud of you. You're doing a

man's job. If he ever fires you, you come and see me. I'll take you to Billings and teach you to trade fat cattle. I'll teach you to wear out two Cadillacs a year packing cattle receipts. Why, if I had your youth and my brains, I could walk on the backs of my cattle to Omaha. Go on out there, Joe, and *bow your damn back.*"

But Joe didn't get the message exactly. He was stirred instead by the romance of landholding that the old man radiated from his cluttered office. And when he and Ellen returned to their little wickiup in the willows alongside Tie Creek, he was less accepting of the plateau that they had reached weeks before. The wickiup was just a place where they had artfully bent the willows into an igloo shape and lashed them down. Ellen had read somewhere that it was the way the Indians had once sheltered themselves. The wickiup was an easy walk from the house and perfectly camouflaged. They were so secure in this shelter that they calmly went on with their activities even when Otis Rosewell rode past a few yards away. They lapped their tongues while the backs of their heads moved in vague figure-eights. They repeated "I love you" and tried to key their utterances to blissful peaks or reflective sighs. A long silence, a sigh, and an "I love you" indicated they had foreseen an extensive future with all its familiar appurtenances and had taken the phrase "I love you" as a kind of shorthand. Joe ached with meaning. Ellen undid the metal snap in back of her brassiere and her breasts were revealed. Either he would sweep his hand slowly up her rib cage and encompass them, or he would unpack them carefully. They were full handfuls with graceful small nipples. And once when Ellen was doing a handstand, Joe made out the faint blue veins underneath. No matter what position Ellen was in, they stuck straight out. If he mashed them gently, they resumed their perfect shape upon release. If he pushed them to one side and let go, they sprang back. They were practically brand new and the feeling Ellen insisted upon was that they were so wonderful they canceled any further expectations.

Joe overflowed with feeling for the girl in his arms. He had never felt such strong emotions. Everything meant something bigger. He could look at her for hours from only a couple of inches away.

5

Together Joe and Ellen began to adopt the mopey love-struck postures, the innocent paralysis of young lovers in small towns. On Saturdays, they took one of the ranch trucks and drove into Deadrock for a swim at the city pool. Instead of yanking at each other and yelling by the poolside, they demonstrated the depth of their feeling by quietly working on their tans in fingertip proximity, or eating quietly by themselves at a shady snow-cone franchise. Joe could accept this because he knew the necessary crisis was coming. Gliding along on these parallel paths, feeling vaguely upset in this atmospheric filigree, watching the others thunder past barefoot at poolside, hot on the heels of screeching females, or crammed in fleshy heaps within sun-scorched automobiles, was almost acceptable to Joe because he was being swept along by something thrilling that he had no interest in understanding.

But when Saturday night came around, Joe watched in astonishment as Ellen rolled out the ranch road in Billy Kelton's flatbed truck. Billy and Joe had been best friends until that day ten years ago when Billy beat Joe senseless. Joe was still not over the sense of injury. For his date with Ellen, Billy hadn't even removed the stock rack or taken his saddle out of the bed. His filthy old chaps, lashed to the crosspiece behind the cab, flapped away carelessly. "That sumbitch must be harder than hell to steer," Joe shouted as they went past waving, "the two of you having to sit under the wheel like that!"

But the truck came back up the road at ten. Joe saw them through the bunkhouse window. He had been pacing around, expecting to be up half the night. He dove to extinguish his light. In a short time, Ellen tapped at his door.

"Who is it?" Joe called.

"Ellen. Can I come in?"

Joe conquered the wish to let her in. "I've got a lot to do tomorrow."

"Joe, I've got something to tell you."

"Tell it to the Marines. Tell it to Billy Kelton. I think you two should be very happy together."

She cried outside the door for a while. Finally, she said, "Good night," and Joe fell asleep.

Otis Rosewell generally stayed in town with his wife, but when things ran late, he bunked with Joe. He and Joe had a nice, easygoing relationship based on Joe's looking up to Otis, and admiringly asking for advice. One night when they were musing about cows and horses and smoking cigarettes, Otis tossed an old screwdriver in his hand as he told about an older cowboy he knew who had worked for the Padlock and for Kendricks' in Wyoming; this man, Otis claimed, would go out by himself for weeks at a time with his bedroll and a lariat and would single-handedly rope, brand, vaccinate, and castrate hundreds of calves. "It took a hell of a horse to keep that rope tight, naturally," Otis went on. "But this old boy slept on the ground with his head on his saddle and hobbled his pony and went from one end of the herd to the other! He was born in a damn hurricane, this feller was—" On the far side of the bunkhouse, a rat ran up out of the woodpile about three feet up the wall. Otis threw the screwdriver toward the woodpile and it turned over in the air and speared the rat to the wall. The rat expired. Joe stared. Otis retrieved his screwdriver, threw the rat out the door and sat down.

"Let me see you do that again," Joe said.

"Run up another rat," Otis said.

When the time came, it came quickly. Joe went, hat in hand, to Mr. Overstreet in his office and, conscious that he was triggering the fall of his daughter's virginity, said, "Mr. Overstreet, I'll be going back to school soon. I think I'll finish up and head out." Word of his imminent departure would speed through the ranch. Awful Mrs. Overstreet would rub her daughter's nose in it. Joe was getting ready to run up another rat.

Overstreet stood in the door of his office, which was dim except where the old gooseneck lamp lit the desk, holding a fountain pen poised in front of his chest, and said, "We'll send your dad a good report. You've been a great deal of use to him and to us. I hope we haven't seen the last of you."

"In case I don't bump into Ellen or Mrs. Overstreet, please tell them how much I have enjoyed the opportunity of being here this summer."

"Well, you'll have to tell Ellen yourself," said Mr. Overstreet. "She's soft on you. Even an old-timer like me can see that. Do this family a favor and let Ellen hear from you once in a while." Joe savored the peculiarity of this departure, the old man contemplating the free labor, himself laying the fuse to carnal dynamite.

Late that afternoon, Ellen flung herself onto the floor of the wickiup and began to weep quietly. Joe hung his head. He wasn't really cynical. He loved Ellen. He'd had the best summer of his life with her. She was like a merry shadow to him, superb with horses, incapable of worry, able to freely get around the back country that surrounded the ranch. She knew all the wild grasses as well as she knew the flowers, and could tell before they rode over a rise if that was the day they would come upon newly bloomed shooting stars or fields of alpine asters that weren't there the previous week. She could spot a cow humped up with illness from literally a mile off, or a horse with a ring of old wire around its foot from even farther. Every walk or ride they'd taken, every middle of the night trip to town made under the noses of her tedious parents, led to this moment.

Joe kissed Ellen through her tears and began to undress her. With a languorous and heartbroken air, she helped him until finally she slid her jeans down over her compact hips. She was nude and Joe thought his heart would burst. There was a baffling mutual tragedy in this nudity. He got undressed. He had never known air in such cool purity. The air around them and between them had a quality it could never have again. When he took Ellen in his arms, her absolute nakedness was such a powerful thing it frightened him. He had to return to familiar kissing, familiar strokes of her hair to bring things back to dimensions he could absorb and dispel the sense that he had hit some kind of thrilling but finally overpowering wall. He had to collect himself; but when he drew back, Ellen was once again full in view, no longer even sitting up to accommodate his movement, but remaining supine while he cleared his head of voices.

He moved onto Ellen and simply lay atop her with his knees against hers. Gradually, the pressure of her knees gave way and one of his slid between them. She let her legs part so that his knees touched the blanket underneath them. Then he felt her spread her legs. He tried to lift up on his arms to see but she held him strongly and wouldn't let him. He slid his hand between the points of their hips, held himself until he was started inside her, and pushed. He'd only entered a moment before he emptied himself in scalding shudders. He felt lost.

Otis took Joe to the train in Mr. Overstreet's truck. When they got to the station and pulled up in front of the columns, Otis let his eyes follow a porter pushing an iron-wheeled wagon along the side of the tracks. "You take care, Joe," he said over the roar of the wagon wheels. There was a bright September sun shining down on the world.

"I will, Otis. You too."

"I think you done Mr. Overstreet a fine job."

"I appreciate that."

"I'm sure they'd always be work for you if he was to get the place off your old daddy."

"Is that what his plan is?"

"I'd say so, Joe. He don't figure on you to fight for it."

"I'd rather fight for it than come back and work for old man Overstreet."

"He's a cheap sonofabitch," mused Otis. "Well, Joe, we'll be seeing you. And good luck."

No sooner had Otis pulled out and Joe had started dragging his duffel bag toward the passenger cars than Billy arrived in his flatbed with all the stuff still in back and climbed out. He stopped on the gravel and gestured to Joe. He took off his hat and put it back inside his truck. There was a white band of forehead against his sunburned face.

"Come here, you," he said, with his hands on his hips.

Joe didn't want to walk over at all. He felt almost paralyzed with fear but knew he couldn't live with himself if he didn't walk over. This was going to be a fight and Joe didn't know how to fight. Billy had whipped him a decade earlier and it looked like it was going to happen again. He started to walk over, feeling he might turn and bolt at every step. He stared back at Billy, at first out of a doomed sense of duty and then with increasing isolation until all there was before him was the gradually enlarging figure of Billy amid the uproar of the railroad station and town streets. Billy dropped him with the first blow and Joe struggled to his feet. He wasn't upright before Billy slugged him again and Joe himself could hear the fist pop against the bone of his face. As he struggled to his feet once more, he heard a passenger cry out that enough was enough, but now he had Billy by the front of his shirt and was hauling him toward himself. As Billy began to chop into his face with short, brutal punches, Joe saw Billy being pushed back at the end of a policeman's nightstick. The policeman stepped between Joe and Billy. They stared at each other with the dismay of strangers meeting on the occasion of a car wreck. "Good luck in Vietnam," Joe said bitterly. He looked at Billy, who was glassy eyed with hatred, and then Joe turned to head toward the train. When he bent to pick up his duffel, he fainted.

6

It seemed Joe would always spend plenty of time unraveling misunderstandings with women. The following summer, when he was eighteen, he'd hitchhiked to Mexico and wound up in a small town in Sonora. He remembered cattle trucks going between the adobe walls on the edge of the town and kind of careening around the fountain too fast, like in the movies. He remembered the constant murmuring of mourning doves and the First Communion girls in white clouds in front of the church. He remembered the century plants and ocotillos with their orange blossoms and gaunt cattle that seemed to walk so hopelessly. He remembered a shirtless man standing next to a hanging side of beef, cutting and weighing pieces of meat for passing customers and rolling the pesos nervously around his forefinger. Joe remembered the town being a dusty grid, poor animals carrying things for the poor people, insignificant things to our eyes like bundles of sticks. It made him ashamed to have anything.

He was led by two boys into a cantina and up to a prostitute, a nice-looking girl who was very tall for a Mexican. He went upstairs. She gave herself to him and Joe responded by falling in love with her and spending every effort to think how she could be reformed and taught English so that he could make her his wife. Joe sat all night in the cantina, a shrunken presence, entertaining her and allowing her to peel his roll of pesos like an artichoke. They danced. They arranged to be photographed at their table. When Joe left for the States, he had the picture, the shirt on his back, and a stricken heart.

In the fall, when he was back in school, Joe's mother found the photograph. She was holding it between her two hands, staring at it, when she called him to her room.

"Joe," she said, "I'm *so* ashamed of you." Joe didn't know what to say. Nothing was appropriate. She lifted her eyes until she had him. "Here you are"—she returned her gaze to the photograph—"with this lovely young woman"—she looked up at him in penetrating disappointment—"and *your shirt is out!*"

Joe's mother taught everyone to play bridge, and about this she had a sense of mission. There was some kind of opiated cough medicine available with which she had dosed Joe, aged four, so that his antics would not disrupt the games taking place in front of the big sixteen-pane window that looked out on the low bluffs that still had the bones of buffalo exposed by spring rains. And Joe daydreamed the bridge afternoons away in apparent bliss. His mother played bridge every week, deeply bored by her companions, the lumpish locals. She thought of her fellow Montanans as humped figures limited by the remote flickers of undeveloped consciousness. She had hoped against hope that her son Joseph Starling, Junior would set out and find culture somewhere, uplifting companionship, make a name for himself, and more or less stay out of town.

As an only child, Joe had been most divided by the contrasting claims of his parents. His father still had the Westerner's ability to look into pure space and see possibilities. His mother saw traditional education as a tool for escape, an escape she couldn't think of making but one which her son could somehow make for her.

Joe graduated from the Kentucky Military Institute and to his father's great satisfaction was accepted by Yale. That happiness quickly disappeared at Joe's decision to study art. When Joe's father visited him at Yale and saw

34

displays of student work and, worse, the crazy-looking building where art was taught, he told Joe they would have nothing to say to each other if this kept up. Joe painted landscapes but they were so austere that they approached not being there at all. They deepened his father's suspicion that this was, despite the endorsement of major institutions, a complete swindle.

His conviction was not altered when Joe got out of school, moved to New York, and became a successful painter. Though it was a career, it was apparently not enough of a career. From Joe's point of view, something wasn't sinking in. The next thing was he couldn't paint. It didn't seem all that subtle psychologically; and he had a good grasp of it. He had always painted from memory and for some reason he couldn't seem to remember much of late. He hoped it was temporary but at the moment, he didn't have anything to offer anyone, even the gallery owners who were practical enough and who knew what was called for. He seemed to have folded his tent and that was that.

But before this, before his love of paint and painting deepened to a kind of dumb rapture, his relationship with his mother grew closer. She resumed a long-buried girlishness. Eventually, this closeness applied to more serious matters. One summer after the family had moved to Minnesota, Joe was staying on the ranch, painting and doing most of the irrigating. His mother, having announced the seriousness of her mission, flew out from Minnesota for a visit.

Joe made iced tea and they went out and sat at a picnic table under half a dozen flowering apple trees; the trees hadn't been pruned in years but sent forth flowers in drenching volume among the dead branches. There was a telephone pole in the middle, which took something away from the scene; and, just beyond, a wooden feed bunk for cattle with four tongue-worn salt blocks. A handful of pure white clouds floated overhead without moving. Joe and his mother had sat right here in the same spot when he was a child discussing sack races, nature, wild flowers, life, anything that came up. His mother still twirled her hair with her left forefinger when she was thinking, while Joe went on lacing his fingers and staring at them until a thought would come. They had always called the desired outcome of events "an amazing voyage," as in "It would be an amazing voyage if you passed physics this term."

"Make a long story short," said Joe.

"It's inherently a long story."

"Try your best."

His mother drank some of her iced tea. She ran her fingers through her hair, pushing her head back to look up in the sky. She made a single click on the picnic table with an enameled fingernail. "Dad is going to have to be dried out. He has had serious problems with his diverticulitis which surgery would cure, but surgery is out of the question because he will go into the DTs before he can recover."

Joe thought for a moment. "Maybe he should just go through the DTs and deal with the rest of it afterwards."

"At his age and in his state, I am assured that he will shake himself to death if he goes into the DTs unless he does it in a clinic."

"Can he live with the diverticulitis?"

"No."

Beyond the orchard, the beavers had dammed a small stream and the cattails had grown up. A dense flock of redwing blackbirds shot out, followed by a goshawk in tight pursuit. The goshawk flared off into a cottonwood and watched the blackbirds scatter back among the cattails. At a certain point, it would start again.

"I have a feeling you can make this story shorter than you're letting on."

"This part I can condense. You have the best chance of getting Dad into the clinic."

Joe leaned one elbow on the table and rested his face on his hand. "Does he even like me, Mother?"

"Not particularly."

"In that case, maybe I do have a chance," he said, as

though elated at a glimmer of light. In fact, he was quite
wounded. And in the end it was to no purpose.

That summer, Joe's father went bankrupt in Minnesota.
But he saw it coming and signed his ranch over to his
sister Lureen to protect it from receivers. Speaking directly to Lureen, confirming that conversation in a letter
and sending a copy of the letter to Joe, he expressed his
intention to one day take the ranch back and finally to
leave it to his son Joe. But he never got the chance: He
died driving his car to bankruptcy court, a black four-door
Buick coasting through Northfield, Minnesota, with a
corpse at the wheel. This ghastly scene dominated the
local news for a month.

His father had played around with his wills so often
that none of them was binding and for all practical purposes, he died intestate. The property in Minnesota went
to Joe's mother, and sufficient investments had with-
stood bankruptcy proceedings that she was able to live
comfortably. Lureen never offered to give her the ranch
back. She made it clear that she was holding it for Joe.
She and Joe's mother had known each other since the
days in the two-room Clarendon Creek schoolhouse
when they were both girls. They never liked each other.
Joe's mother said, "Lureen has been a wallflower and a
cornball since kindergarten." Lureen said Joe's mother
had "enjoyed all the benefits of prostitution without the
health risks and the forced early retirement." It was the
sharpest statement Lureen made in a long, quiet life; and
it had so tremendously amused Joe's father that he had
repeated it to Joe with delight. To this day, Joe didn't
know what to make of it, or know why it had delighted
his father, the banker and former cowboy. A year after his
father died, his mother died—connected events.

Joe and Lureen had never failed to communicate with
perfect clarity on the matter of the ranch. Lease payments were made to her; she deposited them and sent a
check on to Joe. A separate account was opened to compensate Lureen for her increased taxes as well as a management fee for discussing arrangements with the Over-

streets once a year. Lureen lived on her teacher's retirement money and on social security. She owned her home and lived in it simply and comfortably. Joe offered to help out with her needs. She didn't seem to want that, and often remarked that she saw it as her mission to properly attend to the business which Joe's father had placed in her hands. At some point, the matter of transferring it into Joe's name would be taken care of; and that would be that. Unfortunately, Smitty developed pride of ownership.

After a couple of years in New York, Joe moved to Florida where it was always warm, and soon he met Astrid, riding the front of a 1935 Rolls-Royce, wearing nothing but gold spray paint. She was going to a costume party as a hood ornament. When they danced, he got gold paint on his clothes. This much he could remember about their first kiss: the instant it was over, she said, "You're driving me crazy." He had been dating a girl he'd met when he delivered a specimen for his annual physical, a big-voiced Hoosier girl whose tidy apartment was decorated with Guatemalan molas and posters from gangster movies. She didn't stand a chance against Astrid, who went everywhere with a train of dazed men who hated themselves for being so drawn to her. Astrid scalded them with her Cuban laugh or sent them on demeaning errands.

Not long after the costume parade, Joe and Astrid spent an entire evening making death masks and Joe propped his next to his place at the dinner table, and then so did Astrid. She said, "You look incredibly old in your death mask." He had been uncomfortable breathing through a straw.

Joe said, "Yours doesn't look so good itself." He stuck his tongue through the mouth hole of her death mask. "The other thing is, I've got an empty feeling," he said.

After they began living together, Astrid used to ask him why he didn't paint. He asked her, "Paint what?"

After a few years, she quit asking.

*   *   *

To make a living, Joe became a freelance illustrator of operation manuals. This attainment, through his perfect draftsmanship, had at the beginning peculiar satisfactions. He went to work for his old school friend, Ivan Slater, now a successful businessman. Ivan was not interested in art; Ivan was interested in making others understand how things ran. Ivan would tell them how things ran and Joe would show them. He felt he was selling something real. He had nothing more neurotic to concern himself with than meeting deadlines and his vision of people he hadn't met operating diverse gadgets. The big catch with this work was that it always involved Ivan Slater, Joe's most annoying friend, who had failed upward to a considerable personal fortune. Joe wasn't the least bit jealous and was even flattered that Ivan construed it an act of friendship to try to lure him away from what he considered his fairly dopey earlier life.

The first thing Joe showed Americans how to run was a battery-powered folding hair dryer. The former landscapist made the instrument jump out at you, its operating features so vivid as to be immediately understood. On the bright curve of the instrument's side, Joe let the outer world suggest itself in a little glint. Joe poured his heart into the glint. The glint contained tiny details of his ranch in Montana and gave the impression that the hair dryer was right at home in fairly remote circumstances. It made him happy and it in no way impeded the new owner from acquiring knowledge of drying his or her hair. The company comptroller cut Joe a check. Joe went on with his life. The grazing lease allowed him some selection in the jobs he took. Astrid blamed the lease payments for his not painting; she called them his food stamps.

Joe showed people how to operate an electric lazy susan, a garage door opener, an automatic cat feeder, a board game based on geopolitics, a portable telephone so small it could be pinned to one's clothing, a radar detector for cars, and a gas-powered fire log. For a long time, Joe built up his interest in these projects by imagining that he was working for a single prosperous family, five painfully stupid yet happy people who wanted to be able to run this worthless shit they'd paid good money for.

Ivan Slater had consolidated a lot of solid-state and semi-conductor information and come up with a "portable secretary" brand-named "Miss X," a laptop computer powered by batteries, the same size as the average briefcase. Miss X was complicated to use and complicated to describe in that her functions were so diverse—typing, dictation, filing, and more. Ivan Slater was an ingenious technician but a poor salesman, and dragging Joe by the sleeve through the trade shows of a dozen cities, Ivan made the same startling pitch time after time: "Miss X will do everything but suck you off back at the Ramada!" Ivan saw himself as one of the new "hands-on" industrialists, a growing class of powerful men led by the owners of Remington Shaver and Two Thousand Flushes Toilet Cleaner, who appeared in their own television commercials excitedly demanding your business; Ralph Lauren, casting himself as a cowboy in his own print ads; and the king of them all, Lee Iacocca of Chrysler with his immortal "I guarantee it." These men were Ivan Slater's heroes and he did not defer to them in forcefulness.

At a trade show in Atlanta, Joe had an opportunity to taste the resistance among some of his peers which Ivan Slater had generated. They were set up in a booth of their own at a convention center near Peachtree Plaza. The style of their industry was such that a curiously sedate atmosphere prevailed. At an automotive or homebuilders show, it would have been pandemonium. But these were the businesspeople of a new age; restraint and an ambiguously intellectual tone made it a ghostly crowd. Joe stood behind a table upon which rested a mock-up of the laptop secretary. He had a stack of brochures and, since he had not finished the instructional drawings, he was there to explain the machine in his own words. Ivan had long since driven himself into the middle of the crowd.

A man approaching sixty made his way toward the table. He was tall and dressed in a well-tailored gray pinstripe suit. He stared at Miss X without taking a brochure. His left arm was wrapped around his waist and his right hand held his face as he thought.

At last, he spoke: "Is this the one that does everything but suck your dick?"

"Yes, but we're working on it," Joe said.

A week later, Joe was back in Florida. He called Ivan in New York and admitted that he didn't think he could go on with Miss X.

"Miss X," said Ivan, "is history."

Joe believed that he had lost all control of his fate. He knew he couldn't stand one more liaison with someone with irons in the fire. Whatever it was that had pushed him from one place to another was not going to push him any farther. He couldn't understand why when he looked within as he had done for so long in his apprenticeship, he found nothing he could use.

Within a week, Ivan came to Florida. He took Joe and Astrid to lunch at a restaurant so heavily air conditioned the windows were fogged.

"It goes like this," Ivan was saying. "Miss X was a classic example of *not* actually having an idea, of trying to synthesize what was already out there. And it was a good synthetic but its prospects were limited and, hey, I don't blame you for being bored by it. At its center was a complete lack of originality. To invent Miss X, I had to turn myself into a committee and it showed."

"I gather the reason you're so cheerful is that you have a better idea," Joe said.

"I looked out and asked myself, What is the one thing that most characterizes our world? What one thing? The answer is 'distrust.' "

Astrid said, "That's true."

So Joe said, "It's true."

"I set myself the task of inventing a machine that addressed itself to distrust, that my Chinese friends could make with microcircuitry, and that I could sell grossly marked up by the carload. A man once told me that the perfect product costs a dime to make, sells for a dollar, and is addictive. This is along the same lines."

41

"What is it?" Joe asked, annoyed by the long buildup.

Ivan lifted his glass. A smile played over his lips as his eyes shot back and forth between Joe and Astrid. "A home lie detector," said Ivan.

"Have you brought it with you?" Astrid asked anxiously.

"Not to worry. It is only a twinkle in my eye. But the projected cash flow on this one looks like a pyramid scheme. It's going to be as universal as television. It's going to shrink white-collar crime. It's going to drive cheating housewives into the streets by the millions. The President and the First Lady will be gangster-slapping each other on the White House lawn after an evening with the product. A worldwide defrocking of priests will stun believers. Fundamentalist preachers will be turned out of their Taj Mahals by the grinning hordes that placed them there. Four officials will remain in Congress, all truthful morons. It will be necessary to staff our hospitals with veterinarians. Farriers will pull teeth. Canned goods will be sold without labels by word of mouth. *America* will stand *revealed*."

"Will this be difficult to operate?" Joe asked feebly. He felt disgraced as Ivan's stooge.

Ivan massaged an imaginary ball in the air in front of him. His delight at Joe's cooperation was boundless. "Difficult to operate! It's only got two buttons: 'true' and 'false'! It's as simple as the cross they crucified Christ on. It's got everything that's been missing from modern life in two eloquent buttons. By the time this baby makes its third pass through the discount stores, it will have produced a cleansing fire. I mean, the little things! The waiter in Fort Lauderdale who hands you three-week-old cod you ordered as snapper and says 'Enjoy.' I mean, you *follow* the sonofabitch to the kitchen and strap this baby onto him—"

"Wait a minute," said Astrid. "Wait a minute, wait a minute, wait a minute. You can't use this thing like a gun. You can't hook a waiter up to a lie detector while you are ordering in a restaurant."

"You will be able to once society has accepted it," said Ivan with a wounded look.

It was at this point that Joe, and maybe Astrid too, realized Ivan had some problems, that the whole idea was not completely reasonable, any more than Miss X was reasonable, and that what they were seeing here was desperation. In fact, when Joe caught Astrid's worried eye, they managed to communicate that some humoring was in order. And for a moment, they enjoyed the closeness that spotting Ivan's disease implied. Then Joe thought, Maybe they're humoring *me*. Ivan and Astrid had developed what was to Joe a cloying camaraderie, a nauseating chumminess that produced periodic bursts of advice, often directed at Joe.

Ivan felt the awkwardness. His volubility had vanished. "The air is so humid," he said.

"You get used to it," Astrid said, as though interpreting the situation, yet sitting back to watch him handle it.

"What do people do around here?" he asked.

"Oh gosh," Joe said, "the usual things."

"Barbecues?" Ivan asked. He was back in control.

"Oh, no. Much more than that. They have movies and their clubs," Joe said, struggling with each of these replies.

"Clubs? Name a club."

"The Moose."

"The Moose? That's a club?"

"Yes."

"That they go to?"

"Yes."

"Do you go to The Moose?"

"No."

"But what do *you* do, Joe?"

"What do I do?"

"Am I putting too much pressure on you?"

"Not at all," Joe said. "But that question is completely hypothetical."

Astrid lit a cigarette. Now she was watching Joe.

"Hypothetical? 'What do you do?' is hypothetical?" Ivan asked.

"I think it is."

"Joe, *no you don't.*"

"You guys mind if I turn that down?" Joe asked, pointing to the air-conditioning register. He held his throat with his thumb and forefinger, swallowing emphatically. "I'm not sure how healthy those things are, actually."

7

Now Joe was seated at the end of a bar. There was a ball game on TV. He looked into the bottom of his glass for a big idea. He was sitting with a guy named Mack thinking about the ranch, about Smitty and Lureen, about his childhood enemy Billy Kelton, about Ellen and old man Overstreet, about the hills and all the moving water. It wasn't just nostalgia; the lease money had quit coming in. And he wasn't getting along with Astrid.

"It's a tie game," Mack said, staring over the silhouetted heads at the screen. "You think you'll go up and see who?"

"My aunt and uncle. They live in our old house in Montana. I might just go on up there."

"Call first," said Mack. "They could be dead."

"Don't you ever feel like seeing your relations?"

"I think it's all this roots thing. My kids go out and tape the locals. I must not be the right guy for this one. It's a little off-speed for me. That's three thousand miles!"

Joe went back to the apartment. Astrid had tied her black hair back with a strip of blue cloth. She smiled at Joe. Something was in the air. Astrid was not a worrier and you couldn't make her worry if it didn't really come to her on her own. She looked at him, held his eye. Silence fell over the room. He came over and kissed her

45

slowly. She was sitting in a chair at the end of the dining table and he was standing over her, kissing her. She undid his pants and held him. When he stopped kissing her, she took him inside her mouth. He had one hand on the back of her head and supported himself with the other on the table. The mail was piled there and most of it was bills. He tried not to acknowledge that he had seen the bills but it was impossible, there were so many of them. He moaned and she sucked harder. He looked at the gas bill. Knowing it would be enormous, he moaned with particular feeling. She gripped his buttocks with both hands and tried to take him in farther. He shuffled the mail with his free fingers and came to a letter from American Express. Surely their card was going to be canceled. A particularly expressive wordless cry came from his lips and Astrid tried for it all. He could feel the irony all the way to the center of his stomach. He stood as long as he could, then sank faintly into a chair.

After a moment, Astrid said, "What do you have in your hand?"

She pulled the crumpled letter from his grasp. Her brow darkened. "They're dropping us, huh?"

"Who?"

"Are you pretending you haven't seen this?"

Joe shook his head.

A peculiar look flickered across Astrid's face. "Has this been a great blow to you?" she asked.

"I can't win," said Joe. The thing was, he loved Astrid. And he could have brought out better things in her than he had. He brought out things in Astrid that were bad and went around disliking her for them. He sat in his chair and mused about his own unfairness as the wind pressed green masses of Florida holly to the window. "My character," he said, "is composed almost strictly of things I hate in other people."

They were under a new pressure. They were going to have to live on less because of Joe's difficulty with his work and the sudden termination of the lease money. None of the explanations Joe received from his Aunt Lureen made sense or persuaded him. He was suspicious that his Uncle Smitty was somehow getting the money from his sister. At first, he'd felt that if it meant enough to them to just take it, they could go ahead and do so. Though it was a technicality, the ranch was in Lureen's name and, as a technical thing, she could do as she pleased. But that was not the understanding she had with Joe's father, blood to blood, and she knew it. On this note, Joe could get indignant. Sometimes it passed. Sometimes it embarrassed him and sometimes the whole thing made him feel guilty. The worst part of it was that Ivan would come to sense that Joe had less choice about whether or not to do his projects. Ivan said it pained him to see an old friend refuse to abandon himself to the fiesta of consumption that was our national life.

Astrid came over and sat next to him. "Don't be so hard on yourself," she said.

"I always promised myself that in the future I would quit living in the future. But I may have to do a little planning now."

"Joe," she said, "why don't you call some friends? I'm going out. I'm tired of this. Or at least, I'm not interested in this. It's time to do something."

Joe made a few calls to people he knew out West. About the time he got off the phone, Astrid was back carrying packages. She set them down, picked up the hall rug, and gave it a pop. She popped the rug as if she was in a bullfight. Joe's mood had sunk even further since he'd been calling around Montana.

The next time Ivan came down from New York, he took them out to dinner. By the time they got to the restaurant, which was situated next to the ocean on its own band of seagrape-shaded beach, the sun had gone down and the sunset watchers had finished their drinks and were heading home for dinner. Astrid wore her hair up, pinned with a rose-colored enamel flower. Joe accompanied her with his hand lightly rested in the pleasant curve in the small of her back. Ivan Slater seemed to be rushing, though he walked no faster than they did. "I hope I'm not late," he said. "I got caught up watching TV,

Oprah Winfrey squeezing the shit out of some little white lady." He wore a blousy Cuban shirt and had rolled his pants up in some ghastly sartorial reference to peasantry; instead of appropriate sandals or huaraches, he wore the lace-up black street shoes of his more accustomed venues in New York. Nevertheless, he bounded along confidently without actually going faster than his companions. He was marketing a thing called "The Old Vermont Dog Mill," which was a treadmill exerciser for overweight suburban labradors that also served to grind coffee and provide the power for a kitchen knife sharpener. It seemed impossible that he didn't see the ridiculousness of this but he didn't; he saw only opportunity. When Joe thought of the developing problems with the grazing lease and imagined he could be reduced to working with Ivan on the Old Vermont Dog Mill, he was chilled deep within.

They got a table on the deck under the seagrapes and immediately began to look into their menus as though they had a job to get through.

"That's not good conch salad," said Joe. "It's chum."

"Don't start in," said Astrid.

"Are stone crabs in season?" asked Ivan.

"Who knows," said Joe. "I don't know."

"The tone is burn-out plus," said Astrid.

"Ivan," said Joe, "why don't you get your own girlfriend? The waiter thinks this is a ménage à trois. Ditto the maitre d'."

"You've asked this same question since our school days."

"Never getting an answer."

"I do have girlfriends but they are never presentable."

"You could present them to us," said Astrid. "We would be prepared to understand almost anything."

"You talk brave," said Ivan.

"We could take them if they were truly awful," Astrid said. "It's the little things that suck."

When their dinners came, there seemed to be almost nothing on the plate. Joe understood that this was in response to current views on cuisine held in France; and of course that helped to justify the price, but Joe was hungry. He tapped the tines of his fork all around the empty areas of his plate as though probing for food. Astrid was annoyed with him and gave him furious looks, and the waiter sighed operatically.

"If you were back in Montana," she said, "undoubtedly they would put a great haunch before you and you would be happier."

"That's right."

There was a whirlwind of activity as Ivan began to eat.

"Joe," said Astrid, "I've been here all my life and you are a classic snowbird. After basking in the sun for a couple of years, you got ironic about everything."

"He's homesick," said Ivan through his food. "When you're homesick and home is three thousand miles away and you're broke and there's a gulf of communication between you and the faggot waiter and the plate is half empty before you half start, your heart is sore afflicted."

"Thank you, Ivan," said Joe.

"You like a quality of care and selection in your life, Joe. I like life bulging at the seams," Ivan said.

"I like it with loud music and hot sauce," said Astrid.

"Because you're Cuban," Joe said.

"That's racist, actually," Astrid said.

"I'm serious, Joe," Ivan said. "Don't be so meticulous. Quit weighing things out. It's neurotic. Man was made to consume. Say yes to fucking well everything."

The waiter looked significantly at Astrid. They were friends. In three years, Joe had not gotten used to Astrid's friends. The waiter accepted the little illness of her hanging around with straight men. A bright wave caught the lights of the restaurant and rolled obliquely onto the beach. The restaurant was beginning to fill. Joe felt the smile on his face fade pleasantly. Astrid put a cigarette in her mouth and waited for Ivan to light it. Joe enjoyed their friendship. He loved the sight of Astrid smoking, while angry people at neighboring tables waved into the air around them.

Astrid's uncompliant nature made her the only woman friend of Ivan's life. Joe watched with approval.

Sexless friendships reminded him of children. Quite lovely until someone whipped it out.

So once again Joe and Ivan were going to work together. Ivan was inspired by this work he was doing; Joe was trying to accept its necessity. At one time he had painted and had some acceptance; but he painted so slowly at the best of times and was so seldom sufficiently moved by an idea that he had to take work that did not depend upon strong feelings. Lately, he wasn't really painting at all. He was trying to "face it," a phrase Astrid found overpoweringly bleak. He told her he had sold out; she said he lacked sufficient mental health to sell out. "I'm going to face it," he said.

"Don't face it, for Christ's sake," she said.

Now Joe watched gloomily as Ivan paid the bill. When the waiter went off with his credit card, Ivan asked, "What's twenty percent of ninety-three dollars?"

Joe groaned.

"Crass!" called Astrid.

Out in front, intensity was building. The hostess had gold-rimmed glasses hanging on her bosom from a chain. She only put them on to check dubious reservations in the big book on the stand. There was a line and Joe was pleased they had eaten early. They walked onto the street where the suave shapes of automobiles, parked on the fallen palm fronds, glowed in the streetlights. The breaking surf could be heard and Joe admitted to himself the tremendous romance this seemed to imply, though it always seemed to remain in the world of implication. He felt like an old steer with its head under the fence straining for that grass just over there.

They got into Ivan's rental car. Ivan did not start it up immediately. The streetlight shining through the coconut palms lit up all six of their knees. "Joe," Ivan said, "you're very quiet. And I know you, Joe. You are my friend since we stood shoulder to shoulder in the school lavatory popping zits, betting our pride on the hope of hitting the mirror. But this quiet, this looking off, is a calm before the storm, which I know and have seen before, Joe. I only ask that you remember a few commitments and that you be a gentleman about it, if it kills you. I say all this knowing it may be well out of reach for you."

Ivan looked straight ahead through the windshield. Joe looked straight ahead through the windshield. Astrid looked at Joe.

Joe said, "Start it up."

8

In offering Joe the use of her car the next morning, a small pink convertible, Astrid had naively said to get a pound of snapper fillets and a choice of two vegetables and Joe had said he'd be back in a minute. Now clouds settled in the upper curve of the windshield, slowly wiped around, and disappeared. The yellow center line ticked in the side mirror. Lizards and tropical foliage managed to survive in the atmosphere of a New York subway. The traffic on the great divided parkway moved at a trancelike evenness maintained by the Florida Highway Patrol. He wanted to keep moving in case Astrid reported her car stolen.

In the end it was a day that was missing from Joe's life. He didn't turn on the radio until he left his motel near Pensacola the next morning. He realized he was about to hit the real torso of America and his spirits rose. He crossed into Alabama and took a few minutes out to view an arts and crafts fair in a vast baking parking lot. It was as if a thousand garages had been emptied onto a runway. Solemn people stood behind tables that held wan attempts at art in oil and ceramics and a twentieth-century history of appliances. Portraits of Elvis on black velvet. He pulled out onto the highway and resumed, having to go very slow for a mile until he could pass a pickup truck full of yellow lawn chairs. Battered, rusted cars passed with hard faces framed by Beatles-type haircuts. It seemed that before he even reached the Mississippi line, the sky had begun to grow, to widen: at the Escatawpa River the pines strained upward against a terrific expanse of blue sky. The highway was empty. The clouds stretching down to the horizon majestically ruled the scene. Joe was filled with a mad sense of freedom, free to eat fast food, free to sleep with a stranger. Instead of solving his problems, he had become someone without problems, a kind of ghost.

He passed a little bayou where a young fellow in knee-length surfer shorts covered with beer commercials watched a bobber rest on the mirror surface of water. This plain scene held a great mystery for him. There was a lovely waterland around the Pascagoula River with silver curves showing through the sea grass for a great distance while the road crossed in low, loping arcs. He stopped and watched fishermen unloading crab boats. He walked down and sat on a broken-off piling. A woman handed an old fisherman a pint of whiskey in a paper bag. She said, "If you beat me up like you did last weekend, I ain't going to buy you no more of that." Joe heard this with amazement.

He went to sleep in a motel. Outside in the parking lot, a couple leaned up against their car and listened to James Cotton sing the blues. "I don't like white and white don't like me." Joe thought about that as he lay in bed. He couldn't quite understand why, lying in this unknown motel in this unknown place, he felt such a desperate joy.

At seven in the morning, he was rolling through Danville Parish, Louisiana. Pine forests stood on the high ground between the bayous, pine pollen filling the air so that the car was covered with pollen and the air was so heavy with pollen there were times he thought he ought to turn on the headlights to see. But rush hour in Shreveport was different from other rush hours, the thickness of humidity, the crazy songs on the radio, flirtation between speeding automobiles. Secession had worked! The marquee in front of the Louisiana State Fairground announced county pig champions and English rock and roll bands. The radio advertised bass boats, fire ant control potions and the Boot Hill Racetrack.

Joe thought that crossing into Texas and getting past the Red River would give him the feeling of being back out West but it didn't happen. The thunderstorms lashed the highway and it still looked like Louisiana with all the gums and hickories and tupelos. A home repair truck passed with a sign on its side that said, "Obsessed to serve the customer." Nothing halfway about the South. Someone shot up behind Joe in a little Japanese car, face pressed against the windshield, passed, then lost his motivation. Roostertailing through the rainwater, Joe had to pass him again. The cloudburst intensified and a mile or two down the road toward Longview, Texas, a pickup truck went into sideways slow motion, slid across the meridian and went into the ditch. Three men got out and stared at it. These men seemed to feel their pickup owed them an explanation. Once he reached Longview, he could see back to the thunderstorm, see its grand and sculptural shape, its violent black underside. The radio said they were glad about the rain because it would keep the pollen down and people could get some relief from their allergies and wasn't that what people wanted, some relief? Joe liked it for the feeling of dropping a curtain between him and the past, a welcome curtain. This was the highway and he was a ghost. It was a relief.

Somewhere past the Sabine River, Joe started to spot the little oil patches, the active ones with bright painted pumps, bobbing away and pumping oil. And oil patches that had seen better days, with their pumps stopped and the paint rusted off like a field full of giant grasshoppers that had died or reached some eerie state beyond normal death. The radio had used the phrase "nuclear winter" and increasingly Joe was relying on the radio to shape his thoughts. He was still thinking about fire ants. Fire ants in the nuclear winter.

Van Zandt, Texas, was blushing green in a deeply wooded succession of gentle, rolling woodlands. For thirty-five seconds, Joe ached to live there. Then by Terrell, glad to no longer live in Van Zandt, he was out of the woodlands and in an ugly cattle country that looked like Iowa where there were no fire ants and pollen and mulattoes in convertibles, and no race music on the radio. Joe went blank and stayed that way until he came over a big long ascent and there below him was a cloud of mesquite and telegraph wires and glittering buildings. The hard angles of light on each surface seemed to communicate that the West had begun and he was on his way home. The sky picked up the white edges of the ravines, rocks and subdivisions equally. The skyscrapers cheerfully said, "We see you passing, you ghost! So long, Joe-Buddy!" This was Dallas!

There was a perfect Texan urban river bottom at Grand Prairie with scrub willows whose roots gathered trash in the flash floods that shot through new neighborhoods. Joe was maddened by joy at being in the country of the West. He felt that he would find a restored coordination for his life here. This was the West's job. Gustav Mahler of all people was on the radio. Great Southwest Parkway! Lone Star Homes! Texas Toyota! A subdivision of multifarious grandeur, half-timbered Tudor homes baking in the dry air and clinging to the hillsides. A sign in front read *From the 80's.* Joe could not understand the message because he thought they were talking about the decade of these homes; then he realized they meant the price of the units. Holy fire ants! Little places like that?

He crossed the Trinity River in a bright sun that made approaching traffic flash its windshields in a stream of glitter, along the edge of the Fort Worth stockyards. A radio preacher shouted, "Satan is playing hardball!"

On an awful-looking scrapped-off former mesquite flat north of Fort Worth, he passed "Fossil Creek, The Community on the Green. Next right, Blue Mound, Texas." Getting on toward Wichita Falls, the radio briefly stilled, there began to be well-kept ranches, lots of horses, the houses on elevations with windmills to catch the breeze and fanciful entryways welded together out of rod and angle iron. Fetishistic paved driveways. There were things here in Texas that made Joe nervous, but he blamed it on whatever produced that radio religion, fire and brimstone delivered at a nice dance tempo.

It began to grow stormy looking and the conflict of spring and winter produced a cascading immensity of light that Joe felt levitate him as he drove in and out of vast shadows. State Highway Department trucks were ignited from within by a tremendous yellow light. The signs shone fiercely at him with their brusque messages. Railroad track crews were lit up like the cast of a Broadway show. A windy squall separated itself from the general pattern and arose before him like a dead king in an opera. A battered farm truck passed with a tuxedo hanging in the rear window. There were flattened armadillos on the road. The weather looked worrisome—worrisome and bad enough to drive him back to Astrid. Or, if it wasn't for the awkwardness of driving her car, he could have given her a call. He could have said, "I'm en route!"

So, he stopped at Henrietta and ate pinto beans and corn bread and listened to a distant kitchen radio issue fairly dire weather forecasts. The restaurant had wooden booths and a few young men in work clothes sat sideways in them with their arms over the back and spoke in courtly tones to the black-haired, aging waitress.

Back on the road, Joe saw at a considerable distance the British flag emblazoned on a solitary billboard. But when he drew close, it turned out to be an ad for Beech-Nut chewing tobacco. Tumbleweed blew furiously across the road near an old brick high school that stood like a depressing fortress against the distant horizon and slate, moving clouds. There were cotton fields and, here and there, cotton wagons were drawn up on the side roads. The sign in Quanah said, "Stop and Eat with Us. Willie Nelson Did." Joe noted that the goofy faces of the Deep South, the tragic and comic masks donned down there, had been replaced by a kind of belligerent stare. The highway signs said, "Don't Mess with Texas." It didn't look too damn friendly out there. Maybe it was the weather.

Right after he crossed the Prairie Dog Town Fork of the Red River a train approached from a distance. When it came close, all that was visible was its windshield; the rest was a vast blowing mound of snow and ice. What's going on here? Turn on the radio, my friend. He got another preacher, this one explaining that the mind does not work the exact-same as a Disposall and we cannot grind up the filth that goes into it. We must be careful not to put filth into it in the first place.

Suddenly, he was driving on a solid corrugation of ice in a whiteout. It just dropped from the heavens and put an end to visibility. He hunched over the wheel as though to examine the road even more closely than he could in a normal seated position. The outer world was filled with phantom vehicles, some floating by at eye level, others sunk to one side plainly disabled. A human silhouette arose and vanished. It was terrifying. It was a regular bad dream. He thought, I am being punished for stealing, for doubting the truthfulness of my aunt and uncle in withholding my lease money, for not painting and for walking out on a good woman.

He came up behind a twenty-year-old luxury sedan heaving along sedately. He clove to that sedan. It had a bumper sticker that said *XIT Ranch Reunion* and Joe tried to tag it as it appeared and disappeared in the snow. He passed an old tractor-trailer rig full of fenceposts and woven wire jackknifed in the ditch. Then he lost the sedan; it seemed to dematerialize in the whiteness and he was alone. He slowed to ten miles an hour and felt his insides labor against the white indefinite distance before him.

A fashion center for babies was advertising on the radio. They had a special for those hard-to-shop-for preemies. Including diapers for their little thumb-size bottoms. Then all of a sudden, a great miracle occurred, simultaneous with news of these glorious infants. The sun came out on a perfect world in the middle of which, surrounded by hysterical people, a Greyhound Vista-Cruiser lay on its side: red, white, and blue with tinted windows, in the ditch. Joe crept by in case he was needed, but the passengers were having their moment as they watched the driver set out orange cautionary cones, and they didn't seem to need or want Joe, who had not been with them when it happened but rather with the well-dressed babies of the radio.

A little way past the town of Goodnight, he could see cattle running the fenceline in wild amazement at nature. A truck went by like the home repair truck back in Louisiana but this one said, "Don't sleep with a drip—Call a plumber!" The day was almost done. Joe flew through the slush to Amarillo, took a room, ate in a Japanese restaurant and went to bed. He felt like he was breaking his back trying to get through Texas. This ghost wanted to go home.

9

The next day, before he was fully awake, before he had had any opportunity for banishing thoughts, he was in Cimarron County, Oklahoma, where the wind blew so hard the shadows flew on the roadway and where, stopping on the edge of a plowed field, he had to lean backward into the wind to take a leak and even then it just sprayed from his dick like sleet. The radio said that Kansas steer prices were down because several of the packing plants had been closed by blizzards. Joe drove on. Near the horizon, there was the most overcrowded feedlot of Black Angus cattle Joe had ever seen. He stared at it until he overtook what turned out to be a vast depot of worn-out automobile tires, extending over many acres.

He began to see mountains and his spirit rose with the accumulating altitude, kept climbing until it sank again around Monument Hill and new snow and population; finally he was in the Denver rush hour, which caused him to sink into complete apathy as he took his place in the teeming lanes.

He cleared out of north Denver, traffic thinning about the time he passed a vast illuminated dog track, amazing against the darkening Front Range. It was dark and wild and cold after that, after the St. Vrain River and the Wyoming line. A genuine ground blizzard was falling by the time he got to Cheyenne, so he stopped at a place called

Little America, the home of fifty-five gas pumps, and slept like a baby, knowing all that gasoline was out there. There was enough gasoline for a homesick person to drive home millions of times. Joe was hugely annoyed to have had this thought.

He was gone before daybreak, following a Haliburton drilling equipment truck with a sign on its rear that said it braked for jackalope. Joe's sense of mission had reached a burning pitch and he tailgated the big rig over sections of road varnished by the manure that ran out of the cattle trucks. The two vehicles went down through Wyoming in a treacherous eighty mile an hour syncopation.

Wheatland, Wyoming, had sentimental Spanish haciendas out in the windswept tank farm at the edge of the sage. A somber and detached-looking herd of buffalo stared out at the highway across five strands of barbed wire. Tonight was going to be Olde Southe Gumbo Night at the restaurant in Douglas where Joe released the Haliburton truck and stopped for breakfast. There was an array of condiments that suggested people ate at all hours here. Joe examined the salad dressing. It looked like the styling gel in a beauty parlor. Buddy Holly sang "True Love Waits" from a red and chrome speaker at the end of his booth. While he ate, the sun burst out like a hostile and metallic stunt. Beyond the window, the land of the jackalope shone under a burnishing wind.

Back on the highway, a sheriff's car shot past with a little gray-haired prisoner in the back. Joe drove until he reached Kaycee, not much more than a small depression in the ground east of the highway: gas station, quonset buildings, a few houses. He stopped and bought some homemade elk sausage from a man he knew there. He was getting close.

The Tongue River was green and low and clear. It was the last thing he noticed until he crossed into Montana. At Crow Agency a sign said, "Jesus Is Lord on the Crow Reservation." Loose horses were also Lord on the Crow reservation. An ambulance tore off down a dirt road, its red light throbbing like a severed artery.

Three hours later he drove through his old hometown,

Deadrock. He took a left by the switching yard and took the dirt road south toward the ranch. He followed the river bottom back to his house. Before long, the cottonwoods would make a cloudy tunnel for the racing stream but they were just now beginning to leaf out; and where the stream broadened out and flowed in flat pastures, its every turn was marked by an even growth of willows. The light flashed on the shallow streams that fed the river where they emerged from their grassy tunnels; and in the marshy stands of cattail, blackbirds jumped up and showered down once again. A rancher went alongside the road, a great fat man on a small motorcycle. He had his shovel and fabric dams lashed behind him and his felt hat pulled down so firmly against the wind that it bowed his ears out. A small collie lay across his lap as he sputtered along. Some of the fields had great splashes of pasture ruining yellow spurge. The ditch bank along the road was a garden of early spring wild flowers, shooting stars, forget-me-nots, lupine. Snow still lay collected in the shade. You couldn't really tell you had left one ranch and gone onto another. A cattle guard marked the actual boundary but the rolling country was the same in every direction. The house sat down in some trees, old trees that were splotched with dead branches. There was a seasonal creek underneath the trees but it had dried up now into nothing but a wash. A half-acre had been fenced to enclose the place but the cattle had beaten the ground down right to the boundaries.

The door was unlocked. Joe went in and looked around. There wasn't much for furnishings but there was enough. There was a woodstove, an old Frigidaire, and two army blankets on the bunk. The toilet bowl was stained with iron but it worked. Someone had fixed the well. There was a table in the kitchen. And the phone worked. Not owning or even caring about any of it made this seem blissful. His nights wouldn't be interrupted by bad dreams. It was going to be all right.

10

When Joe's father began leasing the pasture to the Overstreets, the ranch began to go downhill. The house started toward its present moldering state; the fences were kept in what minimal condition would hold cattle but where the property adjoined the lessors, the fences were allowed to fall and be walked into the ground by herds of cows. The pastures were eaten down year after year until the buck brush, wild currants and sage had begun to advance across their surfaces, with the result that the carrying capacity dropped and with it, the grazing fees. Evaporation from the stripped ground reduced the discharge of the good springs to trickles; the marginal springs had long since been milled to mud by cattle and finally the mud itself had dried up and sealed the springs. But the worst problems of the ranch existed at the level of paper, where liens and assumptions clouded its title.

At first, it hadn't mattered. Joe had had a good enough career painting; he had found handy equivalents with Ivan Slater and others, all somewhat in anticipation of his desire to resume his work.

Joe had sometimes felt that it would be a great relief to give up on recovering his talent; and now he was facing, in the confines of approaching maturity, the fact that he was broke and there was nothing new, nothing at the edge of things, nothing around the corner that would save him. He hoped he wouldn't soon be known as the man who evicted his own kinfolk from their ancestral pasturage.

Joe had come to believe from reading books that in many landholding families, there existed perfect communication between the generations about the land itself. He noticed how many Southerners believed this. Even if they were in New York there was always a warmhearted old daddy holding out for their possession and occupancy an ancient farm—viewed as a sacred tenure on earth rather than agriculture—whenever they should choose to take it up. Price of admission? Take a few minutes, after the soul-stirring train ride down yonder, to make friends with the resident darkies. Where had people gone wrong in the West? In the latest joke, leaving a ranch to one's children was called child abuse. But Joe couldn't really take that view. He had to go see Lureen and straighten things out.

It had gotten too quiet in the neighborhood. There used to be a roar of roller skates on the sidewalk. The small garage next to the house was empty. It had once held his Uncle Smitty's Ford, a car he called his "foreign car." "It's foreign to me," Smitty explained. Many years ago, Smitty came home from the war. He never left after that.

Joe walked around to the side entrance of the house, the only one anyone had ever used. The front door opened onto a hallway and then into a large sitting room that was reserved for the high ceremonies of the day. He remembered how the furniture was kept covered, dreadful shapes, the drapes drawn until life could resume on a special occasion. Children, who were allowed every liberty in the other rooms, including the right to bay down the laundry chute, build matchstick rockets, and even play in the avalanche of coal in the cellar, were frightened in this room. Joe's grandmother sat for weeks here after her husband died as though the dream of respectability they had shared was alive in its sad furnishings, its curio cabinet, its damask-covered love seat and its solitary volume of Elizabeth Barrett Browning. When the silence of his grandmother's mourning overpowered the rest of the family, Joe was sent to see her. She sat with her hands in her lap and her feet crossed under her chair. He moved to her side and she didn't respond. He knew he had to say something but he could smell new rain on the sidewalk and know that already things were going on that consigned his grandfather to the past. His mind moved to that miracle. "I was wondering," he mused, in his little-old-man style, "if Grandpa happened to leave me any gold." Joe's grandmother stared, and began to laugh. She laughed for minutes while he examined the postcards, fossils and pressed flowers in the curio cabinet, ignoring her laugh and thinking about the curiosities and the miracle of rain, of opportunities beyond the funereal door. There was a ring of keys fused together by fire that he held in awe. His grandmother got up and looked around as though recovering from a spell. She walked straight back into her life, revitalized by the cold musing of a child.

Joe knocked. In a moment the door opened and there stood his Aunt Lureen in a blue flowered dress and white coat sweater. She held her face, compressed her cheeks, and cried, "He's back!" A cloud crossed her face. The sight of Joe seemed to produce a hundred contradictory thoughts.

"Yes," Joe said. "I'm back, all right!" For some reason, he whistled. A maladroit quality of enthusiasm seemed to penetrate the air and the sharp whistling brought it up to pitch.

Joe hugged Lureen—she was small and strong—and followed her self-effacing step into the house with its wooden smells, its smells of generations of work clothes and vagaries of weather, of sporting uniforms and overcoats, straight into the vast kitchen which more than anything recalled the thriving days when they had watched game shows from behind TV trays. Joe's oldest memory was of his Uncle Smitty standing up in his army uniform and announcing, "I for one am proud to be an American." Joe had a photograph of Smitty from his army days, a hard young face that seemed to belong to the '40s, the collar of his officer's tunic sunk into his neck, Joe's grandparents beaming at him. There was nothing in that picture to hint that little would go right for Smitty.

Aunt Lureen carried the tea tray into the dining room. You could see the drop of the street to the trestle for a train that used to cancel talk in its roaring traverse. She had never married, never even had a beau. She had radiated duty from the beginning, a duty which lay basically elsewhere, a broad, sexless commitment to vagary, that is, to others.

"Weren't you an angel to come see us," said Lureen, staring with admiration. Joe poured the tea, thinking, That's just a pleasant formality and of course there is no need for me to reply specifically. Around them the halls and rooms seemed to express a detailed emptiness. "What have you been doing, Joe?" The words of these questions fell like stones dropped into a deep well. Joe thought if he could just get some conversational rhythm going, this wouldn't be such a strain. He had long since lost his nerve to ask about the lease.

"I've been on the road. That's about all I've got to say for myself."

"Doing what?"

"Little deal going there with the space program." What a childish lie! The space program was all he could think of about Florida. That and coconuts. If he had been doing anything there, he wouldn't be here. He had struck a void but he could scarcely tell her he no longer knew what he was doing.

"How did you enjoy working in the space program?"

"Well, I got out in one piece," said Joe. He thought this peculiar reference to himself in an atmosphere which included the explosion of a space shuttle would add solemnity to this occasion. In the world of coconuts, there would be no real parallel. But Lureen missed the gravity of his remark. She bent over in laughter. It was as if he had picked coconuts after all. How painful it was!

Everything was magnified. Lureen's chaste little paintings were on the wall. It had been her escape during decades of school teaching; the bouquets, the curled-up kittens, the worn-out slippers next to the pipe and pouch, the waterfall, all made a kind of calendar of her days. Her pictures reflected her tidy view of a family life she hadn't had.

Smitty could be heard coming in through the kitchen, a lurching, arhythmic tread on the old wooden floor, whistling "Peg o' My Heart." Then he roared; but this was from afar, a great and bitterly insincere braying. His appearance was anticlimactic, his carefully combed auburn hair, his ironic face, his handsomely tailored but not so clean blue suit, making one wonder as he appeared in the parlor, who *did* roar in the next room, surely not this person whose face swam with indecision. Smitty had spent many years now in what he called "study" and his shabby-genteel presence was entirely invented. What had become of the hard-faced soldier of the '40s?

"Joe, my God it's you."

"Home at last."

"A good tan, I see."

"Pretty hot."

"Your late lamented father could have used a trip or two to the Sun Belt. He might have lived longer."

Joe didn't say anything in reply.

"But when you've pulled yourself up by your bootstraps, palm trees seem to be thin stuff. Will you join me for a drink?"

"Not right now. Lureen and I are having a visit."

"Ah," said Smitty. "Then this must be my stop."

Smitty suggested by sheer choreography that an appointment awaited him. When he'd gone, Joe said, "Smitty hasn't changed."

"No, we can count on Smitty."

"Has he gone out for a drink?"

"It won't amount to much. No money."

"Well, that's good," said Joe, making the remark as minimal as possible. A quick look of annoyance crossed Lureen's face. There was something here Joe couldn't quite follow. He felt like a parasite. He might as well have said, "Smitty is drinking the lease."

Lureen said, "We've done the best we could."

Smitty stuck his red face in the doorway. "Joe, may I see you a moment?" The face hung there until it was confirmed Joe would come.

Joe got up and followed him into the parlor. There was a small desk with a leather panel in its top and a chair behind it. Smitty pulled an armchair up for Joe and seated himself opposite, at the desk. He was agitated as he drew some old forms out of the drawer and placed them on the desk top. Joe could hear children bouncing a rubber ball off the side of the house. Lureen would attend to them shortly. She viewed children as other people view horse-flies. Her gentleness disappeared in their presence. They feared her instinctively. Joe heard the shout and the ball bouncing stopped.

"Joe," Smitty said, "I'm right in the middle of a deal that will produce my fortune. We make our own luck, don't you agree? It's funny that after years in the insurance business I should have come up with this! But to my own astonishment I find myself getting into seafood, which is all the rage in this diet-conscious time, shrimp to be exact, Gulf Coast shrimp which I am going to import into Montana! Et cetera, et cetera, but anyway, do you have life insurance?" Smitty clasped his hands on top of the papers in the manner of a concerned benefactor. "I know it's a far cry from shrimp!"

"No."

"Can you appreciate that I am an agent for American Mutual? That is, until that mountain of crustaceans begins rolling North!"

"No, actually, Uncle Smitty, I didn't know that."

"Well, I am. And while I disapprove of nepotism, the smoke-filled room and scratching one another's backs, I am in a position to enhance the advantages you already possess by virtue of your youth." He began to write on one of the forms. "I think I can spell your name," he chuckled. "Don't worry, lad! You're not buying life insurance! And I can find out from Lureen what you're using for an address these days!" Joe began to relax again. "This is just a request to quote you some rates, which will be mailed to your home, sometime . . . hence." He folded up the papers decisively and placed them back in the drawer.

"Thank you," said Joe in a wave of relief.

"You, sir, are welcome."

"I look forward to going over those rates."

"At your leisure, at your leisure. I'm certainly in no rush, what with an avalanche of pink headed my way from the Texas coast!"

Joe clapped his hands on his knees preparatory to rising.

"Shall we?"

"One small matter," Smitty said. Joe froze. "The rather small matter, of the filing fee."

Joe slapped at his pants pockets. "I'm not sure I—"

"Have your wallet? I can help there. You do have it. And the filing fee, which is nominal by any civilized standards and which does not begin to recompense me for the time I will have to put in, comes to twenty dollars."

Joe got his wallet out. He peered at the bills like a timid card player.

"There's one!" said Smitty, plucking a twenty into midair. He was immediately on his feet, an expression not of triumph but of horrible relief on his face. "With any luck, and assuming you pass the physical, you will be able to direct a windfall to an heir of your choice. In your generation, where the act of procreation has been reduced to a carnival, you might have your hands full picking a favorite! And now I excuse myself." He shot out the door.

When Joe returned to his aunt, she said, "Did you give him any money?"

"I'm afraid I did."

"Well," she said, "I'm sure he needed it for something important."

It was a formality with Lureen, when short of other topics or in any way embarrassed, to deplore Montana's failing industries. She started in today on the collapse of the cattle industry, the ill effects of the Texas and Midwestern feedlots, the evils of hedging and the betrayal of the agricultural family unit by Secretary of Agriculture Earl Butz. She attacked the usurious practices of the Burlington Northern Railroad, the victimization of the Golden Triangle wheat man and the sabotage of the unions by neo-fascist strawmen posing as shop stewards. It took her out of herself, out of her meekness; and it made Joe extraordinarily uncomfortable to watch her form a timid oratory behind this array of facts. When she was through, she folded her hands like a child who has just finished playing a piece on the piano.

Joe tried to look out the window, anywhere.

"Joe, right after you got back, Mr. Overstreet announced that he was dropping his lease with us," Lureen said.

"I wondered where it went. My check hasn't come in a long time."

"Even before that, we, Smitty and I, had got into some, uh, some projects. Which we expect will do just fine. I don't know what came over Mr. Overstreet. We've had that arrangement for *so* long."

"Well, who else can you get?"

"I really don't know. Overstreets have us surrounded. I really don't know who else would want it. It's kind of unhandy. And the grass is good this year. I'd even buy the yearlings if someone would run them for me." Joe was paralyzed by sudden excitement.

"You mean, you'd need someone to just run the place for a while?" Joe asked.

"Now that Overstreets have let it go, I really don't know anyone out there I could ask. Do you have any ideas?"

"I'll do it!" Joe said. "Let me do that."

"Would you really?"

Smitty banged through the kitchen and entered the room once again but with an air of tremendous renewal. Joe was frustrated. Smitty had donned what seemed to Joe to be a fairly astounding outfit: two-tone leather evening slippers and a jacket of English cut, a kind of round-shouldered smoking jacket in pearl gray wool, tied with a royal red sash. He had a drink in his hand and a large book, which he reached over to Joe. He sat down in a Windsor chair next to Lureen, lacing his fingers around the drink and resting his chin on his chest while his eyes burned in Joe's direction. In this cheap house, in a modest town, he had achieved a tone of specious artifice usually available only to the very successful. Joe felt the excitement, the need to be wary.

"This is a book," Smitty intoned, then seemed to lose his train of thought. "This, sir, is a book," he began again.

"I see that it is," Joe said.

Smitty delivered a weary sigh, Lord Smitty peering from a dizzying aerie.

"It is Roget's"—what satisfaction it seemed to give him to intone the two voluptuous vowels of "Roget's"!— *"Thesaurus."* This last was said with such abrupt concussion it was like a sneeze. "And it is a gift from me . . . to you."

"Thank you," said Joe.

"Here is how Roget's Thesaurus is to be employed. First look up the key words you wish to use. They will all be big ones. But this book will tell you the *little plain words* that *little plain people* like your aunt and I know and in this way you will be able to make yourself understood to us. Neither of us is in the space program."

"I expect it will come in very handy," said Joe. He reached out and accepted the book from Smitty's hands. Smitty gazed at him with what looked like all the world to be hatred, then made another of his formal departures, raising a forefinger to level one of Lureen's watercolors.

"I wonder what brought that on," said Joe. A sharp tinkling sound was heard repeatedly from the direction of the kitchen, almost the sound of Christmas decorations falling from the tree. Joe looked at his aunt; she looked back. They headed for the kitchen. There they found Smitty with a tray poised over one shoulder like a waiter. It held a quantity of crystal stemware that had belonged to Joe's mother. With his free hand Smitty took up each glass by its base and hurled it to the floor, where it burst. His auburn hair was flung out in every direction and it reminded Joe of some old picture of the devil.

With a pixieish expression, Smitty's gaze moved from Joe to Lureen and then back. He held a glass by its stem.

He paused. He turned his eyes to the glass. In slow motion, the glass inverted and began its descent to the floor. Joe watched. It seemed to take a very long time and then it became a silver star to the memory of Joe's mother. It disappeared in the debris of its predecessors. Smitty sent the remainder of the glasses to the floor with a motion like a shot-putter, even tipping up on one slippered toe. Then he relaxed. Nothing had happened really, had it? All for the best, somehow. Still, thought Joe, it makes for a rather long evening.

"Why don't I show you your room," said Lureen, "and we can get caught up on our rest." Because it had become ridiculous to let this pass without remark, she lowered her voice to say that "everyone," meaning Smitty, had problems which Joe couldn't be expected to understand because he hadn't been around. Smitty stood right there and listened blithely.

"Taking this all in?" Joe asked Smitty quietly.

"Mm-hm."

"You know," Lureen mused desperately, "Duffy's Fourth of July at Flathead Lake was a hundred years ago." Joe had no idea what to do with that one other than take it as an obscure family reference intended to restore the intimacy she had withdrawn. Duffy's Fourth of July at Flathead Lake. What was that?

"Joe doesn't know what you're talking about," sang Smitty. Then he turned to Joe. "You are among friends," he said gravely. "Think of it: your own flesh and blood." He leaned his weight in the pockets of his robe like an old trainer watching his racehorses at daybreak. All his gestures seemed similarly detached from his surroundings. Smitty walked up to the barometer and gave the glass a tap. This seemed to give him his next idea. "I think I'll head for my quarters now," he said. "The artillery has begun to subside. Another day tomorrow. One more colorful than the other."

When Smitty left the room, humming "The Caissons Go Rolling Along," a queer tension set in. Joe knew now his arrival was an invasion, his presence abusive. He thought of making up alarming lies about the space program, ones he could deliver tearfully, accounts of loyal Americans shredded by titanium and lasers. If some sort of guilt based on an unimpeachable national purpose could be held over Lureen, possibly this miserable tone could be altered. "I delivered the little things to the space shuttle that made it a home, the nail clippers, the mois-turizers, the paperbacks, the tampons . . ."

But the tension didn't last. He went back into the kitchen and helped her clean up the broken glass. Lureen held the dustpan. Joe tried to sweep carefully without letting the straws of the broom spring and scatter bits of crystal. He wanted to ask Lureen why she stood for it, but he didn't. They swept all around the great gas stove. As Joe knelt to hold the dustpan, he saw that its pipes had been disconnected. It was a dummy, a front for the mean little microwave next to the toaster.

"A service for twenty," Lureen said, referring to the broken crystal. "Who in this day and age needs a service for twenty?" A laugh of astonishment. Who indeed! My mother needed it, Joe thought. From each window of the kitchen, each except the one that opened on the tiny yard, could be seen the clapboard walls of the neighboring houses, the shadows of clotheslines just out of sight above, duplexes that used to be family homes. A service for twenty! They laughed desperately. How totally out of date! And finally, how removed from the space program! I don't feel so good, he thought.

"Joe, Smitty and I have made not such a bad life for ourselves here," Lureen said after they finished cleaning up. "We never have gotten used to the winters. And you know what we talk about? Hawaii. It's funny how those things start. Arthur Godfrey used to have a broadcast from Honolulu. He had a Hawaiian gal named Holly Loki on the show. Smitty and I used to listen. We kind of formed a picture. Someday, we thought . . . Hawaii! Well, Joe, let's really do call it a day." Lureen led him up the narrow wood stairs to the second floor. Joe tried to think of surf, a ukulele calling to him from the night-shrouded side of a sacred volcano, of outrigger canoes. He tried to put Smitty and Lureen in this scene and he just couldn't. Nothing could uproot them from their unhappy home. Not even a no-holds-barred luau.

Joe's old room looked onto a narrow rolling street. Lureen wanted him to spend the night before going back to the ranch in the morning. You could make out the railroad bridge and the big rapid river beyond. There was a stand next to his door with a pitcher of water on it. Joe's bed had been turned back. The room was sparely furnished with a small desk where Lureen stored her things: paper clips, Chapsticks, pencils. Joe pulled open the drawer as he'd loved to do thirty years before to smell the camphor from the Chapsticks. The pencils were in hard yellow bundles, the paper clips in small green cardboard boxes. The train went over the bridge like a comet, the little faces in the lighted windows racing through their lives. Joe's father had been raised here; his uncles had gone to two world wars from here; educations and paper routes and bar examinations had been prepared for in the kitchen here. Everyone rushing for the end like the people on the train. Smitty came home from the war after a booby trap had killed his best friend and stayed drunk for two years in the very room he occupied now. Joe's father used to say, "I went over too." And Smitty would say, "You didn't go over where I went over."

"Good night," said Lureen. Family business had worn her out. Instead of acknowledging her exhaustion, she had nominated Hawaii, whose blue-green seas would wash her all clean.

"Good night, Aunt Lureen," Joe sang out with love.

Joe stretched out in the dark, under the covers of the squeaking iron bed. He had slept here off and on his whole life. But now he felt like someone trying to hold a tarp down in the wind. He smoked in the dark. It was perfect. Smoking meant so much more now that he knew what it did to him. But in the dark it was perfect. He could see the cloud of his smoke rise like a ghost.

He must have fallen asleep because when he heard Smitty's voice, it was its emphasis that startled him; he had not heard what had gone on before. "For God's sake, Lureen, we're in a brownout! Keep the shade drawn."

73

Joe struck a match and looked at the dial of the loud clock ticking away beside him. It was after midnight. A husky laugh from Smitty rang through the upstairs, a man-of-action laugh. Joe had to have a look.

Lureen's room at the end of the hall was well lighted. Smitty and Lureen stood in its doorway like figures on a bandstand. Smitty wore his lieutenant's uniform and impatiently flipped his forage cap against his thigh. "We move at daybreak," he said.

"The bars closed an hour ago," said Lureen wearily.

"We pour right in behind the tanks and stay there until we get to Belgium," he insisted.

"Smitty," said Lureen, "I heard the radio! Truman said it's over!"

Smitty scrutinized his sister's features. "Can you trust a man who never earned the job? Harry The Haberdasher never-earned-the-job."

"You can trust the radio!" Lureen cried. Smitty stared back.

"I should have listened, Lureen. I should have listened to you. The nation has probably taken to the streets. Am I still welcome?" Their figures wavered in the sprawling light.

"The most welcome thing in the world," said Lureen in a voice that astonished Joe with its feeling. Smitty gave her a hug. Joe watched and tried to understand and was choked by the beauty of their embrace. He wondered why he was so moved by something he couldn't understand.

11

This sale yard was a place ranchers took batches of cattle too small to haul to the public yard in Billings. You didn't go here in a cattle truck; you went in the short-range stock truck in all the clothes you owned because the cab heater went out ten years ago. Some went pulling a gooseneck trailer behind the pickup. You could unload either at one of the elevated chutes or at the ground-level Powder River Gate, which opened straight into a holding pen where the yard men, usually older ranchers who had gone broke or were semiretired, sorted and classed the cattle for that day's sale. Joe stopped and looked back out into the pens to get an idea of the flow of cattle. It looked pretty thin and there was a cold rain blowing over everything. The yard men leaned on their long prods and stared out across the pens into nowhere.

Joe went inside. A secretary typed away, filling out forms, and Bob Knowles, the yard owner, manned the counter. Through a pane of glass behind his head, the sale ring could be seen as well as the small wood podium from which the auctioneer called the sale and directed his stewards to the buyers. Bob Knowles had been here since the years Joe and his family were still on the ranch. He peered at Joe with a smile.

"How long you back for this time?" he asked.

"Damned if I know. But Lureen lost her lease. I told

75

her I'd watch some yearlings for her this summer. She had a grass deal with Overstreet and he dropped her. How's it look for today?"

"Dribs and drabs," said Bob, lifting his feed-store cap to smooth back his sandy hair. "All day long. What are you looking for?"

"Grass cattle, but everyone's got so much hay left over."

"That's it. We just don't have the numbers," Bob said. Joe completely trusted Bob and moreover, he didn't want to hang around here all day every Tuesday buying cattle ten at a time.

"Bob, you want to sort up some cattle for me and just buy me what you can? Then just lot them till we get a couple of semiloads."

"Tell me what you want."

"Big-frame fives and sixes for under sixty-five bucks a hundredweight. Sort them up so they look like a herd."

"That's a tall order. Maybe too tall. How many do you want?"

"Two hundred and fifty head and I'd take some spayed heifers in there if it had to be."

"I can't do it in one day," Bob said decisively.

"Can you do it over four weeks?"

"I can get pretty close."

"Let's do 'er then. I'll get my banking done. And don't hesitate to make me some *good* buys." By this point, Joe was enjoying himself so much he was just hollering at Bob and Bob was hollering back.

Imagine, thought Joe, a world in which you could trust a man to buy you a hundred fifty thousand pounds of beef with your checkbook when he is getting a commission. A particular instance of the free enterprise system running with a Stradivarian hum.

Darryl Burke, the banker, had known Joe so long and liked Joe so well and was so glad he was back in town that he would have liked to see him skip this business with the cows and, as he said, "orient his antenna to the twentieth century." Joe sat in his bright vice-president's cubicle surrounded by tremendous kodachromes of the surrounding countryside.

"Cut the shit and give me the money," Joe said. He enjoyed viewing Darryl in his suit because it gave him the curious ticklish surprise of time passing to see an old pal of the mountain streams and baseball diamonds actually beginning to blur into "the real world." Joe was without contempt for "the real world"; it merely astonished him that any of his old friends had actually succeeded in arriving there. Joe leaned over and said in a loud whisper, "Does your secretary actually believe this act of yours?"

Darryl grimaced and waved his hands around. He knew of course that life was a trick. But it wouldn't do to have the secretary find it out. Joe hated having to sit somewhat outside and spot the gambits. But he sustained a slight fear that whatever carried people into cubicles and suits would deprive him of his friends. There did seem to be a narrowing as life went on. An old fishing companion who threw the longest and most perfect loop of line had become a master of the backhoe. He dug foundations and sewer lines more exactly than the architects drew them on paper. He had become his backhoe. He either rode the backhoe or he drank beer and thought about perfecting his hands on the levers. He suffered from carpal tunneling. He was never out of work. His family had everything they needed as the beer helped him swell toward perfect conjunction with the yellow machine. Was this the same as the cowboy who was said to be part of his horse?

"I'm sure you know that we are not in good times for these ranches."

"Yes, I do," called Joe.

"Nationally, we're looking at a foreclosure every seven minutes. If your dad was here, God bless him, he'd tell you all about this."

"You know the old saying, it can't happen to me. Besides, it's Lureen's. I'm just the hired man."

Darryl groaned. "Some of these fellows slip off into the night with the machinery. I can't say that I blame them. The FHA is topsy-turvy. We're no different. We're having to go after some of our best operators. Incidentally, I know about Lureen's arrangement. I know all about this ranch. And anything you do, she's going to have to sign."

"Well, don't worry. I'm going to be doing so little. One Four-H kid can do more than I'm going to do with the place. I'll scatter these yearlings and ship in the fall. It's not even really ranching. Anyway, like I say, I just work for Lureen."

"As long as you understand that every move drives you deeper. Lureen's going to have to come in." It surprised Joe that everyone seemed to know the arrangement. They considered it Joe's place. Maybe more than he did.

Joe bent over the papers, making a show of studying them. "Your nose is whistling," he said to Darryl. "Control your greed." Darryl sighed. When Joe finished, he looked up and said, "Let 'er buck. I'm back in the cattle business."

"But you're happy," said Darryl with a kind of crazy smile. "That's it, you're happy."

Joe knew he was going to have to buy a horse. So, he skimmed a few hundred from the cattle pool and went way out north of town to see Bill Smithwick, who broke ranch horses and used to work for Joe's father. He lived down along a seasonal creek, a place just scratched into the mainly treeless, dun-colored and endless space. Red willows grew down the trifling watercourse; and alongside them, as though they were a grove of ancient oaks, Bill had placed his home. It was an old, old travel trailer shaped like a cough drop and swathed in black plastic sheeting to keep the wind out. A black iron pipe brought water by gravity down to the half of a propane tank that served as the water trough; it was primitive, but a bright stream of clean water ran continuously. He had a big pen for loose horses and a round breaking corral. It was the bare minimum but it was fairly neat with the hay stacked right, the lariats hung up, the saddles in a shed and the old Dodge Powerwagon actually parked rather than left.

There was a born-again bumper sticker on the truck's bumper that said: "The game is fixed. The lamb will win. Be there."

Bill Smithwick stepped out of the trailer. He wore suspenders over a white V-necked T-shirt and had a beat-up Stetson way on the back of his head like an old-timer. He was a tough-looking forty with white arms and sun-blackened hands.

"Well, God damn you anyway, you no-good sonofabitch," he barked in a penetrating hog-calling tenor.

"I'm back."

"To stay?"

"I'm just back."

"You want to come in?"

"It's not big enough in there."

Smithwick reached behind him and got a shirt. He pulled it on and came into the yard. He shook Joe's hand like he was pumping up a tire. "Hey, what's the deal on your old place? Them neighbors been rippin' your aunty off something awful."

"We took it back. I'm going to run some yearlings there, till I see what's what."

"You and your aunt?"

"No, me."

"Come on, Joe!" shouted Smithwick in the hog-calling voice.

"Really," said Joe, sincerely.

"You're running yearlings and you need a horse."

"Yup."

"What are you going to do with that no-good, low-bred, yellow-livered, whey-faced, faint-hearted Smitty?" Bill shouted.

"He's part of the cost of doing business on that particular ranch."

"I foller you now."

"What you got around here in the way of a broke horse?" Joe asked.

"Well, all grade horses. And no appaloosas! Know why the Indians liked appaloosas?"

"Why?"

"They was the only horses they could catch on foot. And by the time they rode their appaloosas to battle they was so mad it made them great warriors."

"I have four hundred dollars I will give for a gelding seven years of age or less that you say is a good horse."

"Done."

Joe looked off at the pen of loose horses. "What did I buy?"

"Your purchase is a five-year-old bay gelding with black points named Plumb Rude, a finished horse. He's as gentle as the burro Christ rode into Jerusalem. How about a dog?"

"Have one, a dilly."

"I got two I could let go. One's fifteen and one's sixteen. The sixteen's the mother of the fifteen. The fifteen's got a undescended testicle but not so's a man'd notice."

Joe gave him the four hundred, which he had already rolled up in his shirt pocket with an elastic around it. Smithwick stuck it in his back pocket next to his snoose can.

"Let's go look at him," said Smithwick. He pulled his lariat down and they walked to the bronc pen. Plumb Rude was in a bunch of eight horses, easily spotted by the way he was marked, and by his habit of walking sideways and pushing other horses out of his way. He wasn't very big.

Smithwick made a loop and pitched his houlihan. The rope seemed to drop out of the sky over the head of Plumb Rude. Smithwick drew the horse up to him with the rope. The horse must have been caught this way regularly; he didn't seem to mind. "Appear all right to you?" The gelding looked like a horse in a Mathew Brady photograph, long-headed, raw-boned, with sloped, hairy pasterns.

"Looks fine."

"He's a little cold backed but that ain't gonna bother you. Saddle him and let him stand for a few minutes and he'll never pitch with you. And he's hard mouthed 'cause I got hard hands! Haw!"

"Bill, I don't have a trailer. Can you drop him by when you get a minute?"

"Where'll I leave him, in your dad's old corrals there?"

"That'd be fine."

Smithwick turned around and put his hands on his hips and gazed at the pen of broncs. He was the very picture of what Joe took to be happiness. "Lemme see," Joe heard him say, "who am I gonna mug today?"

12

About a week later, the year-
lings started coming in on partial loads, eastbound. They
never could get it together to make up a whole semiload.
Joe just had to pick them up as they arrived. The truckers
left them at the stockyard in Deadrock and stuck the
receipts and brand inspections under the door at the scale
house. Joe went out there with a stock trailer in the evening and an old irrigator's cow dog he had borrowed for
the day. The low buttes on the prairie to the north of the
stockyards were ledged with hot weather shadows, and
blackbirds were lined up on the top planks of the cattle
pens. Joe's cattle were bunched around an automatic waterer at one end, a mixed batch of light grass cattle. Joe
backed the trailer to a Powder River gate and used the dog
to load the cattle. He closed the door and looked in along
the slatted sides of the trailer where the wet muzzles
pressed out. He took his time going back out the river
road and hauled them right through the wire gate on the
south pasture. He stopped and opened the trailer just at
dark. A few yearlings craned and looked out into the
space; then one turned and stood at the rear edge of the
trailer looking down. The others crowded in front,
bawled, and the one looking down jumped. After a pause,
the rest poured out to look at the new world. They scattered and began to graze. Joe felt something inside him

move out onto the grass with the cattle. It was thrilling to feel it come back.

The house was below the level of the immediate surrounding hills. Before sunrise, the tops of the cottonwoods lit up as though they were on fire, while the lower parts of the trees and their trunks continued to stand in the dark of night. Gradually, the conflagration moved downward, revealing the trees, and finally raced out along the ground, emblazoning the horizontal sides of the ranch buildings.

Into this bright scene came old man Overstreet on a bony little grulla mare, and wearing an overcoat. Alongside of him, a middle-aged man hurried to keep up. He was wearing hiking boots and a buffalo plaid shirt. Overstreet gazed around the buildings from his trotting horse until he spotted Joe.

"Joe, I'm tickled to death to see you back. This here is Mr. Prendergast of the town of Philadelphia, Pennsylvania." Joe shook Mr. Prendergast's hand. He had a horsy, eager, well-bred face. "Mr. Prendergast is writing about our area for . . . for what?"

"For a German travel magazine," said Mr. Prendergast.

"How are you, Mr. Overstreet?" Joe shook his hand. The old man had aged startlingly to a kind of papery fierceness like a hornet.

"Where's Otis Rosewell?" Joe asked.

"He rode a sedan to the bottom of the Gros Ventre River. Otis has been gone for years."

"I'm sure sorry to hear it." Joe was startled that he had never heard this before.

"I've been seeing these mixed cattle coming in. Who do they belong to?" Overstreet asked crossly.

"Really, they're Lureen's steers. I'm taking kind of a break. I told her I'd watch them for her."

"Why didn't she come to me?" Overstreet demanded.

"She said you had given up your lease."

"I had, I had! But I didn't expect her to cut off communications!"

"I don't think she meant to do that, Mr. Overstreet. But like I say, I was willing to watch them for her. And the grass was already coming."

"Let me tell you something, young man. This outfit sets slap in the middle of me. I would have had it long ago if it hadn't galled me to let your dad stick me up. But you people need to clear some of these ideas with me before you go off half cocked."

Joe was not happy with the phrase "you people."

"Mr. Overstreet," he said, "we don't need to do any such a thing."

"I'm only interested in what's neighborly," said Overstreet, turning to go. "That's how the West was won." Prendergast laughed uncomfortably and the two of them went off, Prendergast having to jog to the horse's walk as old man Overstreet shouted, "Prendergast, write that down!"

There was a dog living underneath the house, a mass of gray fur living in solitary misery. Joe had glimpsed it three different times, just at dusk when it sat on a low ridge, looking out over the empty country north of the ranch. He began to leave a pan of kibble on occasion to see if he couldn't get this dog to accommodate itself to some degree to the human life of the ranch. But it was pretty clear he was going to have to shoot it; skunks were showing up with rabies and an untended dog like this would be held responsible for all depredations on local livestock.

Joe sat on a nearby hill with a rifle watching the pan of dog food, often drifting off into a nap during which he inevitably had bad, guilty dreams about shooting the dog. It was a job Joe didn't want.

Once he shone the flashlight under the cabin. Exposed teeth glistened in its beam. The dog snarled without ever taking a breath, a continuous, bubbling drone. Joe could have shot it where it was. Getting the corpse out was one thing, but the idea of killing something which had retreated to a final crevice not one other creature desired was insupportable.

Sometimes Joe sat outside the cabin until the dog thought he had gone. Then he would hear the dog moaning to itself, a whimpering agony as its parasites gnawed away at it. Joe put a piece of meat on a pole and shoved it up under the cabin so that he could feel the jarring of the feeding dog, and its agony resumed like a great outside force.

He went to the vet and bought an aerosol can of boticide, antiseptic, and a pair of sheep shears. He now had forty-three dollars tied up in the dog. Then he bought a T-bone. That brought it to almost forty-nine. He drove out to the cabin.

When he played his light underneath the building, the wolfish eyes burned yellow. The dog growled on, both inhaling and exhaling. Around its face, a thick corona of matted fur extended for half a foot in all directions. Joe pushed a pole up in there at the end of which he had arranged a noose of broken lariat. The dog shuddered back to the ultimate inch of recess, driving dust forth in a swirl around the beam of light as the pole approached. It snapped with lightning speed at the end of the pole but the loop kept on coming forward until it was around the brute's neck. Joe tightened the loop slightly, then slipped the pole out. Now holding the nylon rope, he could feel the throb of life at its end. A peculiar quiet reigned in the dusty yard as Joe looked around in an attempt to foresee the consequence of pulling the creature into the light of day. Maybe the dog had the right idea. But Joe had grown up with dogs and this one had lost all shadow of the old alliance with mankind and had become an instrument of secrecy and fear.

The time had come. Joe began to pull. A scrambling could be heard from within and a faint dust cloud rolled out, accompanied by the most piteous tone, a pitch of voice rendingly universal. Joe was about to overwhelm all of the dog's accumulation of temper and habit and to drag him out into the daylight.

The rope was as hard as a stick in his hand. It yielded a degree at a time. Sweat poured from Joe. It runneled down his laugh lines. It stung his eyes. As the dog advanced to meet its fate, it occurred to Joe that he didn't know what it looked like, except for that big wedge of muzzle. For a split second, a part of him wondered what would happen if the dog weighed a thousand pounds. Joe regained enough rope to be able to coil it at his feet. He made one coil, then another, and while he was making the third, the dog shot out from under the cabin, hit the end of the rope and snatched Joe onto his face. Joe held on while the dog ran baying in a great circle, its hindquarters sunk low to scramble against the restraint of the rope.

Joe got to his feet with the rope still in his hands, his palms burned and stinging. He retreated until he reached a pine tree that once shaded the yard of the cabin. Here he was able to take a couple of turns around the base of the tree, and bracing his weight against the rope draw the dog to the tree and snub its head against it. Joe's heart ached at the suffering of the animal in its captivity, the misery which broad daylight seemed to bring. The dog lay there and howled.

Joe bound the dog's mouth shut with twine, narrowly avoiding being bitten, and began to clip the fur with the sheep shears. As soon as he broke the surface of the matted fur, he hit a bottomless layer of pale, thick maggots and felt his gorge rise. He drove back his loathing until he had clipped the dog from end to end, down to its festering skin. He got an old rusted gas can from the shadow of the cabin and went to the small creek that ran past to fill the can with water. He rinsed the dog over and over while the dog, thinking that it was drowning, renewed its moans. Once Joe was sure the dog was clean, he sprayed it with antiseptic and then finally a blast of aerosol with the botfly medicine. The dog lay panting.

Joe cut the twine binding the dog's mouth, placed the T-bone within reach and freed the rope. The pink medicated mass of the dog, whose wounded pride found voice in a sustained howl, bolted across the dirt yard past the eloquent T-bone and into the hayfield, where it sat and poured out a cry and lamentation for the life in the dark which it had lost.

Joe spent the rest of the morning sealing up the space

underneath the cabin with rocks. The dog sat in the field and watched him, making small adjustments in its position toward the steak. Joe noticed these adjustments and, as he walked back toward the ranch, he felt that, given time, the dog would sell out. He thought he knew how the dog felt. The phone rang. There was some excitement about getting his first call. A small voice came over the line. "Joe, this is Ellen Overstreet. Do you remember me?"

"Why I sure do. How are you, Ellen?"

"I'm just fine, Joe. I was excited to hear you were back."

"Where are you living these days?"

"Until recently, outside of Two Dot. But we're separated. I think we'll work it out though."

" 'We,' who is we?"

"Actually, I'm Ellen Kelton now. Do you remember Billy Kelton?"

"Are you kidding? After all the thumpings he gave me? Is he still the wild cowboy I remember?" Joe's question was polite in the extreme.

"Well, not nearly. He's gone to ranching."

"Are you all going to make it through this dry spell?"

"I honestly wonder," said Ellen in a musical voice. "We have had such dust pneumonia in our calves from following their mothers down these old cow trails to water. We've lost quite a few of them. Billy's spent all his time doctoring."

"I can't tell you how nice it is to hear your voice. It *sounds* like you're as pretty as ever."

"I'm not!" Ellen laughed. "On the other hand, nobody puts on weight around here. But let me get to the point."

"All right," Joe said warmly; but the truth was, a nervous feeling had invaded his stomach, something which had just crossed time from where he used to be to where he was now.

"I just thought—and I don't know how easy it will be to do—but I just thought you might like to see your daughter."

"*My* daughter? You say *my* daughter. Well, yes!

What's her name?'' Joe watched the wind toss an end of the curtain into the room. He knew what was meant when people talked about time stopping. He felt his hand moisten on the telephone receiver.

"Her name is Clara."

"Clara. Where did you get that?"

"It's Billy's mother's name."

"I see. Kind of an old-timey name. I guess I'm going to see her, huh?" A sudden intimacy descended with the crisis. "I mean, why in hell don't you just tell me what I'm supposed to do, Ellen."

"That's up to you, Joe. I'm just making the offer."

"Anybody know this?"

"I told Dad."

"You did? And what did he say?" His mouth had gone chalky. "You told your father?"

"He said, 'Good,' 'cause Clara will get it all when you people's place is part of his and it all makes a perfect square."

"Well, this just kind of floors me. And well, Ellen, what about you? What happened to your plans?"

"I teach. I teach at Clarendon Creek."

"That's where I went! That's where my Aunt Lureen taught."

"The first four grades."

Joe could smell the sweat pouring through his shirt. He felt like he was burning up. He felt as if the rickety logic of his new life had just disappeared.

"I would like to see her," Joe said. "Any arrangement that you would like suits me."

"I just wanted to find out if you were interested," she said in the same musical voice. "I'll be in touch!"

13

An old man named Alvie Butterfield who irrigated for the Overstreets came through the ranch yard to change the water in his head gate. He had with him the border collie Joe had used as his cattle came in. Alvie was on a small battered Japanese motorcycle wearing his hip boots. He had his shovel fastened down with bungee cord and his blue heeler balanced on the passenger seat. Joe was walking to the truck with a load of outgoing mail and stopped to talk. They ended up talking about Zane Grey. Alvie's old face wrinkled and his eyes looked off to unknown distances. He said, "I believe everything in them books. When them cowboys are in the desert, I'm hot. When they're caught in a blizzard I send the old lady for another blanket. When they run out of food, I tear down to the kitchen to make a peanut butter sandwich." Even recalling these moments with his nose in Zane Grey caused rapturous transformation in Alvie, and the reality of a life directing muddy water downhill was made tolerable.

"I'm supposed to put out new salt," said Alvie, "but I'm too goddamn tired. You wouldn't think about doing that for me, would you?"

"Sure I would," Joe said.

"You can still find your way around up there, can't you?"

"I think so," said Joe.

"I'm mighty grateful," Alvie said. "Like I say, I'm wore out."

Alvie wandered up the creek and Joe loaded the truck with blocks of salt. He drove up through the basin, got out to lock the hubs, put it in four-wheel drive and climbed into the clouds, passing the Indian caves and the homesteaders' coal mine, before he tipped over into the summer pasture. There were cattle scattered out on the hills in all directions. He could just make out the three small white structures of the salt houses in the blue distance. A velvet-horned mule deer ambled out through the deep grass ahead of him and bluebirds paused on the cedar fenceposts. The only sign of human life was an old sheep shearing engine abandoned half a century ago and looking in the dry air as though it would still run. It was vanity to think about owning this sort of thing. Joe could not exactly understand property. We want things when others want the same things. Still, looking out at pastures that ran to threadlike rivers at eye level, Joe could feel his bones blowing in the wind of the future, and it was a cheerful feeling. All his feelings were currently askew because of Ellen's call, but this was still a good one.

He loaded all the salt out and checked the two main springs. One was reduced in volume because of the winter's low snowpack at the heads of the coulees, but the cattle were still using it. The northern fence line was barely standing, held up by the sagebrush through which it ran, but it held all right and nothing seemed to be going through it. Joe had built that fence. When cattle got out, they just drifted into space and it was an easy thing to get them back in. There was grass everywhere, even on top of the wind-blown ridges where he and Otis had dynamited fencepost holes so long ago. He remembered now what a good gaining pasture it was and how his father, who was a grass man, used to say, Just take care of it and it will take care of you.

He left the truck and walked. The pasture lay in three broadly defined planes that tilted separately and disappeared into the sky. He walked toward a tall rock formation that had once figured in a dream of his boyhood, a dream he had never quite figured out as to all its sources and details and implied perils. But this dream had left him with a high degree of respect for the operations of the subconscious.

In his twenties, many years after the rock episode, he had eaten peyote and had the pleasure of a long conversation with thousands of irises, tulips, and roses at a commercial flower garden. He could *still* remember their nodding concern at each of his questions, their earnest weaving around on the ends of their stalks. As ridiculous as this experience came to seem, it enlarged his respect for flowers; and he sometimes found himself entering someone's property with a sidelong and deferential nod to the garden.

When he reached the great banded rock chimney, something went through him with a signifying interior chime as powerful as looking at an empty bed where a parent once died. A cloud of birds set forth into the wind. Joe sat down and let himself go back.

Joe's nearest neighbor of his own age had been Billy Kelton, already a great big strong boy who was, in those days long before the family moved to Minnesota, Joe's best friend. Billy's father owned the Hawkwood Store. The two boys both had part-time jobs during the school year and ranch jobs in the summer. One day, when they were both thirteen, Billy had come to visit Joe and they got into an argument pitching horseshoes. Joe's father came out and said, "You'd better settle this like men." Joe didn't think he had a chance, and while he stalled Billy sensed not only the opportunity but the peculiar energy coming to him from Joe's father. He landed a roundhouse blow in Joe's face that bloodied him and brought him to his knees. Joe's father ordered Joe to his feet, but when he stood Billy flattened him with a blow to his right ear that sent pain and shame scalding across his vision. A roaring noise seemed to come up around him. Through it all, he could hear his father cheering Billy on. He looked up and saw his father's incredible animation as he shoved the suddenly reluctant Billy toward his son's collapsed form. Even now the memory was terrible.

Joe's father had said, "You'll think about this for a long time. You'll think about what people are really like. That wasn't your enemy that did that to you. That was supposed to be your friend. You think about that just as hard as you can."

Joe ran away that day just long enough to climb to this pasture. He came straight to the banded rock chimney where he sat down and wept for his defeat, wept for his father's collusion in his defeat, wept for the loss of a friend, and the feeling which he never quite ever again escaped that life had as one of its constant characteristics a strain of unbearable loneliness.

As far as he was from the house, he still felt too exposed to the world that day. He touched the altered shapes of his face with his fingertips. Beneath the striped rock was a deep fissure, like a small cave, and Joe crawled into it and lay down in the cool dark. Peace came over him and, as he began to sleep, he plummeted into a dreamy abyss.

Indians poured out of the base of the rock and Joe was one of them. They were anonymous in paint and dyed porcupine quills and trade bead chokers, behind shields illuminated with the shapes of eternity. They moved like a school of fish and swarmed up on their horses. Concentric red circles of ochre were painted around the eyes of Joe's horse and its body was covered by the outlines of human hands. He rested his lance against the horse's neck. The raven feather tied at the base of its point fluttered against the shaft as they galloped over the rims to the small valley below where the white people had built their cabins. Though it was his family's home, Joe could not even remember it in the dream. A man and a woman ran out to meet them, to try to talk; they were blurred unrecognizably by the direct glare of the sun. It was too late for talk. The Indians rode right over the white people in a sudden tension of bows and sailing of arrows and lances. The dust from the horses settled slowly on their absence. The buildings burned as sudden as phosphorus, sparkled and were gone. Everything was gone. Even the stony white of foundations and bones was gone. The wild grass resumed its old cadence.

Joe's mother watched closely over the days it took for the swelling to subside in his face. She let this concern speak for itself and carefully avoided any discussion of the event. Joe said nothing either, though whatever was in the air seemed strong enough. Finally, when only the greenish shadow of a bruise at his temple remained, she asked without seeming to expect an answer, "Your father has made a pretty big mistake with you, hasn't he?"

He didn't answer. He just stared in silence and let her work her way through her changed allegiance.

14

His first free afternoon, Joe stopped by the Clarendon Creek school. Ellen stood on the edge of the small clearing that served as a playground, her sweater tied around her waist and wearing a pair of tennis shoes so that she could double as a physical education instructor. She was urging four tiny children in running laps out around a two-story boulder and back. Their books and papers were weighted with stones next to the lilacs.

"Hi there," Ellen said with an enormous smile.

"What do you know about this?"

"It's pretty wild," she said.

"I couldn't wait."

"You're looking well, Joe."

"Thanks. And you."

"Do you mean it?"

"I do."

"How's your painting?"

"I'm in the space program actually."

"What a shame. You used to write to me from school, remember? About your painting. You were going to be a new Charlie Russell. I saw one of your paintings finally. I really couldn't understand it, Joe. It looked kind of like custard. Next to a house, sort of."

"That happens to belong to one of the Rockefellers,"

Joe said defensively, but the name, he saw, didn't ring a bell.

"Let me make it quick. I've got to go back inside. Clara is with her dad this month."

"On the same old Kelton place?" Joe asked, feeling awkward.

"Yes, but don't go there. I'll try to work something out. And look, please be discreet. Billy is a wonderful father and I don't want to disturb that."

"How about dinner?"

"You what?"

"Would you like to have dinner?" he asked.

"Your face is red!"

"Nevertheless, the invitation stands."

"Yes!" The four children completed their lap and Ellen drifted toward the schoolhouse with them. "Call!" she said. "For directions. We can have a scandal!"

He recognized that there was an unworthy basis to his extreme present happiness. His life was taking a turn that would help push Astrid out once and for all. He already felt the freshness and the simplicity of Ellen as an antidote, though he semi-admitted to himself that that was not what people were for.

He picked Ellen up at six, at her apartment. The length of day had advanced so that it seemed the middle of the afternoon. She came down the outside stairway, skittering to the ground level, looking as fresh as though it were first thing in the morning, in a dark blue summer dress with minute white stars. She had braided her mahogany-colored hair and pinned it up.

"I'm starving," she said, inside the car. "I got so wound up talking to the children about Lewis and Clark I must have burned a lot of calories. I had fun trying to make them see the part of the expedition that went up the Missouri. I tried to make them realize that for Lewis and Clark it was like going into space. I told them the Missouri was the great highway for the Indians and all the tributaries were neighborhoods with different languages and different histories. The little turkeys would really rather hear about war but the unknown gives them a shiver too. Or what they all call 'the olden days.' I'm going to split the difference with them. I'll show them Clark's camp on the Yellowstone and then take them over near Greycliff to the graves where the Blackfeet massacred Reverend Thomas and his nephew. By the way, I'm learning to play golf. I'm going through a difficult time and about a hundred people have recommended golf. I'm glad they did. By the second lesson, I preferred golf to marriage!"

Joe looked at her as long as he thought he could. What a feeling this was giving him! He was driving through a nice neighborhood. In one yard, a man shot around his lawn on a riding mower in high gear. At the next house, an old gent stood in the opening of a well-kept garage with its carefully hung collection of lawn tools on the wall behind him. On most lawns, a tiny white newspaper lay like a seed. American flags cracked from the porches. On the last lawn before Main Street, a rabbit sat between two solemn children.

They walked into the lobby of the old Bellwood Hotel. The bar off to the left was full of after-work customers. Two cowboys came out with their drinks to have a look at Ellen while they waited for their table. "Yes?" she said in her best schoolteacher's manner. They shot back inside.

"I'll have the sixteen-ounce rib-eye," said Ellen before she'd had a look at the menu. The waitress came and took their drink orders: a draft beer for Joe, Jim Beam on the rocks for Ellen. Joe decided on some pan-fried chicken and ordered for both of them. The dining room was half full. A schoolteacher was kind of a celebrity in a small town like this, so they got a few glances. It was too soon for anyone to have put much else together.

Joe was trying hard to relate the present confident Ellen to the early version he had known. He felt he had to do it quickly because the present Ellen would soon eradicate the one he remembered.

"Someone told me you people were getting ready to lose the place," said Ellen. "Dad keeps trying to figure out how to get it. He's only been doing that for forty years."

"It's hard to say."

"Although I don't know what good a ranch is anymore. My dad has been getting jailbirds to help put up hay because they're the only people desperate enough to work. To get somebody to fence you have to find an alky who wants to be in the hills to dry out. Plus the grasshoppers and Mormon crickets are about half ridiculous. I think my dad might just go to town. I don't blame him."

Joe listened intently. It gave him a chance to stare at her without having to talk. He knew Overstreet would never go to town.

"By the way," she said, "let me ask you this, okay? Don't you have a girlfriend?"

"I did."

"Well?"

"She died in a fern bar stampede."

A look of tolerance crossed Ellen's face. Joe tried to remember Astrid charitably but all that came up was her pushiness, her health fetishes, her fascination with cosmetics. Astrid had taught him the field strategy for the aptly named war of the sexes. She had also taught him the charm and drama of picnics on the battlefield. It was a provisional life with this Astrid.

Ellen was as good as her word. When the meals came, she made short work of her big steak. Once when her mouth was too full, she grinned straight at Joe, and shrugged cheerily. This appetite amazed him. And when she was done, she flung herself back in her seat and said, "Ah!"

"Now what?" said Joe, putting down his own utensils. He was thinking about a cigarette. The tension of not mentioning the child was getting sharper.

"Would you like a suggestion?"

"Sure."

"I'd like to go out to Nitevue and hit a bucket of balls."

"I'd rather talk about Clara."

"I'd rather hit a bucket of balls."

★ ★ ★

They were the only two people on the range. It was a green band in the middle of prairie, glowing under flood-lights. Nitevue was situated just off the highway east. It was an open shed with places to sit, three soft drink machines, a golf cart, and a small counter where one arranged for the clubs and balls. Ellen asked for a number-four wood and Joe asked for anything that was handy, which turned out to be a thing called a "sand iron." The concessionaire looked just like a local farmer in a John Deere cap and overalls. He made it clear in every movement that his class background had taught him to despise all sport and waste such as this. He handed over balls, clubs, and tees with an air of ancient loathing.

Ellen stood up on a kind of rubber mat and began firing the balls out through the bug-filled flood of light, almost to the darkness beyond. At first Joe just watched her. There were gophers speeding around, running, stopping, looking, whistling, trying to fathom life on a driving range.

Joe took three whiffs for every time he hit the ball. But even when he did connect, it just went up at a high angle and landed a short distance away. He took a somewhat mightier grip and swung hard; this time the ball almost towered out of sight, yet fell just in front of them. Quickly absorbing the spirit of this unusual game, he shouted, "Sonofabitch!" and examined the end of his club for manufacturing deficiencies. He went back and demanded another club; this one was a "two iron." With it, he managed to scuff the ball along the ground in front of himself, while Ellen drove one long clean shot after another. What's more, his arms ached from inadvertently fetching the ground itself blow after blow.

When she had finished driving her last ball, Ellen walked over to where Joe was sitting on a bench. Her cheeks were flushed with high spirits. Joe thought that it would be a very strange individual who didn't find her lovely.

"You don't seem to have much of a gift for this," she said.

"I'm afraid I don't. Actually, I tried it a few years back. I'm about the same. My dad took it up late in life. I always found something sad in that. Couldn't put my finger on it."

"Tell you what, why don't you drop me at my place. I've got papers to correct and I make an early start. Probably by the time you get out of bed, I've been hitting a lick for two hours."

Joe took a leisurely drive along the river and then turned up her street. There just didn't seem to be any pressure anywhere. When they reached her house, he walked her to the bottom of the outside stairs to her apartment. She turned suddenly, reached to one of his hands, gave it a kind of rough squeeze, bounded up the stairs—"I enjoyed it!"—and was gone behind her door. He stood there vaguely happy, vaguely conscious that they had never made a real plan to see his daughter. He was ashamed to admit that it seemed too much. And the mention of Billy Kelton as a good father galled him.

15

The great window in the front room hung halfway open, the iron sash weights visible in their wooden channels. Cliff swallows ascended to their mud nests under the deep eaves of the old house. Joe thought, Man, I'm getting lonesome; let's have a look at the young people. There were times when the views from his windows seemed full of undisclosed meaning, of tales waiting to unfold. But today their views were as flat as reproductions. He had a tubular glass bird feeder hung outside the sitting room window and the seeds it had scattered on the sill just seemed unkempt. The birds didn't seem to care if they ate or not. He looked at the phone and it rested in its place as though its days as an instrument were finished. He felt there was nothing for him to do. Whatever was next, he hadn't started. His old life smothered him.

He took the highway east over the foothills, passing a spot where you could shoot a buffalo and put it on your credit card. When he stopped for gas, a boy cleaned his windshield and poured out his heart to Joe. He said that his mother had been married more than ten times and that he and his brother had lived in nineteen cities. The boy couldn't remember the names of all the husbands but said, "We had to call every one of them sonsofbitches

'Daddy.' " All Joe could think of was good solid ways of putting his old life to an end.

While the youngster cleaned the windshield and checked under the hood, Joe used the pay phone. It was late in New York.

"Ivan, hi, it's Joe."

There was a long pause. Joe pictured Ivan in his bathrobe, his thick, effective shape like that of a veteran football lineman, characteristically pressing a thumb and forefinger into his eye sockets.

"Why are you calling me in the middle of the night?"

"Because I need to see you."

"I don't like this, Joe."

"Will you see me?"

"Of course I'll see you. Where are you?"

"Montana."

"*Look Homeward, Angel.*"

"Sort of."

"Find what you expected?"

"More."

"How did you leave off with Astrid?"

"I just flew the coop, adiosed it. I don't feel too good about that, actually."

"I'll check in with her."

"So, if you tell me it's okay, I'm coming."

"Sure it's okay. Are you a cowboy again?"

"You know, Ivan, I sort of am."

"It's a riot," said Ivan.

Joe slept all the way to La Guardia. After missing the whole night on the ranch, he watched the sun rise over the Atlantic Ocean.

He took a cab into the city, his small duffel bag on the seat beside him. The skyline of New York, with his cab pointed straight at it, filled Joe with excitement. The unpronounceable name on the cabbie's license, the criminal style photograph, the statement on the grill that separated him from his passengers about his having less than five dollars in change, the omnipresent signs of crowd control measures excited Joe beyond words. Protected by their cars, motorists boldly exchanged glances on the freeway.

He checked into the Yale Club. The lobby was full of younger graduates and their dates. There was a wine tasting announced on a placard in the lobby and a Macanudo cigar sampling in the Tap Room. There were new regulations about jogging clothes in the lobby. There were serious conversationalists around the elevators and two harried bellhops with mountains of luggage on their carts. Four Southerners in their early thirties hooted and pounded one another. "Anybody catch the secretary of commerce doin' his little numbah on the TV?" asked one lanky young man in a Delta drawl. When neither of his fellows answered him, a tight-faced man at the next elevator did. "I saw him," he said, "and he was right on the money." There weren't usually this many young people around. It was a yuppie *Brigadoon*.

Joe carried his own bag to his room, walking down a hallway hung with crew pictures and ambulance-service citations from the First World War. Three Filipino maids chatted in the open doorway of a linen closet, greeting him as he passed. His room was really good, like a room in an old home, though he had to sidle around the bed to clear the dresser, the radiator, and the writing desk. The room had a wooden smell. Joe remembered staying here when he was in school, riding down from New Haven on the train along the seaboard of battered buildings and grassless lots; sometimes he caught glimpses of the exhausted ocean or the odd things that had been thrown out, old window frames, a child's toy bugle, wired bundles of newspapers, cars parked so long their tires were flat, all of which used to stir Joe. Sometimes it seemed superior to the space and quiet of the West.

Leaving his bag unopened on the bed, he went downstairs, back through the lobby and across to Grand Central Station. He walked down into the vast hall of railroading to buy a newspaper. He stared at the schedule boards overhead and noted that it was still unbelievably possible to go to White Plains.

He decided he would walk for a while. Still amazed at

the unreturned glances of the crowd, he felt himself swept against the windows of the shops. He felt a growing desire to be better dressed. He sympathized with the men selling stolen and counterfeit goods from the curb; he thought it must take an exceptional individual to wrest himself from the anomie and become a customer. When cars were stopped in the intersections by traffic signals, he trusted the pattern of his fellow humans in pouring through the narrow gaps between bumpers. Yet it was hard to forget that with a slip of the clutch one was legless. Part of his sense of liberation in New York was the impression of human volume and the consequent trivialization of his problems. If an individual ran out into the crowd from a doctor's office to shout, "I've just found out I have cancer!" it wouldn't have much effect. New York really took the pressure off the basics and Joe felt this liberation in his buoyant stride, his desire to be better dressed, and his inclination to try the cuisines of all peoples. His single year of life in the city taught him that fun at sex, there for the asking, was the steady undertone. Its utilitarian savor ran the risk of all pleasantries.

"The trouble is," said his then roommate, Ivan Slater, after a year of this, "you end up buying them a fifty-dollar dinner. And the more indistinguishable they get, the more it's like having some show dog in your pants that can't live on ordinary kibble."

"Stop!" Joe said. "Stop!"

His room was on the ninth floor but he mistakenly took the elevator to the seventh, got off, and had to press the call button and wait once again. A woman in her early thirties came along and pressed the down button.

"Hi," said Joe. She had a sunny, outdoors look and wore a green-checked dress that suited her pretty figure.

"How are you?"

"I pressed the wrong button."

"You mean you're going down?"

"No, I mean in the lobby. I meant to get off at nine."

"Your face is red," she said.

He said, "I'm lonely."

They had leapt through layers of intimacy with this exchange. He could have said anything. He could have asked her to have sex with him and gotten an uncomplicated yes or no response. But an elevator arrived, and she stepped aboard, saying, "Ta-ta." Presently, his own elevator came and he was on his way to his room. His message light was on. How had she gotten his room number? But it was only Ivan confirming their dinner hour. He stretched out and watched television for a while. His bones ached. He let his mind follow the sirens from the street below. He imagined living here and the thought was a happy one. He could go upstairs to the library or take squash lessons. He could breakfast here every morning before venturing into the street. Finally, a kind of sight which lay buried inside him, stunned to blindness not only by open country but by the sea, would awaken to something he never could have predicted. And he would choose to depict it. Out would come the brushes and paint. Dab, dab, dab.

Joe put on a clean shirt and a blue-and-green-striped silk tie. His suit jacket was rumpled but it was of such acceptable tailoring that he thought it made him look either hard-working or scholarly. He rather liked the figure he cut. When he got to the foyer of the dining room on the twenty-second floor a few minutes before eight, the girl from the seventh floor was there waiting for a table by herself.

"So, we meet again," he said, a remark so deplorable to him that he immediately understood why she furrowed her brow and smiled formulaically. The intimacy of a short time ago was withdrawn. "So sorry." The smile changed and became genuine. She turned her wonderful almost Mediterranean face to one side and regarded him. She is about to ask me something, and something big, he thought. She may ask me if I'd like a loan. I don't know yet but soon I will.

The silver doors of the elevator opened and Ivan Slater stepped out, wearing the latest Italian fashions, wide shoulders, a kind of one-button roll, really an old-fashioned hoodlum suit but made in the bright shades of a discount carpet barn. The shirt was green and the tie was red. He wore great spatulate suede shoes and his pants were held up by what appeared to be a pajama string. His proximity to the fashion centers entitled him to spend a fortune to look like a fool.

Ivan's round, pumpkinlike head and piercing black eyes seemed to say "Stop the music!" while he regarded his illustrator. Joe remembered when he and Astrid used to stay in New York at Ivan's apartment, making love by the second-floor glow of streetlights, mantis shadows climbing the walls.

"Hold it right there," said Joe, turning to the young woman. "You were saying?"

"I was saying?"

"Weren't you about to say something?"

"I wasn't but I will if you like. I can see you'd like me to."

Ivan, watching close, pounded Joe on the back with a sharp laugh. "I see you haven't lost any of your speed," he said in a voice that swung the headwaiter around from the middle of the dining room. "Not you," Ivan called to the headwaiter, jabbing a finger up and down in midair over Joe's head. *"Him."*

When the headwaiter came, Joe deferred to the lady. She said she was waiting for someone. Joe and Ivan took a table near the middle of the room and Ivan ordered a margarita and buried his face in the menu. Joe asked for a bourbon and water, thinking it seemed like a vaguely out-of-town drink.

"I can't wait to hear about what you've done for Miss X," said Ivan from behind the menu. Joe was baffled: he thought Miss X was dead in the water.

Right after the drinks arrived, the young lady came to her table, the next one over, by herself. "I've been stood up," she said and grinned. She pulled the corners of her mouth down in a sad-face. Joe shook his head sympathetically and insincerely. Then her embarrassment looked real, the sort of vulnerability one galloped into like a hussar.

While they drank and waited for the waiter to take

their dinner order, Ivan brought Joe up to date on the manufacturing problems he had hurdled since they last met. Some of them were quite considerable, having to do with separate manufacturers using different quality-control procedures for each of the components, so that holy terrors existed at the assembly end. With Ivan, personnel matters tended to be "love feasts" while manufacturing matters were "blood baths." Ivan had been through this before on simpler things and with purely industrial products involving robotics in the garment industry, which had made him unpopular but had made him money while putting others out of work. But this time it was different. This time it was a blood bath disguised as a love feast. To offset its effect, he said, "What made you want to go back to Montana?"

"Nothing else seems to be home."

"Is that important?"

"It is to me."

"At this point, right?"

"I think it's generally important," said Joe.

"Aw, bullshit," said Ivan. " 'Home' is a concept whose importance rises when people are down in the mouth. Healthy minds don't give a big rat's ass whose country they're even in. How's my friend Astrid?"

"She hasn't seen fit to join me as yet."

Ivan and Astrid frequently spoke on the telephone and even wrote letters. They would have made an ideal elderly couple. Joe sometimes wondered whether it was only sarcastic brutes like Astrid and Ivan who could rise to uncomplicated fondness.

The soup came, saffron chicken. Joe dipped his spoon in it. Ivan looked quite crumpled in his fashions of the hour. By sitting in his slumped position he caused the shoulders of his jacket to stand straight out beneath his ears. Industrial leadership from this man seemed out of the question. The well-bred diners all around them paused to look twice at Ivan, though as he himself would be quick to point out he could easily buy and sell any one of them. Their vague curiosity was felt by Joe as a pressure. He had seen Ivan burst into a chorus of "I'll-buy-you's" before and it wasn't pretty.

Joe had ordered a piece of scrod and a dinner salad. Ivan had ordered a steak, after inquiring which one was the biggest. Their meals came and this seemed to cheer him. In fact, after a brief moment's thought, Ivan seemed to be emotionally restored. Ivan was a hearty, life-loving man, and it wasn't long before he was greedily passing hunks of steak into his mouth. He had to raise and lower his eyebrows with every mouthful to show how good it tasted. A shadow crossed his features while he thought about death, or so Joe assumed.

"The key to me," Ivan said, "is solitude. I have no family. If I had children, all would be different. I've always known that. Alas, my personal miniseries is somewhat different. I continue my wolfish roaming in the capitalist forest. Indeed, right now, I'm having a big love feast with the Chinese. They're our kind of guys. No malarkey about work being their only natural resource, as per the Japanese. In their plant management practices, they do not live in romantic illusions about inventory control. I greatly prefer them to Japs. Japs are racists. Japs like to set you up in business so they can later steal whatever business you capture. But now the Japs are growing hubristic. Their society is changing. Their kids are narcissistic pukes like ours are. They think they can kick back and take it easy but they don't have the resource cushion that permits Americans to take dope, watch TV, and get out of shape. As soon as they lose a couple of steps of that big speed, their former allies are going to call in their marks. Meanwhile, the Chinks are in the passing lane with their balanced attitude, their cultural depth, their emerging talents, the scum of communism just beginning to be rinsed from their eyes"—the sedate dining room was quite concentrated on Ivan now—"and they're looking across the Sea of Japan at their ancestral enemies and crying out, 'ALL RIGHT YOU FUCKIN' SLANTS, STAND BACK FROM YOUR TELEVISION SETS! WE CHINKS ARE GOING TO WHIP YOUR FUCKIN' ASSES!' " People stopped eating.

Ivan put a huge piece of steak in his mouth and all at once turned blue. Joe gazed at him a long time before noticing the color change, so great was his relief at the pause in his speech. The girl at the next table stared at Ivan.

"Is he all right?" she asked. "He's blue."

At that point, Ivan struggled to his feet and holding his throat, began making a sound like a seagull. Joe understood then that a piece of steak had lodged in his throat. Ivan started to stagger through the tables of diners before Joe could catch up to him. Joe knew the Heimlich maneuver and got behind Ivan, taking him around the waist below the rib cage and giving him as powerful a squeeze as his considerable strength would allow. Joe saw he had been successful even from this vantage point by the way the old Yalies jumped back from their tables. The thick bolus of beef, trailed by a yellow wing of vomit, flew across a couple of tables, and that was that. A dozen diners who had been seated were now standing, holding their napkins.

"Good as new!" crowed Ivan, returning to their table. But Joe could tell that he was deeply embarrassed. Suddenly, his thick frame in the latest fashions seemed less bold than sad. Ivan peered around from under his brows and saw that they were all still discussing him. He finally sat silent, smoldering, looking straight out at the diners now.

"That can kill you, y'know. Maybe those goddamn blue-blooded geeks don't know that. Maybe coupon clipping has kept them from learning that," he said in a piercing voice. Turning to Joe, he said, "Let's get a drink and the check." The waiter danced over at the first signal. He was able to make a minor modification of the bill and leave it immediately. Joe signed it and slipped it under his water glass.

"Ivan, the reason I came to town was to tell you, face to face, that I'm not going to do the project. I'm not going to work with you anymore."

"I know, Joe."

"Oh."

"You told me a long time ago," said Ivan, "that you were getting out of real art so that you could come to feel as replaceable as the next guy."

"Yeah . . . ?"

"Well, you were right." Ivan got to his feet. "You're replaceable. All the luck in the world to you, Joe." Ivan was probably the closest thing to a real friend Joe had ever had. These words stung. Ivan stood up and went straight out, shedding his discomfort with every step. Joe rested his head in his hands, staring at a few square inches of tablecloth. When he lifted his head, he felt dizzy for just a moment. But when his eyes cleared, there was the girl at the next table.

"Join me for a drink?" she said. He looked at her clearly. She was beautiful.

"I'm sorry," said Joe, "but I'm afraid I don't know you."

She looked at him and smiled. She said, "What a relief!"

16

Joe and Ellen sat in the park, across from the drinking fountains, under a great blue Norway spruce.

"What's the problem?" Joe asked, brow furrowed in concern like some state-funded psychologist on autopilot. Ellen scrutinized him dubiously for a moment.

"I don't honestly know," she said. "But we've darn sure hit a fork in the road. Billy's had a tremendous amount of problems. After you left, he went in the Marines. He just seems to want to ranch, period, out in the hills doing his thing. And me, I'm about as quick to show sympathy over this Vietnam business as anybody. But it's not real cheerful, the way he goes about it. And like I say, he was in the Marine Corps and it seems to have started there. Being called maggots and stuff when they're just kids."

"Was he in some kind of combat?"

"Uh-huh."

"Do you still see him regularly?"

"We confine it strictly to matters concerning Clara. I don't encourage him. I finally put one of those little observation holes in my door, like an apartment. I had to put it in there because of Billy. Maybe I shouldn't say anything. My mother is seventy years old. She drives all the way in from the ranch to see me. I find myself looking at her through the little eyehole while she stands there with something she baked for me in her arms."

"What about when you want to see Clara?"

"Are you asking why she doesn't stay here with me in the apartment?"

"No, not at all," said Joe. He could see she was getting angry.

"Don't you think it's a little small? Don't you think I work hard enough?"

"No, I—"

"Have you ever heard of latchkey kids?"

"Yes, and that's not at all what I was talking about," Joe said. "I just thought this was a place I could see her. The ranch, with Billy and everything, isn't ideal."

"You're just going to have to be patient," Ellen said, then after a moment added, "I've still got an hour."

They dropped Ellen's books in the return slot at the library and went on with their stroll. Joe felt a strange tension in his stomach, the kind of thing that is communicated. They walked perhaps a block and the lack of a plan was creating enormous pressure.

"Let's go to my place," said Ellen quietly. It nearly paralyzed Joe. Her house was about three blocks away. Since he couldn't quite speak, he tried subtly changing his course. He could see the shiny auburn top of Ellen's head, the tan, freckled bands on the tops of her cheekbones. His agony lasted only the half a block of progress it took to confirm that that indeed was where they were headed.

A nerve-shattering cocker spaniel jolted toward them on four stiff legs attempting to turn itself inside out with a paroxysm of barking. They tried to ignore it, but the dog stole up from behind to bite. Joe turned around and kicked at it as the owner in a V-necked white T-shirt came out in the yard. "You want a cop?" yelled the owner. "Kick the dog and I get you a cop." The dog yelped back to the owner as though injured. Joe kept moving, though he felt his posture had rather collapsed. "Go on," bellowed the owner, "make my day!" But the next block took them into a quieter place where clothes billowed on a line and radios played merrily on window-sills.

The house Ellen lived in could be seen over neighboring rooftops a full block away. As they approached, it seemed to rise and enlarge.

"Come on up, it's unlocked," said Ellen. As she went up ahead of him, he was relieved to detect a lascivious thought at the angular motions of her hips under the cotton dress. What if I didn't have a lascivious thought? he wondered. What if I only thought of that character I met in Miami who burst into an Irish brogue at the moment of penetration? What a relief I'm not thinking of her! The "character" he was thinking about had been fascinated by her own Irish heritage and, during lovemaking, had cried, "Joe me lad, give it yer all!" He had never really gotten over it.

All he could think of was the character with the Irish brogue. He clutched the handrail as Ellen disappeared into her doorway. Good Christ. If I blow this one, I'll hang myself. I must turn into a wolf this minute or I'm lost; crude groping is the only thing that can get me beyond this impasse.

"Joe, what's holding you up?"

"Something in my shoe . . ." He sat on the stairs with his shoe in both hands, shaking it madly. "Just slip out of your little things and I'll be with you in a moment," he said in a gruff voice.

Ellen reappeared on the landing. "You what?" Joe was close to the limits of his endurance. He felt the flood building.

He rolled stomach-down onto the steps and let the laughter burst through him. He felt desperate as it ripped across his mind like a fire. He felt Ellen sit beside him.

"You know something?" she said in an admiring tone. "That's really funny, it really is. Are you all right?" Calmness began to pass over him, slowly, then it took hold. They agreed. It was funny. He was covered with sweat. He staggered to his feet, coming back to the world from an enormous distance. He could take her hand with simplicity. They could agree on going into her place.

"Here I fuck her brains out!" came the thought and he was on his stomach again.

"Joe, the neighbors are going to think you've flipped." He kept laughing. I'd just like to get me a little, was his final thought, recited in the decade-old voice of Slater as she stepped over his convulsed body and went back to work.

He didn't really want to think about the source of these hysterics. He knew down inside it was Astrid. She was using that santería on him from afar, that Cuban voodoo. She had left her prints in his mind and they weren't to be removed that easily. He did feel foolish. He felt that way for a week. He didn't try to see anyone. He didn't want to overdo his certainty about the cause of all this inadequacy. Then Ellen came on Saturday and took him touring. They went west for a couple of hours, with the sun behind them, in her car. She pretty much took the situation in hand; she got the room and they made love very happily. She didn't come across to him as starved or needy but a strong appetite was very evident. He was more used to the intricacies of staging and circumstance.

They were driving home in a distinct aftermath. Joe turned onto the main highway, bearing his palm down on the wheel and giving it a stylish whirl.

"Is this a good time to talk about Clara?" Joe asked.

"No, it is not."

The weather vacillated between blowing rain and infrequent openings of the sky to a higher world. Along the lower Madison, the hills angled toward the southeast were reared up into the oncoming weather and the wet clouds hung over the lower mesas and plateaus near the channels of the river. A cement truck labored along the frontage road.

Then the sun came out and in a short time there was not a cloud in the sky. But the road was still soaking wet and the car filled with the smell of rain and summer.

"I just can't understand why I did that," said Ellen, "when I'm trying to make a sincere effort to save my marriage."

They drove on for a while. Joe turned on the radio but it immediately seemed offensive and he shut it off. There was a great long bench at the south end of the Crazy Mountains that looked like a partly opened scallop shell. You could see all the blue of haze and sage and ditch-burning from here and minute sparkles of runoff from a distance, water carrying everything downward.

"Stop someplace," Ellen said, "I want to do it again." Joe took the first ranch exit and spiraled up above the interstate until he could see out in all directions for miles. The wind had the grass laid flat and a band of antelope drifted like a shadow of clouds. They undid each other's clothes and Joe slid toward her away from the wheel. She straddled him and pulled him into herself. "Jesus," she said, "I can't seem to stop." There was a delicious grotesquery as she pounded into him. He could see his hair and forehead in the rearview mirror jarring with her motion. He was being levitated. He couldn't keep his eyes off the sky, the distance, out of his memories. "Watch my face," she said. Her eyes seemed to close and sink as he joined her. He felt a wet circle of bone and sinew stretch down over him. Her mouth fell open and a groan of despair arose from far inside her.

When they got onto the highway again, she said in an exhausted voice, "Just drive."

This was enough to set Joe on a kind of dream in which the details of the road, the steadily expanding immediate memories, the cornucopia of bright new prospects all flowed together in a sort of narcosis. Joe pictured, in an extremely vague setting, a kind of life with Ellen and Clara. There seemed to be a convenient flow of pavement from the interstate to their exit and from their exit to Ellen's street. Indeed, they were nearly to the house when she cried, "Stop!" in a voice so startling that Joe slammed on the brakes. "It's my husband," she said. Joe expected a sinking feeling but got none. He was actually excited to get a look at Billy again.

But then the car in front of Ellen's house pulled out.

"I guess we're safe," Joe said. "He's leaving."

"Follow him," said Ellen.

"Follow him?"

"You heard me."

This last seemed so peremptory that Joe started after the car, a Plymouth Valiant, in a very uncertain state. They went down past the city park and turned toward the river. They left the older, prim homes of the town and entered a district of split levels and unfinished wood, of newly sodded lawns with dark green seams where the strips met the day lawn arrived. Billy's car stopped and Joe stopped, perhaps a half block behind. Ellen was slumped to dash level.

"He's after that bitch again," she hissed. "And look how he's dressed!"

Billy Kelton threw his legs out, then unreeled himself from the car. He was still the striking-looking, lanky cowboy Joe remembered, and he looked as capable as ever of giving Joe a good thrashing. Joe couldn't see anything abnormal in the way he was dressed. He loped to the house. He had no chance to knock on the door: a slender arm thrust it open and he vanished without any change in his stride. Ellen unlatched the door to Joe's car.

"I've had it up to here," she said. "Can't thank you enough."

Ellen got out of the car, walked up in front of the house as forthright as a hostess and got into Billy's car. She started the engine and blew the horn. In a moment, Billy emerged from the house and walked over, eyes downcast. He lifted the straw hat from his head, wiped his forehead with his shirt sleeve, and replaced the hat. He stood by the car. He talked without raising his eyes. He rested the tips of his fingers on the side of the car and his eyes started to elevate. Some relief was in sight. He bent slightly and looked inside. He smiled suddenly. He leaned inside for a kiss. Then there was a bit of distress. Ellen had evidently rolled his head up in the electric window. The car pulled forward and Billy was dragged a few yards. Then the car stopped for more negotiation. He was dragged once more and released. Rubbing his neck and turning his head to one side, he walked around to the passenger's door and got in. As they drove away together,

Joe watched the car intensely, certain that it would stop again, and Ellen would get out. But it just didn't happen. At least, Billy hadn't spotted him.

That night, Joe reflected on all this as he watched the Miss Universe contest. Miss Chile won. As the other contestants, in their terrible feigned happiness at her victory, covered Miss Chile with kisses, leaving red marks like wounds, her tiara was knocked askew. The camera caught the brief instant in which Miss Chile looked like a buffoon, a moment deftly corrected when Bob Barker rearranged the tiara with a self-deprecating shrug and grin, and with the nonchalance of one who adjusted ten thousand tiaras a day. It was late and Joe was tired.

17

Ralph of Ralph's Repair died. Joe couldn't exactly remember him but evidently he'd repaired some things for him in the past. Lureen called and said that she and Smitty had legal business in Billings and would Joe be kind enough to represent the family at the funeral. Ralph was cremated and an old couple in almost matching light blue pantsuits came out from Yakima for the jar. "Do you know those people?" asked Mary Lynn Anderson, the piano teacher from Rapelje. Mary Lynn had recently been dried out at the Rimrock Foundation in Billings and she had this maddening energy, a real born-again quality that was entirely trained on making up for lost time. She wore a cotton checked shirt of pale green that set off her tanned arms. She used to look religious when she was drinking, spiritually enraptured, but dried out she looked oversexed.

"Who are those people?" she asked Joe specifically, looking at the old people.

"Some kind of connections of Ralph's," Joe said.

"His folks?"

"Beats me. Somebody told me when I came in that's who they were."

"I sent some flowers to the family. I wonder if they got there."

"I don't know."

"Well, I don't want to put them under pressure but I'd

sure as heck like to know if my flowers ever got there. There was a note too."

The memorial service was being held at the little Carnegie library. Joe hadn't been to one of these since his Uncle Jerry was run over by a uranium truck. There were nine people there and five of them were browsing in the stacks. They had agreed to avoid a conventional service as being unsuited to Ralph's memory. The result was that nothing was happening. And in fact, Mildred Davis was trying to renew her library card and her husband Charlie was reading *Field and Stream*. Charlie was famous from opening up on his fourteen-year-old son with his fists for being in town without his cowboy hat on. Terry Smith had a Bible but he was completely furtive about it. Billy Kelton came in wearing his yellow slicker. He stared over at Joe, trying to remember him; Joe didn't help. Then Billy must have recalled their childhood differences, and he looked off in embarrassment. Joe still burned at those memories. Everyone went to the window to watch the new rain. "God, we needed that," said Alvie Skibstad, his gleaming white forehead contrasting with his dark face. "Take some of the fun out of it for the hoppers." Jim Carter came in the door soaked. He was only nineteen but his father had Alzheimer's and Jim had been running the ranch since he was fifteen; he bore the kind of weariness people rarely have at that age. "Headgate burst and run out over Main Street. The dry goods store is flooded." Charlie Davis looked up from *Field and Stream*, and said, "It happens every year." "Naw, it don't," said Jim, tired of old-timers' bullshit, tired in general.

"I hope this doesn't sound disrespectful," said Mildred Davis, "but we're sure going to miss Ralph when things are broken." The only place she had been able to find to sit was behind the counter where the librarian usually sat. She wore a dark blue dress and a pillbox hat from which a piece of starchy lace projected, as though subtly indicating the prevailing wind. The old couple from Yakima looked around like a pair of immigrants.

"Nope," said Charlie. He licked the ends of the first two fingers of his right hand and began madly leafing through the magazine as though he'd left his social security card in there somewhere. "It doesn't sound disrespectful."

They all sat around vaguely, unmotivated; heads began to hang at odd angles. Nothing is an emergency around here, Joe thought, and I'm not so sure that's good.

"I wonder if we ought to say something about Ralph?" Joe asked. Billy was now staring at him. Nobody said anything. A couple of people looked like they might have wanted to but couldn't quite come up with the right idea. "Well," Joe said, "I don't mind saying a few words. For all these years, when we have had things broken, little things, important things, things which allowed our lives to flow, Ralph was there to set them spinning along again and with them, our lives too seemed repaired, whether it was a toaster, a television, a tractor, or a tire."

"You're thinking of Ralph's over to Lewistown," said Billy Kelton.

"I am?"

"Yeah, this one only did appliances."

"Well, I think appliances have become central to our lives," Joe said.

"Forget it."

A silence fell. Billy looked around. He caught the eyes of the connections from Yakima, and then addressed them. There was fire in his eyes.

"The Bible makes us the promise that our dead ones will live," he told them in a clear and direct voice. "They will rise up. 'The righteous themselves will possess the earth and they will reside forever upon it.' I don't know who exactly you are to Ralph but you may feel the lamentation of King David at the death of Absalom. And if so, we remind you that God did not originally intend for us to die. But because of the Adam and Eve business, he pretty much had to let us all return to dust as a payment for sin. But what we expect around these parts is that at the time of the Resurrection, Ralph's got a better than even chance of being called and that's about all you can ask. We knew him fairly well." It got pleasantly quiet as everyone took this in.

People began to leave. "I'll lock up," said Mildred Davis. Joe went out. For some reason, the smell of newly turned gardens along the street reminded him of the ocean and impressions came back of heat and rain, of docks steaming after a cloudburst. He thought of the repairs of Ralph. He couldn't quite seem to place Ralph. He guessed he had made that fairly clear. I've got to get out of this fog, Joe thought. He just couldn't believe he'd gotten the wrong fucking Ralph.

18

Dear Joe,

I am really enjoying pursuing our relationship through the U.S. Mail. Your letters are concise. There is the illusion of decision. The dime store Hamlet you so frequently seemed to be is nowhere in sight. Instead of the oscillating and confused so-called thinker, I have the image of a man struggling to hold on to family land, to lend his best efforts to the creation of vast beef herds. Joe, this ties you heart and soul to every hamburger stand in America. And I think you need that. I think it will humanize you to know your life depends on mob whimsy because your poetic detachment is enough to make me throw up. Maybe this will cause it to go away. Maybe arguing with normal people who want to do something different with your family place will help you see that there are other criteria in human relationships than whether or not people agree with you.

If by some remote chance, all of this has the effect of returning you to the human race, it would make me happy if we could see one another again.

Love,
Astrid

Joe let this soak; then, to heat it up, he wrote back a few days later. As he wrote the letter, he felt an inexplicable, mad, tingling ache.

Dear Astrid,

Your letter seems to take the position that it is in reply to a letter from me. I have not written you. But it is nice to have yours anyway. As for here, it is not so bad. I am leading a baffling life but I am suited to that. I have barely had a chance to look into the sort of shooting we may expect this fall; and in fact all the little pleasures have gone by the way, not because I am so busy but because I am apathetic from being unable to completely understand what I am doing all this for. I wonder if you remember the great number of mountain hippies we used to have around here. Well, they are all running tax shelters for environmentalist organizations and I plan to meet with a few to see if we can save a buck or two as well as take the fun out of breaking this thing up for my greedy connections. Why haven't they moved away? I have found on my return that going out to seek your fortune no longer has the prestige it once had. Now on return they give you that fishy look and ask, "Back for the summer?" This proves to me that it is the rats who *do* stick with a sinking ship. No reference to you of course darling. I have had numerous opportunities to confirm that in fact I trust nobody. Which has its distorting effect. But we all live beneath some sort of lens and no true shapes can be discerned. I think it is quite enough to be able to tell someone what is on your mind, even if the delivery is nervous and sidelong. Therefore, this letter, my ideal recipient.—Still not getting any. How about yourself?

Joe signed it "With suspicious affection," licked the envelope, and threw it on the kitchen counter for the next trip to town. But before he could get it into the mail, he received yet another letter from Astrid, a short one. It said, "I hate you. You stole my car. Now I hate all men." He fired back one more.

Dear Astrid,

God made women because sheep can't cook.

Joe

He sent this latest with a gleeful and almost breathless air, reflected in the enormous cost of sending it by overnight mail. He must have known that it would have a big effect. He must have planned this bit of explosive infantilism without a hint of innocence. Because in four days flat Astrid, wearing enormous dark glasses, dragging more luggage than she looked like she had the strength to carry, walked in the front door and said, "Take it back, motherfucker."

He was so happy! He loved her with his whole heart. And then tears came into his eyes.

"Met anyone nice out here?" Astrid asked.

"One. But I already knew her, really."

"Get anywhere?"

"I would."

"Only what?"

"I keep laughing at the wrong time."

"I *see*."

He couldn't fathom her. It was like Jackie O at the funeral of Onassis. One suspected the sunglasses concealed twinkling eyes. When Astrid wished to tell him something important, she would grab his forearm the way children do to each other in the scary parts of movies. She did that now. "Do try to remember the week we had," she said. "All those funny things that weren't funny."

"Like what wasn't funny?"

"Farting in time to music."

"What else?"

"Calling me drunk at three a.m. and shouting, 'Don't pay the ransom, I've escaped!' Joe, you were a hoot!"

A certain formality was agreed upon without discussion: Astrid would have her own room. As it happened, the two bedrooms were on opposite sides of the kitchen and so the sense of division was fairly complete. It was Joe's plan to make this arrangement clear to Ellen as soon as he could. He didn't think that that was absolutely required; and in fact he meant to be sure his explanation did not imply a deeper responsibility to Ellen than necessary. He just wanted it clear. Astrid settled right into the arrangement without particularly indicating whether she was there for a day or a year. Joe didn't plan to ask. He didn't mention his daughter because he wanted to make certain a reasonable plan for visiting was in place before he got down to the specifics of an arrangement.

He was immediately fascinated by Astrid's city ways, which he hadn't even noticed before. She folded her things in her dresser and hung her blouses carefully in the closet. She got a glass from the kitchen to put in the bathroom cabinet and set a bottle of French perfume on the dresser where the brassieres were folded one cup inside the other. She tied the curtains in their middles to let in light, stretched the bedspread taut and placed a travel-battered paperback next to the bed. Joe noticed all this as breezily as he could, but since he had no real routines in this house, no routines anywhere really, it was hard to make a single natural movement at the same time he was observing Astrid. He simply felt her presence swelling and seeping throughout the house and found himself less and less able to even act as if he was ignoring it.

As they passed in the short corridor, he reached his hand out to her arm. She stopped at exactly that distance and said, "Yes?"

"Hi," he said, smiling, and feeling shockingly stupid. She said, "Hi."

They passed going in opposite directions. Joe thought that to keep this business from degenerating at a very rapid rate, he was going to have to have something to do other than absorb the impact of Astrid.

He turned back from the living room and stretching his arms across the doorway, spoke down the corridor toward Astrid's room. "I'm going to run in and get a few supplies before things close."

"Bye," she called, "use your seat belt."

He sped to Ellen's bearing some peculiar force because she simply let him rush into her house and make love to her, bracing her pelvis while she scrutinized this demented, ejaculating person. Joe felt withered by her quizzical stare. He dressed so quickly afterward he had to pry

124

himself back into his shorts. "I have to talk to you," he said, underlining this vagary with a powerful, fixed look. "You know what it's about. I feel I'm being strung along."

Ellen said, "You've got a lot of nerve after what we've just done."

"I mean, is this it? We're just going to sneak around like this?"

"It depends," Ellen said.

"Depends? On what?"

"On how I feel. God, Joe, you never changed! Can't you take one day at a time?"

"No," Joe said so loud it was almost a shout. *"I want to see my daughter!"*

He went to the IGA store and threw things arbitrarily into the shopping cart. He got stuck in the only checkout line that was open. A small, heavy woman in front of him, with a dirty-faced infant riding the cart, unloaded small items piled as high as her head. He stared at the front page of the *Star,* at the headline RABBIT FACE BABY HAS TEN INCH EARS, and read as much as he could of the text before he had to check out with his items: the dieting mother had binged on carrots during her final trimester.

As he unloaded his groceries in the kitchen, Astrid glided past him and said, "I smell what you've been doing."

He slowly turned in her direction, the burn of deep conviction; he was a bit too slow: she was already back in her room.

"When are you turning in that rental car?" he asked loudly.

"As soon as I can get to the airport," she said. "You can follow me."

"Why would I follow you?"

"So you can fucking well give me back my car."

Joe had once gone out with a girl who was just breaking up with her live-in boyfriend. He had quite fallen for this girl and had already begun worrying about the depth of his involvement. The boyfriend had recently moved out but he stopped back from time to time to bicker with the girl about the ownership of the stereo and the health of the bamboo plant he claimed to have nurtured to its current size, and to laugh sarcastically at the clean house she was currently keeping. As Joe watched the progress of these small nagging encounters, he began to suspect he was witnessing a preview of his own life. Detachment set in. Now, years later, he placed similar hopes on the pink car. Some nagging, the exchange of a few receipts, some appropriate body language, whirling departures or loud footsteps on the wooden floors of the ranch, and the slave chains could be gently lifted.

19

A few days later, he set up his drawing equipment in the kitchen, where the light was good and the coffee was close. But he knew it was a lie and he put it all away again. It was as if he was posing these materials. Astrid came in wearing her wrapper drawn close around her with one hand and carrying a cup and saucer in the other. She went to the sink and looked out the window. Joe felt that there was something brewing: the set of her mouth, her silence, something. He managed to watch her without being intrusive. As she looked through the kitchen window, her expression began to fill, to bloom, and he knew an emotion was cresting, an exclamation was at hand.

"Get a load of that ghastly dog!" she screeched. Joe jumped.

"Is he out there?" Joe got up and went to the window. The dog, lightly blurred with new fur, sidled over the lawn, glancing at the house, his corkscrew tail shifting metronomically over his back.

"I never saw one quite like that," said Astrid.

"I can't believe he's just out walking around."

"He's like something from outer space," she said. "I want to go see him."

"He'll be back under the house the second he sees you."

Joe watched from the kitchen window. He saw the

dog react to the motion of the inside kitchen door. His tail sagged to the horizontal. His lower jaw dropped slightly and his ears clenched into a suspicious knot on top of his head. Then Astrid appeared in the picture. She said something to the dog. She patted the tops of her knees. The crown of the dog's head smoothed as his ears dropped adorably. He bounced back and forth, then bounded to Astrid and licked her face. She found a stick for him to fetch; but when she reared back to throw it, he yelped and ran under the house. Astrid went over and lay on her stomach to plead with the dog. Joe wound open the kitchen window and hauling himself forward over the sink and faucets was able to look straight down on the lower half of Astrid's torso; the rest of her was under the house. She had let the wrapper slip up so that the hard shape of her buttocks was visible up to where they were sliced from view by the clapboard siding. "Aw, come on," she was saying, "whaddya say?" Joe's face was only a matter of feet from her bare loins and he could feel himself swelling abruptly against the sink. Astrid began to back out from under the house. He was terrified that she would discover him hanging out of the kitchen window, and he grappled his way inside, managing to hit one of the faucets in his rush, and soaking the front of his pants. By the time he was standing flatfooted on the kitchen floor once more, Astrid walked back in, stared at his wet bulging crotch, and said, "What have you been doing" in an uninflected voice. It was not a question. She sighed deeply and went into her room.

"Let me see if we can't just drop the rental car right in town," he said into the bedroom doorway.

"Give her my regards," said Astrid, in a kind of trill.

"You can reach me at my aunt and uncle's," he called back. "The number's by the phone." He paused in the doorway, soundless, in case anything could be heard from her direction, any little thing. But it was quiet.

He shot into Smitty and Lureen's. He didn't really want to stop, hadn't intended to. As soon as he got there, he called the ranch. "It occurred to me," he said to Astrid, "that the number might actually *not* be there—"

"It is."

"Okay," he sang, "that's all I had in mind."

"Bye."

Smitty was alone. Lureen had gone to do something at the rectory. Smitty sat at the kitchen table, his hands clasped on its top. He wore the familiar suit pants and his shirt was buttoned right up to his throat. He seemed to stand before some final and invisible inquisition as he wailed, "Here I am living on leftover chicken salad and baked beans! While Lureen dusts for that double-chinned preacher!"

It might have been his present mood or his recollection of his gingerly first night here, but Joe said, "Then why don't you get up off your ass and cook something?"

After a long moment, Smitty said, "I have decided that I didn't hear you. You have still got, by special dispensation, an unblemished record in this house."

"I just wanted to check in and see if you and Lureen are getting along okay."

"We are, if you think so. We're not complaining. The Overstreets are not happy about you running those cattle. I don't know what we, or at least Lureen, are going to live on."

"I think you're going to be fine," said Joe and went out.

"You forgot your thesaurus!" Smitty called from the stoop.

"I'll be back!" Standing in front of the two-story blue expanse of clapboard in the perfectly centered doorway, Smitty reminded Joe of a cuckoo clock. Smitty used to be a man about town, but there were only one or two apertures in the building in which he appeared now: the front door and his bedroom window.

Joe drove down Benteen Street and turned on Fifth, went a couple of blocks in an old neighborhood whose telephone wires came through heavy foliage and slumped low over the street. Plastic three-wheelers were parked on the sidewalk. A woman smoked and seriously watched her dachshund move along the band of grass between the sidewalk and the street. Another woman stood

in the street and waved her husband on as he backed his
Buick slowly from an old garage. At a certain point, she
flattened her palms in his direction, the car stopped, she
got in, and they drove off. There was a five-cent lemon-
ade sign but no stand. Finally, with a flourish, Joe arced
Astrid's rental car into Ellen's driveway. As soon as he
had stopped, the engine still running, the passenger door
opened and Billy Kelton climbed in.

"Hi, Billy."

"Let's take a ride," he said.

Joe put the car in reverse. "Any spot in particular?"

"You pick."

Joe crossed the neighborhood the way he had come.
He made a point of greeting people with a small neighborly wave. Most responded as from long acquaintanceship except the lady with the dachshund, who was sufficiently possessed to remove her cigarette and squint after
him with irritation. Billy exhibited a lazy athletic grace.
He was dressed more conventionally now in a pair of
Wranglers and a blue work shirt. He had a hardbitten,
thin-lipped, fairly handsome face, and a husky voice.

"I don't know what to do about the fact you've been
seeing Ellen . . ."

Joe looked out to the oncoming street. He set his head
to one side as though about to speak. Then nothing came.

"I fought for a country I'm not sure I care to live in.
But while I'm here I can find a few ways to make it my
own. If you follow me."

"Not completely. And I thought your marriage was on
the rocks. Weren't you seeing someone just the other
day? But yes, Billy, I missed the war in Vietnam."

"Well, there you go. That's about it, isn't it."

Joe could nearly feel the heat of his stare. They drove
on down past the wool docks alongside the railroad
tracks and then curved on up toward the courthouse.

"I don't want to just go to spelling things out here,
pardner, but there's this little country of my own where I
make all the laws. Do you believe me?"

Joe pulled up in front of the glass doors of the sheriff's
office. They could look through the windshield, through

the door, and see law officers. It would be an easy thing to honk on the horn. Joe tapped it lightly; two officers glanced out and he waved them off as though he had bumped the horn accidentally.

"Why wouldn't I believe you?" Joe said bitterly. "If you'll admit being in that war you've got nothing to hide. Now, do you want to walk, or shall I? I don't care, this is a rental car anyway."

"I'll walk, thanks. But just take me pretty serious here. It's important. Ellen and I haven't given up. And we have a sweet little girl that's worth any sacrifice we might make."

20

"And B," said Astrid, "it's time you potty-trained your mind. Especially as relates to me and my activities."

He didn't dare ask what A was. She was drinking and had *been* drinking. Nevertheless, she looked quite attractive with her dark hair still wet from the shower, its ends soaking the light blue dress at its shoulders. It was very rare for Astrid to drink too much. This was just fascinating. Everything she did fascinated Joe.

"I don't know much about your activities," said Joe coldly.

"Did you see the little chiquita?" Astrid inquired. Joe couldn't understand why in this age women in the throes of jealousy always used these ghastly diminutives on one another. The chiquita, the cutie, the little woman, the wifette.

"You know, I missed her. Isn't that a shame?"

"I think it is a shame," Astrid wailed, "that you can't have everything you want every minute of the day. You once employed all your arty bullshit to make me feel that I fulfilled something in you."

"We grow."

"You grow. I don't."

"Careful now. We want to avoid the emetic side of boozy self-pity."

She gave him the finger with one hand and raised her

glass to her lips with the other. "Joe Blow," she said with a smile, "the man in translation."

"My God! We throw nothing away! We never know when we might need it!"

"You lost that round, dopey. Go make some dinner. My stomach thinks my throat's been cut, or whatever they say out here."

At first he didn't think he would cook, because she suggested it. He then decided that that in itself indicated lack of independence and went to the kitchen to begin. As he cooked, he watched to see if she would make herself another drink. She didn't. She watched the news (excitement about medium-range missiles). She was looking out into the world. He was looking into the sink. It had just gotten real slow. The terrible slowness was coming over him. He lifted his face to the doorway and there she was, fast-forwarding world news facts into her skull with the television. It didn't seem to matter that she was drunk; it wouldn't make any real difference. It wouldn't turn medium-range missiles into long-range missiles. It wouldn't sober her up unless the actual TV blew up in her actual face.

"What are you cooking?" she called.

"Couple of omelets. Not too much stuff in the fridge."

"No rat poison, please!"

He chopped up some bell peppers and crookneck squash and scallions. He made everything astonishingly uniform. While he beat the eggs, Astrid came in and refilled her drink. She watched him cook. As he heated the skillet, she said, "No, you don't want sex with me just now. You were too busy jacking off while I tried to make friends with your dog." She went back into the living room and fell into her chair. Joe overcame his inertia and finished cooking. He finally got things on the kitchen table and called Astrid. She came and sat down. "I have just seen something very interesting on television," she said, avidly eating her omelet. "This is good."

"What did you see?"

"A report on grizzly bear attacks. It's so exciting here

in Montana! The victims tend to be menstruating women!"

"That's not so hard to understand."

"Ha ha ha. He tips his hand."

"I didn't mean it as a joke," he said.

He couldn't eat. His omelet was a folded yellow fright. His hands were sweating. The glare on the kitchen windows was such that you wouldn't necessarily know if someone was looking in. A shining drop of water hung on the faucet without falling.

"Here's my exit," she intoned. "I get my period. I go hiking in Glacier National Park."

"Let's hope it doesn't come to that."

She started laughing hard and loud. She stopped. Her chin dropped to her chest. A guffaw burst through her nose. She covered her mouth and twisted her face off to one side. "I'm so sorry—" She threw up on the kitchen floor.

"That's enough for me," said Joe and got to his feet.

"Don't put any more miles on that rent-a-car," she shouted as he went out the door. Immediately, he could hear her crying.

"The things alcohol makes us do," he thought, walking across the yard. "Leading cause of hospitalization, leading cause of incarceration"—he began marching to this meter—"leading cause of broken families, leading cause of absenteeism, leading cause of half-masters, leading cause of fascination with inappropriate orifices, leading cause of tooth decay, leading cause of communism, leading cause of Christian fundamentalism, leading cause of hair loss, leading cause of dry loins, leading cause of ulcerated chickens, leading cause of styrofoam. Ah, mother and father," he wheezed, out of breath. "Time to arise. Time to buck some bales up onto the stack." Moonlight dropped upon him. He walked out into the prairie whose humming had stopped at sundown. A fall of frost had begun and the grassy hummocks were starred with ice. The gleam of canine eyes caught the moonlight.

21

Joe spent the following day with the state brand inspector, trying to organize all his cattle receipts. When he got home, Astrid was in bed. She was running a high fever and had sunk into a glumly witty state of disassociated illness. She looked so helpless, so dependent, so unlike anything he'd ever seen before in Astrid that he felt an abounding sweetness well up within. He was sorry that it seemed so inappropriate to mention his declining fortunes. He was under a momentary spell of amicability. People at full strength were better able to sustain their loathing, and avoid these vague and undrained states.

"My darling," said Joe.

"Do you know who's been just swell?" she asked, propping herself up in bed. She looked like a pretty nun without makeup and with her hair pulled back.

"Who?"

"Smitty."

"Smitty? How do you know Smitty?"

"He's been by. And I mean swell."

"That's quite strange."

"He seems so concerned! He's concerned with everything. He just trains this concern on things. What concern is shown by Smitty!"

"What about Lureen? She been by?"

"She was here too. Now that one isn't sure about me.

But Smitty is so lovely. He thought he might be able to get me some insurance."

"You didn't go for it, did you?"

"No, but I gave him fifty bucks for some kind of filing fee."

"I know that filing fee. It's called Old Mr. Boston Dry Gin."

"I couldn't say. I went for his story. It charmed me. I'm already bored. I wish I was back in Florida, fucking and using drugs. It's easy to grow nostalgic in a situation like this."

"Oh, darling, just stop," he said, annoyed by his own reaction. He thought of vigorous, robust Ellen, ranch girl, heartening the next generation with teaching. Difficult to imagine her saying in the middle of lovemaking, as Astrid once did, "Now I'd like it up my ass." He had prevaricated, he recalled, then ultimately brooded about the prospects of a second chance.

"You know it's funny," said Joe, wondering why he didn't appreciate Astrid any more than he did. "I've had such a thing for this schoolteacher."

"Do I have to hear this?"

"I'm trying to keep you entertained. We're beyond any little ill feelings along these lines anyway, aren't we? Besides if I tell you this in a sarcastic way and make it good and trivial I can write 'finis' to the sonofabitch." It wasn't true. He wanted to hurt her. He was laying in stores to hate himself.

"Knock yourself out. I really don't care."

Joe believed her. There was malice in his continuation of the story. It was temporarily beyond him to take stock of the gravity of their situation. It was an awful moment.

"Anyway, I've been drawn to her innocence, whether or not it exists. It may not exist. But I took it as a working proposition that the innocence was real."

"Did you stick it in?"

"I'm afraid I did."

"She can't be that innocent."

"But we had these wonderful little skits. I knew her

136

years ago. We hit golf balls together. We discussed her background on the ranch."

"You stuck it in."

"We stuck it in. We had meals together in an atmosphere that combined lightheartedness and high courtship. We went for a long drive."

"This is to puke over," said Astrid.

"Now, Astrid. There was something quite delicate. A picture had begun to form." Joe felt like a vampire.

"I can see that picture."

"But wait. I had decided to marry her. We would live together in the picture that had begun to form. I flew to New York and quit my job with Ivan. I was exhausted. When I was flying home, the country unfolded beneath the wings and it all came to me that—I don't like that smile, Astrid—I would marry this lovely girl. And I must say, that is a very nasty smile, indeed."

"I shouldn't laugh," said Astrid. "I am in the dreary mental situation in which sneezing, laughing, coughing, calling the dog, or ensemble singing are equally uncomfortable. Anyway, what happened is that you thought it over and upon consideration, upon the most serious consideration you—"

"No. Not this time. I called and before I had the chance to propose, her husband went for a ride with me and told me that they were working it out."

"There's a husband?"

"And a right odd one at that. He used to thrash me when I was a boy, beat me like a gong."

"Well, if you'd had any conviction, you'd have argued with him. If you'd had the kind of conviction that it would take to go back to your painting, you'd have told that hubby off. Now what've you got? A trashy-mouth Cuban who doesn't appreciate you."

"Oh, darling," said Joe in a flat and uninterested tone, "don't be so hard on yourself."

Astrid's weeping was real. Joe could scarcely remonstrate with her. She had every right to this. His position had eroded and he could not say a thing. Instead, he gazed through the window at nothing and came to appreciate how wonderful much of the world could seem.

Collecting herself, she said, "Well, what am I to do?"

"I'm not good at this," said Joe.

Astrid tried to shift her weight slightly. She sighed. "Given my desperation, I wonder if you'd have time to murmur some smut in my ear."

"Astrid."

"Something about the schoolteacher possibly. Anything. There was a fly in the room earlier. You can't imagine my absorption in watching its confused circuit of my room."

"I hope you're resisting ideas like that."

"What easy ideas have you resisted?"

"I hate you."

"I hate you too."

The sudden bitterness of these remarks was stunning. Literally, they were both stunned by what they had said. They had heard it before and it was still utterly stunning, as stunning to hear as to say.

He rose to go. "We don't mean that."

"We don't?" said Astrid. She looked exhausted. He was horribly sorry that he hadn't headed the moment off. But they had been in this intense snare for so long. It was hard to keep things from just running their course.

22

The next day Lureen was on the phone at seven.

"Joe, I don't know if you realize this but Smitty has been bringing seafood up from Texas in a refrigerated truck. I mean, he's brokering it, not physically doing it himself, and he has run into a hitch."

"Which is?" Joe asked, knowing that he had just learned where the lease money had gone, some of it anyway.

"I hear your suspicion already. Now, I want you to give this a fair hearing."

"Sock it to me, Lureen."

"Well, a big load of it spoiled."

"That's a shame. I'm sorry to hear it."

"But it was insured."

"When did this happen?"

"Three weeks ago."

"How much was it insured for?"

"Thirty thousand."

"Wow, that's a powerful load of shrimp. Did he collect?"

"Not yet. But I'm sure he will."

"So what's the problem?"

"The problem is that the insurance company has initiated an investigation. They want to actually *view* the spoiled shrimp. Smitty said, It's a little late now, I buried

139

it. And the investigators said, We want to see the spot. So, Smitty very graciously took them out to the place—"

"Wait a minute. Where?"

"*There*. You were in New York. And up by the burn pit, he showed them the empty boxes, but they wanted to see the shrimp. Smitty couldn't believe his ears. The what? he said. And real rudelike, the chief investigator says, *The shrimp, the shrimp, the shrimp!* It's been three weeks! Smitty told him. They have decomposed! You got it? But—and it's a big 'but'—this horrible man, this investigator said, Nope, there'd still be shells. I don't know where this all leads but, Joe, for my own peace of mind, I know you've spent time down in the Florida—"

"Right, Lureen, I've seen a world of shrimp."

"Would there still be, after all these weeks, any indication—I won't say *evidence*—that there had been any shrimp?"

"Yes. Shells. Tens of thousands of them, by the sound of it."

"Joe, we've tried so hard to be nice to you and make you feel to home . . ."

It was too late. She had already signed for the cattle. Joe put the receiver down slowly and carefully. At first, he was contrite: he could have said something more reassuring. But, like what? He was entirely limited to exaggerating the speed at which shrimp shells decompose. How else could he explain Lureen's belligerence? Surely she was not one hundred percent taken in by Smitty, the bounder. She must know he meant to glom the ranch, mustn't she?

Joe actually saw Smitty drive up. Smitty wasn't going very fast when he came in the driveway, but he stabbed the brakes so that the blue and white Ford skidded a little on the gravel. He sort of threw himself from the car, flinging the door shut behind him. At first, he seemed in a hurry but he lost a little speed by the time he actually got to the front door.

"Smitty," said Joe, opening the door for him. He

reached out his hand. Smitty gave it a glance before shaking it.

"Have you got a minute?"

"Sure I do, Smitty. Coffee?"

"No, I'm fine. Where can we sit?"

They went into the living room. Smitty glanced around at the books, the family pictures, the braided riata that hung on a hook by the door, the college diplomas, the brands burned into the wood, the chunks of quartz that old settler had mortared into the fireplace. They sat down.

"What's the deal, Joe?"

"Sir?"

"The deal. What are you doing back here?"

"Well, I just wanted to come back."

"You did."

"And I thought, somewhere along the way, we might do more with the place. The spotted knapweed and spurge are kind of taking over. Russian thistle. The fellows who lease it don't care about the old ranch. Fences falling. Springs gone."

"Leasing is the only money there is left in these places."

"The money? What money? So far as I can tell, the grazing fees aren't even making it to Lureen."

"We're listing it as a receivable. We've had some problem collecting. If we can't collect it, we can write it off. We all need that."

"To write it off you're going to have to sue the man that owes it to you. The government requires that."

"Whatever."

"Maybe the rancher you were dealing with needed to be examined more closely."

"He's over twenty-one. What can I say?"

Smitty put a cigarette in the exact center of his mouth and with a book of matches in his hands, rested his elbows on his knees, looked off into space and thought. "Joe," he said and lit the cigarette. "Why don't you kiss my ass?"

"Because I have preserved my options, Smitty. One of

them is to keep an eye on you." Then he added, "I know the seafood business hasn't treated you well. You must be under pressure." Smitty's eyes flicked off to the wall.

Well, thought Joe, at least it's a beginning; we'll gradually move old Smitty into position and then do the right thing. He watched Smitty and tried to get to the bottom of the combined helplessness and guile, without much luck. The signals of an old boozer like Smitty, thrown off by the cheesy deliquescence of the brain itself, were seldom instructive.

The glow of Astrid's cigarette in the twilight of her room looked as cheerful as a Cub Scout campfire to Joe as he finished telling her the whole story. He leaned over from his straightback metal chair and lifted the cigarette from her lips. He hadn't had a cigarette in almost a month. He was tempted to take a drag and told Astrid so. "Don't," she said. "It's so hard to quit." He could feel her easy thought. "God," she said, "that's a wonderful story. But you must have such complicated feelings about all this."

"I'm working on it."

Astrid began laughing. She was really laughing too hard. He leaned over and gripped her shoulders to steady her. The laughter made him nervous and he took her cigarette. He had to stick her cigarette way out in the corner of his own mouth to keep the smoke out of his eyes. Then her face began to glisten with tears. Anyway, she wasn't laughing anymore. Joe sat off to one side, holding her cigarette for her.

"One of these days," he said, "it's going to get cold. And that beautiful white snow is going to come floating down."

Joe arranged to buy an old iron woodstove from a rancher up toward the Musselshell River. It was in one of the livestock papers and he bought it very inexpensively, but he had to haul it himself. He took the flatbed truck and drove up through a vast expanse of bluish sage-covered hills. He went through two isolated hamlets, huddled with their Snow Cats and hay sleds piled outside in the heat. One little town had a bar the size of a single-car garage and a log post office that seemed dwarfed by its wind-whipped flag. He drove up to the edge of a stand of lodgepole pines bordered by a big buffalo grass pasture. Someone was burning ditches and high above the column of smoke a blue heron soared, trailing its legs, looking for its accustomed lowlands. Old black automobile tires hung on the fenceposts, painted *Keep Out* as a small log house was approached. The house sat low and defensive behind a field of discarded machinery: old iron wheels, wooden spokes, and last year's winter kill dragged out among the disarray—hides over skeletons, decomposing calves.

An old man answered the door, a glass of whiskey in one hand, his stomach hanging over the top of his pants and chew dribbling out the corners of his mouth. He had hairy nostrils and small, crinkled eyes. "Here for the stove?"

"Yeah, I am." Joe got the money out of his shirt and reached it to him.

"Thank you much," said the old man.

"There's a Farmhand on the Minneapolis-Moline. You load that thing on your own?"

"You bet."

The old man narrowed the doorway. He scrutinized Joe. "Sonny Starling wouldn't be your daddy, would he?"

"Yes, sir, that he was," Joe said. The old man nodded and thought.

"He was a hand, really what you'd call a pretty hand."

"That's what I've heard," said Joe.

"But the bank took all the pretty out of your old man."

"Yes, sir."

"He come in and ruint me in 'fifty-six. I never made her back. That bank just took Sonny and made him into an entirely different feller."

Joe had heard this sort of thing before.

"Well, let me get loaded out of here," he said.

"That's a hell of a way to get ahead in the world."

"Maybe," said Joe, "but anyway, he's dead."

"Good," said the old man.

Joe threw himself into loading the stove. He lowered it onto the flatbed with the Farmhand and boomed it down with some chain he had brought along for the purpose. Evidently the old man didn't need it anymore. He had a better one or he'd gone to electric or gas. Joe started back. When he was nearly home, he saw a pickup truck pulled off the interstate next to the barbed wire. A man stood next to a horse whose head hung close to the ground. The man looked quite helpless and Joe sensed the horse was at the end of the line. It was at this point that his eyes finally filled with tears.

23

Joe drove to Billings on Tuesday to meet with an attorney for the Continental Divide Insurance Company. He dressed in a coat and tie and parked the old flatbed far enough away to dissolve association with it by the time he reached the office. He was early.

He walked into the Hart-Albin store to use up a few minutes and collect his thoughts. He strolled through the toiletries section, admiring the beautiful young women who sold perfumes and intimate soaps, and who tried the delicate atomizers on one another. He sprayed some sample cologne on himself. The glass display cases revealed an Arabic world of indulgence. He tried more cologne. He invented biographies for the salesladies. Reared on hog farms or in the families of railroad mechanics, each greeted her discovery by the perfume manager with an effulgent blossoming. He politely tested one last cologne with a sweaty squeeze of the bulb. A musky, faraway penumbra engulfed him, quite startling in its power.

Time to go to the lawyer. He crossed the street, walked half a block north, and entered the offices. He announced himself to the secretary and immediately the lawyer, Gene Bowen, appeared at his door and gestured Joe inside with a handful of papers. Bowen was a lean, harried-looking man, plainly bright and short of time.

Bowen moved around behind his desk. Joe sat in a

comfortable chair in front of it. Bowen rested his chin on his hands and let Joe begin. "My Uncle Smitty, Smith Starling—"

"Yes," said Bowen decisively, suddenly wrinkling his nose. Joe was astonished at the lawyer's reaction to the mention of Smitty's name. "Is that you? What is that?" Then Joe understood Bowen's reaction.

"Canoe."

"You what?"

"Canoe. It's a cologne. And a couple of others. Musk was one."

"Very well. Go ahead. Didn't mean to interrupt."

"My Uncle Smitty—"

"Would you be offended if I opened a window?"

"Not at all."

Bowen got up and struggled with the window behind his desk without freeing it. "I'm gonna end up with a fucking hernia—"

"Here, let me help."

They got on either side of the window and heaved upward as hard as they could. Bowen pulled his face to one side and wrinkled his nose fiercely. "It's not as if it was some kind of animal droppings," Joe said.

The bottom of the window casement tore free; wood fragments and dried putty flew across Bowen's desk. His finger was bleeding. He walked around and opened his door. "Let that air out while I get a Band-Aid."

The secretary poked her head in. "What's going on in here?"

"We had a little trouble with the window."

"I'd better ring up maintenance." Turning to Joe, she asked, "May I ask what you're wearing?"

Joe was getting angry. "I mixed a few scents, trying them out. But socially speaking, I've had better luck shitting my pants."

Bowen returned and went straight to his desk. "Leave that open, Mildred," he said to the secretary, pointing at the door. "Let's try to bear down and get through this as fast as we can. Okay, 'Smitty' is your uncle. Smitty's got his tail in a crack. You want to help Smitty. Why?"

"I have an aunt who I like very much. She depends on him. They are like a little couple."

"They are."

"Yes."

"And what does she do?"

"She is a retired schoolteacher."

"So, she has a pension?"

"A small one, and a small income from a small family ranch."

"Which belongs to?"

"Uh, to Lureen. To my aunt."

"And Mister Smitty got his stake in the shrimp business by?"

"Mortgaging the ranch."

Bowen sucked on a paper clip pensively.

"It's none of my business, Mr. Starling. But why don't you let this wonderful fellow just go to jail?"

"I'm pursuing my aunt's interests, as I see them, as best I can."

"Okay," said Bowen, dropping his hands to the desk decisively. "I sense that we can speak to one another with candor."

"I sense the same," said Joe earnestly.

"May I be very direct with you?"

"Please."

"Joe, your aftershave stinks to high heaven."

"I really can't do anything about that now."

"As to Mister Smitty, yes, we can try to get the charges dropped. Yes, I foresee that being a discussable possibility. Under this scenario, Smitty fails to recoup the thirty thousand. *In addition to which*, the insurance company is out of pocket, I am guessing, another thirty, in fees, and in ascribable overhead."

"What overhead?"

"They've got twelve floors in Denver."

"I see. Well, look, let's examine the cost of dropping this. You get me some specifics and I'll try to sell it to my uncle."

"But remember, he doesn't have to buy it," said Bowen. "He can go to jail."

"I admit it's tempting," said Joe.

"The first time he stoops for the Lifebuoy in those big showers, he's going to meet some very nice Indians."

"Like I say," said Joe, "the temptation is there."

24

It was a long drive back. He listened to a local radio station for a while and absorbed himself in the community announcements. Money was being taken up to purchase bibs for senior citizens. A truculent Boy Scout made the following statement: "This week we decided what badges we are going to do. The two main ones are Tending Toddlers and Science-In-Action. And we are going to bring dues of twenty-five cents even if we are sick." After that a member of the Lions Club explained the problems they had had building a concession stand for Little League games. They had to find out if the neighbors would object. Zoning ordinances required it be a certain distance from the street. That meant they had to move the backstop. A building permit would have to be applied for. To meet Class A Residential zoning requirements, the concession stand would have to go between the pitcher's mound and first base. The planning board granted a special-use permit. So, after five years, they were now prepared to build the concession stand. Finally, before Joe shut the radio off, the fire chief said they were sick of putting out prairie fires started by the railroad.

Oh, this is an odd little life, he thought, turning onto Smitty and Lureen's street. Great shafts of sunlight came down between the old trees that lined the badly cracked sidewalk. A newspaper boy jumped the curb with his bicycle and a man in a wheelchair, wearing a tam-o'-shanter and smoking a cigar, coasted down the slight incline of the sidewalk serenely, the spokes of his wheels sparkling in the afternoon sun. Two young carpenters with a long plank resting on their shoulders, made a wide turn at the corner and disappeared. Pigeons poured out of the abandoned Methodist church like smoke and ascended into the sky; they were the reincarnated souls of miners, railroaders, and ranch hands. Things seemed so right to Joe, he was able to enfold himself in the breaking wave. Ambiguity was at a safe distance now; it was not necessary to have an opinion about anything.

Lureen led Joe into the parlor. She set out tea. He cast his eye over the curios and the lugubrious draperies that declared this an inner world. He felt he had arrived.

"I've been to see the lawyer for the insurance company."

"Oh," said Lureen, "I wonder if that was a good idea."

"I think it was. We talked about the possibility of dropping the charges."

"Let them charge him. He's innocent. They can take it to court. I almost prefer it. It's in the rumor mill anyway. It might be good to have Smitty's name cleared publicly."

"Are you certain this is your wish?"

"My wish is that it had never happened. But since it has, it has to be cleared. You know, I blame my own mother for this. She doted on me and I'm grateful for that. But to her dying day, she went around town saying, 'My daughter is an angel from heaven, but my two boys' —Smitty and your father—'are common swindlers!' Words like this from a mother hang on in a small town for years."

Looking at Lureen as she poured the tea and thinking of the multitude of first- and second-graders who had gone on from her bare schoolroom greatly strengthened by her attentions, he couldn't help thinking his grandmother had been partly, and maybe entirely, right.

He was so fond of Lureen that, against his own inclinations, he said, "If you change your mind and I can help, let me know."

Lureen looked off and thought for a moment. "When you were a little boy, you sucked your thumb. You sucked your thumb until you were seven years old. And the orthodontist said it had given you a severe overbite and that if you didn't quit immediately, it would have to be corrected by surgery. Remember? It was in August and you were such a desperate little boy. But it was Smitty who sat up with you at night when you cried and put a sock over your hand and stayed up night after night with you—for a week!—until you succeeded. Night after night! He never had a drink until you quit. These people who want to put him in jail don't know anything about that side of Smitty."

Motoring along, unable to sort out his feelings about his aunt and uncle, he mused about his early days with Astrid—the high flying, the courtship, the glands titrating explosive juices into their systems, followed one noon by Astrid's announcement that she was considering suicide.

Later, she rejected it, saying, "Suicide is far too peculiar for me. It's something that should be done by science majors or Mormons. It should be done by people we know little about, like ship brokers and risk arbitragers."

They were so chipper then, embedded in time. Joe could paint blindfolded. They moved in the direction of their intentions as quickly as figures in cartoons. He remembered thinking it was swell past measuring. But somehow it got less juicy. Somehow it got annoying. Astrid never mentioned suicide again. She was far too bored to commit suicide. And they were both beyond something. He couldn't wait to see Astrid and try to sense whether or not it was true they were beyond everything.

He went to her, held her face in his hands, bent over and kissed her softly. "I've never stopped loving you," he said.

"Oh, great!" said Astrid. Joe felt the ache of tears come.

25

A man from the Soil Conservation Service came out in the morning and Joe walked him up the hill to show him where he wanted to put some concrete turn-outs and drop lines for his irrigating water. The man kept stuffing his lower lip with Copenhagen and staring out at the edge where the sagebrush breaks reached the brilliant green of the alfalfa. He had recently been through a divorce, he explained, and wasn't all there. Joe just couldn't stand to hear this. He was counting on this man to represent the real world right this very minute.

"We'll have to survey the ditches in again because we're burning up on the tops of all those knolls," Joe said. "I don't think they were ever in the right place."

"She took me to the cleaners," said the ASCS man, elevating the brim of his cap with a rigid forefinger. "She left me a purple pickup and one clean pair of jeans and that was all she wrote. Propped up in front of the game shows smoking weed all day and this baldheaded old judge says she gets the works."

"I hear you," said Joe absently, and tried to get back to his subject, which was an aging alfalfa field and a ditch that leaked because of all the shale. "The thing is, I've got some backhoe and concrete work that has to be done and it's going to be expensive."

But before he could enlarge on his subject, the government man said, "We'll pick up seventy percent on all irrigation projects whether you shit, go blind, or piss up a rope. But you're going to have to come to town and fill out some forms."

That was what Joe wanted. So he commenced a laying on of hands, murmuring effectively about the victim's life in America. The ASCS man told him the working man don't stand a chance. They walked down through the alfalfa, the white flowers just beginning to come, the shadows curving toward them over the plateau. A hawk flew levelly across the space toward a single tree; just before he got there, his line of flight took a deep sag and he swooped up to his perch.

Joe's cattle were such a sorry, mixed bunch, under such a variety of brands, that it was imperative to get them in and rebrand every one of them. The state brand inspector practically ordered him to. "You better have you a branding bee," he said to Joe when they looked over the receipts.

Joe branded a hundred and thirteen yearlings on Sunday. Astrid left early to tour Yellowstone. She had heard about branding and was determined, she said, to go through life without ever seeing it. Two strong neighbor boys, Ellen's nephews, came down to wrestle. Joe roped the whole time off his gelding, enjoying the good job of breaking Bill Smithwick had done. Old man Overstreet, his plaid overcoat safety-pinned across his chest, showed there were no hard feelings by helping Joe at head and heels as they worked the yearlings in the pole corral. But Joe remembered the old man had been told about Clara. Joe was a little uncomfortable.

Joe thought, I've been away too long. I feel sorry for these animals. A tall sixteen-year-old in a red shirt, which had rotted out in the center of his shoulders, followed the dragging cattle behind Joe's horse and grabbed a front leg so they would drag more smoothly. The other boy put a knee on the head and crimped a foreleg around. The sixteen-year-old sat on the ground holding one leg and subdued the other with his feet. Still, they got kicked. Old man Overstreet applied the irons, J-S, Joe's father's brand. When the smoking metal seared into the flesh of the steers, they stretched their necks out and opened their mouths; their gray tongues fell forth and they bawled. Joe could hardly bear it, though he let no expression cross his face. The sixteen-year-old freed Joe's lariat, and the boy's mother, a silent, rawboned woman of fifty, applied the iron and gave shots to the ones with hoof rot or bad eyes. It went very smoothly in an increasing cloud of smoke. When they had all the cattle penned in one place, old man Overstreet, looking like an undertaker in his long tattered coat, started to go through the cattle with his cutting horse.

Joe thanked his helpers and went back to the ranch to do the paperwork on the soil conservation cost-sharing application. There were black thunderheads up the valley and occasional sparks of lightning; the day could quickly get shortened. He cracked a beer and went out on the porch to watch the weather. This may be the principal use of a cattle ranch in these days, he thought: watching the weather. He daydreamed. Holding his cold can of beer, he remembered an old radio ad he had heard years ago in some city, an ad that was recited in a stylish, hip shout: *"Jet Malt Liquor! Acts much quicker! It leaves you flying at thirty thousand feet!"* Can't ask more of a beer than that. And now came the butterflies, drifting across from the orchard, fritillaries, sulphurs. Little messages from above. A mixed blessing, an easy life. It seemed unbearable that Astrid didn't enjoy this. A car surged past far across the fields on the highway, a big American flag streaming from its antenna.

26

There had been days down south, amazingly long and durable, the days of Joe and Astrid letting down their guards, that turned upon ordinariness. The wonderful times in the produce department of the supermarket, shopping for dinner; the same cheerful black woman sprayed mist on the bins of vegetables and it was like being on a pleasant, intensive truck farm. Or they sailed out to the swampy, uninhabited islands drifting past the bird-crowned mangroves, whose small white blossoms were aswarm with honey bees. They watched the tourists photograph the pelican. They watched the international white sea clouds arrive from Central America on southerly winds.

Sometimes they had helped each other home from bars where a stunned, reflexive criminality disclosed itself in the hungry night life. To have no plan, in the serene near-darkness, amid papery flowers that emerged at sundown, seemed all that they could desire. He had wanted Astrid to understand him. It frightened him to think he might not hate her. This pain seemed quite physical. He had begun picturing Astrid day and night. He had begun to be terrified for her well-being. It was horrible. He resumed cigarettes.

But the time came when it all seemed unhealthy. They withdrew to Green Turtle Cay. There they met a land surveyor from Ohio in a borrowed boat, who was thrown up on the beach by a gale. They sent the home-made local postcards to everyone they knew. They walked the beach at all hours and on Sunday stood in front of the local churches to hear the singing. From the telegraph hill, they could watch yachts move along the coast of Great Abaco, the passenger ferry's regular plying and the periodic advent of the tomato boat. On Wednesday, it was possible to observe the fabulously grotesque scuba lessons behind the one popular resort hotel. Coconut or fruit trees which had proven reliable had steps nailed to their trunks. Each day, swimming became more important. Joe wanted to stay in the cottage and have sex, while Astrid wished to paddle out a few yards for purposes of gaining contact with the drop-off. Finally, it threatened to spoil their vacation and they went back.

Joe made it a habit to ride through the yearlings every day. They were pretty well scattered out and it always took an entire morning. But he enjoyed saddling his horse in the dark and then to be rolling along as the day broke to count and check the cattle. Behind this was the knowledge that he really couldn't afford any death loss. The country had had several dry years; cattle numbers were down across the state, and in the Midwest it was rumored that stored feed was at an all-time high. Unless somebody fooled around with it and the futures boys manipulated things out of all reason, Joe thought his cattle would be right valuable by fall.

The great pleasure came from the grass, traveling through it horseback: the movement of the wind on its surface, the blaze of sunrise across its ocean curves. As the full warmth of day came on, the land took on a humming vitality of cows and grass and hawks, and antelope receded dimly like something caught in your eye. Joe always rode straight into at least one covey of partridges which roared up around his horse. After the first burst, the little brick and gray chickens cast down onto a hillside and resumed feeding. Joe's horse watched hard, then went on traveling. Instead of being someplace where he waited for the breeze through a window, Joe had gone to where the breeze came from.

One day, walking into a dell in search of the head of a small spring, he sensed something in the chest-high grass and serviceberry patches. He stopped to listen. He looked straight up into the brightness of the afternoon sun as something stirred. Suddenly, two cinnamon cubs sprang upright into the glitter, weaving to scent him. As Joe began to back out the way he'd come in, the mother bear rose on her haunches, swinging her muzzle in an arc. The sun behind her made the edge of her coat ignite in a silvery veil. The cubs hastened to their mother's side and the three of them went up to the top of the spring and disappeared into the berry bushes. Joe was out of breath. He couldn't believe his luck in receiving such a gift.

The yearlings began to gain visibly. Joe cut back the chronic pinkeye and hoof-rot cattle until he had them cleaned up and returned to the herd. There was everything in this motley set of cheap cattle: blacks, black baldies, Herefords, Charolais, some Simmental crosses. It didn't matter. He and Lureen had kept their costs down and if the deer flies and nose flies didn't run the yearlings through the wire later on, they ought to do all right.

Most of the cattle were concentrated in the north-facing coulees where the snow had lingered late in the spring. Another mile toward the Yellowstone was the end of the property and the beginning of wild short-grass country, intersected by seasonal watercourses and cottonwood breaks. Here, three different times, Joe found his gate open, thrown defiantly out on the ground. He had a feeling Billy Kelton had passed this way. Luckily, the cattle never found the gap.

Astrid got sick to her stomach and then the sickness just went on and on. They both got nervous about it and finally Joe suggested she go in and see a doctor at the hospital. She hadn't been particularly healthy since she arrived. Nobody was on duty, so, in the end, she stayed at the hospital overnight.

Joe slept poorly, imagining the worst. He picked her up first thing in the morning. She fluttered her fingers in the doorways of other patients she had become acquainted with. In one room, an old man danced around wildly with a smile on his face. "He's on a natural high," said Astrid as they passed the room. Another patient, a woman over eighty, had been parked in a wheelchair and left near the pay phone. She stared at a fixed place in front of her and her eyes never moved when people passed before her. There was no way to tell that she was still alive. "She's so unjudgmental," Astrid said as she made her way fixedly toward the sunlight. Joe held a hand at her elbow and walked her down the sidewalk along the little dotted plantings of potentilla in the cool yellow sun. "I just can't tell you," she said. Joe could feel the thrill of release in her tremulous sighs. "Wouldn't it be something to go straight to the ocean? It was the last stop for some of those people. I felt it. I felt the time we're wasting."

Joe had to navigate the truck intently. The sun shining through the windshield heated up the cab, and the windvane hissed over the country-Western station.

"Have you been in touch with anybody?" Joe asked. There were a lot of phone calls on the bill when he checked Astrid out of the hospital.

"I called a few people last night. Then I quit. They were going to charge out here for a laying on of hands."

"Anything new?"

"Patti and G.J. got busted."

"No surprise there," Joe said.

"Mark Perkins bought a sportfisherman at the federal drug-boat auction. Supposed to have been a good buy."

"So what did the doctor say?"

"He said I've got colitis. He said it's from stress. They have some cortisone thing they can do but I said forget it, I'll try to deal with the causes. Big talk. Joe, I don't have any business being here."

Joe stared straight at the spot above the road where it all turned blue. "You're going to see the point of this soon," he said.

"That's why I came up here."

"Are you okay?"

"I don't know."

At the ends of the roads to the small ranches, people stood by their mailboxes looking through the mail. When Joe and Astrid were nearly home, they came upon a band of sheep swarming on the road. An old man with a long white beard followed the sheep on an ancient horse; his dogs swept back and forth keeping the sheep under control. A younger man walking out at the edge of the herd saw Joe and ran over. Swinging his arm for Joe to follow, he went up through the sea of sheep, causing a channel as wide as the road to part through the wool surface. Joe was able to drive through this as the sheep closed behind him, and in a minute he was beyond the band and up to road-speed again. Astrid watched with a smile. You could never tell what Astrid would like.

They drove into the ranch yard. The dog retreated to a juniper and stared indifferently. Joe jumped out of the truck and, crossing in front of the hood, turned to face Astrid through the windshield. Joe felt she'd been away for years. He spread his arms in welcome. A terrific smile consumed his features. Astrid lit a cigarette and pushed the windvane open while she watched Joe.

"Baby, we're home!" he cried. He thought the pain of his love for Astrid would be more than he could stand.

27

Joe arranged to meet Smitty at the dining room of the Bellwood Hotel and got a table off to themselves. From the lobby, Joe had watched Smitty drive up in a Cadillac. The car was so astonishing and had such power to undermine any subsequent conversation that Joe hurried into the dining room to prevent Smitty's knowing he had seen it. In this small town, a new Cadillac was an item of almost exaggerated splendor and dimension and had the effect of a cruise liner on remote native populations. Joe feared that Smitty had been unable to live up to this new vehicle, and under Joe's gaze would slink from its interior in defeat.

But Joe was wrong. Smitty appeared in the doorway to the dining room, chucked the waitress under the chin, and waved the leather tab of his car keys at Joe. "Joe boy," he called, waltzing toward him. "Am I late?"

"Oh no, Smitty, you're not late. You're on time."

Smitty hung his coat over the back of his chair and sat down with a bounce. "Who do you have to fuck to get a drink around here?" he inquired, letting his eyes drift to the royal elk over the entryway to the kitchen. A waitress emerged and Smitty arrested her with a grin. "My nephew and I would like a sarsaparilla." The waitress took their orders and when she was gone, Smitty said, "There's a side to my drinking, I admit it's small, that I really enjoy. Isn't that surprising? After all these years? A

160

side to this disease that I'd hate to see changed." This moment all but took the wind from Joe's sails. When the drinks arrived, Smitty held his glass of sour mash to the light and said, "You have no idea what this looks like to me. I do not see an instrument of torture. I see something more golden than any casket in the Theban tombs. Knowing that it will kill me in the end, I see the purest, most priceless ambergris of the Arctic cetaceans, the jewel in the crown, the pot of gold at the end of the rainbow. Does it bother me that I will die in abject misery, shaking myself to death in delirium? I have to be honest: *not right now it doesn't.* It's a strong man's weakness."

"I've been to the insurance people," Joe said. "We're going to have to settle with them."

"Why?"

"Because you'll go to jail if they press charges. The insurance company still won't pay. Lureen would be miserable without you. And it is not customary to serve cocktails in jail."

"What do you think, Joe?"

"I think you're guilty. Lureen's your ace in the hole."

"Yours too, Joe."

"I don't think so."

"Don't you? Whose ranch is that?"

"Mine."

"Really?" said Smitty. "Say, I knew your father very well and I don't really buy all this. He didn't like you much, my friend." Smitty's incredibly wrinkled, almost Eurasian face split into laughter. Joe thought of the word "dynamite" as it was used a few years ago. He thought that Smitty had a dynamite laugh, except that it made Joe want to dynamite Smitty. He was weary of trying to understand Smitty. He had just seen a child abusers' support group on television. It seemed society didn't understand their need to beat children. It was getting harder and harder to be understanding. It had always been a problem but now the problem was almost out of sight. Smitty was capable of love, he'd heard; but Smitty's great drive was to get out of the rain. It was hard to understand Smitty

161

completely and not hope his dynamite laugh blew up in his face.

"Let me ask you something, Smitty. Did you borrow the money for the shrimp against the ranch?"

"Yes I did," he said smartly.

"And is there any left?"

"Not much!"

"I see." It was going to have to be a great year for cattle. A century record.

"And I presume you'd just as soon concede that the insurance company has a point."

"That'd be fine."

Of course, thought Joe, let's be honest. Smitty had challenged Joe's claims to the ranch. He didn't know whether or not he cared; but at least he knew he should care. Moreover, he'd be damned if it was Smitty's to decide. On the other hand, as the booze hit Smitty and began its honeyed rush through his bloodstream, he slumped into vacancy and into the great mellow distances past judgment. Joe had been around alcoholism all his life but didn't really understand it. Liquor was just a pleasant thing to him, possessed of no urgency; he would never have resisted Prohibition. It just didn't matter to him as it did to his parents or to Smitty, who was bound for glory.

When Smitty resumed speech it was in a mellifluous tone. "I knew with the loss of the lease," he said, "something had to be done. And you were the one to do it. I also knew that it was not necessary, technically, for you and Lureen to consult with me—"

"You were much occupied with the seafood business—"

"—but I am family, and I would like to be kept abreast of things."

"You will be."

"Our vital interests are now tied together, at least emotionally, and when you buy cattle with the ranch as collateral, I should be told."

"Hereafter, you will be."

"And when you sell those cattle—"

"Yes."

"Just tell me."

"We will."

"I would like to accompany those cattle to the auction yard."

"You may conduct the sale yourself," Joe said feelingly at the sight of Smitty's twitching face, the watery blue eyes seeming to plead for a stay of execution. "Once we bring those cattle down off that grass, I will have done all I could."

Smitty rested the nail of his right forefinger on the rim of his glass. "Along about when?" It was only then that Joe suspected Smitty's intentions exactly.

"October fifteenth," said Joe. There was now no one else in the restaurant; the two sat in its streaming vacancy as though they were in a great train station on the edge of empty country. "Lureen and me," said Smitty, musing. "I don't know. Our mother was a saint, an uncrowned saint. And our father. Um. A short-fused man with a little white mark in his eye. Kind of blind in that one, he was. He used to whup your dad till he was black and blue. Supposed to have made a man out of him. What's that mean, anyway?" Joe didn't know. He wasn't thinking of the question, really. He had just had a presentiment of disaster.

28

As Joe drove home, his mind wandered back a year or so and, as though for the first time, he could see Astrid, her very real beauty, the peculiar elegance of her every gesture, the air of mystery lent her by a gene pool across the Gulf Stream, the saddest river of them all, where some of the world's most interesting races fell into the sugar kettle together. As he dodged the small cattle trucks on the way, he asked himself if he was remembering this right, about Astrid's presence, if that was what it was, her aura, her allure, and if it was still there at all, through the intervening history.

When he drove into the yard, Astrid was knocking apples out of a tree with a stick. She stopped and leaned on the stick to watch him come in. He looked at her. It was still there.

Astrid felt good enough, it seemed. Joe had to take the position that the stress and colitis were gone and now she was better. She immediately made an attempt to fully inhabit the house, to rearrange it, and make it her own. This produced a pleasant feeling in Joe and he was happy to move furniture as instructed and even to dust the tops of tables and bureaus, and the surfaces of the venetian blinds. Astrid had been raised in a conventional Cuban-exile household in Florida, had duly celebrated her *quince* in the tarted-up strumpet costumes that suggested the elders were putting their daughters on the open market. Her life until then had made a regular little wife-prospect of her, but an American high school and four years at Gainesville had flung her into the future. Astrid's latinity became a romantic feature as she went from hippie spitfire to a goddess of the Florida night. Anglo girls in her company always seemed to feel both hygienic and anesthetized. Astrid liked that. She called them "white girls." Now she was up on the sagebrush prairie getting over a broken heart. In a short while, they would both be on social security, trying to eat corn on the cob with ill-fitting dentures. If there is reincarnation, Joe thought, I want to come back as a no-see-um.

They sat down to dinner right after sunset. Coyotes came down close to the yard and howled back and forth. Astrid put the serving dishes on the table: black beans, yellow rice, chicken. Joe lit the candles. "That would be your coyotes?" Astrid asked, at the latest uproar outside the windows. Joe nodded. "You know," she said, "I'm sort of beginning to appreciate this place." She looked off. "Sort of."

"Good," said Joe, gazing in rapture at the tropical food.

"But this country, it's the big romance in your life, isn't it?"

"For what it's worth."

"The mountains?"

"I don't particularly like the mountains," said Joe.

"You like all that other stuff. The stuff that doesn't look like anything. The prairie."

"Yep."

"Because why? Because it makes you feel big or because it makes you feel little?"

"Jesus, Astrid, how should I know? You don't necessarily like things on the basis of the size they make you feel."

"Very well," said Astrid. Joe looked at her blinding and mischievous smile. He could feel his pulse racing.

"What a meal," said Joe. "Like we never left."

"Really, you left," said Astrid.

"I guess."

"I followed."

"It's sweet, isn't it."

"Because you stole my car."

"Yes . . ."

"And because you hated me," Astrid said.

"You followed because I hated you?"

"Hated me enough to steal from me."

"Oh, let's not make more of this than there really is. I needed to get home and my sense of style precluded catching the old outbound dog. Do you mind if we finish this nice meal before we pursue this?"

"You can't hate and eat at the same time?" Astrid asked.

"I can if I have to."

They were nearly finished eating. The rich dishes had left a lovely sheen on the plates.

"I wonder if there is some way we can have sex," Astrid said. Joe felt a sudden tension in his stomach.

"It's really up to you, I—"

"My God, Joe, you're hard already!"

"Not for long, my darling."

Astrid covered her face and let out a Cuban-coyote laugh of extreme merriness. When she was quiet, she allowed her eyes to gaze back. "It's still there."

"Astrid."

"The unsightly bulge of legend," said Astrid. "We'll have to be very gentle."

"Look!" Joe shouted as he stood up and pointed to his trousers. "This time it *is* gone!"

Joe began to clear the table. He didn't like all these jokes. He rinsed off the dishes and thought how he disliked sharing chores. And he'd long since decided it was easier to eat out than show gratitude for home cooking. He'd rather do it all himself, or have somebody else do it all while he did something entirely different but complementary and useful. He wouldn't mind looking after Astrid but he preferred doing it all. In general, he was appalled by the various duos: Butch Cassidy and the Sundance Kid, Bonnie and Clyde, the Reagans. He looked around him and all he saw were these duos. It was like needing the prescription changed in your reading glasses; the world was made incoherent by duos or by people trying to cook side by side.

By the time Joe followed Astrid into the bedroom, she had undressed and was stretched out on top of the blankets. There was a small lamp in one corner with desert scenes depicted on its shade that gave only a small amount of light. He undressed and lay beside her. He put his hand on her and she closed her eyes. The light seemed to waver as he felt the wetness begin around his fingers. She tipped her legs open. He heard the coyotes start in again. He slipped down between her thighs and put his tongue inside her. When he moved up, she said, "You may now enter," and he did. She pressed upward and shuddered; he sometimes felt that the Latin woman in Astrid was revealed in the indignation of her orgasm. Then he came and it was suddenly almost impossible to keep his weight off her, the feeling of an external force using then discarding him.

"I'm hungry again," Joe said after a bit.

"Real hungry?"

"For a snack."

"Make some toast. There's some preserves in the fridge."

"I love the word 'fridge.' "

"Make me a piece too."

"*Like a fridge over troubled waters*," sang Joe.

"How can you be so happy with someone you hate?" Astrid said.

Joe looked at the toaster with its astounding automotive shape, its haunted black slots now showing the faintest smoke of the toast inside. He examined the glints on the toaster and found little curved details of his house. When it popped up, he buttered the toast and spread strawberry preserves. He headed back to the bedroom. Every other woman he ever knew now bored him.

"You ought to put on some pants," Astrid said, "if you're going to serve food."

"You can't please everyone."

"It's waving around."

"It's not 'waving around.'"

He went to the window to look at the full moon. Everything was so clear, it was as if he was right out there with the moon. The stars showed in great sheets like the spray from a breaking wave. Beneath them were the curves of the prairie. Joe ate his toast and jam in the window and watched. He didn't think it made man seem small to see the vastness of the natural world. I'm just going to stand here, he thought, drained of sperm, my brain in the constellations.

"I don't know if I ever told you this, Astrid," Joe said, turning back toward the bed. "But I used to be a pretty darn good caddy. I was captain of all the caddies when I was sixteen years old. Carried double with those big old leather bags. Nine out of ten of those golfers let me pick their clubs. I never played myself. I was saving up for college. My father could afford to send me to college but his drinking had made him so erratic, I wasn't sure he would keep it together until I got there. Sure enough, he went tits-up on a land development deal and I was lucky to have my caddy savings. One time, I tried to help him. He was such a good fellow when he was sober that I was sure he had no idea of how he acted when he was drinking. So I bought a tape recorder and spent the evening with him. He went crazier than usual. The next day, while he was still hung over, I brought the tape into his bedroom, set it up on the dresser and turned it on real loud. Well, it should have worked. As a theory it was very much in the ballpark. But the actual sound of his own ranting and raving was much more than he could deal with. He bellowed. He smashed the machine. He kicked me out of the house. Not long afterward, he drank himself to death. Possibly, that is where he was headed. Sometimes I think I murdered my father with his own voice."

"What got us started on this?"

"I look out at the stars and wonder if my folks are out there."

"I see."

"All their troubles gone."

Joe got in under the covers next to Astrid. He turned on the bedside radio. A man was describing his visit to the great mall of Edmonton, Alberta. Joe lay with Astrid considering this mall in their warmth. The man couldn't fully express the size of the great mall to the listening audience. He had picked out a shirt he liked in a men's store in the mall. He went out to be sure that there wasn't another shirt in another store, in another part of the mall, he might prefer. He concluded that it was the original shirt, a blue Western-cut shirt with snap buttons, that he wanted more than the other shirts, many nice ones—there's no disputing taste!—he had seen. But the great mall of Edmonton, Alberta, was so vast, so labyrinthine, that he could never find the store again that sold the shirt he preferred. Question for the listening audience: can a mall be, somehow, too wonderful, too big? Specifically, does the great mall of Edmonton, Alberta, so surpass our hopes that we are no longer satisfied by it? Stay tuned.

Joe and Astrid were asleep.

29

Joe wondered what brought these tranquil eras on. There hadn't been many of them. He'd once had one that lasted a whole winter in the Hotel Dixie in New York. He'd been painting; he'd had a nice plant, girlfriends, no vices, clients, tickets to fights and shows, surprising acquaintances. Then homesickness struck. The plant which had seemed so companionable turned into a vile hothouse puke overnight. Suddenly, he was stoned day after day. The girlfriends were reptiles. When they made love, all he noticed was their frightening shadows on the ceiling from the streetlight outside the window. The fights, shows, and companions were maddeningly predictable. Some of his work seemed senseless no matter how much it was accepted. He even tried to capture the white hills. The era of tranquillity dissolved and his wanderings began anew. He hoped the present state wouldn't disappear the same way.

The cattle looked so fine scattered out on the grass and the springs were flowing at such a good rate, that Joe, out of pride, gave Lureen a tour, driving through the pastures in the truck and noting the atmosphere of renewed prosperity. She peered peakedly out at the ranch, her face low in the window of the truck.

"How much are they going to make us?" Lureen wanted to know.

"We'll find out when we get to the sale yard."

"But they always used to tell me ahead of time. I could just call that nice Mr. Overstreet and he'd tell me."

"That was a lease, Lureen. We didn't own the cattle. And Mr. Overstreet isn't what you think he is."

"I just don't know," she said. They drove on past the sheepherders' monument to the low breaks that looked off toward the Crazies. Some cattle were brushed up in the midday and a coyote angled away from them, stopping every few yards to look back. The truck labored in first gear and Lureen held on to her seat with both hands. There were two short-eared owls coursing over the sagebrush for mice and one distant hill had the outline of a band of antelope serrated on its crest. What am I saying by this, Joe wondered. That it is mine? The owls curved on around toward the truck, their pale, flat faces cupped toward the ground. Their wings beat steadily and they moved at the speed of a man walking.

"I could have done without this," said Lureen. "Your father pushed me around when he put it in my hands. In a way, I never wanted it. I worked all my life. I didn't want to be pushed around. Then Smitty had so much bad luck. The war hurt him. The war all but killed Smitty. And I had to help him, more than I could have without this."

"Does Smitty realize the war is over?"

"I really couldn't say."

"What does he want, Aunt Lureen?"

She thought. She looked out through the windshield at the country Joe liked so much. The country seemed to wither as she looked at it, the springs stopping and the steady wind carrying the life out of everything.

"I think Smitty would prefer to be somewhere where he could be warmer. He thinks a lot about falling on the ice."

That would be about right, Joe thought.

"Do you see how fat those yearlings look?" he asked.

She looked blank. Fat cattle were the local religion. They were the glow, the index of this place. If one didn't care about fat cattle, this was not the place to be. It should not have been necessary to find words for it. It was annoying to find yourself trying to communicate the glow of a particular country to someone with a blank look on her face.

Lureen kept looking out the window and trying to be interested. She put a finger to her cheek when they passed a few yearlings standing alongside the road and said, "Mmm!" like someone tasting a candy bar in a commercial.

When he got back from dropping Lureen off, a bundle of steel posts and barbed wire in the back, Astrid was down alongside the creek looking into a pool. "I can see the fish!" she called. Joe parked and walked down beside her. They sat on a sunwarmed boulder. "This is pretty nice," Astrid said. "The birds shoot back and forth across the creek. It's like there are two bird countries and they visit each other. There's also one that walks down the bank and disappears under water. Am I hallucinating?"

"It's a dipper."

"Well, no one lives quite like the dipper. Give me a hug."

Joe squeezed her. She slid down from the rock and stood embracing him, her face turned sideways on his chest. She held him that way for a moment then pulled her dress over her hips and pressed against him. "Here?" he said.

"I think so," she said. As they made love, he felt with his fingertips where the warm granite was pressed against her flesh. Later they dressed and followed the stream up for a couple of miles. There were teal in the backwaters and they saw a young mink darting in and out of the exposed cottonwood roots along the bank. Joe told Astrid what it was and she wanted to know how many it took to make a coat.

"Have you noticed something?" Astrid asked.

"What?"

"I'm still here."

"I did notice that!"

★   ★   ★

The Butterfields down the road past the Overstreets had a siege of dust emphysema go through their calves, and everyone chipped in to doctor. Joe helped move cattle down the alley to the chute, and afterward he spent a few hours hunting arrowheads. Joe remembered the time he fell down a hole, knocked himself in the head, and dreamed that he was an Indian attacking his own home. When he looked for arrowheads, it was with a ticklish feeling that he was searching for part of his own earlier life. He stopped at eighty-year-old Alvie Butterfield's little house to ask permission to hunt in his recently spaded-up garden. Alvie's garden happened to be a camp where Indians had dropped projectiles from Folsom points all the way up to Winchester cartridges from the Victorian age, continuous occupancy for thousands of years. It was just a garden to Alvie, who was getting ready to join those warriors in what the Indians called "the other side camp." Standing reedily in a baseball cap, Alvie Butterfield waited for the end.

"I left 'em all for you," said Alvie.

"Attaboy."

"You got a TV?"

"Yes, I do," said Joe.

"What's it supposed to do?"

"Rain by Wednesday."

"Good."

"You need anything, Alvie?"

"Not really, no."

Joe went out to Alvie's garden spot. There were the weedless hand-spaded rows. There were the curves of earth where the shovel had left them in the ancient camp. Many a rare plan was laid here. The new sun was sucking the moisture from around the eloquent flints. Joe began to walk the rows like a stoop worker at a lettuce farm. Each row unraveled beneath his eyes slowly, the approximate straight lines of Alvie's shovel converted to amazing canyons, the clay banding the loam wherever it fell, numerous rocks. Joe had never much cared for rocks. They were merely the increasingly magnifying context of what man had not made. Too many rocks were annoying.

Joe had been dutiful about going around with a field geology guide but it had not taken. The rocks and soil were just the old land as received. His mind filled with their tumbled shapes as he made his slow way up and down the rows with intermittent hops over stones that had accidentally split. A circle of warmth expanded between his shoulders. Alvie's radio played from afar. A band of birds went through the air like a cluster of buckshot. He found places where Alvie in his weariness had rested on the shovel, the blade penetrating without lifting. For a long time, Joe felt himself to be in a place in the earth where no one had ever lived; a few flakes of brighter, prizeable stone like a thin pulse began to turn up and suddenly life surged: *an arrowhead.* Joe picked it up and blew the grains of dirt off of it, a bird point, notched, shaped, a little weight in the palm, something he wanted to close his hand around to feel the life in it. He was as possessive as the man who had lost it. It was just a moment, as if they could feel each other through the stone.

Then some of Joe's cattle got through the fence and traveled a couple of miles to the bottom of a big coulee where they loafed in the ruins of an old homestead. Joe tried to bring them back but ended up having to get Freddy Mathias and one of the Lovells' high school kids to help him. It made a nice day horseback, whooping and riding through the rough country, the yearlings running erratically in front of them with their tails straight up in alarm. The southern migration of birds of prey had begun and there was an archival assortment of hawks on the crooked cedar posts. A golden eagle towered over the ranch, slipping from lift to lift till he went through the roof of heaven. The high school boy took a header at a gallop, a burst of dust; the tough kid scrambled to run down his horse and remount. Freddy went past Joe at a conservative trot and, when he saw the youngster snatch up his horse, said, "Oh, to be young again!"

When they pushed the yearlings back through the gap in the fence, the cattle quit running so hard and seemed to admit they knew they were back where they were supposed to be. Joe looked around. They were only a few thousand feet above the old homestead but it seemed like the roof of the world. He could look off not so far and see the granite verticals, the permanent snow. The world here seemed like a real planet and not just the physical excrescence of civilization.

When the youngster rode up, Joe said, "You break anything?"

"Naw."

"What happened?"

"Sonofabitch lit in a anthill."

Joe thanked them and everybody split up on their shortcuts home, the three horses quickly disappearing from each other in the back country. Joe returned to patch the hole in the fence and started back. The scent of ditch-burning was in the air, like burning leaves in small towns in the fall. The country just seemed to drop away from the horse in a pleasant way. Joe picked up the old wagon road for the last mile and a half, and jogged back down to the buildings, arriving at the moment the night-hawks swarmed into dusk.

At Lureen's request, he stopped in to see her in the blue house that lost more of its power to haunt him the longer he was home. The ghosts of cellar and attic were eclipsed by the need for repairs, and the oversize kitchen stove only emphasized Lureen's paltry cooking talents. As he drove up to the house, he saw Smitty's face briefly in the window. He knocked and Lureen came to the door.

When Joe asked after Smitty, Lureen said he was in Wolf Point visiting Sioux and Assiniboine members of the Veterans of Foreign Wars. They sat down to tea. Lureen wasn't saying much but she looked scared. On a table next to the dining room door was a substantial pile of new clothes, men's and women's, curious because they were strictly for tropical wear. "Sale items," said Lureen, seeing Joe look. He had never seen such colors in this house. It was as if the coconuts of the space program had come back to haunt him.

"I have something for you," Lureen said and left the

room. While she was gone, Joe tried to guess what gruesome family memento would soon be his. He drank the tea he had never liked. He looked at walls which had first defined interior space to him, then had filled him with a lifetime's claustrophobia. He looked out the high windows beside the kitchen door to the blue sky and felt all over again that freedom could very well be at hand.

Lureen came back in and placed a file folder on the table. He suddenly knew what it was. It was the deed. In her own way, Lureen was making every cent count. She knew Smitty was going to take the check for the yearlings. Joe was filled with nervous excitement. Smitty and Lureen were going to Hawaii with the check. Between that and the money lost on Smitty's seafood venture, the place would be bankrupt. And he held the deed in his hands. "The transfer is in there, and it's been notarized."

"How can I thank you?" he asked. Slipping eye contact, a tremor crossing Lureen's face, and the dissolute nephew receiving a family holding, in vacuity, with hands he hoped expressed as much sincerity as the praying hands on Christmas cards. All in their way were the last detectable tremors of the life of a family. Joe looked down at the empty document, thinking it might contain a single ounce of meaning or reality or possibility by way of naming or holding a place on earth, and he was suddenly and absurdly elated. He looked at Lureen, divested of the ranch, and he saw in her eyes a dream lighter and more ethereal than Hawaii itself. It was as if in this room where the hopes of generations had just collapsed, the roar of warm surf could be heard. He couldn't keep the mad grin off his face, the goofy and vaguely celebratory grin that Lureen observed in astonishment.

30

It was just starting to get cold. The local weather forecasts were revised twice a day as the weathermen of three different channels strove against one another in explaining the Rorschach shapes of storms in the Gulf of Alaska. Joe concentrated on the fates of these storms as they threw themselves on the mountains of Washington and Idaho, and expired. One of these days soon, they were going to slide down through Alberta, catch the east side of the Rockies, and turn Joe's world upside down.

He took this time to cut firewood and spent days on end in the cottonwood groves taking out the standing dead and transporting the wood to a pile next to the house. The growth of this pile fascinated him. He sensed it was in his power to make a pile bigger than the house. He moved along the creek and cut up the trees the beavers had felled. While he worked, he could see trout on the redds, swirling after one another and fanning nests into the gravel. The eagles had started coming in from the north and were standing high in the bare trees along the stream. Their rapine, white-tailed, dark and monkish shapes showed from a quarter of a mile away.

He sat down in the autumn forest, an old woodchopper with his hot orange chain saw. I am posing for eternity, he thought. He was desperate. He was desperate because the constant companionship of unanswered questions was affecting his nerves and suggesting that it was the absolute final and daily condition of living. He was no longer interested in remaining in the space program.

The irrigation water stopped running and the springs were down to a bare minimum. He moved the yearlings every few days, an activity that took him to remote pastures on horseback. He enjoyed his horse's sure-footedness. He could travel on breathtaking sidehills you could barely negotiate on your own feet in a kind of skywalking perfection as the cattle flew forward in coveys. In this motion and vastness, he could actually think about life, beginning and end, with equanimity, with cheer. Joe thought he was vaguely bigger than everything he saw and therefore it would be tragic and for all nations to weep over, if anything happened to him. But here in the hills, he would feed the prettiest birds. As promised by all religions, he would go up into the sky where his folks were.

Joe felt the return of love and remorse, like a bubble of gas rising through crankcase residue. The slowness of the bubble's traverse seemed to express the utter gallonage of his desire as well as the regret that made it something of a rich dish and gave this emotion its peculiar morning-after quality.

"I think we're missing something," he said.

After a moment, Astrid said, "I know what you mean."

She bit her thumbnail in thought and looked off. Joe examined some carpet. The white hills, the departing dream, the impending embarkation for Hawaii only illumined the plight. He had heard nothing from Ellen and felt she didn't want him to see Clara. When you're young and think you'll live forever, it's easy to think life means nothing.

Astrid stood up and stretched, then stopped all motion to smile at Joe. She went to the door and opened it, letting in the clear, balsamic breath of foothills, of sage and juniper and prairie grass. She stood on tiptoes to stretch and inhale.

"Joe," she said deliberately, "this isn't for me."

Joe didn't hear her. He turned on the radio. First he got a semi-intellectual cornball on FM and then a wonderful song from 1944—what could that have been like!—about a cowboy going East to see the girl he loves best. "Graceful faceful" went the chorus, "such lovely hair! Oh, little choo-choo, please get me there!" It was sung in the kind of voice you'd use to call a dog in the dark when you really didn't expect the dog to come. It disturbed Joe because it suggested that the Americans of the recent past were insane foreigners. Then an ad for a local car dealer filled with apparently living objects: "Cold weather is coming and your car doesn't want to face it. You need a new one but your wallet says 'No'!" Joe thought, Is anyone following this? Astrid was still in the doorway. What was it she'd said?

There was no great problem in getting the criminal charges against Smitty dropped. Once Joe relieved the insurance company's fears of damage claims, once those assurances were documented and in place, the ripple of society's desire for retribution expired on the bench of the small, local courthouse. Nevertheless, a few motions had to be gone through. Joe drove Smitty to the hearing as though he were his child and had been involved in a minor scrape. There was only the judge, dressed in the plaid wool shirt in which he had been raking leaves, and his secretary. Smitty appeared in his uniform and stood at attention throughout the questioning. So great was the judge's pity for this foolish person that he concluded his inquiry with the question "Can I count on you to avoid this kind of thing in the future, Lieutenant?"

"Yes, sir! You can, sir!"

The judge gazed down at Smitty with a melancholy smile. "Smitty, Smitty, Smitty," he said. "You're kind of dumb like a fox, aren't you?"

"Possibly so, yes, sir."

"Thank your lucky stars, Smitty, that you live in a

small town where we know you for what you are. Adjourned."

Driving along to his meeting at the bank, Joe remembered his happiest period as a painter. One summer, he had gone on the road to do portraits of Little Leaguers. He set up a table at ballgames all over Montana and saw the rise and ripening of the great mountain summer from a hundred small-town diamonds. Instead of pumping gas or choking on dust behind a bale wagon, Joe turned out bright portraits of children in baseball uniforms. It was an opulent spell that Joe remembered now with a kind of agony.

Darryl Burke, Joe's banker, leaned back and laced his fingers behind his head. He wore a great blousy pin-striped blue and white shirt. "How's life on the haunted ranch?"

"Great for me. I'm a ghost myself."

"Bankers don't believe in ghosts. Bankers believe in the enforceability of contracts."

Joe didn't think this was the time to depict his dream of letting it all go back to the Indians by way of atoning for a century of abuses; nor to unleash his misogyny on family matters.

Darryl, his chair tilted back on two legs, pitched forward on four. "Do you know why Lureen lost her lease with Overstreet?"

"Not really. I figured everybody had all the grass they wanted."

"They lost their lease because Overstreet heard you were coming back."

"I'm not following this. What's that have to do with it?"

"Well, old Smitty had a double deal going there with old man Overstreet. When he couldn't get that ranch off your dad, he tried to get it off Lureen. Smitty wanted to make a deal but all he could control was the lease. As long as you weren't around. A lease for Smitty and a lease for Lureen. His was bigger."

Joe thought for a long moment before saying, "That's

awful. I mean, I know it's awful. But if you and I were to go dig into it, we'd find out that Lureen was just looking the other way, happy that Smitty was staying busy. Still, you don't like to hear a thing like that."

"Of course you don't. And we're talking property here, man. When are you going to ship the cattle?"

"Pretty soon. But I'm hesitant."

"Hesitant? Now is the hour! This is the best the market is ever going to be."

"I think they're going to run off with the money."

"Who?"

"Smitty and Lureen."

"No, Joe, you don't think that. You just think you think that. That's crook time."

"They already have Hawaiian costumes. I've seen them."

"Come on. You mean that's where you think they're headed?"

Joe had his hands close to his chest and he pantomimed the playing of a ukulele. "Surf's up," he said grimly. Darryl stood and pulled down part of the venetian blinds so he could look out toward the drive-up tellers.

"Smitty will never run out of ideas," he said. "He's a fart in a skillet. But this is way past him. I don't see him making such a big move."

"He is concerned about falling on the ice. He wants to be warm."

"But," said Darryl, "when you get right down to it, if that's what they want to do, they can do it. They can. It might be the end of the ranch. But they can do it. If that's what they want. We covered our bet when we loaned money for the cattle. If Lureen wants to exchange those yearlings, and the money she borrowed for Smitty's shrimp deal, for the ranch itself, she can do it. Don't look at me, look at your father. I just keep score."

Suddenly, it came to Joe. "It's not fair!" he said. He decided he wouldn't mention that the deed, together with all its liens and encumbrances and appurtenances thereto, was in his pocket, thick as a week's worth of junk mail. In some opaque recess within Joe, a worm was turning. Property!

"I better get going," he said. "Thanks for visiting with me about this."

"Glad to, Joe. It's pretty clear, anyway."

"Try to come out and see us before it snows."

"What happened to summer? It's really hard to believe it could snow already."

"Do you actually notice such things from in here?" Joe asked. Darryl stared.

"I get out once in a while," he said.

31

In the dream it was summer and when he awakened he remembered the lazy sound of a small airplane and the sight of a little girl too far away to see clearly, picking chokecherries on the side of a ravine. The prairie spread into the distance and its great emptiness was not cheerful. It woke him up with sharp and undefined sadness. He tipped his watch, lying on the table beside the bed, so he could see its dial against the vague light coming in the window. It wasn't quite five yet. He lay back and felt the warmth of Astrid beside him. He knew he had to see Clara. He couldn't wait. He had thought his situation with Ellen would sort itself out and an appropriate introduction would ensue. But it seemed now that might never happen. He couldn't wait any longer.

He would go to the end of the Keltons' road and watch Clara get on the school bus. He arose slowly and began to dress. His stealth awakened Astrid. "What is it, honey?"

"I've got to get receipts for those cattle. I'm meeting the brand inspector at the scale house."

"When will you be back?"

"Before lunch." He felt something sharp from the deceit.

Joe left the truck almost two miles away from the Keltons' road just as the sun began to come up. He hurried along the oiled county road straight toward the lime and orange glow that in a matter of minutes would be the new day. When the sun finally did emerge, Joe was safely concealed in the scrub trees opposite Ellen and Billy's mailbox. He had a feeling he couldn't uncover. Waiting for his little girl to catch the school bus, he was as close to whole as he had felt in memory. It was several blissful moments before the absurdity of his situation, his concealment, his uncertain expectations, dissolved his well-being. The chill of morning crept in. Finally, the yellow school bus rose upon the crown of the hill and went right on through without stopping, as though it never stopped here. Did Ellen invent Clara? Joe thought of that first.

He crossed the county road and started up the ranch driveway, walking as quietly as he could so that he could hear if anyone approached. As he went along, presumably getting closer, his nervousness increased and he began to picture alert dogs bounding at him, a family bursting from the front door to confront a stranger.

By the time the house was visible, a modest white frame house, neatly tended, a few yards from its barns and outbuildings, Joe could see in a small grove of wild apple trees the perfect place to hide. A rooster crowed. And when he got inside the trees, his concealment was so perfect that he arranged his sweater against a tree trunk as a pillow and prepared to spend however long it took to watch every single human being who lived in that house, who used its front door, who walked in its yard, who did its chores.

The rooster crowed again and in the near distance a bull bellowed rhythmically. Past the house was a small corral. A solitary paint horse rolled and made a dust cloud, then stood and shook. In the sky above the house, just now ignited by sunrise, were clouds which must have hung there in the windless air all night long. Joe felt himself drift into this serenity as though, not merely hidden, he was incorporeal and free as a spirit.

The door opened and a little girl ran out, pursued by Billy. He overtook her, turned her, and rebuttoned her cloth coat. He pulled her straw hat down close on her head and she tipped it back again. He pulled it down and she tipped it back. He swept her up. He held her at arm's length where she hung like a rag doll with a grin on her face. She acted almost like a baby with Billy though she was far too old for that. Above all, she clearly resembled her father, Billy Kelton. Joe scarcely had time to track his astonishment. It was enough that Billy's olive skin was there and the distinctive, inset brown eyes. But the minute Clara spoke, asking Billy to let out some chickens, Joe knew from her crooning voice that Clara was feeble-minded. Billy planted her where she stood and went into a low shed. There was an immediate squawking from within and then four or five hens ran into the yard. Clara ran after them. Billy came out and deftly swept up a small speckled hen. Clara took it in her arms. Billy removed her hat, kissed the crown of her head, and replaced the hat. He went back into the shed while Clara stood bundling the hen and rubbing her cheek against it. The little chicken sank her head between the shoulders of her wings. Billy emerged with some eggs held against his stomach with his hand.

"Let's eat, kid. Put your friend down."

"I want take my hen!" Clara crooned.

"Mama won't let us, angel," said Billy, wincing sympathetically.

"My friend!" she pleaded.

"Okay, go on and take her in the house," said Billy gently. "What d'you think Mama's gonna say? I'll tell you what Mama's gonna say. Mama's gonna say take that chicken on out of here."

Clara shrugged and followed Billy toward the house, defiantly carrying her hen. Billy went in and Clara hesitated. When the coast was clear, she set the hen down and made a haughty entrance to the house. The speckled hen shot erratically back to the shed. Joe didn't move. He felt compassion sweep over him, not for Clara, whom he did not know, but for Billy in all his isolated, violent ignorance. It was this Joe had waited for: something that would cross his mind like a change of weather and leave a different atmosphere behind.

32

The sun couldn't quite penetrate the pale gray sky. It looked as if it might rain; if it did, it would be a cold rain, close to snow. Everything about the morning said the season was changing fast. When Joe awoke, he felt a lightness that approached giddiness, almost a gaiety. It seemed so beyond sense that he thought he must immediately put it to use.

He got on the telephone and began calling truckers to haul his yearlings to the sale yard. He got a mileage rate, a loaded rate, and a deadhead surcharge. He arranged a dawn departure. The only thing to slow this cattle drive down was going to be the speed limit.

He spent the next day on horseback. Overstreet's nephews came up from their ranch as they had done for the branding and helped him gather his pastures. A small herd formed, then grew as he traveled forward, downhill and toward the corrals. The horses loved this and tossed their heads, strained at their bits, ran quartering forward, and generally hurled themselves into the work of sweeping the land of beef. Every now and again, a herd-quitter gave the men the excuse of a wild ride to restore the yearling to the mass of its fellows. By nightfall, the dust-caked nephews with the thin crooked mouths of their grandfather had started down the road home on lathered horses, and the cattle were quiet in the corrals. Overstreet himself was there to count the yearlings, mouthing the numbers and dropping his arm decisively every ten head. Looking at the backs and heads of the crowded cattle, the myriad muzzles and ears, the surge of energy, Joe was reminded of the ocean when it was choppy. He thought he knew why Overstreet was being so helpful.

Joe put his hot horse in a stall out of the wind and gave him a healthy ration of oats, which roared out of the bucket into the tin-lined trough. The little gelding always looked like he was falling asleep while he ate, and Joe watched him a moment before going out to check his gates.

Joe had become so preoccupied with getting the cattle shipped that his communications with Astrid almost came to a stop. She seemed to sense something and they rather politely stayed out of each other's way.

They loaded the cattle in the morning by the yard light. The metal loading chute rocked and crashed under their running weight. Joe went inside the trailer to help swing the partitions against the crowded animals. Their bawling deafened him. At the end of each load, the rope was released from the pulley and the sliding aluminum door flew down to a silent stop in the manure.

The first truck pulled off while the second one loaded. There were three frozen-footed steers that were crippled and hard to load. They went up last and the two trucks pulled out, their engines straining in low gear at the vast contents of living flesh going down the ranch road in bawling confusion. From beneath the bottom slats, the further green evidence of their terror went on flowing. Joe watched the back of the trailers rocking from side to side with the mass and motion of big trawlers in a seaway. In a moment, the red taillights had curved down past the cottonwoods and disappeared.

By three that afternoon, the cattle went through the sale at seventy-one and a half dollars a hundredweight and the money was sent to Lureen's account in Deadrock. And of course the ranch was Joe's. Mainly, it filled in the blanks in the painting of the white hills. A homeowner, a man of property. He sat in the living room with the deed in his lap. He showed it to Astrid. He fanned himself with it. He tried to make it a joke, but she didn't laugh and neither did he. He wondered what Smitty would do with the money.

Sometime after midnight, Joe was awakened from sleep by someone knocking on the door. Once he saw the clock and knew how late it was, he was filled with sharp panic. He got up without turning on the lights and eased into the kitchen. In the window of the door, he could see the shape of someone standing. He thought first of not answering the door and then wondered if it might not be a traveler, someone with car trouble, or a sick neighbor. And so he went into the kitchen and turned the light on. The minute he did that, the figure outside the door was lost. He opened the door on the darkness and said, "What is it?"

There was no reply. Joe had made out the shape of the figure. It looked like his father. The glow from the yard light, so recently cloudy with insects, was sharply drawn on the cold night. Joe wanted to say, "It's a clean slate." Surely this was a dream. It must have been a traveler.

Joe closed the door as quietly as he could but left it unlocked. There was no sound anywhere. He went back to bed and lay awake. He felt the cold from the blackened window over the bed. He had begun to suspect that by coming here at all, he had taken back his name. He remembered the sense of paralysis having a particular name had given him in the first place. He had loved moving into a world of other people's names. He had even tried other names and had felt a thrill like that of unfamiliar air terminals and railway stations, places where he could abandon himself to discreet crowd control. Finally, this took such vigilance it was wearying. He wanted his own name. And yet, the ride home through spring storms, through unfamiliar districts, had a quality that was independent of where he was coming from and where he was going. He had a brief thrill in thinking that all of life was about two things: either move or resume the full use of your name. But the idea slipped away when he tried to grasp it.

It was still dark when he got in the truck and filled it up at the fuel tank next to the barn. Then he began to drive. He drove to White Sulphur Springs, Checkerboard, Twodot, Judith Gap, Moccasin, Grassrange, Roundup, and home, four hundred miles without stopping.

By the time Joe pulled up in front of the house, he was exhausted. The lights shone domestically in the dark, illuminating parts of trees and the white stones of the driveway. It seemed that a placid, sunshot existence must be passing within.

Joe opened the door and Ivan Slater rose inelegantly from the deep, slumped couch while Astrid, standing a certain distance from one undecorated wall, tried to hang the moon with a smile that was both radiant and realistic.

"What are you doing here?" Joe demanded. "Where did you come from?" He smelled a rat. Ivan had been called in as Astrid's chief adviser before.

"Joe." She may have said something before that but Joe didn't hear it. Then she said, "I need to talk to you."

"I know," Joe said, noticing that whatever was in the air suspended Ivan's promotional bearing so that he stood exactly where he had arisen, taking up room. It was exactly the moment one would ordinarily say, "Stay out of this."

"Joe, let me run this by you," said Ivan. "Astrid isn't suited for this, somehow. She has asked me to help her get resituated. I'm Astrid's friend and this is what friends are for. P.S. We're not fucking."

"That's fine, I hate her," said Joe experimentally.

"Now Joe," Ivan said, "you've had a long drive."

"You knew I wouldn't stay," Astrid said. "What's this about, anyway? I don't know. But I do know I'm getting out of here. And it's a joke to claim you hate me."

"The fucking Cuban geek," Joe offered.

"Punch him in the nose, Ivan," said Astrid.

"That will do," Ivan said to Joe without emphasis.

"Take the dog with you," said Joe to Astrid. "That's the worst dog I ever saw. It'll be perfect for your new home."

"Okay, but don't generalize about me. And what is this about a new home?"

"I used to like dogs," Joe explained maladroitly.

"I had a lot to offer. I still do. Not for you, obviously. But who does? All I need to know is that it's not me. And I loved you. So, good luck. Good luck with the place. All the luck in the world with the cows. Enjoy yourself with the land. Happy horses, Joe."

"I used to like women!"

"I'm not like that dog, Joe," Astrid said.

"Don't jump to conclusions. I want you both out of here right away. I need a quiet place to sleep."

"Joe, it's late," Ivan said. "You're not in your right mind. As if you ever were, in fact."

"This advisory role you cultivate, Ivan, is unwelcome just now. I dislike having my time wasted."

"You're not that busy," sang Ivan. Joe sighed and looked at the floor. He wanted to collect his thoughts and he feared a false tone entering the proceedings. He wanted to leave off on a burnishing fury and empty out the house. It was hard to see that he'd had the intended effect; Ivan was scratching his back against the doorjamb. Astrid was smiling at a spot in midair. She was a fine girl. They had feared all along that they couldn't survive a real test. It had been lovely, anyway. It was a provisional life.

While they packed Astrid's things, Joe watched TV. As luck would have it, it was a feature on farm and ranch failures with music by Willie Nelson and John "Cougar" Mellencamp. He remembered leaving the deed in the truck. He might have left the windows open. Pack rats could get in and eat the deed. The wind could get the deed.

They came into the living room with their suitcases.

"This is pretty interesting. It's about farm and ranch failure," Joe said. "Can you go during the commercial?"

"No," said Astrid, "we're going now. Were you serious about that dog?"

"What next!" said Joe without taking his eyes off the screen.

"May I see you a moment, Joe?" Astrid stood in the

doorway to their bedroom. Ivan studied the backs of his fingernails in the open front door, buffing them occasionally on his left coatsleeve. Joe met Astrid in the bedroom and she shoved the door shut. She gave him a long look and took a deep breath.

"Let me tell you something, sport," she began, "you don't fool me with this tasteless display we've just witnessed."

"I don't."

"No, you don't."

"What sort of display would have struck you as less tasteless?"

"A sincere remark or two about your plight. A word of hope that you'll come to life soon. Your life."

"All whoppers!"

"I'm just gonna step back, and let you choose."

She went out the door. Joe followed her. Ivan was still in the same spot. When Joe went over, Ivan deployed his hand as a kind of handshake option, Joe's choice. Joe shook.

Ivan and Astrid went into the night. He heard them call the dog and when he saw the lights wheel and go out, and he knew the dog was gone, he at last realized how blithely things were being taken away from him. He went to bed and contained himself as well as he could, but the pillowcase grew wet around his face.

His sleep produced the need for sleep, for rest, for deep restoration from this masquerade of sleep in which all the tainted follies had opportunity for festivity and parade. He had Astrid in his arms and his inability to distinguish love and hate no longer mattered because she wasn't there in the light of day.

33

The cool spell passed and it was hot again. Joe was going to take a good long look at the white hills. He was going to start at the beginning. He got in the truck and drove toward the drought-ravaged expanses east of town where the road looked like a long rippled strip of gray taffy; on the farthest reaches of the road, looking as small as occasional flies, were the very few vehicles out today. Dust followed a tractor as an unsuccessful crop was plowed into the ground. Joe could picture the cavalry crossing here, following the Indians and their ghost dogs. Sheep were drifted off into the corners of pastures waiting for the cool of evening to feed. Ribbed cattle circled the tractor tires that held the salt. Old stock ponds looked like meteor craters and the weeds that came in with the highway gravel had blossomed to devour the pastures. It was neither summer nor fall. The sky was blue and the mountains lay on the horizon like a black saw. A white cloud stood off to one end of the mountains. In a small pasture, a solitary bull threw dust up under himself beneath the crooked arm of a defunct sprinkler. The thin green belt beneath the irrigation ditches contrasted immediately with the prickly pear desert that began inches above. The radio played "Black roses, white rhythm and blues." Astrid used to say, "I thought Montana was so unlucky for you. I can't understand why you want to go back." And he had said with what seemed like prescience and laudable mental health, "Yes, but I'm not superstitious!" And she'd said, "Wait a minute. You were pretty clear on this. You said it was unlucky for you and it was unlucky for everybody else."

Joe said, "That's my home!"

He stopped the truck at the bottom of a long, open draw and walked for almost an hour. At the end of that walk, he reached the gloomy, ruined, enormous house that he had long ago visited with his father, the mansion of the Silver King, a piece of discarded property no longer even attached to a remembered name. It was a heap out in a pasture and if you had never been inside it the way Joe had and felt in the design of its chambers the anger and assertion of the Silver King himself, the mansion didn't look good enough to shelter slaughter cattle until sale day. Grackles jumped and showered in the lee of its discolored walls and the palisade of poplars that led from the remains of the gate seemed like the work of a comedian.

Joe walked to the far side of the building and sat down close to the wall out of the wind. The mud swallows had built their nests solidly up under the eaves and wild roses were banked and tangled wherever corruption of the wall's surface gave them a grip. Concentric circles in the stucco surrounded black dots where stray gunfire had intercepted the building, adding to the impression that it was a fortress. Joe thought about how his father's bank had repossessed the property. His father was gone—even the bank was gone! He was going to go in.

A piece of car spring in the yard made a good pry bar, and Joe used it to get the plywood off one of the windows, leaving a black violated gap in the wall. He made a leap to the sill, teetering sorely on his stomach, then poured himself inside. He raised his eyes to the painting of the white hills.

Joe walked across the ringing flags to get a view of the picture. He could feel the stride the room induced and imagined the demands of spirit the Silver King made on everything. Such people, he thought, attacked death headlong with their insistence on comfort and social leverage. It was absolutely fascinating that it didn't work.

But the painting was still mysterious; it had not changed. "The only painting I've ever understood," said Joe's father after he had showed it to his son. "Too bad it's fading." The delicacy of shading in the overlapping white hills, rescued from vagueness by the cheap pine frame, seemed beyond the studied coarseness Joe's father leveled at everything else.

It was a matter of dragging an old davenport across the room and bracing it against one corner of the fireplace. He stepped up onto one arm, then to its back and then up onto the mantel. He turned around very slowly and faced the wall, to the left of the painting. By shuffling in slow motion down the length of the mantel he was able to move himself to its center.

There was no picture. There was a frame hanging there and it outlined the spoiled plaster behind it. It could have been anything. It was nothing, really. Close up, it really didn't even look like white hills. This of course explained why it had never been stolen. Joe concluded that no amount of experience would make him smart.

His father must always have known there was nothing there. The rage Joe felt quickly ebbed. In his imaginary parenthood, he had begun to see what caused the encouragement of belief. It was eternal playfulness toward one's child; and it explained the absence of the painting. It wasn't an empty frame; it was his father telling him that somewhere in the abyss something shone.

34

He was driving a little too fast for a dirt road, tools jumping around on the seat of the truck and a shovel in the bed beating out a tattoo. He was going to see Ellen, sweeping toward her on a euphoric zephyr. He knew how intense he must look; and he began doing facial exercises as a preparation for feigning indifference. The flatbed hopped across the potholes. Antelope watched from afar. "Hi, kiddo," he said. "Thought I'd see how you were getting along." He cleared his throat and frowned. "Good afternoon, Ellen. Lovely day. I hope this isn't a bad time." He craned over so he could watch himself in the rearview mirror. "Hiya Ellen-baby, guess what? I'm gonna lose that fucking ranch *this week*. YAAGH!" A sudden and vast deflation befell him and he slumped in the front of the truck and slowed down. When he got to the schoolyard, the children were gone and Ellen was walking toward her old sedan in her coat.

She saw Joe and walked over toward him. She said, "Well, what do you know about that?"

"I wanted to see you," said Joe.

"Here I am."

"Have you been thinking?"

"About what? My phone bill? My cholesterol?"

"Your phone bill."

"I think about it every time I lift the Princess Touchtone to my ear. Incidentally, my husband and I are anxious for you to know how happy we are to have worked everything out. I realize I'm kind of repeating myself. But it seems we have to do that with you. Joe, I don't want to be this way."

"Can we take a short drive?" Joe asked.

"How short?"

"Five minutes."

"I guess it can be arranged," said Ellen and climbed in. Joe noticed how closely she followed the rural convention of going from an amorous interest to a display of loathing; in the country, no one broke off an affair amicably. Ellen looked out at the beautiful fall day, directing a kind of all-purpose disgust at falling aspen leaves. This was the sort of thing Astrid never put him through.

Joe drove back toward town and quickly approached its single stoplight; he was heading for the open country to show her the white hills, both the painting and the ones beyond, and explain enough about his life that he could, if necessary, close this chapter too.

"Where are we going?" Ellen asked in alarm. "Stop at this light and let me out." The light began to turn red. Ellen tried the door handle. Some pedestrians had stopped to look on. Joe ran the light. Ellen pushed the door open and shouted, *"Help!"* and Joe hit the gas. The bystanders fluttered into their wake. He watched in the rearview mirror as they started to go into action.

"We'll just take a little loop out toward the Crazies and I'll drop you back at the school. What in God's name caused you to yell that?"

"I wanted to be dropped off. Joe, you have to learn to take hints a little better than you do."

"I'm going to show you something and we're going to talk."

"About what? My husband and I are back together. We have resolved our differences. We're happy again. We're a goddamn couple, got it?"

"Why did you lie to me about Clara?"

She studied him for a moment in a shocked way. Then he saw she wouldn't argue.

"Billy and I had hit this rough spot in the road."

"I still don't follow you."

"It was Daddy's idea actually. He had worked it out on the calendar. I have to admit, it wasn't that far-fetched. But he's got that big bite missing from his ranch and he kind of put two and two together."

"You ought to be ashamed of yourself."

"Whatever." She turned to him suddenly. She made little fists and rolled her eyes upward. "You don't need to understand me. Billy knows everything there is to know about *me*, and he loves *me*."

Joe wished he had time to think about this. She had a point. It was about lives that were specific to each other. It wasn't about generalities. It wasn't about "love." "Love" was like "home." It was basic chin music.

Joe drove along slowly, as though adding speed would only substantiate the appearance of kidnap. Since he was pouring with sweat, he now merely wished to add a few amiable notes and get Ellen back to the schoolyard. This had all turned into something a bit different from what he had hoped for. At that very moment, he began to realize how much he wished he had Astrid advising him right now. She would say something quite concrete like "Hit the brakes" or "Don't do anything stupid. That way nobody will get hurt."

"Here they come," said Ellen.

"Here comes who?"

"Look in the mirror."

A small motorcade had formed a mile or so back; a cloud of dust arose from them and drifted across the sage flats. Joe picked up speed but couldn't seem to widen the gap. Perspiration broke out on his lip. "Are you going to clear this business up with that mob, if they catch us?"

"Let me get back to you on that," said Ellen with the faintest smile. Ellen had become so strange. It was more than indifference—it was a weird fog. He imagined her thinking how badly she wanted to get shut of this jackass and back to the husband and daughter she loved. This perception reduced Joe's account to virtual sardine size. He felt too paltry to go on taking the wheel.

He flattened the accelerator against the floor. The

truck seemed to swim at terrific speed up the gradual grade toward the hills. A jack rabbit burst onto the road ahead of them, paced the truck for fifty yards and peeled off into the sagebrush. Nothing Joe did seemed to extend the distance between himself and the cluster of vehicles behind.

"Have you been doing any fishing?" Ellen asked.

"I really haven't had the time."

The truck skidded slightly sideways.

"Somebody said there's a Mexican woman staying with you." So that was it. A bird dove at the windshield and veered off in a pop of feathers.

"An old girlfriend," Joe said candidly. "It's a very sad thing. She couldn't stick it out. She'd had enough, and she was very patient in her own way. If she'd lied to me more I'd be with her today."

Ellen mused at the rocketing scenery.

"I've got a teacher's meeting in Helena," she said wearily. "On Tuesday. That's another world."

"Who will substitute for you?"

"An old lady who doesn't make the kids work. It makes me look like a bum." Somehow, Joe got the truck into a wild slide going down a steep grade into a gully. The truck turned backward at about sixty miles an hour. "This is really making me moody," said Ellen. They plunged into a grove of junipers and burst out the other side in a shower of wood and branches. Some of the foliage was heaped up against the windshield and it was a little while before Joe could see where he was going. The vigilantes were still bringing up the rear in a cloud of dust. One of them dropped back, a plume of steam jetting from the radiator.

It was hopeless. He couldn't outrun them in this evil, weak farm truck. All he wanted was a brainless chase that could last for weeks. He stopped, backed and turned around. Deadrock was visible in the blue distance. The machines advanced toward him. "You've really got a bee in your bonnet," Ellen said.

"Shut up, you stupid bitch, you rotten crumb."

"I *see*," said Ellen. "The idea being that I got you into this?"

Joe said nothing.

"After the big rush, I am now a 'stupid bitch.' This may be the first serious conversation we've had since we met. Are you telling me that it is possible I could mean more to you than pussy or golf lessons? Let's have it, Joe. I could actually rise in your esteem to the status of 'stupid bitch.' Oh, this *is* romantic. I had really misjudged the depth of feeling around here. And I've gone back to my husband when I could have enjoyed these passionate tongue-lashings."

At the approach of massed cars and trucks, Joe just stopped. Twenty vehicles wheeled all around them and skidded to a halt, dumping a small crowd of armed civilians, the State Farm agent, a mechanic still in his coveralls, a pharmacist in a white tunic of some kind, a couple of waitresses. They were still pouring out and a few guns had been displayed, when Ellen threw open her door and cried, "This is all a terrible misunderstanding! It was supposed to be a joke!" She climbed out of the truck. One of the mechanics, in coveralls and a gray crewcut that showed the crown of his head, came to the truck and held a gun to Joe's temple. Joe looked over to see Billy Kelton emerging from a Plymouth Valiant he should have recognized. "A complication," Joe said. "Here comes Billy."

"Son," said the man in the crewcut in a startlingly mild voice, "this is where she all comes out in the wash." Joe had a sudden feeling of isolation as Ellen walked over and joined her husband at a distance from the cluster of people and vehicles. Billy shoved her away from him and began to walk toward Joe's truck. Joe wondered what the shoving meant, in terms of a margin of safety, of an exploitable ambiguity.

"That's Billy," said Joe's guard. "He's getting ready to have a fit."

"What's he going to do?"

"Do? He's going back to Vietnam!"

The mechanic smiled like a season ticket holder. The blood beat in Joe's face. Joe thought that was the time to grab the gun but he just thought about it with a kind of longing, knowing he wouldn't have any idea what to do with it.

Billy came over with a bakery truck driver at his side, a blond-haired man with long sideburns and an expression of permanent surprise. "Something to tell the grandchildren, ay?" Billy said to the mechanic. "Get him out for me, would you?"

The mechanic opened the door and dragged Joe out. He and the man from the bakery held his arms, shoving him up against the car. Billy got so close, Joe could only focus on one of his eyes at a time. But it was enough for Joe to recognize that Billy didn't have his heart in this. Twice he had punched Joe years ago and apparently that was enough. "Time is hastening, Joe. You need to cut it out." Billy turned and spoke to the others. "You guys can go." They hesitated in their disappointment. "Go on," he said more firmly. They began to move off. "The show is over," he said, making what Joe considered an extraordinary concession.

"Is that it?" asked the mechanic.

"That's it," said Billy without turning back. "Ellen, take my car back to the house."

"He really didn't do anything, Billy."

"Probably not. Just go on back now with Vern and them."

Ellen moved away from them. A breeze had come up and the clouds were moving overhead rapidly. The air was cold enough that the exhaust smell of the vehicles was sharp. Billy turned to Joe once more. "We'll just let Ellen go on back to town with Vern and them. If she goes, they'll all go. They're upset because they couldn't lynch you. You and your family sure been popular around here. All them boys banked with your dad."

"Which one is Vern?" asked Joe without interest.

"Fella with the flattop."

"Oh." Joe's eyes drifted over to Vern, who was returning reluctantly to a car much too small for him. Joe couldn't see how he could even get in it. But he elected not to report this impression.

"Let me drive," said Billy, opening the door to get in. Joe slid over.

"The keys are in it," Joe said with a sickly smile.

Billy was wearing old Levi's and wingtip cowboy boots nearly worn through on top by spur straps. He smiled at Joe and started up the truck. Joe could see that the cars and trucks which had followed them were almost out of sight now. As the various members of the community who had come out to help returned to town in their cars, something went out of the air. Joe said, "I saw on the news they're having a potato famine in Malibu."

"I don't have too good a sense of humor today, Joe."

They drove on, and Billy was a careful driver. They took the road that went around to the south, which eventually connected to the ranch. "Am I the biggest problem you've got, Joe?" They both followed with their eyes a big band of antelope the truck had scared, all quick-moving does except for one big pronghorn buck who rocked along behind in their dust cloud.

"Not really."

Billy sighed. Joe looked out the windshield but saw nothing. Joe remembered one time he and Astrid were dancing to the radio and she called him "sweetheart." She had never called him that before and never did again. Everything takes place in time, Joe thought, wondering why that always seemed like such a heartbreaking discovery.

Suddenly, Joe wanted to talk. "My old man used to say, 'If you ain't the lead horse, the scenery never changes.' Now it looks like I might lose the place. I need to get out front with that lead horse. I feel like I've been living in a graveyard."

Billy looked at him. Joe watched Billy deeply consider whether or not the fraternization was appropriate. It was clear that there was insufficient malice in the air to warrant this drive on any other basis. What a day we're having here, thought Joe.

After a resigned sigh, Billy started to talk: "When I come home, I pretty much come home to nothing. Except that we already had a kid. And then we got married. Old man Overstreet never let me forget I come into the deal empty-handed, just had my little house. He always introduces me, 'This here's my son-in-law Billy. He runs a few head of chickens over on the Mission Creek road about two and a half miles past the airport on the flat out there.' Never *will* let me forget. And I ought to punch you but I can't really. Life used to be so simple."

It was a long way around. It seemed as if the mountains toward Wyoming stayed the same size ahead of them, sharp shapes that curved off toward the Stillwater. You could be under traveling clouds and off toward the mountains the clouds would seem stopped. And the mountains looked like a place you'd never reach. On top of that, nobody seemed to want to get there much anyway. Billy must have felt Joe look over because he turned on the radio only to get the feverish accordion of Buckwheat Zydeco shouting out the bright nights of New Orleans. He turned it off and said, "I want to go back to work."

It seemed to Joe to be the most glowing of all thoughts. It went with the day and it went with their situation.

"I don't seem to understand what it means to have something," Joe said. "I don't seem to get what I ought to out of it. I feel like that place still belongs to my dad."

"It ought to belong to whoever's been working on it."

"Which is you, I suppose."

"It was when Overstreet had it leased. When you took it back, I had to go up to the house. That was when me and Ellen started to have such a wreck. We ain't over it yet. We may never get over it. She was raised up to think I ought to have something, and I don't." Joe remembered long ago when Billy had punched him out at the railroad station, and he thought he might have understood even then how the dispossessed are quick with their fists. But now Billy seemed to have lost even that capability. Joe thought that at the narrow crossroads in which Billy Kelton lived, the use of his hands had been cruelly confined to a kind of unchosen service. Lack of his own ground indentured him to people smaller than himself.

"That place of mine," Joe said, "has got serious debt against it but a man who wanted to stay and fight it ought to be able to hang on to it." He stared at the beautiful prairie and wondered if anyone had ever owned it. "I don't want to stay and fight it. That's just not me."

Billy slowed the truck. "Have you seen my father-in-law's map?"

"The one with the missing piece?"

"Do you have any idea what it would mean if I had that little chunk of the puzzle? Even for five minutes?"

"I probably don't," said Joe. "But we're all so different."

35

Joe had dinner with Lureen at her house. She didn't feel like cooking, so Joe stopped off for some chicken, a carton of cole slaw, and some soft drinks. She greeted him in the doorway, then went right back inside and sat under the kitchen window with her hands in her lap. Looking at her, Joe wondered if it wouldn't be the kindest thing he could do to burn her house down.

Joe walked around opening cupboards, looking for dishes and utensils and glasses, then set the kitchen table for the two of them. He got Lureen to come over and they sat down to eat. She didn't seem to want to eat much. Joe bit into a drumstick, then watched her over the top of it while he chewed. He tried the cole slaw. It was sweet and creamy like a dessert.

"Good chicken," he said.

"Delicious."

"You haven't tasted it yet."

"I will. Thank you for bringing it."

"Look at it this way," said Joe. "It's not beef! Ha-ha!" She took it in listlessly. A bird hit the window and they both looked up.

"It's all right," said Joe. "Didn't hit that hard."

Then he noticed Lureen's tears falling in the cole slaw.

"You must have foreseen this," he said.

"I didn't, Joe."

He chewed on the drumstick, trying to have a perception.

"But didn't it ring kind of a bell after it happened?"

"No."

"It was a bit of a crooked scheme for all parties concerned," Joe pointed out, actually enjoying this store chicken.

"*I know!*" Lureen wailed, throwing herself back in her chair.

"Long ago, my father, your brother, your *other* brother, told me never to take my eyes off Smitty."

"It's going to be hard to watch him in Hawaii," Lureen sniveled with an extraordinary, crumpled misery that Joe had not only never seen before in her but never seen in anyone of her age.

The phone rang and Joe answered it. The lovely and cultivated voice of a young woman explained that he, as the head of the household, was a finalist in a multi-million-dollar sweepstake. Joe cut her off. "I'm not the head of a household," Joe said and went back to Lureen.

"Wrong number," he said.

"Was it those sweepstakes people?"

"Yes."

"They're used to speaking with Smitty," she said and began to cry again. Joe's heart ached to see his poor little aunt in this condition even if she had brought it upon herself. He could see a tulip glow from the setting sun high in the kitchen windows. And then the perception came.

"Lureen, I'm going to tell you something and I want you to listen carefully." She stared at him like a child. "You know our Smitty," he said and she nodded her head up and down in a jittery fashion. "He'll spend all that money. You know that and I know that." He let this sink in. "And it won't take long." The nodding stopped. She was listening raptly. Joe was now ready to drop the panacea. "*And then he'll be back.*"

Lureen stopped all motion. She looked at Joe's face with extraordinary concentration.

"Are you telling me the truth?"

"Yes."

"And it won't take that long?"

"Not that long at all."

"I ask myself if he's really secure in Honolulu. You read from time to time of racial problems there. The Hawaiians are quick to throw a punch and they are absolutely enormous."

And it's unrealistic to expect another thorough bombing by the Japanese, Joe thought. Lureen picked up a wing and seemed to admire it. "You're one hundred percent right about his inability to handle his finances," Lureen observed in a comparatively lusty voice. "I might just as well start resigning myself to the reappearance of his little face at the screen."

"Not a moment to lose," said Joe tonelessly. "Start resigning yourself today." He gave her a confirming gesture with his bare drumstick which was reminiscent of the heads of corporations Ivan admired so, the ones who promoted their own products on television. Then he looked up to the band of sky in the window. He had seen that band when his grandfather died and he had asked his grandmother if he'd left him any gold.

As the principal lien-holder, Darryl took in hand the matter of working out the closing, the ritual exchange of a dollar bill so crumpled it took two paper clips to attach it to the documents. Joe accepted that the substitution of a born-to-the-soil type like Billy Kelton for a drifter like himself was equal in favorable impact to keeping it out of the hands of an opportunistic schemer like Overstreet who never borrowed from banks anyway. The picture of this hard-working cowboy with an honorable service record holding a gun to Overstreet's head would be applauded throughout the community and give them something to discuss other than the *Dead End* sign the state had put up on the road into the cemetery. Overstreet paid Joe one visit, waving a checkbook and making one or two ritual threats which were windier than his usual succinct style. It had been years since Joe had heard the phrase "rue the day" and he mulled it over until the words dissolved into nonsense.

The mineral rights were briefly a hitch. Joe couldn't at first face that his father had long ago placed them in trust for a caddies' college fund in Minnesota. But when he realized this, he knew finally that his father had really said goodbye to the place even before his soul left his body in that four-door Buick. He borrowed Darryl's phone at the bank while the principals still sat around the contracts in a cloud of cigarette smoke, and called Astrid to explain his latest theory, that they could work it out. Astrid's reply was typical, almost vintage, Astrid.

He drove toward the ranch that was no longer his. It was hard not to keep noticing the terrific blue of the autumn sky. The huge cottonwoods along the river had turned purest yellow, and since no wind had come up to disturb the dying leaves, the great trees stood in chandelier brilliance along the watercourses that veined the hills. Joe had to stop the truck to try to take in all this light.

The branches were heavy with early wet snow. Joe looked out from his kitchen window and felt his unshaven face. The light on the snow-edged world was dazzling. He used to feel this way a lot, almost breathless. He quickly started a pot of coffee and returned to the window to look at the snow starting to shrink in the morning sun. There was a soft mound of it on his woodpile, and on the ends of the logs he could see that water from snow melt had sunk into the wood. A sudden memory came back across the years: his father cleaning grouse at the sink in the ranch kitchen, a raft of feathers on darkened water. "I wish I was a vegetarian," he laughed. "You never have to pick number-eight shot out of a tomato!" The sky was blue and the air coming from under the slightly opened window so cool and clean that he admitted to himself that his spirits were starting to soar. He thought he'd begin to get his things together. He stood in the window a moment more and looked out at the beautiful white hills.

What Astrid had said, more or less, was that they would pretty much have to see.

NOBODY'S ANGEL

This book is for my beloved Laurie,
still there when the storm passed

"I love hell. I can't wait to get back."

—MALCOLM LOWRY

1

You would have to care about
the country. Nobody had been here long enough and the
Indians had been very thoroughly kicked out. It would
take a shovel to find they'd ever been here. In the grasslands that looked so whorled, so cowlicked from overhead, were the ranches. And some of these ranches were
run by men who thought like farmers and who usually
had wives twice their size. The others were run by men
who thought like cowboys and whose wives, more often
than not, were their own size or smaller, sometimes
quite tiny. The farmer-operators were good mechanics
and packed the protein off the land. The cowboys had
maybe a truck and some saddle horses; and statistics indicate that they had an unhealthy dependence on whiskey. They were not necessarily violent nor necessarily
uneducated. Their women didn't talk in the tiny baby
voices of the farmer-operator wives nor in the beautician
rasp of the town wives. The cowboys might have gotten
here last week or just after the Civil War, and they
seemed to believe in what they were doing; though they
were often very lazy white men.

The town in the middle of this place was called
Deadrock, a modest place of ten thousand souls, originally named for an unresolved battle between the Army
and the Assiniboin—Deadlock—but renamed Deadrock
out of some sad and irresolute boosterism meant to cure

an early-day depression. To many people Deadrock was exactly the right name; and in any case it stuck. It was soon to be a major postcard.

Patrick Fitzpatrick lived on a ranch thirty-one miles outside of town. He was a fourth-generation cowboy outsider, an educated man, a whiskey addict and until recently a professional soldier. He was thirty-six years old. He was in good shape; needed some crown work but that was about it.

2

The yard light erect upon its wood stanchion threw down a yellow faltering glow infinitely chromatic falling through the China willow to the ground pounded up against the house by the unrepentantly useless horses. Patrick Fitzpatrick glided under the low branches on his mare as the band circled into the corral for salt and grain and water and the morning's inspection for cracked hooves, lameness, splints, bowed tendons, lice, warbles, wire cuts, ulcerated eyes, wolf teeth, spavin, gravel, founder and worms.

Near the light's edge the dogs watched him pass: Cole Younger, yellow, on his back, all four legs dangling, let his eyelids fall open upside down; Alba, black, in the sub-shadow of mountain ash, ready to run; Zip T. Crow, brindle, jaw alight on parallel front legs, considered starting a stampede with his hyena voice. Thinking finally of the consequences, he fell to dreaming as the last horse, a yearling running at an angle, jog-trotted into the corral to drink in the creek alongside the other shadowy horses deployed as regularly as a picket line. Zip T. Crow slunk over behind some relic of a walking cultivator and dropped into its confused shadows like a shy insurrectionist. This was the day to ride up to the airplane.

3

In very early spring before the creeks flooded, before the first bridges washed away and the big river turned dark, before the snow was gone from the rugged shadows and the drowned livestock tumbled up in the brushy banks, Patrick found the airplane with his binoculars—a single ripped glimmer of fuselage visible a matter of hours before the next flurry concealed it for another month but not before Patrick had memorized the deep-blue ultramontane declivity at the top of the fearsome mountain and begun speculating if in May he could get a horse through the last ten thousand yards of deadfall and look into the pilot's eyes. Patrick was the son of a dead pilot.

Then in May Patrick walked up the endless sloping nose and saw the pilot quite clearly. He climbed past him to the copilot's seat and found fractured portions of granite, parts of the mountain that had poured like grapeshot through the fuselage clear into the tail section, leaving the copilot in innumerable pieces, those pieces gusseted in olive nylon, and the skin of the aircraft blood-sprayed as in a cult massacre. Farther aft in the tapering shape where the beating spring sun shone on the skin of the plane and where viscera trailed off in straps, fastening and instruments, it stank. Arms raised in uniform, the pilot seemed the image of a man in receipt of a fatal sacrament. The oxygen hose was torn away, and beyond the nautiloid effigy, Patrick could see his mare grazing on the alpine slope. Unable to differentiate flesh and electronics, he was avoiding the long-held notion that his father had died like a comet, igniting in the atmosphere, an archangelic semaphore more dignified than death itself. For Patrick, a year had begun. The inside of the plane showed him that life doesn't just always drag on.

4

Patrick left the sidewalk through the door between the two angled windows. It was cold, but when he hung his coat inside and glanced onto the street, it looked like summer. Purest optics. There was a stock truck parked at the hotel with two saddled horses in back facing opposite directions. Many saddle horses spend the day parked in front of a bar, heads hung in sleep. Can't get good help anymore, Patrick thought. Even if you could, who wants to tell people what to do?

Two steps up at the poker table was an old man with a diamond willow cane pushing chips onto the green felt. There was a belton setter at his feet, two strangers and a girl dealing cards. Not strangers, but he couldn't remember their names.

"Afternoon, Patrick," said the old man, whose name was Carson. That was his first name.

One stranger said, "Hello, Captain"—Patrick had been in the Army—and the other said, "How's the man?" Classmates with forgotten faces. But Patrick was rather graceful under these conditions, and by the time he'd gone through the room, the setter was asleep again, the players were smiling and the girl dealing was reading his name off the back of his belt.

The bar was nearly empty, populated solely by that handful of citizens who can drink in the face of sun blazing through the windows. Patrick ordered his whiskey, knocked it back and reconnoitered. Whiskey, he thought, head upstairs and do some good.

He called, "Thanks so much!" to the bar girl, put down his money and left. It was hard to leave a place where God was at bay.

He walked all the way to the foot of Main, straight toward the mountain range, crossed the little bridge over the clear overflow ditch and went into a prefabricated home without knocking. The windows were covered with shades, and once his eyes accustomed themselves to the poor light, he could see the prostitutes on the couch watching an intelligent interview show, the kind in which Mr. Interlocutor is plainly on amphetamines, while his subjects move in grotesque slow motion. They were dealing with the fetus's right to life. On the panel were four abortionists, five anti-abortionists and a livid nun with the temper of an aging welterweight.

"Hello, girls."

"Hello, Patrick."

"No game on?"

"College basketball. We're watching this fetus deal."

"Anybody make a profit?"

"Loretta did."

Loretta, a vital brunette with tangled hair and a strong, clean body, beamed. She said, "Trout fishermen. Doctors, I think. One had a penlight. He said he always checked for lesions. I said clap. He said among other things. I said four- to ten-day incubation. He says which book are you reading. I said I don't read books, I watch TV. So he gets in there with this penlight. I could've swatted him."

"Free checkup," said Patrick. "Look at the good side of things."

"Who's winning?" Loretta asked. She came from Deadrock, looked like a nice farm girl.

Deirdre, from Great Falls, always literal, said, "The fetus." This nun was packing the mail.

Patrick asked if they were betting. They said no. He

said that as he was a Catholic, he would kick in the set if the fetus lost.

"There's a Catholic," said Tana as the camera isolated the apoplectic nun shouting the word *"Sacred!"*

"I've seen better ones," said Patrick.

"Well, there's one, is all," she said doggedly.

Andrea, the young, bright blond, was from the High Line. She said, "I was with this rancher on his place. He wanted to go again. All the lights went out. I said that's Rural Electrification for you. He said that's Montana Power. I said well, I can't see nothin. He said it's hydroelectric. It comes off the grid, out of Columbia Falls. So I said what's the deal? Do we go again? He said not if I can't see. And just then, like God was on my side, the power came back on and I doubled down for fifty bucks. Thank you, Montana Power! Thank you, Columbia Falls!"

"Jesus," Patrick said. "That nun is going to blow her stack." He was staring at the screen.

"She's no help to the fetus team," said Loretta. The moderator kept saying, *"Sister! Sister!"* but nothing could slow her tirade, which continued to feature the word *"Sacred!"* repeated at very high volume.

"I'm glad I don't have any money on this one," said Patrick. Andrea got up and went to the kitchen to make iced tea. Loretta, from Deadrock, had gone to grammar school with Patrick, had been a medical secretary, then been not quite happy with that and tried prostitution, a respected job in Montana because of its long utility during the settlement of that region. Loretta's rural good looks made her prosper, particularly among visiting sportsmen.

Deirdre, from Great Falls, said, "That nun could use some eye shadow." Deirdre was best with closing-time stumblebums. Patrick asked Loretta if he could have a word with her privately.

The two went into the kitchen as Patrick fought back a little tingle. Loretta hiked herself up on the counter and Patrick sat in a ladder-back chair. There were coffee cans on a low shelf, each labeled with one of the girls' names;

and in front of every can was a kitchen timer. The cans held each night's earnings and the clocks foiled dawdling or inappropriate enthusiasm.

"Loretta," said Patrick. "You're prettier than you were at homecoming." Only an officer. She'd actually gone downhill.

"I've got a better life now. When did you get back?"

"Not too long ago. In the winter."

"You home to stay?"

"Trying to be. It'll depend on what I can get going. We're still running pairs and I've got a few outside horses to break, if I can remember how. I guess my grandfather has just had to pick up whoever he could. So a lot of things have kind of gone downhill."

"He had that one Indian for quite a while. Supposed to have been a good hand."

"What Indian?"

"He was, you know, a friend of Mary's, the way I had it." Mary was Patrick's sister.

"Well, Mary is why I'm here."

"What's the trouble?"

"No trouble. I just can't find her. I mean, I thought you might know."

"She got out of this work a long time ago, Pat. The Indian is the best way to find her I know. He was supposed to be real different. Used to shark pool at the Corral, just take everybody's money and never say a word. You know, an *Indian*."

"Well, I'm not going to go hunt her down or anything. But if you see her, tell her I'm home."

"I sure will."

"Boy, you look good, Loretta."

"More!" She put on her "It Girl" smile and spun on her toes.

Patrick walked over to the can labeled "Loretta," wound the clock in front of it and turned it loose real slow.

"Gives me a vicarious thrill," he said. She waved as he went out the door into the sunlight that bounced from the high walls of granite around the town.

5

Patrick was ticking off obliga-
tions. He walked back outside under the heartless blue
sky. He was searching for his grandfather, who had left
the ranch early that morning. Patrick feared a binge. But
as he had just left the Army and was not yet used to being
home, he was rather like someone out of stir, trying to
establish a pattern in a new world. For example, this
morning after feeding the horses, he had thought very
seriously about moving to Madrid. He had learned Spanish at the Monterey language school, but the Army made
him a tank captain in Germany. Nonetheless, he often
daydreamed of an ancient walk-up in Castile with a stone
kitchen, a cook he could afford and a stream of interesting characters who could understand that what had begun as scholarship had precipitated him into cold-war
mongery, *not* a desire to drive a bulletproof dump truck
on the East German line. Patrick had read widely, could
break horses and did not, as yet, live in Spain. In any case,
he would never reveal his love for the tank. He was tall,
single, had lost his father and looked after a grandfather
who now drank too much. Patrick drank a little too
much. His father had been a test pilot for Boeing. His
mother remarried in California. Lately, Patrick was having trouble answering letters, especially the prying ones
from the family about the finances of the ranch, which
were precarious; and with each arrival of the mail it had

become a real Mexican standoff between hiring a secretary and embarking for Castile.

Angled on the corner of Big Horn and Main was the Part-Time Bar, where Patrick went to have a George Dickel and water as a way of staking the place out for his grandfather. The Part-Time was an old-timers' favorite. The homemade soup there took a little of the edge off the binges and sustained anyone hungry in search of company. This hunger struck at all hours.

Patrick walked in and it was busy. He surveyed the room; no sign of his grandfather. At the bar many aging backs hunched in concealment.

"Anybody seen the old man?"

About fifteen nopes.

Patrick got his whiskey at the bar, sat down in the row of older faces and thought: This is the kind of place that makes you want to grow old, just sit here and eavesdrop.

Down the bar:

"I was born in 1904."

"Here?"

"Evidently."

Cigarette smoke moved horizontally toward the EXIT-TELEPHONE-REST ROOM sign.

Every time someone entered, "What d'ya know?" in a hearty voice; and the reply: "Not much." The "o" in "know" carrying the drawn-out local dipthong.

Patrick sipped in deep contentment. Underneath the murmur of conversation and easy laughter was the continuous slap of plastic chips from the poker game in the corner.

An elderly man next to Patrick in a John B. Stetson hat and blue suspenders said, "Colder it gets, the more a guy'll notice." He stared fixedly at the commemorative bottles. A pretty girl in a blue sweater dealt poker and in a firm voice repeated the rules. The new players feared her.

"Fifty cents to a buck on the deal and before the flop.

There's a three-raise limit on each round, no cutting.
Twenty bucks to buy in."

The old man next to Patrick was adjusting his butt on
the stool, improving his angle for a conversation. The
bartender shot past to the glass-and-wood cooler that displayed five kinds of beer at knee level. Patrick tried to
read the farm-auction poster from twenty feet; thought,
Used to could do that.

A voice from the corner: "Can't draw no goddamned
clubs."

The bartender collected more orders—Sunny Brook,
Cabin Still, Old Grand Dad, Canadian Mist, another
George Dickel for Patrick.

"Hungry?"

"No," said Patrick.

"We got three kinds of beef jerky—King B, Big Slim
and Rawhide Ranch."

"I don't think so."

"Plus beer nuts and smoked almonds."

"Who shot that six-pointer?"

"I did, Pat. Right after Korea."

The old man asked the bartender, "What bets've I
got?"

"You got the Pirates and the Tigers."

"Buck a square?"

"Yup."

"What kind of cigars you got?"

"Everything from White Owl to R. G. Dun."

"Gimme an R. G. Dun."

Patrick thought that in a moment the old man would
tell him where his grandfather was; he was warming up
and didn't want to be a squealer. Patrick pointed to a
bottle of Hiram Walker chocolate-mint liqueur and
asked, "Ever try that?"

"No."

The old man knew Patrick knew. He was going to
play it silent. Down the bar a heavy woman in her sixties
squinted and started describing commemorative bottles
in a lungful of Lucky Strike smoke: "Illinois Gladiola
Festival, a 'Ducks Unlimited,' an Australian koala bear,

Indian chief, Abraham Lincoln, the Kentucky Derby, Am Vets, a telephone—"

"Barkeep, what's it say on that model train?"

" 'Jupiter.' Says just 'Jupiter.' "

"I don't know what in the hell that means. Why don't somebody scrape that junk down from offa there?"

The old man pivoted to Patrick. "Your grandfather is trying out for a movie."

"He what?"

"Read the poster on the inside of the door."

CASTING CALL
for HONDO'S LAST MOVE, *a feature film.*

WANTED
Men, women and children for bit players, extras, et cetera.

ALSO NOTE
In order to reflect the hardships endured in the West in the 1880's, we would especially welcome the physically eccentric, those with permanent physical injuries, such as scars, missing teeth, broken limbs, broken noses, missing limbs, etc.

CONTACT
Arnold Duxbury, Casting Coordinator, Room 115–17, Murray Hotel. Interviews commence daily at 10:00 A.M.

Patrick thought, The old bugger has scars, missing teeth and evidence of a broken nose. That is where we shall find him. One episode too many of Wagon Train, dog-food ads masquerading as life.

Rooms 115–17 were, respectively, reception, waiting room and Duxbury. There was a considerable lineup of the maimed. The worst was a five-year-old boy whose pet wildcat had recently clawed out his eyeball. He wore an oozing patch and steered his head around, trying to figure out what he was doing there. His mother, a telephone operator who moonlighted at the Tempo Supper Club, respected her son's injury enough to bark *"No cuts!"* at Patrick when he tried to move up the line and look for his grandfather. The mother indignantly steered the little boy forward by the arm, and Patrick sheepishly got at the end while the halt, lame and maimed glowered at him, thinking, It's the bloody tank captain from the Heart Bar Ranch, trying to throw his weight around. But the sound of crutches and labored breathing grew behind him, and soon he stood at the desk of Marion Garland, who said, "What brings you to the geek show?" *Streets of Laredo* poured from a neighboring room.

"I'm looking for my grandfather—"

"What's your grandfather's name?"

"Frank Fitzpatrick."

"Francis X?"

"Yes."

"He's with Mr. Duxbury now."

"I'll just go in and get him."

"That's not our procedure—"

"It is now."

Patrick walked past her into Arnold Duxbury's office. Duxbury was a youthful forty. Every single thing he had on was denim, including his boots, which Patrick did not think was possible; treated rubber, perhaps.

Francis X. Fitzpatrick was showing a mule kick by taking off his pants. Duxbury explained that that would be unnecessary, as we were dealing with family entertainment. The crooked upper thigh was the old man's trump card and he wouldn't take no for an answer. Finally Duxbury said, "Hey, relax, you're in the movie." The old man shot his sleeves confidently.

"On the basis of what?" he demanded.

"The nose and your age."

"Well, write my name down."

"I already did."

"I'll see you on the set," said the old man, fastening his trousers. "Y'know what I mean? You better spelt my name correct."

"Come on, Grandpa," said Patrick. "I need you at the place. You mind?"

* * *

Duxbury and Garland signed up eighty-seven permanently injured Americans for *Hondo's Last Move* and returned to Los Angeles. The film was already in trouble; the distributor was thinking of pulling out to do something more in the Space line, as Westerns were beginning to show signs of what he called in a *Variety* interview "metal fatigue."

Nobody ever saw Duxbury and Garland again. As it turned out, Patrick's grandfather would never quite get over it. His heart was on a movie poster, however close to the bottom. There were still small wings on his shoes.

6

Patrick gave his grandfather a good lead, then got in the Ford and started home. The yellow truck shot along the river road against the amphitheater in the Absaroka range between Case Creek and Sheep Creek. A summer storm hung in the deepest pass above the truck, and lightning volleyed in silence. Patrick glanced at his knuckles, looked up, dodged a pothole, admired a hawk circling in a thermal against the limited storm now evaporating like steam on glass. The truck sucked down into the creek bottom. The storm dematerialized and left the hawk in empty blue.

Patrick stopped at the calving shed a mile below the house and played Ornette Coleman on the machine, wondered why Ornette always had a white bass player and why he made you think so hard. Patrick decided that because Ornette was such a thorough master of bebop, he knew a white man could be expected to play melodic bass and not worry too much about time. Was Ornette as clever as the Yardbird? Why was there not a statue of Charlie Parker in Washington? When Patrick thought of Ornette Coleman running an elevator in Los Angeles with a roomful of scores and his mother sending him food from Texas, he developed grave doubts about the District of Columbia.

Patrick daydreamed on with unimpeded high energy. Lenin's girl friend Inessa Armand died in 1920 of typhus in the North Caucasus. Patrick read that in a Mexican comic book while preparing for flight to Castile. He read that in the vague interior light of a high-speed American tank in Germany. He was a security measure. He liked whiskey. Most of the other security measures preferred pharmaceuticals. With their dilated pupils and langorous movements, they were there to help save the West from the East, should the occasion arise. Patrick felt they had already gone East. But then, he was a captain, and being an officer had slowly sunk against the grain until finally, strangely, he was actually an Army captain, if you could see around the matter of the Mexican comic books.

I will work the claybank mare. She has taken to running through the bridle. She does not fall off to the right as well as she does to the left. I want her to drag, lock down and turn around when she needs to. We are not trying to make trail horses. We are not leading a string of dudes to a photo view of Scissorbill Peak.

Next to the barn a cat ran through three shadows without touching the sunlight, then emerged triumphant in the glare, mouse crosswise in its hard domestic mouth. After a motionless instant the cat started toward the green lawn and the house, where, in front of the sink, it would leave the minute head and vermiculate insides of the mouse.

The horses, maybe twenty head, were all in a pod on the far side of the corral, shaded by cottonwoods. Wild rose bushes grew right to the poles, and the sides of the corral were like a tall hedge, illuminated by the pale-pink blossoms. The claybank mare was in the center of the band, nearer the side of the corral, really; and as Patrick closed the gate to walk toward the horses, the mare, butt toward him, shifted her head slightly for better rear-angle vision—out of a very real sense that it was she who was going up to the pasture with Patrick and not the other roughly nineteen. She looked like a shoplifter.

In this bunch there were no kickers, and so Patrick murmured his way gently through the big bodies, feeling their heat and watching the quizzical movement of the claybank mare's head and ears. Some of the horses kept sleeping, the good old saddle horses, lower lips trembling in massive dreams, one or another rear foot tipped up, weight transferred from muscle to ligament in that horse magic of standing sleep; one or two craning, ignorant yearlings, and Patrick's hand touched the mare's flank, which twitched involuntarily, as though he'd shuffled across a carpet and given her a flicker of static electricity. He said softly, "Hey, now," as he moved toward her head. "Care to go with me to Spain? Little walk-up deal with a cool stone kitchen?" And he had her haltered, turned around and headed for the gate, the mare flopping her feet along, knowing she was going to school.

Patrick brushed her thoroughly, watching the early light go through her coat. Claybank and grulla were his preferred colors; claybank, just like it sounded, a blur away from a copper dun, or a copper dun that had been rolling in alkali dust, then run for a mile until the color started through once more. *Grulla* was Spanish for blue heron. Grullas had better feet than claybanks and were said to stand the sun well. This far north it didn't matter. Patrick irrationally believed that anything dun, claybank or buckskin had more cow sense.

He saddled the mare with two Mexican blankets. You had to kind of rub the blankets up onto her or she'd try to pull the hitching rack out of the ground. She was young. And when he pitched the saddle up on her, he held the cinch, girth and billets so that nothing would slap and start her pulling back. Today he tried her in a grazing bit to get her nose out a little; he had been riding her on a higher-ported bit, and she was collecting her head too much, tucking it up like some fool show horse from California. Patrick liked them with their faces out, looking around, their feet under them, not like something in front of the supermarket that takes quarters.

This mare was searching for a reason to be a bronc, as perhaps they all were; so Patrick walked her in a figure eight to untrack her, stood in one stirrup for a moment, then crawled on. By your late thirties the ground has begun to grow hard. It grows harder and harder until the day that it admits you.

Then a half mile in deep grass and early light, time for a smart young horse to have a look around, scare up some meadowlarks, salivate on the copper mouthpiece, get a little ornery bow in her back and get rid of it. Patrick changed his weight from stirrup to stirrup, felt her compensate, then stopped her. She fidgeted a moment, waited, then let the tension go out of her muscles. He moved her out again to the right. All she gave him was her head; so he stopped her, drew her nose each way nearly to his boot, then made a serpentine track across the pasture, trying to get a gradual curve throughout her body in each of her turns. The rowels on his spurs were loose enough that they chinked with her gaits. Patrick used spurs like a pointing finger, pressing movement into a shape, never striking or gouging. And horseback, unlike any other area of his life, he never lost his temper, which, in horsemen, is the final mark of the amateur.

Patrick broke the mare out into a long trot, dropping her back each time she tried to move into a lope. She made one long buck out of irritation, then leveled off like a pacer eating up ground and slowly rotating the cascading hills, to Patrick's happy observation. I love this scene. It has no booze or women in it, he rejoiced.

He set the mare down twice, liked her stops, then blew her out for half a mile, the new fence going past his eyes like a filament of mercury, and let her jog home while he told her continuously how wonderful she was, what a lovely person she was becoming.

Black coffee and a morning breeze through the paper. Martinsdale Hutterites had recalled three hundred contaminated chickens. Cowboys for Christ was having a benefit. Billings fireman captured with three pounds of methamphetamines. Poplar man shot to death in Wolf Point; Bureau of Indian Affairs investigator and tribal police arrested two men as yet unnamed. Half million in felonious cattle defaults. Formerly known as bum deals, thought Patrick. A new treatment center for compulsive gamblers. Lives shattered by slot machines. Wanted or for sale: TV stand, green-broke horse, ladies' western suits, four-drawer blond dresser, harvest-gold gas range, three box-trained kittens, nonleak laundry tubs, top dollar for deer and elk hides, Brown Swiss, presently milking, Phoenix or Yuma to share gas. When Patrick's father went down testing an airplane, fast enough that its exterior skin glowed at night from the friction of the air, the hurtling pulp which had been his father and the navigator and which had passed through the intricate molecular confusion of an exploding aircraft at its contact with eastern Oregon, the paper identified him as Patrick Fitzpatrick of Deadrock, Montana, and the navigator as Del Andrews of Long Beach, California. Great space was given to the model of the aircraft and speculation about a declared salvage value. As so many people have had to wonder, Patrick thought, if my father is dead, how can I be alive? In this way Patrick lost much of his own fear of death. The crash had provoked none of the questions usual to accidental death. There was nothing to identify.

Patrick's grandfather walked into the kitchen, opened the refrigerator, stared about at the contents, settled for a handful of radishes and sat down.

"What's the cattle market doing?"

"Haven't had the radio on," said Patrick. "Somebody sold a bunch of bred heifers in Billings yesterday for a twenty-seven-hundred-dollar average."

"Bred how?"

"Shoshone or Chandelier Forever, forgot which. You want me to make you some breakfast?"

"I can rustle."

"Here, sit down. What do you want?"

"Couple of soft-boiled eggs."

Patrick started getting them ready. "In Europe there'd be these restaurants that put soft-boiled eggs in little porcelain holders, and they'd cover it with a knitted thing to keep the egg hot."

"That's the silliest thing I ever heard. I have no desire to see Europe."

Patrick served the eggs and some toast.

"Down there, there in Oklahoma, they've got a toll-free number for the cattle market. I hate having to listen to all this deal on the radio to find what steers brought."

"Steers aren't going to make you anything," Patrick said. He put some English on that.

"Feeding out seven months ain't going to make you anything."

"I never said ranching was any good."

"Talk like that," said his grandfather feistily, "and you won't want to fix nothin.'"

"Well, just let her fall down then," Patrick said.

"It ain't even historical."

"That's right." Historical? That was a first from the old souse.

"And where would you be running this remuda of yours?"

"On the damn forest service."

"Try it."

"I may."

Patrick's grandfather returned to his eggs, smoldering. Patrick was going to let him make his own tomorrow.

"You ought to back your horses more if you want them to get their butts down," said his grandfather.

"Don't tell me to back my horses. I get their feet under them by making them want to stop."

"They aren't tanks, Patrick."

"I rode some colts you broke twenty years ago. Couldn't turn them around in a twenty-acre pasture."

"Why don't I just cook my own eggs tomorrow? Seems like a little favor spoils your temperament. I remember some of them colts and they turned on a dime. Why, you bugger, I broke Leafy's mother!"

"You cook the eggs."

When he was away Patrick's daydreams fell easily back twenty years to summers riding in the hills, spooking game in the springs and down in the blue, shadowy draws, swimming in the gold dredge, girls present, the cold sky-blue submersion a baptism, the best place for the emerging consciousness of women to grow in suitable containment. Even, suddenly in a West German dance hall, remembering the flood of tears at twelve when he'd killed a spike buck in the same little grove where he and his father always cut their Christmas tree. Before that, hunting coyotes, his grandfather had crawled into a cave near Blacktail and found a ceremonially dressed, mummified Indian warrior on a slab of rock. His grandfather refused to tell anyone where the corpse was, and Patrick wore out two saddle horses looking for it. A friend, Jack Adams, later found it over on Mission Creek. "You do not disturb the Old Ones," his grandfather had said. Then Jack glommed the mummy, making everyone cross. And Patrick himself, on the North Rosebud, had found the scribblings of the phantom ancient Sheepeaters; he had slept in eagle traps and in the coffin-shaped hole in the rock the Crows had made above Massacre Creek. He had seen the skeleton of a Cheyenne girl dressed in an Army coat, disinterred when the railroad bed was widened. Her family had put silver thimbles on every finger to prove to somebody's god that she was a useful girl who could sew. After his father went to work for Boeing and split up with his mother, Patrick lived with his grandfather and ate so much poached game that the smell of beef nauseated him. He lost the tips of three fingers in his lariat heeling calves in the spring and never went to the movies except to meet girls. He could shoe horses, beat a hunting knife out of an old file, throw a diamond hitch, fix windmills, listen for broken gate valves in the well; and masquerade enough in town to occasionally get his ashes hauled, though he still preferred the sinewy barrel-racers he first met at the gold dredge whose teasing country-ruthless sensuality was somehow smokier than the ten-speeders just learning to roll a number. At sixteen he was jailed twelve times in a row for disorderly conduct; and his father, in the year that he died—a circumstance that left Patrick permanently dented with guilt—borrowed against his share of the ranch and sent Patrick to a preparatory school in the East which thought that a rebellious young cowboy would be a colorful enough addition to a student body that included a Siamese prince with a Corvette, a West German, five Venezuelans and one Negro that they would overlook his poor grades and boisterous history with the law.

They taught him to play soccer. Once again he was in short pants. For a long time he could see his knees in the corners of his eyes when he ran. It made him miss the ball. It was one of the troublesome ways he couldn't escape his own mind. Later, it got worse.

7

Evidently someone passing through Grassrange had given Mary a ride as far as Roundup, then dropped her with a social worker there. The conditions that moved this person to, in effect, turn Mary in were ones that produced concern and not fear: Mary wasn't making sense. The tough district court judge at Roundup had Mary hauled to Warm Springs, which is Montana's state mental institution. She had been detained. But the primary problem was that no one could identify her and Mary wasn't helping. She said that something was always happening to her, but she would tell no one what it was.

Patrick was her custodian once she relinquished her name. He took her home, cruising the interstate in his truck on the intermittently cloudy day. He looked over his sunglasses; he was trying to seem old.

"What'd you read?"

"Two books, over and over."

"What books were they?"

"Books of poetry, Patrick. I read the poems of Saint Theresa of Avila and the poems of Saint John of the Cross. That car has Ohio plates. How many Ohio songs can you name?"

"You make any friends?"

"One trouble with loony bins is you make friends and then you make enemies, and there are these referee-doctors who don't seem to be able to stop this seesaw deal between the two. All they do is keep the patients from savaging each other." She leaned to see herself in the rearview.

"What's the matter with you, anyway?"

"Evidently I can't see life's purpose."

"What do you mean 'evidently'?"

"I mean that that's what they told me. I didn't come up with the idea myself."

"I don't ever think about life's purpose," said Patrick, lying in his teeth.

"Lucky you," she said. "We got enough gas?"

"We do, and there's more where that came from."

Mary was, Patrick thought, such a pretty girl. And she didn't have the neurasthenic glaze that produced what passed for looks among people who would rather raise orchids. Mary had a strong, clear face, a cascade of oaken hair and a lean, athletic figure. But she also had, Patrick thought, a bad attitude. Certainly no bell-jar lady, though.

It made him worry. He was open-minded and interested in other tastes than his own, normally. But, for instance, being Mary's older brother produced, just now, the following question: Who is Saint John of the Cross? I thought Jesus was the one with the cross. It was as if the cross was a party favor, a prize for the most serious face.

"Want to stop at Three Forks and get plastered?" Mary inquired. Her hands made laughing shapes in the air, foretelling gala Three Forks. A saloon conjunction of the Missouri headwaters.

"It isn't the day for that."

"There's another one with Ohio plates."

"I don't care."

"Our home state is being deluged by those of Ohio."

"It's fair."

When the universal shitstorm seemed to mount its darkest clouds, Patrick always said that it was fair. Mary fell silent. Her trouble was she thought it *wasn't* fair. They'd had words about this before. Mary had said his calling everything fair made him more fatal than any

Hindu. People like him, she accused, refused smallpox vaccine. Who did he think he was with this fairness? The truth was *nothing* was fair. That's where I've got you, said Patrick.

But Mary's travails had today deprived her of fight. She fixed a stony look upon I-90. She didn't think any of the signs were funny and she stopped counting Ohio plates. Patrick began to worry. He could hear her breathing.

When they spiraled down the Deadrock off-ramp, Mary said, "The other thing is, I'm in a family way." The blackbirds shot across the lumberyard, and they both decided that watching them veer between the sawdust stacks was quite the best thing to do.

They passed the smoking waste-burner and log reserves of Big Sky Lumber in silence; and similarly Madison Travertine, where water-cooled saws made weird pink marble slabs out of million-year-old hot-spring mineral accumulations. They crossed Carson's Bridge over the big river while Patrick considered his next question and the mysterious sign painted on the rocks under the high falcon nests:

PLEASE STOP IT

Nobody knew what the sign meant. In place of direct attention, Patrick accumulated roadside information: ROCK SHOP—AGATES, TERRI'S BEAUTY SHOP, YUMMEE FREEZE, HEREFORDS: MONTANA'S GREATEST TREASURE, U-NAME IT WE'LL FIND IT, a white barn in the turn with a basketball net, a rough-breaks sign, white crosses in Dead Man's Curve, and the broad, good pastures, defined in the earth slits of flood irrigation. A farmer with a shovel watched the passing water.

"Who's the father?"

"Not telling." Drawing a lower eyelid down with her forefinger: Share God's joke on us.

"Okay."

"Do you have any babies in Germany?"

"I don't believe so."

"Little visits you might have made?"

"Who said I made little visits? I was busy in the tank. You need a shower."

"Boy, do I."

"I should warn you, Mary."

"What?"

"Mother's visit coming up soon."

"Whew."

"So . . ."

"I don't know. Tough it out, I guess."

"Are you stable?" Patrick inquired.

"Terribly. I wouldn't have given them my name otherwise. I let them circulate my fingerprints while I caught up on some reading." She patted her satchel of books.

Patrick glanced over at Mary, glimpsed the eczema-like condition that left her hands cracked and red from the nervous attacks. They fluttered under his gaze.

"How's Grandpa?" she asked.

"Just a little bit remote. You catch him at the right time and he pours it all out. Otherwise, he's kind of floating around." He was slipping toward Mary.

"That's because he's old," said Mary. "And because he knows he's going to die soon."

Patrick could supply no refutation: He was in midair; he had no family and he wasn't in love. He did try to make his sigh as significant as possible. Mary arched her brows.

"What have you been doing for a living?"

"Let's not go into that," said Mary.

"Where have you been?"

"I was in Belle Fourche, then Denver. I was in Texas for about a month. I was in Grassrange and Moccasin for quite a while, but I *will* not talk about that."

"What'd you think of the Texans?"

"They're like Australians. They're great, actually, as long as they don't talk about Texas. Can we fix up my room like it was?"

"It hasn't changed."

"Is the blue reading lamp still there?"

"Yup."

241

"Bulb work?"

"At last examination."

"Any rules?"

"As a matter of fact, yes," said Patrick. "We do not allow Negro field chants after three in the morning."

"There's always something," said Mary as they turned up the road that carried them to the ranch and the hills. The wild roses shelved green in the bends, and the demarcation of light and shadow on the dust seemed artificial. Patrick looked over at Mary. She was staring up the road toward the ranch and her eyes were not right. He had certainly made his little joke knowing that she would not look right when he turned, in the hopes of deflecting that moment. Patrick didn't know what he saw in her face—it was pale—but forced to name it, he would have called it terror. Well, fuck it: Basically the whole thing was terrifying.

"I could use your help in gentling some of the yearlings," he said, but he got no reply. The air rushed in the wind vanes.

"Mary, remember the jet that crashed last winter up in the Absarokas?"

"Yes . . ." She stared at the ranch yard as Patrick glided toward the turnaround at the barn.

"Well, I found it with my binoculars. I could see a wing sticking out of the snow, just the tip. It's behind Monitor Peak. I went up there."

She coddled her satchel. "One book I wouldn't take to a desert island is a family album."

"Now, what's that supposed to mean?" he asked.

Mary turned and looked full at him. "It means," she said, "that Daddy's not in that plane."

8

On Sunday, Patrick was invited to the Z6 for luncheon, and for some reason he went. This required a long drive nearly to McRae, where, past the West Stoney River, the Z6 road angled into sweeping foothills. The hills were dry and blue-green with sagebrush, here and there illuminated by small bands of liquid-moving antelope as easy-traveling as sun through windy clouds. The land here seemed the result of an immense and all-eradicating flood, which left rims and ridges as evidence of ancient cresting seas.

The Z6 was what remained of an old English-based land-and-cattle company, the kind that once flourished on the northern grassland, with headquarters in London and Edinburgh; but it had shrunk to the absentee ownership of American cousins, a few of whom contrived to audit its profits and losses from New York City. In July and August the American cousins bought Stetsons and headed west, clogging first-class on a big jet. One cousin, though, Jack Adams, nearing sixty, had been on the ranch most of his life. A good operator, he was a rowdy frequenter of the Montana Club in Helena and a high-speed evader of radar traps. A lot of the people came because of him; but in general they were just day drinkers gathered on a hard green lawn under the inhuman blue sky. Things would grow less intelligent as the day wore on.

Jack came out to meet Patrick as he pulled his truck

243

alongside the cars in a small turnaround facing the lawn and the fine old log buildings, which looked low, solid, somehow refined with their cedar roofs and wood smelling of linseed oil. Patrick admired him because Jack was a cowboy and a gentleman, and so he was pleased that Jack came out carrying him a glass of bourbon, knowing it was Patrick's favorite drink, but knowing also that Patrick, like himself, would drink anything and that, strictly speaking, neither of them drank for fun.

"I hoped you'd come," said Jack. "Anna's made a few gallons of real good Marys, full of nutrition. I thought a little of this with water would help graduate you into nutrition."

"Thank you, sir," said Patrick, slamming the truck door. "To your health."

"Yours. No sense in getting your granddad out today?"

You could see the people, the strangely stylized, bent-at-the-waist postures of people socializing on a lawn.

"All he talks about is the past and the movies. I need to get him back on some middle ground before I can show him. Besides, he doesn't like anybody."

"People go through phases," said Jack. It was not, perforce, banal. "We've all taken a spell or two."

Deke Patwell, the editor of the Deadrock *News*, started toward Patrick. Patwell had left graduate school with little but the habit of dressing in the ill-fitting 1950 seersucker that characterized his professors; but by the time he established himself in Deadrock, he decided that it was the place where the last stand of just folks would take place. This sort of fanciful descent was a kind of religion and had been something of a vice among the privileged classes for centuries, Marie Antoinette being the most famous example. Patwell had as little use for Patrick as he had for the poor and dispossessed. He was a champion of the average and he meant to make it stick. This attitude and Patwell's capacity for hard work made the *News* successful. It was a legitimate success.

"How's Patrick?" he said.

"Not bad, Deke."

"Enjoying the gathering?" Deke was always rakish when he managed to leave his wife at home.

"Oh, yeah."

"Anything newsworthy up your way?"

"No, it's been awful quiet."

"We thought it best to ignore Mary's little run-ins."

Patrick felt his blood rising. "Like what?"

"Well, you've been away. And like I say, we didn't see fit to print." Little homecoming presents. Lawn war.

"I appreciate it," said Patrick as best he could, wondering why Patwell was establishing this debt. Maybe just the husbandry of someone who daily had to call in the repayment of small favors.

"Time for my refill," said Patwell. "And call me if you get anything up your way."

Patrick walked toward the lawn. The lawn was Anna's idea. Anna was Jack's wife. Anna did not belong to the dude-ranch-wife set with the shaved back of the neck and boot-cut Levis; there were certain perquisites for having raised children and done well that she regarded as indispensable. One was a lawn; others were New York clothes, a restaurant-size gas stove, a Missouri fox-trotter horse and a German Olympic-grade .22 rifle to shoot gophers with. The first time a luncheon guest shoved a Ferragamo pump into a gopher colony, Anna ordered the rifle. In early summer she sat upstairs beneath the steeply angled roof in her bathrobe, moving the crosshairs over the rolled green expanse, looking for rodents in the optics. Jack learned to use the back door as he came and went to the pens and barn, the report of the small-caliber rifle becoming, year by year, less audible.

The Bloody Marys were in a huge cut-glass bowl, which rested in a cattle-watering tank filled with ice. No one had fanned out far from this place and Patrick got a quick survey: a few people he already knew, Anna, who just winked, and a handsome young couple he'd never seen. The husband wore a good summer jacket and a pair of boots the height of his knee, outside his pants. An oilman, Patrick thought. Oilmen, whatever else they might wear, needed one outstanding sartorial detail to show that their oil was on ranches. And by God, if there was enough oil, they'd go ahead and put cows on those ranches and wear their boots like that. You wanted to be sure no one thought you were a damn parts salesman.

Patrick still had his bourbon and had planned a slow approach, but Anna swept him in, introducing him with the "Captain" prefix. Deke Patwell was deftly escorting an inheritrix from Seattle named Penny Asperson and interviewing an orthodontist-land speculator from Missoula via Cleveland named, believe it or not, something-or-other Lawless. All Patrick could remember was that last name. And there was the couple, sure enough oil: Claire Burnett and her husband, whose real name was John but who was already, in his thirties, called Tio, which is Mexican for uncle and is a rather flattering nickname for one who aspires to be a *patrón*. But Tio was vivid anyway, piercey-bright, oilman feisty, and his wife was a knockout. Patrick knew their name, a little bit, because of horses.

The conversation was lively already. A boy had been shot and killed on a ranch recently for trespassing. Claire and Tio looked baffled at this bit of local color. Deke Patwell slid comfortably into his local-expert mode and sternly explained that only the ranchers' reputation for being trigger-happy kept them safe and their way of life intact. Then playfully he tugged at her sleeve and said, "Claire, you do horses so well. Let me and Tio do current events. Later you do house. Anything else is just five-o'clock news."

"Where is the dead boy's family?" Claire asked. Tio then scooped down into Bloody Marys. Deke caught his glance and they walked over under the cottonwoods. Claire turned to Patrick. Tio had bought Deke's views.

"I'm not going to ask you what you think."

"Yes, ma'am."

"People side up with Tio because they want his business."

"I don't want his business."

"What are you captain of?"

"Tanks."

"See, they know how shocking their thinking is. They just want it to set them apart. Has nothing to do with that boy—Tanks?"

Patrick tried to decide whether good country living, money, self-esteem or the kind of routine maintenance that begins with pumice-stoning the callouses of one's feet and ends somewhere between moisture packs and myopic attention to individual split ends produced Claire's rather beautiful physical effect. Claire said she didn't know who meant what anymore. Baseball players had Daffy Duck haircuts sticking out from under their billed caps, rock 'n' roll stars all wore sateen warm-up jackets like the baseball players', and the President was passing out in a foot race while Russians installed nerve gas around ballistic-missile silos. So who could tell whether or not that little old editor was copping an attitude or whether Tio was just kicking back into his good-buddy act because he was in someone else's state?

Patrick said, "I don't know."

She said, "What do you mean 'I don't know'?"

"I don't know and I don't care."

"Let's go to the house and refill your bourbon. I can see you casting a funny eye at those mixed drinks. Did you train a mare named Leafy?"

They started toward the house.

"Yes, I did."

"What do you want for her?"

"Well, she's just my horse."

"I saw her at Odessa."

"She was there."

"Did you ever breed her?"

"No."

They walked into the cool wood-chambered living room with the buffalo rugs and the Indian blankets and the peyote boxes and the beaded parfleches on the deeply oiled logs.

"Would you ever breed her?"

"If she let me know she wanted to have a baby."

"You ought to breed to our stud. I presume she's cycling."

Patrick just didn't reply. He looked up from his freshly drawn glass of sour mash, a smile on his face that crossed all the silence of immediate conversational aftermath.

He took a long, kindly look at this young woman, thought of their banter, saw in her confidence that she enjoyed it, too, the way grade-schoolers like to slug each other out of sheer attraction. Then he wondered if he would find Tio less estimable the next time he saw him, which would be in a few moments, or if he would gather that Claire was just in a world of her own, set out upon one of the ineluctable trajectories of conflict that can be blamed upon something long ago, a book, a parent, an aging nun, a baton dropped in front of a sold-out stadium. I don't know, he thought, and I don't care. Yes, I care, but I won't.

"Ever hear the joke about the escaped circus lion down in Texas? He nearly starved to death. Every time he growled at one of those Texans, it scared the shit out of him. And when he jumped on him, it knocked all the hot air out. So there was nothing left to eat."

She said, "I'm from Oklahoma. My God, is that a joke?"

"Let's go inside. I could interpret the wall hangings. They're Northern Cheyenne."

"Thanks," she smiled, "but we done had Comanche down at home." She dropped her chin and examined him.

He thought he could see perhaps the tiniest acquiescence, though not quite anything he could hold her to. He found her engaging and probably as strong as he was, that is to say, not particularly strong or, rather, strong in the wrong ways.

"We're more fun than the luncheon guests," said Claire bravely as she went into the hard glare over the lawn, gone in her bounding step toward the people at the tank. It could be said that Patrick's mild stalling, giving Claire a lead, came from a very slight sly motive in him, one that he recognized and resolved to give a bit of thought to. The stalling left him among the mops in the front hall, hooks holding worn-out hats, irrigating boots, a pair of old dropshank spurs and a twelve-gauge: a basic tool kit.

Then when Patrick stepped onto the lawn, Tio was walking resolutely toward him, long-strided in his tall calfskin boots. What's this? Well, for one thing, thought Patrick, it's the first time I've seen eighteen-karat-gold oil-derrick blazer buttons.

"Patrick."

"Tio."

"They say you're a horseman."

"Something of one," said Patrick, thinking, Your wife was too friendly. He was a little ahead of himself.

"Do you like good cow ponies?"

"Yes." Were there people who didn't?

Tio plunged his hands in his pockets, then leaned the full weight on his straightened arms, tilted slightly forward from the waist, weight in the pockets. Tell you what I'm gonna do. One knee moving rapidly inside its pant leg. "Claire say I got a stud?"

"Yes, she did."

"Tell you much about the old pony?"

"No—"

"Say he was good?"

"She thought I ought to breed this cutting mare of mine to him."

"Well, you should, old buddy. This pony'll cut a cow, now. I mean the whole bottom drops out and he's lookin *up* at them cattle. He traps his cattle and just showers on them."

"Well, I'm gonna ride this mare another couple years yet. She's my number-one deal."

"*Plus*, this pony comes right from the front of the book. Peppy San out of an own daughter of Gunsmoke. It idn't any way he can get out of traffic fast enough to keep hisself from being a champion."

Patrick wasn't much interested. He said, "Well, when I get something to breed, I'll take a hard look at him."

"I want you to breed that old Leafy mare. This stud of mine is young and he needs mares like that to put them good kind of babies on that ground. You know how long Secretariat's cannon bone is?"

"Sure don't."

"Nine inches. So's this colt's. That's what makes an athlete. That'n a good mind. This colt's got one of them, too. His name is American Express, but I call him Cunt because that's all he has on his mind. He's a stud horse, old Cunt is. But I'm like that. You were always lookin for a smoke, I'd call you Smoke."

"What d'you call Claire?"

"Claire sixty percent of the time, and Shit when she don't get it correct, which is right at forty."

Patrick thought, I wonder if they'll ever teach him English. Maybe he doesn't want to learn. Maybe you can't be an old buddy and speak English. Patrick would rather hear a cat climbing a blackboard. And he didn't like what Tio called his wife forty percent of the time. In fact, he just didn't like Southwesterners. It wasn't even cow country to Patrick. It was yearling country. There were no cowboys down there significantly. There were yearling boys and people who fixed windmills. After that, you put in dry wall on the fourteenth story of a condo in Midland, where some cattleman did it all on a piece of paper with a solid-gold ball-point pen and a WATS line: a downtown rancher, calling everything big he had little and old, and calling his wife shit; the first part of the West with gangrene. Dance the Cotton-Eyed Joe and sell it to the movies.

Here came Jack Adams with another bourbon; probably spotted that look in Patrick's eye and sought to throw fat on the fire. People often have this kind of fun with problem drinkers. But Patrick was determined to be somebody's angel, and they wouldn't catch him out today. Instead he started back to the company, excusing himself. Made a nice glide of it.

Deke Patwell and Penny Asperson were passing a pair of binoculars back and forth, trying to find the property lines a thousand yards uphill. "Not strong enough," said Deke, putting the glasses away. "We'd have to walk up there, and we know how we feel about that." His mouth made a sharp downward curve.

Anna said, "We use the National Forest anyway. So I don't know what that property line's supposed to mean." She gave the Bloody Marys a thoughtful stir.

"You will when the niggers start backpacking," said Deke Patwell. "Oh God, that's me being ironic."

"Anna's the lucky type," Patrick said. "She'll get O. J. Simpson and an American Express card."

Claire said, "You sprinkle this much?"

"After July," Anna said. "It's a luxury but we've got a good well. If it was Jack, we'd be waist-deep in sage and camass and just general prairie, and the ticks would be walking over us looking for a good home."

The buildings, which made something of a compound of the lawn, moved their long shadows, lengthening toward the blue sublight of the spruce trees; but the real advent of midafternoon was signaled when Deke Patwell passed out. Everyone gathered around him as his tall form lay crumpled in his oddly collegiate lawn-party clothes. He was only out for a moment, which was too bad, because he had grown strident with his drunkenness, especially as to his social theories. He had been drawing a bright picture of Jew-boy legions storming the capitol at Helena when his eyes went off at an angle and he buckled.

Then he was trying to get up. He rolled mute, imploring eyes at the people surrounding him, threw up and inhaled half of it. It was like watching him drown. Jack bent over, stuck a hand in his mouth and said, "I'd say the Hebrews got the capitol dome."

Anna said to Jack firmly, "Go inside and warsh your hands." Deke let go another volley and said he didn't feel so good.

Minor retribution crept into Patrick's mind. He said, "Maybe a drink would perk you up." Deke cast a vengeful glance up to him, said he would remember that, then tipped over onto one shoulder on the lawn and gave up. His plaid summer jacket was rolled around his shoulder blades, and a slab of prematurely marbled flesh stood out over his tooled belt.

Patrick ambled toward the little creek that bordered one side of the lawn. Perfect wild chokecherries made a topiary line against the running water, which held small wild trout, long used to the lawn parties. But then Penny Asperson followed him, and when he looked back, he caught Claire's observation of the pursuit. In his irritation he thought Penny was thundering toward him. There were yellow grosbeaks crawling on the chokecherry branches, more like little mammals than birds.

"Bloody Deke," said Penny. "If he'd had the gumption, we'd be up at the boundary. He'd be sober and the air would be full of smoldering glances." Penny's broad sides heaved with laughter. *"Now* look. And he smells." Patrick wished to speak to her of carbohydrates and chewing each bite twenty-seven times. But she was, after all, a jolly girl.

"The smell's the worst of it," Patrick said agreeably. "I thought Jack was courageous to free his tongue."

"It takes a man to do that."

"And Jack is a man," said Patrick, a little tired of the silliness. A pale-blue moth caught one wing on the water and a cutthroat trout arose beneath it, drifted downstream a few feet, sucked it in and left a spiraling ring to mark the end of the moth.

"Did you forget your rod?" Penny winked.

"Oh, what a naughty girl."

"Patrick."

"Penny. Let's go back."

"I think we should," said Penny Asperson. "Or we'll start talk." They walked back to the tank, Patrick doing all he could to control his gait, to keep from breaking into a little jog. Tio was talking firmly with Claire, knocking her lightly in the wishbone with his drink hand, for emphasis.

As Patrick passed, Tio said, "Wait a sec, Captain. This goes for you." Patrick joined them, trying to see just as much of Claire as he could with his peripheral vision. He wanted to put his hand on her skin. Tio went on in a vacuum.

"I need to have this little old stallion in motion," Tio said. "I travel too much to keep him galloped, and besides, I don't like to ride a stud. Cousin Adams tells me you can make a nice bridle horse, and if you can get this horse handling like he ought to, that'd be better than me having to mess with him every time I get off the airplane. You're in the horse business, aren't you?"

"Sure am," said Patrick. Claire shifted her weight a little. "Can I change his nickname?" Claire reddened.

"You can call him Fido's Ass for all I care. Just get that handle on him. I'm going in to look at old Jack's artifacts. Supposed to have a complete Indian mummy he found in the cliffs." He strode toward the house in his tall calfskin boots. "We gone try and give that mummy a name."

Anna appeared in the door.

"Patrick!" she called. "You've got to take Deke home. He's spoiled a storm-pattern Navajo and now he's just got to go home."

"Coming!" called Patrick, and Claire was halfway to the house—in effect, fleeing.

Patrick undertook the loading of Deke Patwell. Anna apologized for making Patrick accept this onerous detail, adding that otherwise it would have to be Jack and it was sort of Jack's party. They locked Deke's door where he slumped, and turned the wind vane in his face. His lip slid against the glass.

For the first couple of miles toward town, Deke tried slinging himself upright in a way that suggested he was about to make a speech. He slumped back and watched the hills fly by while the hard wind raveled his thin auburn hair.

"I didn't like your comment, buddy."

"What comment?" Patrick asked.

" 'Have another drink, perk you up.' I don't like getting a raft of shit like that just because I want to cut loose on the weekend." When he tried to spit through the wind vane, it came back in on him.

"I probably shouldn't have said it. It was a joke."

"It wasn't funny." They passed the corrals, scales and
loading chutes of the local livestock association. There
were a couple of horses and an Australian shepherd in
one section, waiting for their owners to come and do
something with them. Patrick let a little silence fall.

"You come home," Deke went on, "just pick up
where you left off. Goddamned officer."

"Well, I wasn't much of an officer."

Patrick was mostly successful in shutting Deke out of
his mind, like listening to the same day's news on the
radio for the second time. They were driving along the
switching yards, and probably because of Deke, he began
to think of the old rummies who used to be such a part of
a big yard like this. Electric engines, good security lights
and cross-referenced welfare lists stole our bums, thought
Patrick. When the American West dried up once and for
all, those migrant birds, the saints of cheap Tokay, began
to look bad to the downtown merchants, to the kayakers
and trout fishermen, even to the longhairs with tepee
poles on the tops of their Volkswagens, who thought the
rummies were like the white men who had corrupted the
Indians with whiskey in Bernard De Voto's *Across the
Wide Missouri*. Anyway, they were gone.

Deke was still maneuvering for an insult; but they
were nearly to his house now on Gallatin Street. Deke
knew his time was running out, and Patrick was hurrying
a little because he had begun to find himself paying a bit
of attention, starting with a slurred polemic against his
grandfather, which didn't work because it listed things
about the old man Patrick liked. They pulled in front of
the brick house as Deke started in on Patrick's sister
again. And for the first time Patrick thought, This is going to be close. Deke Patwell must have thought so too,
because he opened his door before announcing the following: "She's *immoral*. And I have every reason to *believe*
she uses drugs." It was quite a delivery.

Patrick kicked him through the open door onto the
sidewalk. Deke's head snapped down on the concrete but
recovered, leaving him on all fours, blood in the corner of
his mouth and vomit on his period costume. He kept

printing the blood on the palm of his hand to be sure he'd been injured. Mrs. Patwell appeared in the door. The tab-leau was a basic stacked deck illustrating Patrick's penchant for violence. "You'll live to regret this," she said with a compression between her eyes. Two children appeared on the sidewalk, and one of them, unable to make much of these grownups, could think of nothing more salutory than to sail his frisbee over the recumbent form of Deke, yelling, "Catch it, Mr. Patwell! Catch it!" It seemed appropriate to Mrs. Patwell to go after the kids, who scattered into the wilderness of back lots and yard fences. She didn't have their speed, their quickness. Patrick headed home. He felt quite giddy.

9

Patrick wound along to the east of the river. It burst out blue in segments whenever a hay or grain field dropped away. Also, there were tall mountains and a blue sky. But they only go so far. Patrick would have liked a silent, reverent involving of himself with Claire. In another era he could have been her coachman. "Might I assist, Ma'moiselle?" She can't help but notice how good he is with the horses. One must put aside one's silk-bound missal and duck off into this grove of elms. The horses graze; the springs of the little coach can be heard for miles. Screeching like fruit bats.

Patrick approached the ranch as though in an aircraft, sitting well back, making small adjustments of the wheel with outstretched arms as the buildings loomed, moving his head with a level rotary motion. We are making our approach. The stewardesses are seated in the little fold-down chairs. Claire is alone in first class; the surface of her gin and tonic tilts precisely with each directional adjustment. And now we are stopped and the dogs are gathering. Lilacs are reflected in the windows. Grandpa dashes to the truck. Must be with the ground crew, perhaps a baggage handler. That or a fucking woodpecker. Turn off the ignition. Engine diesels and quits. Opposite door flung open by Crew Chief Grandpa. This man is excited.

"Your sister has gone mad!"

"What are you talking about?"

"I smelt turpentine," the old man roared. "I went down to her room and she was painting everything. She was painting curtains! I couldn't get her to listen to me. She just talked on like I wasn't there." Patrick's heart sank. "When I went back, she was gone."

"Where is she now?"

"That's it. I don't know!"

They were hurrying toward the house.

"Why are we walking this way, then?"

"Well, maybe she's back in her room. Pat, what the hell's the matter with her?"

"I really don't know." He didn't, either.

They hurried up the walkway and went in through the kitchen. Patrick could smell the paint and turpentine from here; and as he went down the hallway, it got more intense. He expected for some reason that she would be in her room, and his grandfather, pressing behind him, seemed to agree. Patrick knocked and got no answer. So he opened the door. She wasn't there. If it wasn't for the fact that the paint was blue, the room would have looked like the scene of a massacre. A house-painter's broad brush soaked blue paint into the bedclothes. The up-ended gallon can directed a slowly moving blue tongue under the dresser. There was no turpentine in sight. The curtains had begun to dry stickily, with a cheap surrealistic effect, around a window full of sky and clouds.

They went back to the kitchen. But by that time the barn was already burning. It was visible from the kitchen, a steady horizontal pall moving downwind from between the logs. Patrick started for the doors. "Call the Fire Department! I'll run to the barn."

Patrick sprinted around the bunkhouse to the barn. He climbed the wooden strakes into the haymow. Mary sat under the rafters. The hay was on fire and the wind blew through the separations in the logs, creating innumerable red fingers of fire that worked through the bales, collided and leaped up into longer-burning lines, a secretive, vascular fire.

"We are without tents. We'll do anything to stay warm. There are tracks in the drifts. We used to have a chairlift to get us down, but my mother interfered with the mechanism and confiscated my lift pass. She put rats in the last empty gondola."

"I'll get you down," said Patrick. "But we must go now. And stop talking like that."

"Yes," said Mary. "We must think of the baby."

The volunteers arrived in a stocky yellow truck, threw the intake hose into the creek and doused the barn inside and out. Steam roared into the sky and cast shadows over the house like storm-driven clouds. The firemen were dressed in yellow slickers and had plexiglass shields in front of their faces. They guided the heavy canvas-covered hose inside their elbows and against their backs, like loafers leaning on a village fence. Only one man aimed the nozzle into the smoke and flames. Patrick thought that he could see in their expressions that this was an unnecessary fire. Perhaps it was his imagination.

Afterward the phone rang; it was Deke Patwell, still somewhat blurred. The phone in Patrick's hand felt like a blunt instrument.

"Understand you've had a barn fire."

"That's right, Deke."

"Any suspicion of foul play or is it all in the family?"

"It's all in the family," said Patrick.

"Hope like heck it stays out of the papers."

"Thank you, Deke. I'm one hundred percent certain that it will. You know what I mean, Deke? I'm really that sure."

It did seem, though, that Deke was intoning some small, minatory announcement and that it might have been better if Patrick hadn't kicked him onto the sidewalk. But weren't there a few things one was obliged to do? Perhaps he hadn't paid enough attention to Mary over the years. He might have written more often. If he had, Patrick considered, the kick might have been vague or symbolic and not shooting some ass-pounding moron onto the sidewalk. And Mrs. Patwell pursuing the children like a wounded pelican—that, too, would have its consequences. The Patwells had the solidest marriage in Deadrock.

10

Patrick stood at the counter at Farm Needs and bought ten iodized-salt blocks, five hundred pounds of whole oats and a thin twenty-eight-foot lariat. Standing at the counter, he could stare across the street to the grain elevator, the railroad tracks; and coming out of the east, he saw the Burnetts' car; and when it passed, he saw Claire at the wheel. He followed the car with his eyes and without moving his head.

"Let me just take my slip," he said to the salesman. "I'll swing through for the oats in a bit."

He followed the car discreetly, thinking, She doesn't know this truck anyway, left at Main, up a few blocks until she stopped. He parked in front of J. C. Penney's; he saw her get out of her car and walk into the MyWay Cafe. Patrick slapped his pockets for change. The meter maid was two cars away. He had no coins and here she came.

"I'm afraid I'm out of change."

"I'll give you time," she said.

"That's all right."

"My gosh, it'll save you five dollars." Her grab on the facts was evaporating. The meter itself seemed like a joke.

"Write me up," said Patrick, jauntily heading across the street, the meter maid staring at him with her pad of tickets. She began to write. She wrote hard and she wrote mean.

Patrick sauntered along the MyWay front window; but then when he gave his eyes one cut to the interior, he found himself locked in gaze with Claire. He waved, then mimed may-I-join-you? As though talking to a lip reader. She just *smiled*. In we go, thought Patrick; my back is to the meter.

The MyWay is sandwiched between the Wagon Wheel western store and Good Looks, ladies' fashions. It's kind of a shotgun arrangement, white inside with orange tables. It has a clock that reads twelve o'clock, three o'clock, 7-Up and nine o'clock. It has a reversible sign hanging in the door that says, OPEN, but from the customers' view reads, SORRY, WE'RE CLOSED. It has candy in a display called Brach's Candyland. It has a Safety and Protection on the Job poster, a dispenser for black hair-combs guaranteed for ten years and still only thirty cents. A huge box of S.O.S. says it will cut grease quicker. It's an A.F. of L. union house and smoking is permitted. It seemed ready for a nuclear attack.

Patrick stood next to the waitress while she finished telling Claire something. Claire cut her eyes over to him, smiled, then paid polite attention to the waitress.

"My brother can lie his way out of anything," she was saying, "but not *me*. I ain't sayin I wasn't in the wrong. My pickup was flat movin, comin around that old canyon. I'll tell *you*. But this smoky says, 'You wanta pull it over or drive fifty-five?' I shoulda outrun his ass. Okey-doke, let me get this. How bout you?"

"Black coffee," said Patrick, and sat down.

"How're you-all?" Claire had eyes that shone.

"Never better."

"Bite?"

"No thanks. I came to town for grain."

"I was hoping you were following me."

"I'll follow you next time I see you." To the waitress: "Coffee is all."

"Where can you get something to eat in Deadrock?"

"You're eating now."

"How can you tell?"

"You can feel it in your throat."

She chewed slowly and watched Patrick a moment before speaking again. He started to get jumpy.

"May I share my impressions with you about Montana?"

"Oh, but you can," said Patrick in a tinny voice.

"An area of high transience. But while folks are here, they are proud of it. I have seen no marches to the state flag yet, but I have noticed your extremely direct state motto: *'Oro y Plata.'* I know that stands for gold and silver. It shows a real go-getter attitude."

"Is that good, Claire?"

"Back where I come from, your shoe salesman strikes oil in the side lot and starts a ranch with headquarters in the Cayman Islands, then he buys a show horse, the bull that wins the Houston Fat Stock Show and a disco."

"Whoever did that?"

"My father! I'm *nouveau riche!* We're just not old family. The foundation for old families in Oklahoma is early-day stealing, before the advent of good records."

Patrick changed his mind and ordered pumpkin pie. He could see upper torsos passing the front window. He could see newspaper readers at other tables, revealing only their hands, which seized either end of the newsprint and stretched it to their eyes.

"What got you to come to Montana?" Patrick was growing tired of hearing himself ask these sap questions. Still, he couldn't break out of it. I'm no sap, he thought.

"Tio sold the cabin cruiser. We had it in Corpus. It was to go to Padre Island. Padre Island is kind of a redneck Riviera. It has great birds. But Tio kept running aground. Tio has kind of a health problem. So when the Coast Guard said they wouldn't rescue us anymore, Tio said, 'That does it. I'll spend my money in another area. The northern grasslands, for instance.' "

"Has it been a good move?"

"The jury is still out. Tio's starved for conversation. Nobody does much oil here, not to mention cattle futures, row crops or running horses."

"Did Tio inherit his money?" I've had enough of Tio. Why am I asking this?

"Let's say he got it somehow. But he's done right smart with what he got." It was a hollow advertisement.

"I see."

"And in some ways he's a very private person. About the only way somebody'd get his telephone number at home is if one of his bird dogs run away and they got it off its collar."

Patrick moved upon the pie, ate half of it, swigged some coffee and asked (this will get her off balance), "When was the last time you blushed?" He blushed. Sapland.

"At my wedding." It didn't get her off balance.

"Really."

"Oklahoma girls are trained to pull off one of those in their lives. After that, they are never required to do it again."

"I blushed at my First Communion."

"Are you a Catholic?"

"I consider myself one."

"You mean you aren't practicing."

"That is correct."

"Than why do you consider yourself one?"

"It makes me feel I'm just that much less of a white man."

"Aha!"

Patrick managed to pay for the ice cream and walk Claire to her car. He held the door for her. She ducked in and, talking to him, made a blind reach for the climate control, then the sound system. Four speakers boom in Jamaican: *"Natty don't work for no CIA."* She grinned.

"Amo shuffle on home," she said. "Babylon by Cadillac."

"Can you give me a lift to my truck?"

"Get on in."

The cool interior was wonderful, the simulated-walnut dashboard reassuring in that someone cared to keep up appearances. No high tech here, just plastic that ached for ancient hardwoods.

"Take your first right." They cruised up Main and turned. "Sure is nice and cool in here."

"I don't imagine that's much of a problem in Montana. What in the world do people do in the winter?"

"Just hang around the salad bars. There's nothing quite like Green Goddess at thirty below. Take another right."

Two more rights and they were back where they started, in front of Patrick's truck. Patrick opened the door. "Thanks a lot."

"Sure enjoyed circling the block with you. And say, the conversation was great."

"Same to you goes double."

Claire smiled. "I like dragging Main in the heat of the day. Been crazy about it since I don't know when."

"Good-bye."

"Good-bye."

Patrick thought, This is more horrible than a glint of bayonets in the concertina wire.

11

The next day, Patrick thought that a good meal might help Mary. His grandfather was bitching about the cuisine as well. So he drove to town for some supplies. He thought first about tea-smoked duck but remembered that all the ducks left in the freezer were green-winged teal—too small, really, for what he wanted. He recalled the advice of the master chef Paul Bocuse: Shop first, then decide what you're going to make; attend to the seasons—no strawberries for Christmas dinner, no game for Easter.

He entered the IGA store already primed, then excited once he had the shopping cart. He found black mushrooms, cloud ears and Szechwan peppers without a hitch. He was on a run. He found a fifty-pound bag of beautiful long-grain South Carolina rice effortlessly. The huge-cloved California garlics and fresh ginger set him on his heels; so that when he found the strong, perfect leeks bound together with paper-wrapped wire, smelled the earth in the darkened roots and felt their cool bulk against his hands, he knew the enemy had been driven from his fortification. Three fat chickens, small projectilelike cucumbers, fresh spinach to make streamers to mark the depth of his clear pork soup, a case of Great Falls Select from the cooler and yes, a bit of help to the truck would be nice. Put the leeks up front with me. I'm a captain, good-bye.

The grandfather and Mary sat at the round kitchen table while Patrick worked. He boned and skinned the chicken, then sliced it all into uniform strips. He had first cooked on the lid of an old Maytag washing machine —a basic utensil in the mountains. But now he had a south San Francisco hard-steel wok, restaurant-sized.

"What in hell you been doing to support yourself?" Grandfather asked Mary.

"I worked for a veterinarian."

"What happened?"

"I lost the job."

"For what?"

"I was fired for taking animal tranquilizers."

"You *what?*"

Patrick made a rectilinear pile of the chicken slivers. He mashed the garlic with his cleaver, removed the pale-varnish papery skins, then minced the peppers; the same with the ginger—both arrayed alongside the chicken. He broke up the serrano peppers and spilled the rattling minute seeds into the sink.

"What else have you been doing, Mary?" asked Grandfather in a yelp. Granddad under stress always grew dog-like.

"Well, let's see. Got pregnant and, uh, went to Warm Springs. You know, *the big nut house.*"

"Oh, well, great, Mary."

Using the cleaver, Patrick split the well-washed leeks into cool white-and-green lengths, dividing them on the steel. He could feel the animosity through his back.

"I hear you've gone into the movies, Grandpa."

"I was just having a look around. Anyway, nobody knows where that damned movie went to. I certainly don't, but I'm darned mad about it."

Patrick fired up the wok, the cooking shovel resting inside. He poured in the oil. In a moment numerous small bubbles migrated vertically through it.

"Then I joined up with some communists from Canada."

Patrick turned from the stove. "Can it," he said to Mary. "And *you,* shut up about the movies."

He dropped the garlic in, then the ginger, then the Szechwan peppers, then the serranos. They roared in the oil and cooked down gorgeously. Arrayed around the wok were leeks, chicken, yellow crookneck squash, soy sauce, rice wine, salt—everything *jingbao*, explosion-fried. He raced about setting the table, put the wok next to a six-pack and served with the cooking shovel.

"Do I have to use chopsticks?" the grandfather wailed.

"You better if you're going to China."

"I'll bring my own utensils. Say, who said I'm going to China?"

"Use the chopsticks, Gramp. They won't let you take silverware through the metal detector at the airport. Y'know, because of international terrorism."

"Tomorrow can we have chili?"

"No, you're having a can of tuna and your own can opener, you goddamned sonofabitch."

"I like water-packed tuna, but no oil for me, please."

"Eat what I made you."

Mary stared into her plate, held each piece up as though trying to see through it, then returned it to her plate. She went to the kitchen for a glass of water and was gone a little too long. Patrick returned to his own meal: She ought to be darling when she gets back.

"Used to be a real stockman's country," said his grandfather, eating quite rapidly once he forgot the chili and tuna fish. "No one retained mineral rights in a ranch trade. No farm machinery." Mary came back. "Strange people here and there. One man with a saddled horse tied under his bedroom window at all times. Southern man with his boys chained up at night. Irrigator from Norway hiding in a car body from the hailstones. Me and old what's-his-name buying hootch out back at the dances. Pretty schoolteacher used to ski to them dances, packing her gown. This Virginian used to do the nicest kind of log-work'd get tanked up and fight with a knife. Old Warren Butterfield killed him and buried him past the Devil's Slide, only not too many people known that at that time and Warren's at the rest home, fairly harmless I'd say. Virginian needed it, anyhow. I could show you the spot.

Shot him with a deer rifle. Virginian couldn't remember pulling the knife out on Warren at the dance. Warren told me that couple days later and he went up to shoot him, that Virginian couldn't figure for the life of him why. It gave Warren second thoughts, but he let him have it. Everybody was pleased, big old violent cracker with protruding ears, ruining the dances. Nicest kind of logwork, though, used a froe, chopped at them timbers between his feet, looked like they'd been through the planer down to the mill. After that, everybody went to frame. No more Virginian."

Mary said, "Kill, shoot, whack, stab, chop."

"Well, that's how it was."

Mary looked up past Patrick and said, "Who are you?" Patrick stared at her an instant and turned. It was Tio, standing in the doorway. He suspended his Stetson straw horizontal to his stomach.

"Knocked, guess nobody heard me. I see you, Pat?"

"Surely," said Patrick, getting up and leaving his napkin and following Tio outside.

"I'll be listening to murder stories," Mary said. Tio looked back, made a grimacing, uncomprehending smile, which she received blankly. "How y'all?" Tio tried.

"Say, thanks for dinner," bayed the grandfather. "And don't forget: Water-packed, or n-o spells no!"

Outside, Tio asked, "You cook, Pat?"

"Yeah, sure do. I like it a lot."

"Make chili?"

"Yup. My grandfather just requested it."

"Like a tejano or this northern stew-type deal?"

"Tejano."

"I make Pedernales chili à la L.B.J. Crazy bout L.B.J. Eat that chili in homage, old buddy. Y'all through eatin, weren't you?"

"We were, actually."

"What'n the hell was that?"

"Chinese food."

"Old boys have got more oil than anybody thinks."

"Who's this?"

"Chinese. We sit here?"

"Sure, this'd be fine." They sat on the wood rack where water had once sluiced to cool milkcans not that long ago, before the supermarket. Patrick could see the big anthracite Cadillac nosed up to the straw stack.

"It's a hell of a picturesque deal out here," said Tio, looking all around. "Has to be an escape. About a month of this, though, I'd start missing my wells and my travel agent, in that order. Getting to where I can't hardly stand a vacation. The same time I'm looking to farm everything out. Supposed to be delegating. But delegating for what? Got everything a guy'd ever need. We knocked off work and redid an old sugar refinery down in the islands, then moved to Saint-Barts. Every time we went down to dinner, we'd be lined up behind these Kuwait sand niggers waving three different currencies at the waiter. Me, I took the old lady and went back to Tulsa, got her a little hidey-hole and a bunch of charge accounts, and threw her to fortune. I'm not saying I farmed *that* out. But I figured this: If nature's going to run its course, an intelligent man best stand back from his television set. Well, nothing happened. By the time I got a hundred million in help on a little offshore daydream of mine, she'd bought maybe two dresses and was back breaking colts like somebody supposed to call you sir. Still now, Pat, my conscience is a-nagging at me all the while. Hell, look at you. 'What's the point of all this falderal,' ole Pat is asking hisself."

"You read my mind." Patrick thought, I must have a stupid, vacant face for people to run on at me like this. I must have big jug-handle ears.

"Well, the point is, good buddy, I took my chances. And there wasn't any chances. Old Shit is bulletproof. You could drop her anywhere and she'd land on her feet. *Plunk.* She could run a ranch while Tio saw to his oil and radio stations and stayed out on that road to where *his* nature could take its little course. If you had enough Catholic churches up in this country, I could put her on a few sections with half a dozen top kind of wetbacks. They're like Brahman cattle—it takes quite a little to hold them, and it's them churches that'll do it. And really, a guy'd rather leave his wife with them than white trash. See, a Mexican will know where he idn't posed to mess, where your white trash might have him some delusions of grandeur. Some of them been President."

"Are you telling me she's not going back to Tulsa with you?" Patrick needed a translator.

"I'm just saying I'm gonna be traveling all summer. Look, we don't have children. We can't have them. At first, I took it like a man. I said it's all my fault. I've got an undiagnosed situation with my nerves that could be passed on. I was set to send her to California to one of these Nobel prize-winner sperm banks. Then we found it was her. Some kind of lady's plumbing problem that's to where you can't just go on in and fix it. Then my doctor at home told me the nerves was nothing to worry about. It was iron-poor, tired blood."

"I don't quite see what this has to—"

"Lookit here. I'm not saying Tio's going to do no replacing. But here's this fortune settin in Tulsa getting bigger daily. Where's Tio's son and heir? How's this dynasty supposed to happen? Well, maybe it doesn't happen. But a realistic Tio is a Tio who keeps his buns in circulation in case something magic comes out of the woodwork; and you can't be haulin your old lady on trips like that. She don't haul good to start with."

Patrick thought hard to understand why this warranted calling him away from dinner. "Did you want me to help out in some way?"

"Truthfully, she's gonna have to have someone around. You've both got interests in common with these fool nags. Plus I'll back every horse prospect y'all might unearth. But I just want you to be kind of a big brother to the little gal. Old Jack Adams tells me you're solider than a pre-Roosevelt dollar and you'd be the guy, especially if you watched your drinking. She's gonna need company and it's almost never gonna be me."

"How in the world could you ever arrange a thing like that?" Patrick used the word "arrange" on purpose.

"I just did! Trust Tio's fine Italian hand. Movin people from one place to another has always been my best lick."

Patrick hoped that it would work. He badly wanted

just to be around Claire. But he said, "I'm already some-body's brother. And I've never really understood the job."

"You can take the weight, Pat. You've got fabulous shoulders. Big old, strong old . . . *tank captain!*"

"Well, she's a fine lady. If she wants anything at all, she's sure welcome to come by." Patrick reflected that he had to be at the dentist by nine.

"Any horses you particularly like I could pick up for you?"

"No thanks."

"One thing I guess I better say. Big thing from my point of view, and hell, I'm a hunch player or half them wells'd still be just a star in Daddy's eye. Big thing is, I know you're cowboy enough to keep it in your pants." Tio raised his hands against any further words. "That says it all."

12

News of a family visit to the ranch—Patrick and Mary's mother, her second husband and their son, Andrew—was sending Mary into one unearthly disjuncture, cycles of recollection, some assertions of a nonexistent past; and producing, for Patrick, the question, How in the world will she raise this child? He was now quite frightened; and his love for her prevented him from considering anything that would actually be a solution to her troubles. He kept on with his patchwork of concern, trying to stay available when she seemed to be slipping. His grandfather had been terrified by the barn fire, as Patrick had. And the lingering picture of the smug volunteers troubled Patrick, as though, for him, it was they who had set the fire. But then, that was a little simple, too.

When Patrick first returned to the ranch, he didn't quite know what he was doing there. Yet he couldn't look back on his years in the service as a period in which things had made much sense. His tank-driving lay somewhere between an update on a family tradition and the dark side of the moon of a highly camouflaged scholarship program. Still, he blamed himself because he had let things drift, and he now occasionally noticed that not only was he not in his teens, he was actually at an age when a certain number of people died of heart attacks. Heart attacks! He knew he was under stress but he didn't know stress of what. Maybe it was just the jaggedness-of-the-everyday. He thought of the term "stress-related" and he wondered if that was why he behaved sometimes in ways he wished he hadn't. He didn't, for example, like drinking as much as he did; yet he liked and approved of *some* drinking and the occasional comet binge with all bets off. But lately he was waking up in the dark with his heart pummeling its way through his chest and a strange coldness going through his body, waking nightmares in the dark; and he didn't know where it was coming from. He tried the trick of counting blessings like sheep, but the personal components would not cohere. He loved his sister and grandfather and horses; he loved the place. But he couldn't help thinking that it was edges and no middle. And as soon as he'd had that thought, he began to doubt it, too. He worked hard for the conclusions, then evaporated them with doubt. Worst of them all, though, was the one he called sadness-for-no-reason.

He had come home hoping to learn something from his grandfather. But the old man was still too cowboy to play to nostalgia for anyone; though as a boy he had night-hawked on the biggest of the northern ranches, had seen gunfighters in their dotage, had run this ranch like an oldtime cowman's outfit, building a handsome herd of cattle, raised his own bulls and abjured farm machinery. Still, he got closer to the past in recollection: "It's not like it used to be. They've interfered with the moon and changed our weather. That's why the summer clouds sail too high to rain on our old pastures. The goddamned sonic booms have loosened all the boards in the houses, and that's why we have all those flies. Didn't used to have those. Things up there affect us. Like when you have an eclipse and the chickens fall asleep. Something happens inside and we don't know what it is. And the ground water is going in the wrong direction . . . twisting, turning sonofabitch. I had a surefire witch out here try to douse me a well for a stock tank. He said, 'I can't help you, Fitzpatrick, the inside of the world is different.' Used to be I'd have that water witch out and the bark would peel off that stick and that old willow butt would jump and buck with him and hell, we'd go fifty feet and have more gallons a minute than a guy could count." Ground water danced in his eyes.

"I thought it always changed."

"Go up on Antelope some night and look down at the yard lights. Used to be coming off any these mountains it was dark. Just throw the reins away and let the horse take you home. When that sheepherder went crazy in 1921, Albert Johanson, who was sheriff, went up to Hell Roaring and shot him between the eyes and left him. I packed in there and took the stove and tent down for Albert and then I had to put this dead Basque on a mule and pack him out. Well, it got dark. I come clean out at the west fork of Mile Creek and I could see maybe one light on the flat. But I didn't know whether I had that stiff or not till I got to Wellington's ranch and we got a lantern. I had the herder but my hitch had slipped. I had him face down on a little Spanish kind of a mule with a cross mark on his back, but the hitch slipping turned his face up, rope laid acrosst his gums like he's snarling. Old boy killed a young rancher's wife with a sickle, rancher name of Schumbert, down to Deer Creek now, older feller now. He finds this herder trying to pour cement over his wife in the cellar. Her head's set over next to the scuttle where the sickle took it off. He's so stunned the Basque taps him and he's out. He wakes up and his man is gone to the hills and his wife is waist-deep in soft concrete with her head setting on a small deal of firewood scantlings. Schumbert goes to town, notifies Albert, calls the funeral home and puts hisself into the hospital. Directly Albert goes to tracking and finds the herder's camp, just a wall-side tent and a barrel-headed horse with his front legs coming out the same hole, and old Albert, he hallos the camp. Directly here comes our Basque, packing a thirty-thirty with a peep sight, and cuts down on Albert and Albert puts him away. Then me, I'm Albert's friend. Albert has had enough for one day: He don't want to pack that camp to the valley. So I'm Albert's next victim. I hated packing that stiff because he scared the mule and

all I had was a basket hitch with nothing really to lash to.
When I got to Wellington's I was surprised we still had
our man, and I guarantee you this: We had that mule
broke to pack *anything*. That was one mule you could
call on. *God*, what a good mule." The mule had replaced
the ground water and sleeping chickens in the grandfather's eyes.

Patrick saw this man, his grandfather, with no pity for
himself and less for others, touching the kitchen match
to a cold kerosene mantle—ignition and the wavering
light on the dead man—thinking then as he would now
that it was a matter of available light, a matter of seeing
what one had achieved, whether one had successfully descended the mountain from Hell Roaring without losing
the load, and at the same time imagining that he was
illustrating a story about how there were now too many
lights on the valley floor and that it was better when you
had to hang the lantern in front of the spooking mule to
catch the grimace of face distorted by a single lash rope
crossing the mouth of a murderer and looping around the
girth of a mule whose scarred flanks were decorated with
stripes of blood like war paint. Had this all really disappeared?

As then, when he felt the old man's past, or when he
went among the ancient cottonwoods that once held the
shrouded burials of the Crow, Patrick felt that in fact
there had been a past, and though he was not a man with
connections or immediate family, he was part of something in the course of what was to come. None of which
meant he'd failed at ambition, but only that its base was
so broad he could not discover its high final curves, the
ones that propelled him into the present, or glory, or
death.

"How'd they get the wife's body out of the concrete?"

"Hadn't set yet."

"What'd they do with the head?"

"Propped it where it was supposed to go once they had
the box. Who cares."

"What happened to the husband?"

"He wrote away for another one."

"Another what?"

"Another wife."

"What do you think happens when someone dies?"

"They can't do nothin anymore. Most religious sum-buck walkin couldn't persuade me that they can do much. Don't add up. God created an impossible situation."

Patrick thought that this was a dignified appraisal, no Ahab railing against mortality, but simply the observed, which in the end was harsh enough: that for one who could stand it, those who sought to strike the sun for an offense seemed like cheap grandstanders; and they were certainly in no shortage.

Now his grandfather took down his daily missal from above Patrick's shelf of cookbooks and pint-size bottle of sour mash, a bottle old-timers called a mickey. He sat down in the one comfortable ladder-back the kitchen had, and said, "What's for dinner?" Patrick thought, Is this our religion? He remembered a clever young tank-gunner with a year at the university who pasted the picture of a new swami above his observation port every month. He wanted war with Communism, then exciting visits to ashrams. He wanted to find himself, but first he wanted to smash Communism. He thought swamis stood for that. His name was Walt. He had records by Carlos Santana but called him by his assumed name, Devadip or something. Walt loved Santana Devadip-or-something for inventing swami rock 'n' roll. He wanted to go to Santana's hometown, but he had heard San Francisco was now commanded by fairies and therefore he thought the next thing was to smash Communism, then go on a swami tour of the Orient. Walt had luxurious sideburns that looked suspiciously as if they'd been permanented. He liked Germany but he wanted to raid the East. Some-times when Walt's ambition had been fortified by mystery substances, especially the one he called "mother's little helper"—by all accounts something invented to keep advance-reconnaissance rangers awake for three days at a time—sometimes then Walt asked Patrick to hack a left into what he called Prime-time red, cross the

276

border, head downtown and shell the home of the East German mayor. On such occasions Patrick referred to the gently fatal attitudes of his heroes of the Orient, urging Walt to cool his heels, at least until mother's little helper wore off. It was '76, the bicentennial. The East Germans had won forty-seven medals in the Olympics and Walt didn't like it, was real bummed out, said "Fuck it" all the time.

But that was long ago and far away, as so much eventually was. Patrick was still midway in the accumulation of his scrapbook, and paramount in that was what he thought of as a less lonely life. For now, bereft of his German girl friends and base-employed bachelorettes, the cowboy captain felt stranded on the beautiful ranch he would someday own, land, homestead, water rights, cattle and burden. He had no idea what he would do with it.

This had not entirely been necessary. There had been nice girls, beautiful girls, German dynamos with degrees who desired to be cowgirls when the captain returned, girls who could do English in the inflection of Tek-Ziz, New York or the late President Kennedy. It had been a long go on the line of the Soviet bloc and it had included paternity suits, arrangements and affection. He had tried Spain on leave, but the Spanish girls wouldn't go to the beach and the English secretaries on holiday behaved like beagles in heat at a guard-dog show in Munich. He began using an electric razor. He began not to care. He began not to brush between meals. He began to brood about the high lonesome and the girls at the gold dredge and their desire to be barrel racers and then make little babies. By now they'd had bunches of them and the babies were all in 4H. He read Thucydides and asked about soldiers' homecomings. He heard Marvin Gaye sing the national anthem at the heavyweight championship fight, and that was that. He quit the Army. He had never fired a shot, but he was going home to Montana to pick up where he left off—which was a blurred edge; blurred because of boarding school, the death of his father, the disappearance—intermittent—of his sister and the remarriage of his mother to a glowing, highly focused businessman from California who owned a lighting-design center in Santa Barbara and was a world-class racquetball player.

Now, home for a time and with no good reason to support his feeling, what had seemed the last prospect in his vague search for a reason to come home and *stay* turned out to be a subliminal inclination toward another man's wife; which was plainly unrequited if not without charm, and pointless.

Can't help that, thought Patrick. He turned his thoughts to what could be helped, most of which consisted in learning the particulars of the ranch which he had always assumed he would run but which he never had run and which, in fact, no one had ever run, except his grandfather. Patrick's father had gone off to test airplanes, and the man before his grandfather—an Englishman with the papers of a clergyman too finely scripted to be doubted by the honyockers and illiterate railroaders who settled the town—that Englishman never lifted a finger except in pursuit of Indian women and in operatic attempts at suicide in the six inches of running water from which the place was subsequently irrigated. He did leave, however, large academic oils that he had commissioned as decoration in the dining room, depicting smallpox epidemics among the Assiniboine from the point of view of a Swiss academic painter in his early twenties, eager to get home and tend to the clocks. The paintings showed all Indians in Eastern war bonnets, holding their throats in the paroxysms of dehydration, popularly assumed to be the last stage of that plague. It had never, to Patrick, seemed the right thing for the dining room. At the same time it did not deter anyone from eating. Today Patrick felt a little like the Englishman who had commissioned the paintings.

But he did have a thought. He went into the pantry, where his grandfather had hung the telephone, and being careful to stay loose, dialed and got Claire.

"Claire," he said, "this is Patrick Fitzpatrick."

"Well, hey."

"Say, I'd just remembered, I never gave Tio an answer about that colt."

"Fitzpatrick! That you?" It was Tio.

"Yes, it is."

"You callin regardin that colt?"

"Yes, I—"

"You gonna take him?"

"Yes, I'd like to."

"You should, he's a good colt. Bill us at Tulsa. Honey, you still on?"

"Sure am. Where're you?"

"I'm down to the granary with the accountants. Can you load that horse yourself?"

"Sure can."

"Carry him out to Fitzpatrick. Listen, I gotta go. Bye." Click.

Patrick said, "Do you need directions, Claire?" He was happy. Then Tio came back on.

"You oughta breed ole Cunt to that mare of yours, Fitzpatrick. Think on it." Click. Pause.

"Uh, yes, I will need directions."

Patrick said, "Let's just wait a second and see if Tio comes back on."

There was a pause, and then Claire said, with a little fear in her voice, "Why?"

"I hate repeating directions," said Patrick. His was an odd remark. He had no such attitude. He was starting to make things up. The last Army officer in this area he could think of who did that was General George Armstrong Custer.

279

13

Intermittently behind the corrugated trunks of the cottonwoods Patrick could discern a sedan with an in-line trailer behind it. He was replacing planks on the loading chute, ones that had been knocked loose while he was gone; and he could see down to the road from here, to the sedan, the dust from the trailer and the changing green light on the metal from the canopy of leaves overhead. Cole Younger was the first dog to detect the car turning in, and his bellowing bark set Alba and the hysterical Zip T. Crow into surrounding the outfit. Patrick left the spikes and hammer at the chute and started down the hill. Once past the orchard he could hear the horse whinny inside the trailer and he could read the word "Oklahoma" on the plates. Was that Sooner, Hoosier or Show Me? The door of the sedan was open, but glare on the window kept him from seeing. He could make out one dangling boot and nothing else. Claire kicked Zip T. Crow very precisely and without meanness as the dog stole in for a cheap shot.

The car looked like it could pull the trailer a hundred in a head wind. Patrick had a weakness for gas gobblers; and a rather limited part of him, the part that enjoyed his seventy-mile-an-hour tank, had always wanted to rodeo out of a Cadillac like this one. He took a hard look: oil-money weird, no doubt about that. Like Australians, loud with thin lips, hideous Protestant backgrounds, unnatural drive to honky-tonk as a specific against bad early religion and an evil landscape: bracing himself against Claire.

She got out wearing knee-high boots, washed-out Wranglers, a hot-pink shirt and a good Ryon's Panama straw. Long oak-blond hair disappearing between the shoulder blades in an endless braid.

"Hello," he said. "How are you, Claire?" The dumb grin forms. No drool in the mouth corners yet.

"Just right," she said. "And you, Patrick?" There was sweetness in her inquiry. Claire just kind of stood there and let the sun hit her, only her thumbs outside her pants.

"What do we have in the back?" asked Patrick.

"Got Tio's horse."

"Aged horse?"

"Four."

"Is he broke to ride?"

"He is," she said, "but he's rank."

"What's he do good?"

"Turn around," she said. "He's real supple."

"What's he do bad?"

"Bite you. Fall on you. Pack his head in your lap. Never has bucked. But it's in him."

"How do you like him shod?"

"Just double-ought plates. Had little trailers in the back. We skipped that. He'll run and slide. He's still in a snaffle bit. You do as you like. But don't thump on him. He can get right ugly."

"Why didn't you take the horse to one of the guys around Tulsa?"

"We're gonna be here most years. We wanted to be able to see how the horse was going. Plus Tio wanted someone who was staying home with his horses." The advent of the husband into the conversation dropped like an ice cube on a sunbather's back. Could Claire have known the extent to which the horse was part of the arranging?

"How come you call him American Express?"

"Tio billed him out as ranch supplies. We named him after the card."

"Right . . ."

"Tio would give you what you wanted for your mare. You could go on and bill the accountants in Tulsa."

"She's just not for sale. But I appreciate it."

"How's she bred?" Claire asked.

"Rey Jay."

"That can't hurt."

"The only way blood like that can hurt you is if you don't have it."

You had to reach through to get the butt chain, past the dust curtain and the levered doors. Through the interstices of a green satiny blanket, the horse's color could be seen: black and a mile deep. Looked to be fifteen hands. Squeezing his butt back till the chain indented a couple inches: a bronco. She said, "This colt can look at a cow." She said "cow" Southwestern style: "kyao."

"I believe I'll unload him, then, and put a saddle on him and put him before a very kyao."

She said, "If he don't lock down, give him back." Patrick thought: I won't give him back if all he can do is pull a cart.

The stud unloaded himself very carefully, turned slowly around on the halter rope and looked at Patrick. A good-looking horse with his eyes in the corners of his head where they're supposed to be; keen ears and vividly alert.

Claire looked at her watch. "Y'know what? I'm going to just let you go on and try the horse. If I don't get back, Tio's going to pitch a good one."

"Well, call me up and I'll tell you how we got along." A rather testy formality had set in. The electric door at closing time.

She scribbled the accountants' address in Tulsa for training bills and then she was gone, the clatter of the empty trailer going downhill behind the silent anthracite machine to the great space toward town. Patrick tried to conclude something from the aforegoing, rather cool, rather unencouraging conversation, then suddenly grew irritated with himself, thinking, What business is this of mine? I'm just riding a horse for a prosperous couple from Oklahoma. Nobody else even knows I'm out of the Army. I shall do as instructed and bill the accountants in Tulsa.

Patrick absentmindedly led the horse toward the barn, trailing him at the end of the lead shank, the horse behind and not visible to him. And in an instant the horse had struck him and had him on the ground, trying to kill him. Patrick cradled his head and rolled away, trying to get to his feet, the stallion pursuing him and striking down hard with his front feet until Patrick was upright, hitting him in the face with his hat. Patrick stood him off long enough to seize the rake leaning up against the tack shed and hold the stud at bay. The horse had his ears pinned close to his head, nostrils flared, a look of homicidal mania that will sometimes seize a stallion. It was Patrick's fault. He was in pain and he blamed himself. The horse's ears came up and he began to graze: He had no recollection of the incident. Patrick picked up the lead shank and led him correctly to the barn, the horse snorting and side-passing the new shapes in its interior, until Patrick turned him into a box stall and left him.

He hobbled toward the house, and Mary, who had heard or sensed something, came out. Patrick knew it was less than serious injury; but it hurt to breathe and he wanted to know why.

"What in the world happened?"

"New stud got me down."

"What's wrong with your voice?"

"Can't get my breath. You take me to town?"

Mary drove the Ford while Patrick scanned the road for potholes. She had some theory, some fatal Oriental notion, that this horse represented an intricate skein of influences which had already demonstrated itself to be against Patrick's best interests. Patrick couldn't help thinking that it was the horse Tio sent him.

"Mary, you haven't even seen the horse."

"That horse is employed by the forces of evil. You watch. The X-rays will show something broken."

Patrick sat on the bench outside the X-ray room, his green smock tied behind. Mary had gone on and on about the horse and its relationship to Patrick and the universe; and about how Patrick had to think about these things and not just go off and drive tanks or break any old horse or see the wrong people. Patrick sorted through his incomplete knowledge of the world's religions and, as he awaited his X-rays, tried to think just what it was she was stuck on this time. He began with the East, but by the time the nurse called him, he had it figured out: Catholicism.

The doctor, staring at the plates, said, "Four cracked ribs."

They taped Patrick and sent him home. In the car Mary said, "Now do you understand?"

"No," he said.

"There-are-none-so-blind-as-those-who-will-not-see."

"Yeah, right."

Patrick, apart from hurting considerably, disliked the monotonous pattern he had long ago got into with Mary, bluntly resisting what he saw as signs of her irrationality. He had to think of another way, though the burdens of being an older brother impeded his sense. And something about his own past, the comfort of the Army, the happy solitude of bachelorhood, the easy rules of an unextended self—some of that came back with the simple pain, the need to hole up for a bit. For instance, a friendly hug would kill him.

14

The Northbranch Saloon is a grand spot in the afternoon, thought Patrick. There will be no one there, there will be the sauce in the bottles and that good jukebox. And he could start getting Claire off his mind and just sit at the bar and think about her; *then* go about his business without this distraction with her *off* his mind and his mind thereby liberated for more proper business. At this point he knew his father would have asked, "Like what?"

"Hello, Dan," he said to the bartender on duty. "George Dickel and ditch, if you would." There was a TV on top of the double-door cooler. The host was getting ready to spin the roulette wheel. A couple from Oregon stared, frozen, at his hand. Patrick gripped his drink and looked up at the "North Dakota pool cue" overhead—it had a telescopic sight; he preferred it to the "North Dakota bowling ball," which was simply a cinderblock. Claire puts her hands in her back pockets. Around the top of the bar are boards with names and brands on them. American Fork Ranch, Two Dot, Montana. There's a machine that will play draw poker against you. Hay Hook Ranch. Raw Deal Ranch. Bob Shiplet, Shields Route, Livingston, Montana. Clayton Brothers, Bozeman, Montana. I also don't think she is being accorded treatment commensurate with her quality by that Okie hubby. And what's that ailment he's supposed to have?

She could be the queen of Deadrock, like Calamity Jane, an early Deadrock great. She could be Calamity Claire. Maybe not such a good idea. Maybe bad. There were three views of the original Calamity on the north wall. In one she is dressed as an Army scout. In another she leans on a rifle and wears a fedora on the back of her head. The last is an artist's rendering on the cover of a dime novel, a Victorian heroine of the kind Patrick was crazy about.

DEADWOOD DICK ON DECK,

OR

CALAMITY JANE, THE HEROINE

OF WHOOP-UP

Oh me oh my. "Make that a double, Dan." Dan moves past the cross-buck saw, the set of Longhorns, the old-time handcuffs, the horse hobbles, singletrees, ox yokes and buffalo skulls; and fetches the big bourbon. I thought whoop-up meant to get sick to your stomach. Patrick declines to order a Red Baron pizza. He looks out on the empty dance floor, the drums and amplifier, wagon wheels overhead with little flame-shaped light bulbs. Romance. Lost in the crowd, we dance the Cotton-Eyed Joe. Mamas, don't let your babies grow up to be cowboys. Hear that, Mamas? Don't let the sonofabitch happen. Lost souls on the big sky. Hell in a hand basket.

Ease past the L. A. Huffman photos of the old chiefs toward that jukebox, now. Get something played, vow not to stay here too long and fall down. No sick-dog stuff.

Jack Daniels, if you please!
Knock me to my knees!

"Dan, triple up on that, would you?"
"Sure about that, Pat?"
"Damn sure. Got troubles."
"Well, get the lady back."
"Never had the sonofabitch. I'm just panning for gold."

"Beats wages. Beats havin' your thumb up your ass."

"You haven't dragged that triple up to me yet."

"Not going to."

"Oh dear . . ."

"Come back tonight when there's some company to drink with."

"Oh, piss on it. Is that how it is?"

"That's how it is. You're on the allotment."

"Well, goddamn you anyway."

"See what I mean?"

"Go fuck yourself." The front of Patrick's brain was paralyzed with anger.

"Tried all my life."

"Good-bye, Dan, you sonofabitch. I'll see you."

Patrick pulled off into the IGA parking lot, suspended in the heat against distant mountains with a special, silly desolation. He got out and walked toward the automobiles, four rows deep, clustered around the electric glass doors with labels protecting the unwary from ramming their faces.

He squeezed between a new low Buick with wire wheels and a big all-terrain expeditionary station wagon when suddenly a great malamut-German shepherd crossbred cur arose behind the glass to roar in Patrick's ear. He thought his heart had stopped. Then his head cleared. He leaned inches from the window: fangs rattled against the glass, spraying the inside with slobber. Patrick looked around and crawled up onto the hood, growling and knocking his own teeth against the windshield wipers. The monster tore around the interior in an evil frenzy, upending thermoses, a wicker picnic basket, a jerry can, clothing, backpacking gewgaws and a purse. Patrick clambered over the car until the beast's eyes were rolling; then he went inside to buy a six-pack, feeling happy among the pregrown ferns, vanilla extract and Mexican party favors. The summery youngsters seemed especially healthy as they gathered around the newest rage—alfalfa sprouts—heaped cheerfully next to the weigh-out scale, plastic bags and wire ties. As if to confirm his good fortune, he went through the six-items-or-less line with nobody in front of him but without having had any success in guessing the identity of the dog owner. So he sat on the curb and tipped back a can of Rainier while he watched the expedition vehicle. He felt a criminal tickle at the base of his neck.

In a moment an extraordinarily well groomed couple came out with one bag and a magazine, the man in the lead, and went straight to the car. He opened it, yelled "MY GOD!" and quickly shut it. The beast arose once again in the windshield, revealing a vast expanse of whitening gum, and sized up his owners.

"Are you sure that's your car?" Patrick called out in a friendly voice.

The husband whirled. "Absolutely!" he shouted. His magazine fluttered to the pavement.

"I'd let that old boy simmer down," Patrick suggested unoffendably. The wife pertly noted that sled dogs were a little on the high-octane side.

"I can see that!" Patrick cried like a simpleton.

Something about that challenged the husband, and he pulled open the door of the car. The rabid sled dog shot between the two and landed huge and spraddled in front of Patrick, gargling vicious spit through his big, pointed white teeth.

I must be close to death, thought Patrick, feeling the Rainier run down the inside of his sleeve. I always knew death would be a slobbering animal, I knew that in Germany and I knew that upon certain unfriendly horses bucking in the rocks. It is every last thing I expected.

He did not move his eyes. The owner was coming up slowly behind the dog, murmuring the words *"Dirk, easy, Dirk"* over and over. And death passed by like a little breeze: Very slowly the lips once more encased the teeth while Dirk, double-checking his uncertain dog memory, seemed to lose his focus. The owner reached down and gently seized the collar with a cautious "Attaboy."

"Buddy," said the owner, "I feel real bad. Is there anything I can do to make it up to you?"

"I'd like some money," said Patrick.

"You what?"

"Money."

"How much money?"

"Enough for one Rainier beer in a can. And you buy it. With money."

The owner returned Dirk to the all-terrain vehicle. His wife waited, not wanting to go in there alone. The husband headed into the store, and Patrick gestured to her with the rest of his six-pack. He made her a toothy grin. "Want a beer, cutie?"

No reply.

In a few minutes, the Rainier appeared in Patrick's vision. He took it without looking up. "That fucker needs a sled."

"He's got one," the owner shot back.

"I mean your wife."

No fist swung down to replace the Rainier in his vision. All Patrick had to watch was the slow rotation of a bright pair of hiking boots; there was the sound of cleated rubber on blacktop, the door, the V-8 inhalation and departure. The high lonesome will never be the same for them, thought Patrick, however Dirk might feel. The sky will seem little.

I've been through quite an experience, perhaps the number-one Man-Versus-Animal deal for many years here in the Rockies. But I better get myself under control before it's lights out. God has made greater things to test us than ill-tempered sled dogs; God has made us each other.

15

When Patrick was fifteen and in need of reasons to stay in town late, he invented a girl friend, whom he named Marion Easterly. Claire reminded Patrick of Marion. Marion was beautiful in mind and in spirit. He pretended to be hopelessly in love with Marion, so that when he rolled in at two in the morning, he would claim that he and Marion had been discussing how it was to be young and had merely lost track of time. His parents, vaguely susceptible to the idea of romance in others, bought the Marion Easterly story for a year. Patrick had typically been up to no good in some roadhouse. He created a family for Marion: sturdy railroaders with three handsome daughters. Marion was the youngest, a chaste and lively brunette with a yen for tennis and old-fashioned novels about small-town boys in knickerbockers. When Patrick got locked up, Marion was never around. So gradually his parents began to view her as a good influence on their son. If he would just spend time with Marion Easterly, the disorderly-conduct business would fade, boarding school would seem less obligatory and Patrick would grow up and become . . . a professional.

In July, Patrick roped at the Wilsall rodeo, then joined the rioters in front of the bars. He'd tied his calf under eleven and was considered quite a kid, one who deserved many free drinks right out on the sidewalk. Patrick and his friends sat on the hoods of their cars until the sun collapsed in the Bridger range. By three in the morning he was back at the ranch, careening around the kitchen, trying to make a little snack. He banged into a cabinet, showering crystal onto the slate floor. A pyramid of flatware skated into fragments. He dropped the idea of the snack.

Patrick's mother and father popped into the kitchen in electric concern. Patrick reeled through the fragments in his cowboy boots, crushing glass and china noisily. He looked at them, his mind racing.

"Marion is dead," he blurted. "A diesel. She was going out for eggs." His parents were absolutely silent.

"I just don't give a shit anymore," Patrick added.

"You can't use that language in this house," his mother said; but his father intervened on the basis of the death of a boy's first love. Patrick waltzed to his room and passed out.

After ten hours of sleep ruined by guilt, booze and the presence of all his rodeo-dirtied clothes, Patrick awoke with a start and was filled by a sudden and unidentified fear. He cupped a hand over his face to test his breath, then smeared his teeth with a dab of toothpaste. He ran to the kitchen to clean up his mess; but he was too late. He really was.

His mother and father were waiting for him. The kitchen was immaculate. His father wore a suit and tie, his mother a subdued blue dress. It seemed very still.

"Pat," said his father, "we want to meet Marion's folks. We wanted to help with the preparations."

Patrick's mother had thin trickles of tears glistening on her cheeks. But they fell from eyes that were wrong.

"We can't find Easterly in the book."

"They don't have a phone."

"Could we just drive by?"

"I don't think they could handle it, Dad. I mean, this soon."

The ringing slap sharpened Patrick's sense of the moment. *"You were blotto at Wilsall,"* his mother said. *"Marion Easterly doesn't exist!"*

"Kind of embarrassing, Pat," said his father. "We went to the hospital, the morgue, the police. The police in particular had a good laugh at our expense, though the others certainly enjoyed themselves too. I'm afraid you're kind of a no-good. I'm afraid we're sending you away to school."

"It's fair," said Patrick.

"I'm afraid I don't care if it is or not," said his father. No unscheduled landings for that test pilot.

16

This was daring but it had required two bar stops: the front door flickered open.

"Tio, where's your wife?"

"Pat, d'you just walk in?"

"I drove from my place and walked the last forty feet."

"God, what an awful joke. This your first time up here?" The effect of Patrick's joke still hung on Tio's face.

"Yes. A beautiful spot."

"It's all lost on me."

That seemed a strange piece of candor to Patrick. The ranch was beautiful, a close dirt road lying in a cottonwood creek that arose to find old stone buildings, then meadows that spread above the ranch to adjoining cirques at the edge of the wilderness. It had the quality of enamel, detailed in hard, knowledgeable strokes, a deliberate landscape by an artist no one ever met.

Somehow the handsome oilman seemed harried, stranded on this picture-book ranch in his bush jacket and as anxious to be back among his oil-and-gas leases as Patrick had been for the loud bar.

"Claire is gypping horses in the round pen. Just go back the way you came and around the old homesteader house. You'll see it in the trees."

"I guess if I'm going to be looking after her, I'd better get the hang of it."

"That's it, good buddy. I'd fall down dead with my hand raised if I told you I couldn't get off of this vacation fast enough. You two go out and play. You can take her anywhere. She's more adaptable than a cat. All I do is dream of crude."

"You sure know your own mind," Patrick said, fishing for sense in Tio's remarks.

"Yeah, I do."

"Anything else?"

"Not really."

Claire appears to him as follows: at center in a circular wooden pen a hundred feet in diameter. Deep in river sand, it seems a soft, brown lens in the surrounding trees. Claire directs a two-year-old blood-bay filly in an extended trot around herself, the filly's head stretched high and forward, the flared and precise nostrils drinking wind on this delightful, balsamic and breezy flat.

It was on enough of an elevation that you could see the valley road mirroring the river bottom, the switchbacks to the wilderness, the flatiron clouds, the forest service corrals and the glittering infusion of sun-born seeds moving with the brilliant wind. But you couldn't see the house, and from the glade of young aspen, you couldn't see anything.

"Hello, Patrick."

"Hi, Claire."

"How are you?"

"I'm fine. Drank a bit too much, I'm afraid."

"You like this filly?"

"Sure. Isn't she deep through the heart?"

"I think she's great."

"Go for a walk with me."

"You rather ride?"

"I'm too dumb today to get a foot in the stirrup."

Claire left the longeing whip in the sand, and the filly swung gracefully forward, ears set, watching Claire leave the pen.

"Where are we going?"

"Where does this path go?"

"An old springhouse at the top of these aspens."

"I'd like to see it."

"Why?"

"I want to talk," said Patrick, "and it's easier if you keep moving, and to keep moving you need to be going somewhere."

The smallest aspens jumped up along the path with their flat leaves moving in a plane to each touch of breeze. When Claire went ahead, Patrick stared at the small of her back, where the tied-up cotton shirt left a band of brown skin.

The springhouse, now in complete disrepair, had been used to cool milk. A jet of water appeared from the ground and flowed into the dark interior of the house, gliding disparate over cold stones and out of the house again. Inside, the cold stones chilled the air and seemed to cast a dark glaze on the wood floor and sides. There was one old tree shading the house and minute canyon wrens crawled in its branches. But the wet stones were what you sensed even looking outside.

When they went inside, Patrick tried to seize Claire. Then he sat down on the plank bench, and over the water and the round river rocks their breathing was heard, as well as the catches in their breath. Patrick stared at his open hands. Claire gazed at him, not in offense or terror but in some absolute revelation. She now wore nothing but her denim pants; the shirt was in the dark stream that brightened the stones. And Patrick's face was clawed in five bright stripes. She finished undressing and made love to Patrick while his attempts to remember what it was he was doing, to determine what this meant, seemed to knock like pebbles dropped down a well, long lost from sight. He was gone into something blinding and it wasn't exactly love. Patrick supported himself on his arms, and splinters of the old floor ran into the tension of his hands. In a moment they were both shuddering and it was as if the four old windows above had lost the transparency, then regained it. And details returned: the mountain range of river stones against the wall, the electrical cord approaching from the ceiling, old saw marks and hammer indentations around the nail heads and, finally, the beautiful woman's tears running onto the coarse planks.

"You ought to get out," she said.

"What's the matter?"

"I don't do that kind of thing."

"You just did."

"I know. I bet when we're old it makes us feel lonely and empty." This could be a long, slow wreck.

They heard Tio call: "Anybody around?"

From the southwest window his distant figure could be seen trudging to the sand pen. Claire said, "I'm going straight down to the house around behind him and get a shirt. If you can think of a good cause for those scratches, you're welcome to join us."

"I wish I hadn't done that," came Patrick's contrition.

"It'll pass. It better. I'm just sick."

"Where is everybody?" came Tio's voice. Claire disappeared and Patrick followed her. About halfway down the hill, they heard him call out, "Come on, you guys! I'm getting insecure!" They rushed along in the trees. Claire was giggling.

"This makes me nervous," said Patrick as he went, realizing how preposterous the situation was.

"You shouldn't do this to me!" Tio called from afar as Patrick started his truck. Claire looked up toward the springhouse.

"He's such a little boy," she said with affection. "Listen," she added quite suddenly, "won't you have dinner with us tonight? I insist, and it's the least you could do."

Patrick drove off, thinking once again of the little walk-up in Castile, the stone counters scrubbed concave. He wondered why that came to him at these times or during summer war games at seventy miles an hour with the self-leveling cannon, the hurtling countryside on a television monitor. In the Castilian walk-up an unfuckable crone has the say of things and brings vegetables.

He cut down Divide Creek and went the back way around Deadrock. No supplies needed. Coming from this direction, you could see the ranch's high meadows cross the river bottom. You could see the old schoolhouse road and used-up thrashers and combines, drawn like extinct creatures against the gravel bank. Then this way you could run along the curving rim to the ranch itself, seeing now from above the original plan, a little bit like a fort and old-looking. Though around here nothing was really old. A woman in town was writing a book called *From Deer Meat to Double Wides* to chronicle the area and show it was old. There was a chapter on Patrick's ranch as well as one on high-button shoes, plus prominent Deadrock families, all written at very high pitch. The ranch chapter had a romantic version of the foray against Aguinaldo's insurrection, as well as of Fourths of July celebrated with dynamite. When Patrick grew older, the ranch meant less. The trouble was, he had charged it with meaning while he was in the Army, and left without benefits. He wanted his heart to seize the ancient hills, the old windmills and stock springs. Now all he seemed to care about were the things that lived and died on a scale of time an ordinary human being could understand. Then he wanted to know what those things were there for, taking every chance for knowledge about that. Nor was he about to press his grandfather about death's nearness. But he would watch him for accidental revelations. He had a feeling that the little churches around Deadrock, all of them so different, were trying to duck this question. He was tempted to attend every one of them in a string of Sundays to see how this fatal ducking worked.

He knew that one reason he still felt so incomplete was that his father had farmed him out, left him as crow bait to education and family history. And his grandfather hadn't given his father much. All that cowboy rigidity was just running from trouble. Patrick had wandered away and Mary had flown into the face of it, the face of it being the connection they never had, an absence that was perilously ignored. The connection had not been in the

airplane on the mountain; it had not even been a sign.
Mary in pursuit of the ghosts was close; Claire was
nearer. But he had been indecent. Had she? He was inclined to think she'd been worse than that.

17

Patrick and Claire sat next to each other in the deep old leather couch. There were chunks of Newfoundland salmon that Tio had caught, in a silver bowl, and toast points made from bread Tio had baked the previous day. Then Tio brought them a superior cold pumpkin soup and pressed upon them yet another bottle of St.-Émilion before returning to the kitchen. Instead of an apron he had a worn-out hand towel tucked into the top of his tooled belt and he moved at very high speed. He said they did not have many minutes to finish the bottle and move to the dining room. Patrick was impressed. But he felt he was in a madhouse.

"Will dinner be as good as this?" asked Patrick.

"Dinner will be great," Claire said.

"And he caught these fish?"

"Oh, Tio is a sportman. Got a bunch of records and all. He shot the ninth largest whitetail to ever come out of Texas." Patrick studied her eyes, hoping he would not find real pride in the bagging of the ninth largest whitetail. He did think he saw a little pride, though. Above all, he saw the beauty of beveled face with its gray-green eyes and ineffable down-turned Southern mouth.

"How does he ever find the time to be a fine cook and record-holding sportsman?" He sensed something aggressive in his own question.

Claire looked up at him. "What else has he got to do?" she inquired.

"He's got businesses to run and a lot of money to look after."

"Tio don't have any money. *Doesn't* have any money."

"Well." Patrick was finding some embarrassment in this. Claire's amused and corrected bad English was also a moment he'd liked to have gone back over. "It seems you live well and it seems you can do as you want."

"We do. But I support Tio."

"How?"

"Inherited Oklahoma land." Stated flat. "Including mineral rights."

Patrick looked straight at her in silence.

"Tio told me," he said deliberately, "that he had a world of leases and row crops and wells he had to get back to and he couldn't mess around up here in Montana any longer."

"Tio has this little problem, Patrick."

"Which is?"

"He thinks he has those things. It's not his fault. But he gets carried away. And in some respects Tio isn't completely healthy."

"What else does he think?"

The door flew open and Tio brought in a plate of roast lamb chunks with currant jelly. He bore the mad vanity of an Eagle Scout.

"Thinks he's got a jet plane and a jillion Mexicans."

Patrick stared at Tio in shock.

"Who's this?" Tio asked.

"Guy in Houston," said Claire. She pointed toward the gulf coast of Texas.

"Oh, yeah? Well, finish them lamb and come eat dinner. It a be on in five minute."

Tio's manners and his cooking were equally fine. Yet in the tall wavering of candlelight, the conversation— ranch history and oil—carried, against what Patrick now knew, some echo of calamity, something that lingered. "You get a deal," said Tio, "to where what you're looking

300

for is the actual lifeblood of the machine age, and this junk pools up where it gets trapped and where nobody can see it in the middle of the earth, and all we're doing is running little needles downwards toward it. Unless of course you're some old farmer with a seep. And the last one of them I know about was mounted and hangs over the dining room table at the Petroleum Club. But a man has to suspect his traps before he runs his drill in on down to where Satan is gettin out his book matches. And you got to know your domes." Then he looked around the table with matchlessly overfocused wide eyes. "I just don't care to be around people interested in other fuels. They make me sick." His eyes compressed to refocus on a forkful of perfectly prepared lamb.

"Go on ahead and eat that," Claire said quietly.

"What happened to your face, Pat? Get scratched tryin to get you a little?"

"Had a colt run through the bridle in some brush."

"Didn't know a colt had a hand on him like that."

"It was the brush that did it."

"Boy, amo tell you what, you couldn't carve a more perfecter piece of brush for that job, now, could you?"

"Say, after all this wine, I'm finally seeing what you're getting at: I try to rape some girl and she claws me. I guess I had a better day than I thought."

"Aw, good buddy." Real disappointment, moral disappointment, floods Tio's face: A man don't talk like that in company. In the flashing silence Patrick gave himself the liberty of remembering Claire beneath him, one thin arm reaching into the cool quiet, the aerial motion and breath. They ate quietly for a long time. Then he saw Tio's studying eyes deep against his own; they were, somehow, certainly not normal.

Claire got up. "I don't like to eat when it's like that."

"Food not right?" Tio asked. "Anybody says I can't cook is dumber than Ned in the First Reader."

"I'm going to sit in the living room."

"What about you, Pat?"

"I'm going to finish this good dinner."

"I'm heading for bed. I've got some studying up to do.

Then me and about five of my best old buddies around the country are going to hang all over our WATS lines and make a couple of bucks."

"Well, good night, I guess."

"Good night. Don't get scratched."

"I got my colts rode earlier. What a day."

The lamb had been defatted the way they did in France. Patrick could see Tio's shadow when he came to the top of the stairs to look down to the first floor. That kind of came in intervals while Patrick went through a lot of Bordeaux. Then the shadow of Tio stopped coming and producing its simple effect. So Patrick went to the living room, where he penetrated Claire with a peculiar vengeance, noting, only at the clutching, compressive end, the ninth largest whitetail deer ever killed in Texas.

"What'd I do with my hat?" asked Patrick. "I've got the whirlies." Claire sat up, a broad snail's track on her thigh, and in her molten eyes was something Patrick had never seen before because it had never existed before, not exactly.

Patrick managed to get dressed, walking back and forth across the front of the stairs, feeling a sick and depressed giddiness, not even rememberable from the Army years, of having threaded a miserable, shivering, narrow trail to wrath and humiliation, for which he knew hell fire in one of its uncountable manifestations would someday be handed on as silver a platter as the one that held Tio's dinner. A headache set in behind his temples and he was rather in love and in a bad mood. Claire stopped him in the yard, where he walked in his socks, carrying his tall boots, staring in a dumb, fixated way at his drunken target.

Claire's small, strong hand turned him around blank by the shirt, and he looked once more into the pained eyes, forcing his own off as one awaiting a lecture. "Cruelty is something I hadn't seen in you before."

"I saw it in you. I thought I was treating you for it. I thought I was the doctor." Patrick's anger, partial product of his damages and certainly of his drinking and his indirection, formed thickly in this inconsiderate remark.

"No, I'm the doctor," Claire said. "And Tio is the patient. And you are a cruel outsider."

She walked back inside and Patrick knew which of them had lost and what had been lost. As he drove off he saw all the upstairs lights clicking on in series and he was in genuine retreat.

18

His eyes were swollen shut from the butts of the cues when the chief of police shoved him into the drunk tank. "I don't know which one of you snakes bit the other first. It's all cowboys and Indians to me. But you're in my house now. And you're for sure snake bit."

"Yeah, right," said Patrick.

" *'Yeah, right,'* " laughed the policeman. "Shit, you can't even talk! Look at it this way: This is probably the only bunk in town where they won't keep beatin on you. You'll get breakfast and we'll see you on home."

"I'm sorry," said Patrick, angling for the narrow bunk catercorner to one other amorphous form, foreshadowing, Patrick thought, his future. "Nothing to read. Someday I'll be a dead bum."

"I'll tell you what: You just as well throw in with me, mean as you are."

"Am I mean?"

"You're plumb mean."

"Oh, that's terrible," Patrick said in simpleminded drunkenness. "Oh, I wish you couldn't say that about me."

"Well, I can!" said the chief of police brightly.

And the lights dropped to minimum observation, just enough to get a vomiter's tongue cleared or keep some whitecross detox bozo from beating his head on the fixed steel table where, it was intended, one would eat, play cards and be polite about the finger paints. As Patrick fell off to sleep, he felt that it was a good jail, one where they preferred your being a civilian to your being a jailbird, suicide or rising crime star.

Patrick didn't know whether he was dreaming—he didn't think he was—when he heard the chief's voice, coming in through the alpha waves and alcohol, say, "The lady left your bail."

As for now, his belongings, his keys and directions to his truck were what he most required.

The note from Claire read:

> Patrick,
> Tio flew to Tulsa early this A.M.
> Stop/call for details as needed.
> Claire.

Oh shit oh god oh now what. Can this be more sad-ness-for-no-reason? Pig's conduct is what I'll stand accused of, you can bet your hat on that. And my feeling is that the chaps who have made such a stretch of bad road out of my body with their cues are, at any other time or place, universally considered good fellows who never reverse their cues to beat on a human and who, all agreed, had been driven to the limits of their patience and who, moreover, when the jury returned, were universally acquitted and not a little applauded by all familiar with the particulars of the case. Except that Patrick couldn't remember anything about it. Therefore he would join the cheering throng in its endorsement of each lump's administering; for though he was the recipient, democracy did call for backing one's fellows, even on limited information.

19

Grandpa was discovered kneeling above the kitchen sink, killing yellow wasps against the window with the rolled Sunday Deadrock *News*. This seemed a little tough in one of our older cowboys, thought Patrick; this could be sadness-for-no-reason, although well short of harbinger-of-doom. There were dirty dishes containing glazed remains. Patrick's thought—that he'd only been gone a day—had a minute hysterical edge. What would he find with a week's absence? It seemed his grandfather had become unnaturally dependent upon him since his return. Before that, he could help, hire help, ask for help or do without. But now, silhouetted behind stacks of dirty dishes, he crawled after wasps, backlit brilliant yellow on the glass, and swung at them so hard he was in danger of losing balance and rolling to the floor.

"Did you get that editor?"

"No."

"Over to some woman's."

"Exactly."

"See you had a night in the hoosegow."

Patrick stopped. "Where are you getting this?"

Grandpa slung his legs down and unrolled the wasps'-guts-encrusted *News*. There Patrick reviewed a photograph of himself being removed from the Northbranch Saloon by the police. A lucky motorist from Ohio got the photo credit. The small crowd did not look friendly and the police looked like heroes. There was only a caption, no text; it read:

WAITING FOR RAIN

It's fair, thought Patrick.

"Well," he said to his grandfather. "Let's tidy this joint up." His heart soared with the thought of stupid little projects.

Deep in the grain bin the mice swam fat and single-minded while Patrick's coffee can sliced around them to fill the black rubber buckets. The young horses turned at the pitch of tin against oats and moved to the feed bunk, first in disarray and then in single file; and then snaking out at each other, rearranging the lineup as the yellow granules poured from the bucket.

The laminations of heat-and-serve yielded to the hot suds rising about Patrick's reddening forearms. He looked at the pleasant inflammation and thought: It proves I'm Irish. Then, with the bucket and brush, he could better see the undersides of the table as well as scrub the floor.

Here's something new: He's wetting the bed. And where does that lead? Is it a little thing, as incontinence? Or is it a nightmare with the impact of a cannon, rending and overwhelming, that would soak the tunic of the bravest grenadier? We will not soon have the answer to this. As of the here and now, we have a bed that needs changing.

At the very moment the Whirlpool goes from rinse to spin, it bucks like a Red Desert Mustang and would continue to do so if Patrick didn't heave a great rock on top of its lid, a rock that, as an interjection to its cycling chaos, restores order to as well as performs the last cleansing extraction of Grandpa's socks, underdrawers, shirts and jeans. This recalcitrant jiggling is, Patrick's old enough now to know, the deterioration of bearings and the prelude to a complete collapse—not necessarily an explosion of Grandpa's soiled linens around the laundry room, but certainly, in a year of poor cattle prices, a duskier and less fragrant general patina to this two-man operation. So Patrick views the rock as a good rock, keen stripes of marble and gneiss, a rock for all seasons.

"I have no idea what he saw. But it's sure enough undignified."

"Let me put it another way: Why did he go to Tulsa?"

"What he said was, his quail lease had come up for renewal and his father is sick, which I know is true."

"Your note said to stop by for the details."

"I guess I just wanted you to stop by!"

"Of course I *would*. And I owe you for bail."

"Anyway, what is this?"

"Damned if I know."

"It's sort of got this painful side to it."

"I know."

"Maybe nothin but ole remorse."

"Yeah, ole *remorse*."

"At least you're—whatchasay?—'unencumbered.' "

"I decided to marry my grandfather yesterday morning. As I am doing all that a wife could do for him, there's but little sense in our not making it legal. So don't go calling me unencumbered."

All of this was said, and nothing more, through the screen door of a porch, silhouettes freckled by afternoon light; they barely moved.

20

Heading home, Patrick nearly had to go through Deadrock or around it; and despite that he wanted to avoid stopping in a place renowned for its money-grubbing, bad-tempered inhabitants, a place whose principal virtue was its declining population, he needed an economy-size box of soap powder for the floors. So he went through Deadrock. He pulled off into a grocery store where he and its only other customer, Deke Patwell, ran into each other in aisle three.

"I see I'm in the papers."

"Yup. Real nice type of fellow heading for Yellowstone. Little Kodak is all it took."

"You write the caption?"

"Sure did."

"Very imaginative."

"Thank you. How's the head?"

"Not at all good, Deke. You know those pool cues."

"Only by reputation. They say one end is much worse than the other."

"Thicker."

"That's it, thicker."

Patrick pulled down a large box of soap.

"Floors?" asked Patwell. Patrick studied the contents.

"Exactly."

"Comet's a mile better."

Patrick got a can of Comet.

"And you'll want a little protection for the knees," Patwell said, and went to the cash register with his impregnated dish pads.

Patrick followed him. "I'd use rubber gloves with those hands of yours, Deke. Dish pads are full of irritating metal stuff."

"God, I wouldn't think of forgetting the gloves. My hands just aren't tough enough with the job I've got."

Outside:

"That been a good truck, Patrick?"

"Fair. Had the heads off first ten thousand miles."

"Tell me about it. This thing's been a vale of tears. I'm going Jap."

Waves. Bye-byes. Patrick noticed, though, from two blocks away, Patwell giving him the finger. He considered it extremely childish.

21

By Friday, Patrick thought he'd mended enough to ride Tio and Claire's stud. He had him in an open box stall with an automatic waterer and a runway. The horse had been on a full ration of grain all week with very little exercise. Patrick expected him to be hot. This young stallion spent most of his day looking out on the pasture in hopes of finding something to fight. When any other horse came into view, he'd swing his butt around against the planks and let out a blood-curdling, warlike squeal. So Patrick went into his stall cautiously. The stud pinned his ears at Patrick, bowed his neck and got ready for trouble. Patrick made a low, angry sound in his throat and the horse's ears went up. Patrick haltered him, took him out to the hitching rack and saddled him. He was a well-put-up horse but he looked even better under saddle. His neck came out at a good angle; he was deep in the heart girth and in the hip. Patrick bridled him with a Sweetwater bit, put on his spurs and led the horse away from the rack, got on and took a deep seat.

He rode up to a round wooden pen sixty feet across. Inside it, a dozen yearling cattle dozed in a little cluster. When Patrick rode in and closed the gate, the yearlings stood up, all Herefords, about five hundred pounds each. The stud was kind of coarse-handling, no better than cowboy broke. He smiled to think it was Claire who put this using-horse handle on him. But Patrick cut himself a cow and drove it out around the herd. The yearling feinted once and ran across the pen. The stud tried to run around his corner instead of setting down on his hocks and turning through himself. So Patrick just stopped, turned him correctly and still had time to send him off inside the cow. He set him down again in correct position. The stud reached around, tried to bite Patrick's foot and lost the cow he was supposed to be watching. Patrick didn't think he liked this horse. Nevertheless, he galloped him hard to get the nonsense out of his mind. That took two hours. This time the stud, having soaked through two saddle blankets, paid attention to his job. Patrick worked him very quietly, never got him out of a trot, but did things slow and correct.

In a sidehill above the house was a root cellar made of stone and with a log-and-sod roof. A horse fell through into the cellar one winter and Patrick built another roof, dragging cottonwood logs into place with the Ford gas tractor. He used it as a wine cellar and sometimes as a place to put vegetables if someone maintained the garden that year. In Germany he had raised tomatoes in nail kegs, and the big, powerful red tomatoes sunning on his balcony often touched his lady friends, who found the plants too piquant for words in a NATO tank captain. "You grew these?" "Yes, I did." "How *sweet*. You *are* sweet." At that point Patrick would know this was no dry run; post-coital depression was already in sight, no bigger than a man's hand on the horizon. Once Patrick picked up the nail kegs to make room for the lady, now keen to sunbathe, and midway through the effort, his face in tomatoes and vines, he said, "I'm homesick, homesick, homesick. I'm just homesick. Montana has a short growing season, but I'm homesick, just homesick . . ." After he'd done this for a while, the lady sought her dress and departed. "I don't want to see you again," she said. "Ever."

"It's fair."

Anyway, Mary headed for the root cellar to avoid a

conversation, just at the moment, with the grandfather. When Patrick found her, she was moving down the rack, giving each bottle a half-turn to distribute the sediment, an almost aqueous shadow play on the ceiling, the sun reflecting on the orchard grass that grew to the cellar door. A narrow foot trail wound down the hill to the house.

"Grandpa isn't drinking that stuff, is he?"

"Once in a while. I've been cooking for him. He'll drink a little then. He seems to be taking the cure."

"Let's have a bottle of champagne."

"Very well."

Patrick found a bottle of Piper Heidsieck and un-corked it. They sat on crates in the half-light and passed it back and forth. It was nearly empty before either spoke. Mary sighed continually. Patrick felt that junkie light go up his insides.

"I'm sick of going around with my nerves shot."

"I get mad."

"Well, I get the creeps. I get bats in the belfry."

More silence. Patrick examined the sod and rafters. He decided he'd done a good job.

"Why did Grandpa try out for a movie?" Mary asked.

"He wants to be better known, I guess."

Mary said, "That's more nails on the blackboard."

"I myself would like to be extremely famous, larger than life, with souvenir plaster busts of me available at checkout counters."

"I'd like to be ravishing. I'd like to put on the dog." Her hands were shaking.

"What's the matter with you?"

"Whew . . . uhm . . . whew."

"What?"

". . . speechless . . ."

"Here. Don't try. Have some more of this." She took the champagne. "Horse fell through. Up there. Didn't find him for two days. He ate a hundred pounds of pota-toes." Mary's breathing was short and irregular. "He didn't want to leave. Then he heard the irrigating water and gave in. Didn't I build a good roof?" Mary nodded rapidly. "Anything I can do?" She shook her head. "Be better if I leave you alone?" She nodded her head, tried to smile. Patrick left. He wanted to be quiet going down the hill. God Almighty, he thought, she is a sick dog.

22

Patrick's grandfather seemed to be returning from a long trip. One imagined his hands filled with canceled tickets. It had rained a week and now the sun was out.

"Just take and put the mares with colts on the south side. Everybody else above the barn. The open mares will fight across the wire."

"I did that," said Patrick to his grandfather.

"That's the boy," said the old man, and closed the door; then, through the door: "You better look for your sister." Patrick was tall and the old man was short and looked a bit like a stage paddy, an impression quickly dispelled by his largely humorless nature.

Through the kitchen window Patrick could see his mare sidestep into the shade. The old Connolly saddle looked erect and burnished on her chestnut back. She tipped one foot and started to sleep.

"Mary's all right," he said, and went outside and mounted the horse with an air of purpose that was at odds with his complete lack of intentions. The mare, Leafy, was chestnut with the delicate subcoloring that is like watermarks. She had an intelligent narrow face and the lightest rein imaginable. Patrick thought a great deal of her. So she had not been ridden while he was away in the Army. A captain of tanks on the East German line in 1977 who comes from Montana has unusual opportunities to remember his home, and apart from the buffalo jump, where ravens still hung as though in memory, Leafy was the finest thing on the place. Downhill on a cold morning, she would buck. Like most good horses, Leafy kept her distance.

When Patrick got to the spring, its headgate deploying cold water on the lower pastures, he found Mary reading in the sun. The glare of light from the surface of the pool shimmered on the page of her book, and she chose not to look as Patrick rode up behind, leaned over and guessed she was reading one of the poet-morbids of France again, enhancing her despair like a sore tooth. Over her shoulder, on the surface of the pool, he could see Leafy's reflection and his own shimmer against the clouds.

Mary said, "Patrick, when Grandpa slapped the senator, was it something he said to Mother?"

Patrick said, "What brought this up?"

"I've been reading about mortal offenses."

"Grandpa slapped the senator for saying something about the Army, and the senator put Grandpa out of the cattle business."

"That hardly seems like a mortal offense."

"It does to an Army man."

"How do you feel?"

"Better by the minute."

"Do you miss your tank?"

"I miss loose German women."

Patrick got down and sat by the spring, holding Leafy's reins. He glanced at the book—De Laclos, *Liaisons Dangereuses*. I could very well figure out who these corrupt French bastards are, he thought, but it plays into the hands of trouble.

Patrick pulled some wild watercress and ate the peppery wet leaves, covertly looking up at Mary with her pretty, shadowed forehead. Cold water ran on his wrists.

"What are we to do, what are we to do?" He smiled.

"I don't know, I don't," she said. "We get the family this month. That will be a trial by fire, me with child and you without tank."

"I shall fortify myself with whiskey."

"The last time you did that, you went to jail. Furthermore, I don't believe your version of Grandpa slapping the senator. The Army never meant anything to him."

"Actually, I don't know why he slapped the senator."

"He slapped the senator," said Mary, "because the senator disparaged the Army. You just said so."

"And you said the Army never meant anything to him."

"That's right, I did." She looked off.

Perhaps, thought Patrick, being a captain of tanks for the Americans facing, across the wire, the captains of tanks of the Soviets has not entirely eradicated my own touchiness as to such disparagements. Although now I'm in a tougher world.

Patrick rode away. Mary turned anew to the French, and the trees at the spring made one image on the water and a shadow on the bottom. It was a beautiful place, where the Crow had buried their dead in the trees, a spring that had mirrored carrion birds, northern lights and the rotation of the solar system. It was an excellent cold spring and Patrick liked everything about it. Ophelia would have sunk in it like a stone.

When he was young, and one of the things he was managing now was the idea that he was not young, but when he was very young, a child, he and Mary picked through the new grass in the spring of the year, when you could see straight to the ground, for the beads that remained from the tree burials. Their grandmother, who was still alive then and who remembered that the "old ones," as she also called the Indians, had at the end died largely of smallpox, made the children throw the beads away because she was superstitious, superstitious enough to throw her uncle's buffalo rifle into the river on the occasion of the United States' entry into World War Two. The family had had this absurd relationship to America's affairs of war, and the Army had been a handy place of education since the Civil War. The great-grandfather went there from Ohio, and from a gaited-horse farm now owned by a brewery, only to die driving mules that pulled a Parrott gun into position during the bombardment of

Little Round Top. It is said that the mules were the part he resented. Later, with the 1st Montana Volunteers, he helped suppress Aguinaldo's native insurrection.

Apart from his death, there was the tradition of rather perfunctory military service, then, starting at Miles City in 1884, cattle ranching, horse ranching and a reputation of recurring mental illness, persistent enough that it tended to be assigned from one generation to the next. Mary seemed to have been assigned this time. The luckier ones got off with backaches, facial tics and alcoholism.

The family had now lived in this part of Montana for a very long time, and they still did not fit or even want to fit or, in the words of Patrick's grandfather, "talk to just anybody." They would bear forever the air of being able to pick up and go, of having no roots other than the entanglement between themselves; and it is fair to say that they were very thorough snobs with no hope of reform. They had no one to turn to besides themselves, despite that they didn't get along very well with one another and had scattered all over the country where they meant nothing to their neighbors in the cities and suburbs. Only Patrick and Mary with her hoarding mind and their insufferable grandfather were left to show what there had been; and when they were gone, everyone would say in some fashion or another that they had never been there anyway, that they didn't fit. As for Patrick, numerous things were said about him but almost nothing to his face, and that was the only deal he cared to make.

Patrick spent the remainder of the day fixing fences at the head of the big coulee, where the ranch adjoined the forest service. In the deep shadows under the trees, small arcs of snow had persisted into the early summer. The mountains, explained his grandfather, were U.S. territory, and below them were all the people he would see in hell. There was some theater in this remark. But the old man loved his coulee. In years past they had dragged big kettles behind draft horses to make a course for match racing on Sundays, when the dirt savages were at church.

You couldn't see the race, which was illegal, until you got to the rim of the coulee.

Patrick and Mary's mother, Anita, married Dale in Long Beach and had a son, now eleven, named Andrew. Anita had been in Long Beach to comfort the wife of the co-pilot, Del Andrews, after the crash. The two widows met Dale in a Polynesian after-hours club and did not speak to each other again after the engagement. Anita, Dale and Andrew were coming on the weekend. It was Friday and Mary had not emerged from her room in days. Dale had connections in Hawaii for winter vacations; but now it was summer, and once Anita got over the matter of Mary's pregnancy, they could have a super holiday in the mountains.

"If you quit carrying her food to her," said Patrick's grandfather from the stove, "she's gonna have to come out." The grandfather still made coffee like a camp cook —with eggshells in the grounds and cold water dripping from his fingertips to make it precipitate.

"I don't believe she will," said Patrick. He had made a tray for Mary, very domestically, with French toast and orange juice. He really didn't think she would come out.

Today Mary had armed herself with the New York *Times*, illuminated from the window facing the juniper-covered slope. The light fell equally upon the nail-head bedspread and the vase of broad orange poppies from around the well pit. The room was carefully and comfortably arranged, a case of battening down the hatches. The family was coming.

Mary stopped the coffee cup at her lips, angled slightly, and said, "I don't want to deal with them, Patrick."

"It's not a matter of dealing. Don't think like that." He watched her twist up the corner of the bedspread and watched her eyes. Then the light in the room moved.

On the wall was a painting by Kevin Red Star which except for its hallucinatory colors Patrick would have liked, but which seemed, as furnishing for a troubled girl's room, to be throwing fat on the fire. More to his liking was the perfect Chatham oil, five inches across, a juniper of shadow on snow and bare ground. The blue paint from the day of the fire was cleaned up and gone.

The truth was that Mary and Patrick thought a lot of themselves at the worst of times, and of each other. This air, despite breakdowns or shooting, earned them the sarcasm of the townies. They each loved the open country where they lived, and big, fast cities. Booster hamlets failed to hold their interest. Town was for supplies.

"I didn't sleep much," said Mary. "Perhaps I should avoid the coffee so I can sleep this afternoon. What's Grandpa up to?"

"He's writing a letter of complaint to an importer of Japanese horseshoes which includes veiled references to the sneak attack on Pearl Harbor. Yesterday he was bitching about me not making my Easter duty."

"Oh, yeah? What'd you tell him?"

Mary pressed the tines of her fork into the French toast experimentally. "I said I could buy everything but the Holy Ghost."

"I'd have guessed the Holy Ghost was the only one of the three you *would* buy."

Patrick peered at her, then went down the hall and got an old Bud Powell ten-inch from his endless bebop collection. He came back, played "Someone to Watch over Me," and the two drifted off for a moment. How could a sick man like Powell bring you such peace, he wondered.

Patrick said, "I wish I could do something that good just once." Indicating Bud Powell.

"You will, now that you've picked another way of expressing yourself than tank driving."

"I sought to destroy communism."

"While despos took over America."

"Despo" was a word Patrick and Mary had—from the song "Desperado"—to describe the hip and washed-up effluvia of the last twenty years. The song itself, which now seemed to belong to the distant past, was the best anthem for a world of people unable to get off various freeways. Mary had invented the subcases: *despo-riche* and *despo-chic.*

Mary was getting jittery. Now she would ice the cake. "In bathing suits," she said, "I prefer D cups, split sizes and matching cover-ups. I love warm-up suits in luscious colors. Even though I'm expecting out of wedlock, I'm heavy into my own brand of glamour. Few days see me without intensive conditioning treatments, Egyptian nonpareil henna, manicures, pedicures and top skin-care products."

"Are you all right?" asked Patrick.

"I'm in stitches," said Mary. She began to cry but checked herself and grinned bravely.

When the record finished, Patrick asked if he should turn it over. But she gazed toward him in the concentration of someone trying to overcome stuttering, concentration or paralysis, it was hard to say.

"Try to sleep," he said. "Please try."

23

"All I want to know," said his mother, "is what tribe?" Her eyes lifted to cut across the original buffalo grounds.

Dale, her husband, took the Igloo cooler out of the back of the station wagon, desperately surveyed the ranchstead with the rectangles of snow-line meadow between the buildings and said:

"High, wide and handsome!" His smile revealed that if no one was buying this, he wasn't selling it.

But Patrick's mother in her hearty kilt was steadfast. She locked down on tan, angular calves.

"What tribe?"

"I don't know. We will have to wait and see."

Dale said, "Anita, I thought we had an agreement about this."

And Anita said, "You're right, of course." She was still establishing Dale. Dale didn't care. His original enthusiasm had flown the coop. Now he was with his screwy fucking in-laws.

If it wasn't my mother, thought Patrick, I'd swear it was Shrew City Sue. It goes without saying that Andrew had a cap gun and that he fired away with it like a rat terrier yapping around the feet of an arguing couple. Patrick thought his mother would club Andrew, but she had turned her attention to unloading the wagon onto the lawn. Dale accompanied everything with a stream of chatter. He sensed his wife's short fuse. Dale, Patrick thought, was giving it his best. It was kind of not much.

Patrick's mother and her husband had matching snake boots. Of all the people on the ranch, it never occurred to Patrick that he in his knee-high M. L. Leddy cowboy boots and tank captain's shirt was the most anomalous. Besides that, he was now sick of America.

"Lordy, lordy," said his mother, stooping for her camera bag. "I'm going to have to control myself, if only with respect to promises I made to Dale." She'd build up Dale if it killed her.

"I think you are, Mother. Mary is a little shaky."

Dale said, "The old days seem never to have died." He wore a fixed expression memorized from a hairstyle illustration in a barbershop.

Mary's disease, if that could be said, was, Patrick thought, an insufficient resistance to pain of every kind. When she was a child, the flyswatter could not be used in her presence. Patrick watched tears stream down her face in the supermarket as an elderly couple selected arthritis-strength aspirin with crooked hands. Some of this ought to have been noticed and remembered by his mother.

The grandfather made his greetings somewhat perfunctory. After all, this was only his former daughter-in-law. His son was dead. He didn't ever pay attention to Dale and he detested little Andrew. He couldn't really understand what they were doing here. He smiled and said, "It's a big ranch. We can all damn sure keep out from underfoot if we half try."

"What's *that* mean?" asked Andrew.

"Why don't you stay out in the bunkhouse?" roared the grandfather, senility kicking in like rocket fuel.

"I think it would be nicer being near the kitchen etcetera," said Patrick's mother with a taut smile. It was clear she saw her former father-in-law as someone to be humored.

"Not a damn thing wrong with the bunkhouse," his grandfather barked. Dale started off with the bags straight for the main house, right in the middle of the conversation. Andrew was galloping, and Patrick helped with a great sagging valise that felt like it had a thick dead midget inside. They fanned out toward the house, resisting a very insistent silence. Patrick walked behind his grandfather and watched his rolling gait. Dale and his mother were in his periphery. It was a movie with the sound track gone. Andrew now bore a wretched face; his fake gun dangled at his side. For him, the West stank.

They were winding down to seeing Mary. There was the luggage, the general greeting, the formal exclamations about returning to the ranch, and then it would be faced. They rushed into the kitchen. Patrick's mother tried the cupboards; Andrew asked where he could find an arrowhead fast. Down the wooden hallway, bebop poured from Mary's room.

"Make your own," said the grandfather.

"I can't make an arrowhead," wailed Andrew. "I'm no Indian!"

When Patrick said, "Let's go say hello to Mary," a kind of familial smile not unlike saying "Cheese" befell the little group. They followed Patrick through the narrow hall toward a drum solo coming from the farthest door.

They lost the grandfather right away. Then Dale detained Andrew. Patrick and his mother arrived as the applause began at the end of the drum solo, recorded live at the Blue Note, and the room was empty. The sheet on the bed was drawn taut, and Mary had outlined herself in ink, life-size, carefully sketching even the fingers. Across the abdomen she had traced the shape of an infant; and she was gone. Patrick went to the window; he could see across the meadow to the forest. She was either in the forest or at the spring.

"Orphanages," said Patrick's mother, "were made for good and sufficient reasons." Dale ducked his head in shame.

Then Patrick had a thought that dazed him and he panicked. He ran to the corral and caught his mare, but twisted the cinch and had to start over. Leafy felt his bad nerves and kept side-passing away from Patrick until he got a foot in the stirrup and swung up on her. She started running before Patrick could touch her with his feet, carrying him into the cold wind from the trees. Thus the ground, the sky, the vaulting motion of the horse against a static earth, seemed like life itself. The ground resisted the speed that Patrick desired, like history.

24

Once past the coat hooks, the plan of the funeral home is clear. This place can handle the lapsed of all religions. There is a corridor on the left with perhaps three rooms leading off perpendicularly. In every one of these rooms is someone dead. Over the door of each room is the last name of the goner: Symanski, Westcroft, Fitzpatrick. Just at the point of division between this set of rooms and the large room to the right, where services are held, is a small stand holding a kind of guest register; it has an attached light. A discreet brown cord trickles over to the wall outlet. The owner stands behind the guest book and flags the dalliers by the coat-rack; he is dressed somberly, but not grimly. His is the air of riding out a good franchise. Here and there are his assistants, that odd breed of Recent Graduates in smart suits and razor-cut hair who have decided to spend the rest of their working lives driving hearses and standing in attendance at funerals with their hands just so.

Patrick, the blood rising in his head, circled past the casket with the other mourners; he took one look at the barbaric effigy constructed from his deceased sister and decided: I have no attitude toward this. He was still far from knowing what had happened to him.

They sat in the front row: Patrick, his mother, Dale, his grandfather and little Andrew. Little Andrew had wanted to touch the body. He got a good snatching for

that. The grandfather gaped around and smiled at his con-
temporaries, all of whom, Patrick felt sure, were thinking: Odd for a person so young to go when it's usually one
of us. Patrick wondered if these old people didn't feel a
little edge, thinking time was not so reliable a force
against the living that it could be utterly counted on.
There was always mishap, the unexpected; and in this
case, the perils of one's own hand. Few had the nerve for
that and, all in all, went uncounted, as they were easily
dismissed as mental cases. The old people gazed around:
this was just social. Of course, there was death. The middle-aged worked on the theater of doom, many of them
with dramaturgical mugs that wouldn't pass muster at
the local playhouse. The very young craned around like
the very old; and all were surrounded by the funeral
house staff, including the altogether depressing Recent
Graduates. Patrick was getting angry. Mary was gone and
this bit of drill seemed superfluous. Moreover, the audience included a substantial group of townies eager to see
the family on its knees, which Patrick could have stood
for, except that there was no family anymore. The
mother was divorced and gone, Patrick was in disgrace,
his father long dead, his sister was ridiculed before she
died; and his grandfather despised everyone. Patrick was
growing more incensed by the second.

The Ford dealer bowed his way down the aisle, holding a narrow-brimmed and piquant fedora, obsequious before a couple of hundred prospects. His wife stared into
infinity, her cylindrical hat indicating a level stance in
the face of mortality. A tiny wino brakeman slipped in
because he'd seen the gathering. The preacher materialized in the wings, counted the house and withdrew to
await the swelling crowd. Deke Patwell was on hand to
report the loss. A lip reader from the stationery store sat
front and center with her own missal. The song "Chapel
in the Moonlight" came dimly from invisible speakers.
There were five Indians with hard Cheyenne features,
two of whom were young enough to be suspects as
Mary's paramour. Andrew had a cast-metal articulated
earth-mover, which he rolled quietly back and forth

between his feet. His mother moved her shoe to block its progress and Andrew looked up at her with no expression whatsoever.

Scattered around the audience were people never before seen in town, friends of Mary's from all over the Rockies. They were uniform in age but staying well away from each other.

The minister began to move under the arcade of flowers past the casket toward the Recent Graduates pushing the lectern at him from the opposite direction. "Chapel in the Moonlight" diminished and disappeared. Patrick's mother drew back the silk string from her missal and raised the face of one who, as the mother of a suicide, had nowhere to hang her next glance. Dale seemed to be saying, This is how it is.

The minister gazed for a long time at his own little volume; and when the moment came at which its pages could best be heard, he turned it open, gazed, then abruptly closed it again: he would speak from the heart. That was a good one, and everybody looked at him, even the Recent Graduates, sharpening expressions in anticipation of something daring.

"Young Mary Fitzpatrick," he crooned, "was a free and delightful spirit . . ." He paused. Perhaps he never should have paused, or paused so long, because the fury Patrick had feared arose in him and he spoke.

"*Shut up,*" said Patrick in a clear voice. "*We knew her.*" The quiet was like undertow.

The minister's head fell with patience. Patrick arose. His mother's face turned in horror. Nearly half of the audience got up and started to the rear. The editor-in-chief gazed back at Patrick, then led the group out. Aaron Clark, the prosecutor, stayed close alongside the editor. Dale, after a moment's reflection, left with them. Patrick's grandfather pulled Andrew onto his knee. The Indians milled and went, leaving one frightened young man in a Levi jacket and carrying a broad-brimmed uncreased straw. That's our man, thought Patrick, but I won't talk to him. It's all disgrace. Patrick walked up to the minister and demanded to know where he had gotten the business about the free and delightful spirit. "You never met her. That was an unhappy girl and she isn't going anywhere. She's just dead." What remained of the audience stirred at this ghastly speech.

Patrick turned to go and spotted the Indian. He changed his mind about talking to him. They looked at each other hard and Patrick asked him to wait outside. Patrick watched him turn slowly and go into the blind light at the door, affixing the straw hat as he did so, causing a sudden deep shadow to reveal his face as he stared back in the glare, his expression very much that of something cornered and awaiting necessity, grave and shy at once.

"Have you had enough?" He saw his mother. He was blank. "Have you had enough, I said! I *said*—"

"I heard what you said." She was right into his face. He gazed off at the casket and thought about that Indian in the sidewalk glare, the angular, expressionless face lit by the dark under his straw hat. "You said nothing."

Between the pews Patrick's grandfather led Andrew to the rear. The old man looked upon Patrick with a sadness he'd never allowed to be seen before. Patrick couldn't understand the expression at all, not at this time.

"Take it easy, Pat," he said. "I'll bring little Andrew here. It's just best for you to go on out of here. Andrew wants an arrowhead. So I'll try to find him one. And then they're going to bury her, see. And what I'm saying is it's just best if you go on out of here, Pat."

"Did you happen to notice the newspaper editor?" His mother inquired. She walked off, leaving no time for a reply, though in an instant of stunned, relieving giddiness, which shot through his grief like a tiny spark, he almost told her that he read only the sports page. Then he thought of his grandfather and walked toward the light. He knew and felt the people's close watch on him. He had always understood that to observe the burying of other people's dead was one of the few things that made their lives palatable.

But best of all the agony of those who remained. Aha! There had not been a good death like this one in Patrick's

329

family for some time. His father's death in the desert of the Great Basin had seemed remote. There had been a dry spell. But Patrick knew, too, that he had not learned; his grandfather had walked out and given them nothing. There was nothing in the old cowboy's face, his straight-backed walk toward the door, to give them anything. And Patrick had raved. He had raved for nothing. So this was a good one. This was one of the best ones they had ever seen.

25

The Indian was on the sidewalk, cars disappearing fast around him. He dropped his face slightly at Patrick's appearance in the door and then looked once behind him. Patrick saw something guarded and ready in his stance, the clear, round, pale brim intersecting his delicately modeled forehead.

"Do you need to see me?" Patrick asked.

"If there is something between us."

"What's that supposed to mean? Is that Indian talk?"

"I don't know."

"What's your name?"

"David Catches."

"Well, they're going to bury my sister. Will you be going?"

"You'll make another speech. I don't want to hear that kind of thing."

"Then why don't you come to the house tonight?"

David Catches followed a police cruiser with his eyes as it rounded the corner and vanished at low speed.

"What time?"

"Before the sun goes down and we lose our light. That way we won't be stuck inside. Do you know the way out there? Do you know how to get to our place?"

"Of course. I helped your grandfather."

"I guess I knew that."

"You were in the Army. At that time your grandfather

didn't take care of himself. I didn't have any rattles. I had a Goldenrod fence stretcher and a slick-fork saddle. Mary brought me there to make him an Indian. I punched cows and peeled broncs for a couple of years. But I saw a way to get out one night and I was gone. I got away just before I learned to think like him."

An old man walked by, leading matched springers. He walked his dogs according to the National Bureau of Standards, so that people could set their watches by him. In Deadrock there were children who thought one told time by dogs.

"When did all this occur?"

"We went to Grassrange and I worked for an Indian who ranched on Flatwillow Creek. A guy sent me some horses to break, from over at Sumatra. Mary came with me! We had a trailer house down in the trees. We had a good dog and four good saddle horses. We were happy. Then something must have gone wrong. Anyway, Mary was gone, one day just gone."

"She turned up in Roundup."

"I don't know."

"Then on down to Warm Springs. Hey, I'm giving you the details."

"I just don't know."

A silence fell over them, an unresisted silence like a trance. Then David Catches said, "You've got to go now. I will see you tonight." To Patrick it seemed a moment later that the silence resumed. Except that this time an arrangement with straps and pulleys lowered Mary into the earth between panels of artificial turf that covered the scars that the machinery had left making the hole. Only the family was there, and since Patrick was responsible for the absence of the priest, it was felt he should say something by way of a benediction. He said, "I'll never see her again."

It required three cars to carry the family. The cars were parked down on a blacktop crescent below the mausoleum. You could see the foothills from here and a few farm buildings along the base of the escarpment, like curious physical interjections in the landscape. Patrick viewed this all helplessly as Mary's habitat, knowing that on this broad hill, picked for its view, gale-driven snow stretched immense drifts toward the west, over everything, over stones and monuments, and that there was nothing that could be done for that. On the upper end of his own ranch, a miner had, years ago, filled coffee cans with cement and pressed marbles into its surface, picking out the name of his three dead children. So anyway, except that there was nothing new in this, it was the one thing that was always new.

26

It was pitch dark. "I am Marion Easterly," said the voice. "You never let me exist. I am not allowed to let you rest. But one night at the proper phase of the moon, a neither-here-nor-there phase of the famous moon, I will arise in the face of our mother and our father and I will be real and you will not have been sent away to school and the proper apologies will be made and you still will have won the roping drunk at the Wilsall rodeo; and all, all will be acceptable." Patrick turned on the bedside lamp and there was Mary, grinning and buttoned up in a navy peacoat. "Take away the offending years," she said, "for they have ruined us with crumminess and predictability."

"Go to bed," Patrick said to Mary. "Anyone can see you've gotten yourself altered."

Dale turned around in his front seat to look straight at Patrick. The driver, never seen before, presented himself as a concerned friend of the cemetery franchise. He offered to drive and they let him. The other cars were driven by concerned friends of the cemetery as well.

Dale said, "That was quite a deal you put on, Pat."

"How long did it take you to pump yourself up to say that, Dale?"

"No time at all." By his own scale, Dale was dauntless.

"Well, if my grandfather would have the courtesy to

334

die, it might mean something to you, even as a lease deal. Why don't we pull the other car over and find out just how long Grandpa is going to pull this business of not dying?"

"Stop this," said his mother. Patrick's batty conduct made her practical.

"Driver, detain that car."

The driver said, "This isn't a patrol car."

"I say stop that car. Remove the offending mystery."

Dale said, "This will not continue."

"My father is dead as well," said Patrick. "But he's no use that way, is he? He's no use to Boeing aircraft and he's no use to us—Driver, pull that car to the shoulder. I accuse its occupant of lingering."

Patrick could tell that he was ignored like a bad drunk. Beautiful scenery rolled past the windows and was of absolutely no use or comfort to anyone. He looked over at his mother, stranded in horror, and thought, What is the use of my going on like this? And there is no repairing what I've done, nothing to be helped by apology. No use.

But when he got to the ranch, he was quite astonished to see the broodmares pasturing the deep grass, their foals moving like shadows next to them, twisting their heads up underneath to nurse. That was one thing that seemed to go on anyway, something that helped, unlike the baleful and unforgiving mountains. He thought, I hope Andrew will find an arrowhead. And if he doesn't, that Indian will make him one, if he's any kind of an Indian.

What could I have done? I might well have canceled the reproving-older-brother performance. I might have done better than that. And was there anything to the remark heard over the years that Mary had "that look," that she was doomed? We shall quiz the Indian as to doom. We are encouraged to think they are the only ones with coherent attitudes on the subject. It's the worldwide aborigine credit bureau.

The dinner table was set and there was food. Patrick didn't know how it got there and he had no idea how the five people converged at the same time while the late-afternoon sun blazed through the windows. It was clear that no one but Andrew was going to do anything with the food. Funeral meats, thought Patrick. Where does that come from? I'm afraid of the thought.

"How do you like that dinner?" he asked Andrew.

"It's great," said Andrew. "Except for those things, those Brussels sprouts."

"Well, eat up."

"Gonna."

Then Patrick's mother began to sob. She sobbed bitterly and deeply, as though a convulsion was at hand. Dale looked across at Patrick. "Are you happy?" he asked. Patrick shook his head. He was wrong again. Dale wasn't even gloating.

"Aw, come on, Mama, please stop," Patrick heard himself say.

". . . can't . . ." In her grief she looked strangely like Mary.

"It's over. Nobody could do anything."

"It isn't true," she choked. "It's not."

Andrew looked from face to face, as if he were at a tennis match. Dale stood up. He wasn't an impressive man, but he seemed to have a right to his disgust.

"I'm going to the bunkhouse," he said. "I'll have the car ready in a bit. We're going to leave immediately." He turned to Patrick. *"What have you and your sister done?"*

"What have my sister and I done!" Patrick repeated in an astonishment that faded easily.

Dale lifted his wife to her feet. "There are things you don't do. Andrew, let's go." The pale lighting designer had gotten indignant. Patrick felt an odd strength in it.

"I'm still eating!"

"We'll stop on the way. Get up!" Andrew raised his hands and shrugged philosophically. Then he stood. When the three went through the dining room door, Dale had one more thing to say: He said, "You've shed all of it you're going to on my wife. It was an old trick of your father's. But don't you start."

Dale left, crazily brave in his elastic-waist vacation pants and loud shirt. Patrick did note that he stood up for his own. And what do I stand up for? You better think of something fast.

27

Patrick's grandfather, mashing peanut butter onto an unheated English muffin with the back of a spoon, watched a wasp cruising the honey jar and asked Patrick if he wanted to unload the ranch. He was sure that a pigeon in the form of a deer hunter from Michigan would appear.

"What else would we do?"

"I don't know. Get on out of here maybe."

"It seems like I just got back."

"We could go to the Australia."

"I don't think so."

"Country like this used to be. No sprinklers, no alfalfa, no yard lights, no railroaders, no nothing."

"I don't know," said Patrick. "I don't want to go to Australia." He visualized Limey prison descendants photographing koala bears in vulgar city parks.

"This country used to be just nothing and that's when it was good. And they say the Australia is one big nothing. I'm telling you, Patrick, I bet we'd do good out there. You can run a spread with just your saddle horses."

Then it got quiet again. There was nothing further to be said about the Australia. There was not even anything to be said about the departing station wagon, whose lights wheeled quickly against the house.

"Tell me about David Catches," said Patrick.

"Oh, yeah. Well, he was here for a while. It wasn't

right, but your sister had him here and he was of some use."

"What kind of use?"

"He was good with stock. Worked a long day. But then after that was done, he'd try to tell you how it was. I think Mary made him do that. I don't think he wanted to."

"What did you do about it?"

"I told *him* how it was."

"How long did this go on?"

"Couple years."

"How come I never heard about it?"

"Like I said, I didn't feel it was right. I mean, here's this Indian. And what was Mary up to? I just didn't feel it was my job to explain it."

"Maybe it is." That's what the jailer thinks, thought Patrick: Throw in together and save the world.

"Anyway, he went to making an Indian out of me and it wasn't in the cards."

"Why did he try to do that?"

"He had Mary about halfway made over and I guess he figured to start in on me."

"Did you believe any of it?"

"Some of it."

"Like what?"

"I don't know."

"I mean just for instance."

The old man twisted about. "Well, Patrick, this guy'd give you the feeling he'd know where Mary had gone." Now there was absolute quiet. In a moment the old man spoke again: "Pat, what you said today did not absolutely one hundred percent wash with me." Here it comes.

"Well, I don't know. I don't know if I've ever done anything right anymore. I already feel a little bad about the way they left out of here. Do you feel good about anything anymore?"

"I feel good about the Australia and the movies."

"Come on."

"Well, I like what I had, the way I used to live. There's nothing to do anymore, but I'm too old to do much anyway. I can go out in the hills, but I got to take a horse I'm a hundred percent sure won't buck me down. Who wants to go in the hills on a horse like that? So I think about something I don't know one thing about, like the Australia. And that works pretty good. I recommend it. I say it's good. I'm not saying it has to be the Australia. It could be just an animal you've never seen." The old man changed his gaze. Patrick turned to see David Catches in the doorway, his hat removed and held with both hands, his black straight hair swept back. Catches smiled and nodded. "You could think about that Indian," the grandfather continued. "I don't know any more about him than I do the Australia." Patrick got up from the table.

"Be back in a sec, David, I've got to get a few things." Patrick hurried off down the corridor.

"You been staying busy?" asked the grandfather.

"Pretty much."

"Doing what?"

"Punching cows."

"Where's this at?"

"Different places. Roundup, Ekalaka, Grassrange, Sumatra. Different reservations. Up on Rocky Boy."

"I'm hardly ever horseback," the grandfather said angrily. "Time was, irrigated ground was considered modern."

Patrick walked in. He was carrying a small valise. His grandfather went to the window.

"Are we ever going to eat?"

"I don't want to."

"Catches, what about you?"

"I stopped in town and got a hamburger."

"You know what I can't remember?" asked Patrick. "Whose idea was it we talk?"

"I don't know," said Catches. "Doesn't matter. What d'you got in the sack?"

"Whiskey. Number-one kind of bourbon."

"Okay," said Catches.

"That way we've got a shot at some actuality, medicine man. I mean, this isn't going to be the sweat lodge."

"You're not gonna do your well-known mean-drunk

340

thing, are you?" asked Catches. Patrick gave him a long look.

"All it is, is for loosening tongues and to make sure we don't have any mystical ceremonies."

Catches put his hat on and walked over to the sink. He twisted the faucet, cupped his hand under the stream, drank, turned off the water and wiped his face. "No more cracks. I tried to save her too."

Patrick sat down. "Save her from what?"

"You people and her own thoughts."

"I don't want to talk about this," said the grandfather.

"Stay where you are," Patrick ordered. "Have a seat, Catches." Catches drew a chair with the same fatal gesture he extended to the hat. Now the hat was foursquare on his head and he was looking at the whiskey Patrick unloaded on the table. The yellow electrical light contained the three of them in the dying day. Catches couldn't keep his eye off the bag. Patrick filled a jug with cold water and set three glasses on the table. He filled the glasses nearly full with whiskey. "The ditch is in the jug, boys. We're all throwed into this mess. So make yourself brave."

Catches tilted the whiskey back to his face and, pausing very momentarily, produced a wicked little knife from its leather encasement, a narrow blade with dark, oxidized steel, a maple handle with stars and silver faces. He didn't seem to mean much by the gesture.

"Is that anything special to you?" Patrick asked. His grandfather got up and walked out. "Spooked the old boy. Well, is it?" They could hear the grandfather slamming doors down the hallway.

"Just a little knife. I cut binder twine with it."

"Uh-huh."

"Do you think you helped Mary an awful lot, being an Army officer who kind of looked down on her no matter how much she thought of you?"

They drank another glass of whiskey before Patrick answered: "Is that what happened?"

"You didn't save her. I am saying that."

"Maybe *you* should have saved her," said Patrick.

"And I didn't look down on her. I neglected her. It's different."

"You didn't do jack shit."

"This is a pretty state of affairs," said Patrick. "Who's to pour our whiskey?"

"I'll do it." Catches refilled the glasses.

"I have something you can take to the powwows," Patrick said. "You'll be the talk of the town." He left the room for a moment.

It was the sheet Mary had painted of herself and the baby. He draped it over the shoulders of David Catches.

"This was Mary's way of saying, *'Adiós, amigos.'* I want you to have it for whatever gala occasions you chaps have down on the reservation, social events that inevitably produce the Budweiser flu and well-known Cheyenne jalopy crashes. Having said that, we will now drink heap more deathbed whiskey. You didn't take care of her."

"What care could you take of her? She was a grown woman." Catches stopped. "Besides, we are now to the place where one of us is inclined to kill the other."

Patrick moved very slightly in his chair.

"On the basis of what?"

"On the basis of two men revenging themselves upon each other for what they haven't done themselves. Boy, I don't know what that means."

"You came close."

"I know," said Catches, "but I fell on my ass."

"More sourmash for my lieutenants," said Patrick. "Away with the offending mystery."

"As you wish."

"Catches, are you an educated man?"

"I certainly am. Let's drink at high speed."

"Okay."

"We have a shot at murder tonight. I'll wear this sheet to remind me of your insult."

"I think that would be appropriate."

"What do you have for a weapon?"

"I have my skinning knife," said Patrick.

"Get it," said Catches.

"I am in considerable pain." Patrick found his skinning knife in the hallway. It had a deeply curved blade and a worn birch handle.

"Not a bad knife," said Catches.

"It is designed," said Patrick, "for disheartening an aborigine."

"But what's at issue?"

"Oh, dear. The noble savage displays his vocabulary. At issue, let me see. At issue is whether you caused Mary despair."

"I thought it was like flu."

Patrick stared at this arrogant Indian whose infuriatingly expressive hat drew a jaunty line above his eyes.

"What do you think about us getting drunk?" Patrick asked.

Catches said, "A warning has come to me that there is no escape."

"I've had no such warnings. Everyone hears footsteps. But no sacred eagles bearing messages."

"How much of that is there left?"

"Another bottle."

"Brought out this sheet, did you?"

"How do you like the fit?"

"A little long in the back."

Patrick asked, "Do we each have a fair chance?"

"Depends," said the Indian. "But not if it's up to me."

"Last Indian I remember making the papers was a Northern Cheyenne named Paul Bad Horse who killed that supermarket clerk, cold blood, for what was in the till. Paul wasn't charging the cavalry. Paul got our clerk in the back of the head."

"Stop this small stuff." They topped off water glasses with brown whiskey. Patrick thought, This Cheyenne is going to buckle under the sourmash. He thinks he's got something for me to buckle under; but it's going to be a cold day in hell. I'm going to ice this redskin.

"See, where you're just exactly one pickle short of a full jar, Tank Captain, is that you think you're going to come to me as my equal in matters concerning Mary. Besides, you are less educated a man than me."

"She's dead and we're not."

"Neither of us is wily," said Catches. "Neither of us is getting paid to do this—Give me a refill . . . thanks. But if it went just right, one is prepared to kill the other. We should have a complete agreement about that."

"I think that's real fucking boring and obvious."

"I can't help that."

"We can't bring Mary back."

"No, we can't," Catches began, tears gleaming down his face.

Patrick's grandfather appeared in the kitchen doorway dressed in his long johns. He was in a red-faced rage.

"I'd like you two to go. All right? Go away. Go to the barn. Go anywhere. Go away. I've listened to as much of this as I will. It's terrible. *It's terrible what you both say, pouring that out.* But on this place the answer is no. Take it away, take it to such-and-such a place, but get it out of here."

The two younger men went outside. It was a cold night and the stars crowded down upon them, the buildings of the ranchstead scarcely visible in their light. Patrick was utterly lacking in anger. All he wanted to say was the right thing. "Don't know just where to go here. David, you bring the bottle?"

"I got it."

Patrick thought he could see him gesture with the whiskey. They were already drunk, and Patrick had it in his mind to get down to a thing or two if he could think just what those things might be. Then it struck him with a shock that it might have been no more than that he was still trying to get close to Mary.

"Let's get us a couple of horses," said Catches. "Ground's all beaten down around here. We'll get up in those hills. We've got one and a half bottles of whiskey to go."

"Nobody says we have to drink it all."

"Only that's what's going to happen."

They'd already diverted toward the corral, where the barely shifting shapes of horses moved at their sound. There were stars over the horses' backs and you couldn't see where their legs reached the ground. When his mare Leafy turned to him, though, he identified the space between the glints her eyes made; and the sound of her relieved exhalation at recognizing his approaching shape helped Patrick sort the horses.

"Here's my mare. Why don't you go in there and grab that claybank? I'm supposed to been riding her more." Patrick saw Catches' halter flip up around another horse, a bay.

"I got one I broke."

The two saddled up in the deeper darkness in front of the saddle shed. Patrick could hear the steady, rapid preparation of Catches, the heavy noise of the saddle slung up on the bay's withers, the slapping of billets and latigo, then the tight creak when he cinched up. They swung into their saddles and each rigged a bottle against the swells with the saddle strings. Catches still had Mary's sheet.

"North Fork suit you?"

"That'd be fine," said Catches.

"What do you carry that little knife around for?"

"You know Indians: homemade tattoos, drinking and knife fighting."

"That kid Andrew wanted an arrowhead. You might have got him a yard rock and chipped on it a little."

"I was relaxing at a dinner party," said Catches. "Life is more than just work."

Remove the offending silliness, Patrick thought. Make it all fair. But then he felt even sillier. They went through three or four gates before they hit the forest service trail, trickling up through the trees in the starlight while Patrick felt sillier and sillier, looking back every now and again to see the floating white shape of Catches' hat above the dark form of the moving horse.

"I like this whiskey, David."

"You bet."

"I like it in bars as well as out here in the widely promoted high lonesome."

"Right, Patrick."

"But in the bars—watch that deadfall—but in the bars,

a fellow tends to act up because of the social pressures. After you act up once, you're expected to act up again. Grown men on crying jags, pistoleros wetting their pants—" An owl fled rapidly up the trail on beating, cushioned wings, and they watched it go. "I would like to build myself a big stroller," Patrick continued. "Like babies have, y'know, shaped like a doughnut with a sling seat in the middle. Wheels that let you go in any direction. It would have drink holders and cups for poker chips. You could just scoot around and not worry about falling."

"That's quite an idea. You ought to write that down. Yeah, I'd get that one on paper."

The air currents changed and then the smell, cool and balsamic, came from the high draws in the darkness on either side of them. Sometimes when the trees were closed solidly overhead and they moved in absolute blackness, Patrick could tell the direction of the trail only by feeling the mare's body turning beneath him. When the trees opened once again like a skylight, Patrick stopped and offered Catches the bottle. Each of them took a deep pull, rerigged the bottle to Patrick's saddle and moved on. Patrick inhaled deeply through his open mouth, carbureting the sourmash and piny air into a powerful essence. A peculiar feeling rose through him, seemingly a glimpse of time's power: roping, soccer, Germany, the ride on I-90 with Mary, even the fine mare creaking underneath him. Then that evaporated and the Indian floated behind him on the bay.

"We could use a couple of those strollers you mentioned," said Catches. "Perfect for going down the mountain."

"One time when Mary and I were small—"

"Look back at those lights."

"I know. One time when we were small—"

"See how they drop into the groove the trail makes as we go up? There's only four left. Now three."

"Then can I tell my story?"

"Okay."

Patrick kept riding until the last ranch light dropped into the trail.

"We shared the same room, see. And my folks came back from a party at Carlin Hot Springs. And they were having words. Well, my dad gets out his duck gun and blows away the plumbing under the kitchen sink. They used to just endlessly do stuff like that, you know, really hating each other. And we'd lie in bed thinking, Please don't get divorced, please please please. That and the atomic bomb were our big scares. So anyway, the water is running everywhere and my grandfather comes in, smacks my father in the face and disarms him. So my mother just shrieks at my grandfather, who's trying to fix the plumbing. My father keeps saying, 'Sorry, Pop, sorry.' And pretty soon my mother comes down to our room and opens the door. The water was right behind her. She turns on the light and sees we're awake. She's real drunk, but she gives us this long looking-over. Then she announces, 'Why don't you two just get out? Why don't you just get the hell out and quit causing all this trouble?'— How's that for a family tale?"

"I thought your dad was supposed to be so terrific."

"Well, we're up here on a truth mission, aren't we? He wasn't so terrific. But when your father dies he becomes terrific through the magic of death." Patrick thought, with releasing clarity, Especially when he falls out of the sky in flames. Wow and good-bye.

"Y'know," Patrick mused, "some things are like a watershed. They mark between the before and the after."

"Name one."

"Like the first time . . . the first time you put your shirttail between the toilet paper and your ass."

"Aw, for crying out loud."

Then Patrick thought what he really meant and his throat hardened and ached and it was necessary for some time to ride in silence to combat sorcery and recollection through the metronomic sound of horses.

They dropped down into a swampy spot, the horses drawing their feet heavily from the muck; and as soon as they stepped up the other side, they woke a half-dozen blue grouse, who thundered off and scared the horses into staring and motionless silhouettes. Then once again they were going.

"If it was daylight, we could've shot a couple of them to eat at our powwow."

"Do you have a gun?"

"Nope."

God Almighty, Patrick was thinking, I am indeed away from the tank and must, as I had said I would, begin anew or at the very least go on to the next thing undaunted by either failure or death, neither of which I have mastered, though I cannot be accused of facing them with fear; but what did you know about them, relieved in fear at the arrival of adrenaline, relieved in death at the arrival of the embalmed dummy, relieved in separation by the dazed and unremitting sense that there had never been connection, not with people and not with places? What had Germany been? Three or four colors, twenty vulvas and strudel? Growing up, as life blind-sided you with its irreversible change, the heart pleaded for rituals that would never come: the West, the white West, a perfectly vacant human backdrop with its celebrated vistas, its remorseless mountains-and-rivers and its mortifying attempts at town building. Patrick longed for a loud New York bar.

When they reached the slope where the ranges divided, it looked like an enormous open lawn in the dark. There were the shapes of animals out on this expanse, deer or elk, and those shapes drifted away as Patrick and David picketed their horses, then sat facing the slope that elevated darkly to sky. Stars disappeared as the black shapes of clouds cruised the bright space. And for a while, all you could hear was the drinking.

"Had this cat living in the trailer at Grassrange," said David. "Could walk upside down on the acoustic tile all the way to the overhead light and kill moths and eat them and, y'know, like let the wings stick out of the corners of his mouth up there next to the light."

"Think the glare would get to him."

"He wouldn't even take his shot. Just hang there alongside the bulb and pretty quick a moth would fly into his mouth. Fat sonofabitch and I never seen him mousing during moth season. Then in the winter he'd move out of the trailer into this Amoco barrel used to be a dog's house there at Grassrange and hunt mice. He snagged one bat at the light in two summers; otherwise, it was all moths. He had to get down on the floor and fight that bat, though."

"What did Mary do while you were there?"

"She'd just be reading, mostly; cooking. Then people'd bring her young colts to halter-break and gentle. She had chickens. She took a lot of pictures of that cat on the ceiling, but we never had the money to get them developed. I could drop the film by, if you're interested. I mean, if you felt like getting them developed. Mary was afraid the light bulb would overexpose the film and we'd've spent our money on nothing at all. Really, we didn't have no money." Catches started crying.

"Jesus Christ, David."

"I don't know."

"Come on now."

"I just don't know."

"Sit up there, old buddy. I can't stand it. Come on, now, you're gonna get me going."

"Well, what's the fucking use?"

"I don't know."

"What's the use?"

"There isn't any use. I thought Indians knew that."

"Somebody steered you wrong, Fitzpatrick."

"Well, you better figure it out. There seems to be signs everywhere that there's no use."

"Spoiled my fucking hat tipping over on it."

"See?"

"I don't take it as a sign."

"It's a sign that there's no use. Well, let's take aholt here. Let's show them different," said Patrick. It was about as strong as he ever got. All he wanted to do was shriek, Demons! Zombies! The dead!

The Indian was trying to restore the crease in his hat. "My chapeau," he said and laughed. "You should have written her more."

"I know," said Patrick.

"Drift in bad here in the winter?"

"Oh, yeah. We had some cattle trapped in the Moccasin draw one time and the bears raided into them, got 'em all. Bears just padded over that snow and started killing cows. Quite a wreck in there when it thawed. Looked like a Charlie Russell painting of the '86 blizzard, these half-gnawed skeletons up against the rocks . . ."

"Hunh."

"I have to throw up," said Patrick.

"If you're loud about it, crawl off away from the horses. I don't want to walk home."

Patrick got off a way, his hands deep in the lichen, and let it pour everywhere.

Catches continued in a louder voice: "My dad was a great one for throwing up on his horse and going on a blind-ass bronc ride into the cattle."

By the time Patrick found his way back, navigating by the white hat and the shapes of the horses when he couldn't find the hat, Catches was getting pretty choky. "See, she was what I had and she left me about thirteen different times and all this was, was the last time. And that's it. That's all she wrote. But she was crazy and I'm not. And sorta like you said, I won't be getting her back. All I'm going to say is this, and it might be the thing we fight over: She was more to me than she was to you." Catches got out his knife. High above them, a heavy moon turned the scree brilliant as miles of quartz, and every so often something would come loose and roll, making a noise light, dry and clear as a single piece of bone.

"Do you deny what I said?" asked Catches.

Patrick followed the serration of forest, divided at the pass, and the vertical curve to the south of unearthly luminous granite.

"I don't deny it," said Patrick, absolutely letting

something break in the name of some small, even miserable decency, something in its way perfect and unmissed
by David Catches, who said, "Thank you."

The rest was the ride home.

28

Both Patrick's desire for privacy and his mistakes in human judgment sprang from the same vague feeling that things were very sad. This feeling had predated the death of his sister by some time. Still, he had not always felt this way. Now he did seem to always feel this way. And so he tried to stay on the ranch or make some blind attempt to get rid of the feeling that everything was sad-for-no-reason. The latter seemed to fail with absolute regularity; whereas staying on the ranch and working would just do. And he still thought Claire could change it all. Sometimes he felt that she had to. It made him uncomfortable.

Patrick got up suddenly, feeling he wasn't reacting appropriately to anything, that he wasn't doing any good. He heard the spring creak on the kitchen door and wondered who had come in. He shot the front of his shirt into his trousers with his hands, wobbled his head about and acted in general like someone trying to renew his concentration. This was getting to be a quieter house and the steps in the hallway, now plainly his grandfather's, were clear; but Patrick thought they were slow, and when the door opened, revealing Patrick standing in no particular place in the room and his grandfather exactly in the doorway with a newspaper, Patrick knew there was something not right. "Have you read this?" his grandfather asked, revealing little in his face to give away what was

to be seen. Patrick started to read, then sat down. The
newspaper had reported the funeral on the first page in
unbelievable detail, including Patrick's rash remarks.
The tone was unmistakably satirical and in the patented
style of Deke Patwell. Basically it took the position that
Patrick and Mary, long a local variety act, had pressed on
amusingly after death.

"What did we do to them?" asked his grandfather. "I
don't know."

"Patwell wrote that."

"Oh, I know."

"Where're you going, Pat?"

"To see Patwell."

"I think you better. I think this has to be fixed."

Strangely enough, nearly his first thought was, If they
send me to jail, I'll never see Claire again. And finally,
the almost infernal concentration of anger, the numb and
almost stupid feeling in the front of the brain. His grandfather came down the front hall and gave Patrick a revolver.

"I don't want that," Patrick said.

"You ought to take something."

"I'm taking me, Grandpa."

"I think you ought to shoot the sonofabitch until you
get tired of it."

"Well, I'm going to go down there and that's about all
I know about it."

Patrick left the house and went to the barn and got an
English blackthorn cane that had an ingenious ruler
which slid out to measure the height of horses in hands.

The appointment desk lay in the eyeline of Patwell's
open door, so that Patwell, sighting over the blue-washed
Deadrock crone at the phone bank, could see Patrick had
arrived. There were about ten reporters and secretaries in
a large blond room without a view and a wilderness of
baked-enamel office equipment in soothing gray. Patrick
stared back at the faces and was refueled in his anger to
know that these were the typists and copy editors and
that they possessed a little glee that didn't belong to
them.

Patwell called out, "What took you so long?"

Patrick just strolled around the receptionist into Patwell's office. He felt cold and peaceful.

"You want to close that door, Pat?"

"Not really, Deke. I just came by to find out why you wanted to talk about us in public like that."

"I run a newspaper and I thought you deserved it."

"Is that how it goes in editing? You give what you think people deserve?" He seemed to be helping Deke with his explanation.

"Yeah, that's pretty much how I feel. It's an old-fashioned newspaper."

"I feel you deserve that, you cuntful of cold piss," said Patrick, caning Patwell across the face. It took Patwell off his chair. "Get up," said Patrick. "Get back to your chair quickly. If I begin flailing your bottom with this thing, I'll lose my self-control." There was a livid mark across Patwell's face as he scuttled to his swivel chair. "Now," said Patrick, "that was meant to correct your attitude. You have hurt my feelings with your filthy fishwrapper and you have hurt my grandfather, who is an old man. Do you follow me so far?" Patwell nodded hurriedly. Patrick wondered how many fingers in the outer office were dialing the police. "People just kind of live their lives, Deke. Y'know, they're not out there just as cannon fodder for boys with newspapers." Patwell nodded furiously. Patrick stared at him, feeling Patwell turn into an object again, one that had managed to besmirch his dead sister, and he could feel the crazy coursing of blood that he knew, unchecked, could turn him into a murderer. But then the police arrived, among them the chief of police, who demanded an explanation, and handled his gun.

"Deke wanted me to act out the Ronald Colman part from *The Prisoner of Zenda*. Isn't that so, Deke?"

The chief of police turned eyes of patented seriousness to the editor. "Do I arrest him?"

"No."

"Why?"

"Because he'll be put in jail."

"He's been before."

"When he gets out he'll kill me."

So something, after all, got through. Patrick just departed; when he passed through the large room with numerous brave-dialing employees, he said, "When this doesn't make tonight's newspaper, you'll know what kind of outfit you work for." They wrote that down, too; they were untouchable.

The cop caught up with him outside. "What else you have in mind for the day?"

"What's it to you?" Patrick asked, about a half-inch from the chief's face. It was turning into a Western.

"I don't know. You're still packing that cane and you aren't limping." The chief meshed both hands behind his head, thrusting forward an impervious abdomen.

"Don't let that throw you," said Patrick. Then he withdrew its inner slide. "See? You can measure your horse. This would be a Shetland pony and *this*—this would be Man o'War!"

"Well, thanks for the explanation, cousin."

"Anytime."

"I hope you don't need no help of any particular kind in the future."

Patrick smiled. "Not a chance. Not unless my car doesn't start or something. I might borrow your jumper cables."

The impact of Catches' love of Mary was driving him in circles. Even after Mary's death, it meant more than anything he had. Patrick was closest to it with Claire, and that was not very close.

29

At one end of the granary was an open shed with big tools hanging on its walls, truck-sized lug wrenches, a scythe for the beggar's-lice that grew tall around the buildings and got into the horses' manes. There were also old irons for brands that the ranch owned, ones they quit using when they finally got a single-iron brand. There was a stout railroad vise, and Patrick's grandfather had been at it all morning, making a skinning knife out of a broken rasp.

"I'm going to kill me one more bugling bull, skin him with this and move to town."

"That's your plan, huh?" Patrick was kneeling on the ground, crimping copper rivets that had gone loose in the rigging of his pack saddles. That morning there had been a stinging fall breeze, and gear needed going through if he would make it to the hills before winter. "Got a spot picked out in town?"

"Those apartments across from the library."

"Sounds awful nice," said Patrick. "This has sure gotten to be a can of worms." Patrick wondered what he meant by that. The place wasn't at fault, but maybe something about it had begun to smell.

"That's what any ranch is, and this is a good one. It's got two hundred fifty miner's inches of first-right deeded water, plus a big flood right and the adjudication—y'know, if a guy cared to irrigate."

"I'll wait for some farmer to chase that water. My horses would rather be on prairie grass any day than wallowing around in alfalfa." They were starting in again.

"Well, I'll kill the one bull. Then look out town, here I come. After that, you can irrigate, not irrigate or piss up a rope."

"And you can be a star at the lending library."

"What?"

"Nothing."

Patrick worked away on the pack rigging, oiled the straps, coiled his lash ropes and canvas manties. It seemed crazy on a cool day, the two men polishing away on things they needed in order to get out, to go into the hills, to disappear. And yet Patrick didn't really want to disappear. All recent losses drove him to thinking of Claire. And he had no sense she did the same. Living on the ranch, which from his tank had seemed a series of bright ceremonies, was now more like entrapment in a motel on the interstate. Nor was he filled with a sense he could do something about it. It had stopped meaning anything.

30

Claire came to the side door at Patrick's knock, and he was astonished to see how genuinely stricken she seemed. "Patrick, I haven't any idea what to say to you."

"It's all over. There isn't anything to say." Then he added, with ungodly bitterness, "The angels came and took her away."

He walked into the house and got his own coffee as though he lived there. Claire circled the kitchen in a preoccupied way, knocking cupboard doors shut. Patrick felt somehow choky when he looked over at her, so extraordinarily pretty in a yellow wash dress that seemed to belong to another time, like some unused memento of the dust bowl, something a girl driven off her bridal farm in Oklahoma and since gone on to old age in some anonymous California valley might have saved.

But the daughter of a desperate man of 1932 might well have worn such a yellow dress on a pretty day like today or worn it in hopes of seeing someone she loved. What if that turned out to be me? Well, a person could work at it. And then what? Then-what equals implications and I don't know what they are. I'm getting to know very damned little.

"When do you suppose Tio will come back?"

"It's a mystery."

"You still haven't talked to him?"

"No, and I've tried to. He showed up in Tulsa for a short time and now he's gone from there."

"Does this make you nervous?"

"*Yes.*"

"Me too. But I'm not sure why."

"If you knew Tio better, you'd know why."

"I would?"

"You certainly would."

The phone rang and Claire got up from the table in her yellow dress to answer it. She answered twice and put the phone down. "Whoever it was hung up," she said, trying not to let that seem significant.

Suddenly she grinned. "Can you press your weight?" she asked.

"No."

"I can. One fourteen." Patrick thought about a hundred and fourteen pounds in a yellow wash dress.

"Can you do the Cossack Drag?"

"I never tried."

"I did. I almost got killed."

They went up a stretch of white, chalky-looking road into a beautifully fenced pasture, almost a paddock; there were half a dozen old-time quarter mares with colts at their sides. Claire ran down their pedigrees; it was all front-of-the-book: King, Leo, Peppy, Rey del Rancho, Zantanon H and a granddaughter of Nobody's Friend. Patrick looked at them with their deep hips and shoulders, real cowman's horses of a kind that seemed to be vanishing, the kind that made you think of Shiloh, Cold Deck, Steel Dust, and Rondo, all legends of border fighting, match racing and the trail drives.

"Where did you find this set of mares?"

"Well, one by one, really. They were all scattered and neglected because they wouldn't raise running horses for Ruidoso. They're all old horses, and I bred every one of them to a last son of Poco Bueno, who's a three-legged fifty-dollar cripple in Alice, Texas, who belongs to a scrapmetal dealer. I figure those colts are a half-century old the day they're born. That chestnut mare is blind. Her foal will stand off by itself and be perfectly still just to tease her mother. Her mother will keep nickering because she can't locate her. Then that baby speeds up and nurses, and the crisis is over.—Why aren't you married?"

"Me?"

"Yes."

"Never came up."

"Have you had girl friends?"

"Oh sure, lots of those. But I didn't have a good picture of home life. I think that has kept me from settling down. Also, I can't get my own intentions straight. First I was a kid growing up. Then I was cowboying for a while, riding around in sedans from place to place with a saddle in the trunk. Then I was in school, out of school and in the Army. Now I'm on the ranch. I don't have an orderly approach. I don't see me with a Nobel prize or managing a Houston heart clinic."

"What about running your beautiful ranch?"

"Got my doubts there, too. I'd like to just see to the horses, but it ought to be farmed up quite a bit more. I always thought farming was a highly evolved form of mowing the lawn."

"It is."

The wind changed directions, gusting around the pasture, warm and piny, with the faint cool afterbreath of fall.

"Are you superstitious about things," Claire asked, "that have to do with life and death?"

"I haven't been so far."

"My grandmother lived with us in our old house near Talalah. And one day the nails in the walls started falling out of their holes. That same day my grandmother died. There were nails all over the floor."

"I've never seen things like that. I don't believe my eyes are open to that sort of occurrence. Mary saw things like that. My experience with death was, it was real bluntlike and didn't send any calling cards." Suddenly gloom dashed in on him like some palpable dismal animal. They walked past the horse pasture with the deep-bellied mares grazing with their shadow colts, all the way to where the jack fence changed to steel-posted five-strand barbed-wire cattle fencing; and uphill of them, yearlings drifted along a hill to escape the flies in this new cool breeze.

The irrigation water came through a gap in the hillside like a bright tongue, and south of that a few hundred yards, they crossed into a piece of old meadow, full of original prairie flowers, all sweetly angled back toward the foothills by the prevailing wind, the same wind that swept Claire's yellow dress close around her long legs, the same dress that Patrick folded on the ground, the only thing that she had been wearing, so that she shivered and watched his gentle folding of the yellow cotton upon itself, then let him make love to her in something of the same way. Afterward, he glanced over and saw the one flat shoe, almost a slipper, she had crossed on the other, pinning a pale scarf in the light ground breeze, and with death and superstition and signs one could not read temporarily at bay, he felt a sweeping ache that in a child would have been the prelude to tears.

He said, "Leave everything and come with me." He was the one with the conviction. It scared her for a moment.

Immediately it struck Patrick that this attempt to spark his intentions across a gap not yet measured would never succeed. Nor was Claire shocked. Maybe she could have said the thing herself. Properly speaking, neither of them thought so. But Patrick felt like a sap—not a sap like the gland puppets of sudden love, the first-sighters and the stars of the one-night stands; but a sap of the heart, the amorous equivalent of someone who throws his clubs during a golf tournament.

"It should never have gotten this far."

"Why?" he asked.

"Because it's just to where it maybe could be extremely shattering. Besides it's . . . everything is . . ."

"What? Everything is what?"

"More than just coming home from the Army."

"No, it's not," said Patrick. "Everything *is* coming home from the Army."

"Okay, let's break it up. Boys, I want you to come out clean and punching."

"Don't be sarcastic."

"Well, we're down to that."

Suddenly there were details, tree trunks to bump into, rocks to trip over. In a Norway spruce next to the door, an old strand of Christmas lights deteriorated.

"I wish it could be like in books," said Patrick. "I wish it could be a big simp love story."

"I don't want to be in a big simp love story."

"My job would be to save the ranch."

"You're thinking of Gary Cooper."

"I guess there's a difference."

"A big difference. Gary Cooper saved the ranch. He had simp romances, too. Gary Cooper had his in barns. Book romances often take place in Europe. Cafés instead of barns. Me and Tio been to Europe. He brought his own ketchup and Pepto-Bismol. It was a gourmet tour."

"Sounds like quite a guy."

"He is," she said plainly.

"Well, I don't want to hear about him."

Inevitably Patrick drove home listening to a professional reminiscer on the radio who did Western topics twice a week:

"The awesome force of men and animals belittles all the images etched into the retinal filmstrips of my mind . . . The arena dust! . . . Churning hoof sounds . . . a truckload of hogs! Magnifique!"

31

Patrick was back the next day. He was losing it. It was late afternoon and their throats ached. He thought that there was fire in the daylight.

"We could fall in love," said Patrick, sickeningly swept past all reason.

"And then he'll hire a detective."

"What?" From the trance.

"Have you been listening?" She flicked a fox-spur from his hair. "We pull this and it's 'Katy, Bar the Door.'"

"What?" Where was he?

"Put on your boots. If we can keep walking, I won't feel so nervous. My God, what is this we're doing?"

Down toward the stream that swept past the fine old house, the heavy-trunked cottonwoods seemed to hold their dismaying branchloads of greenery in the awkward and beautiful whiteness which at a distance gives the valley river bottoms of the West almost their only sentimental quality. The rest consisted of towns with the usual franchise foreshore at either end; or in the case of Deadrock, the whirring elevations of the interstate, quiet only when the arctic storms of middle winter feathered every concrete radius with snow. Patrick felt drunk. The house hung over him. Claire pulled herself against him in the warm air. He panicked at the driveway. There might have been too many cars. There might have been chartered aircraft or police. There might have been dead people or banshees to militate against this surge that held him in its force.

They were in a bed in a room with a south-facing window that the sun crossed like a bullet. When the horses whinnied to be fed at the end of the day, gathered below the darkening window in a plank corral, Claire's tears chilled all over Patrick's face. The old dive-bomber comic they found in the trunk was crumpled under the pillows. A pale star had bravely arisen to follow the sun across the window; brave, thought Patrick, because it privately knew it was two hundred thousand times the size of our solar system, though its millennial flames are the only thing that would stop me now. All it is, is this small evening star. The horses are hungry. We are sore. Saying she loved me made her cry. In the iron-cloistered control station of the fast American tank was the glossy photograph of a German princess's strangely expressive anus, and beside that the release buttons for the rockets. The whir of treads on deep Teutonic sod brought peculiar memories. Marion Easterly, the mystery heartthrob, the archangelic semaphor known as the Dead Father and now the snowy grid beneath which his sister would lie forever were all contained in that upendable shallow bowl, the rim of which divided past and future. I am finally outside the bowl.

32

Patrick drove home in the night. The yard lights were strong in the blackness of the valley's gradual elevation southward like the scrambled approach to a bridge. After he had said to Claire, Leave everything and come with me, she had asked, Where? And at first he had been hurt, searching, as men do, for blind love, but then, even to his credit, he did indeed wonder where they could go and it became clear that he still, as of the Army, hadn't exactly returned to the ranch and they might just as well go there; and that that in turn might give him the handle he had long sought on his situation there, might carry him back to the sense of purpose his great-grandfather had had upon his return from Aguinaldo's Native Insurrection, the dynamite firecrackers on the Fourth of July and the general feeling of being able to see farther than your nose in front of you. He nearly strangled on his last idea, as though Claire should provide this firelight; he felt ashamed. There was a porcupine waddling across his turnoff; he stopped the truck, stared at its awkward purpose and wondered if the porcupine had anyplace to go. Patrick ached. He thought, literally, that he was aching like a fool. Chest pains. Incapable-of-judgment. The best thing would be for us to move to the ranch together. Nevertheless, he imagined the center of his mind looked like an asshole taped on the dashboard of the tank.

He walked into the dark kitchen and turned the light on over the stove ventilator. He made himself a drink. He didn't know what time it was and he felt guilt but could not pin it down. He would rather have felt the guilt than the sadness-for-no-reason. The latter was a ball breaker, whereas guilt was easily anesthetized with not all that much bourbon. Then the phone rang and of course it was Tio.

"Tio, where are you?"

"Can't let on, Pat. *Where are you?*"

"Right where you called me. In my kitchen."

"Well, I was just settin here wonderin if anybody there in Montana had got so eat up with the dumb ass they life was endangered."

"I can't see that they could be."

"How's my stud colt?"

"He's rank and squeally. He's going to make a great gelding."

"Well, Fitzpatrick, I'm down here shootin quail and thinkin about things. We got good dogs and a bunch of Mexicans to shag dead birds. It's the life, but they practically raise snakes and you can't get through that blackjack and cat's-claw with a horse. So you're down among them. You're down among the snakes, Fitzpatrick. You follow me?"

"Yes, I do." Patrick tilted his glass until he no longer saw movement among the ice cubes. He was getting nervous.

"I suppose I shouldn't be leavin Claire to fend like that. Most generally a man's a fool to leave one that Cadillacky to its own devices."

"How did you get down there, anyway, Tio?"

"In a Bell helicopter with full avionics and a walnut interior. Had to fly around all them bullshit mountains up there to get to a place fit for human habitation. I knew that colt was dumber than Fido's Ass, but I want you to turn him back to me double tough. I expect that. And if Claire's lonely, call her and give her that Dial-a-Better-Day exchange in Deadrock; I'll be back when I get back."

"Okay."

"Fitzpatrick, life is a shit sandwich and I take a bite every day. You do too. But if you had to eat it in one swallow, you'd choke on it and die a very unpleasant death." He rang off and that was that.

Patrick stood still and then trickled whiskey down the inside of his glass like a chemist in a high school play performing an experiment; and in fact the glazed look on his face did seem very much like bad acting. " 'Okay,' " he said aloud. "Why did I say okay? That Oklahoman shit-heel suggested that I give Claire the Dial-a-Better-Day number. And I said okay!" But he looked up Dial-a-Prayer in the directory and made the call. With God, it turned out, every loss is a gain. Hello. Thank you for calling Dial-a-Better-Day. Disruption and sadness will be banished. I wonder if they're thinking about that sadness stalking me, that evil ferret sadness that ingests five times its weight each day. Hearts will be healed and God will lift us up. Garlands instead of ashes. Sixty-first chapter of Isaiah. God will see you in the next reel. He is Our Projectionist. I will wring His Little Neck if I get another instance of sadness-for-no-reason.

"Darling?"

"Yes."

"It's me."

"I know it is. Oh God."

"What are you doing?"

"I'm in bed. I'm here, scared of the dark."

"Should I come over?"

"I don't think so."

"Guess what."

"What?"

"Guess."

"Tio called," said Claire. Panic was in her voice.

"How did you know?"

"It was easy. Where is he?"

"He wouldn't say. He was quail hunting. All he'd say was that life was a shit sandwich and we had to take a bite every day."

"He was being very intimate with you. Normally he

saves the sandwich speech until much deeper into the situation."

"What do you mean by that?" Patrick demanded, thinking this had happened before.

"I mean like in an oil deal or something. By the time they've cased the well, fractured and done their logging— y'know, kind of late in the game—he tells some new-comer in the business up north here in the Overthrust or something that life is a shit sandwich etcetera. Just when the guy is hanging on by his teeth. So he is either being intimate with you or he thinks you're hanging on by your teeth."

"I think I'm following."

"Did he menace you?"

"I'm not sure."

"How not sure?"

"Well, he said that if you had to eat the sandwich in one bite, you'd choke to death."

"He was menacing you."

33

Patrick lay in bed and stared around at the furnishings of his room. There was only one lamp and, overhead, a moth-filled milk-glass ceiling fixture that gave off an awful light. The bedside lamp was a real must. How many things, he wondered, shall we call real musts? What about ball bearings? A real must in defending one's self against the natives was a handful of stout ball bearings. The 2nd Division went up against Villa with only their uniforms and their ball bearings; without a belief in The Maker, a real must, all there would have been to show would have been the ball bearings, while Villa took his false gods to Deauville for the races. Jesus Christ, he thought, let us turn our thoughts to Claire; the mind is no boomerang. Throw it far enough and it won't come back.

Did Tio in fact smell a rat, or only a quail? Was Patrick the Montana version of the Tulsa hidey-hole, where ole Shit proved bulletproof? He felt ashamed of having had this thought. Shamed and chilled. Himself as part of a test of sexual allegiance. Maybe he meant to out-Tio Tio, to get just hopelessly Western about this situation, this fix, to see who, just *who*, was the standup gunslinger of the two. It is typical of me, he thought, to foresee a major showdown well before an acquaintanceship has been struck between the principals. Am I not rude? I am.

He hadn't been rude yet, but he would have to cut

back on his drinking or it was going to all burst forth in a clenched and dangerous teetering toward love, requited or otherwise. This was the sort of isolated dam break that Patrick was susceptible to. When he could identify it, he thought it was ridiculous. He didn't see anything now at all and he was therefore wide open to any repetitious mistake, precisely at a time in his life when he could least stand repetition. But then, where was the repetition; and couldn't this just be a fear, as guilt is a fear, of something that didn't exist?

He drifted away. One of the first lines he ever learned from a song was, "I got a hot-rod Ford and a two-dollar bill." He was hitchhiking from Two Dot and he heard it in the back seat of a hot-rod Ford. He had never seen a two-dollar bill. Up front an older boy necked with his girl. Patrick could smell something . . . well, something. He had not imagined that there would be anything to smell. He tried not to stare or draw breath through his nose. Breath through his nose, he knew, would be a mortal sin. He looked instead at the sagebrush flats and streaks of water running from spring-flooded culverts in the creek bottoms.

"How far you going?"

"What?" Seal off that nose, she's wriggling.

"Where you getting off at?"

"Deadrock."

"We ain't going to Deadrock. I'm shutting down this side of Harlowton—You ever seen a rubber?"

"Yeah." He hadn't. He was mouth-breathing and gaping into the sagebrush.

"Ever seen one like this?" It was a Ted Williams brand and it had the ball player on the label, ready to pound one out of Fenway Park.

"No, I sure haven't."

"Came out of a machine," said the girl. "In Great Falls because of the air base. It's a year and a half old. It's give out and it's still in the wrapper. That's about how I was raised, buddy."

"Up around them bases," said the driver, "a rubber don't have a long life to look forward to."

"It does in Harlowton," said the girl doggedly.

"I ought to rape your ass!"

"You and what army?"

The driver went into the hot-rod slump, left hand fingering the wind vane, upper body wedged between the wheel and the door. It worked; she crawled on over and Patrick craned at the landscape, wondering if this was going to end up in confession, then finally filling his lungs with the immemorial musk that fogged the interior of that hot-rod Ford, thinking: Purgatory at the very least.

He would have to go back to that, just to find one level of the power Claire had come to have for him. At the very minimum she was the lost ghost of the gold dredge.

34

Today was going to require a departure, a mighty departure, from the recent pattern of thinking, drinking, funeral attending, cooking, baby-sitting his grandfather, caning editors and tampering with love. Because the ranch was falling apart. It was somehow terrific to rediscover that the ranch was not a dead, immutable thing. He could see from the upper road where one headgate had washed out, and there was a great mean scar where the water had gouged at the pretty hillside, and the topsoil from that particular part of the ranch was now in the Yellowstone River on its way to North Dakota. That had to be fixed. There were four places where the wire was down on the west-division fence; that would have to be pulled up and restapled. Things were a mess and he was getting excited. He was going to need his fence stretcher and fencing gloves and it was still going to be tops in mindless. But if he had any luck at all, this was going to last for years. It was like the heart trouble he wished for and never got.

He started hurting about halfway through the day. He hauled salt and mineral blocks, ponying a second horse up to the forest line. Then gathered thirty black yearlings from the brush along the creek where the flies had driven them from their feed. He gathered them into one end of the corral and he penned them off with a steel panel. He hung the heavy spray canister from a canvas strap over the sore muscles of his shoulders and waded among the fly-swarming backs, pumping with one hand and directing the nozzled wand with the other. When he was nearly done, one white-eyed steer flicked out a rear hoof and kneecapped Patrick, and he had to go sit down until the pain subsided and the knee swelled up tight within his jeans. He sat on the dirt of the corral, the canister still in place, tapped one dirty boot with the spray wand, looked through the steel panel at the milling steers as they felt the flies' liftoff; like them, he rolled fool eyes to heaven and thought: Claire, my knee hurts.

He hung the sprayer on a corral post and rode back down to the ranch. He was so tired that when he unsaddled the horse, he just drop-kicked the saddle out of his way and threw the bridle in a heap. He grained the horse and kept her down for the next day and went inside.

Then, while he was making dinner for his grandfather, who was sorting a shoe box of assorted cartridges, he noticed through the kitchen window that everything was covered with a thin layer of dust.

"Did the wind blow real hard here today?"

"No."

"How come everything is covered with dust?"

"A helicopter landed in the yard."

"What?"

"Helicopter."

"Who was in it?"

"Nobody got out. Here's an old Army Springfield round."

"How long did it stay there?"

"Oh, bout an hour. Made quite a racket. They never shut that big propeller off. I really didn't want to walk near it." Tio had made an aerial visit under power and Patrick had missed it: a lost effect, like rabbits jumping from a top hat in an empty room.

Patrick had given up on his cooking since his grandfather had gone off his specialties. So now he made dopy chicken casseroles or things he could cook all day in a crock; and today he had prepared, of all things, a big bowl

of red Jell-O to set beside the aerosol can of Reddi-Wip;
and it was in its tremulous surface that he first detected
the return of the helicopter, a faint sound, a drumming,
like one's pulse; then rapidly magnifying as it moved
toward them. Its horizontal motion could be felt to stop,
and high above the house the waves of sound centered.

Patrick walked out the front door and could see the
great insect shape high above the ranch. It made him nervous. The moment he stepped into the yard, the helicopter began to move toward the mountains, disappearing
finally through a narrow pass. Patrick went back inside
and thumbed open *The Joy of Cooking.*

"I wish that movie hadn't gone away," said his grandfather. "Maybe there was movie people in that helicopter."

"I doubt it."

"They could have been scouting locations."

"I suppose."

"Everybody loves a Western."

"How do you know it was a Western?"

"*Hondo's Last Move?* What else could it be?"

"The word around here was it was about a child mo-
lester named Hondo."

"I didn't know that. God, I didn't know *that.*"

"Can you eat chicken and dumplings again?"

"Sure. Can we go to the movies?"

"I'm pretty tired, Grampa."

"Or there's one with Greer Garson on TV. It's about a
factory, I think."

"Maybe that would be better. Besides it'll be late once
these dishes are cleaned up."

"I'll help."

"Okay."

"Tomorrow can we look at apartments?"

"Sure."

"I can't remember which rifle this went to," said his
grandfather in disgust, placing the cartridge next to the
Jell-O. "I think it was that one that the horse fell with
coming out of Falls Creek with Arnie."

"I didn't know Arnie, Gramp." Patrick was sick of

these unreferenced tours of memory. Fucking Arnie, any-way.

"He was the scissorbill from up around Plentywood. I don't know. Anyway, I know it's gone."

"You want a drink?"

"No. That was a funny-looking machine, that helicop-ter. Shame Mary couldn't have seen it. I didn't have my hat and my hair was blowing all over. I got dirt in my nose. It went straight up and I lost it in the sun. It was exactly like the movies. Maybe it was full of prisoners and there's this guy who didn't shave, with a tommy gun."

Patrick was getting depressed as he cooked. Tio, he guessed, was home. He literally pined for Claire and there wasn't anything he could think to do about it. And there was something about his grandfather's running on, which didn't usually bother him, that was getting at his nerves. Still, he could fall back on the day's work, a new regime toward bringing the ranch back to order. There was some warm memory tugging at him that he couldn't quite iso-late; and as he cooked, he searched his mind for it, feeling that it would cheer him up. Then it came: It was the velvet hydraulic rush of his tank over Germany, the or-derly positions of the crew, and being the captain.

"Fitzpatrick."

"Hey, Tio."

"Awfully sorry about your sister."

"Thanks for saying so."

"And remember, it was her right to do that. She's the only one to know if it was a good idea. It can be just the thing; I'm persuaded of that."

"Okay."

"Say, how much do you want for your ranch?"

"It's not for sale, Tio."

"I just went down and dumped that Cat-Track joint that was such a thorn in our sides, that quicksand trap on the north Canadian, and the money's burning a *hole* in my pocket."

"This is my grandfather's and my home."

"Well, move ass to town. I want to spend this *dinero.* The old man tell you I came and looked at the place?"

"Were you in a helicopter?"

"That was me. That you come out in the yard at suppertime?"

"Yup."

"I thought so. Say, are you sleeping with my wife?"

Not a word in reply.

"Leafy, am I not thoughtless? I am. Left you in a cold corral with no kisses. Here is a kiss. What a beautiful horse you are." Leafy exhaled and changed weight on her feet. It seemed so extraordinary to Patrick that this water-marked mare with eyes like tide pools could also be twelve hundred pounds of orchestral muscle, could trust and work for you, could ride the continually moving hands of the mortal clock with you, could take you in the hills, help you win a rodeo or work cattle, could send you gliding with new tallness on a part of the earth that was worth all the trouble. "What do you know of trouble, Leafy? Or do you take the position that it is my department?"

Onward to the restoration of order: mucking stalls, wheelbarrowing the manure across the road onto the rich pile that would be so useful to a determined gardener with a nice ass. Then he went up on the metal roof of the granary before it got too hot and tarred over the nail holes as he had to each year. He had put the roof on and had nailed in the troughs of the corrugation instead of the lands, as one is supposed to, and so it had to be tarred yearly. He was determined to ride Leafy today because he thought he glimpsed sadness-for-no-reason in her eyes. When Leafy was born, her mother dropped her in the last piece of snow in a spring pasture. Patrick found the foal, a clear, veinous membrane around her shoulders, shivering in the snow, her seashell hooves just beginning to harden in the air. He put an arm under her butt and one under her neck and lifted her out onto the warming prairie grass while the mother nickered in concern. Then he drew the membrane down off her body and let the mare lick her dry. The watermarks in her coat were like leaves and Patrick named her while the mare contracted and drove out the afterbirth; Patrick lifted the placenta, shaped like the bottom of a pair of long underwear with one short leg, and scrutinized it for completeness; a missing piece retained in the mare could be fatal. Leafy wobbled to her feet after pitching over a few times and stood, straight-legged, springy-pasterned, with her exaggerated encapsulated knees. Patrick put iodine on her navel stump, which made her leap. The mother stood and Leafy ducked under to nurse. The mare kept lifting a rear leg from the pain of new milk; then the two, big and little shadows, glided away to their life together. Patrick went off through the orchard; and by the time he had started down the hill to the house, he could hear the birds arguing in the afterbirth. In his mind he had marked the foal for himself.

"At least can we look for apartments tomorrow?"

"I promise. I'm just tired, Grampa. Besides, you want to see them in the light."

"They have lights, Pat. They have electricity, for crying out loud. They're about two blocks from the movies."

"Still, you want the outside to be nice. You want to look around."

"If I was worried how they looked on the outside, I'd stay on the ranch."

"I don't know what this bee in your bonnet is, anyway. Why *aren't* you staying on the ranch?"

"Because I see things I can't do anymore, and in an apartment I won't. I won't have to watch you do things worse than I did them. I'll be protected from such a sight." Patrick was angered this time by his grandfather. But even irritated, he dreaded seeing the apartments.

35

The lights wheeled against the house and stopped. Then Patrick could see only the darkness. But when the car door opened after quite a long moment and its interior lights went on, he saw that it was Claire. He raced down the stairs to the front door. He turned on the hall light and stepped outside. When she got to the door, Patrick felt the ardent flush of blood through his chest.

He said, "I had a sore knee," then held her and kissed her. She seemed limp or exhausted.

"You what?"

"I wanted to tell you yesterday I had a sore knee. You weren't here. It's not sore anymore, but I wanted to be a baby about it."

Claire followed Patrick through the doorway, past ten year's history of overshoes, overshoes with lost buckles, overshoes covered with the manure of cattle long since vanished through takeout windows, and overshoes of drunks who failed to return. They sat in the kitchen and Patrick found her request for whiskey an inspiration; so now the cheerful label of George Dickel's bourbon was between them, and if it had not been for Claire's strangely stricken look, all would have been not just happy but beyond belief. It was the middle of the night and they were alone together on Patrick's ranch. He knew there was something going on; but he was determined to turn things into his first impression no matter what.

"He's home."

"I know. I talked to him."

"Well, I don't know what his problem is."

"What's he doing?"

"He's just kind of raging around. He sent his pilot into town. First he was going to sleep in the helicopter. I kept saying what's the matter, and he says it's boring. I'm bored. I said I was sorry. When he goes down there and they get on those phones, a lot of them start using pills and they get very cross. But this time I don't know. He used to be so sweet. I think he must know something. Then he came inside and said we were going to forget it; but first he just wanted to know what in the hell I had achieved in his absence. I said nothing and he said he didn't think so. Well, we even got over *that*, which maybe was too bad"—she refilled her drink one-handed, leaning on the other, the pale thick braid coming over her shoulder across her pretty breasts—"because when we went upstairs, he grew extremely nasty with me."

Patrick's stomach twisted. "How?"

"Never mind. It was simply too coarse for words. It was nasty." She took a long breath. "So what I told him was he had the wrong person. He needed someone you just pay, because he sort of saw it as I was to do as I was told. So Tio yells, 'Are you talking about a whore? Fine! I'd like three!' He said that I was a whore in every way except the one that counted. So that's where I am."

"Where?"

"Trying to find three whores for Tio!"

"Are you serious?"

"Absolutely. And I told him so." She smiled weakly. "I was hoping you'd know where I could find them."

"Is he safe?"

"Oh sure. It's just that he can get right repulsive with me. He'll treat them like queens and overpay, too—"

"Are you calling his bluff?" Patrick felt as though he'd fallen in the middle of a dispute wherein he feared discovering some passion. This had some of the signs of revenge and he was not entirely happy to help.

"I'll help," he said.

So instead of being alone together on the ranch with the dwarf owls drifting across the yard through the yard light, the coyotes trickling down out of the hills toward dawn when the cool inversion changed the smell from cottonwood to evergreen, instead of that, they were barreling through the night toward a Deadrock cathouse. At least, thought Patrick, we are in her car and I'm damn well going to insist on a ride home. Purgatory at the very least.

Once again—that is, not since he had first come home and sought rumors of Mary and had overcome his resistance to the facts—once again, this time with Claire, he crossed the footbridge over the clear-running ditch and knocked on the whorehouse door. He remembered the television debate as to the fetus's right to life, the coffee cans naming the girls, the kitchen timers. The door opened and David Catches greeted Patrick and Claire. Patrick introduced Claire to David and they went in.

"What are you doing here, David?"

"What are you doing here?"

"I can't give you the instant replay. The story's a little hard to tell."

They passed into the living room; the television was on and girls were scattered in teasing fragmentary bits of clothing. Loretta, the former homecoming queen, wearing almost nothing, gave Patrick the kiss of a very old friend; but still he felt something tighten in his crotch. There were somewhat brutal sounds continuously to be heard in neighboring rooms; and Patrick thought, This wonderful spot is good for our town! Loretta's playfulness had taken some of the sting from his situation.

"I met Mary here," said David. "I guess I came back, y'know . . . old times. Anyway, I make sure everything is okay. In other words, I got a job."

Suddenly a door opened and a very happy, inebriated man of fifty pirouetted into the room. He was naked and tumescent and he had spotted Claire. "Where were you when I ordered?" he demanded to know.

"She doesn't work here," David said politely.

"Someone's trying to hog her," he said. "I'm a good customer and I won't stand for it."

"She's with the police," said David. Patrick couldn't take his eyes off Loretta, and the shadowy, lounging figures watching television were getting under his skin.

"That's just great," said the drunk. "Now I've lost my hard-on. Where my shoes?" He stumbled disconsolately toward the door he'd emerged from. "Where'm I gone get nother? Can't get nother. Only hard-on I had. But who cares? None of you care . . ." He drifted away. "You're all women's libbers," he added.

Once the situation had been explained to David, whom the girls called Cochise, and a cash settlement made by Claire, they were ready to head for Tio Burnett's ranch. "Let's get a head count here!" David called as the three girls pulled on revealing one-piece quick-draw dresses. Claire noticed Patrick staring. She was very slightly and most delicately irate.

"You think they're pretty, don't you?" she said very close to his face. His heart soared.

"Well, they *are* pretty."

"I thought the best things in life were free."

"This is the major exception."

Patrick, Claire, Loretta, Deirdre and Tana went out through the door, Patrick shaking hands once more with Catches, considering that friendship was somewhere possible, and in the mixture of perfume, mysterious sounds behind doors, weak drinks and TV, he thought he had seen Mary's ghost for the first time in a form he didn't believe would kill him.

Claire gave the girls a wide and too-sunny smile, the lightest crow's feet at the corners of her slate eyes, and said to the women, "Get on in." The three climbed into the backseat; Claire got in and Patrick prepared to drive. No amount of air-conditioning could daunt the garden of scents that filled the interior of the car. Patrick felt thrilled.

"Where exactly we going, Pat?" Loretta asked.

"Remember the old Leola Swenson place in the Crazies?"

"Yeah."

"Well, there."

"You two know each other?" Claire asked.

"Yes."

They headed up north on Main Street. The brick false fronts, the glitter of the bars and keno parlors, the sight of the grand old stone railroad station's arcades lit only by passing cars, seemed to make things extraordinarily cheerful. Patrick could hear the polishing of silk stockings on shifting legs in back, and it occurred to him that he hardly knew anyone who wore them anymore; they were worn to be removed.

"Is this a Cadillac?" Deirdre asked.

"Yes," said Claire.

"I was going to get one. Montana has such tough usury laws you can make great deals with General Motors' financing plans. But I wanted front-wheel drive. So I got a Toronado."

Tana said, "I'll never pass the driver's test. I can*not* parallel park."

"That's because you refuse to pull up even with the car in front of you. That is absolutely the only way it will work," Loretta said.

"It gives me the creeps to pull up that far. I keep thinking someone will get my spot."

"They get your spot anyway, because *you* never get it."

"Who is this person we're going to see?" Loretta asked.

"My husband," said Claire. The car was silent. Shapes passed the window in that silence: sawdust burners glowing in the night, various spots of lights on the remote hills like beacons, patterned somehow, as though they were to be read from space.

Deirdre piped up innocently, "You sure are under-standing!"

"Thank you," said Claire grimly.

"Will there be any rough stuff?" Loretta inquired.

"No."

"Good. I sure wouldn't want to cross that sagebrush in the dark."

Tana asked, "Will you be with us, Claire?"

"I'm sorry, no," said Claire. This was really getting appalling to her. The impulse, it seemed to Patrick, had long since disappeared into the gritty logistics.

"I think, ladies," Patrick said, "that it would be best, all things considered, if nobody saw me tonight."

"Mum's the word."

When they got to the bottom of the road, Patrick turned off the lights and crept toward the house. There were low brushy willows at one side of the road, and they glowed in the moonlight with an extraordinary pallor. The darkness, the glow of the instruments, the invisible female presences, made Patrick think of the Army. Or the inside of aircraft. It seemed to him that Claire was sitting extremely upright and that that was somehow dis-tinct from the warm, crowded people in back. She was lit by instruments.

"You'll have to walk from here," said Patrick. "Just to be safe." The house, emerged from the elevation to the road, was completely lit from within; but nothing other than windows were illuminated, a crazily assorted series of panels in the darkness itself. It looked unfinished, like a sketch for something unearthly. Nobody crossed one of the panels; it was a terrifically detailed emptiness.

"I'll pick you up in three hours, ladies," said Claire.

"Here?"

"No, I'll drive up."

They watched the women walking toward the lights until they were absolutely perfect silhouettes, moving like three black flames to the house.

Patrick turned the car around and started downhill. When he had gone far enough, he turned the lights on and glanced over at Claire. Her face was shining with tears.

For three hours, they were on their own, the thud of freedom. Patrick thought of, and rejected, numerous simple
questions before he spoke. Then he asked, "Why did you
marry him?" She turned quickly to look at Patrick.

"Because I loved him," she said; she was angry.

At the bottom of the hill, you could turn north or
south on the pavement, or west toward the Bridger on the
country road. "Boy, this is a quiet car," Patrick said, then
stopped to think. He turned left to get closer to his ranch
and to calm his nerves. They were nearly to Deadrock,
circling slowly above the lights on the interstate, before
Claire spoke: "Will we wake anybody up if we go back to
your place?"

"No."

"It will be quiet there?"

"Could be a little too quiet."

The interstate kept curving into them, fanning the
lights of Deadrock farther and farther northward. The
trucks eastbound in the night mounted from the valley
and rolled with a peculiarly fatal motion until they were
out of sight.

They made love in Patrick's bedroom. They had simply
not spoken. There had been a temptation to leave the
motor running. Claire's breath shuddered and she held on
to Patrick rather than held him. He was overcome with a
blind tenderness. They each smelled like the women in
the car. He held her hips and turned his forehead into her
fragant neck and felt his own throat ache pointlessly.
Suddenly it was out of their control, like a movie film
that has come off its sprockets, leaving vivid incompre-
hensible images. Then stops, awaiting repair.

"Can you breathe?"

"Yes."

"Like this?"

"Yes, I can breathe fine."

"Sun'll be up in three hours."

"I know it."

"But you'll still be driving in the dark."

There was a very long spell of silence.

"I'll be driving home from here in the dark." Then she burst into convulsively merry laughter. "The sun should be up by the time I get back from dropping the ladies— *Oh God!*"

Patrick burned, watching her dress. There were things Claire did, not entirely necessary to the simple restoration of her clothes. The braid lay in the channel of her back. She leaned to kiss him good night before she had covered her breasts. Her eyes had now a velocity, an intention and loss of weakness that made him know that although there time was gone, she wanted him again.

"Amo shuffle on home."

"I think you should."

"Natty don't work for no CIA."

"That's clear."

"I have chores."

"Right . . ."

"No car pool up that way. Babylon by Cadillac."

"Seems like a shame."

"What?"

"Hit and run. Nothing eventual."

She said, "It's what we have."

36

In the three hours Patrick slept, a foot of snow fell. It must have fallen on an almost windless night, because where it cleaved at roof's edge the angle was perfect and vertical. Some of it fell in powdery sheets onto the still-green lilacs. But the world was white as Christmas, and the Absarokas beyond seemed a subtle interstitial variant of that same whiteness, a photograph with two or three planes of focus. The first thing that Patrick heard was a rifle booming into silence; and when he went to the window in his drawers, he could see down into the yard, where his grandfather, head shrouded under an immemorially weathered John B. Stetson hat, was sighting in his old Winchester. He had dragged a table into the yard and was firing toward the elevation of earth beneath the orchard. Patrick took down the binoculars from on top of his dresser to see what he was firing at: an old Hills Brothers can, with the man in the yellow caftan drinking coffee, wedged in the bank. As Patrick watched, the caftan disappeared, round after thundering round, until only the head and fez remained; then in one resonant crack that rolled down the creek bottom, they were gone too. The old man restacked the empties in their box, removed five live rounds, put those in his shirt pocket and stood up on the one good leg and the one slightly crooked, mule-kicked leg that had nearly got him into movies.

By God, thought Patrick, the bastard can still shoot.

Once Patrick got downstairs, he could smell Hoppe's number 9 powder solvent, one of the most sentimental fragrances in the land. Before he turned the corner into the kitchen, he could make out the muscles in the old man's forearm as he raced the cleaning rod in and out of the barrel; he stopped and watched the patches accumulate from gray-black to white, heard the minute amphibian sound of the oilcan and the swish of cloth. Then when he heard the rifle stand in the corner with a solid thud, he imagined it would be safe to reveal himself without making any promises about hunting trips.

"Good morning."

"Good morning, Pat."

"That you shooting?"

"Yes. The old smokepole will still drive a tack."

"What were you shooting at?"

"I was shooting a little tin. I shot it till I got tired of it. Then I quit."

"I suppose you want to go hunting."

"No, I don't. I want to look at apartments. You take me. I can't be arguing with landlords. I'm the ramrod of the Heart Bar."

Arnoldcrest Apartments was built in the twenties and, architecturally, made more than a passing bow to the phantom district known as Constantinople. There was something secretive about its ground plan, a suggestion of courtyards and fountains that never materialized from the beginning, arched entryways and recessed windows— all once the hope of a man dreaming of the deserts of the East, but quite another thing to the widows and pensioners of the Northwest, flattened by snow, fixed incomes and a hundred thousand newspapers. On the other hand, one could hang out an upstairs window, perhaps a little perilous for the octogenarians, and see nine Montana bars. That was not all bad. They could be reached in five minutes at a walk, three at a trot, round-trip times to the contrary notwithstanding.

They walked from the parked truck. Patrick thought,

It's Istanbul, not Constantinople. Why did Constantinople get the works? That's nobody's business but the Turks'. This is what the yellow man in the fez was trying to tell me: We've got everything here but the harem.

Mr. Meacham, the manager, had been in the merchant marine and wore his khakis and T-shirt and crew cut with the same directness of statement—washing versus pressing, cleanness versus grooming—that Patrick imagined had been the measure of the man on the high seas. He had two further thoughts in a row: One, is this how you dress if it is a regular part of your job to take Arnold-crest clients out the door feet first? Two, is this how you dress to set up a disciplinary contrast with old cowboys and ranchers who do not maintain up-to-date standards of personal hygiene? In other words, does Mr. Meacham batter a door down with his crew cut when he suspects bed wetting? This was a little like packing lunch for Junior's first school day. Patrick was extremely nervous.

First they explored a one-bedroom. It had plaster walls and milled wainscoting that must have been done on a production line fifty years ago. The sockets were waist-high, and there was an overhead fixture in the livingroom with green glass cherubs. The steam registers bracketed the one decent-sized window, and the window gave onto a view of the Emperial Theater and the Hawk, a little bar that sold cheese and cigars.

"Who's living in the building?" asked the grandfather.

"A number of people like yourself," said Meacham. "Some terrific people. A number of former cowboys."

"Any Indians?"

"Yes, Mr. Stands-in-Timber is just down the corridor with his mother, who is said to be a very good cook. They speak sign language to themselves, and so they're very quiet neighbors indeed."

It *was* fairly quiet, though the lonesome sound of daytime television came from behind brass-numbered doors. Meacham stood at ease, awaiting a decision.

"We're a hop, skip and a jump from the hospital," he threw in. "Lots of folks feel there's something nice about that. It would take all day to list the churches. Some people like to worship with the radio, but me, I'm for getting out and doing it if you're able."

The two-bedroom looked vast, though it might have been its emptiness that made it seem so. It faced the back lots of small homes with children, high garbage output and racket, which made these vacant rooms seem sad to Patrick. He was afraid there would be too many reminders of the years now lost to his grandfather; though his grandfather might know the children weren't going to get anywhere, either. Nevertheless, he pressed for the one-room with the view of the theater. And he arranged for additional basement storage for guns, saddles and panniers.

"You have any girl friends, Mr. Fitzpatrick?"

"Don't be so goddamned stupid."

The snow had turned to slush in the street, and people passing the Arnoldcrest had their overcoats drawn around themselves in defense less against this one soggy day than against the five months of winter just now easing itself out of the Arctic. Patrick struck a bargain for his grandfather's new home. He'd move in after elk hunting.

They stopped at the cemetery. It was Patrick's first visit, although, to his surprise, his grandfather had already been, once to remove an ensemble of funeral decorations and once to see if the grass was going to get a start by winter. Patrick thought it was preposterous to view this as a "visit"; but seeking to calm down, he was increasingly bent on imitating the actions of ordinary civilians. The snow had covered the grave and that seemed somehow a friendly fact, a mantle over someone troubled in ways he had never been able to understand, unless it was just the sadness-for-no-reason. Near them an old woman in a heavy twill overcoat sorted flowers by their stems, turning three half-dead bunches into one pretty bouquet and one bundle of waste vegetation. She sternly planted the doomed flowers in snow over her grave, returned to an old Chevrolet she had left idling, and departed, throwing the flowers that hadn't made it into the backseat. She looked very practical in the flying snow; and Patrick thought there was something to be emulated in that, as to one's arrangements. Old people, he imagined, daily put their shoulders to a wheel that would break every bone in a young man's body.

But this cemetery was a strange place, a prime piece of land, with Views. And in all respects it was best seen as real estate. The land holdings were small, especially by the standards of the West. For some reason you had "plots" instead of "lots." It occurred to Patrick that as his home country cooked down into smaller and smaller pieces, "plots" were going to be the finale of the land swindle.

"Pack saddles in good shape?"

"Yes, they are," said Patrick.

"What about the lash ropes?" His grandfather stared at the neat stacks of gear.

"Yup."

"Manties?"

"Plenty and in good repair."

"We still have those canvas britchens?"

"I had them changed over to leather. They were galling the horses. And I changed to wider cinches on the deckers so we can get away from circulation sores."

"The game is going to move in this snow. We ought to start thinking about heading out. If I get a good elk, I can rent a locker at Deadrock Meat and walk down every day for my game. I'll have all of the good and none of the bad. How you plan to shoe that string?"

"Two of them are plates, like Leafy. I'm just going to reset them. One's that gelding I pack salt on. Who you going to ride?"

"Harry Truman. I want heel and toe calks on him."

"I'll shoe him today, then, so you can get him rode a little before we take him in the hills. He's been turned out all summer."

The grandfather went up top with a halter and bucket of grain to catch Harry Truman. Like his namesake, Harry Truman was half thoroughbred and half mustang. He was a good horse and the last horse the old man broke.

While Patrick looked for his apron and shoeing tools, he tried to think about Claire. He had to assume she was not in trouble; but returning to a home after having called your husband's bluff with three prostitutes was not to arrive upon an exact bed of roses. Then, too, it was she who had to drive them home, laminating her own guilt with their doubtless enthusiastic tales of comparison as to their evening with Tio, a man who waited in an empty house for her return. With this thought Patrick *was* worried, and he was heartsick.

"Hello?"

"It's Patrick. Can you talk?"

"No."

"Okay, good-bye, but call me."

"Thank you so much! We have all the subscriptions we can handle!"

She hung up.

Well, she's alive and in good voice, I would say. The snow kept falling. The bunkhouse looked increasingly like some bit of Holland ceramic, its hard angles sentimental in the white down-floating crystal. Who could be against that? Patrick was slightly against it because he had to shoe Harry Truman. But Harry was a good horse, a big strong roan with just a touch of mustang jugheadedness, but strong in all quarters and surefooted to the last degree. Shoeing him, feeling the smart horse balance on three legs, as opposed to him hanging all over you like a less bright horse, Patrick felt that he could entrust him with his grandfather to the farthest, stormiest ridge.

Peculiarly, his love of the disagreeable old man emerged in the task. He used a hoof gauge to shorten the angle of the horse's front feet, so that they would break over easier, make the horse handier. He rasped everything off to the gauge and pared out the inside of the hoof, tapering his strokes to the contours of the frog, sensing with his knife the extraordinary blood-pumping dome beneath. He shod with Diamond oughts all the way around, calks at heel and toe. And when he walked him on his lead shank, the horse traveled out balanced and square.

Patrick's back was sore, but he knew his grandfather could fork old Truman without concern now and spend his whole mind on the Absaroka he loved.

In Patrick's life, at times of crisis, he had sometimes wished to throw up and go to sleep. He had often wondered about this; but as he was one who despised psychiatry, no easy explanations were available to him. He thought he felt a little queasy as he dialed Claire.

"How are you?"

"Fine. Now can you talk?"

"Yes."

"I want to throw up and go to sleep."

"What?"

"It's snowing."

"But what did you just say?"

"I"—clears throat—"you."

"You what me?"

"Nothing."

"Hey, buddy, you're a phone crank."

"Just wanted to call."

"The telephone is an instrument which can be abused."

"Well, here's me."

"Come on, Patrick." Then she just said, "Patrick."

"I don't know. Took Grandpa to town. I'm just feeling, uh, weird."

"Why?"

"Why! The answer is . . ."

"The answer is what, Patrick?"

"Stress-related. I fear purgatory at the very least."

"But what *is* it?"

"I'm looking for a reason."

"I'm looking for a reason too."

"How did Tio take to the wall of hookers?"

"Not at all."

"What? Incidentally, where is he?"

"Right outside this window. He's trying to read my lips. He's shoveling the walk. No. Where was I? Oh, right, he wouldn't have anything to do with them. He stayed upstairs and watched Johnny Carson. *They* made quiche Lorraine and *I* had to clean up the mess."

"Well, I really never saw why we were bringing your husband three hookers."

"And it bothers you . . ."

"I think so."

"It bothers you in a way you can't quite put your finger on?"

"That's it," he said.

"I can answer that for you. Despite that it was a gesture which I thought would best help him to see how I thought he was treating me, the main thing you're worried about was whether or not it indicated some lingering passion between Tio and me."

"The crowd jumped to its feet as his teeth soared into deep left."

"What?"

"It's fair."

"What've you been smoking, son?"

"I ain't smokin. I can barely get out of my own tracks. My foot is stuck in the spittoon. I can no longer sneak up. They can hear the spittoon ringing from a mile out. By the time I get there, all that's left is tracks. And you can't smoke tracks."

Thus another one seemed drain-bound.

In the beginning was sadness; immediately after that was sadness-for-no-reason; and beyond that was the turf of those for whom the day-to-day propositions for going on at all seemed not at all to the point. Patrick, the tank man, took the middle ground: He didn't know why he felt as he did.

Why do I feel as I do?

She hung up on him. A dangerous lip-reader was shoveling her walk.

37

Dear Mother,

Well, things are still in kind of a wreck around here. I have not been feeling entirely right about my behavior and I think that Dale was correct in saying that that rests upon my shoulders. Still, with us, all was not as it should have been. And I can't help but think that Mary paid the biggest part of the price. I'm not saying anybody killed her. But couldn't we have done a better job? I mean, it was quite hard to find anybody to talk to around here. It still is. Grandpa is about as chatty and agreeable as ever.

I don't know what Mary had. I had Marion Easterly but she was invisible. Afterwards I had soccer and my tank. But these things don't add up always. I met Mary's close friend of the Cheyenne persuasion and I couldn't help but thinking he had done rather more for her than her family.

He met her in a whorehouse where she had a job.

Also, I don't think Dad's airplane stunts, including the whopper in the end, were that funny.

I've been thinking about throwing in with more oil-type people, one in particular, as this high lonesome

394

plays out right after its use in calendar photos, funnies and radio serials. I've met a nice girl.

I've found a lovely flat for the Granddad. There's a sign-language study center next door and a monorail to the emergency room. His movie hopes run higher than ever. I've persuaded him of the need of a regular physical, as well as a long hard look at the daily stool. I think he's listening up pretty fair.

Well, this is no more than an apologetic valentine to you and Dale. Tell Andrew that I feel very strongly that he will never find an arrowhead.

Think of us!

Love,
Captain Fitzpatrick

38

"Tio?" Patrick held the phone slightly away from his head.

"How's Patrick?"

"I'm fine."

"What can I do you for?"

"You know when we talked earlier?"

"Yes," said Tio. "Sure do. But we finished that conversation."

"Well, not entirely."

"Yeah, we did. Now, don't y'all be stupid. I've got to ease up on this beast with my rocks and sling. So don't go to jumping me out with some Yankee love of truth. Guy in my position needs to exact some teeny form of retribution without resorting to a bunch of bald statements and unusual self-righteous Yankee speeches, calling me up in the middle of the day with y'mouth hanging open, this man-to-man horseshit, which you have my invitation to give back to the Army."

"I can't understand this."

"Myself!"

"How does it turn out?"

"You just shake and it's snake eyes time after time. They're loaded."

"Meaning what?"

"You never answered me about Claire."

Patrick was not used to this form of evangelical yammering, if indeed anyone was. The best gloss of Tio's speech he could come up with went: There are things one doesn't say; in which case, they had just had a rather traditional moment together, man-to-man, in vacant splendor.

39

In times of great tribulation, a visit to Marion Easterly often seemed important. Mary claimed that Marion had been his greatest love, that no one would ever equal her in Patrick's eyes. But Patrick was sure that they had been apart long enough now, that the Miss Palm side of Marion had sufficiently diminished and that his new and real love for Claire was deep enough that a chat with Marion wouldn't do all that much harm.

Marion was living with a Lutheran clergyman on Custer Street. They had a white marriage and a view of the mountains. An irrigation overflow babbled through the childless lawn. Or, rather, a trout-filled brook. Anyway, babbled.

"Heck," said Patrick. "You're only a hop, skip and a jump away from Loretta's place."

"I know, but I'd be afraid those little dickenses would . . . ensnare me!"

"You could be right." Patrick had made a big Dagwood sandwich. He was trying to eat this three-decker in the fetal position without getting mayonnaise on the bed.

He told Marion that he was in love. He told her that his lady was married to a man of the oil. He mentioned that they had gone all the way and that he thought that the man of oil knew this. Marion raised her hands to the sides of her face, pretty as a picture. "Oh, oh," she exclaimed. "I fear very much for you at the hands of this person of oil."

In the afternoon Patrick expelled two West Coast coyote hunters from the ranch. They had started out on the Mojave, hoping to set a record that would make one of the gun magazines. They were, respectively, a Sheetrocker and a Perfataper. They had been taking amphetamines for four days and had nearly filled their powerful Land Cruiser with dead coyotes. The Sheetrocker did most of the driving, while the Perfataper stood through a "shooting station," which was kind of a sun roof. He had a two-sixty-four magnum and his best lick was blasting. They were four pelts shy of the record and were just working their way east, broadcasting the squeals of dying rabbits from speakers mounted behind the grill. They hadn't had a good day since the Wasatch range in Utah. They were losing weight, running out of money and pills. The Sheetrocker said that he just wanted to touch one off. And the Perfataper said not just one; we're taking a hard run at the statistics.

"Well, your dead-rabbit record is scaring my horses."

"So?"

"And you're on my land."

"So?"

Patrick thought about mayhem; but again, that could cheat him of Claire. He directed the coyote hunters up to Tio's ranch. The yellow Land Cruiser rolled off and in a moment began spitefully broadcasting the deathsqueals of the rabbits again.

Patrick wondered why he had sent them to Tio's ranch. It was not to create further trouble, certainly. Searching his mind, he decided that it became impossible to call over there again; and just maybe he could elicit some response with these yo-yos in the Jap land-gobbler.

Very generously, Catches had had the film developed of the cat stalking moths in Grassrange. In most of them the cat was a light-struck incubus figure, the light something like a separate galaxy, and the moths strangely technological creatures, as aerodynamic and systems-ridden as ICBMs. Patrick thought this was a lovely gift and hoped that the wherewithal had come from the night of Loretta, Deirdre and Tana. The letter said, "What are you doing?"

Patrick decided that in the Castilian walk-up he could go native. He would wear his hair swept back from the forehead and hold his black tobacco cigarette out at the ends of his fingertips. He would bring the pimentos back in the oiled paper, the anchovies and the terribly young lamb. He'd go to the odd mass or two, not in *preparation*, as he might now in the remorseless West; but in the healthy, ghoulish attendance of Spain, to stare at the wooden blood and pus of the old Stations of the Cross. He could have fun there and not have foreboding. He could have the time of his life making smart salads by the stone sink. It could be tops in mindless. He could duck the English secretaries like the plague, as each had already been hopelessly wounded by her own London travel agent. In any case, his crude post-coital bathrobe slopping about was sure to cause *no harm* to anyone; and the question of smelly imbroglios starring oil-minded Southwesterners could not happen to him, stainless in Madrid, with day help. The black olives in the salad would have wrinkles like the faces of men who have lived a long time, innocent of violence.

"What have you done!"

"Oh dear."

"I have narrowly escaped with my life!"

"I see it now. I said the wrong thing." Patrick was thinking of his conversation with Tio.

"You sure did."

"Give me the headlines."

"Well, they rolled in and shot everything that moved. They're in the living room now, knocking back Turkey and getting too close to Tio for comfort."

"Wait a minute. What are you talking about?"

"The coyote hunters."

"Have you talked to Tio?"

"Not yet. But he's crazy *about* them. He's in there

yelling First Amendment and States' Rights. They're real drunk and it's getting crude."

"You haven't talked to him . . ."

"I talked to him right up till the coyote hunters and that was all she wrote. He said he might make a trip today in the helicopter. But if he didn't, I'd of wished he had."

"Did you know that Tio and I spoke?"

"No, I didn't."

"I'm not sure what was said. But I think we agreed you and I were sleeping together and we wouldn't talk about it."

"Do you really think that?" Claire asked in an exhalation of terror.

"I'm afraid I do."

"I better start running, then. I better clear out."

She rang off in panic. Had Patrick endangered her? He thought to himself, I'd better not have. That would have been well beyond the jaggedness-of-the-everyday.

Something was making him feel that he had touched something he didn't completely understand. He had once, washing dishes, reached deep into the suds and been flattened by electrical shock. The root system of the China willow had carried a power line into the septic tank. From Patrick's point of view, the tree had nearly electrocuted him. It took a plumber and an electrician to explain the occasion. Patrick said, "I was only washing dishes."

The plumber said, "When lightning flew out your ass."

Something about Tio was like washing those dishes.

40

Claire arrived and said that the ranch wouldn't do. The same applied to hotels, motels, rest stops and locally notorious zones of cohabitation.

"How about a johnboat?"

"No."

"Wait a minute, wait a minute. Did I do the wrong thing? Can't you say you want to be with me?"

"I just don't want to get nailed in the crosswalk."

They ended up at the line shack on Silver Stake. Patrick rammed and jammed his way in there, missing the vacant shafts, in his truck. Meadowlarks showered out of the buckbrush at the advent of grill and bumper. The combination to the lock, hanging on the warped plank pine door, was that of Marion Easterly: four zeros, easy to remember. The roof was made from sheets of aluminum used in the newsprint process. A practiced eye could invert them to the unweathered, unoxidized side and find the same old crap in aluminum immemorial. Dog eats baby. Indiana woman gives birth to five-pound bass. Silver Stake was on the Heart Bar allotment. The walls were made of the miserable little east-slope logs with their millions of pin knots. It had a patent heater and a pack rat bunk. It was kind of a cowboy joint, hidden upside a terrific wilderness. Patrick missed his Charlie Parker records.

He missed Bud Powell as well, despite recent associations. He did have the following to protect Guinevere from storm and flood: one sledge, two splitting wedges, a double-bitted axe, kitchen matches, Winchester, twenty rounds Remington Core-Lokt 140 grain, Pabst Blue Ribbon (a case), potatoes, onions, stew beef, fifty-pound sack of pinto beans ("I've got to stock up for fall roundup! I am *not* making an assumption!"), peppers and pepper derivatives—Frank's Louisiana hot sauce, ancho peppers, chilipiquines and Tabasco. Blankets: five-line Hudson Bay, two. Artilleryman's gloves. Harry Truman biography: "When I hear them praying in the amen corner, I head home to lock the smokehouse." Something like that.

"Why do we have all this stuff?"

"It's our new life!"

"What!"

Drip-baste cast-iron pot; skillet *con* giant flapjack flipper; and the requisite lid from an old Maytag washing machine. Soap: laundry, dish and personal. Steel wool. Dry rack, dish set with bluebirds, and percolator.

"It looks like we're here to stay! And we're not!"

Patrick gave the lock the full zeros and they were inside. Rat manure and newspaper bits were strewed on the adzed floor timbers. From the window one little turn of Silver Stake Creek turned up to the right and disappeared like a live comma. It was a world that yielded only to a broom, flung-open windows and wood smoke. They threw the flypaper out in the snow with its horrid quarter-pound load of dead flies. Thermal inversion pushed the first smoke down the chimney, and then the flue heated and sucked. There were empty cartridges on the windowsill, a calendar that didn't work this year and a coyote skull for a soap holder. Next to the sink was a cheap enamel pitcher, in flecked white and gray, for dishwater.

"God, I don't know," said Claire. "Are we preparing a moonlit rendezvous?"

"I really don't know, either. You said you wanted to get out of town."

"But this has the earmarks of a shack-up. What I had in mind was my life. Saving of same. I wanted to miss the initial flash. Hold me. There. Oh dear, Patrick. What in God's name did you do?"

Patrick split up the small fatty pine chunks for the woodstove. "I've been trying to think why I did that. Honestly, I thought it was what you would have insisted upon. Not a shack-up. I know it's a shack, but . . . well."

"Again."

"What?"

"Hold me." He could feel her wary, wild shape through her clothes.

They stood in the cool cabin, the pine beginning to catch and the fog of condensation starting to spread on the cold windows; the awful, clear mountain light diminished and modulated its measuring-stick quality, its cartoon illumination of human events. The cabin filled with golden light, finally; the stove crackled and the cold fall sun hung, suspended and inglorious, in the steamy glass. The minute bough tips of evergreen touched the same glass, casting spidery black shadows in the steam.

Sling the mattress over on the coil springs, to the side upon which no pack rat has trod. Claire made up the bunk with the woolen blanket so that it looked like a Pullman berth on a silver shadow train flying through the Carolinas in last light. Claire was a bow beneath him, thumbs indenting his arms, intense this side of screaming. Then her face tipped to one side. And Patrick stared down at her strong bare body as he entered again and again. He wanted to say that sufficiency rather than salvation was at issue. Then, jetting into her, there swept over him an indifference to their danger. Therefore, he shut the hell up and for the moment was glad to be home.

Blanket over his shoulders, Patrick attended to the interior of the little ship set against the hard evergreens, now throwing the peculiar pulsing light of a pressure lantern through the imperfect windows. He took the claw hammer and, clutching the blanket around himself as though modesty continued to be an issue, battered down the exposed nails that years of frost had heaved up out of the flooring. He put perhaps more effort into this than it entirely required.

"Patrick, Tio was my neighbor in Oklahoma. His mother virtually raised me. We'd hit it pretty good and there wasn't time for us kids at our house. There wasn't a thing wrong with him, there really wasn't. Anyway, I married him. And then after that—and maybe this is where I feel like I broke with something I never should have—after that, I took up with my people's views. Which is not necessarily bad in and of itself; but the situation was that I had all the leverage and pretty soon we weren't in high school and we weren't at A & M and then we weren't even in Tulsa. And pretty soon it was pretty damned fast and I had broken his heart one too many times. But by the time I was sorry there was something there in him that was gone for good."

"How had you broken his heart one too many times?"

"That will never be any of your business."

Patrick thought, You are in your perfect little cabin, which you have seen as a ship on an empty sea; and the light and the air seem to substantiate your happiness as you putter around in your wigwam blanket tapping back nails. And then there is something not unlike the blind flash experienced by those whose homes have suddenly been illuminated by the voluminous and unwelcome light of a flamethrower, or some self-immolating madman who picked your yard, or a bad wire, a meteor, an act of God . . . gasoline.

Patrick said, "That's enough for me. I don't want to hear any more."

"To start with, Tio was all right. But he's not all right anymore."

"What was all right about him? I don't want to hear this."

"He had just so much talent but he busted a gut for that. And about the two thousandth storage tank my people tried to shove down his throat, his mind quit that little bit, and in Tio's mind he was an oilman. Then he had airplanes, stewardesses and guns. He learned to farm things out. He bought everything he wore at Cutter Bill's in Dallas. He never rode a horse but now he couldn't miss Ruidoso. He began to speak of his daddy. His daddy was what you'd call an Okie with a capital O, little ole thin-lipped Ford parts manager out at the four corners. Despite his redneck ways, he always wanted Tio to buckle when it came to those tanks, however many fourflushers, missed connections or falsified airline tickets that might have entailed."

"This has grown too heavy. This is becoming quite brutal. And anyway, all I wanted was your ass." His throat grabbed.

"C'mere, Mr. Wretch."

"No, now wait a minute."

"For what. Give me the blanket, anyway." She began to sing. It had become obvious that she was, to a highly refined degree, hysterical. " 'I've been to Redwood, I've been to Hollywood—' "

"Oh, stop this. Stop!"

But by then she was crying and Patrick could only stand by, stove heat to his back, wrapped in his dopy blanket.

"Please stop."

So a night passed without much sleep; then just before light a lynx screamed in the rocks and Patrick got up to fire the stove once again, preparing to make breakfast. He stopped to reach under the blanket, which was pulled over Claire's head, and with the morning hands of a sleepy cook, examined her entire body, just to do that, before she could wake up. He held his hands against his face, then cracked the eggs one by one, watching them drop into the white bowl. He stared at them. The vague anticipatory birds, too small to shoot, the ones that ruin all-nighters, began to make specific announcements from the surrounding brush. When he went out to the creek to fill the percolator, the stony air stung Patrick's skin. And as soon as the first brown bubble appeared in the glass top, he slipped back under the blanket to rediscover Claire's expectant and dreaming heat.

* * *

Patrick put breakfast on the table. The cabin was warm now. He could think of only one fact: Nobody knows where we are. But we've been here overnight and that is a declaration.

"This is extremely wonderful, Patrick."

"Thank you."

"I'm worried."

"I know you must be. But if we could suspend that—"

"Let's try. We shall see us try."

They made a decent attempt at making an island of the place, like an English couple eating marmalade in an air raid. Patrick had parked the truck nearly against the cabin in case the lantern inside didn't work; but when he glanced up and saw the one headlight in the window, it frightened him for an instant. He thought, With all my reputation for independence and for being warlike, it would seem I'm afraid of everything; it was one of the secrets he had that he had never cared to keep. But now he wanted to be courageous, because without it he had no chance of holding Claire. There were so many questions about her existence that would have to have help; and it was Patrick who had brought everything to a head with his codified silences with Tio. Hiding in the woods wasn't going to do for long. Lastly, he realized it was the headlight of his own truck.

"Let me ask you something," he said, testing his bravery. "Do you love me?"

"Yes."

"Very well. I know what I'm going to do. I'm going to go see Tio."

At this point there were no gestures that could accompany such extreme statements. It just had to be said across the table. Anyway, Patrick was going. He didn't look sure of himself and Claire seemed too depleted to respond.

41

Patrick's heart was pounding when he climbed from the truck. He deliberately walked past the front window so that he could glance inside. The Cadillac was tilted up on the slope to the lawn, and he remembered that that was where he had seen it last—a precise parking habit. But mainly he noticed the huge tire prints of some powerful machine across the new lawn in a big arc that took them out of the place—not down the road but directly out through the sagebrush. Then, he noticed the flies on the window, thousands of them.

He knocked without getting an answer. So he knocked again. He craned to see past the angle of the hallway into the kitchen, but could discern nothing. He tried the door and found it open. He walked in among coatracks festooned with deluxe sporting clothes and was overpowered by some awful smell. He was completely frightened, but he worked his way into the kitchen, calling out Tio's name ahead of himself through the kitchen and into the living room.

The living room was ruined with broken bottles and glasses, turned-over furniture and, worst of all, the carcasses of coyotes, some skinned so that they looked alive, veined and bug-eyed, in reaching-out postures so distinctive as to suggest they ran even in death. Hides, curled up and stinking, one hanging on the ninth largest whitetail ever killed in Texas, all swam under a mantle of flies. Patrick rolled open the windows and turned the heat off.

He started upstairs; and by the landing he could see Tio's boots, toes down over the top step. Patrick thought, He's dead. He climbed the rest of the way, and as he moved around Tio's rumpled body, the body moved, the head turned up for a look. "Fitzpatrick."

"What's the problem here, Tio?"

"Had some bounty-hunter friends on a visit. Godamighty, did I sleep here?"

"Evidently you did."

Tio struggled into a kneeling position and let his head hang for a long moment. "Godamighty. Last thing I remember, we was trying to get them coyotes skinned. We was a little far gone." Tio got up. "I was shooting at something in the fireplace. I guess they panicked. Up till then, our plan was to hunt you down like an animal. Which is all you are. Then I had kind of a fit and they run off on me."

Tio wandered toward the bathroom and closed the door. Patrick expected him to emerge with a gun. He looked around the room for the weapon Tio had mentioned and didn't see it. He began to be sure that it was in the bathroom. Then he heard the shower running. In the eerie situation it sounded like some kind of weather behind the closed bathroom door, like a distant storm that ended suddenly. Patrick then thought of Claire, on the chance his minutes were numbered.

The bathroom door swung open. Tio, wrapped in a towel, was drawing broad stripes through the shaving cream on his face. Still standing at the top of the stairs, Patrick could hear the sleepy drone of the flies downstairs. Tio spoke to him, shaving accurately and without a mirror.

"Eat up with the dumb ass," he said, grimly.

"Looks like it."

"*What . . .* in the fuck are you doing here?"

This sent Patrick spinning: Was it to lay claim to the first thing he seemed prepared to fight for since coming home? Was it to bring to closure a mystery he couldn't bear in all the tranquility of the cabin? He really didn't know; but he understood that those were the questions.

"Well, Claire got kind of frightened by your guests."

"That's not it," said Tio, leaning over the sink and scrubbing vigorously at his teeth. I've got it, thought Patrick, I'll tell Claire I shot him. No, Christ, that's hysterical. Tio stood and turned toward him. "You could drive to my house, but you couldn't tell me the truth. Pitiful. I'm supposed to need professional supervision, but you're pitiful." He threw the towel behind and wandered naked to the closet, where he took the utmost care in picking his wardrobe for the day: Levis, a green chambray shirt and his tall boots. The buckle on his belt had the cattrack brand overlaid on it in gold. It was Claire's family brand. Patrick was relieved he'd gotten his clothes on. And he was still thinking about being called pitiful. He felt his blood rise.

"I love Claire," he said.

"Oh, I bet you do."

"That doesn't seem important to you?"

"I'd hate to see you get her killed. *That's* important to me. I'm crazy about the girl."

"What are you talking about?"

"Well, you say you're in love with her. How would you like some clown putting her life in question?"

"I wouldn't."

"Well, as the lady's husband, I'm here to tell you that that is exactly what you're doing. Nothing will happen to you. You're not important enough and nobody is going to *make* you important enough. Otherwise this little turn with Claire would look like it meant something, and it don't. It's just a momentary case of the dumb ass. Basically, we're up north on vacation and maybe it got a little rowdy. Oklahoma can be brutal hot in the summertime. But it's starting to cool off now. It's time Claire and me headed home. So you fetch her. Tio's gonna carry her back to where being with her people makes her feel bullet-proof again."

Patrick started down the stairs ahead of Tio, and just as they moved to the level of the flies, he heard a sudden noise behind him, one that revealed the fear within himself, and the gasped word *"Fitzpatrick."* Patrick turned and saw Tio half-seated, half-sprawled on the steps above him. He was changing color quickly and had lost control of his body. A stain spread at his crotch and Patrick could see in his struggling eyes that he now could no longer speak. Patrick remembered Claire's words: *"I'm the doctor and Tio is the patient and you are a cruel outsider."* Was this it?

Tio was lighter than Patrick had expected. He carried him to the truck in the crazy daylight and felt the gusts of Tio's malady. Then, on the drive to the hospital, Tio twisted up against his door and his teeth began rattling against the window. Patrick pulled him upright and kept on driving.

They wheeled Tio through emergency. The doctor on call said they'd had him once before, explaining this while he tapped the nail of his forefinger on the crystal of his wristwatch. He held the watch to his ear and directed Patrick to the lobby to check Tio in. Tio glided off, wheeled by an orderly, his tall boots immobilized by a retaining strap. His face was locked in some terrible rictus, but his eyes blazed toward Patrick; Patrick would never forget their blaze.

Patrick checked him in, writing Claire's name under "Next of Kin" and his own on the bottom line.

42

On the way back to Silver Stake Creek, Patrick stopped at his ranch and put the stock rack on his truck. He loaded Leafy and Box L, saddles, picket ropes and a hundred pounds of sweet feed. He went inside to see how his grandfather was doing and found the place in good order. He discovered the old man in the living room watching Houston play Denver.

"Hey, Grandpa, I'm running—"

"Where?"

"I'm spending time with a real great lady."

"I'm glad to hear that."

"But look, I want to make early elk with you. So will you do me a favor? Will you buy us our groceries? I'll be back to get us packed in four or five days."

"What do you want to eat?"

"You decide. And get me a box of 270's. Hundred thirty grain."

"How long you plan to stay with this young lady?"

"I told you, four or five days. Nothing is forever."

Then he headed south. He could see Leafy's mane streaming in the rear-view mirror, Box L turning his forehead into it. Sixty-mile-an-hour horses with a highway unraveling behind them.

The mountains paralleled the valley and the snowy peaks were extending with fall to the valley floor. Patrick wondered seriously if this country had ever been meant to be lived in. Right now he could only imagine small hot spots of survival, winter seemed so imminent. He could imagine lying in bed with Claire and he could imagine seeing after his grandfather on the ranch and diligently looking after his warm animals so that the cold didn't sweep them away. But the country lacked the detailed human regimen he imagined he could find in his Castilian walk-up, daily human rituals of coffee, cigarettes, wine, newspapers. The Deadrock region was just exactly the dumb fucking dehumanized photogenic district that would require a bunch of American reformed Protestants to invent. His mood had begun to show.

Patrick was getting sour; he was getting ready to cheat. He drove up into the brush once more. There was still some smoke at the head of the chimney; so he'd done that right. He unloaded Leafy, then Box L. He drove picket pins out in the meadow and hobbled them so they wouldn't cross lines.

And then he went inside. Claire had taken down the Hudson Bay and was curled, undressed, in front of the wood stove.

"Tell me," she said.

"He's gone."

"Gone? Gone where?"

"It said Tulsa."

"*What* said Tulsa?"

"The note. It said he would be back by hunting season. I'm taking my grandfather in the hills then. And you can go. Or whatever you decide." All Patrick could think in the indescribable panic that touched him was, I'm sure he's getting the best of care. He's going to have to live a few days without her at the side of his bed.

Claire smiled. "Then we have some time together," she said.

"I wish we had a lot of time together."

"We don't, darling. Let's not pine for what we don't have."

Patrick thought, I've lied my way into this. What ever happened to the officer and the gentleman? He concluded that it had never been the case. The hell with it. "What are we to make of this?"

"I think we're going to have a perfect time," said Claire. "I'm real encumbered, but I'm falling in love with you."

"That's what's happening to me."

"Isn't it so nice?"

"I don't know if those are the words," he said.

Shortly thereafter, packing saddlebags to take some limited supplies to the divide, the horses tied nose to nose at wind-twisted spruce next to the creek, Patrick knew that he was going to have to say something. But he was determined not to say it now. Otherwise the police or the papers or some blind, abstract party would do the work for him. So he was going to have to say something.

When they got to the top of the world where the lichen made free, unearthly effects, as though the rocks were stained by sky, they tied the horses once more, loosened cinches and made love on cold ground where spring flowers were blooming in the mouth of winter. Then they tied a knot at the corners of the Hudson Bay and enclosed themselves in it, though the blanket now smelled of the four-thousand-foot pull just made by Leafy and Box L.

"The thing is this: When I got to the house, the thing is, Tio was there, actually."

"He was? You say he was there?"

"And at first things seemed quite normal. He just insisted that I be removed from this situation and that way this would never have happened. I didn't think I saw him overwrought. He showered and changed. And suddenly he'd fallen and it was kind of . . . a fit."

"Why didn't you tell me?"

"I wanted the time with you."

"What's the matter with him? You liar!"

"I don't know." He was stung.

"Did they get him to the hospital?"

"I took him."

"You were there when he fell apart? He's not going to like that."

"Does he always come out of these?"

"Yes. I wish you hadn't lied to me."

"Well, I just did," said Patrick angrily.

"Is he hurt?"

"No, and the doctor on emergency had seen him before. So I thought they'd know what to do."

"They will. But it doesn't show up on the brain scan or in blood tests. And it never happened before we married."

"That could just be coincidence."

"It's not. But you didn't tell me the truth."

"Are you entirely guilty for these fits? Is that your opinion?"

Patrick's question sent Claire on a jag, as though somehow it all had to be pinned down immediately or their own fortunes would be swept under by the same malady.

"My family persuaded Tio that I had married beneath myself. I could have prevented Tio from believing that. I assure you he was a very nice boy and he bought what my family had to say. Tio never looked up from the work my father had set him to do until he had proven he was a genuine Tulsa *patrón* just like my father. It took years. And when Tio returned his attentions to me, I just wasn't really there anymore. He began saying peculiar things. And when my father was dying, Tio hung around his hospital room. He said he wanted to be in at the death. He succeeded, the only one to see the so-called final gasp. Then, sir, we went on a tear: Ruidoso, Santa Fe, Vail, La Paz. I didn't know whether he was happy or sad. He didn't know if I was there with him or not, and it just lingered like that until we started on home from Palm Springs. Tio stood up in front of the in-flight movie and went haywire. He was horrible and superhuman and we had to make an emergency landing in Phoenix. They had this center where they could study him, and let's see, I think it was there that he asked me whether or not I was going to let him go under. And I said I wouldn't. Two days later, he was pounding that WATS line. And like I said, it's not on the brain scan or in the blood tests. But I did say I wouldn't let him go under. I hope you've got that clear."

They didn't come down from the divide until darkness had fallen and the shining mantle of stars had rotated into the night. The stars looked like matches. There was some word for matches that was very close to the word "lucifer." They looked like lucifers; and the horses picked down over the blasted rocks. You couldn't see their legs and down in the trees Patrick and Claire couldn't see each other and the lucifers were hidden behind the branches and even in the cold you waited for the lightning. "It would be hard for us to be much of anything with that hanging over us," Claire said, almost asking. Patrick felt the sickness overcome him, the sickness he had known, one way or another, would come. "Tio knows me very well. He studied very closely and saw me falling in love with you. And I'm the one who made him so mean." Leafy slid on the granite veil that caught the vague light of stars; and sparks streamed from her iron shoes. "What do you wish?" Claire asked.

"I wish you'd shut up."

43

Loitering before the hospital seemed not the ideal thing. Pacing like an expectant father, he had less than the routine beatitude upon his face. Presently Claire emerged, and from an unofficial doorway, suggesting familiarity with the place.

"He's resting. He's completely conscious."

"What did he say?"

"He said that he was surprised to see me and that he thought I had come because I found sick people amusing."

"He's lost none of his sense of humor. Did he tug at your heartstrings?"

"Somewhat." Her eyes clouded over as she turned to gaze at Patrick. A doctor arrived on a ten-speed bicycle and shot past very close, so that for a moment the air was filled with bay rum.

"Let's go."

They drove toward Claire's place. Patrick told her about the condition of its interior, the carcasses, the bottles.

Claire turned on the radio. *"The girls all look prettier at closing time."* "I wish things would lighten up," she said. "I know we're grown and all. But I'd like to dance my ass off."

"Tell me about it."

"We'll survive this. But what is that worth?"

Patrick remembered Germany when the drugged girls were carried screaming from the cafés, the sense of flames in the doorways, the nerve net hanging vulnerable in empty space. Now the space was turning to enclosure and that was probably what Claire meant by wanting to dance her ass off. He wasn't sure; but it had her quality of saying the right thing.

She was not prepared for the inside of the house. While Patrick raced around filling plastic bags, Claire flung open the windows, upstairs and down. Soon the wind coursed through the place, carrying flies and stink to blue eternity. When Patrick went upstairs he could see a shadow below, just as when Tio had paced the night of their dinner. At the top of the stairs was a photograph of Claire's wedding. She looked quite the same, except that in the photograph she wore her hair in an old-fashioned chignon; but perhaps that was just the style of wedding pictures, the photographer hoping to give his work a lasting quality by suggesting the newlyweds had died some time ago.

The curtains in the big bedroom stood straight out the window in the breeze. Reports fluttered under paperweights. Claire made the bed with fresh sheets and said, "Would you like to stay with me tonight?"

There was no sense that her husband haunted the room, and Patrick said yes. Then they stopped the chores and sat in the window seat holding hands. They could see down to the meadows. The hay had recently been mown and lay in windrows drying and waiting to be baled. They looked at the varied yellow triangles as closely as if they awaited something crossing them. What could that have been? No telling; but it did seem the setting for a mythical creature or a fugitive.

"May I see your breasts?"

Claire smiled and undid her shirt, dropping it around her waist without untucking it from her pants. Patrick's heart pounded. They were small and definite, like a girl's; and their pallor against the tan of her shoulders and face made them seem secret and powerful. She pulled her shirt on. "Chilly."

"Thank you."

"Hadn't you looked before?"

"I was swept away."

"I see. So was I."

"Does one ever just say the hell with it?"

"The hell with what?" she asked.

"The consequences."

"Some people do," she said, without much warmth for those people.

"Did you ever want someone so much you didn't make love because you'd be too close to see them?"

"That hasn't happened, but I think it's not impossible. I guess that would be adoration."

A harrier hawk flew low against the meadows, banking and casting on new angles in the wind.

"How much of you is there left?" Patrick asked.

"I'd be the last to know. How much of you is left?"

"Well, my major foray into self-pity is the belief that it's all left," Patrick said.

"I certainly don't have *that* belief. You have to have lost a thing or two along the way."

"Please don't say that."

"Okay, but you're a very silly boy. And certainly don't embarrass yourself for me by listing the things you've lost and left behind."

"It's fair."

"So it's agreed, we're going dancing."

"I'd love to," said Patrick, lying reversed on the bed, leaning on his elbows, facing Claire's closet. Claire was trying on clothes for him. She had immense vanity, enhanced by the sunny pleasure she took from it. Patrick thought, *I could never make this up.* He tried to puzzle out the pretty petulance of women picking through their clothes, as though every blouse, every slip or dress, seemed to personally let them down a little. Claire held a spangled silk blouse up to her eyes and said, "What in the world could I have been thinking?" Finally she lay on the floor to pull on a pair of tight jeans. She put on a pair of rose-and-silver high-heeled shoes, a silver belt and a loose

silk top with short sleeves. This had all been quite measured. Patrick was cotton-mouthed.

"And you mustn't get terribly drunk."

"I won't."

"And if I see you starting, I will ask you to stop."

"How?"

"As proof of your love. As proof of how mortally serious it is to go dancing."

"Then it will work. Where shall we go?"

"The Northbranch."

That was the spot all right; but it would make an unmistakable announcement that would fly through
Deadrock.

"It's not exactly a hideout."

"I'm not ashamed."

Unless you're on the dance floor under the wagon wheels
and lights, you have to walk sideways in the Northbranch on a Saturday night; and inevitably, to get a drink
you have to wedge into the service bar and irritate the
barmaids. Then when you dance you have to leave your
drink on someone's table, and it is considered to be in the
tradition of the West for others to finish your drink for
you while you are away.

No amount of lovemaking replaces dancing, though
there's a connection. The band played "Faded Love,"
then "Please Release Me" and "The Window up Above."
Patrick and Claire slow-danced to a fiddler with a smoky,
reminiscent style and to the singing of a short man
whose Stetson couldn't quite hide all his baldness and
whose voice was fine and deliberate and haunting as
trains in distant night.

Claire seemed strong and light as Patrick held her,
curving his hand around her back and holding her hand
rather formally and elevated. She rested her face straight
against his chest. A few people stared; but the dancing
continued, the whole crowded floor graduating slowly in
a circle. Young cowboy couples with their hands in each
other's back pockets and toothpicks in their hat brims;
older people in fox-trot postures with crazily fixed

expressions; indifferent couples counting the house or watching Patrick and Claire; a drunk in a green suit, his hand upraised, his index finger extended, trying and failing to cut in: these and others were bound to the slow circle toward the music. Patrick could feel Claire's back expand now and then with a sigh. Then some gruesome story-song commenced about dogs and children and watermelon wine. They left the floor.

They managed to find a spot at the bar. In the mirror Patrick could see Calamity Jane and remembered being here last: love and death: Claire and the sled dog Dirk. The bartender came up.

"Man wants to buy you both a drink."

"Thank you," said Patrick and ordered. "Who is it?"

"He phoned it in from the hospital. Man down there's gonna cover for him."

Man down there was Deke Patwell. Weak waves, Deke with a little painted grin. I don't know and I don't care, thought Patrick. Claire had been watching. Deke must have phoned the hospital with the latest.

"Do you want to throw up and go to sleep?" she asked.

"Not at all."

"Shall we dance?"

"Yes."

They were back in the dense wheel, a hundred faces strangely anesthetized by three cheating songs in a row. It seemed unlucky.

"How are you holding up?"

"I'm going to be able to stand it," said Claire. "Just."

"Won't you go with me somewhere a long way off?"

"No."

The little flame lights overhead lent the place a peculiar ecclesiastic air. Patrick couldn't remember why. It seemed in the Bible there were always flames dancing over things and that the flames were meant to be a positive sign. These dusty light bulbs weren't going to be quite all that. But there, after all, was Claire's imaginary precursor, the impossibly ugly Calamity Jane in the clothing of a scout. However, the latest song from the bandstand referred to two-timers as snakes crawling in the night. Patrick remembered Tio calling over the phone that he was down among the snakes; and that when you threw the dice they always came up snake eyes.

"Claire, do you fear Tio?"

"I know him too well."

"Most people are murdered by people they know well. Do you think you're in any danger from him?"

"If I am, there's nothing I can do about it."

"You sound like my sister," said Patrick; then he remembered that he had it exactly wrong, that it was Mary who had accused him of being more fatal than any Hindu. "Actually, I'm not right about that," he said. "You're more like me."

They danced from cheating to trucks to lost love to faded love again, which seemed sadder than lost love, to the green grass of home, double beds, jobs you could shove, a ride to San Antone, yellow roses, the Other One, caring and trees. Claire put her arms around him and began to cry. She said, "Oh baby, do something." When the first, most ardent wave had passed over him, he thought, and not without fear or confusion but still shot through with ardor, This is it.

"If we could only remember . . ." Patrick trailed off with the quality of dramaturgical preplanning; but then, helplessly, having at this moment seemed inauthentic even to himself, he just doggedly fell silent, because he was certain that if they both could remember any of their original intentions, *something* would occasion a rescue, something astral; but not, certainly, this assaying of present requirements. A former captain of tanks encounters a former Oklahoma golden girl still actively married to a current person of the oil, with difficulties, none of which appear on the apparatus: What values shall we assign to each, that is, from loyalty to practicality to romance? Do we subtract for the premature curtailment of tank? Do we dock for nonamplification of golden-girlism? Do we quantify our reservations as to the nondocumentable nature of oilperson's helpless flaws? How about this: Altruistic cowboy tank captain rescues princess of the Cimarron from mock-epileptic oil-and-gas-lease scoundrel. No, well . . . no. But if we could only remember. Anyway, Claire caught that, knew the long thought was genuine, even if the deck was stacked and, for her as for practically everybody, the matter of remembering first intentions was as reproachful as anything could be. The road to hell has seen more paving materials than the Appian Way, I-90 and A-1-A combined.

"Okay, let's buck up here now."

"Very well," she said.

"Are we at the crossroads?"

"I have no idea."

"Can one have fun at the crossroads?"

"I have had no reports as to that," she said.

"For instance, having disguised myself as a nurse, shall I pull Tio's various life-support connections?"

"There are none."

"But if there were."

"There aren't."

"Ball breaker."

"Now, now."

Of course, they were trying to work themselves into a reckless state of mind, a form of play in the face of grave consequences familiar to the bandits and thrill-killers of history. This time it wasn't working. It was undemonstrated that Claire lacked love for Tio. It was not clear that Patrick had a plan. Most of all, everything with respect of the heart's grave and eternal sweep seemed at odds with the constant machine-gunning of the age.

"I do love you," she said so fatally as to put it beside desolations he had already come to know, ones which played human hope against arithmetic and impossibility. Meanwhile it seemed that not only was Patrick drunk but he was about to break down. Who wanted to go dancing and put up with this?

"I know what you're thinking. But you're going to have to pull yourself together."

"What do you mean?"

"Cheer up." It was the only thing she could have said to return Patrick to the ground and make him stop circu-

lating with ghosts and faulty desire. A car crashed outside and there was a long jingle of glass, a stuck horn.

"They're playing our song," said a revitalized Patrick, sweeping Claire to the floor for a turn.

44

At closing time she wanted to be taken home; and it was clear she meant to be dropped off, that Patrick was to go to his own place. He said that he didn't understand. They were both slightly drunk. Couples swarmed past, carrying plastic to-go cups. One bartender had moved next to the door opposite the bouncer, who was sitting on a Naugahyde-and-steel kitchen chair. His thighs pressed together all the way to his knees, and he reviewed departing customers as though they were only going on parole.

Patrick started the engine. "What is this?"

"What is what?"

"Just dropping you off?"

"Time to think. I mean that, Patrick."

"You mean as if there were an answer."

"That's just what I mean."

"Well, you'll have to outgrow that," said Patrick. He meant nothing enigmatic by his remark, and in fact the notion hung over the entire ride to Claire's ranch, suggesting there *was* something to it. Therefore—though it had been a superb evening, given the time and place, most of the immediate gloom kept at bay—Claire went straight to the house. Patrick wheeled the truck's lights against the scattered buildings and suppressed an urge to go back into town and look for some kind of trouble. He was beyond that; he headed home to the Heart Bar Ranch

—that is, his inheritance with its increasingly vacant buildings and rooms.

By nine in the morning he had reduced the broader effects of his hangover by ruthless scrubbing in the shower, harsh versions of the remaining ablutions, clean clothes and coffee with his grandfather.

"I forgot to send in the meter reading. So they came out and did it and charged us." His grandfather delicately tested the layer of cream on his coffee with the tip of his spoon; then he gave it a stroke and it all twirled to color. He sipped. "One guy to drive the truck. One guy to read the meter and write it down. There'll be a third person to bill us for the extra, which is five dollars. The electric company is gonna be fifty bucks in the hole."

"Everything else all right?"

"Seems so. I've been out on Truman. Everybody looks sound. One yearling pulling up a back leg. I don't see a stifle there or anything to be concerned about, though. I've paid no attention to the irrigated ground. I shut off the wheel line and the hell with it. Seems like Truman's gaits have improved. That old dogtrot's practically a rack now. Wish I could take him to town."

An hour later, ignoring official visiting hours, he was sitting next to Tio's bed. Tio said, "This is just foolish."

"Maybe not."

"You reach a certain age, I think, when you haven't got your house in order and you start seeking out bad situations."

"You think that's what I'm doing?" Patrick asked.

"I see you as some character who joins the Foreign Legion hoping to be killed by Arabs because his dog has died. And if everything goes well and they put a bullet in him way out there on the desert, the dog is still the only one to feel sorry for."

Patrick was silenced, not simply by the creeping appropriateness of the speech, but by the glimpse of that in Tio which had drawn Claire: the character, the oil-field voodoo.

"Who do we feel sorry for in your life?" Patrick asked.

"Always been hard to say. I had begun, *once* I began, to figure out who'd had who. Got close, I mean extra close, when—snap—I started my rigor mortis routine. Never been much in the long run. Casts its little old shadow on things. Course, from a cold-ass business point of view, a guy doesn't want to weigh in as a nut. But some things can't be helped. And if I could help this, then what could I do? Kill you? Kill her? Kill myself? God works in mysterious ways, I'm a bald-ass liar if he don't. Nothing more ruinous to my expectations in life than waving a pistol around or farming out crimes that point an accusing finger at me. Slow grind don't set you in your place, then I'm a nigger aviator. Just remember this, Fitzpatrick: I've got a gadget-filled mind. And I've got a gadget for every situation."

A brilliant light—brilliant suggesting something momentary, as a flare—fell upon Patrick, who staggered very slightly and acknowledged acquaintances with a quick sideways tip of the head, a gesture he had not formerly used in America. At Front Street in the clangor of the shunting yard, he grinned to himself and thought: Rue Northern Pacific . . . Calle Caboose. Perhaps this *is* the caboose. The noose of the caboose. The last car before the vanishing rails, a view entirely different from that from the engine.

Everything from finding the truck to returning to Silver Stake seemed to happen at half speed. Why in a movie camera did you have to run the film through at high speed to produce slow motion? Why couldn't things happen "in a wink" as they did in the books he read as a boy? The desire to use up the road in a wink is the way the high-speed camera of the drunk's brain produces accidents, the mad wish for change.

In the last mile before camp, perhaps some admission was at hand, no sheepish acquiescence to the occasion, but an actual acknowledgment of all the signs and semaphors and general messages from headquarters that the very thing he had begun to hang his fatigued hopes upon was out of the question.

He opened his jackknife to cut the black twine on the baled prairie hay. He separated that into flakes and fed them into the small corral so that the horses could eat well away from one another. He knocked the grain pannier to scatter possible mice and brought Leafy a bucket of oats. He sat down rather heavily before her and held the bucket. She exhaled across his head and face questioningly before dropping her muzzle into the grain. She ate with the regularity of a horse who will be fed again; and when Patrick held his hands around the strangely delicate pasterns, feeling the heat that arose from the coronal bands of hoof, she stopped, pricked her ears forward, stared with the black and endless eyes that had made him cut her out from the other foals numerous springs ago and went back to eating. Patrick had imagined she was worried about him, that he was somebody. Then the patterned movement, observed from this crazy angle of legs —hoofs all as different as seashells—and the disappearance of everything into the dark: the orderly rotation of big animals according to their decorum from feed to water to standing sleep, a movement throughout the night that never disturbed Patrick, sleeping face down in the mountain corral.

Claire found him there, not before he had awakened but before he'd had time to reconstruct and too late for him to jump up and pretend to be doing anything else. Storewide gala on mortification of the flesh. Patrick was sick of it but couldn't think what there was to be done.

"I wanted to see if you were all right."

"Of course I'm all right."

"I see."

He sat up and gazed around the corral: horses, poles, the crowding evergreen slope; how absurd, the sort of thing to give you the sweats. Claire's hands seemed to plunge deeper into the pockets of her blue dress. Beautiful as usual, thought Patrick angrily. In the meanwhile I've become a laugh.

"What are you doing today?" she asked tentatively. It was as if they were starting all over again.

"Reading a book."

"What book?"

"It's called *The Life of Marion Easterly* and it's by all three Brontë sisters."

He thought, I shall not be tempted by any of this. I prefer the concerned breathing of my horse upon my much-abused head in the night—though Claire would have seen to it that I went to the cabin. On the other hand, waking up and seeing there was nothing to eat, I would have gone on my own.

Creeping in was a new light-heartedness. Patrick ruefully considered that Claire might get away with this one. Just as well head indoors, then, and tidy up.

The broad-bottomed tin kettle sent clouds of steam into the room, and the stout wood stove beat gentle heat against Patrick's bare knees. There will be shaving; there will be brighter eyes. The wandering part in his hair would be rediscovered and traced to the crown of his scalp. Teeth only the madmen at Ipana could dream of. A nice shirt from the clutches of the Armed Forces in Europe. But it was pathetic.

Soon, however, they were shouting.

"Tio seems very used to your indiscretions."

"He's not."

"It seems he is."

"Shall I just go, Patrick?"

Now he was sorry, at first because of his shouting. Then he remembered her shouting and he was less sorry. Besides, the way moods swept back and forth over lovers like tide seemed now to Patrick a humiliating process. I love you I hate you I'll kill you I can't live without you blah blah blah. This last thought took him to the final button of his shirt. He dropped his hands to his sides, watched the steam carry to the door past Claire and believed he felt like the Ancient Mariner at an abandoned bus stop. Then Claire stirred together some breakfast—a rather scientific attempt, he thought, to raise his blood sugar, going to Jerusalem with a Bible and a soil-test kit. I

should start shouting the moment I've eaten my breakfast. I mean *shouting*.

"Can we ride again?"

"Let's load up and get the fuck out of here."

"This has been so lovely out here. Are we about to be
actual?"

"We'll quit while we're ahead. I've got things that
have to be done." What if she asked for examples?
Change the cat's whisker on Grandpa's crystal set? Milk
the elk?

Leafy kept testing the floor of the trailer with her fore-
foot, then finally loaded up. Delicate as she seemed to
Patrick, the trailer set down on its springs. Panniers, lash
ropes, spoilable food, all were piled in the truck.

And now a simple dialogue between the two engine
exhausts, G clef by Patrick, revving a bit between ratios
as he swung about and headed the rig down the mountain, manifold resonating in the gee-haw of faded romance. One of the West's last and smallest wagon trains,
he thought; an observation that exhilarated by its brief
coldness and necessary stupidity. The two vehicles separated and headed into the distance.

But by the time he reached the ranch, the phone was
ringing and she was asking without any introduction,
"What *can* I do? What am I *supposed* to do?"

"I don't know."

"But you just don't do anything you please. Do you?"

"Of course not."

"That's all I wanted to know."

She rung off and left Patrick even less enlightened. He
decided that it was partly the phone's fault; that even
notepaper was inadequate to such an enigma. He played
bebop and cooked Chinese food. It seemed the only answer. He wouldn't see love to its senescence without a
middle period.

Then she called again. He was eating a trout, curry
and rice invention wrapped in won ton skins and playing
the Jazz Messengers so loud he almost didn't hear the
phone ring.

"Tio's home. But he's so demoralized, it's not like him."

"I don't know what to say to you."

"I wanted to talk to somebody. He's a sick dog."

"There are bigger things than pairing off," said Patrick.

"Like what?"

"Life and death."

"Take the easy ones, cowboy."

"Well, I asked you to leave with me."

"That's another one. You're going downhill. People promise people, Patrick. How is it with you—strand people with all your speeches? Some of us still own up to the ones we made on homecoming day, for crying out loud."

"That bad?"

"That bad."

"Well, I'm getting off before you ruin my dinner." And he did.

Then, to make up for it a little, he took Tio's stud out to ride in what light was left. His food had begun to digest, and the smell of the horse was obviated by the smell of hoisin sauce and curry. They went up the road, the stud spooking about in the shadows but advancing into new darkness with the pressure on his sides. A partridge dusting in the pale light went off at an angle, and the stud watched bug-eyed, side-passing through the spot in the road just vacated by the bird. My God, what a stupid bastard, thought Patrick. He once had a farrier who claimed that the two most ignorant things a man could do were to refuse to cut a stallion and to turn down a drink of whiskey. Then Tio's stallion gave out a terrific scream as if to tell any mares in earshot that he feared no bird. As for Patrick, his love of Claire kept him, with some struggle, from acknowledging that the thoroughly faulty Tio was coming to seem human. It wouldn't do.

And anyway, it wouldn't last; that is, it didn't. Coming back down the road in nearly complete darkness, past one small ranch with its generator thumping in the cow barn, Patrick found it necessary to two-hand the horse once more, like a colt; his muscles felt short and bunched. If he could have gotten his head down, he would have bucked.

He took the saddle off, hung the bridle and closed the stud up when Tio materialized from the next, empty, stall; he must have been sitting on the feed bunk.

"How'd my stud go?"

"He went all right. We didn't do much."

"I've got a gun."

"Oh, great."

"You can't see it, can you?"

"No. Are you going to threaten me?"

"I don't know what I'm going to do! Been made to feel pretty poorly about myself and that leads direct to your doorstep."

"May I sit down?"

Tio nodded affirmative, but with a crazy, loose-necked gesture. Patrick sat on the bench next to his forge, hiking up on his hands and swinging back onto it. Unconsciously, he looked about at the things with handles: chisels, screwdrivers, hammers.

"Are you drunk, Tio?"

"No."

"What's the deal?"

"You tell me."

"I don't know what it is."

"Except it ain't right."

"I guess not."

"We go' make it right."

Patrick sighed. "Okay." He guessed he wanted it made right; and he could find nothing actual in this suggestion of gunplay. He didn't think Tio could, either. At the same time, he didn't want to be some dim, surprised bozo who couldn't read the cards and got shot.

"Not like you think."

"Why don't you just get rid of the gun so that we can talk?"

"There's no gun."

"Why did you say there was?"

"I thought it would have a different effect."

"I can see that," Patrick replied.

"Gun's like a big car. Just something to arrive in. Real anger you do in your shirt-sleeves."

Patrick got up, uncomfortable, pulled the lamp on over the forge, took the bench brush and tried to be busy, for Tio seemed to bear real forward motion, anger, humiliation, whatever. It was hard to say.

"Usually I get a nap," said Tio.

"I don't follow."

"A nap. I missed mine today."

"Right . . . ?"

Tio looked dead. "So I'm shot. I gotta go home. I gotta sleep. The restoration process. Let's pick up where we left off. I'm suckin wind. A big nap will solve that."

"Well, as you wish."

"This is me," said Tio. There when they drove the golden spike, his arms held wide. "Hand in hand with nature. The big snooze."

Patrick discovered where Tio had parked when the Cadillac pulled out, lights high, from between the oldest cottonwoods. He hung his chaps under the yellow bug light and considered: *He missed his nap!*

The other thing is, I've got to get this bad-minded horse back to his owner. Every time I ride that bastard, I feel like a monkey fucking a football. That's not a good feeling. And you don't want to get caught at that.

At evening he was heading for Tio's ranch with the stud behind in the trailer. By the time he went under the big hanging gate, he could see Tio's helicopter, and by the time he got as far as the house, he could see Tio inside the helicopter behind its tinted bubble. Patrick felt nervous about this; but he didn't want the horse around, he didn't want the business connection, and he didn't want the excuse for Tio's visits. Anyway, Tio didn't bother to look up. Patrick could see vaguely that he had the headset on—probably getting a weather report on the VHF.

So he unloaded the horse and led him carefully, thinking at first, This is this canner's last chance to get me; recalling Mary's view that the horse was an instrument of the devil. Leading the horse was like flying a kite: He was just a bad-hearted, bad-minded, uncoordinated canner. And the devil had better instruments.

He put the horse up and stepped out of the stable, a kind of West Coast shack with doors on runners and air-conditioning. Claire was on the porch of the house in her yellow dust-bowl dress, one hand dug into her thick hair.

"Come up here, Patrick!"

"I've returned your horse!" he called.

"I see that!"

When he got to the porch, Claire was shaking and her eyes were drawn inward as though to lengthen their focus to eternity.

"He wasn't any good, really."

"I couldn't get him to do anything. As you can imagine, it's best I return him."

She stared at Patrick and laughed, either ironically or bitterly—stopping him. Certainly nothing was funny at all.

"Can you come in?"

"This is getting crazy. I don't understand. I never have understood."

"Just come in."

Patrick was lost—lost passing into the house, then lost in its rooms, whose opaque human shadows stood sourceless and eerie as the shadows birds cast by starlight. He sensed Claire in her cotton dress no more than he sensed Tio getting his weather forecasts a hundred feet away in an aluminum-and-plexiglass capsule as hermetic and sacrosanct as the Oval Office, Lincoln's tomb, the seal on bonded liquor, virginity.

"Come here to me." She shoved the door closed behind him.

"Claire!"

"Shush!" She seized him hard, and by the time he kissed her throat, it was wet with tears.

He whispered, "What's going on?"

"It's none of your business."

"Is that true?" Patrick asked emphatically. They each seemed to him terrifyingly unconnected.

"That's true. Don't worry about Tio until you go and

fetch him." She pulled—or, rather, twisted—him down onto the divan; and she was barefoot.

She said "Baby" and lifted to slide her yellow dress under her arms. Patrick thought, This is as good a place to die as any. He was not so far gone as not to note that the West's last stands were less and less appropriate to epic poetry and murals.

"Should I call you baby too?"

"I didn't mean that. I wasn't calling you baby. That's not what it meant." She was naked now and Patrick awaited a bullet.

"I've got to hear what you meant."

"Last chance."

"Last chance . . . Am I going to get killed at this?"

"I don't see how. *I'm* not going to kill you."

Drawing this particular blank, Patrick, in mortal confusion, made love to Claire, who seemed, spasmodic and weeping, finally more martyred than loved. Patrick heard himself a mile off and incoherent.

Then acknowledgment of everything external moving in upon his consciousness appeared as an ice age. He wasn't a captain or a cowboy. He thought for a moment, literally thought, about what he had set out for; and he knew one thing: he was superfluous.

"Why," he asked, "have we been put up with?"

"By whom?"

"By your husband."

"Ask him. I'm through. But you could ask."

"I *will.*"

"Do."

Tio was dead, exhaust piped into the bubble until the smothered engine quit and Tio went on to the next thing. He hung forward in his harness as though starting the international freestyle; it looked like a long swim indeed. Around his dead face earphones whispered news of a world cracking; but Tio was spared. Lust and boredom provided no such indemnity. It made thrill-killers of nice people.

"Do you think we can fly this thing?"

"Oh, Patrick."

"Are you shattered?"

"Not really."

"Did you love him?"

"Sure."

"I wonder what happened."

"No, you don't."

"I think I really do."

"We fucked him to death."

"Don't talk like that."

"And you thought he was a bad man. You thought if you pushed him hard enough, he'd put you out of your misery, like your sister did for herself. But he wasn't a bad man."

"I mean, is it the main thing to be put out of your misery?"

"Are you miserable?" Claire asked.

"Are you?"

"No. I'm in mourning. I wanted to celebrate it with you before you got miserable again. That part of you deserves to live. The rest should be in there with Tio. You might enjoy him like this." She laughed a high, uncontrolled laugh, one that masked not tears but something wild and unreachable. Patrick felt, as he looked into the bubble, that he looked through the bars of a prison; and that in some terrifying way, the voice of Claire was the bright music of the jailer's keys fading in the corridor.

"Would you like to go back in?"

"I really don't think so."

"Scared."

"Yes."

"All you know is what *I* knew when we went inside before."

"I realize that."

"No guts, no glory," she said.

"I'm not going in with you."

Claire stretched her arms over the plexiglass and stared inside. "I guess if I've done nothing else, I showed one of you how to carry the weight and not go to pieces. I didn't go to pieces. He did and you're about to. I've got this feeling I don't want to lose that. The love was real in each case."

You could see the house in its own lights. It looked like an ad for a paint that was weatherproof and that banished evil. It looked flat.

"Is the love gone?" he asked.

"What if it is?"

"I don't know."

"It's nothing you can do anything with. It makes you go around proving you're not rotten or spoiled by sin— Look at him."

"I thought love was all that mattered."

"Well, it's very nice. Taxes awful high in that neighborhood. You know what I set out to do? In my little quiet way? I set out to have been around."

"Get it done?"

"Well, I've been around."

"You learn anything that could help us? See, I'm real in love with you and I'm sort of stuck."

Claire never seemed morbid, cynical or flippant. Patrick could not see how she had been made into this. Her rakish femininity had first drawn him to her; but now her absolute female power, which men fear will finally be turned upon them, was at hand. He was sure she hadn't wished this or wanted to be competed for. But the two of them had made a major purchase on a long-term plan. She at least acknowledged the cost, while Patrick compressed it to a dead husband. She wasn't being cold; she intended to pay.

"I think you should go in with me."

"Why?"

"For a couple of reasons."

"What are they?"

"One is it will never happen again. We have to give him that."

"And the other?"

"You'll have a real good time."

Patrick went. She made it seem easy.

★　★　★

Had the love been real? Patrick thought so. He never specifically changed his opinion. Too, he gave Leafy to Claire. He must have meant something by that. In life, he later thought, shoot anything that moves. Otherwise, discouragement sets in. Tio at least had gotten the latest weather.

Patrick's grandfather shot the best elk of his life. Patrick packed it out for him and arranged for it to be mounted and hung in the Hawk Bar, the place the old man could see from the window of his apartment.

Patrick and Claire corresponded for some time after he went back into the Army and she returned to her childhood place at Talalah. Once she sent a picture of herself, but he didn't like keeping it around. After that, the correspondence trailed off.

Anyway, his share of the lease money from the ranch allowed him to buy an old second-story flat in Madrid. He spent all his leave time there. Deke Patwell had it from someone who knew someone who knew someone that he had a woman in Madrid, an American named Marion Easterly; and that when she was with him, he was a bit of a blackout drinker. There were some people in Deadrock who had liked Patrick; and a few of them thought, At least he's not alone.

In any case, he never came home again.

THE BUSHWHACKED PIANO

This book is for my mother and father.

When the sea was calm
    all ships alike
Showed mastership in floating.
                    —W.S.

1

Years ago, a child in a tree with a small caliber rifle bushwhacked a piano through the open summer windows of a neighbor's living room. The child's name was Nicholas Payne.

Dragged from the tree by the piano's owner, his rifle smashed upon a rock and flung, he was held by the neck in the living room and obliged to view the piano point blank, to dig into its interior and see the cut strings, the splintered holes that let slender shafts of light ignite small circles of dark inside the piano.

"You have spoiled my piano."

The child would remember the great wing of the lid over his head, the darkness, the cut wires curling upon themselves, the smell of spice and the sudden idea that the piano had been sailed full of spice from the Indies free of the bullet holes that would have sent it to the bottom, resonant with uncut strings, its mahogany lid slicing the wind and sheltering a moist and fragrant cargo of spice.

What an idea.

After that, wisdom teeth, a perfect horror: one tooth slipping out as easily as an orange seed popping from between your fingers; the other less simple, requiring the incision of a flap of skin and the chiseling through a snarl of impacted roots and nerves, the tooth coming away in splinters and his very mortality flashing from the infected maw.

Then: a visit to his grandfather's farmstead. Abandoned. The windows glinted blank on a hay field gone entirely to pigweed. Wingnuts made soft black moons in the punky wood of ruined shutters. When he shielded his eyes at the front porch window and saw into the old kitchen, he perceived the pipes of myriad disconnections, jutting and pointing into space; and, in the half-light of a far corner, a white enamel water heater, a rash of rust broken out on its sides, crouched like a monster. When he kicked in the front door, it swung wide and wobbling; its lock spilled screws far too long. He started to explore but quit at the bathroom where a tub poised lightly as a dancer on cast-iron lion's feet, its faucets dry, bulbous.

Years away but, he thought, in direct sequence, a woman sat on a blue stool striking at her hair with a tortoise-shell comb. And behind, on the bed, Nicholas Payne, her seducer, sighted between the first two toes of his right foot, wishing his leg were a Garand rifle.

There were any number of such things from that epoch, but a handful seemed to make a direct footpath to lunacy: a stockbroker's speckled face, for example, his soft, fat eyes and his utterly larval voice.

He was too young to have to make such connections, rolling across an empty early-morning city, red-eyed in an eggstained bathrobe, a finger in each corner of his mouth drawing it down to a grotesque whitening slit through which he pressed his tongue. Since they found him curiously menacing, the attendants supplied a canvas coat with longish sleeves. It was insulting and unnecessary.

That was some time ago now, and he recovered at home. When he was being odd, he would sometimes, at night, go to his bedroom window, ungirdle, and urinate on the walnut trees radiant below him in the moonlight. Sometimes he boiled eggs on the electric range and forgot to eat them or went into the closet and stood in the dark among all the dusty shoes. He had an old cello, painted blue, and he often sawed upon it. One night he took the pliers to its strings and that was that.

His family said that he could not be trusted around a musical instrument.

Then, just when he was doing so well in school, he lit out on a motorcycle. And nowadays that trip would come to him in happy little versions and episodes. Anyone could see that he was going to pull something like that again. Even his mother's friend who had managed the Longines Symphonette could see he was fixing to pull something. She taught piano, and Payne took from her.

But all Payne could remember was that first cross-country trip. He was on an English Matchless motorcycle and headed for California. Nebraska seemed so empty he sometimes could scarcely tell he was in motion. Those were soil-bank days and you had to watch out for pheasants on the road. Payne felt intuitively that a single, mature rooster could disable an English racing machine. Later, he recalled two cowboys outside of Vernal, Utah, in a windstorm, chasing a five-dollar bill across a feed lot.

A girl rode with him from Lordsburg, Colorado, to Reno, Nevada, and bought him a one-pound jar of Floyd Collins Lilac Brilliantine to keep his hair in place on the bike.

And California at first sight was the sorry, beautiful Golden West silliness and uproar of simplistic yellow hills with metal wind pumps, impossible highways to the brim of the earth, coastal cities, forests and pretty girls with their tails in the wind. A movie theater in Sacramento played *Mondo Freudo*.

In Oakland, he saw two slum children sword fighting on a slag heap. In Palo Alto, a puffy fop in bursting jodhpurs shouted from the door of a luxurious stable, *"My horse is soiled!"* While one chilly evening in Union Square he listened to a wild-eyed young woman declaim that she had seen delicate grandmothers raped by Kiwanis zombies, that she had seen Rotarian blackguards bludgeoning Easter bunnies in a coal cellar, that she had seen Irving Berlin buying an Orange Julius in Queens.

In the spring of that year, San Francisco was dark with swamis. He didn't stay long. Until that fall he lived north of San Francisco in a rented house, in the town of Bolinas. The memory of that now isolated these months to a single morning when he had turned out at dawn and gone to the window. Looking across the meadow that was the southern end of the low, vegetated mesa he lived upon, he could see the silver whale shape of fog that lay in from the sea, stilled, covering Bolinas, the lagoon and the far foothills. The eucalyptus around the house was fragrant in the early wet sun and full of birds. Firing up the motorcycle, he went spinning down Overlook Road toward the ocean rim of the mesa, straight toward the wall of fog at the cliff. Shy of the edge, he swung down onto Terrace Road and dropped quite fast through the eucalyptus and cedar, really as fast as he could go, through repetitive turns, the smells by-passing his nose to go directly to the lungs, the greenery overhead sifting and scattering shadows, the dips in the road cupping sunlight, the banked turns unfolding his shadow, the whole road flattening out, gliding along the base of the Little Mesa, down the corrugated concrete ramp onto the beach where he found himself in the fog with the sun melting it into streamers and the beach dark, streaked, delicately ridged like contour plowing; and everywhere the rock underpinning nosing through the sand and Payne obliged to steer a careful fast course with the front wheel swimming a little, until he reached Duxbury reef where he once caught a big, blushing octopus the color of any number of slightly gone-off tulips, as well as gunnysacks of monkeyface eels, cabezone and cockles—provender. He set about now getting mussels, snatching them off the rocks impatiently with less philosophical dedication to living off the land than to eating mussels at intervals of twice a week steamed in sixty cents a quart, third-press mountain white, and fennel. When he finished his work, he sat on the largest boulder at the end of the reef, the base of which was encircled with drifting kelp, weed and the pieces of a splintered hatch cover. The fog retreated to an almost circular perimeter within which a violet sun shone. The sea stood in a line of distant mercury. The sanderlings raced along the edge of the sea in almost fetid salt air. And Payne, thinking of home and knowing he would *go* home, saw with some concision that, as a citizen, he was not in the least solid. In a way, it was nice to know. Once he began to see himself as societal dead weight, a kind of energetic relaxation came over him and he no longer felt he was merely looking for trouble.

The homecoming itself was awash in vague remembered detail; the steamer dock on Sugar Island looked draped in rain. He remembered that. It was a wet, middling season in Michigan; he forgot which one. There were a number of them. And this: the condemned freighter *Maida* towed by tugs toward a chalky wafer of sun, toward the lead-white expanse of Detroit River, black gleaming derricks, slag—the whole, lurid panorama of cloacal American nature smarm debouching into Lake Erie where—when Payne was duck hunting—a turn of his oar against the bottom brought up a blue whirring nimbus of petroleum sludge and toxic, coagulant effluents the glad hand of national industry wants the kids to swim in. This was water that ran in veins. This was proud water that wouldn't mix. This was water whose currents drove the additives aloft in glossy pools and gay poison rainbows. This was water the walking upon of which scarcely made for a miracle.

Moping on an abandoned coal dock, Payne rehearsed his imagined home. He tried by main force to drag back the bass-filled waters he actually remembered. He dreamed up picturesque visions of long packed lawns planing to the river and the lake in a luminous haze beyond. He recollected freighters and steamers sailing by, the side-wheeled and crystal-windowed palaces of the D & C Line that had so recently gone in stately parade up the Canadian channel, the sound of their orchestras borne across the water to Grosse Ile.

But this time the *Maida* toiled before him on the septic flow, vivid with arrows of rust thrusting downward from dismal scuppers. On deck, a handful of men rather specifically rued the day. Life in the U.S.A. gizzard had changed. Only a clown could fail to notice.

So then, failing to notice would be a possibility. Consequently, he fell in love with a girl named Ann who interested herself in the arts, who was quite beautiful and wild; and who, as no other, was onto Payne and who, to an extent that did not diminish him, saw through Payne. In the beginning, theirs was one of those semichemical, tropistic encounters that seem so romantic in print or on film. Ann had a beautiful, sandy, easy and crotch-tightening voice; and, responding to it, Payne had given her the whole works, smile after moronic smile, all those clean, gleaming, square, white teeth that could only be produced by a region which also produced a large quantity of grain, cereals and corn—and stopped her in her tracks to turn at this, this what? this *smiler*, his face corrugated with the idiocy of *desire* and the eclectic effects of transcontinental motorcycle windburn, a grin of keenness, blocky, brilliant, possibly deranged. And stared at him!

He went to her house. He croaked *be mine* from behind the rolled windows of his Hudson Hornet which in the face of her somewhat handsome establishment appeared intolerably shabby. He felt a strange tension form between his car and the house. The mint-green Hornet was no longer his joy. The stupid lurch of its paint-can pistons lacked an earlier charm. The car was now spiritually unequal to him. The wheel in his hands was far away, a Ferris wheel. The coarse fabric of the seats extended forever. All gauges: dead. The odometer stuttered its first repetition in 1953 when Payne was a child. A month ago he'd had a new carburetor installed. When he lifted the hood, it sickened him to see that bright tuber of fitted steel in the vague rusted engine surfaces. The offensive innocence of mushrooms. A thing like that takes over. A pale green spot on a loaf of bread is a fright wig inside of a week. These little contrasts unhinge those who see them. The contrast between his car and her house was doing that now. He could barely see through the windshield, but clear glass would have been unendurable. The world changed through these occlusions. Objects slid and jumped behind his windshield as he passed them. He knew exactly how a building would cross its expanse progressively then jump fifteen degrees by optical magic. Don't make me go in that house. Just at the center of the windshield a bluish white line appeared like a tendril turning round itself downward and exploded in a perfect fetal lizard nourished by the capillaries that spread through the glass.

Gradually, he worked himself from the machine, went to the door, was admitted, went through to the back where Ann Fitzgerald was painting a white trellis and, paint brush in her right hand, dripping pale paint stars in the dirt. "Yes," she said, "I will." Indicating only that she would see him again. "Stay where you are," she said. An instant later she photographed him with a large, complex-looking camera. "That will be all," she smiled.

The steamer dock, the former property of the Sugar Island Amusement Company, defunct 1911, was a long balconied pier half-slumped under water. Near the foot of the pier, abandoned in the trees, was an evocative assortment of pavilions, ticket stands and stables. There were two carved and lofty ramps that mounted, forthright, into space. And the largest building, in the same style as the pavilion, was a roller rink. This building had come to be half-enveloped in forest.

It was nighttime and the ears of Nicholas Payne were filled with the roar of his roller-skated pursuit of the girl, Ann, at speed over the warped and undulant hardwood floor. He trailed slightly because he glided down the slopes in a crouch while she skated down; and so she stayed in front and they roared in a circle shuddering in and out of the light of the eight tall windows. Payne saw the moon stilled against the glass of one unbroken pane, gasped something like *watch me now* and skated more rapidly as the wooden sound sank deeper into his ears and the mirrored pillar that marked the center of the room glittered in the corner of his eye; he closed the distance until she was no longer cloudy and indefinite in the shifting light but brightly clear in front of him with the short pleatings of skirt curling close around the soft insides of thigh. And Payne in a bravura extension beyond his own abilities shot forward on one skate, one leg high behind him like a trick skater in a Dutch painting, reached far ahead of himself, swept his hand up a thigh and had her by the crotch. Then, for this instant's bliss, he bit the dust, hitting the floor with his nose dragging like a skeg, landing stretched out, chin resting straight forward and looking at the puffy, dreamy vacuity midway in her panties. Ann Fitzgerald, feet apart, sitting, ball-bearing wooden wheels still whirring, laughed to herself and to him and said, "You asshole."

2

It was one of those days when life seemed little more than pounding sand down a rat hole. He went for a ride in his Hudson Hornet and got relief and satisfaction. For the time allowed, he was simply a motorist.

After the long time of going together and the mutual trust that had grown out of that time, Payne had occasion to realize that no mutual trust had grown out of the long time that they had gone together.

He had it on good evidence—a verified sighting—that Ann was seeing, that afternoon, an old intimate by the name of George Russell. There was an agreement covering that. It was small enough compensation for the fact that she had lit out for Europe with this bird only a year before, at a time when the mutual trust Payne imagined had grown up between them should have made it impossible to look at another man. Afterwards, between them, there had transpired months of visceral blurting that left them desolated but also, he thought, "still in love." Now, again, George Russell raised his well-groomed head. His Vitalis lay heavy upon the land.

The affair of Payne and Ann had been curious. They had seen each other morning, noon and night for the better part of quite some time. Her parents, Duke and Edna Fitzgerald, were social figments of the motor money; and they did not like Nicholas Payne one little bit. Duke said he was a horse who wasn't going to finish. Edna said he just didn't figure.

But Payne and Ann saw each other morning, noon and night. A certain amount of that time was inevitably spent up to no good. For Payne—and for Ann too—the whole thing seemed one of life's maniacal evocations, a dimensional reach-through, heaven.

Once, for instance, they were on Payne's little boat; he was in the cabin, adjusting the flame on the parabolic butane heater. Ann was on the bunk beside him, Payne in a Jesuitical hysteria of cross-purposes. Ann, clearly, prettily, waited for it. And Payne gave her one too, just like that. He looked underneath as he mounted her: a herring leaping from bank to bank, a marine idyll. Ann, for her part, should have never told him to hold on to his hat; because for an alarming instant he just couldn't get going at all. She patted him with encouragement and told him we were a big boy now. She slipped her ankles up behind his knees. Payne felt as though he were inflating, becoming a squeaking surface that enlarged getting harder and paler, a weather balloon rising through the stratosphere, merely a collapsed sack at the beginning, growing rounder and thinner with altitude, then the burst and long crazy fall to the ocean.

Afterwards they watched a Lake Erie sunset together; a bleached and watery sun eased itself down on the horizon and broke like a blister, seeping red light over the poison lake. They could count the seven stacks of the Edison Electric Company. They smelled with affection the effluents of Wyandotte Chemical. They slept in one another's arms on the colloidal, slightly radioactive swell.

Next day, he had a little hang-over. He smoked grass and consequently had the notion his chair was singing in a languid Dick Haymes voice. Outside, he was convinced the sky had been vulcanized. He tried to call Ann and got her mother who was cool to him. She reminded Payne that the whole family was packing to go to the ranch in Montana and that maybe it would be better if Payne called at the end of the summer.

Payne still could not believe that Ann would spend a minute with the other one. It broke his heart to think so. Her family hated him. She was always reluctant because of that to have him in the house at all. They knew he wasn't working. They had seen him on motorcycles and felt he had thrown his education away. Now, on the phone, Ann's porcine mother had it in her heart to tell him to wait until the end of summer to call. Payne doted on the pleasure it would bring to shoot the old cunt in the spine.

"Bartender," Payne said, "my glass is leaking." He looked at the flashing sign of the Pontchartrain Bar, visible from in here. "Have you ever tasted cormorant?"

He didn't know George Russell, the other, but he didn't hesitate to call him on the phone. "Listen George," he said, "I demand a cessation of stupidities on your part."

"Oh, Payne," George said with pity.

"I want to help you."

"Ah, Payne, please not that."

"I remember you said once George that you could not live without lapels."

"I didn't say that," said George with a debonair tone. *"I cannot live without lapels."*

"That's not true. Are you drunk or taking dope?"

"Whether it's true or not, why did you say it?"

"I didn't say it."

"What could it mean?"

"I didn't say it."

"What could that mean? 'I cannot live without lapels'?"

"Payne," George interrupted. "Can you live with this: Ann has been seeing me. Can you?" All Payne could remember about George was that he was what dentists call a mouthbreather. He had decent teeth which he had bought at an auction of Woodrow Wilson's effects. George hung up. Payne had one foot in the abyss.

Someone put some change in the jukebox. Two couples who knew each other materialized in a sentimental jitterbug. It was the kind of thing sailors did with each other and with brooms when they were brokenhearted on aircraft carriers in World War Two, flight deck jitterbugs with the kamikazes coming in for the coup de grace; it was the very dance a bosun's mate and a chief petty officer might have done a hundred and fifty-three miles out of Saipan with an eighty-five piece Navy orchestra playing Flatfoot Floogie on top of four hundred thousand tons of high explosives in a state of being approached by a religious Japanese in a bomb plane.

Payne headed back to his table, but some oddball had glommed it. "Who's the oddball?" he asked the bartender.

"You are."

"I saw a sign in the urinal that said 'Please do not eat the mints.' This goes for you." The bartender forced a laugh, throwing back his head so that Payne could examine the twin black ovals divided by the stem of his nose. He went to his table anyway, carrying a fresh whiskey. "Tell me about your family," he said to the oddball.

"Three of us is all," smiled the other, "two dogs and a snake." Payne looked at him, feeling his brain torque down into its first focus of the evening. The man picked up one of his galoshes from the floor and held it to his own ear. "I can hear Akron, Ohio," he announced. Payne was enthralled.

The man was sloppy and stretched-looking. Seeing Payne look, he boasted of having been most monstrously fat.

"Guess."

"Two hundred," Payne said.

"Close. Five years ago, I weighed four eighty. C. J. Clovis. You call me Jack." He pushed himself up. He was missing a leg. Then Payne saw the crutches. Clovis was neckless, not burly, and his head just sat in the soft puddle of his shoulders. "I lost more weight than I can lift!" He directed Payne's attention to the various malformations of his skeleton produced by the vanished weight. The hips were splayed, for example. "My feet went flat! I had varicose veins popping on me! Danger looked from every which way!" He told Payne about his two friends in the Upper Peninsula who both weighed over four hundred and who, like Clovis, were brokenhearted because at that weight they couldn't get any pussy. Therefore, they took a vow to lose all their excess. He dieted under the care of a doctor; his friends went on crashes of their own design. In the beginning he had reduced too fast and, consequently, as his body fed off itself, gave himself gout.

"Then I got this old fat man's disease, gangrene, and lost my leg."

"How long ago was this when you lost your . . . leg?"

"A month. But I'm going to get me an appliance and I'm as good as gold."

"They say a missing limb continues to hurt."

"Oh, naturally yes. Of an occasion."

"How did these other fat guys make out?"

"How did they make out?"

"I mean how did they reduce?"

"They reduced all right," said C. J. Clovis, looking angrily toward the bar.

"What do you mean?" Payne asked.

"They're dead!" Clovis looked around fidgeting, looked out the window and fidgeted furiously before looking back at Payne suddenly. "I'm going to get me some appliance!" His hands flew aloft like fat birds.

"I believe that you are, Jack."

"I'll be rockin and a rollin," he said with religious glee. "I'll be good as gold! I'll have a time! Do you understand, God damn it?"

". . . yes . . ."

"Stay a while and see me smile! Give me a chance and I'm gone to dance! I'll do the backover flip every trip! I'm gone to be reelin off the ceilin with a very happy feelin! *I'll be good as gold!*" Jack Clovis locked his eyes in position throughout the recital. Payne was locked in a paroxysm of embarrassment. "That is my pome," said Jack Clovis. "You take it or leave it."

"I'll take it."

"I could turn pro, Buster. You remember that." Being called Buster was the only part Payne didn't like.

"At what," he asked baldly.

"Why after I get that appliance I might take up an instrument. I could go a hundred different ways. You'll be able to hear me laughin a mile off and performin on some God damned instrument." He swung his head angrily through a hundred eighty degree sweep. "When I think of them other two fat boys and what they're missing. Shoot! they too smarted themselves that time." Payne thought of the two fat boys ballooned against the insides of their coffins while his old friend schemed about an artificial limb, entirely magic in its pink plastic and elastic hinges.

The two men sat in a field of formica and did not speak. Payne could not accept the relief of an electric pinball machine that bloomed for him. Even without his gratitude, it spilled its pastel clouds and rang its bells while an unmoved player draped two fingers on the plunger and waited for it to get his victory out of its system.

"May I have your ear?" asked C. J. Clovis, a disturbing question from an amputee. "I need your confidence. You have heard haven't you of farmers who bring ten citrus fruits to bear from a single tree. You have heard of winter wheat. You have encountered, possibly, forced vegetables. I cannot go into it at this time; but let me say only this. There is a special application of these wonders that applies to the life of bats. And the potential? Top dollar. I will say no more.

"My own appliance," he continued to say, "which I mean to have in no time flat will be itself a natural wonder. I have confidence in it. It will have more actual articulations in it than a real limb. Though I will still be a monopod, this aluminum wonder will fetch me from spot to spot. Your name and address?" Payne gave it to him. "Let me drink in peace, sonny. And one last thing. Remember, won't you, that I am in the Yellow Pages."

"Yes, sir."

* * *

You do meet some people in a bar, thought Payne who continued drinking. Gradually, he ceased to think of the unimaginable C. J. Clovis; and to nurse, instead, his obsession with the possible infidelities of Ann. He thought of calling the house but knew his fears would be heard in his voice. He was, moreover, a little intimidated by her parents. They were good at their world at least; and he seemed bad even at his. Darling be mine I love you. More Black-Jack Daniels, he said, and make it snappy. I am the customer. It was brought. "I pay," he said lashing simoleons to the countertop. "I own a chain of wurlitzer chicken parlors and every Grade-A fryer has my brand on its ass." Later, some entirely theoretical argument with the bartender ensued during which the bartender thrust his face over the bar at Payne to inquire how anybody was going to wage trench warfare on the moon when every time you took a step you jumped forty feet in the air. Payne reeled into the night.

He was standing in front of the Fitzgeralds' door, in the dark, with no good in mind. Ann would be asleep. Inside of him, where all secrets were borne in darkness, a kind of Disneyland of the intestines went into operation, throwing forth illusions, mistimings and false alarums. Payne had a moment of terrible littleness. He pulled his sleeve back to learn the time and discovered he no longer owned a watch. He felt better. He saw again how he might be illustrious. The wrought brass knocker on the recessed oak door said FITZGERALD in stern, majuscule letters; above, heraldic devices worked in the metal itself proclaimed the Fitzgeralds rampant animals of one sort or another; while below—a pause while Payne goes completely out of focus, considers his mortality, our times and the music of the spheres, and refocuses—while below, then, a semicircle of smaller English uncials warned, *"Let Sleeping Dogs Lie."* It had been made to order, Payne surmised, by a microcephalic pump jockey from Burbank.

A stern Payne lifted the knocker as to announce himself, stopping on the upstroke. Its squeaking changed his mood. His thoughts were awash with all the noises he hated; especially Pomeranian dogs, wind chimes and windowpanes wailing under soft cloths. He lowered the knocker and released it.

Then he thought very hard. He stood without moving for a long moment and he thought quite as hard as he could. And when he had absolutely enough of that he turned the door knob slowly and firmly, opened the door, stepped inside and closed the door behind: a felon.

All of the lights were turned out on the first floor and in the living room, though there seemed to be light enough in the air for him to see his way; and crystal shone dully on the end tables. He wandered out of the living room and into the den, shutting the door behind.

In almost the first cabinet he rifled, he found brandy and the most magnificent Havana cigars he had ever seen, the legendary coronas, Ramon Allones Number One. His mouth was watering before he had one lit. With the first blue puff unraveling in the air, he poured himself a tall slug of brandy. He pulled Fitzgerald's Holland-and-Holland shotgun down from its cabinet, threw it up to his shoulder and, in his happiness, believed he saw the big canvasbacks coming in flat, slipping just under the wind and flaring all around him.

Could the Fitzgeralds have heard? Could they have heard him making shotgun noises with his mouth? Big ones? Like a twelve-gauge makes? He went to the door, stood behind it, pushed it open with his foot and jumped into the opening, brandishing the shotgun in the darkness. If anyone had been there, the situation had been clear and they had chosen not to show themselves. Payne pulled the door shut again and, holding the shotgun by the barrels, rested the butt on his shoulder and sat down, staring out of the dark window at the darker branches against it. "Pleasure is not the absence of pain," he said aloud and swallowed all of the brandy. Instantly his eyes brimmed with tears and he ran around the room crying, "I'm dying, Egypt, dying!" Then he sat down again, took off his shoe, put the barrels of the Holland-and-Holland in his mouth and, sight unseen, pulled the trigger with his toe. There was a single, metallic, expensive and rather ceremonial English click. He took the barrels out of his mouth and thoughtfully replaced the cigar.

Feeling his way along with the shotgun, he began to explore the house. He went upstairs in the streaming moonlight. The first room on the right was a bathroom with a sunken tub and a shower nozzle on a pivoting arm. Payne unzipped his fly and began to urinate into the toilet, carefully shooting for the porcelain sides of the bowl. Then—and the gesture was perfectly aristocratic—he shifted his stream to the center of the bowl. It made a lot of noise. Then he flushed the toilet.

Payne tucked the end of the toilet paper in his back pocket, without detaching it from the roll, and returned to the hall. The paper quietly unwound behind him like a cave-explorer's twine. Over his shoulder, he could see its reassuring stripe in the darkness.

At the first bedroom door, he turned the knob. The door caught and would not open freely. He hesitated, then gave it a good jerk. It came free with a small creak. In the gaping space was an enormous double bed, Fitzgerald on his face, his wife on her back facing the ceiling. The enemy. It was some moments before he realized that the door was letting the wind pass through uninterrupted and the organdy curtains were standing into the room and fluttering and making noise. When he shut the door behind, he felt the unmistakable hum of fear. It had set up headquarters under his sternum. He lost track of what he was doing. His coordination departed and he made unnecessary noise with his feet. He still bravely managed to get to the edge of the bed and look down at the muzzle of the shotgun bobbing under Missus Fitzgerald's nose. He had occasion to recall the myriad exquisite ways she had found to make him uncomfortable. He remembered too—looking at her laid out like this—that Saint Francis Borgia had been impelled to his monkhood through horror at the sight of the corpse of Isabella of Portugal. Beside her, and invisible in a ledge of shadow, her husband rotated in the blankets and unveiled his wife. Wearing only a pair of

floppy prizefighter's trunks labeled *Everlast*, her gruesome figure was revealed. It upset Payne to see such a
thing. She began to stir then, and he withdrew the gun. In
the moonlight, he could see where her nostrils had fogged
its blue steel. The room was filled with cigar smoke now.
Under Payne's eyes, the two Fitzgeralds blindly and in
slow motion fought for the covers. She won and left him
shivering and naked. He was as fuzzy and oddly shaped as
a newborn ostrich.

A discovery that Ann was not in her room wrecked
everything. Now the toilet paper, in snarls and strips forever, angered him. He thought balefully of climbing the
old lady just to fix them; but felt, all in all, that he'd
rather not. Free of the paper, he sauntered gloomily
through the blue light tapping ashes on the rug, heartbroken. The bitch.

He bashed around the upstairs, not hearing the
Fitzgeralds stir this time, and headed down to the den
moaning a little. He poured another brandy, relit his cigar, gulped the brandy and smashed the glass against the
far wall.

Finally, the throwing of light switches and the wily
flap of carpet slippers came to his attention. A tongue of
light advanced to the foot of the stairs. Payne scampered
around the room repeatedly imagining he would get off
with a spanking.

It was both of them. Payne was now crouched on the
shelf beside the door. He turned at their sudden voices
and rammed the gun cabinet door with his nose, actually
slamming it. He knew paralysis. A voice: "Is this, is this,
do they, where's the—?"

Then Missus Fitzgerald was in the den fixing instantly
upon the smashed glass, the shotgun on the floor and the
stain of brandy. Her eyes met those of Payne. Startled,
she soon let her joy upon this ruin of him as a suitor be
perceived.

"I'm a person you know," Payne claimed.

"Come."

"With valves."

"You're going to get a crack at cooling your heels in

our admirable county jail," she said, moving toward him. "Do you know that?"

"I want my walking papers."

"No. You're going to jail you shabby, shabby boy."

"Back off now," Payne said, "or what I leave of your head won't draw flies at a raree show." He turned around and faced the bookshelves from five inches. "When I look I want you to have given me room to clear out. I'll count three." In the bookcases he saw, once he had focused at this close range, numerous volumes of interest, not the least of which was Borrow's incomparable *Lavengro*. But he was distracted by La Fitzgerald. By the time he turned and started out, she was screeching and hauling at the telephone. He wormed his way out of the narrow window into the garden; every pleached bush biting at once; dark, bark-packed, red meat bites all over him.

He went on all fours through the garden beds. He went, not like a man on his hands and knees, but with abrupt swinging motions of his limbs, head high for observation, hunting and on the move. This is the veldt, he thought, and this is how lions act.

I am leading the game, he thought, or not?

3

During the night, Payne frequently woke up, overtaken by horror. But nothing happened. He should have foreseen that. Not calling the cops was a precise piece of Fitzgerald snobbery. One's name in the papers.

He had breakfast with his mother who came in from an early round of golf. Her hair in a smart athletic twist, she flapped down driving gloves beside a robust ox-blood purse. Radiating cold outdoor air, she brought their breakfast to the porch. Today she was a lady eagle, Payne noted. She reached for a croissant with her modeled Gibson Girl hand.

They were able to watch the river from here. The table was surrounded by the telescope, bird books and freighter shipping codes with which Payne's father kept track of profitable tonnage on the river. ("There goes Monsanto Chemical loaded to the scuppers! They're making a fortune! Don't take my word for it, for God's sake! Read about it in *Barron's!*")

Through the top of the glass table at which they ate, Payne could see both of their feet splayed on the terrazzo. He watched his mother probe daintily at her cheerless breakfast of champions awash in blue skimmed milk. And he knew by the warm detachment of her smile that she was about to spring something on him.

"What is it, Ma?"

Her smile soared up out of the wheat flakes, inscrutable and delicate. "You know Dad," her voice rich with inflections of toleration, of understanding. "You know how he is, well, on the subject of you doing something a tiny, well, the tiniest bit *re*gular or res*pec*table, you know how he, how he, how he—

"I know but stop that."

"What?"

"How he, how he."

"How he wants you to simply take advantage of your most obvious advantages and join the firm; and it's not—"

"I will not subject myself to a career in lawr. I had my little taste of lawr in lawr skyewl."

"I see."

"Yass, lawr skyewl."

"Yes, well I do think you ought to know that if you repeat that speech to him—" She said this simply and very wisely. "—it would be useful to plan on your having your hash settled. Uh, but good, I'd say." She raised one thin arm emphatically, holding aloft her spoon; and a drop of milk, like a drop from the pale blue vein on her arm, quivered on the hand then ran into her palm. She turned her eyes to it. "You sneer at a man who offered to give you—"

"Strings."

"—to give you—"

"Too many strings attached."

"To give you, never mind, to hand over to you the finest law practice in the entire Downriver."

"Altogether too many strings attached to the finest lawr practice in the entire Downriver."

"But no—"

"But no I wanted to do something all by my lonesome possibly not even in the Downriver at all."

"Really, Nicholas, shut up, wouldn't you." Payne put a piece of hot glazed almond roll into his mouth and stopped talking. Maybe Duke Fitzgerald was hiring someone to kill him at this very minute and he was sending almond roll down a gullet that was doomed. He looked fondly on as his mother lifted her spoon again and dipped a chunk of bread and yolk from her egg cup.

"You think that your allowance is to be resumed."

"Okay, please, enough. I always supply my own funds."

"I couldn't go through it again," she went on doggedly. "Like last Fall. Your father working and you duck hunting every day of the week and filling our freezer with those vulgar birds. And the year before riding up and down the country on the motorcycle. It makes my head swim. Nicky, it makes my head swim!"

"I have to keep on the qui vive for spiritual opportunity."

"Oh, for God's sake."

"I do."

"And poor Ann. I sympathize with her and with her parents." Little do you know, Payne thought. I've got to bear down hereabouts.

"Mom," he inquired. "You want my motto? This is some more Latin."

"Let's hear it."

"Non serviam. Good, huh? My coat-of-arms shows a snake dragging his heels." His mother started giggling.

There was nobody here to make him see the world as a mud bath in which it is right tough to keep showing a profit. He invented a joke to the effect that blood was always in the red and death was always in the black; and thought: What a great joke!

By the time his father got to him that evening, Payne, by careful examination, found himself adrift. The two men each had a drink in hand. His father had had his annual physical and was in an already exacerbated mood. He'd had a barium enema. If you had an intestinal impaction, he claimed, "that barium bastard would blow the son of a bitch loose." Payne said he would keep it in mind.

There had been trouble with the furnace. Since the house had been in his mother's family for four generations, that whole sector was implicated by the mechanical failings of the furnace. Mister Payne presently insisted that the machine had been salvaged from the English Channel where it had received the attentions of the German U-boat corps in 1917. "It was installed in our cellar with all its brass and corrosion intact and in its earliest glory. The touching ships' wheels by which the heat is adjusted have all seized in position so that the only real regulatory control we have is opening the doors and windows. I have been increasingly unamused during winter months in creating a false Springtime for six cubic acres around our house. The Socony Vacuum and Oil Corporation's fee for this extravaganza customarily runs to three thousand per diem."

"I understand how you feel," said Payne lamely.

"No you don't. I learned yesterday that the breakwater is sloughing at inconceivable speed into the river. I'm afraid if I don't pour a little concrete in there, we'll lose the pump house this winter."

Payne held his cold glass to his forehead. "I saw it was crumbling myself." He crunched an ice cube; an illusion of his own teeth shattering.

"You don't realize the cost of these things," his father mentioned drily, his eyes leaden with authority.

"But if it has to be done."

"Of course it-has-to-be-done. But you regret the cost of it. The *cost* almost overshadows the *value* of the pump house you're trying to *save*."

Payne gave this a moment's quiet thought.

"Perhaps you'll let it go then," he said.

"And lose the pump house! With an irreplaceable pump!"

"Just what do you want me to say?"

"I want you to advise me. I would like to hear your ideas."

"Sell the house and buy an A-frame somewhere very far inland."

"Oh, well, if you're laying for something."

"How much sense does that make?"

"And maybe you ought to go easy on that stuff," said his father, lordly in the precision of his tailored livery. He jabbed a finger at Payne's drink, now splashing, then running, off the wall. "And if you don't want a drink, don't pour yourself one. The solution is not to pour yourself a drink and then throw the drink against the wall. It may be a solution in some circles; but it is not one I mean to finance."

"I bought this drink in a bar. I am its proprietor."

"I have attempted to talk about this breakwater, this ailing breakwater which, if it isn't healed, is going to drop my high-priced pump house into the Detroit River, irreplaceable pump, tightly built clapboard shed and all. I scarcely need mention that it will break your mother's heart. Her family has been in that joint for ten generations; and that pump house has borne witness to a hell of a lot of their hopes and fears. And I'll be God damned if I am going to play host to a squadron of union cowboys at six bucks apiece per hour just to keep the Detroit River out of the lawn and I suppose, ultimately, the basement."

"All right," Payne said, "I'll fix the breakwater."

"Don't do anything that's too rough for you."

"I've had enough hectoring now," Payne said. "I'll fix your breakwater but I've had enough of the other thing as of right now."

"You do as you wish, my boy." He gave the smile of love and understanding that is done primarily with the lower lip. "You have your life to live. Otherwise—"

"Other than what?" Payne interrupted, having become, some time ago, an expert on these lawyers' jumps by which a grip is obtained upon the testes, an upper hand as it were.

"Other than your performing some reasonable duties around here as a basis for our providing, gratis, your keep, I don't see how we can let you go on."

"You've muffed it now," Payne said. "I would have done it anyway. That's too bad."

"I've smiled through any number of months of your aimlessness, punctuated only by absurd voyages around the country in motorcycles and trash automobiles. I just find the Rand McNally approach to self-discovery a little misguided. I want you to know that I won't let you lie doggo around the house awaiting another one of your ter-

rible brainstorms. My rather ordinary human response
has been to resent having to go to work in the face of all
that leisure. I, of course, stupidly imagined that this leisure has been not possible without my going to work.
Once I had seen *that* I knew I could at least have the
pleasure of being the boss. I know it's idle; but it gives me
a cheap and real thrill."

"You make it pretty clear," said Payne with admiration.

"In other words," his father said pleasantly, "fix the
breakwater or get out."

"Okay."

"Are you going to fix it?"

"Oh, not at all."

"You'll have to go," his father said, "you'll have to get
out."

They strolled around. It was a pleasant evening and
the garden beds smelled better than they would later on
when they were grown over with summer vegetation.

The next morning, they talked in the driveway. Now his
father's mind was on his briefs again. And the talk didn't
please Payne as the one the day before had. His father,
then, stood, hat in hand, bored to tears. "You're through
here now," he said with muffled alarm. "Now what are
you going to do? I mean . . . what? In terms of your education you're perfectly set up to . . ." His face looked
heavy and inert as though you could have carved from
eyebrows to chin and removed the whole thing without
hitting bone. ". . . to . . ." He looked away and sighed,
rotated the hat ninety degrees in his hand and looked at
the door. ". . . you could . . ."

The boredom was infectious. "I could what?"

"I could find you a slot as a publicist."

"Non serviam," Payne said, "I've been reamed."

"What in God's name do you mean?"

"I actually don't have a clue."

They kissed like two Russians. "Goodbye."

The minute his father drove off, Payne's hemorrhoids
began hurting. The same thing preceded the last motor-

cycle trip, commencing with a gruesome fistula that fought eighty dollars worth of Cheyenne penicillin to a draw. Interminable Sitz baths in flimsy flophouse sinks had given him the legs of a miler. Payne knew the showdown was not far away.

Payne felt that he was wrong to always hang in to bitter ends. The current declining note was an instance. He had lived too long with all the irritants of life at home, small contestations and rivalries which inconvenienced his happiness pettily. A kind of drear mountainous persiflage always accompanied such encounters. He ended by being buried in the piss-ant social inclemencies which turned him into the petulant loafer par tremendoso he himself regretted being.

In the past, he had run up and down America unable to find that apocryphal country in any of its details. His adrenalin cortex spumed so much waste energy that a lot of amazing things happened. And he deliberately changed his highway persona day by day; so that, across the country, he was variously remembered for his natty dress, for his opposite of that, for his persistent collection of "data," for his arbitrary and cyclonic speechmaking, for his avowed devotion to his mother and father, for his regular bowel movements, for his handsome rather loosely organized mock-Magyar face, for his tiny library and transistorized machines locked away in ammunition tins, for his purported collection of the breakfast foods of yesteryear, and for his habitual parabolic coursing through the U.S.A. with attendant big trouble, pursuits and small treasured harbors of calm or strange affections along traveling salesman lines, facing enemies with billboard-size declarations of a dire personal animus, cluttering hundreds of small midland streets with regrettable verbs and nouns, sharp ones, heavy ones and ones which made barricades and tanktraps in peaceful summer villages where no one was asking for trouble.

In most ways it had been an awful strain, one he'd been glad to finish. Now, being on the verge of it again, he felt an uproarious tension in his mind.

4

People turn up.

For much too long, he continued to appear dazed. He often thought, "I couldn't have been more of a pig." Interested only in things that provided no morning after, he paid out deceptive conversations that made everyone in earshot fidget.

When he closed his eyes, Ann seemed to speed through a cobalt sky, a lovely decal on the rigid Ptolemaic dome. Every room gave at the corners. And why should anyone in the fat of late spring imagine that winter was not far away, scratching its balls in some gloomy thicket?

He dreamed and dreamed of his adolescence when he had spent his free time watching medical movies, carrying a revolver, and going around, for no reason, on crutches.

He was interested these days in how people listened.

He heard them. Completely buggy in the frame bed, he pawed the wall for the switch. They were down there: dogs. He climbed out of bed, driving a putty-colored shadow to the stairhead. At the bottom, a sea of fur flowed toward the toilet. He heard them taking turns drinking. He was excited and frightened. He felt a long, terrible oblong of space standing out from his chest and going all the way to the first floor.

* * *

The next day, he went to see a World Adventure Series movie of Arabia and talked for hours about Death In Africa. Two thousand years of desert heat turns a man's body into a weightless puffball which can be made into a useful kayak by slitting the paunch. Take it fishing. Show your friends.

He called Ann at the ranch. "Have you been arrested?" she inquired.

"Not yet."

"Oh, well. I didn't know what they were going to do."

"I'll never forget it, Ann."

"I wouldn't think so, no."

"I couldn't have been more of a pig."

". . . well . . ." she said equivocally.

"Things good there on the ranch?"

"There's this new foreman," Ann answered, "he's sort of beautiful and mean."

"I can handle myself," Payne said.

"You apparently thought so," Ann commented, "when you perched on the mantel that night—"

"On the shelf actually."

"—and screamed like a crow—like a crow—at mother. That's something, all in all, for a prize."

"I got one," Payne said mysteriously.

"Nicholas, oh . . ."

"You're crying."

"This call . . . is getting expensive."

"You are crying aren't you?"

". . . I . . ."

"I see you," Payne began clearly, "almost as a goddess, your hair streaming against the Northern Lights. And you tell me that this call is getting expensive. When there's a picture of you in my head which is an absolute classic. On the order of something A-1." In front of Payne's chin three holes: 5¢, 10¢, 25¢; a tiny plunger dreams of a plungette; glass on all four sides, circles of hair oil printed with a million hairlines and underneath, a tan-colored tray, scratched with names, a chain and a directory.

"Nicholas," Ann said, "try to train yourself to have a healthy mind."

"To what end?"

"Happiness and art."

"Oh my God." He concluded swiftly and hung up.

Hit the door and it folds. Fumes and automobiles. I've landed in a part of the American corpus that smells bad. The body politic has ringworm. These women. Really. All of them perfect double-headers. Smile at both ends. Janus. Make their own gravy like dogfood. I've been up against all kinds. Some of them lift an arm and there is the sharpishness of a decent European cheddar. And that art talk. I know what it leads to: more of her excesses in its name. And things like relinquishing underwear to protest the bugging of her phone by the CIA.

Appropriately, a hand-painted sign adorns an opposing brick wall: a weary Uncle Sam in red, white and blue stretches abject, imploring hands to the beholder; a receding chin has dropped to reveal the mean declivity of his mouth, which says "I NEED A PICK ME UP." Payne approached, saw with shock the signature: *C. J. Clovis Signs.* Back in the booth, he splashed through the Yellow Pages and found his name.

Fascinated, Payne started, seeing another, up the alley which ended a quarter mile ahead with a blue gorgeous propane tank; the other end, a little white gap of dirty sky like the space between the end of a box-wrench held, for no reason at all, to the eye, a little space and, in the center, a red quaint telephone booth, where he had spoken. A radio played, its fell music contested by a rabid squabble of "electrical interference." Here was no scene for a happy boy. This was a land of rat wars, a dark fiefdom of bacteria, lance corporals with six arachnid legs.

The far wall, over the propane tank, between drain pipes spangled with oxidation, another sign, this depicting a dark Andalusian beauty, possibly a bit literal. Behind her the municipal skyline arises, tendrils and building pieces, in a total nastiness of habitat; the barest tips of her fingers, palpitant and patrician, rise barely over the lower frame; cheap day-glo letters proclaim her message:

"My hosbin's frans dawn lok me percause I yam an Ees-panidge voomans." The signature—ye gods!—C. J. Clo-vis. Beneath it, his marque, a naugahyde fleur-de-lys.

If Ann were here she would look at him, eyes reeling with meaning. She would never have seen the humor of the sign on the next building which showed five crudely drawn French poodles spelling out PILGRIM COUNTRY over a New England landscape in technicolor dogspew. How would she take the last picture Payne could find which showed a "farmer" attacking a "housewife" whom he has caught stealing, by moonlight, in his vegetable garden? Underneath, *"Here's a cucumber you won't forget!"*

Payne, agog, sped, by foot, away from the area; and ended sitting on a curb. The question was whether he had seen that stuff at all. That was the question, actually.

Cautiously, he returned to the telephone booth and called Clovis' number and listened in silence to a re-corded message: "Hello, ah, hello, ah, hellowah thur, zat you, Bob, Marty, Jan, Edna, Dexter, Desmond, Desilu, Dee-Dee, Daryl, dogfight, fistfood . . ."

Payne was slipping.

To his credit, he asked himself, "Did I hear that?"

The sun fell far astern of the alleyway.

A tired rat picked its way among the remains of an innerspring mattress, determined to find The Way.

A dark brown elevator cable suspending a conventload of aging nuns in front of the fortieth-floor office of a Knights of Columbus dentist, popped one more micro-scopic strand in a thousand-foot shaft of blue dust light.

Certain soldiers took up their positions.

An engineer in Menlo Park pondered possible mail-boxes of the future.

In the half-light of an office, a clerk had a typist; the landlord, spying from a maintenance closet, made his eyes ache in the not good light and thought he saw two Brillo pads fighting for a frankfurter.

"I don't claim to be a saint," Payne remarked.

One leg had gone lame, his pocket itched for his old heater, his old Hartford Equalizer.

Millions of sonorous, invisible piano wires caused the

country to swing in stately, dolorous circles around the telephone booth. Payne felt it hum through the worn black handle of the folding door. The directory, with its thousandfold exponential referents, tapped with the secret life of the nation.

He went off now, thinking of Ann: impossible not to imagine himself and Ann in some cosmic twinning; they float on fleecy cumulo-nimbus, a montage of saints says: It is meet.

And, picturing himself against the high interiors of the Mountain West, he thought of old motorcycle excursions. He looked at the Hudson Hornet and asked, will it do?

5

The Hudson Hornet appears at the mouth of a long bend, a two-lane county road in the Pryor Mountains of Montana. Bare streaks in wooded country, glacial moraine, scree slides like lapping tongues, sage in the creek bottoms, aspen and cotton-wood. Behind the lurching Hornet, a homemade wagon rumbles on four six-ply recaps from the factory of Firestone and Co. The wagon is the work of the driver, Nicholas Payne. With a bowed gypsy roof, the sides are screen with hardwood uprights. Inside are bedrolls, an ammunition tin filled with paperbacks, a stack of Django Reinhardt records, a cheap Japanese tape recorder; banging from side to side in the springless wagon, a sheepherder's stove seems to dominate everything; its pipe can be run up through an asbestos ring in the roof and an awning lowered to enclose the sides. There is a Winchester .22 for camp meat. There is a fishing rod.

Payne walked around Livingston, hands deep in pockets, head deep in thought, feet deep in the dark secrecy of boots. He went into Gogol's Ranchwear and Saddlery to try on footwear. He had no money but he wanted ideas. He felt if he could hit on the right boots, things would be better. His throat ached with the knowledge that it would not be impossible for him to run into Ann in this town. "Howdy!" The salesman. Payne sat.

"Boots," he said.

"What you got in mind?"

"Not a thing other than boots."

"Okee doke."

"Can I charge them?"

"Live in town?"

"I sure do," Payne said.

"Then go to her," said the salesman. "Let's get you started here." He brought a pair of boots down from the display stand. He rested the heel of one in his left palm and supported its toe with the fingertips of his right hand. "Here's a number that sells real well here in Big Sky Country. It's all-American made from veal leather with that ole Buffalo Bill high stovepipe top. I can give you this boot in buff-ruff, natural kangaroo or antique gold—"

"No."

"No, what?"

"It is not right that a cowboy should dress up like a fruit."

"Now you listen to me. I just sold a pair of boots to a working cowboy in pink turtleskin and contrasting water buffalo wingtips."

"You don't have to get mad."

"I sold a pair of dual re-tan latigo leather Javelinas with peach vamps to a real man. And you tell me fruit."

"No one said you had to be a meanie about it."

"Okay, we drop it." The clerk insisted that they shake hands. "Let's get you into a pair."

"Now I want tennis shoes in mocha java."

"I thought you wanted boots."

"If I go barefoot will you tint my pinkies Antique Parmesan?"

"Sir."

"Yes?"

"Gogol's Ranchwear and Saddlery doesn't want your business."

Payne went to the front of the store, stepped up to the X-ray machine, flipped it on and put his eyes to the viewer. There was a handle at its side that controlled the pointer which Payne directed at the memento mori of his skeletal feet on a billiard-cloth green background. He suddenly saw how he would not live forever; and he wished to adjust his life before he died.

Payne took to his room and napped unhappily until evening. He woke up thinking of how he had camped one night on the Continental Divide and pissed with care into the Atlantic watershed. Now he wasn't sure he should have. He tried to imagine he was saying toodleoo to a declining snivelization; and howdy to a warwhoop intelligentsia of redskin possibility with Ann as a vague Cheyenne succubus—the complete buckskin treatment.

But under his window, attendants drifted in a Stonehenge of gas pumps. Fill er up! America seemed to say. A blue, gleaming shaft descended cleanly under the grease rack and a Toyota Corona shot off into the Montana night. Hey! Your Gold Bell Gift Stamps! Poised against the distant, visible mountains, the attendants stood by a rainbow undulance of Marfak.

All the windows were open to the cool high-altitude evening; under the blanket of his rented bed, Payne had the sudden conviction that he was locked in one of the umbral snotlockers of America. On the pine wall overhead, a Great Falls Beer calendar with Charles Remington reproductions of wolves, buffalo and lonesome cowpokes who tried to establish that with their used-up eyes and plumb-tuckered horses they were entitled to the continent. George Washington had tried the same thing: Throwing coins across a river, he had glommed America from the English. Payne could even understand how, in the early days, Indians, oriented to turkeys and pumpkins, were depleted by unfired blunderbusses, sailboats, maps. Just as Payne felt macadam and bank accounts depriving him of his paramour.

It had been, he felt, another migraine spring. He sat up and bit into an apple, a handsome, cold Northern Spy; blood on the white meat; teeth going bad; tartar; sign of the lower orders; drop them at the dentist; refurbish those now you.

Sleep.

* * *

C. J. Clovis, former fat man and entrepreneur of large scale "gadgets" of considerable cost and profit to himself, sat in his Dodge Motor Home, easing a clear lubricant into the bright steel nipple on the upper articulation of his appliance. He smiled admiringly at the machined bevels at its "knee" and saw the little quarter-arcs of ballbearing brighten with oil. Laced neatly to the aluminum foot, with its own argyle, a well-made blucher seemed quite at home.

The built-in television murmured before him: the Johnny Carson show. Clovis flicked it off and rolled out two blueprints on the dining table, weighting the corners with heavy coins of some foreign currency which he produced from his pockets. The plans depicted a model of a bat tower which Clovis would build for America; modern, total engineering of bat enclaves, toward a reduction of noxious insects in the land. On the prints, the handsomeness of the structures was not hidden; they arose with loftiness from formed concrete piers and had stylish shakeshingle roofs surmounting three tiers of perforations through which the bats could enter. The floor plan, if that is what it must be called, was based loosely on the great temple of Mehantapec in the Guatemalan highlands. That is, the "monks" in this case, bats, dwelt in individual but linked sequences of cells roughly oblong in cross section, each of which debouched into a central chute or shitscuttle; the accumulation, a valuable fertilizer, could be sold to amortize the tower itself.

The bat tower involved sixteen hundred dollars in materials and labor. Clovis had slapped a price tag of eight thou on the completed item; and considered himself prepared to be beaten down to five. Not lower. Not in a land where mosquitoes carried encephalitis. Next a note to Payne who had been reamed and would not serve: offering him a position as crew boss in an operation dealing in the erection of certain pest control structures, a highly engineered class of dealie. No holds barred financially. Need aggressive young man with eye on main chance.

Address me Clovis/Batworks, poste restante, Farrow, North Dakota. All the best.

Clovis worked his way toward the stern and made himself a nightcap: eleven fingers of rye in a rootbeer mug, and adjourned to the toilet for a rapid salvo; a fascinating device, the machine used flame to destroy the excrement. Clovis stood in now slow-witted eleven-finger wonder as the little soldiers accepted the judgment of fire. Like toasted marshmallows holding hands, they became simple shadows and disappeared.

The instant before he fell asleep in the comfortable double bed, he commenced to feel sad. C. J. Clovis had every right to believe, as he did, that it was no fun to be shaped like a corncrib under a tarpaulin and to have only one leg. He was already sick of the appliance. He looked out of the high laminated window to Sagittarius on the close night sky feeling the ache of tear ducts under his eyeballs; and thought, soon it will come. . . .

In the early morning, under Payne's window, no one moves at all. All along the curb, cars, pick-ups and stake trucks are angled in. The street is dusty in front of rolled awnings, conventional stores in a region where Montgomery Ward sells roping saddles. The Absarokas tower at the south end of Main Street; east of town a fish in white-washed stones decorates a snuff-colored mountainside, its dorsal exaggerated where children walked too far with their rocks.

At this very moment, Payne should have been seeing Ann. Was it that he feared arrest?

Some time ago, when Payne and Ann had first met and been so interested in one another, Ann went to Spain with one George Russell, a young associate of her father's. She had in Ann Arbor developed a reaction to the ineffectual group of bridge-playing bohemians who hung around the Union and with whom she, as an *artiste*, spent her time. George, who at least seemed decisive as her new friend Payne did not, convinced her to make the trip. Unlike the bridge players, she thought, George was the kind who could receive and transfer power, big G.M. power. Nevertheless, her societal notions were such that she could, despite her infatuation with Payne, conduct a trial run for her European trip, with George, in a Detroit hotel. As far as Ann was concerned, it was just barely okay. George's fiscal acumen was not matched in his bedroom performances. He seemed weirdly unsuitable.

Parenthetically, it was Payne's upset that impelled his first cross-country motorcycle trip. Her departure made him reckless enough that he overworked the motorcycle and blew a primary chain outside Monroe, Michigan (home of George Armstrong Custer, who went West) at seventy miles an hour; and locked both wheels. He went into a long lazy succession of cosine curves before buying the farm altogether in a burst of dirt and asphalt followed by three shapely fountains of gravel; the last of which darkled the fallen cyclist's features for only a single instant of that year. No serious injury ensued; just a lot of mortifying road burn. Nine days later, he hightailed it for the Coast.

Thinking of Ann organized Payne's effort; any enlightenment proceeding from the present freedom of his condition, however irresponsible that freedom may have seemed, would finally devolve happily upon their connubial joys. He would tell her about all his wild days. He would tell her about his motorcycle in the mountains, the blue sheen of Utah glare ice when he rode down the west slope of the Uinta Mountains to fine snowless towns lurid with cold; about eating bloodwurst sandwiches for the three days he was camped in the Escalante Desert and up on the Aquarius Plateau. He would make little mention of the cutie he dogged repeatedly at the entrance of his Eddie Bauer nylon and polyvinyl expeditionary tent whose international burnt-orange signal color brought the attention of a big game hunter down in the timber who watched the fleering fuckery in his 8X32 Leitz Trinovids. The same girl who bought him the Floyd Collins Lilac Brilliantine to hold his hair down on the bike, showed him some American Space outside of Elko,

Nevada, in the bushes near a railroad spur. She liked him to tell her he was a hundred-proof fool who was born standing up and talking back. It had been a beauty autumn with falcons jumping off fence posts like little suicides only to fly away; an autumn of Dunlop K70 racing tires surrounding chromium spokes that made small glittering starscapes in the night. "I'll take a car any day," she had said. "You cain't play the radio own this."

To see Ann now, well, never mind. I'm fundless. I want to be demeaned by postal money orders. Kiss me. I'm not one of your deadbeats.

A stake truck made a huge, pluming trail of dust coming West from the Boulder River. The dust washed out sideways on the scrub pine, rose high behind the truck and turned red in the early morning sun. Payne had nothing to play his Django Reinhardt records on.

He thought of the two of them becoming one and didn't like the idea. The shadow of the Waring Blender. Short of sheer conjugality, he didn't see why that would be any better than the billiard collisions that marked their erratic, years-long circling of one another.

If only he could see her. That was the thing. Not an idea. A thing of a certain weight. They would wander through the bones of an old buffalo jump, picking up flakes of jasper and obsidian, pausing now and again for that primordial rhumba known to all men. She would have a Victrola for his Django Reinhardt records. They would lurch and twitch from the dawnlit foothills to the sweet sunset-shattered finality of the high lonesome.

Held in abeyance, the question of Clovis, whose letter, queerly put, suggested to Payne a chance of productive movement, a set of brackets for this other. But to respond to Clovis' offer frightened him a little, like jumping a train, not for what it vouchsafed immediately; but for what it threatened in the long run. Once started, how stop? How does the foreman of a pest control project retire?

He wrote to Clovis and said, I'm your man; come get me. I have an operating radius of fifty miles, a need of:

clean sheets, alcoholic beverages in reasonable quantities, harmless drugs, one Tek natural-bristle toothbrush with rubber gum massager, sufficient monies to clean or fix four pair Levis, four gaudy cowboy shirts, eight pair army socks, one Filson waterproof coat, one down-filled vest, one sleeping bag in the shape of a mummy, one pair Vibram-sole hiking boots, one pair Nocona Elegante boots with bulldogging heels and stovepipe tops, one scarf by Emilio Pucci, one pair artilleryman's mittens with independent triggerfinger and one After Six tuxedo.

He accepted, in other words, Clovis' offer with a sense that with the addition of this job to his routine, his life could be reconstituted like frozen orange juice.

Implacably, he would bring himself to Ann's attention in a way that reached beyond mere argument and calling of the police.

He would become a legend.

6

It is five o'clock in the morning of the Fourth of July on the fairgrounds at Livingston, Montana.

The day before, Payne sat in the grandstands in unholy fascination as Tony Haberer of Muleshoe, Texas, turned in a ride on a bucking horse that Payne felt was comparable to the perfect faenas of El Viti he had seen at the Plaza Mayor. One moment, stilled in his mind now, Haberer standing in the stirrups, the horse's head between his feet, the hind feet high over Haberer's head, Haberer's spine curved gracefully back from the waist, his left hand high in the air and as composed as the twenty-dollar Stetson straw at rest on his head: a series of these, sometimes reversed with the horse on its hind legs shimmying in the air, spurs making electric contact with the shoulders of the outlaw horse, then down, then up, then down until the time is blown from the judge's stand and the horse is arcing across the sand in a crazy gallop; a pick-up rider is alongside the bucking, lunatic animal, the bronc rider reaches arms to him and unseats himself, glides alongside the other horse—the outlaw bucking still in wild empty-saddle arcs by itself—and lands on his feet to: instant slow motion. Haberer crosses to the bronc chute with perfect composure; lanolin-treated goatskin gloves, one finger touches the brim up of the perfect pale Stetson with the towering crown; the shirt blouses elegantly in folds of bruised plum; faded overlong Levi's drop to scimitar boots that are clouded with inset leather butterflies. Payne sweats all over: *Make it me!*

But at five o'clock in the morning of the Fourth of July in the arena of the Livingston, Montana, fairgrounds, one day after Haberer rode, Payne crouched in a starting position in the calf chute. In the next chute, his quarter horse backed to the boards, Jim Dale Bohleen, a calf roper from the sandhills of West Nebraska, slid the honda up his rope and made a loop. He swung the loop two times around his head, flipped it forward in an elongated parabola and roped the front gate post; then, throwing a hump down the rope, he jumped the loop off the post, retrieved his rope, made his loop again, hung its circularity beside him with the back of the loop held tight under his elbow, leaned way forward over the saddle horn, his ass against the cantle and his spurs back alongside the flank strap. "Any time you are," he said to Payne.

Payne sprinted out of the calf chute, running zigzag across the graded dirt. Jim Dale gave him a headstart, then struck the quarter horse which came flat out from the chute, the rider rising forward, his looping rope already aloft for the moment it took to catch Payne, then darting out around Payne, tightening around his shoulders to an imperceptible instant as Jim Dale Bohleen dallied his end of the rope hard and fast around the saddle horn to flip Payne head over heels, the long thin rope making a gentle arc at the moment of impact, between the saddlehorn and Payne. The horse skidded to a stop and, backing very slightly to tighten the rope, dragged Payne. Jim Dale was upon him now, lashing hands and feet with his pigging string.

Payne lay there, feeling the grit between his lips and teeth. Beyond the judge's stand he saw the Absaroka Mountains, the snow in the high country, the long, traveling clouds snared on peaks. He remembered the record player over yesterday's loudspeaker—"I want to be a cowboy's sweetheart"—its needle jumping the grooves as six broncs kicked the timbers under the judge's stand to pieces.

"Two more," Jim Dale says, lazily coiling his rope between his hand and his elbow, "and I'll teach you how to work a bronc saddle." Payne heads for the calf chute.

The Fitzgeralds had box seats. They were almost the only rodeo patrons who were not in the grandstand and were consequently islanded among empty boxes. Mister, Missus and Ann Fitzgerald sat with Fitzgerald's foreman. He had been hired by the realtors who were managing the Fitzgerald ranch and keeping its books at a hefty fee. This was Wayne Codd. The ranch itself was one of a valleyload of write-offs, being sleepily amortized by the Bureau of Internal Revenue.

Wayne Codd was a young, darkly stupid man from Meeteetse, Wyoming. His eyes, small and close, suggested an alternative set of nostrils at the other end of his nose. It would not be fair to take unexplained peaks of Codd's recent history and evaluate him without talking of his past; it is possible, for example, that he was run over by an automobile quite a few times as an infant.

One of Codd's tricks was to drag his saddle out of the back of his GMC and take it into a bar where he would strap it on a stool, placed in the center of the dance floor, and make some little clerk sit in it all evening by slapping the piss out of him every time he tried to dismount. From time to time, Wayne Codd had been shot and stabbed with various weapons; but had not died.

Codd made no secret of his attitude toward the elder Fitzgeralds. He often said, *"Duuh!"* to Fitzgerald's obvious remarks and sometimes called him Mister Dude P. Greenhorn.

Nor did Codd hide his scratching lust for Ann. The Fitzgeralds had a little bathhouse near the stream from which their ranch was irrigated; and one day when he was supposed to have been repairing the headgate, Wayne Codd lay under its green pine floor, the interstices of whose boards allowed him a searing look at Ann's crotch. Two days later, he blew a week's salary on a Polaroid Swinger which he stored in an iceskate carrying case under the bathhouse.

It seemed to take so long to get through the drearier events. The barrel races, wild cow milking contests, synchronized group riding by local riding clubs often composed entirely of ranch ladies with super-fat asses, wouldn't stop. "Let's hear it for Wayne Ballard and his Flying White Clouds!" cried the announcer after a singularly fatuous event in which an underfed zootsuiter shot around the ring with his feet divided between two stout Arabians.

In the far towering Absarokas, a gopher and a rattlesnake faced off under an Engelmann's spruce. Mountain shadows, saturated with ultraviolet light, sifted forty miles down the slopes toward the Livingston fairgrounds. And far, far above this confrontation between two denizens of the ultramontane forest, a cosmonaut snoozed in negative gravity and had impure thoughts about a tart he met in Leningrad or Kiev, he forgot which.

"Folks," said the announcer mellifluously, "ah wont to speak to you about croolity to animals. We have got the broncs coming up here in a minute or two. And as some of you good people already know, certain bleeding hort spatial intrust groups is claiming croolity on this account. But I wont you good people to see it this way: If you wasn't watching these broncs here today, you'd be lickin the pore devils on some postage stamp." Far, far from the grandstands and box seats, the announcer raised hopeful hands to those who would see.

And announced the next six riders on the card.

The first was Chico Horvath of Pray, Montana. "Let's try the horse, cowboy! Yer prize money's awaitin!" Chico got himself bounced right badly and marred the stately cowboy's retreat with a slight forward bend from the waist indicating damage to the stomach. A clown ran out and collapsed in the dirt, jumped in and out of a barrel, frequently permitting his pants to fall down. Two good rides followed, in the order of their appearances, by Don Dimmock of Baker, Oregon, on a horse named Apache Sunrise, and Chuck Extra of Kaycee, Wyoming, on Nightmare. The fourth rider, Carl Tiffin of Two Dot, Montana, was trampled by a part-Morgan horse name of Preparation H. The fifth rider scratched.

"Our Number Six rider," went the announcement, "is a newcomer and an unusual one. Our cowboy is Nick Payne of Hong Kong, China. Nick spent his early years fighting Communism. Let's watch him now. He draws hisself a mean ole roan some of you know by reputation. Let's watch now, Nick Payne of Hong Kong, China, on Ambulance!"

"A Chinaman bronc buster," exclaimed Wayne Codd. "I have seen spooks and redskins but this here is some sort of topper." The Fitzgeralds, their interest galvanized, competed, clawing, for the binoculars. It was herself, La Fitzgerald, who confirmed their awfulest suspicions.

"It's him," she breathed. Ann raised her telephoto lens to the arena, her hand perspiring on its knurled black barrel.

Giddy with horror, Payne stood on the platform beside the Number Six bronc chute looking slightly down at Ambulance. He could not look straight at the horse. The ears of Ambulance lay back on his vicious banjo-shaped skull and the hoofs of Ambulance rang like gunshots on the timber. A man in a striped referee shirt—falsely suggesting that this was a sport we were dealing with here—ran up to Payne. "God damn it, cowboy! Get aboard!" Artfully, Payne avoided the nazzing of his undies. He looked down at his gloves. He moved as though underwater. Jim Dale had resined his gloves for him and they were sticky as beeswax. Looking, then, at Ambulance he wondered which of them was to end as glue. Everyone was yelling at him now. It was time. The strapped muscle of Ambulance's haunches kept jumping suddenly at the movement of hooves cracking invisibly against timber underneath.

He got on. Friendly hands from behind pulled his hat down so he wouldn't lose it. Payne tried to keep his legs free by extraordinary Yogic postures—inappropriate here at the rodeo—then dropped them into the stirrups and took his lumps. As Bohleen had shown him, Payne wrapped his gloved and resined hand palm up in the bucking rope. When the rope was wrapped to the swell of thumb, he closed his grip and mummified quietly. Then Payne lifted his left hand in the air where the judge could see it was free and clear.

Payne's joy—filling him now—was steady and expanding; and lit the faces of the cowboys sitting on the fences around him, smiling at one whose turn it was now, whose own million-color shirt filled and billowed softly in the wind, whose own sweet and gambling ass rested without deception on a four-hundred-dollar Association saddle having bought a one-way trip on a thousand pounds of crossbred viciousness. All questions of his history and ambition were null and void. Whoever it was had pulled his hat down around his ears would have known that. Payne had gotten on.

He nodded and said as the others had, "Let's try the horse." And someone reached down behind him and jerked the bucking cinch. The gate flew open and the cowboy from Hong Kong, confusing the clangor of the clown's comic cowbell with his own rattling testicles, wondered how, after two terrible plunging bucks, he had not only managed to stay aboard but also—as the horse soared forward onto its front legs so that he feared going butt first down over its head—had made the magic touch of spurs to shoulder, the left hand still sky-high and the right hand way back under his crotch somewhere.

Then the horse stood full length, towering on its satanic hind legs, wriggling and sunfishing its thousand-pound torso, and fell over backwards.

Payne cleared, rolling free of the enraged horse who, still on the ground, actually stretched to bite at him; its enormous legs churned on the opposite side of him as it surged to get to its feet again. Payne, already standing, his joy flooding in blinding rainbows that it was over before it had begun with no evidence that he could not ride a bronc revealed, adjusted his hat beside the flailing horse, took two exquisitely bored steps, kicked Ambulance a good one in the ass, turned and bowed delicately to the cheering crowd now rising to its feet in homage.

The horse finally got its footing and soared angrily away between the two pick-up riders, one of whom reached to snatch the bucking cinch free so that the horse seemed to glide to a stop, flaring at shapes and fences.

Payne smiled to the lingering applause and beat the dust from his Levi's with the borrowed Stetson straw.

7

Wayne Codd drove. Fitzgerald sat in front, not thinking of Payne. He was trying to imagine why all those polled Herefords he bought had calves with horns. He was suspicious that Codd, who had arranged the purchase, had just dehorned a lot of cheapjack range stock and turned himself a tidy sum. It was mortifying to think this throwback could have cheated him.

Ann sat in back with her mother. She burned with love and admiration while her mother merely burned. The four of them rode up the valley of the Shields and stopped when a shepherd drove his band of blackface sheep across the road in a single surge, his two dogs running importantly around their perimeter like satellites.

"You are to be strictly unavailable," counseled the mother in no uncertain terms.

Ann did not answer. She was finding it difficult not to respond to Payne's heroic performance. She still saw him insouciant far across the arena and beneath the judge's stand, a giant, vicious horse soaring over his head. It was too bad, she thought, that she lacked the nerve to call him, if only in her heart, Pecos Bill. It seemed for once his confusions and indecision were invisible and gone as he stood in perfect clear air under mountains—at one with the situation. And this made her think of his refusal

491

to read her favorite D. H. Lawrence novels because he said Lawrence always tried to be "at one" with things.

"We weren't born in a Waring Blender," he told Ann. He called Lawrence "Lozenge" and frequently associated him with devices that made pulp from vegetables.

To the immediate east of them, in the Crazy Mountains, a Forest Service plane stocked a mountain lake with trout, releasing its cloud of fish against the Delft-blue sky.

Ann lay her head back on the tan leather of the Mercedes' seat and did quadratic equations in her head for a while; then rehearsed the skeletal articulations of the Rhesus monkey that she had dissected against Gray's Anatomy. For reasons only she knew completely, Ann was ready for ficky-fick.

Wayne Codd, two years on the job, had certain reservations about his employers. His predecessor as foreman had blown a ventricle and died the previous winter pushing bales of winter feed off the wagon. Codd thought the man was a good old boy and when his request of the Fitzgeralds—that he be buried on the old ranch—was *refused*, Codd signed off on them for good. The foreman had wanted his spot under the big sky, up on the old Soda Butte where he could see the ghosts of retreating Shoshone. Codd, then just a hand, knew he would succeed the old foreman so long as he didn't offend the realtors who were running the place; but the advancement embittered him. It still seemed that—even though the old boy had only worked on the ranch five-and-a-half weeks—his request to be buried up in the high lonesome deserved better than the Fitzgeralds gave him.

Instead, they sent the foreman's body back to the wife and child he had deserted in Wyandotte, Michigan. His union local buried him in his arc-welder's uniform. The casket was draped with leis. The funeral dinner was catered by River Rouge Polynesian Gardens.

Wayne Codd had not only the physical features but the memory of an elephant. He knew that when the chips were down the Fitzgeralds would go South on everything he damn well knew was decent. And that went for Ann. That is why, on hot swimming days, he put in the long, long hours under the bathhouse. At the end of the day, the little Polaroid Swinger seemed to weigh a ton; and for this trouble and the trouble of lying on his back swatting the big striped horseflies, his Stetson dropped over the pointed toe of one boot and the circles of honest cowpoke sweat expanding toward the pearly diamond buttons, he got a handful of obscure little photos of what looked like a field mouse behind bars.

Missus Fitzgerald stared at the first of their own sections, her mood utterly forged by the appearance of Pecos Bill. She had learned to identify the reddish furze of mature cheat grass and had been informed that it would not feed the stock. And though it was the only grass she could identify besides Kentucky Blue, she seemed to be singling it out of some fabulous variety when she cried, "That cheat grass!"

The ranch house, with its downstairs sleeping porch that gave the effect of a lantern jaw, was surrounded by lesser buildings, all log: the barn, stable, bunkhouse and shop. She could see it now at the end of the ungraded road in the cottonwood trees she considered neither here nor there. She was an enthusiastic bird watcher with a mild specialty in warblers. Out here, all the beastly birds of prey that appeared in her Zeiss weighed down her spirits. In fact, she had asked Codd over and over to shoot a big harrier, a marsh hawk, that she could see from the breakfast room, sailing low over the gullies and pockets. From time to time, Codd would blaze away to no avail. And Missus Fitzgerald, seeing the great hawk, felt anew that Nature was diminished by it. It was warblers she wanted, the little pretties.

They drove up front and parked. Fitzgerald looked around at the house and the yard. He looked at the great sheltering willow that had gotten its roots into the septic tank and gone beserk. "Peace," said Dad Fitzgerald. "Ain't it wonderful?"

* * *

The Fitzgeralds' Double Tepee Ranch, whose twin triangle brand aroused local cowboys to call it wishfully the Squaw Tits, sat on a bench of fat bottom land in a bend of the Shields River somewhere between Bangtail Creek and Crazyhead Creek. It was one of the many big holdings whose sale was consummated through the pages of the *Wall Street Journal*. The ranch had been founded, under its present name, by Ansel Brayton, a drover from New Mexico who had brought the earliest herds this far north. It was sold—through the *Wall Street Journal*—by Ansel Brayton's grandson, a well-known Hialeah faggot.

Fitzgerald was proud of his place and often said to his wife, "The ranch is good, Edna." He would stroll along the willows of his river frontage or along the lane of Lombardy poplars, stop beside the lush irrigated hayfields now mowed and raked, with the bales still lying in the combed golden order of the harvested acreage. It was his ranch, not Edna's.

Of course, she wanted as small a part of it as she could. From his G.M. earnings he had set up separate investment facilities for the two of them; and it produced a little happy contention. She had built, with her share, a wig bank on Woodward Avenue for the storage of hairpieces in up-to-date, sanitary conditions. She often compared its profitable records with the slightly scary losses of the Double Tepee. Fitzgerald had visited his wife's operation, walking through the ultraviolet vaults filled from floor to ceiling with disinfected hairpieces. It was not the Mountain West in there. Stunted workmen in pale green uniforms wheeled stainless wagons of billowing human hair down sloping corridors. Prototypes of wig style rested on undetailed plastic heads. No sirree, Bob, thought Fitzgerald, I'll take Montana.

The living room of the ranch house was two stories high with a balcony at the second story. It was all done in a kind of rustic art nouveau: birchbark ormulu and decorated extravaganzas of unpeeled log.

At the north end of the first floor was the library where they held today's meeting. The question at hand was whether or not to call the police. "I don't know," said Missus Fitzgerald, "any use of the police at all down-grades everyone involved."

"They are merely a facility."

"But they mean something tacky," she said.

"They are a simple public facility."

"I know what a public facility is," she said.

"Okay, all right." He waved her off with both hands.

"It's as if something low—"

"We pay for them. We ought to use them."

"Something shabby—"

In 1929 the Fitzgeralds were married. On their first morning together, he bellowed for his breakfast. She called the police on him.

"—merely—"

"—even vulgar or—"

He never asked for his breakfast again. Not like that. Sometimes he got it anyway, in those early days. Now the maids brought it. He bellowed at them, like in 1929. Let them try the law.

"Call the police," said Fitzgerald doggedly. "Tell them the circumstances. They'll hand Payne his walking papers so fast. Or I'll get the bugger on the phone myself. I'll tell him he just doesn't figure. Do you read me?"

In 1929, when two large bozos of the police profession snatched the up-and-coming economist from his breakfast table, he had doubts about the future of his marriage. As the shadow of his struggling form left a bowl of Instant Ralston in uneaten solitude, a vacuum fell between them that later became tiny but never disappeared. "The year of the crash," he often said wryly, meaning his own little avalanche.

Missus Fitzgerald had lost her rancor, temporarily, in the realization that Payne's inroads had been made possible by a certain amount of cooperation if not actual encouragement from Ann. It was so dispiriting. A pastiche of lurid evidence made it clear what she had been up to. Infamy and disgrace seemed momentary possibilities. And though she took a certain comfort from such abstractions, there were dark times when she saw an exaggerated reality in her mind's eye of Payne hitching in naked fury over her spread-eagled daughter or worse, the opposite of that. At those times, Missus Fitzgerald scarfed tranquilizers again and again until all she could think of was heavy machinery lumbering in vast clay pits.

Fitzgerald was thinking he should have slapped the piss out of her in 1929, that rare crazy year. (Sixteen years before Payne was born when his mother and father were touring Wales in a rented three-wheel Morgan; and twenty years before Ann was born. Ann was conceived in 1948. Her mother, already Rubensian, to be generous about it, stood on an Early American cobbler's bench grasping her ankles as the then-wasplike Dad Fitzgerald —so recently the squash champion of the D.A.C.—laced into her from the rear. As he had his orgasm, he commenced making the hamster noises that lay at the bottom of his wife's subsequent sexual malaise. His legs buckled and he fell to the floor and dislocated his shoulder. What neither of them knew as they drove to the hospital was that Ann's first cell had divided and begun hurtling through time in a collision course with Nicholas Payne, then knuckling around the inside of a Wyandotte playpen.) But he never did and now it was too late.

"You wonder about old man Payne," said Fitzgerald.

"Yes, you do."

"He has the finest law practice in the entire Downriver."

"Yes he has."

"He's right up there, you know, *up* there, and he throws this classic second generation monstrosity on the world."

"You wonder about the mother," said Missus Fitzgerald. "She was once the chairman of the Saturday Musicale. She got the Schwann catalogues sent to everybody. How could decent people develop a person in this vein? I ask myself these things."

"Yes, but like all women you fail to come up with answers."

"All right now."

Dad made his fingers open and close like a blabbing mouth.

"I'm sick of the theory approach to bad news," he said. "I'm a pragmatist. In my sophomore year in college two things happened to me. One, I took up pipe smoking. Two, I became a pragmatist."

Mom Fitzgerald began to circle the Dad, her neck shortening under the blue cloud of 'do. "Well, you little pipe-smoking pragmatic G.M. executive you," she said. The hands which banished bad thoughts flew about in front of her. "You're going to give us one of your little wind-ups, are you? Your college history, are you?"

"I—"

"I'll pragmatize you, you wheezing G.M. cretin."

"Your pills, Edna, your pills. You're getting balmy."

"Show me that little trick with your hand, where it tells me I'm talking too much."

"Get your pills, Edna."

"Go on, show it to me."

He showed her the blabbing motion with his hand at the same time he told her, "Get the pills, Edna." She slapped his hand open. He made the blabbing motion again. "Get your pills I said!" Then she nailed him in the blaring red mug and ran for it. He galloped after her grunting and baying as he hauled her away from the desk. She turned then and raked his chest with a handful of ballpoint pens and a protractor.

He tore open his shirt, revealing his chest, and seeing with his own starting eyes the blue and red lines all over it.

"You maniac! You shitbird! Oh my God you piss-face you!"

Wayne Codd, deliriously attracted to this compromising episode, sprinted across the immense living room. "Is there anything I can do?" he asked, looking in on the extraordinary uproar of Dad Fitzgerald stripped to the waist, his wife sobbing on the couch, her bum in view, sheathed in a vast reinforcement of pink rubberized girdle and a systematic panoply of attachments; everywhere

497

it was not held back, terrible waffles of flesh started forward. Codd felt he had them dead to rights.

"Saddle my horse, Codd," said Fitzgerald.

"You want to ride horseback?"

"Saddle that horse you God damn mountain bonehead."

Codd looked at the scrimshaw on Fitzgerald's chest.

"No one talks to me that way, Fitzgerald."

"Oh, of course they do. Now saddle the horse. No cheap talk."

Codd darted for the stable. It was the wrong time for a face-off. He meant to keep a low silhouette.

Fitzgerald turned to Edna.

"Duke," she said. His chin rested fondly on his abstract expressionist chest. Their obsession with Payne was temporarily suspended in a vision of Instant Ralston, cobbler's benches and happy squash tournaments at a time when Europe was beating its way into the Stone Age.

"Edna," he said.

8

Ann troweled around the strawberry sets in her little garden, weighting the corners of each square of net. Sweet Wayne Codd had made her a little irrigating system, a miniature of those in the hayfield with its own little head gate and little canvas dam and little side ditches that went down all the little rows between the little strawberries. Each day Wayne came down and opened the gate, flooding the little garden with clear cold creek water that made the strawberries grow fast as wildfire. How sweet they would be too, she thought, bathed in mountain sunlight and floating in that heavy cream Wayne skimmed and brought up from the barn. Nicholas, are you thinking of my little strawberry garden?

Mister Fitzgerald rode his strawberry roan across the creek, his chest stinging with strawberry-colored tincture of merthiolate. He was on the lookout. He thought of all the sauce the old broad still had in her.

> ". . . what those five feet could do
> has anybody seen my . . ."

Payne towed the wagon up Bangtail Creek and, in an agony from his labors, sat waist deep in his sleeping bag. He leaned over to look at the vast strawberry evanes-

499

cence that was ending the day and yelled at the sky, "I've had more heartaches than Carter's got little liver pills!"

Ann fluttered around her room in her nighty like a moth. It had come to be time to think again about George Russell. She had after all lived with this bird; and in the face of Payne's luminous appearance the day before, it seemed well to review the options. She transported herself to a day on which they had traveled through reasonably intact swatches of Provence, rolling along conspicuous in their Opel sedan among the pie-plate Deux Chevaux. There were the usual laments about American towns not having trees like that; and, withal, a pinched whininess was their sole response to all that was demanded by towns accreted upon Roman ruins. That day they reached the border town of Irun where, over the questions of Spanish border officials and views of the varnished heads of the Guardia Civil, they gazed upon the gray-green wonder-mass of España.

Through the efficiency of the crafty young executive, George Russell, they found themselves at the bullfights in Malaga, a mere day later. Ann's knowledge of that came in pulses, there in the window over the garden, the garden in Montana:

They watched the bullfighter set up the bull for the kill. The bulk of the fight—the queening and prancing—was behind them now. He put away the wooden sword and took the steel one and moved the bull with the cape to uncross his front feet. George beside her had been giving the most relentless play by play: The bull's tongue was out because the picadors had stayed in too long and had piced the bull too far back. The placing of the sticks, George said, had been arrant dancing. The torero's ringmanship had been questionable; he had allowed the fight to continue until the bull's head lolled.

"Nevertheless," George summarized, "everything with the right hand, and I'm thinking especially of the *derechazos*, has been worth the trouble of getting here." Ann nodded and looked back down onto the sand; at once, depressed.

The bullfighter had folded the muleta over the sword, reached out placing the cloth before the bull and, withdrawing the sword, rose up onto the fronts of his feet sighting down the blade. The exhausted animal remained fixed on the muleta. A moment later, it lifted its head from the cloth and the torero stabbed him in the nose to drive the head down. You can bet it worked. Ann looked away. Even art . . .

"Listen to those English," said George. "The bastards are cheering the bull!" The bullfighter went in. The bull made no attempt to charge him. The sword went all the way to its hilt and the bull did not fall over dead. Instead, he turned slowly from where he had taken the sword and began to walk away from the torero. He had his head stretched out low and far in front of himself, close to the ground. Part of the retinue joined the torero following the bull in its circling of the ring. The bull walked in agony, an ox driving a mill, the torero behind, patient, trailing the sword in the sand. The bull stopped and the torero and his retinue stopped as well. The bull heaved and vomited several gallons of bright blood on the sand and began plodding along again. Presently, the hind legs quit and the bull went down on its rear. The torero walked around in front of it and waited for the completion of its dying. The bull lifted its head and bawled and bawled as though in sudden remembrance of its calfhood.

Laughter broke out in the stands.

Then the bull just died, driving the one horn into the sand. The torero stretched an arm over his head in much the same gesture Payne had made in the bronc chute, and turned slowly in his tracks to the applause.

"C-plus," George Russell said. "An ear."

By then, anyway, it was not so easy to sleep. They had been in Spain some weeks now in the small house in the villa district of Malaga's North End: Monte de Sancha. The days were not hot but still clear and the nighttime came prettily, zig-zagging up the sloped system of streets and passages. And when it was dark it would be quiet for a few hours. By midnight, however, the high-powered cars on the coast road would begin their howling at almost rhythmic intervals, now and again interrupted by the independent screams of the Italian machinery, the Ferraris and Maseratis.

George, the employee of General Motors, and guarded car snob, dismissed the "greaseball hotrods"; but often paused in Torremolinos and Fuengirola to caress the voluptuous tinted metal or smile dimly into the faces of the drivers. Ann imagined the noise made him sleep even better; and in fact, coming in from the terrace, a sleepless middle of the night, the long cones of light pushed along beneath the house by a wall of noise rising and falling in sharp slivering of sound as the cars jockeyed for turn positions on the way to Valencia and Almeria, Gibraltar and Cadiz, she would see George, asleep on the big bed, his lip neatly retracted over the Woodrow Wilson teeth in something altogether like a smile.

That day they returned from Seville where George had taken four hundred and nineteen photographs of Diego Puerta killing three Domecq bulls which he dismissed as brave but "smallish."

"Small but bravish?"

"Brave but smallish, I said."

"Then why do you take their pictures."

"Oh, come on."

She had seen in George an unusual, even troubling, interest in the bullfighters, passed off with the same misleading sneer as the greaseball hotrods; but once she had caught him pinching his hair behind between thumb and forefinger, looking at himself sideways in the mirror, and she knew he wondered how it would be to wear the bullfighter's pigtail—even in the clip-on version of the modern "swords"—and cruise the Costa del Sol in his Italian automeringue all the way from Malaga to Marbella where sleek former Nazis teased the flesh on the sun-dappled concrete of the Spanish Mediterranean and sent cards to Generalissimo Francisco Franco on his birthday.

With none of this to endure, the sight alone of George throwing the absolutely limp and filthy wads of Spanish bills at waiters, at the African who bent iron reinforcing rods with his teeth in front of the Cafe España, or at the concierge of the Plaza de Toros in Seville whose undershirted laborer son came to the door inopportunely as George highhandedly tried to bribe the mother; so that George very nearly got it, then and there, just got it; and when at the bars he would say in a loud voice, "Another Ciento Three para me," she would begin vainly to plot her escape and was only stopped when she could not think of any place she wanted to go. Sometimes, too, she stayed because she felt that suffering was good for an artist, the source of his wisdom.

So, then, ever since the grave of Cristobal Colon, and intermittently before, her escape had been to think of Payne. She could not, in her thoughts even, avoid the very beastly and useless things he did. But somehow the thought of his bad drinking, the spilling train of cigar ash always on his front, the ardent nonsense and volcanic cascade of lies and treachery, seemed now, as it had not when the two had been side by side to compare, unobjectionable next to George's calculations.

George was planning another trip now. Starting in Sicily they were going to follow thermoclines all worked out on a thin pad of tissue maps so that they would stay at a temperature and humidity least likely to rouse George's sinuses. Only the scenery would change.

But George was everybody's dream. Once her father and George were talking in the den and Ann listened in.

"How are they treating you at G.M.?" her father had asked.

"Oh, God," George grinned.

"That's a boy!"

"Trying to work me to death," George allowed.

"You ought to know why!"

"Trying to do five jobs at once. They think I'm—"

"You're going to go, George! You're going to go big!"

"—think I'm *atomic powered* or some damn thing."

"*Atomic powered!* Oh, God kid, you're gonna go."

Unable to think of it any more, Ann went out onto the terrace in the dark. Overhead, the standard decal moon of Spain hung under the auspices of the Falange.

Under such circumstances, it was scarcely a bustle of nard.

She had fallen in love with Payne; or at least with the idea of that.

Payne dozed achily in his wagon, the roar of Bangtail Creek nearby. When Ann had come home from Europe she found Payne crazy. They rented a little house for a week. And stayed together.

Payne dozed and woke in completely unspecific exhaustion. Every night the dogs had come into the house. He knew they were down there. He always knew. He watched them for months. He looked for heads but could only see a glitter of eyes in his penlight. He never knew their number. He was not afraid. He let them drink from his toilet. He kept it clean for them. He left food but they wouldn't take it. He was never afraid. One week. She stayed and saw them. She held the penlight and they both saw them. They figured twelve feet and they divided that into four dogs. It could have been three dogs. They thought with terror that it could have been two dogs. Sometimes they giggled and talked about it being one dog. They heard them drink. They didn't know. It made them fastidious about the toilet. They didn't forget to flush in times like that. They knew the dogs were coming. They kept it clean. They made love and talked about the dogs. Payne was trying to put his suspension system back in order. For quite a while there it was okay. He needed to get in touch there again though. It was like some kind of middle ear trouble. He woke up and couldn't tell which way he was pointing, whether it was his head or his feet that were pointing toward the door. When the dogs came he would really start whirling. Maybe he should have shooed them out. He didn't see the point of that. Neither did Ann. He was awfully crossed up and the dogs didn't hurt and later Ann said that there had not been any dogs. He was fielding grounders. It had been hot all day. He imagined that all the leaves had turned. That everything outside was bright with frost. That winter was not far away. He did not know about that. It wasn't that he wanted winter. He wanted to get his white Christmases off a bank calendar.

"It's all in your head," Ann said. Which was exactly right. Not that anyone was ever helped by that kind of idle information. But she tried so hard, so awfully hard. No she didn't. She didn't try all that hard. She always nailed him with that fucking Art. What Gauguin did. What Dostoyevsky did. What Lozenge did. He told Ann everything. True and false. She showed a preference for the false. He told her stories of Grandma making mincemeat in the late autumn up in Alberta with her great tallow-colored buttocks showing through her shabby frock. It was all false, all untrue, all gratuitous. She made a whole view of him out of it. A whole history. A whole artistic story of his childhood.

Then Ann began to catch up. She saw he had invented himself *ab ovo*. She was upset. After the first chink, he pissed away everything. She called him a mirage. That was the end of their week. She really laced into him. Underhanded stuff. Subliminal broadsides. But the mirage business hurt his feelings. There were certain areas where he was not a mirage. Period. There were certain areas where he was implacable, don't you know.

He kicked her out. Ann found out he was not a mirage in a way that brought her up short rather fast. Irony of being kicked out of the house by a mirage. He liked that sense of things. The recoil factor of reality. Now he couldn't see it. That kind of impatience. But he had been pressed. Two years of the most needle-nosed harassment from home.

Ten days later he saw her. A high-school science exhibit. He remembered it exactly. Ann was there. Right where they could see each other. There was a glass-enclosed diorama against the wall. It was supposed to be Patagonia. He remembered one tree full of plaster fruit. Looked like grenades. Hanging over everything on these thousands of fine wires was a cloud of blue parakeets. He left without a word. The most overweening cheap kind of pride. Not speaking. He would pay.

A false spring night. He was out in the garden behind

the house. He had a cloth sack of sunflower seeds. He was drunk. He pushed the seeds into the dirt with his forefinger. The sky looked like the roof of the diorama. This was Patagonia. He was part of the exhibit. He did not consistently believe that. He did not believe it now. But he will believe it again.

At the instance of his mother, a red-beezered monsignor was soon found in the wings, ready to counsel him. The monsignor told Payne that if he kept "it" up he would roast like a mutton over eternal fire. Whatever it was that Payne answered, it made the monsignor leap with agitation. It nearly came to blows.

Payne ascended the stairs of the bank building to the county treasurer's office. He was looking for a job. The stairs circled above the green skylight of the bank on the first floor. Somehow the whole beastly building started to bulge, started to throb. And he dropped his briefcase through the skylight. A file clerk looked up at him through the hole. And Payne saw that it was better to be looked up at through the hole, crazy as you were, than to be the file clerk looking.

He began thinking in terms of big time life changes, of art and motorcycles, mountains, dreams and rivers.

Stay for the sunrise. This dude is the color of strawberry. It creeps up Bangtail Creek and flowers through spruce. It stripes the ceiling of the wagon, tints the porous Hudson, and makes, through the screen, something *wild* of Payne's face.

9

Unbeknownst to Payne, a rare blackfooted ferret, which to a colony of gophers is somewhere between C. C. Rider and Stagger Lee, darted from its lair and crossed County Road 67 between Rainy Butte and Buffalo Springs, North Dakota; not far, actually, from the Cedar, which is the south fork of the Cannonball River. This rare tiny savage crittur came very close to being (accidentally) run over by C(letus) J(ames) Clovis, the round-man of total bat tower dreams, who pressed Westward in his Dodge Motor Home.

In a single swoop, Clovis had justified at least a summer's expenditure. Using only local labor and acting himself as strawboss, he raised his bat tower in the West and provided the first bugfree conditions for the American Legion picnic in Farrow, North Dakota. He had watched with a certain joy the bats ditch their high native buttes and come clouding in along the dry washes and gravel bars, through willows and cottonwood, bats in trees and sky pouring like smoke from their caves and holes, bluffs and hollow mesa dwellings, toward the first Western Clovis Batwork with its A-1 accommodations. At the little "Mayan" entrances, there were bat battles. It was—and had to be—first come first served. For a short time, the rats in the bats prevailed; on the little tiered loggias, fearful bat war broke out. And underneath, a worried C. J. Clovis stood with his first client, Dalton Trude, mayor of

Farrow, and listened to the distant scuffle. Presently, victims of the fray began to fall; black Victorian gloves; deathflap.

But once things settled down and the various freak bats of anarchy were either knocked off or sent back to the bluffs, Clovis could see that the tower would work. Two days later, the picnic was held and at dusk the bats gathered high over the hot dogs, fried chicken and a whole shithouseload of potato salad. Quite on its own, a cheer went up. Hurrah! Hurrah for them bats! Hurrah for American Legion Farrow Chapter Picnic! Hurrah for C. J. Clovis of Savonarola Batworks Inc. Hurrah!

Clovis set out.

He nearly hit a blackfooted ferret. He crossed the Cedar or south fork of the Cannonball River between Rainy Butte and Buffalo Springs, North Dakota.

C. J. Clovis headed for Montana.

A lowering sky carried smoke from the pulp mill through Livingston. Payne looked at rodeo pictures on the wall of the Longbranch Saloon, refused another drink with a righteous flourish. During the night the northwesternmost block of Main Street burned to the ground. The twenty-four residents of the Grand Hotel escaped without harm. A fireman ran in confusion out of a dress shop carrying a flaming dummy, crying, "You'll be all right!" The dummy was not all right. It turned into a pool of burning plastic and gave off noxious black smoke for hours. A pair of chaps belonging to a man who had been on the burial detail at the Battle of the Little Big Horn were lost without trace. So was a Mexican saddletree with a silver pommel. So was a faggot's collection of bombazine get-ups. So was a bird, a trap, a bolo. All that truck, without a trace.

Payne walked around the fire zone. Adamant volunteers capered around the hook-and-ladder, dousing ashes and trying things out. The hotel appeared to be quite all right; but the lack of windows, the unusual darkness of the interior said no one was home. Possibly only a Commie.

Glass was scattered clear across Main. The plate window of Paul's Appliance Mart blew when the walls buckled and the second story fell into the cellar. The prescription file of City Drug was salvaged and moved to Public Drug where orders will be filled as per usual. A precautionary soaking of the Western Auto roof produced unusual water damage. Bozeman sent their biggest pumper and four firemen. Let's hear it for Bozeman. "Livingston teens were helpful in 'cleaning out' City Drug," the mayor said ambiguously. The *Livingston Enterprise* mentioned "raging inferno," "firemen silhouetted against the flames," a "sad day for all concerned" and various persons "bending over backwards."

That, thought Payne, gazing at the wrack and ruin, is the burned-down block of my hopes, doused by the hook and ladders of real life. Some varmint signed me up for a bum trip. And, quite honestly, I don't see why.

It looked like rain. Nevertheless, art had raised its head. Ann brought her books inside, field guides and novels; and stood the field glasses on the hall table. She took her camera out of its case and mounted it on the aluminum tripod before pulling on her slicker and going outside again. She folded the tripod and carried the whole thing over her shoulder like a shovel and crossed the yard, climbed through the bottom two strands of wire and dodged manure all the way to the unirrigated high ground where the sage grew in fragrant stripes of blue. The lightning was shivering the sky and it scared her enough that she prudently avoided silhouetting herself on hill tops. When she finally set the camera up, she had no even ground and had to prop the tripod with stones. She checked frequently through the view finder until she felt she had it plumb and began composing. The view finder isolated a clear rectangle of country; three slightly overlapping and declining hills, quite distant; evening light spearing out from under dense cloud cover. The hills divided the frame in a single vibrant line; and though she thought there was something tiresome and Turneresque about the light spears, she liked the incandescence of the

cottonwoods whose shapes gently spotted the sharp contours of hill. She had trained herself to previsualize all
color into a gray scale so that she could control the photograph in black and white. It pleased her to see the scale
here would be absolute. The white, searing lightning
with its long penumbra of flash, graded across the viewed
area to the pure black shadows in the draws and gullies.
Ann felt this polarity of light with an almost physical
apprehension; the lightning thrusts seemed palpable and
hard. She turned the lens slightly out of focus to exagger-
ate the contours of the composition; then returned it to a
razor edge. She held her breath as though shooting a rifle
and kept her hand cradled under the lens, looking down
at its pastel depth-of-field figures, the three aluminum
legs opening from under the camera like a star. A light
perspiration broke out upon her upper lip as she pared
away, focusing, selecting aperture and shutter speed
toward the pure photographic acuity she perceived in her
imagination. The lightning would have to be in it or the
picture would be a silly postcard. But it was flashing ir-
regularly and she never knew when it would appear. She
wanted it distant and to the left of the lower end of the
hills for decent compositional equipoise. As the storm,
still distant, increased, the bolts of lightning appeared
with greater regularity, a regularity Ann began to feel was
rhythmical. She attempted to anticipate this rhythm so
that she could trip the shutter at the suitable moment; at
each plunge of lightning, at each searing streak, she tightened her muscles and gradually closed in on the interval
until, after a dozen or more instances, she stood away
from the camera with the cable release in her fingers and
moved—very slightly—from head to toe. Her eyes were
closed, it must be said. After some moments of this stren-
uous business, she opened her eyes, dazed, and tripped
the shutter at the microsecond that the lightning shimmered, distant, over the lower end of hills. Black and
white, diminishing grays were, she knew, stilled and
beautiful across thirty-five millimeters of silver nitrate
emulsion inside her little camera.

Ann panted there for some time before gathering the

legs of the tripod and heading back down toward the ranch.

She felt at one with things.

She felt as if, plumb tuckered, she had blown her wad. She knew that inside her box was an undeveloped image awaiting the bath of real chemicals. Her mind and heart rang with these volleys of zickers. Her step was springy. And her desirable little ass was tight and peach-cleft with girlish go. Aristotle says Eudemonia, she thought.

LAUREL, MONTANA
FRIENDLY CHURCHES
COME
SEE
US

It won't be long now, thought Clovis. Billings was behind at last. To the immediate right of the controls was the television. Clovis had turned it on and was watching The Dating Game. An attractive adolescent girl had just won two weeks in Reno with a glandular Chief Petty Officer. She had picked him because his voice reminded her of Neil Sedaka. But when he came out from behind the curtain, the girl was agog.

The summer mountains were the color of cougars. In the foreground, a flippant Burma-Shave antagonism manifested itself. Horses stood in the shade of larger signs and switched. Clovis was thinking of Payne's youthful power. It won't be long now, he reminded himself.

Is this fair, Payne asked himself, is it? He looked out of the window of the Big Horn cafe. There was a crowd in the street watching the wreckage of the fire: cowboys, loggers, businessmen, a camel. A young schoolteacher was having lunch with a promising student. "Once you get the drop on Shakespeare," the teacher said, "you've got the whole deal licked." The mayor arrived outside.

A wrecking ball came through a half-burned building, an old mortician's shop, raining pieces of unfinished headstone, tongue and groove siding, bird and mouse nests. A small group had formed around the mayor who gestured toward the fire damage with one upraised palm. "We're gonna prettify this son of a bitch or die trying," he assured his constituency.

"I don't like my work," Payne told an elderly waitress.

"Never mind that," she said. "Have a bromo, honey."

"I'm unhappy with my lot," he told her.

Ann wasn't small. She was delicately made though and long rather than particularly slender though she was slender too; but what impressed you about her hands, nose and feet was their length and the paleness of her skin. Her eyes seemed very fully open, the upper lid nearly invisible and the lower seeming pared away to a sliver, though without the usual quality of staring. When she smoked, she handled a cigarette with careless precision and could leave a cigarette in her mouth, breathing and squinting through the smoke, and look rather beautiful doing it. She listened attentively even to Wayne Codd who had decided that, after the honeymoon in Paris, they would just constantly be going to operas.

On that appointed day, Payne watched Main Street from the crack of dawn. And at the crack of dusk, the great Dodge appeared, blocking the end of North Main and browsing up the center line with the head of the immortal fatty craning around the inside.

Payne jumped up from his seat in front of the Peterson Dewing building and ran alongside the vehicle. They shook hands through its window and Payne rode on its step while Clovis hunted a forty-foot parking spot.

They camped that night on Bangtail Creek, leaving the Dodge behemoth on the highway. They schemed like Arabs until the morning and rose at first light. Payne built a fire in a small wheelbarrow he found; and in the morning chill, they moved the wheelbarrow around to keep in the sun. They warmed their hands and planned it all.

There was time to go over it later; but, perhaps, Payne

began to see as he had not seen before that in certain important ways his own life, like Clovis', was not funny; or only limitedly so, like cakewalking into a barrage; or better, one of Clovis' horrific signs, the Uncle Sam, for instance, shriveled, asking for a pick-me-up. Payne's indirection took him strangely, as though he were coming down with it, feckless flu. The headlong approach of C. J. Clovis made him, in his vigor and arrogance, the stick in the candy apple of America; it filled Payne with the joy of knowing that expressways are inhabited by artful dodgers, highhanded intuitive anarchists who don't get counted but believe in their vast collective heart that the U.S.A. is a floating crap game of strangling spiritual credit. Write that down.

Clovis saw quite another thing in Payne.

10

C. J. Clovis stood on a bench in Sacajawea Park at Livingston, Montana, haranguing an audience composed of cranks and drifters not unlike himself, on the subject of bat towers. Bats in Clovis' description were tiny angels bent on the common weal, who flittered decoratively through the evening sky ridding the atmosphere of the mosquito. Now the mosquito to Clovis was a simple pus-filled syringe with wings. Was that what you wanted your air filled with? If so, never mind bat towers. If not, contact Savonarola Batworks, Incorporated, poste restante, Livingston, Montana.

"Dear Governor Wallace," wrote Ann to the famous Alabaman. "As an American artist, I would like to offer my condolences for your deceased wife. Rest assured that your darling Lurleen awaits you in Hillbilly Heaven. Sincerely yours, Ann Fitzgerald." Ann was constantly ready to lace into rednecks and right-wingers.

The clear shadow advanced across the parquet floor of her bedroom. She had been in the room since dawn making marks on the floor, every hour on the hour, numbering the shadow's progress to indicate the time. An imperfect plan, she thought, but I'll always be able to glance at it in August and know *quelle heure est-il*. I never come except in August. She sings "Stars Fell on Alabama" in a quiet, pretty voice. Her attitude toward Governor Wallace begins to soften.

Her thoughts of Payne are sporadic and persistent; there has been a pattern. Thoughts of love upon waking in the morning. Thoughts of deprivation then fulfillment on the great unwobbling pivot just before lunch. In the late afternoon, she often thinks of him with anger. Why does he act like that? In the light of the present household tensions, which are terrifically nonspecific, Montana itself begins to pall and subsequently the West, America and so on. As the features of the world recede, Payne is left high and dry like a shipwreck in a drained reservoir. Ann longs to move longingly among his waterlogged timbers, carrying the key to his sea chest. Angelfish, Beau Gregories, tautogs, lantern fish, sergeant majors, morays, bullheads, barracudas, groupers, tunas, flounders, skates, rays, sea robins, balao and narwhals gasp on waterless decks as Ann runs through Payne's bulkheads.

Payne walked across the town to the railroad station where he had left the car. The wagon remained at Bangtail Creek; he hoped not very seriously that it hadn't been vandalized. Underneath the trees on the long lawn beside the station, Pullman porters took the air, chatting with each other and with conductors over the noise of steel-wheeled wagons trucking luggage into the station. Payne wanted to ride the Northern Pacific to Seattle, sitting with Ann in the observation car; perhaps jotting in a pigskin diary: *My Trip.*

I sometimes see myself, thought Payne, in other terms than standing on the parapets with my cape flying; but not all that often.

Payne did not carry a pistol and tried not to limp.

Payne watched Clovis eat. Clovis was a nibbler; not the kind that doesn't like to eat but the kind who tantalizes himself and makes the food last. Between nips, Clovis described the deal he'd made to build a bat installation in the top stage of an abandoned granary. Payne was to do the building by way of preparing himself for larger projects. It was to be called either a "Bathaus," a "Batrium" or a "Battery"; but, in no case, a "Bat Tower"; the latter being reserved for the all-out projects of Clovis' dreams.

The bat installation was being constructed for a prosperous rancher/wheat farmer whose wife liked to shell peas outside in the evening. She was allergic to 6-12 and Off.

"What if these towers draw vampires?" Payne inquired without getting an answer. Clovis nipped and nibbled, occasionally touching the merest tip of his tongue to a morsel and re-examining it before popping the whole item down his gullet.

Payne watched him. He was draped over his bones. The appliance was the only thing that seemed alive. A morbid air radiated from the man, a certain total mortality that made Payne think rather desperately of Ann.

"What are you gulping for?" Payne asked Clovis, who was swallowing air.

"I am filling my air sac."

"Why?"

"Oh, because despair is my constant companion, I guess."

Payne thought: *what?*

"I didn't see any mention of it in the Yellow Pages."

"What's in them Yellow Pages is between me and the phone company," said Clovis.

"Okay."

"So don't throw the Yellow Pages in my face."

"And those loony signs you had signed your name to in that alleyway off Gratiot Avenue."

"Yeah, what's wrong with them?"

"They're unpatriotic!"

In a single violent motion, Clovis pulled the little pistol from the back of his waist band. Payne snatched it away and shot holes in the tires of the Hudson Hornet. "You want to hurt me?" he said. "There! Now my Hornet won't go any place!" His voice broke.

"I didn't mean a thing . . ." Clovis was upset now.

"You didn't? You pulled that pistol!" Payne's throat ached and seized. He thought he was going crazy. Bangtail Creek beside them roared like an airplane. Mayflies and caddises hatched from its surface and floated toward the stars. Two hundred yards above, it formed its first pool where a coyote made rings in the water around his nose.

The noise of the creek had prevented this small member of the dog family from hearing the argument.

Later, they went over to the Dodge Motor Home and watched Johnny Carson. Ed McMahon infuriated Clovis and he yelled at the television. The guests were Kate Smith, Dale Evans, Oscar Levant, Zsa Zsa Gabor and Norman Mailer, the artist. Johnny smiled with his eyes but not his mouth; and did all these great deadpan things. The big thing was that his outfit really suited him to a "T." Then they watched the Late Show: *Diamondhead*; beautiful Hawaii, very complicated, very paradoxical. They actually had cowboys. But what held your interest was this unique racial deal which was dramatized by Yvette Mimieux falling in love with a native who was darkskinned. It occurred to Clovis that since the Johnny Carson show was taped, it was possible Johnny and his guests were home watching the Late Show too.

"Is there no longer any decency?" Clovis asked.

Payne went back to his wagon to sleep. He could see, hanging in the unnatural pallor of moonlight, a heavy flitch of bacon. Vague boxes of breakfast cereal, dull except where their foil liners glittered, stood next to uneven rows of canned goods. Frying pans hung by pots hung by griddles; and in the middle of all these supplies, next to a solid sewn sack of buckwheat, a radiant Coleman lantern with a new silk mantle began to burn down for the night.

When they awoke, Payne made breakfast for the two of them over his camp stove. The deep balsamic odor of the back country surrounded them. Payne noticed the unseemly slouch the Hornet had on its slumped tires and viewed his own pathology with a certain historical detachment.

"These Little Brown Bats are starting to give me a pain in the ass," Clovis said.

"What are you going to do about it?"

"Probably nothing. I had an idea I could make a go with this Yuma Myotis; but its natural range is too frigging southerly I believe. I have seen the bastards in mine shafts as far west as Idaho; but I don't know." He was quiet briefly. "I'm not starting on an exotic God damn bat breed at this point in my life!"

Payne tried for an intelligent remark. "The thing is, you want something that can really scarf bugs."

"Oh, hell, they all do that. I could take a Western Pipestrel and have the little son of a bitch eating his weight in June bugs night after night. This here is a question of style, a question of class. I want a classy bat! And I don't want something that has to be near running water or has to live in a narrow slot or within two miles of eucalyptus or that sucks the wind for rabies. What's the difference. The Little Brown is okay. That goes for the Silverhaired. But no one is going to pretend they're class bats by a long shot."

"What's . . . a class bat, for instance?"

"Well, no Myotis! That's for damn sure!"

"What then?"

"Almost anything, Payne, for God sake. Leafnose, there's a nice bat. Western Mastiff: that sonofabitch will curl your hair to look at him close. The Eastern Yellow is a good one. The Pallid, the Evening, the Mexican Freetail, the Spotted, the Western Yellow." When he paused, Payne handed him his breakfast on a paper plate. When his voice came again it was mellifluous and sentimental.

"I once owned me a Seminole bat. He was mahogany brown and he looked like he had the lightest coating of frost over him. He weighed a third of an ounce at maturity and was a natural loner."

"Did you name him?"

"Yes I did. I named him Dave."

"I see."

The red Texaco star was not so high against the sky as the Crazy Mountains behind it. What you wanted to be high behind the red Texaco star, thought its owner, was not

the Crazy Mountains, or any others, but buildings full of
people who owned automobiles that needed fuel and service. Day after day, the small traffic heading for White
Sulphur Springs passed the place, already gassed up for
the journey. He got only stragglers; and day after day, the
same Cokes, Nehis, Hires, Fanta Oranges, Nesbitts and
Dr. Peppers stood in the same uninterrupted order in the
plastic window of the dispenser. Unless he bought one.
Then something else stared out at him, the same; like the
candy wrappers in the display case with the sunbleached
wrappers; or the missing tools on the peg-board in the
garage whose silhouettes described their absence.

That is why Payne coming at the crack of dawn, rolling a herd of flat tires, pursuing the stragglers all over the
highway, seemed unusual enough that the station owner
helplessly moved a few imperceptible steps toward him
in greeting. "Nice day."

"Yes it is."

"Right in here with them uns. Blowouts is they?"

"Yes."

"I see that now. I hope they can be saved."

"They'll have to be."

The man worked furiously taking the tire off the rim
of the first. "That's one puncture!" There was a rattle; he
fished around. "This tire has been shot!"

"Yes, sir."

The man looked up bemused and went to the next
tire.

"What kind of recaps is these?"

"Six-ply Firestone Town and Country. Self-cleaning
tread."

"This here's been shot too."

"Yup."

The man stood, turning his sweating forehead into the
corner of his elbow. "I ain't going no further."

"What do you mean?"

"What do I *mean*?"

"What do you mean?"

"I mean that there has been a shooting here."

"I just want my damn tires fixed."

"Just fix em, heh, no querstions asked? Like ole Doctor Mudd fixing Booth's leg? Let me ask you this. Have you ever read yer history? Let me ask you that."

"No."

"Let me give you a little background then."

"I don't want any background. I want these tires fixed."

"I don't move without an explanation."

The two men were desperate. Payne had nowhere else to turn. The station owner was dealing with his first customer in some time. Payne initiated the detente.

"I shot them myself," he said.

"That's all I needed to hear." The man wiped his hands on a brick-colored rag. "In fact that's just plain more like it." He commenced putting a hot-patch on the first tire. "Honesty is the best policy," he added.

"Oh fuck you," Payne inserted.

"You can say that if you want now. I got no quarrel with you. But when you come in here and want me to start fixing what is plainly the results of a shooting why, you're starting to eat in on my professional ethics."

"I'm going to start screaming."

"I am not going to a federal penitentiary in order to protect a dollar and a half's worth of repair biness."

"I'm going to yell fire."

"What do these go to?"

"They go to a Hudson Hornet."

The man finished and charged Payne three dollars. Payne told him he thought he had been protecting a dollar and a half's worth of biness. "Rate went up," said the man, "with complications of a legal nature."

"That Hornet," he said, "was quite an automobile. Step down in if memory serves. Had quite an engine. Put your foot in the carb and she'd go apeshit to get off the line."

"Yeah only mine doesn't go apeshit no matter where you put your foot."

"She get you over the road?"

"Barely."

"That's all you want," said the owner, racking his mind for a pun about going over the road barely.

"One day," Payne said, fantasizing aggressively, "I'm going to have me a Ford Stepside pickup with the 390 engine and a four-speed box. I want a stereo tapedeck too with Tammy Wynette and Roy Acuff and Merle Haggard cartridges."

"Sure, but that engine. You crash the dude and it's all she wrote." The owner though had picked up on Payne's fantasy. He wanted the same truck, the same stereo cartridges.

"I want to put the cocksucker on 90. I want to go to British Columbia. I want music on the way."

"You do have something there."

The station owner helped Payne take the tires out of the garage. Payne gave them a roll and the tires raced each other down the incline, peeled away and fell in overlapping parabolas to stop near the pumps. Payne rounded them up and got them all going at once, running and yipping around them like a lunatic. When one tried to streak away, he booted it back in line sternly.

By the time he had ridden herd all the way back to the camp, he had named the four tires: Ethel, Jackie, Lady Bird—and Ann.

It was good to have such spirits today. He had bluffs to call.

11

Somewhat experimentally, Ann let her hair hang out of the second story window. Black and rather ineffective against the logs, her beautiful, oval, foxlike face nonetheless glowed against the glassy space behind her.

She retreated inside and began to clean up her room. Protractors, lenses, field guides, United States Geodetic Survey topographical maps, cores of half-eaten apples, every photograph of Dorothea Lange's ever reproduced, tennis shorts, panties, a killing jar, a mounting board, fatuous novels, a book about theosophy, a bust of Ouspensky, a wad of cheap Piranesi prints, her diplomas and brassieres, her antique mousetraps, her dexamyl and librium tablets, her G-string, firecrackers, bocci balls and flagons, her Finnish wooden toothbrush, her Vitabath, her target pistol, parasol, moccasins, Pucci scarves, headstone rubbings, buffalo horns, elastic bandages, mushroom keys, sanitary napkins, monogram die for stationery, Elmer Fudd mask, exploding cigars, Skira art books, the stuffed burrowing owl, the stuffed, rough-legged hawk, the stuffed tanager, the stuffed penguin, the stuffed chicken, the plastic pomegranate, the plaster rattlesnake ashtray, the pictures of Payne sailing, shooting, drinking, laughing, reading comics, the pictures of George smiling gently in a barrera seat at the Valencia Plaza de Toros, an annotated *Story of O*, the series of telephoto shots of her mother and father duking it out beside the old barge canal in Washington, D. C., Payne's prep school varsity jacket, an English saddle, a lid of Panama Green, Charlie Chaplin's unsuccessful autobiography, dolls, a poster from the movie *Purple Noon*, a menu from the Gallatoire restaurant, one from the Columbia in Tampa, one from Joe's Stone Crab in Miami and one from Joe Muer's in Detroit, and one rolled skin from a reticulated python curled around the base of a stainless steel orbiting lamp from Sweden—in short, a lot of stuff lay wall to wall in a vast mess, upon which she threw herself with energy born of her separation from Nicholas Payne.

Within all of her reflections pertaining to him, some in her fantastic style, some in her rational, there permeated the mood of impossibility. Rationally, she knew her training barred a love affair *in extenso* with a man who could describe himself as a cad, someone who had little enough esteem for the *structure* of her background, anthropologically speaking, to call her father "a jerk-off." But in the back of her mind, a tiny voice told her that Payne was someone whose impossibilities could be adapted to expand her spiritual resources. Nothing happened she couldn't outgrow; but what bothered a little— sometimes—was that Nicholas, through some total romantic frangibility, didn't have quite the same resilience. His emotional losses had a way of turning out to be real ones. It was like in books and made her jealous.

Here, in a funny way, a considerable moral precision was seen in Ann; and it was a faculty that refracted from quite another part of her than that which had her hang her head from the window, hair against logs. And stranger still, it was this part, not the Rapunzel, which made her once so limp with love for Payne, the cad, Pecos Bill; that put her under such a spell that to see him at all would be to cut her moorings forever on a risk no one was recommending.

She read somewhere that love was an exaggeration that only led to others; and she seized on the notion. She wanted a subtler scale of emotions than it offered. She was exhausted by the bruising alternation from ecstasy to despair. For someone who believed she might have been an honest-to-God intellectual, it was humiliating. During that first winter, she and Nicholas would walk on the Lake Erie shore making plenty sure that the desolating wave wrack of human debris didn't touch their feet; involved either in total spiritual merger or agonizing disharmony; remembering it now, she could only think of the lurid, metallic sunsets, the arcs of freighter smoke and the brown tired line of Canada beyond.

And, too, these alternations had a certain cosmic niftiness, a Heathcliff and Cathy finality that gave her a sense of their importance. And the secrecy was good. No one knew they were down in his boat copulating in the rope bunk, night after night. No one knew they launched citizens of their own to the condom-city that had been triangulated between Cleveland, Buffalo and Detroit. No one knew that they had chipped in and sent the Mother Superior at Payne's grade school a tantalizing nightie from Frederick's of Hollywood with the note, "To a real *Mother Superior!*" No one knew, despite Payne's opposition to Lozenge, that she felt transcendentally affixed to every day that passed for an entire winter.

Now, from a handy tree in central Montana, Wayne Codd watched Ann fall upon her bed in the debris-filled room to weep wretchedly, spasmodically. What a sight! He put the binoculars down from his eyes, having banished a rather piddling inclination to self-abuse. The hell with it. They was work to do. He felt the imperial blue of the West form in his eyes. He felt the virile prominence of the cowboy in the mythographical ecosystem of America. Like a sleek and muscular hyena, he knew the expendability of chumps and those who weep, that the predators, the eagles of humanity, might soar. He shinnied down ready for ranching. *He* hadn't cried since he was a child.

For Missus Fitzgerald, the handwriting on the wall was about to appear as a lurching mechanical hysteria which took—in this incarnation—the form of a Hudson Hornet.

For Payne, driving along and listening to the livestock

reports—"These fat steers is dollaring up awful good"—it was not as easy as it looked; a vast fungo-bat of reality seemed to await him in the Shields Valley; to be precise, in the vicinity of the Double Tepee or Squaw Tits Ranch. But it would do to say in his favor that the old fidgeting approach, the old obliquity, was gone. No, frightened as he might be, he would arrive head-on.

Little comfort derived from the slumbrous heat of the day. It was a flyblown hot summer to begin with; but this bluebottle extravaganza of shimmering terrain didn't seem like anything you would call Montana. The animals were running crazy and dead game was all over the highway. The creeks were trickles. Their trout hid in springs and cutbanks. A long mountain bluff ended on the side of the road, the merest tongue tip of a yawning universe.

As he drove, he had a bird's-eye view of his own terror. High, high above the mountain West, Payne saw an automobilicule, microscopic, green, creeping up a hairline valley between wen-size mountains. The driver was too small to be seen. The horizon was curved like a boomerang. Payne "chuckled goodnaturedly" at the tiny driver you couldn't even see who thought his fear saturated everything down to the Pre-Cambrian core. How naughty!

God the Father was out here somewhere; as to the Holy Spirit, he merely whirled quietly in a culvert, unseen by anyone.

Payne turned the radio dial irritably, getting only British rock music. It maddened him. What a smutty little country England had become, exporting all its Cro-Magnon song dodos, its mimsy, velveteen artistes. Payne wanted Richie Valens or Carl Perkins, and now.

Missus Fitzgerald, trying to make up for snippish words and a recent attack involving ballpoint pens, made with her own red hands a rich cassolette of duck and pork and lamb and beans. With her great Parisian balloon whisk she beat a pudding in an enormous tin-lined copper bowl; and set it—trembling—on the drainboard.

* * *

Payne lifted the front gate and swung it aside, stepping carefully across the cattle guard. His hands were trembling. He drove the car through, got out and closed the gate behind himself.

Along the road to the ranch buildings, a small fast stream ran, much diminished, and where it made turns were broad washes of gravel from the spring run-off. Scrub willow grew here, and on the cliffbanks were the holes of swallows. Then came the mixed woodland that Payne could not have known was the last stretch of geography between himself and the house. That it was composed of larch, native grass and bull pine held no interest for him. He had to go to the bathroom quite a lot. A relatively small band of pure American space seemed to throw a step-over-toe-hold on his gizzard.

Payne made no attempt to lighten his tread on the porch and, before thought, gave the door a good pounding. Mister and Missus Fitzgerald opened the door together stretching their arms to him, paternally and maternally. In the long warmly lit corridor Ann stood shyly murmuring "darling." They took him inside, warming him with their bodies; everyone, it seemed, tried to hold his hand. "May we call you son?" Ann cried with happiness. They leaped to each other, kissed with youthful passion, held each other at arm's length. "At last!" A beaming, lusty preacher moved forward as though on a trolley, supporting a Bible with one hand and resting the other on top of it.

Payne made no attempt to lighten his tread on the porch and, before thought, gave the door a good pounding. He heard someone move and was afraid. Frequent nerve farts troubled the silence. He thought: Windex, buffalo, Zaragoza. He knocked once more and the door behind the little grate opened at eye level. Nary a sound was heard. He knocked again, stood quietly and knocked once more. A weary voice, that of Mister Fitzgerald, was heard from the grill. "I hear you, I hear you. I'm just trying to think what to do about you."

"Let me in."

The door opened suddenly. "Right you are," said Fitzgerald. "God help us." He shut the door. "Follow me." Fitzgerald pulled him into the hallway. Payne followed him down to a small utility room. "Stay here." Fitzgerald left.

Payne stood very nearly without motion for ten or fifteen minutes. Nothing. The washing machine stopped and a few minutes later the dryer, which also had been running, whirled to a stop. Payne idly opened the washing machine and saw the still wet clothes pressed centrifugally to the walls of its tumbler. The door opened behind him.

Missus Fitzgerald's voice came from behind him. "Who are you?"

Payne turned, stood, smiled. Her face was more delicate than a casserole.

"GET OUT"

When sophisticated or wealthy women get angry, they attempt to make their faces look like skulls. Missus Fitzgerald did this and looked awfully like a jack-o-lantern. She was that fat.

Payne offered to explain.

"GET OUT!" She just said that. "HE'S IN OUR HOUSE!" she added, taking credit for a discovery that was not hers.

"I can—"

"NO!"

"I can—"

"NO!"

"No, what?"

"YOU CAN'T . . . YOU HAVE TO GET OUT!"

Somewhere along in here she began scoring heavily with a plumber's friend with which she belabored Payne. He shielded himself and sought protection behind the hampers. "You've got crime written all over you," she panted. He seized the plumber's friend, suppressed an itch to beat the living piss out of her with it. Fitzgerald arrived, having allowed a leisurely ripening of the scene.

"You jerk," said Fitzgerald, "you didn't know when a favor had been done for you." He chuckled grimly to himself. "Do you realize," he asked, "that when the Second World War was raging and Hitler was riding high that

I was the squash champion of the Detroit Athletic Club?" This stopped everything.

"What has that got to do with anything!" his wife, Edna, wailed. Fitzgerald started into a long song and dance about the kind of guy he was. And though there was considerable poignancy in his latest fatuity, its effect was to shatter Missus Fitzgerald's primitive stagecraft of shrieks and accusations.

"Ann!" Payne bellowed after some thought, trying to bring things to life. He caught the right note; because Fitzgerald lunged to shut him up. But Payne could not mistake the sound of her skittering descent of the stairs, one hand on the rail, the which seemed to last an eternity.

As she appeared, he commenced cowering before her parents. They melted under her glare. Payne saw her, his spirit twining and tautening. Before him, the one true. They smiled amid the total inutility of this bug scuffle. Discreetly, Ann recorded everything with her camera, including a final blow with the plunger.

"Neutral corners," cried Fitzgerald.

"Are we not ever to be safe?" inquired his wife. Payne quietly turned the washing machine on again.

"I can explain everything," he said with sudden blind joy.

"We don't want to hear!"

"Maybe you should," Ann said, her voice a saffron buffalo trotting to Jerusalem with a pony express mailbag of loving hellos. "Maybe you ought to."

"Are we not ever to be safe from the depredations of this criminal?"

"Edna," said Fitzgerald in the plainsong of common sense.

"Never?" A minute fissure had appeared in her voice.

"Edna," Payne said.

"I want someone to tell me," she said with a noble, judicial mien—as though her voice was making an independent threat to cry—"I'm prepared to make other arrangements with my own life if we are to be repeatedly

and casually displaced by the depredations of this hoodlum . . . Catholic criminal type."

"Oh, now Edna."

"I'm a backslider," said Payne. "There's many an
empty day between me and my last novena."

"I have my wig bank, as silly as that may sound. But
there is work for me."

"No, no, no. Payne will be gone. You'll see."

A flash of hatred as can only be produced by an inconvenienced businessman arced from Fitzgerald's eyes to
those of Payne. Payne wanted so much to have a showdown; but he knew it would come to nothing with Ann.
It was part of her style to present herself as an integral
part of a noble family package.

On the other hand, when her father took Payne by the
throat and attempted to strangle him, it was Ann who
tore free his hands.

This was another mistake for Fitzgerald; its unseemli-
ness even drove his wife from the room. She went out
saying she no longer saw how it would be possible to
inhabit this ranch.

"This hasn't been a satisfactory show," tried Fitzgerald, winningly, "on the part of the Missus and myself."

"Frankly, the part with the toilet plunger left me
cold." It had become difficult to be heard over the washing machine. It shuddered and wobbled in a steam-laden
surge. Engine-driven, Payne imagined, it whirled a sacred
cargo of Ann's little things.

"Daddy," Ann said, "it's too late for this kind of . . .
protection."

"It's hard to face that, honey."

"But you must."

"I know that darling. I see that too. We never interfered much before, did we? Before Payne broke into the
house? Did we darling? And bombarded Mom with filth
when she found him in the library? Did we? But, kids, try
and see it my way, huh? Nick here screaming that Mom's
head wouldn't draw flies at a raree show—that's not
good, is it kids? Or is this a generation deal?"

"Can we leave the laundry room?" Payne enquired.

"Let me just say this," Duke Fitzgerald went on. "Ann, do as you wish. We'll honor whatever you decide. And Mom will back me up. I promise."

"I don't know what I wish!"

"Ann—"

"I don't know, Daddy!" Ann didn't want to pair off. She wanted to play in her room with all the junk for a few more years. Fitzgerald, the ghoul, saw it.

"I mean, look, do you want to get married?"

"No one said that," Ann said. Payne was grievously pained. Fitzgerald raised his palms up, both of them to one side of his face in a gesture of assured noninterference.

"You wanna set up house, I'll get outa the way." Fitzgerald could have had the ball game then and there; but a sudden vision of a house without Ann in it, and of his wife charging in with a fistful of ballpoint pens, made him pull back. He lacked—at that moment anyway—an essential killer's instinct.

But Fitzgerald had shown his right, even in this incomplete thrust, to a room at the top. Now he wanted to round things out. "Nick, there's room here for you. Ann'll tell you when we eat." Even that took some restraint. Fitzgerald wanted to promise Payne that if he turned his back it was going to be angel choirs long before he thought he'd ever see them.

"Fine," Payne said, nodding graciously.

"Okay, kid. We've got a deal."

Fitzgerald went to the door and took its handle. He let his head drop a little without turning to look at them. "G'night, Annie," he said thickly and went out.

When he had gone, Ann said, "He never called me Annie before."

Payne seized her. They grappled lovingly among the hampers. A famous man says that we go through life with "a diminishing portfolio of enthusiasms"; and these, these, these *children*, these these these these *little children* will soon not be able to feel this way about anything again.

12

Wayne Codd eased the bunkhouse door shut behind himself and made his way across the open drive to where Payne was unloading a couple of low, tatty, catch-all suitcases. It was not in the least the kind of luggage Codd associated with top-level arrivals at Gallatin Field in Bozeman. The fourteen-carat buckaroos from Dude City Central Casting that poured out of those Northwest Orient Fan Jet Electras didn't go around with deal luggage of that sorry order. It reassured him.

Then the haircut. You couldn't see the bastard's ears. Codd wanted to go up and flat tell Payne that red white and blue were colors that didn't run. Instead, he took the time to estimate Payne as though he were a chine of beef; and he came up with the dispiriting intelligence that Payne was on the big side. Furthermore, he was throwing gear around the back of the wagon in a way that reminded Codd, by special paranoid telepathy, of himself being abused at some future time. He walked over.

"Nice day," Codd said.

"Yes it is." Payne rolled an Indian blanket and packed it beside the camp stove in the front of the wagon.

"Been sure hot."

"Yes it has."

"You workin here naow?"

"Just visiting." He climbed out of the wagon. "I work

with another fellow. I guess I'll be staying here a bit though."

"How long?"

"I don't know."

"About how long?"

"I surely couldn't tell you." Payne introduced himself and they shook hands.

"You're not workin here then, ay?"

"No."

"And you're not figurin on workin."

"Why? Do you work here?"

"That's right, friend."

"You sound like a man with a situation to himself," Payne declared.

"I am," Codd said. "I expect to keep it that way."

"Well, it *is* nice to be able to lay back without anybody cracking the whip when you do."

"Yeah, only I don't do that."

"That's even more wonderful."

"I wasn't callin it wonderful," Codd said.

"Well, that's even more whatever you've been finding yourself calling it."

"Uh huh."

"Look," Payne said, "you were the one that came over and talked to me."

"That's so. I was."

"Are you the foreman here?"

"Correct."

"Got anything to do right now?"

"Nothin."

"In that event," Payne said, "why don't you buzz back to the bunkhouse and let me get on with the job."

Fitzgerald leaned out of an upper window.

"Wayne, give Nick a hand there if he needs you."

"Run all those suitcases up to the guest room," Payne said, fishing for a cigar in his shirt pocket. "I'll be playing foreman over here at the foot of this tree."

Codd put a forefinger into Payne's chest, prefatory to making a remark of some kind. Payne spoiled his preparation by slapping his hand halfway around his back, establishing specific personal limits.

He lit his cigar and retired to the shade at the foot of the cottonwood. Codd disappeared into the entrance of the house. Fitzgerald smiled overhead . . . at what?

Payne lifted the wagon tongue off the wagon hitch and put his back into moving the son of a bitch under the trees by the tack room where it would be inconspicuous. He planned to use his considerable handiness in helping everyone at the ranch. Then they would all be happy and like one another. Thinking of Ann, of the ranch, of his happiness and good work under the mountains and sunshine, he sings:

> All around the world
> I've got blisters on my feet,
> Trying to find my baby
> And bring her home to me!
> With a toothpick in my hand
> I'd dig a ten-foot ditch!
> And run through the jungle
> Fighting lions with a switch!
> Because you know I love you baby!
> Yes you know I love you baby!
> Whoa-oh you know I love you baby!
> Well, if I don't love you baby:
> GRITS AND GROCERIES!
> EGGS AND POULTRIES!
> AND MONA LISA WAS A MAN!

Ten hours and fourteen and a half minutes earlier, C. J. Clovis had come out of surgery for the removal of his left arm which had been rendered useless and dangerous by a total closure of circulation and the beginnings of gangrene. Whether or not his doctors had been precipitous in the removal of the limb remained to be argued. In any case, they had consulted with his physicians in Michigan, including the singular young surgeon to whom had fallen the unlikable task that ended with lugging the heavy left leg of Clovis across the operating theater to the stainless bin; where it was discarded like tainted meat—which, presumably, it was. As with the amputated leg, the arm, discarded, had shown the baleful, zigzag incisions as though the work had been done with pinking shears.

It took Payne hours to find him in the empty hospital ward, where he rested on that particular fine summer's day. Payne, worse than useless, permitted tears to stream down his cheeks, until Clovis shouted, "Stop it! I may be a goner! Just stop that!"

"I would have stayed up at Bangtail if I had known you were sick."

"I didn't know I was either. This is one fucking mess."

"The doctor said this is the end of it. He said it'll take some getting used to but this is the last thing that's coming off."

"Don't listen to them, Payne. They've scavenged me as it is. I don't know where they're going to stop!"

"They already have stopped."

"But can't you see! With their tin-can optimism they feel no responsibility to be accurate! They just don't want scenes in their waiting rooms! Everybody's going to be okay! And these buggers probably believe it, is the worst of it. They believe everything is going to be okay right up to the point the patient kicks off, then they switch to their famous doctor's resignation in matters of life and death. When those fuckers start in like preachers about doing all that was humanly possible I want to kick their big soft white asses. I want to yell, 'shove your humanly possible! You're dismantling me! My arm is gone! My leg is gone! Now just give me a God damn schedule and I'll know when you're gonna haul off the rest of it!' Here's the kind of deal that floors you, Payne: Where is my arm at this minute?"

After a while, Payne admitted he just didn't know what to say.

"Almost the worst part," Clovis said, "is that I just got a contract for a Batrium."

Payne remembered the breakwater at home.

"I'll do it. I'll build the . . . batrium."

"You don't know how," Clovis said, his face, unbelievably enough, lighting with ambition and greed.

"I'll figure it out."

"I'm so happy. I may as well say it. I am."

Payne sped away with a sense he hadn't had since his paper route. The feeling of the last few days of no longer needing sleep was exaggerated at once.

So, for the next two days, Payne lay upon his back in the top of that silo, in the infraheat of the pure high exposure enhanced by the warmth of fermentation below him. And he carefully nailed, coigned, wedged, buttblocked, strong-backed, mitered and chamfered the passages of the Clovis Batrium, the sweat pouring out of him in a fog. Even pinch-face, the farmer, admitted that it was "crackerjack carpentry"; and there was no trouble collecting the payment in full which Payne delivered to a rather pleased multiple amputee in the Livingston clinic.

Ann's voice from the stairwell, sandy and musical at once, "Nicholas! Supper!"

"Sit wherever you like," said Missus Fitzgerald with cloying joy at Payne's arrival. "Wherever." Payne placed himself next to Ann. It was quite dark already; though a candelabrum of beeswax candles burned an octopus of light in the gloom. As everyone else arranged themselves, Fitzgerald at the serving dishes, Payne believed he saw, in the far end window, the face of Codd rise, gape and vanish.

"Montana," Missus Fitzgerald said in a heavy twang for the occasion, "is a fur piece from home."

"Anything here not suit you, Mister Payne?" said Fitzgerald.

"Nothing."

"Do you like to travel?" La Fitzgerald.

"I do very much, thank you."

"And where have you been?"

Payne named the places.

La said she had been to all those and more.

"Mother," said Fitzgerald, "is a travel fiend."

"A travel what?"

"Fiend."

"I began," Missus Fitzgerald agreed, "as a young girl, traveling in Italy. The Italians in those days pinched the prettiest girls—"

"Mussolini cleaned that particular clock," said her husband.

"And I," Missus Fitzgerald said, "had to leave the country."

"I see," said Payne, nervous.

"A mass of tiny bruises."

"I uh see."

"Italy, this was Italy."

Payne had to comment.

"It must have been a long time ago, Missus Fitzgerald," he groped. The indelicacy of the remark was invisible to him, glaring to the others. Now, once again, Missus Fitzgerald hated his crime-ridden little guts.

"Mother, Nicholas didn't mean *that*."

"No," said the Mum, "you wouldn't suppose ordinarily."

Payne began to see it and, wordlessly, felt plumb stupid. He was quite unnerved by the situation. The last time they'd had him in the house . . . oh, well, what was the use. It was on everybody's mind. King Kong takes a nosedive. A proclamation of emperor. Magister lewdy at the papal bullfights. Stalked through the house, a shotgun to the lip, a brandy for each ear. Mortal coils was the color of his vita. It was as simple as that.

Payne looked at Ann, saddened that he was not always a man who was in his own driver's seat. By flashes, she was enraged too that he lacked George's polish. And Payne wondered: Will you care for me when I'm old? Will you fork over for two adults in the mezzanine when we hit the Saturday matinee? Or make me sit in the smoking loggia with my cheap cigar, bicycle clips on my pants legs and a card that reads: *The U.S.A. social security props this potlicker up every morning. It is yer duty as a citizen to treat him like a Dutch uncle.* Don't make me get old,

Mom. Remember me? The boy that wanted to skyrocket into eternity in a white linen suit that showed his deltoids? Don't permit the years to tire him. But then. Well. Isn't it really time that is the shit that hits everybody's fan? Fess up, isn't it? But Ann, to hold my hand when the others have gone and left me with words of foundationless criticism, after whole epochs, the two of us to face the final ditch spewing exalted thoughts like feathers from a slashed pillowcase. Wouldn't that be a dream the regality of which would shut down the special-order department at Neiman-Marcus?

"There," Payne said with clarity. "I feel so much better." They looked at him. He was suddenly blinded with embarrassment; and his mind slipped away, really slipped away. Past the far edge of the gravy boat, he perceived an Oscar Niemeyer condominium high in the cordillera of the Andes. An elderly Brazilian diplomat stood over a young Indian prostitute, a finger raised, his nose in a manual, saying, *Do that!*

At the same time, he saw curious things happening in the American West. For instance, at the foot of the Belt Mountains, a young man who had earlier committed the stirring murder of a visiting Kuwait oil baron, ate from a tin and barked *"mudder"* at his captors.

A tall summer thunderhead hung over the valley of the Shields River, in fact, directly over the Fitzgerald ranch, certain of the walls of whose main house hid the little dinner party from the view of nobody whatsoever.

Nobody whatsoever would have been much interested in Payne's discomfort which was quite carefully cultivated by two of the three people around him.

"No," Payne said, "I couldn't eat another turnip."

"Potatoes?"

"No," Payne said, *"(ditto) potato."*

"What about some asparagus?"

"No," said Payne, *"(ditto) any more asparagus."*

"Payne," said Fitzgerald, "what do you want?"

"How do you mean?"

"Out of life?"

"Fun."

"Really," said Missus Fitzgerald.

"So do you."

"But," she said, "I'd have hardly put it that way."

"Nor I." Fitzgerald, naturally.

"I would have," said Ann, trying to show her surprise at their remarks. The word "fun" seemed to accrete images of liberation.

"You would have put it," Payne said in a general address to his elders, "more impressively. But you would have meant fun."

"No," said La, "we would have meant something more impressive than fun too."

"You seem to imagine that by fun I mean some darkish netherworld of hanky-panky. Nothing could be farther from the truth."

Fitzgerald shook his head in a wintry smile. The effect, entirely unsubstantiated, was of wisdom.

"What do *you* mean by fun?" Missus Fitzgerald inquired.

"I mean happiness. Read Samuel Butler."

"I assure you we have."

"Do it again."

"Oh, Payne, now," smiled Fitzgerald, his face a study in major Greek pity. "Payne, Payne, Payne."

Payne felt, thinking of his father's furnace, that he wanted to heat the air to incandescence for six cubic acres around the house. "Cut that shit out now," he told Fitzgerald.

Ann, sensing the feasibility of Nicholas' blowing his stack, raised the tips of conciliatory fingers over the table's edge as in steady there, steady now big feller, don't kick over your oats there now big feller there now you.

"I wanted," Payne said, "merely to have dinner in an agreeable atmosphere. Is generosity no longer available?"

"Ah Payne, Payne, Payne."

"Give it to me straight. I can take it."

The mother told Payne that they had had enough of him. "We merely asked what you believed in," she said. "We had no idea it would precipitate nastiness."

"What I believe in? I believe in happiness, birth con-

trol, generosity, fast cars, environmental sanity, Coor's beer, Merle Haggard, upland game birds, expensive optics, helmets for prizefighters, canoes, skiffs and sloops, horses that will not allow themselves to be ridden, speeches made under duress; I believe in metal fatigue and the immortality of the bristlecone pine. I believe in the Virgin Mary and others of that ilk. Even her son whom civilization accuses of sleeping at the switch." Missus Fitzgerald was seen to leave the room, Ann to gaze into her lap. "I believe that I am a molecular swerve not to be put off by the zippy diversions of the cheap-minded. I believe in the ultimate rule of men who are sleeping. I believe in the cargo of torpor which is the historically registered bequest of politics. I believe in Kate Smith and Hammond Home Organs. I believe in ramps and drop-offs." Fitzgerald got out too, leaving only Payne and Ann; she, in the banishing of her agony and feeling she was possibly close to Something, raised adoring eyes to the madman. "I believe in spare tires and emergency repairs. I believe in the final possum. I believe in little eggs of light falling from outer space and the bombardment of the poles by free electrons. I believe in tintypes, rotogravures and parked cars, all in their places. I believe in roast spring lamb with boiled potatoes. I believe in spinach with bacon and onion. I believe in canyons lost under the feet of waterskiers. I believe that we are necessary and will rise again. I believe in words on paper, pictures on rock, intergalactic hellos. I believe in fraud. I believe that in pretending to be something you aren't you have your only crack at release from the bondage of time. I believe in my own dead more than I do in yours. What's more, *credo in unum deum*, I believe in one God. He's up there. He's mine. And he's smart as a whip.

"Anyway," he said mellifluously and with a shabbily urbane gesture, "you get the drift. I hate to flop the old philosophy on the table like so much pig's guts. And I left out a lot. But, well, there she is."

And it was too. Now and again, you have to check the bread in the oven.

An instant later, he imagined he was singing the Volga

boat song. Ann clapped a hand over his mouth. It wasn't the Volga boat song. It was some febrile, mattoid, baying nonsense. No one saw why he should be acting up like this.

"What are you *doing?*" It reminded her of the way people went crazy on TV as opposed to Dostoyevsky.

"Dunno."

He had strained himself.

His feeling was that it was the dining room, the act of eating itself, that dramatized what the Mum, the Dad, had in mind for him. That was what was behind their fierceness over their food; they were pretending it was him, he decided; and he didn't like it from an almost metaphysical plane of objection; to the effect that martyrdom should be represented more strikingly than in platters of meat and vegetables. These things, thought Payne, are not relics. Bits of the true sirloin. He imagined monstrances filled with yams and okra; our beloved smörgasbord has gone on before.

Payne calmed down. He considered the solemn flummery of the Fitzgeralds' departure, the effect that time was not to be wasted on him. He looked at Ann, becomingly leaning on the table with both elbows. A certain hirsute mollusc came to mind.

"Dinner seemed to fall short of one of those civilized encounters of mind we hear about."

"Yes," Ann said, ungratefully adding, "your fault as much as theirs. It just seems completely uncultivated."

"I think so."

"That kind of silliness could be endless. You'll never tire each other out."

"My silliness means more."

"Oh, I don't know."

"I've made it a way of life," Payne said. "That means something."

"But what are we going to do. I'm so tired of this, this—"

"Yes, me too."

"This, this—"

"Yes," Payne said.

"We could run off," she said, thinking that she could take pictures, making the act of running away itself the unifying factor or theme.

"I see it in my mind's eye," Payne said wearily.

"I mean it though, Nicholas."

"The hobo shot. The American road. We sit in ditches covered with sage and pollen. Cannonades of giant mid-American laughter flood the sky around us; it is ours. We are giants in the earth snagging Strategic Air Command bombers in our hair because it is big hair. That goes up. Where bombers are."

There was a disturbance at the door, a small aggressive shuffling, the lout's movement of Codd.

"I was wondering."

"Yes?" Payne said, the dim view showing.

"If there was anything I could do."

"No, Wayne," Ann said pleasantly. "Thanks, not now."

"But Mister Fitzgerald said to come over and see what I could do."

"Nothing, thanks, Codd," Payne said.

"I was sure that—"

"The old dodo gave you a bum steer," Payne said simply.

"I'll tell him," said Codd with the smile there.

"You tell him that you were given a bum steer by him and had received it in good condition."

"Yes, because he said for me to come see what I could do. But I'll tell him from you that the thing was he had given me this bum steer."

"One other thing, Codd."

"No, you one other thing a minute. I'm thinking of busting you in the God damn mouth."

"No, Codd."

"No, what."

"You won't do that. You'll announce it over and over but in the end you won't do it."

"That's your idea, huh."

"Sure is."

"Well if you get it," Codd said, "don't come cryin to

me. Because it'll just be a case of you achin for it and me givin it to you."

"As a guest here I resent the abuse of footlings. Presently, I may be heard to shriek for the management."

"Do it."

"*Peep.* See? My heart's not in it. Codd, one false move and I'll pull your upper lip over the back of your head. And another thing: I love you."

"Then you're a fruit."

"But Ann too, see? It's one of those world brotherhood deals that's liable to end in liquidation. Damn it, I'm washing my hands of you. I'd hoped you'd turn out to be something better than this. Your mother and I had dreamed you'd be the first mate on a torpedoed Nazi destroyer. And I don't know where this leaves us; with our dreams I guess; of what you might have been; if it hadn't been for the war years."

"What you ought to do," Codd said, seeming to know what he was talking about, "is go up to Warm Springs and get yourself certified. Far as I'm concerned, yer too crazy to beat up."

"Yes," said Ann. Her soundest social notion was that everyone in the world was too crazy to beat up.

Codd walked down the hallway, the bulldogging heels of his tiny cowboy boots ringing on the hardwood. With a light feinting gesture of the head, he avoided injury by elk's antler at the corner of the living room; with a low scuttling jump, he avoided entanglement with bearskin at the front of the grotesque travertine fireplace with its iron firedogs and prestolite scented simulogs. Pivoting in a sharp dido around the far entrance to the living room, he was in an identical hallway where, once more, there was the ringing of the tiny boots as his forward bolting posture soon hurtled him through the far screen door. On the lawn, he walked over the cesspool, invisible to him under the sod; among the heavy willows he strode toward his bunkhouse beneath the singular tattoo of Orion.

Hanging, later, upended over the dormer window of Ann's room, he watched her mock burlesque before

Payne, their subsequent entanglement, her compact up-
lift of blushing buttock, his paler flesh and hers flaring in
their seizure, the long terrific prelude and final, spasmic,
conjunctive entry, marked, unknown to either of them,
by the gloomy jetting of Codd against the shingles overhead.

Codd, spent, saw the rooftree sink suddenly in his vision, Orion start up, and realized he was falling. In a terror of being perceived hanging from the lintel, his livery
about his knees, he launched himself into space, plunged
into a lucky willow and merged himself against the
heavy rigid trunk while Payne knuckled up and down the
sill saying I know you're out there.

Satisfied that it had only been a limb falling, Payne
returned to Ann, lying upon her stomach. The peerless,
long back arced up at her bottom; Payne sat next to her
and slid his hand underneath, thinking this is where Dar-
win got the notion of primordial ooze; put a speck of it
under a microscope and see Shakespeare leaping through
time; also, lobsters, salamanders, one coelacanth. He
knelt between her thighs, raised her hips, thrust and
flooded helplessly. My God. How many fan letters could
you seal with that. Enough to get the message across,
perhaps. Mock turtle soup.

Leaving Ann's room and proceeding to his own, he
passed, in the lugubrious great hall of the house, Mister
Fitzgerald, smoking peevishly and adjusting with one
glowing foot an ornate iron firedog.

"Evening, sir."

"Well, Payne, good evening."

"Do you want to speak to me?" Payne asked.

"Not at all."

Payne continued past the stone entry of that really
funny room and into the glossy varnished passageway to
his own quarters. About halfway down that corridor, he
ran into Wayne Codd who, from his position within an
insignificant shadow cast by a large plaster-of-paris penguin, inquired whether or not Payne would care to fight.

"No," Payne said, and went to his room where he admired the drum-tight Hudson's Bay blanket with its four black lines for the indication of class or general snazz. He had locked the door; but it was a short time before the clicking of Codd's skeleton key groping for the indifferent tumblers of Payne's lock was heard. Payne patted the cool surface of the sheet. "This is a happy Western lodge," he said to himself. "I smell elk in this pillow." Then close to the door, he said, "Wait a minute, wait a minute, I'll unlock it." For a long moment, he made no movement. "You'll have to pull the key out."

"Okay." The key was extracted.

"Come in," Payne said. The knob wrenched and the door did not open.

"It's still locked," came the ululating voice, urgent with wrath.

"Hang on. Just a sec." Payne brushed his teeth. "What did you call me?" No answer, but once more the swift perfect failure of the skeleton key. Payne's ablutions were most complete. He brushed first smartly the teeth then smoothly the hair. He never once poured smoothly the buckwheat batter. He adjusted trimly the clavicles and elevated the coccyx at a racy angle like a Masai. By way of preparation, he bounded around the room in what came to seem a perfect frenzy. Abruptly, he flung open the door, knocked Codd unconscious, closed the door and turned in for the night.

Presently, however, a brisk knocking was heard upon the door and Payne answered, expecting to find the drear, abnormally expanded face of the recently comatose Codd. Unexpectedly, he found instead Fitzgerald, at pains not to tread upon his foreman.

"What's with him?"

"Receipt of blow to his chops. The hydraulic effect of that, you might say, toward a reduction of consciousness." Fitzgerald stepped over him and entered the room. "I know why you've come."

"You do?"

"*Oui, mon enfant,*" said Payne, "you want to invite me into your family."

"Do you realize how inexpensively I could have you shot?"

"Yes."

"You do?"

"But I'm alarmed you would maintain such connections."

"Well, goodnight then, Payne."

"Goodnight to you sir. I trust these morbid preoccupations of yours will not trouble your sleep. Look at it this way, I could have you shot as cheaply. I presume the price is within both our means."

"Yes, I suppose. Well, goodnight then, Payne." He went out, taking elaborate pains not to step into the face of his foreman, Wayne Codd. Payne went to sleep, moved by the pismire futilities of moguls—their perpetual dreams, that is, of what could be done with the money.

13

A long gliding sleep for Payne was followed by a call to breakfast. He stumbled into the hallway and found himself in some sort of procession, the whole family moving in one direction, deploying finally in silence around a glass pantry table. They were served by an old Indian lady who maintained a stern air that kept everyone silent. Plates were put on the table with unnecessary noise. Then, when it seemed finally comfortable to eat, there was an uproar in the hallway. Behind Codd, darkling with rage, came the fabulous multiple amputee of untoward bat-tower dreams—none the worse for wear—C. J. Clovis, variously sustained with handsomely machined aluminum mechanisms and superstructures; around which the expensive flannel he affected (and now a snap-brim pearly Dobbs) seemed to drape with a wondrous futuristic elegance. The Indian woman stepped through the smoked-glass French doors in petulant response to the noise. Breakfast was ordered for Clovis. The Fitzgeralds arose, smiling gaily aghast. Admittedly, the rather metallurgical surface Clovis presented to the world would have been intimidating to anyone who hadn't been in on the process.

Payne made the introductions. Codd, sporting welts, bowed out. Payne watched him until his attention returned to the others; he found Clovis already selling a bat tower.

"We don't want a bat tower, Mister Clovis," said La.

"In what sense do you mean that?"

"In any sense whatever."

Clovis gave them the encephalitis routine—mosquitoes as pus-filled syringes, et cetera, et cetera—including a fascinating rendition of death by microbe during which his plump sagging little carcass writhed mournfully beneath the abrupt motions of the metal limbs. From the viewpoint of the Fitzgeralds, it was really appalling. Coffee and toast cooled without interference. Fitzgerald himself was perfectly bug-eyed; though by some peculiar association he remembered canoeing at a summer camp near Blue Hill, Maine; afterwards (1921), he had puked at a clambake.

"Still don't want bats?" Clovis asked in a tiny voice.

Missus Fitzgerald, who could really keep her eye on the ball, said, "Nyao. And we don't want the tower either."

"Where's my breakfast?" roared Clovis.

"We want to live together," Ann addressed her mother. "Nicholas and I."

"How did you pick us?" Fitzgerald asked Clovis.

"I was looking for my foreman."

"Shut your little mouth," Missus Fitzgerald told her daughter, who gnawed fitfully at a sausage. Codd was at the door once again.

"Write my check," he said, "I've had the course."

"We'll talk about this after breakfast," Fitzgerald said to him. "You may be right."

"It's him or me," Codd said.

"Quite right," Fitzgerald said, "but later, okay? We'll have it all out."

"I'm old enough to make this decision," Ann told her mother. Codd went out. Clovis' breakfast came. He scowled at the lady of Amerind extraction who drummed around the table splashing cups full of coffee.

"What did you say?" Fitzgerald, this shocked man, asked his daughter.

"Nicholas and I wish to set up housekeeping."

"You just aren't fussy," her mother accused, "are you."

"And it's time she got started," Dad averred.

"Well, she's not, Duke. She's not fussy and she never was."

"Life has a way of bringing out fussiness."

"Ann," said her mother, "I hate to see you learn to be fussy the hard way."

"I told you later!" said Fitzgerald to Codd who had reappeared. "Now get." Codd shrank away. "Not one bat tower," he said, catching Clovis' eye.

"I can get it for you cheap," Clovis said.

"Tell us you don't mean that," Missus Fitzgerald said.

"I don't mean that." Ann shrugged.

Now Clovis really began to eat as if there were no tomorrow, shooting through not only his own large breakfast, but all the leftovers as well. At one point, he had three pieces of toast and an unsqueezed grapefruit clamped in the appliance. It would be friendly and fun to say that he held the others in thrall.

Payne excused himself with the tiny wink that means the toilet; and escaped. The truth was the blood vessels in his head were pounding in an apoplectic surge. He went outside under the exploding cottonwoods and hot mountain light feeling an upwelling of relief of freedom of space of scarcity of knowing there was the invisible purling descent of mountain water someplace right close. In the watercourses on the side slope he could see green hands of aspen the million twirling leaves. Then he jumped into the Hornet and bolted.

A time-lapse photograph would have shown the palest mint-green band against the mountains and the steady showering of transcontinental earthclods from the dying rocker panels and perforated bulbosities of fender. Behind the spiraling lizard of glass-faults, the preoccupied face of him, of Payne. What did he ever do to anybody?

The man at the Texaco who had excited himself about the bushwhacked recaps said, "Go ahead and use it. Not long distance, we hope." Payne looked around. There was no one else. "We?"

"You and me."

"Oh, no, no, no, no just a local call."

A minute later, Payne asked Codd to give him Clovis. Clovis came to the phone.

"Hello?" he asked warily.

"Me, Payne. Get out of there. I don't want you peddling a tower to my future in-laws."

"Future in-laws. You ought to hear them on the subject of you, pal."

"I have and don't want to anymore."

"A horse who isn't gwine finish."

"I don't need to know that."

"Where are you?"

"The Texaco."

"Are you coming back ever?" So Clovis had picked up the true pitch of Payne's departure.

"The body says yes."

He'd been gone an hour. When he sat down at the table, he could see the Fitzgeralds sniffing the Hornet's fuel leaks. Once Payne saw a picture of André Gide in his library, wearing a comfy skull cap, looking at a bound folio and puffing his Gauloise cigarette. Thinking of that now, Payne couldn't completely see why he should continue to take his lumps here in the presence of breakfast scraps and depleted grapefruits.

"We've been having an incredible conversation with your boss," Missus Fitzgerald said to him.

"Good," Payne said.

"About these oddities, these bat towers, you two are pushing."

"I'm just the simple carpenter," Payne said.

"Mister Clovis says you're going to Key West," said Fitzgerald, unnaturally elated to be able to announce this.

"It's news to me."

"Yup," Clovis grinned, "it's so. Are you ready for the rest?"

"I am."

"I nailed them for twenty G's: one tower and one

only. Naturally, it will be our masterpiece." Payne was pleased with the news; though it pained him to have Clovis use his confidence tone in front of the Fitzgeralds. "One catch. No bats down there. We're going to have to bring our own. Just a detail. And you did hear me about the twenty G's."

"Yes," Payne winced. They conversed as though the room were empty of anyone but themselves.

"You shoulda seen the two-page telegrams I was whamming down there. You didn't know it but I composed the damn queries in that creekbottom. And you oughta seen my literary style. Right out of the adventurer William Beebe whose underwater footsteps I have always longed to trace through the atolls of Micronesia."

"What in the hell are you talking about?"

"Twenty thousand dollars," Clovis said, "and how we got them."

About the time that it became plain that Payne would not only clear out soon but perhaps—even if it was not plain to the Fitzgeralds—take Ann along with him, Codd began to conduct a curious delineation of his own plans all toward asking himself the question whether or not he was willing to go to the State Penitentiary at Deer Lodge and there to manufacture license plates for automobiles, all for the pleasure of busting Nicholas Payne down to size and, in some ultimate manner, *fix* him for good. The question was in the long run one that sprang from a fantasy of himself scuttling out of a low, dense bush, whirring almost invisible out of that bush with his speed, to hit Payne over the head with something of a single ball-peen density sufficient to prevent the rising of Payne again from the spot on anything but a litter for the deceased. He giggled with a thought of Payne afloat in brains and spinal fluid. R.I.P. if you think you deserve it because here's where God takes over! Wayne was a religious boy.

The relief Codd got at having developed a frame of action permitted him to enjoy, as he once always had, his little bunkhouse. On the shelf beside the Motorola, a blue flowerpot burst with poppies grown right from a Burpee's packet. That took tender loving care! His postcards, cowboy writing paper, electric cattleprod, wraparound sunglasses, Model 94 Winchester 30–30, bathing suit (Roger Vadim model), Absorbine, Jr., truss and Philmore crystal set with loop antenna—were all carefully arrayed in the doorless closet next to the TV. His 4-H belt buckle, angora dice, birthday cards (30) from his grandmother and novelty catalogues were all on the dresser next to his great-grandfather's Confederate forage cap and great-grandmother's hard porcelain chamberpot out of which he had eaten untold tonnage of treated grains and cereals from the factories of Battle Creek, Michigan.

And on the walls were many varnished pine plaques emblazoned with mottos. And there were snapshots of girlfriends, bowling trophies, hot cars, a dead eagle spread over the flaring hood of a Buick Roadmaster. In the top right-hand dresser drawer behind the army socks were many unclear snapshots of Ann's twat. Seen from under the bathhouse floor by the impartial eye of the Polaroid camera, it seemed itself to be a small, vaguely alarming bird, not unlike a tiny version of the American eagle lying on the hood of the Buick Roadmaster; alarming to Codd anyway, who, let's face it, never had known what to make of it. What was the use of his getting a lot of pictures of the darn thing if he couldn't touch it?

The bed was just a bed. The chairs were just a bunch of chairs. There was a parabolic heater with black and white fabric cord. There was just a regular bunch of windows—well, only four; but they seemed to be all over the place. One window was close to the door and today it framed the blaring red mug of an unhappy Duke Fitzgerald.

"Come out here a minute, Wayne."

There was just one Wayne Codd in there and he came out.

"Sir?"

"Can't you do anything?"

"He hasn't given me a chance."

"He did night before last. I found you K.O.'d on his step."

"I got sucker-punched, sir."

"Well, Codd, I thought you'd have had your own stake in this."

"Sir?"

"I mean I don't know if you realize what he's got her doing."

A dish dropped and broke faintly in the main house.

"Oh, yes I do, sir," Codd said firmly, "I've seen them at it."

Fitzgerald waved his hands frantically in front of his face. "For God's sake Wayne." Wayne looked down at his boots, remembered Orion streaking up, the lash of trees. "I saw them, sir."

Hideously, Fitzgerald had an agonizing image of Payne as a kind of enormous iguana or monitor lizard, even the beating throat, in rut, over the vague creaminess of Ann. Suddenly, out of the generalized eroticism, he was back in the winter of 1911, lying on his Flexible Flyer on a hill in Akron, imaginatively pitting himself against a flying-V of naked women. He remembered their rubbery collision, the women writhing and squealing under his runners.

"Codd it's rough. Chemistry . . . changing times . . . God I don't know."

"But I will do the job, sir."

"Gee Wayne I do hope so. It's what he ought to have."

"Don't you worry your head, sir. He's going to have it." Codd began to choke a little with emotion at having proclaimed even in so veiled a fashion his dismal loyalty. He was without relations and nobody loved him. This was going to have to do.

"Ann," said her mother, "wouldn't you stay a minute?"

"Of course I will, Mother. You never—"

"I know I'm tiresome and maybe a . . . a little old." The smile. "But just this once."

"You never want me to stay! You want me to get going after meals. 'Why don't you get a move on?' you're always saying! I'd love to sit and talk a minute for crying out loud!"

Missus Fitzgerald fanned all that away, all that sass, all that fearful adolescent whatnot, all that chemistry.

"I'm going to make you a proposal."

The little furrow, only one now, between the tapered eyebrows; the delicately rouged beezer narrowed with the seriousness of it. Ann grew desperate. I'm only a kid, she thought, I want to hightail it; not this thing with papers. She wondered what it could mean anyway, feeling her chemicals boil up the neck of her Pyrex beaker. But the old lady looked bananas as she produced now a red vinyl portfolio with her lawyer's name, B. Cheep, Counselor-At-Law, in gold rubber on its handle. Out came the papers, business papers, girl; papers with which Missus Fitzgerald planned to make a serious obstacle to Nicholas Payne.

"These aren't only for people who go bald," said the Missus.

"What's this? What *is* this, Mother?"

"The wig bank! The wig bank!" The famous lapis lazuli glitter of eyes.

"Oh."

"You say 'oh.' "

"Actually, yes."

"I wonder if you would say, 'oh' in some of the circumstances I have been forced to visualize."

The gnomic tone bothered Ann.

"Maybe I would say something quite different, Mother."

"I wonder if you would say 'oh' if you were a part-time secretary at the bank in Wyandotte who had dropped December's salary on a teased blonde beehive which you had stored all through the summer and broken out for the Fireman's Ball in November only to find that the expensive article contained a real thriving colony of roaches and weevils; so you spray it with DDT or 2, 4-D or Black Flag or Roach-No-Mo and all the bugs, all the roaches, all the weevils run out and the wig bursts into flames by *spontaneous combustion* and the house which you and your hubby—because that's what they call their husbands, those people: *hubbies*—burns down around the wig and your nest egg goes up with the mortgage and it's the end. I wonder then, if you were her and had owned this wig which you had stored privately, I wonder if you would have wondered about a refrigerated fireproofed wig bank after all? Or not."

A little voice: "I would have put my wig in the wig bank."

"I THOUGHT SO. And I was wondering one last thing. I was wondering if the owner of this wig bank came up to you and hinted at a partnership I was wondering if you would shrug with that pretty little dumbbell face and say 'oh.' "

Suddenly Ann wanted to bring in the cane crop in Oriente Province where the work and earth was good all at once and Castro came out in the evenings to pitch a few innings and maybe give your tit a little squeeze and said he appreciated your loading all those *arrobas* for the people; and the cane fields ran to the sea where a primitive but real belief in Art helped people meet the day.

"How can I be your partner?" she asked.

"Come to Detroit with me now."

"But Nicholas I wanted to see more of Nicholas."

"You wanted to see more of Nicholas."

"Don't make fun."

"I had smaller chances for developing standards, my girl. But I developed them I assure you. I was fussy."

"Well, so am I."

"Not to my way of thinking."

"I'll go along with that."

"You control your tone," her mother said.

"You control yours."

"Trying to extort a half interest in my wig bank and not plan on showing up for the work side of things."

"I don't want a half interest in your little bitch of a wig bank."

"You don't have the standards for the job anyway," says the Ma, lighting a Benson and Hedges. "Well, you won't get it I assure you. We need people who are fussy."

When Missus Fitzgerald got rolling scarcely anyone in sight got off unabraded.

Ann went to her room. She was comforted a little by it and by the tremendous number of familiar objects. But the objects themselves brought a special discomfort. In this way: Ann felt that it might soon be requisite for her to go with Payne someplace and she wanted to do that. But she wanted to stay around and play with all the junk in her room and look out of the window and read passionate books and write poems and take photographs that held meaning. And she didn't mind getting laid either if she could sleep at home; but to be out there on the road doing it and not be able to go back and play with all the junk at night. . . . Plus, someday, and this had to be gone into rather systematically, when it became necessary to think in terms of the long run, she did not want to find she had closed the door on George, the rara avis, as her father called him.

Payne knew the time was coming now. He didn't know when precisely; nor did he know that Wayne Codd, former Gyrene and present-day homicidal knucklehead extraordinaire, stalked him from afar, looking for an opening and feeling soundly backed up by the Fitzgeralds senior. Codd himself had no plan. He was just going to get in there and let the worst of his instincts take over. By contrast, Payne, excited about his coming travels, thought of the open roads of America and the *Saturday Evening Post* and its covers by his favorite artist besides Paul Klee: Norman Rockwell. "Make it me who's out there!" He saw spacious skies and amber waves of grain. Most of all he saw the alligator hammocks of Florida and, in his mind's eye, a stately bat tower standing in an endless saw-grass savannah over which passed the constant shadows of tropical cloudscapes; merry bats singled out stinging bugs at mealtime; Payne confronted a wall of Seminole gratitude. And on a high rounded beach the multiple amputee of original bat schemes smiled at a blue horizon.

You'd think he'd never been there.

These frosty mornings put the young wanderer in mind of the Tamiami Trail. He remembered, not uncritically, juice bars where the hookers went to keep up their vitamin C. He remembered a cocktail lounge with aquarium walls that let you see water ballet. He remembered his surprise when girls who had waited on him before appeared behind the glass, streams of bubbles going up from the corners of forced subaqueous smiles. Most of all, he remembered the vivid, rubbery cleavage of one of the girls who swam toward the glass. He wanted to stir her with wrinkled waterlogged fingers of his own. One day, he sat close to the glass and made a simian face over his cuba libre. The girl, who turned out to be a Seminole, laughed huge silver globes to the surface.

He was seventeen. Those were the days when he still went around on crutches for no reason at all and carried a pistol. He was riding his first motorcycle, an early hog, acetylene-torched from the contours of a Harley 74 ("Call it a Harley cause it harley ever starts."), toward Everglades City with the Seminole girl on the back. For the first part of the ten days they traveled together, she seemed as assimilated as an airline stewardess—owned a bikini, ate snacks, screwed with a coy reserve and made, while doing so, the same "bleep" Payne heard subsequently from small weather satellites. He carried the crutches on the bike, the pistol in his pants. By the end of the trip, the coy reserve had vanished and in all respects, Payne felt, she had become an aborigine.

She taught him this: Hold the pistol at the ready, ride the back roads in the 'glades at night in first gear with the lights on dim; when you spot a rabbit, hit the brights, shift to second and "get on it a ton" until you overtake the rabbit, draw the gun, shoot the rabbit and stop.

Then the aborigine would skin the rabbit, make a fire and cook it over little flames that lit their faces, the motorcycle and the palmettos. After that, whiskey drinking and off-color games would set in.

One night she took him to see an alligator the poachers hadn't found: an enormous beauty with jaws all scarred from eating turtles. Miami wasn't far away; but this was a thousand years ago, back when the Harley was already old.

Now Payne meant to show Ann what it had been like. Incipient Calvinism would keep him from divulging the details of the Seminole girl's lessons. Historically, she would be simply an Indian who had guided him in the Everglades.

Payne had no way of knowing that Ann would expand his entire sense of the word "aborigine" with cute tricks of her own.

Codd was summoned to the library, scene of recent ballpoint skirmishes and terminal conferences re: the transgressions of Payne. Missus Fitzgerald smoked contemplatively in the bay window, looking out upon the greedy willow that secretly probed for delicious effluents in the Fitzgerald septic tank. Fitzgerald, turned to the liquor wagon, his back to Codd, his hands doing something invisible like a baseball pitcher adjusting a secret grip on the ball. Abruptly he turned with one of his chunky famous highballs aloft for Codd—thinking, "The foreman is brought in for a drink with the owner"—and said, "Our dear Wayne."

Why not simply accept the fact that the willow is a symbol.

"Thank you," said Wayne.

"What do you think of this Payne?" asked Missus Fitzgerald.

"I dunno really."

"Go ahead," said Fitzgerald, "roll it over in your mind: What do you really think of the bastard."

"I've got my doubts," Codd said.

Missus Fitzgerald chuckled. "You're so deferential, Wayne. That makes us even fonder of you." Wayne thought of automotive differentials, how they accepted the power of the motor and made those wheels turn massively like all those wheels turned massively in grade-school educational movies about the U.S. on the go.

"Wayne," said Fitzgerald, "we've got our doubts as well. But because of Ann, who is essentially just a baby still, can you follow that? still just a baby, Wayne, because of Ann this guy has us over a barrel and we have no recourse at all. He cannot be discouraged. He cannot be sent away. God, I remember when I was wooing the missus, why hell I—"

"Let's not talk about you just now, dear."

"That's right, honey. Let's keep our eye on the ball. — Uh, Wayne, I don't know how to say this—" He turned to his wife. "—but God damn it honey, aren't we getting fond of Wayne?"

Wayne picked up the thread right along in here, about how he was earmarked as the son-in-law. In his mind's eye, he twirls a silk opera hat; beside him in the box, Ann listens raptly as a heavy fellow in a jerkin bays, *"Amour!"*

"Yes, Duke, indeed we are."

"Wayne, let me throw the meat on the table. This bird has kind of got the double whammy on us, what with Ann's being, at this point, little more than a child. And, on the level, the guy has our hands tied."

"This goes way back," says Missus Fitzgerald. "We've had him in the house like a cat burglar, you know, rooting through the liquor cabinet and whatnot." Fitzgerald studied her face for indiscretion. "No, Duke, now," she said, seeing it. "Wayne has to know."

"This is true," Duke acceded slowly.

"Anyhow, we just wanted to fill you in," she said.

"Kind of put the bee in your bonnet," he said.

"And you kind of see what you can come up with," she said.

"Go ahead and finish your highball," he said.

"You've hardly touched it," she said.

"Oh, hell, take it to the bunkhouse and finish it," he said. "And bring back the glass when you're through."

14

C. J. Clovis too was now
asleep in the mobile home; he had removed the two artificial limbs. Since the missing arm and missing leg were
from the same side of his body, he looked, sleeping on his
stomach, like a boomerang. In his dreams, he twitched
with happiness. He saw his towers crossing the country,
none out of sight of the other. He dreamed of a natural
harmony in which the silent war of bats on bugs left a
ground level peace where ladies shelled peas under evening trees. Slivers of white showed between his lids as his
eyes rolled to applause.

Two years ago, George published Ann's poems. It was a
birthday present. The book was reviewed in *Sumac*, a
literary magazine which had assumed the subscription
list of a former publication, *Diesel*, a journal of lesbian
apologetics. Seeing the review again gave Ann such a
sense of her own ability to synthesize hard-edge experience that she lost a good deal of her fear of going off with
Nicholas:

> It is difficult to talk of the work of Ann Fitzgerald
> without mentioning the sense of longing, of time
> and love past, that percolates through her best
> verse. These are delicate moods that survive the
> most concrete—even brutal—details. This, from *A*

Loss Of Petals (George Russell Editions, Malaga, 1968):

> "Beside me on *our* bed
>   his sleep fitful:
> We *lingered* at our lovemaking(s).
>
> And at his tossings
>   his
>   dong
>   flopped
>   wanly
> To the Posturepedic shadows
>   of mice and loss."

At a time when poetry faces schism and a dearth of real gift, Fitzgerald's perfect reveries throb just under the skin of a discredited craft.

She would have shown the book to Payne long ago, if it hadn't been for the publisher's colophon. And she didn't really want him to know how clever she was. Moreover, she had a specific interest in photographing him when he was being most emptily superior, when reflex maleness made him show himself at his worst. Nothing personal, mind you; she was chasing universals.

In the immediate future, she wanted only a dead-level view of the country. She wanted to be along for the ride just like those cowboy's floozies she saw at all hours sitting under the rear-view mirrors of pickups. The simple national archetypes like floozies, bowlers and rotarians seemed suddenly to be rather at one with things, possibly in a way Lozenge could never have foreseen. In an epoch in which it was silly to be a druid or red Indian, there was a certain zero-hour solace in being something large enough to attract contempt. Ann looked forward to being a floozy as another girl might have anticipated her freshman year at Vassar. With almost Germanic intentness, she had set her sights on being cheap and available and not in the least fussy.

She broke out the peroxide, pouted at herself in the mirror and squeaked, "Call me Sherri."

In the quiet of a Michigan evening, Payne's mother tweezed a dog's hair from the meat loaf. A moment later, without warning, she thrust a spoiled cheese into a lidless plastic garbage pail. Payne's father, in the den, stared at a picture of Payne dribbling in for a lay-up. "Mother," he called to Missus Payne, who was trying apparently to thrust that cheese all the way to the bottom of the pail. "Here's that picture of Nicholas dribbling in for a lay-up you asked about!"

Nicholas Payne hunkered in his handmade bow-roofed and screened motor wagon and packed with joy his possessions. He knew that this little driveway he was parked in was hooked up to every road in America; and all those roads ran to the sea.

He slowly packed his mummy bag into its stuff sack thereby closing the parenthesis on whatever fantasies he had had about walking over the mountains that summer. He took the sheepherders' stove to pieces and stored it. He lifted the cookware down from the hooks on the ceiling and rolled the Coleman lantern in a towel.

Wayne Codd sat on the one-front step that his bunkhouse had, watched Payne, and waited for it to get dark. He just wanted to get in there and play it by ear. Afterwards—on those evenings when he and Ann weren't at the opera— they would have two possibly three *hand-picked* couples over for bridge and drinks. Sometimes when they were feeling restless, they would drive out to Gallatin Field to see the kind of people who got off the plane, just to keep a check on that. Late that night, Ann would perform her duties as a wife. Codd troubled over that idea a moment or two, mistakenly emphasizing the word "perform" in his mind; until with exquisite anguish he saw what was essential to the notion. *"Duties!"* he groaned with ecstasy. *"Perform duties!"*

* * *

Dad Fitzgerald was awfully hungry and just prowling around the kitchen and getting in the Missus' way. She ignored him and moved through the room with a certain dirigible grace. When, from time to time, he caught her eye they smiled at each other; until once when he smiled and she just stared back at his face. She came up close to him. "I thought so," she said. "Get back upstairs and groom your nose!"

"I'm hungry!"

"I'm not going to have that at dinner. I told you if you let yourself go I'd go back for bank inventory. Now groom that nose." Fitzgerald started to leave the room. Her voice softened. "Dinner will be ready when you come down," she added to placate the honking auto dodo.

He went back up the stairs of a house built on the ancestral hunting grounds of the Absaroka Indians, with a gloomy certainty that the rotary nose clipper had been left at home. And even though he knew it was irrational, he began to lose interest in the West.

Codd, originally hunkered by the wagon, later hunkered by a bush; and then out of pure feral instinct, moved, unconsciously, under the bush itself until his camouflage was quite complete and only the shiny points of his Mariposa cowboy boots and slow-burn eyes would have been visible to a botanist peering to identify the bush (Juniper).

The point of his left elbow rested upon his knee. His left hand supported his face, tilted to the left to smear slightly the flesh on the Anglo-Mongol cheekbone. His right forearm rested upon the other knee at such a pitch that his fingers dangled all the way to the ground, resting delicately upon the end of an iron sash weight.

If you had photographed Codd and drawn a circle around the picture of him, the diameter of which was a direct line drawn from the tip of one boot to the crown of his head, he would have filled the whole circle with the rest of his body; he was compact, in this posture, as dense and raring as a seamless cannonball.

No one photographed Codd. No one knew Codd was in the bush with the sash weight watching Payne behind the screen of his wagon. Codd could see little more than the movement of a lantern now behind the screens and behind the leaves of his own bush. Rising over the barn in a sky still very slightly blue, the moon made a mark like when your arm is grabbed and a fingernail sinks. A light was still on in the barn. The door was open and a luminous gold rectangle of hay dust was lit from behind. Codd was passing time by guessing weights and distances. As patient and systematic as he seemed to be, Wayne Codd was in the most important ways completely out of kilter. The words "ball peen" pivoted through his mind too ardently for anyone's comfort but his own.

Payne examined the trailer hitch with a flashlight. It was a good sturdy mount with welded struts and a two-inch ball. The trouble was it was necessarily attached to the car. He could see the circle of metal corruption around each of the welds and, looking underneath, whole sections of the frame seemed mechanically compromised and degenerate. The essential horridness of the Hudson was disclosing itself. It had begun to destruct.

He crawled further under the car, examining the places where the steel of the springs had crystallized. The shocks were hopeless. Every grease nipple exuded a fist of gritty sludge. As Payne looked around, he began to develop a fear that the car would collapse on top of him.

How he wished he had his old Matchless motorcycle again with its single 500 c.c. cylinder, its low-end monster torque and simplicity. He was sick of the lurching mechanical hysteria. He wanted to stretch out on the Matchless, his chin on the gas tank, his feet crisscrossed on the rear fender, his hands out in front of him like a man in a racing dive, and listen to that English engine come up on the cam for the purest and most haunting wail he had ever heard since Niña de los Peines.

No more Hudson Hornet seat springs liberating suddenly from the long oppression of upholstery to stick him in the ass. No more steel shriek of brakes and sudden vision of highway through the floorboards. No more gradual twirl of rear-view mirror or wide-open charge down quiet streets even though the foot was off the accelerator and he was now groping on the floor to pull it back.

Payne wanted a Coupe de Ville with mink upholstery. He wanted factory air and four on the floor. He wanted tinted glass and the optional four barrels. He wanted a stingy-brim Stetson and a twenty-three-hair moustache. He wanted the AM-FM with stereo speakers in the back, the tape deck, and the climate control lever that let you have Springtime in the Laurentians forever.

For a long time he lay there with the nine-battery Ray-O-Vac in his hand. It never occurred to him that it was unwieldy and flimsy compared to a sash weight.

Codd saw the light fan out from under the car and started to make his move. He spilled forward onto his fingertips, his face up and forward like a mandril's; and sidled into the evening air.

During the Livingston rodeo, a gopher and a rattlesnake had faced off under one Engelmann's spruce way up in the ultraviolet-saturated shadows of the Absarokas. Only the snake had been able to pay attention. After that the gopher was done for. A goner. What's more, the gopher died a virgin. His own secret genetic message sent a million years ago went undelivered. The message of the snake, however, had gone special-handling first-class registered. Which goes to show: It doesn't pay to scrimp on postage.

Payne was remembering when the dogs were passing the foot of the stairs. Is that what they were? Were they dogs? Yes, he decided, those were man's best friends passing the foot of the stairs. Sometimes he feared going downstairs in the morning that they'd still be there to rip through his terrycloth robe and tear at his inwards.

He looked at the rather vague edge of the Hornet's rocker panel. Thrust under and toward him were the snakeskin tips of Wayne Codd's Mariposa cowboy boots.

Payne understood now. He imperceptibly moved the flashlight off his chest and propped it beside him so that it continued to fan out at exactly the same angle. Codd's placement of his feet, just outside the penumbra of light,

now made sense. Then Payne moved carefully to get out
from under the car at the other side. He looked back. The
boots hadn't moved. The long curves of them were crisscrossed with the shadows of tie-rods. Payne rolled free,
rising slowly to look at Codd through the windows of the
car. Codd's head was bent downward, watching with absolute attention and lack of motion.

As yet, Payne had not specified his alarm, picked his
flavor between terror and concern. He moved very cautiously to the front of the car without alerting Codd and
then watched him for some moments. He spotted the
long billet of sash and felt an indignation of his own that
was entirely dangerous. He studied Codd very closely
then. He could not have missed anything. He did not
miss the soundless motion of Codd's eyes turning up to
see him.

Codd began to move, loose and righteous with what
he had to do. When he was close enough he swung at
Payne. He swung too far because the weighted fist hit
Payne under the ear so that Payne felt something sing
through him but did not fall. Then, when Codd missed on
the next swipe and kicked wildly at Payne, Payne rushed
him and got him over the hood of the car battering him
against the moonlit dihedral of windshield and feeling a
tremendous turbulence inside of himself as he lifted the
ragdoll weight of the shrieking Codd up again and again
to beat him full length over the front of the car. And, as
though Codd were without any weight at all, he began to
no longer hear Codd striking the car but could only see
the head as fragile as a winter melon colliding against the
curving glow of glass making spidery shooting stars in
the windshield at every touch.

Payne released him, sickened, and sat down. Fitzgerald was in full motion running toward him, crossing and
recrossing the rectangle of light from the barn. Then Ann
was coming too, an enormous silver nimbus of bleached
hair around her head.

In complete physical possession, Payne watched the
lolling go out of Codd's head as he came down from the
hood of the car. Codd seemed a moment later to teeter

back from the angle of the Mariposa boots as he raised the sash weight high overhead and brought it down against Payne's skull. Payne felt himself guide its clear descent with his eye. The moment of shock was a single click, as a cue ball touches the triangle of billiard balls, a clean line, a perfect sound, then the balls of color bursting from the center and darkness pouring in until zero.

15

It was quickly apparent that Codd had not given Payne, as it first looked, a blow that was mortal. The question of damage to the brain, however, was not settled. The notion Ann had was that her family would take an upright line in compensating Nicholas. As for herself, she would feel honor bound to do whatever he told her to do.

Now that was an alarming idea. She was filled with a terrifying and delicious vision of living her life out with a man who had been made a feeb by damage to his brain. She saw her parents out of misguided loyalty giving Payne work that he could do. And suddenly a terrible picture of Payne wheeling bins of disinfected wigs in her mother's wig bank came to Ann. For a long time, she had secretly photographed Payne at his worst moments; but pictures of him reduced to idiocy by brain damage would be of merely pathological, rather than artistic, interest. This thought of hers, clear as it was, diminished Ann more than she would ever be able to know.

But, poor girl, she was so undermined at the moment. At the time of the accident, she had seen the complicity between Codd and her parents; one, she assumed, that had got out of hand. Then her mother had spotted Ann's peroxide hair and, even before it was determined whether or not Payne was dead, had screeched, "You little hoor!"

* * *

When Payne regained consciousness, he discovered that he had lost much of his peripheral vision; producing what the doctor described as "vignetting"; it gave him the sense of looking down a pair of tubes. Added to the insane headache he had, it was very disconcerting. No one knew if it was permanent or not.

Ann came often but he could never quite figure if he had just seen her or imagined it. So he lay there in an indescribable air of expectation, most of which turned out to be unwarranted.

Clovis was in and out all the time, displaying his familiarity with the staff. He gave Payne some advice that seemed rather wild-eyed in the beginning and then made sense. Clovis conducted a few arrangements to substantiate the advice and, two days later, Payne was feeling well enough to act upon it.

Summoned by Payne's attorney, sitting beside him now, the Fitzgeralds arrived at the hospital, all three of them. Payne directed them to chairs and they sat, next to the sink.

"As soon as I am able," Payne said, "I am going to Key West to build a bat tower. I plan to take Ann with me. We will of course live together; 'cohabit' is the word, Heath informs me." Payne gestured to indicate Counselor Egdon Heath beside him. "Both on the way and after we get there."

"I'm afraid that won't be possible," La smiled, boiled eggs for eyes. "We don't operate that way."

"Fill them in, Heath."

Heath ingratiated himself with a suggested, if not actual, undulance and a winning meringue smile. The Fitzgeralds were thrown into ghastly discomfort. "There are any number of writs we can serve you with at this time," he began. "I have advised my client to pursue an individual suit in the amount of two millions. Mister Payne has a fetching inability to speculate in terms of such numbers. So I showed him the tax assessor's rather conservative estimate of the value of your ranch and assured my client there would be quite a bit of change left over! I do not hint at avarice by any means when I say that this procedure has had the effect of piquing Mister Payne's interest. And of course we have not given up the notion of going for the wig bank as well. My own point of view is based on the fact that I am here on speculation. And it costs me twenty thousand dollars a week to leave my office in Los Angeles.

"Furthermore . . . a mint?" They shook their heads. He ate one, palming the foil. "Furthermore, a Mister Wayne Codd, temporarily resident in the fearful little city, has signed his name to half a dozen statements of his own composition. My evaluation is that they hint at a criminal dimension to this affair that could be explored with a mind to not only cleaning you out but salting you away!" He muttered insincerely to himself that he must abjure the vernacular, then cried, "Acky poo! I know how you feel about that! In the beginning, I didn't see why I should leave Los Angeles. I just didn't. But there was something that turned me on. Something that thrilled me and I searched it out. I lay in my Barcalounger until it came. And it turned out that it was the fact that we had both punitive and compensatory options in prosecuting this suit that gave me, frankly, a kind of hard-on to represent this man." Then Heath admitted to his voice a dry Episcopal scorn he had learned many years before at the Cranbrook School for Boys.

"Mister Payne has made me promise to say this: He will call me off in the event your daughter goes to Florida not only unhindered but without disapproval expressed through inheritance provisos." Heath was counting on a certain Republican solidity in the Fitzgeralds to keep his case airtight.

"We will not be blackmailed," one or possibly both of the Fitzgeralds said firmly.

"Presumably not," said Heath, "and that point of view fills me with pleasure. I personally never expected you to sell your daughter down the river in quite the manner indicated here."

"Heath," Payne said, "you're chiseling."

"Quite right."

"I told you I wouldn't have any of your damn greediness," Payne said. Heath was chastised.

"You're absolutely correct," he said; he could afford this. Payne had the opposition dead to rights.

"I suggest you drop everything you've said," Missus Fitzgerald announced, looking at the ceiling with a bored recitative air, "while you still have something left."

"There's nothing more to add, madame," said Heath, not only a lawyer, husband and father, but an influential man who had given Los Angeles Episcopalianism its particular sheen. "You know how it stands. I assume we begin suit. Do contact your own attorney immediately; and be sure he's good." Frivolous imitations of generosity by Egdon Heath.

"I should have thought your investigations would demonstrate that we have effective counsel," said Missus Fitzgerald, her words and words only having any conviction.

Fitzgerald himself broke in, chuckling to himself for quite some time. "You lawyers have tickled me for years. You're all pork-and-beaners till the day you die. I don't care if you make a million a day."

"Go ahead. You're bagged. Get in a speech."

"May I go on, Mister Heath? I was saying I really have to chuckle—" He showed how you do. "—when I think of you guys. You never get the human underpinning into your heads. You're constantly trotting out your writs and enjoinders without ever seeing that the law is a simple extension of the most ordinary human affairs."

"That's not true. Go ahead."

"May I continue, Mister Heath?"

"Do that. But you're bagged and bagged big."

"May I go on you fucking shyster?"

"Duke!"

"Daddy!"

"Wildly and emotionally inaccurate. But go on."

Fitzgerald composed himself and said, "What you as a particular lawyer have missed in this particular instance expresses perfectly what I am saying." Fitzgerald sat on his triumph like a jocular playmate. "Our daughter has

already expressed a wish to go off with Mister Payne!"
Missus Fitzgerald joined the fun of a smiling triumph directed at this L.A. pinhead.

"I know that," said Heath simply.

"Then what's the problem?" one or possibly both of the Fitzgeralds asked at once.

"You said she couldn't go," Heath said with even greater simplicity.

"Your small sense of conduct surprises us in a professional man of law," said Missus Fitzgerald. "Any parent would recognize our refusal as a way mothers and fathers have of stalling for time while they make up their minds." Her pronunciation of the words "mother" and "father" was straight out of Dick And Jane. The Fitzgeralds looked at each other. They were winging it together, depending now on their intimacy, their knowledge of each other. This would be a test of what their marriage was founded upon.

"We have decided," said Mister Fitzgerald, looking hopefully at his bride, "that Ann is old enough to make her own decisions. In this case—" Oh, this was beautiful. "—we definitely do *not* approve of her decision."

"But will you stand in her way?" Heath, out of control, pleaded.

"No."

"What! You're opening the door to lewdness!"

"Heath," Payne warned.

"She's a grown woman," Missus Fitzgerald insisted.

Heath began to shout: "There's a question of consortium here, God damn it! It is technically questionable if these people have a right to intercourse. And without that legal right they are fornicators! You call yourself *parents* in the face of this abrogation of decency!"

Payne: "Shut up, Heath. Shut up and get out."

Heath ignored him. "A minor distrainment of your chattels and you sell your child into bondage! Let me ask you one thing. Let me ask you this. Have you questioned the effect of bastardy on the esteem you doubtless hold in your community? I mean, what if there is illegitimate issue? What if there is?"

Payne lay on his side now holding his head. The others were rigid with horror as the white-knuckled L.A. shyster circled them sinfully. "Let us talk reason. Exemplary or punitive damages in this action are extremely unlikely, right? The community has no need to make an example of you. Do you follow me? In equity, the assessment of damages is wholly within the discretion of the court where you will be more likely to get sympathetic treatment than my client. I mean, look at him. He looks like a crackpot. My client is everybody's fantasy of an ambulatory anarchist. Isn't he yours? Ask yourself that.

"Now lastly—and try to get this straight—it is the plaintiff's responsibility to keep damages to the minimum indicated by the tort. In this instance, the multiple of damages actually sustained is difficult to specify.

"I advise that you settle out of court. I advise that you keep your daughter in the home in which she belongs."

"How much?" Fitzgerald asked.

"I'm thinking of a hundred grand."

"The hell with that noise," Fitzgerald said and walked, his wife beside him, with dignity from the room. They would have to buy some champagne and celebrate their victory.

Ann delayed. She leaned over Payne's bed and filled Payne's ear with hot breath when she said, "They've sold me down the river, darling. It's you and me now." She left.

On his own way out, Egdon Heath said, somewhat acidly, to Payne, "I ought at least to nail you for my air fare."

"That's the life of a speculator," Payne said. "Nice try."

Payne was whacked out. He made friends with the nurse who attended him. She had tiny close-set eyes and an upturned bulbous nose. She told Payne her life story pausing upon occasion to break into tears. She had remained unwed through her thirties; then suddenly married an elderly motorist from a nearby town. Recently he told her that it had not in the least been love at first sight.

So there was that for her to cry about. Payne took her hand, seeing her face at the end of a tube, and told her, "Don't sweat it, darling," in his most reassuring glottal baritone.

They didn't do a thing to Payne but take one kind of reading or another, including an X-ray. They took readings day after day. "What's my temperature?" Payne would ask. Or, "What's my pulse?" Or, "What's my blood pressure?" One day, sleepily, he inquired, "What numbers am I, Doctor?"

"Quite a few," the doctor said. "All of us are."

One thing Payne thought of continually was the time he blasted the piano with his .22, the beautiful splintering of excessively finished wood, the broken strings curling away from liberated beams of spicy piano light, the warm walnut stock of his .22, the other spice of spent shells, the word hollowpoint, the anger of the enemy, the silver discs the bullets made on the window, the simple precision of a peep sight, the blue of barrel steel, the name Winchester when you were in America, the world of BB Caps, Shorts, Longs, and Long Rifles, the incessant urge to louse up monuments, even the private piano monument he perforated from a beautiful tree with an almost blinding urgent vision of the miserable thing ending in an uproar of shattered mahogany, ivory, ebony and wire. No more Bach chords to fill the trees with their stern negation. There's no room here for a piano, he remembered righteously. No pianos here please.

Ann sat in the front of the Hudson. Just as in the songs, she had hair of sparkling gold and lips like cherry wine. Perhaps, hair of sparkling pewter and lips the color of a drink called Cold Duck. She looked like an awful floozy. Her eyes had melting antimony edging on their lids. God only knew what she had in mind. She looked as round-heeled as a tuppeny upright after ten years of throwing standing crotch locks on every womb worm that came her way.

His vision, however, had improved; to the effect that the world no longer appeared as a circular vista at the end of a conduit. His urge to ride on the highway was now a quiet, tingling mania.

"Let us hear from you," the Fitzgeralds said when the kissing had stopped.

"Sure will," Ann said, "I'll drop you a line one of these days." Her parents looked at her. They needed the right word and quick. Something had gone entirely dead here.

"Let us know if you need anything," her mother tried.

"Yeah, right." Payne started to back around. "Take it easy," Ann said. And they left.

"I guess," Ann said after they had driven a while, "it had gotten to be time for me to cut out."

"All right," Payne said, "now take it easy."

"Darling, I'm upset."

"Yes, me too. My head is all fouled up."

"I feel like a hoor," she said. Payne felt a distant obligation to contradict her.

They passed through the box canyon of the Yellowstone where the venturi effect of chinook winds will lift a half-ton pickup right to the top of its load leveler shocks and make the driver think of ghost riders in the sky until the springs seat again and the long invisible curves of wind unknit and drive him through the canyon as though his speed were laid on him as paint.

Some hours later, Ann seemed to have fallen into a bad mood. "Where are we going?"

"Bat country," said Payne. That quieted her down.

"You know what?" she asked later.

"What?"

"This damn car of yours is coming off on my clothes."

At Apollinaris Spring, Ann thought: My God, if George ever saw me pull a low-rent trick like this! In fact that's something to think about. She began to record the voyage with her camera.

* * *

They dropped down into Wyoming and headed for Lander, running through implausible country where Sacajawea and Gerald McBoingBoing fought for the table scraps of U.S.A. history.

Coming down through Colorado, still west of the Divide, they passed a small intentional community—people their own age—all of whose buildings were geodesic domes made of the tops of junked automobiles. Payne could see gardens, a well, a solar heater and wanted to go down. But the members of the community were all crowding around down there and rubbing each other. They were packing in down there and Payne felt the awful shadow of the Waring Blender and drove on. Ann was mad. "Why won't you mix, God damn it?" I read Schopenhauer, Payne thought, *that tease!*

They headed for Durango, stayed for a day, then dropped into New Mexico and headed for Big Spring, Texas.

They cut across Amarillo and made a beeline for Shreveport on a red-hot autumn day to Columbia, Florida, where Payne had been sent in the first place by Cletus James Clovis. This was bat country. Payne took a piece of paper out of his pocket. A short time later, he was knocking on the door of a reconditioned sharecropper's house. When the man opened the door, Payne saw the wall behind covered with curing gator skins. "C. J. Clovis said to see you about bats," Payne said. The poacher told them to come in and have something cool to drink.

A day later, Payne, with his biggest hang-over ever, and his companion, the poacher Junior Place, with a big one of his own; and Ann snoozing in the Hornet with an actual puker of a white lightning hang-over and her peroxide beehive full of sticks and bits of crap of one description or another, and the North Florida sun coming in like a suicide; the men paused at the end of the sandy road in the palmettos beside a pile of wrecked automobiles each of which held a little glass-and-metal still—the product of which drew a considerably better price locally than any bonded sauce you could find out at your shopping plaza. Payne was flattered at this confidential disclosure.

They had little distance to go. Junior had loaned Payne a pair of his own snakeproof pants—citrus picker's trousers with heavy-gauge screen sewn inside a canvas sleeve from the knee down. And the two of them crossed the palmettos on a gradually upward incline, near the crest of which Junior Place began to scout back and forth for the mouth of the cave.

He told Payne to feel as best he could for a breeze. So Payne wandered the crest of the hill, feeling for a breeze that came to him shortly as a breath of something cool and watery, something subterranean rising around him. He found the entrance in a cluster of brush from which a solid cool shaft of air poured. He called out its location.

The two men carried triangular nets on long hard-wood poles. Payne had his nine-battery Ray-O-Vac and Junior Place carried a carbide lamp. Junior came over and pushed aside the brush to reveal a coal-black oval in the ground, a lightless hole through which he slid as from long practice.

It proves one thing about Payne that he followed straightaway. He wanted to maintain voice contact. "How do you know C. J. Clovis?"

"Hardly know him a tall," said Place. There was no way of knowing the immensity of this blackness; it sucked away Payne's voice without an echo.

There were things going by his head at tremendous speed. "I had a five-minute talk with the man," said Place. "He is a freak of nature." The blackness pressed Payne's face. "I'd do anything in the world for him. Come up side of me now. Okay, use the lamp." The lights went on. The paleness of the limestone hall surprised and terri-fied Payne. The colliding planes of wall and ceiling ap-peared serene and futuristic and cold. Every overhead sur-face was festooned with bats. They were all folded, though some, alive to the presence of the men, craned around; and a few dropped and flew squeaking crazily through the beams of light. Then a number more came down, whirled through the room with the others; and as if by signal they all returned to the ceiling.

They set the lights where they would give them advantageous illumination; and with the long-handled nets commenced scraping pole-breaking loads from the ceiling. A million bats exploded free and circulated through the chamber in a crescendo of squeaking. They upended the bats in the plastic mesh bags and continued swiping over head. By now, they needed only to hold the nets aloft and they would fill until they could not be held overhead.

Bats poured at Payne like jet engine exhaust; pure stripes and curves of solid hurtling bats filled the air to saturation. The rush and squeaking around Payne were making him levitate. As when the dogs were in the house, he no longer knew which way his head or feet were pointing. He had no idea where the entrance was. Junior Place continued at the job, a man hoeing his garden. Payne whirled like a propeller.

When it was over, Payne had to be led out of the cave, carrying his net and shopping bag. There was an awful moment as the entrance began to pack all around him with escaping bats. When he finally stood outside the hole, he watched a single, towering black funnel, its point at the hole, form and tower over him.

He would have to tell Clovis: a tower actually made of bats.

They liberated the bats in the wagon behind the Hudson. The bats circulated, a wild squeaking whirlwind, before sticking to the screen sides to squeak angrily out at the men. Some of the bats, their umbrella wings partially open, crept awkwardly around the bottom of the wagon before clinging to the screened sides. Soon a number of them were hanging from the roof adaptably.

"Do you have any idea what a hang-over is like in the face of that?" Ann asked the two men.

They said goodbye to Junior Place at the end of the road. Payne returned the pants, gingerly fishing his own from the wagon.

Ann slumped against him and fell asleep once more.

Place, at the end of his white lightning road, waved a straw hat and held his nets overhead at the edge of a palmetto wilderness in his snakeproof pants.

Payne aimed the load for Key West.

> I got ten four gears
> And a Georgia overdrive.
> I'm takin little white pills
> And my eyes is open wide. . . .

16

They woke up in the morning in the sleeping bag beside the car. The bats were running all over the wire. They already knew Payne was the one who fed them: banana and bits of dessicated hamburger.

Across a wet field in the morning in the peat smell of North Central Florida and surrounded by a wall of pines stood a rusting, corrugated steel shed with daylight coming through its sides variously. From one end, the rear quarters of a very large field mule projected; and the animal could be heard cropping within. On the broad corrugated side of the shed itself in monstrous steamboat letters, filigree draining from every corner,

FAYE'S

GIFT

SHOPPE

Payne fed the bats and started coffee on the camp stove while, her hair teased into something unbelievable, Ann shot over to Faye's. By the time the coffee was ready, she was back at the car with long gilt earrings hanging from her ears. "Check these," she said. "Wouldn't they be great for when we went dancing?"

"They would be that."

They could have made the Keys by nightfall. But Ann wanted to stop at a roadhouse near Homestead where she played all the Porter Wagoner, Merle Haggard, Jeannie C. Riley, Buck Owens and Tammy Wynette records on the jukebox and danced with a really unpromising collection of South Florida lettuce-pickers and midcountry drifters. Then Payne got too drunk to drive; so they slept one more night on the road at the edge of the 'glades with the bats squeaking and wanting to fly in the dark, wanting to go someplace, and Payne remembering in a way that made him upset the aborigine of ten years before.

In his liquor stupefaction—and rather woozy anyway from the tropic sogginess and the streaked red sky and the sand flies and mosquitoes and the completely surprising softness of the air and the recent memory of the yanking jukebox dancing—he was just a little alarmed by Ann's ardor at bedtime. She had the camera within reach and he was afraid she would pull something kinky. And then he was just detached from everything that was happening to him; so that he saw, as from afar, Ann commit a primitive oral stimulation of his parts. Engorged, frankly, as though upon a rutabaga, her slender English nose was lost in a cloud of pubic hair. They had the sleeping bag open, underneath the wagon, in case it rained. Ann detected Payne's reserve and aggressively got atop of him, hauling at his private. There was so little room that each time her buttocks lifted, they bumped the underside of the wagon and sent the bats surging and squeaking overhead. She facetiously filled the humid evening with Wagnerian love grunts.

They hit A1A heading down through Key Largo, the mainland becoming more and more streaked with water and the land breaking from large to small pieces until finally they were in the Keys themselves, black-green mangrove humps stretching to the horizon and strung like beads on the highway. Loused up as everything else in the country, it was still land's end.

"What do you think you're doing?" Payne finally asked.

Ann turned a face to him as expressionless as a pudding under the glued, brilliant hair.

"What do I think I'm doing?" she repeated as though to a whole roomful of people.

On either side, the serene seascapes seemed to ridicule the nasty two-lane traffic with monster argosy cross-country trucks domineering the road in both directions. From time to time, in the thick of traffic problems, Payne would look off on the pale sand flats and see spongers with long-handled rakes standing in the bows of their wooden boats steering the rickety outboard motors with clothesline tied to their waists. Then below Islamorada he saw rusty trailers surrounded by weedy piles of lobster traps, hard-working commercial fishermen living in discarded American road effluvia.

In Marathon, a little elevation gave him the immensity of the ocean in a more prepossessing package—less baby blue—and he saw what a piss-ant portion of the terraqueous globe the land really is. They stopped to eat and Payne had turtle. The end of that street was blocked with the jammed-in immense bows of four shrimpers. Their trawling booms were tangled overhead. He could read *Southern Cross, Miss Becky, Tampa Clipper* and *Witchcraft*. On the deck of the *Tampa Clipper*, a fisherman in a wooden chair, his hat pulled over his eyes, and half-awake, gave the finger to a lady who sighted him through the view finder of her Kodak. When she gave up, his arm fell to the side of the chair, his head settled at an easier angle. He was asleep.

Suddenly, they were in the middle of Key West and lost with a wagonload of bats lurching behind them in side streets where it was hard to make a turn in the first place. They passed the Fifth Street Baptist Church and read its motto on a sign in front:

WHERE FRIENDLINESS IS A HABIT
AND PARKING IS NOT A PROBLEM

They ran into the old salt pond and had to backtrack. They cut down Tropical Avenue to Seminary Street down Seminary to Grinnell out Grinnell to Olivia and down Olivia to Poorhouse Lane where they got the car jammed and had to enlist the neighborhood; who helped until they got a good look and backed off, saying, *"Bats!"*

But suddenly Payne was happy to be in Key West. It was Harry Truman's favorite town and Harry Truman was fine by Payne. He liked Truman's remark about getting out of the kitchen if you couldn't stand the heat. Payne thought that beat anything in Kierkegaard. He also liked Truman's Kansas City suits and essential Calvinized watchfob insouciance of the pre-Italian racketeer. He enjoyed the whole sense of the First Lady going bald while the daughter wheedled her way onto the Ed Sullivan show to drown the studio audience in an operatic mud bath of her own devising.

They went past the cemetery, the biggest open space in Key West, filled with above-ground crypts, old yellow-fever victims, the sailors of the *Maine*, as well as the ordinary dead, if you could say that.

Ann sneered at everything, though she had acquired, quite without irony, a rural accent.

"What is this act?" Payne asked, as if his own attempts to extrapolate the land through mimicry of its most dubious societal features were not absurd.

But Ann just watched the beautiful wooden houses go by; each, it seemed, separated from the other by a vacant lot full of moldering and glittering trash or by small, rusting car gardens with clumps of expired fantasies from the ateliers of Detroit.

To Ann, at that moment, America said one beautiful thing after another.

To Payne it said, *I got all pig iron.*

"Which way to Mallory Square?"

"Keep going."

They kept going and hit the Thompson-O'Neill shrimp docks.

They went thataway. From afar, the anodized fantasm of the Dodge Motor Home was peerlessly evident. It sat under the quasi-Moorish battlements of the First National Bank. On the Motor Home, this note: "Payne: I'm at the Havana Hotel. Room 333. Get a move on. C. J. Clovis, Savonarola Batworks, Inc."

* * *

Clovis himself looked petulantly from the window of Room 333 with no certainty that Payne would ever come. He could see the reflecting metal roofs of Key West, the vegetation growing up between and, across town, the Coast Guard and Standard Oil docks. He wanted to play tennis but he only had one arm and one leg.

He tried to interest himself in the builder's plans for the tower which was to be built on nearby Mente Chica Key. But he was upset. He wanted vodka. He wanted a tart. That girl of Payne's was a tart. Why didn't he get rid of her? A rich tart with an old rich tart for a mother and a successful stupid male tart for a father. He should have hit the bastards for a fifteen-level bat atrium.

Clovis was quite upset. He had an ailment.

In a small glowing plastic cube hovered the numeral 3. Payne pressed the cube with his index finger and the doors slid shut and the two of them soared upwards. Presently, they stopped and the doors opened and there was a sign.

←300–350
351–399→

Payne turned left down the corridor, leading Ann by the hand. Ann's prole mania made her strike up conversations with every Cuban chambermaid that were singularly brittle in the vastitude of their misunderstanding.

Finally, room 333. A knock.

"Yes?"

"It's me."

"Come in. I can't come to the door. I've got an ailment."

They went in. Clovis was on the bed, the covers pulled up under his chin. He looked peaked.

"I've got one this time," he said in the chanting voice he always used in speaking of illness.

"What."

"I've got a real dandy on this run," he said.

"The other leg."

"No." Clovis looked out of the window a long time. A tear tracked down his cheek. He did not look back at them. "My heart is on the fritz."

They sat down. This was a sorry way to start the venture. There was work to be done. It was warm. You could go for a swim and all be friends.

"From a fugitive's point of view," said Clovis, pulling himself together, "this is the worst place in the world. You can't get off the highway anywhere from here back to the mainland for a hundred-and-fifty miles. The bastards would have you funneled."

"Are you planning to be a fugitive?"

"No. Payne, how are your hemorrhoids?"

"Fine; thank you for asking."

"Take care of them before they get out of hand. Once they're thrombosed you get impaction and every other damn thing."

"They're already thrombosed."

"Then you're in for a postoperative Waterloo."

"No, I'm not. I'm not having them operated on."

"Well, that's just what I wanted to ask you."

"Ask me what?"

"Whether you wouldn't join me in the hospital."

"No, I won't."

"This time I'm scared."

"I don't care. The answer is no."

"Where is your humanity?" Ann inquired, thinking of how that lay at the roots of Western culture.

"Among the dying grunions," Payne replied, "at Redondo Beach."

They put everything—Hudson Hornet, wagon and motor home—under a shade tree behind the Two Friends Bar. Payne fed the bats and wondered if they missed their home in the limestone cave. It had gotten hot.

Once inside the motor home, Payne drew all the blinds and turned on the air conditioner. It was soon comfortable and they napped on the broad foam bed.

When they awoke, it was dark. Ann was chewing a large wad of gum and sipping from a bottle of whiskey she had bought at the Two Friends Bar while Payne slept. She poured him a drink without saying anything. She was strolling around without her clothes on.

Payne swung his legs over the side of the bed. He looked and felt exhausted. Ann pivoted around toward him, the Nikon to her eye, and photographed him.

It didn't take her long to find the radio. She turned on a Cuban station with its Sten-gun dance music and began to pachanga up and down the aisle in some inexplicable transport. "Dance?" she called to Payne. He declined. The music was discouragingly loud. He could hardly keep his eye on her as she caromed around the inside of the motor home. Once when she shot by he made a grab for her. She kept streaking around, breasts lunging. "Dance?" she cried again. He refused, watching in wonder, and undressed, folding his clothes. "Wallflower!" He thought this painstaking reserve would be good for things. But he had an erection; so he wasn't fooling anyone. It was aimed at his own forehead; and he felt a giddiness as of danger. He suddenly believed that the engorged penis acquires all its blood from the brain. He made Ann come over and sit on it; and she got violently exercised by the procedure. At the supreme time, his whole head seemed to be opaque. "Egad," he barked shortly. Payne really looked at her for the first time that night; she seemed awfully big and the cascade of silver hair disoriented him entirely. When he withdrew, a translucent tendril connected them an instant longer, then fell glistening on one of her perfect thighs.

Payne turned off Radio Havana. Someone was giving the sugar quotas, province by province, *arroba* by *aroba*. He found a brownie with walnuts and ate it, not bothering to dress. He had a little drink. He looked around himself. Ann was lying on the couch next to the settee. Overhead a lighting that felt sourceless but was probably fluorescent shone with a lunar absence of shadows. It was like being in an atomic submarine; perhaps, inside a vacuum cleaner was more accurate. Everything was built in.

Nothing stood clear of the curved walls. The whole inside of the motor home was a variation on the tube theme. They were in an intestine, Payne thought giddily; and digestion was worse than anything the Waring Blender could do to you.

Payne thought that the rug had been pulled out from under his crazy act. Ann's was beginning to look a little more marginal than his, if that was possible. Yet he had— he thought—a purpose behind his and still did; which was, in the vernacular, getting it all together. On the old motorcycle excursion, he had tried to draw a line around it all; now he was trying to color it all in.

From time to time that night, drunken shrimpers beat on the door. "Invasion of privacy," thought Payne. He had nowhere else to put the vehicles; so this activity would have to be discouraged completely. They tried to sleep awhile; but it was never long before the uproar began anew. Then he heard a number of them arguing in some drunk's comedy and one of them tried to force open the door. "Breaking and entering," Payne thought. They knew there was a female in here and had gone entirely doggy. The door of the motor home bulged and Ann was frightened completely if temporarily out of her hillbilly act. Payne got up, rifling through drawers.

He found in Clovis' underwear drawer the revolver he had recently employed to bushwhack the tires on his Hudson Hornet. Payne was wearing only his shorts. Nevertheless, when he opened the door, stepped down and circulated among the drunks with the revolver, he was found to be, in his own way, strangely impressive. The drunks had a leader in the person of a stringy individual with a Confederate flag tattooed on his forearm that said, *Hell, no, I ain't forgetting.* This man proposed to disarm Payne and go aboard. He said that anyone who pulled a gun better be prepared to use it. But when Payne took a handful of his cheek, put the barrel of the gun inside of his mouth and offered to blow his brains all over the Gulf of Mexico, there was a loss of interest in tampering with the motor home or going aboard at all. They could tell that Payne had reached that curious emotional plateau which did not necessarily have anything to do with anger that, once gained, let one man kill another. Payne would never have known until he had done it; but complete strangers could tell beforehand. So Payne went back aboard only wondering why he had not been nervous; and not realizing how near he had been to a most significant human act; while the drunks now squealing, revving, popping clutches and roaring off were all somewhat sobered up with how close it had been.

The owner of the bar came out. "Sorry those old boys took it in their heads to pester you. Sorry as hell."

"No bother at all," Payne said. The man was studying him, trying to guess how much he would put up with. "I do feel you ought to know that the next time it happens I will kill people." Payne thought he was telling a lie. The owner's face whitened.

"I'll pass that on," he said.

"In the end they'll like it that way better."

The bar owner laughed very slightly.

"I expect they will," he agreed. "I will sholy pass it on."

Payne climbed back in and locked the door. Ann looked at him as he put the pistol up. She had photographed him standing in the doorway in his shorts, as he turned back into the artificial light, the revolver hanging by its trigger guard from his forefinger. He looked transported.

"I'm a king bee, baby," he said.

"Have you fed the bats?" she asked.

First thing in the morning, Payne and Clovis met with a Cuban named Diego Fama who would act as co-foreman and interpreter on the tower project. Clovis wanted to use entirely refugee labor. He said he wanted to do his part to make opposition to Castro attractive.

Diego Fama was a muscular contractor type, his Cuban-Indian physiognomy to the contrary notwithstanding. He had startling big forearms which he crisscrossed high on his chest when listening. He did not speak English particularly well; but listened to the planning with heavy, Germanic attention. He already understood the project better than Payne and Clovis. "Easy job," he said precisely when the talk was done.

"How long?"

"Under a week." The news embarrassed both Payne and Clovis with respect to the price they were getting; but not for long.

"How many men?"

"I figure that out," Diego Fama said. "I say now though possibly twenty of these persons."

"Where will you find them?" Payne asked.

"I figure that out," Fama replied balefully.

"And what is your subcontracting charge?"

"Three thousand dollars," Fama said. It was unbelievably cheap.

"That's high," Clovis said, "but we accept. When do we start?"

"Monday in the morning."

When Fama was gone, Clovis wrote out a bill on the kind of pad waitresses carry and gave it to Payne for examination.

BILL

1 Bat Tower	$16,000.00
1500 Standard Bats	$1500.00
1 Guano Trap w/ storage receptacle	$1000.00
1 Special Epoxy Tropical Paint, Brushes and Thinner	$500.00

THANK YOU. PLEASE CALL AGAIN.

"I'm surprised at you," said Ann back at the motor home, "treating the old fart like that."

"Are you?"

"He's scared to death his ailment is going to carry him off."

"How would it help if I went in and had my butt trimmed?"

"Surprised at you," she said, "leaving him in the lurch."

"I'm not leaving him in the lurch."

"The lurch."

"I'm not."

"Explain it if you're not," she said and as he started to rage, she raised her camera to photograph him. He got in a conventional wedding-portrait smile before she could snap it. "Surprised at you," she said.

"I'll visit him every day," Payne said.

Ann had been out photographing trash, gas stations and Dairy Queens. "Leaving him in the lurch." She turned the turretlike lens of the Nikon Photomic FTN and fired point-blank. "You look so wiped out I wanted to get it on film with all this plastic crap around you. It's too much."

"I hope it comes out," said Payne.

"I got one of you last night that was priceless. You were making a drink in your underwear and I must say you were sagging from end to end."

"I'll want to see that one."

"You will."

"Tell me this, are you having a little social experiment here? Is this what was once called 'slumming it'?"

"I don't know what you mean."

"You tell me what it is then," said Payne.

"It's art."

"Well," Payne said, "any more fucking art around here and I'm going to commence something unfortunate. I had enough art at the hands of the Mum and Dad."

"I cannot understand you," Ann said; but she had got a glimpse of what the shrimpers had seen and she knew it was going to be necessary to shut up.

"I can't understand you," she said at a distance.

"Persevere."

Ann left the motor home and skulked around the back of the bar. Payne watched her making desultory photographs of citrus rinds and inorganic refuse. A fat and drunken tourist in bermudas went by and she followed him for awhile, snapping away at his behind, and then returned to the motor home.

She had every hope that her dark night of the soul would be on film.

In the middle of the night, Payne suddenly awoke with a terrible, unspecific feeling of sadness. He waited until he had a grip on himself. Then, he woke Ann. "You're right," he said.

"About what."

"About Clovis. I'll go to the hospital with him."

Ann kissed him. "You're always thinking of others," she said.

"Will you feed the bats?"

17

Payne called Clovis and told him. He could feel his relief over the wire. "I don't want to go it alone this time." Payne felt as if confirmed in his decision; though he was himself frightened by the operation in store for him.

Construction of the tower was going to be in the hands of Diego Fama.

The hospital arrangements were wangled artfully by Clovis who alluded to his own medical history in veiled tones. It sounded gothic and exciting. The personnel were thrilled by Clovis' lack of limbs. He seemed the real thing in a hospital dogged with health and minor problems.

A not unoccupied elevator passed through the building; it carried a solitary patient in gold embossed plastic bedroom slippers and an uncomfortable shift tied around his mottled neck. His hair was de rigueur wino, combed back and close. At the top floor, the door opened and he ran for daylight, radiant with his own brand of hyperesthesia.

After the proctological examination, during which Payne's surgical need was specified as "acute," Payne fell asleep. He had been horrified by the doctor's steering that machine through his inwards like the periscope of a U-boat.

The Monroe County Hospital was an unusual place.

Situated next to a dump ("Sanitary land fill"), the smoke of burning garbage blew through the wards. Meanwhile, Clovis was wheeled around to all the testing facilities. He had a cardiogram, an electroencephalogram, an X-ray. His urine, stool and blood were tested. They took skin scrapings and hair samples. They weighed C. J. Clovis.

The curtain was drawn between the two beds. Payne could hear the doctor and Clovis talking. The doctor demanded to know exactly what the complaint was.

"My body's all aching and racked with pain," said Clovis.

The doctor, a feisty former fighter pilot of the United States Navy said simply, "There isn't anything the matter with you. You are in the habit of illness. You ought to get out."

"What is your name?"

"Doctor Proctor."

"I'll have your ass."

"I've arranged," said Proctor plainly, "to have you put out. You are in the habit of illness."

The doctor passed the screen where Payne lay. There was silence when he was gone. In a while, Clovis hobbled around to the foot of Payne's bed.

"You heard that?"

"Yes—"

"I'll have his ass."

By that evening, Clovis was gone. By the next morning he was back. He had no doctor assigned to him at all. Since there were plenty of beds, they agreed to let nurses run tests on him from time to time and to use him as a kind of training doll. Clovis slept all the time. He was having a holiday. It was rather boring for Payne and bad times were ruining his posture. He walked around in a curve. He looked like a genius.

They never got a girl as pretty as Ann in here. A good number of the women who had come knew what they were getting into and opted for it out of some carnal compulsion. Which is to say that a certain number of gangbangs had originated here; and were remembered. Nevertheless, she held her own at the bar, elbow to elbow with the shrimpers in their khaki clothes and their ineffable odeur of the docks.

When a fight broke out later over who exactly was going to talk to her and in what sequence, she saw the whole bloody mess as an Ektachrome fantasia hanging on the walls of the Guggenheim.

Standing next to the pool table, waiting for his shot and never having glanced up at the fight at all, was a shrimper in his late thirties who looked like a slightly handsomer, slightly more fleshed-out version of Hank Williams or any number of other hillbilly singers, save that he wore khaki fisherman's clothes. He spoiled an easy bank shot and said, "Them cushions is soft. Don't nobody replace nothin here?"

He walked straight over to where Ann stood. "This is no place for a lady," he said. "Have you ever been to Galveston by sea?"

All the next day, Payne and Clovis spent on the telephone. They had decided to let Diego Fama and family go ahead and build the tower. There were many questions of credit to be settled, equipment and ready-mix concrete to be secured. The tensest conversations—and they were Payne's—were with the officers of the Mid-Keys Boosters who had been sold on the thing in the first place by Clovis. They were testy to begin with and grew more so the more money was required of them.

Payne tried to reach Ann at the Two Friends Bar and got unsatisfactory answers.

Diego Fama's mother called and wanted to know what to feed the bats.

Flat on his back, Payne had a chance to fret about Ann. She was going haywire. But he thought he could help her over the phase if he could be with her. His hemorrhoids had seemed to come between them. It seemed hideously unnecessary. What had people done in ages gone by about such a condition? Nothing. And their lives had transpired like a stately pas de deux amid plentiful antiques and objets d'art of real interest to the connoisseur. We each of us know instinctively that hemorrhoids were unknown before our century. It is the pressure of the times, symbolically expressed. Their removal is mere cosmetic surgery.

When he browsed in the hallways it had seemed that the sickrooms full of, in some cases, the most monstrously injured or ailing creatures, should give onto trees, lawns and ruminant cars driven, now and then, by people with nothing in the slightest the matter with them. Nothing.

He pretended that he was among the dying and made himself quite sad with the exercise. The doctor enters. I'm sorry to have to tell you this but all of us sometime. I'm afraid it's. I know, doctor, I know. And the others. Is it known among the others. That I'm to. And the little girls. Will they or would they take in hand the shy item of a man who will not be here?

From his window, which was none too clean, he saw many a scalped tree and sorry palm on an expanse of asphalt. God knows how, but they say you make friends here. Who never forget you. Payne looked around him. My Christ, they'll drive their expensive steel in my fanny. And at the end I am to pick up the tab. There you are, doctor. All those simoleons for what you have done to me.

Beside Payne, asleep, a certain misshapen person, an object of great curiosity: Clovis. He had made a mess of his bed. Payne—still starched and ventilated in his back-buttoned shift—noticed that. Rumple sheets enough and they appeared to turn yellow. Possibly it was the abysmal light that threw so many soft, upsetting shadows. Payne felt his face had elongated. He knew his voice would not be strong.

But Clovis slept on, his face running all over an immense forearm. He lay on his stomach and pushed forward with his leg, sleeping like a baby.

★　★　★

"Close your mouth on the therm." Payne could taste the alcohol. The nurse had that flush, clean prettiness that might have been blown from a single bead of thermodynamic plastic; that beauty so illusively distributed among majorettes and Breck shampoo girls that certain Rotarian interests have attempted to isolate as a national type.

Thinking of what was to come, pain appeared to him in a number of guises, the main one being something minute, an itching follicle, that expanded like a sonofabitch. Why me?

The next time the pretty nurse came, she drew Payne's curtain around him, thus cutting off some incipient conversational gloating between Payne and Clovis on the subject of the bat tower.

The girl plainly came to her profession via the misrepresentations of Nancy Drew. Fluffing pillows. There, doesn't that feel just a lot better now? Roll over. She used his entire can to drive a column of mercury. He wondered why she took his temperature there, when she hadn't before. She was building to something.

He rested his head, wan. Around the top of the curtain, a white painted pipe bisected the ceiling. He could hear Clovis next to him fold a newspaper roughly; its shadow jerked on the ceiling.

The nurse laid out her instruments on the cloth-covered tray beside him: the thermometer, some sort of shaving materials, and a dire rubberoid article with chambers, petcocks and tubes. Payne ran scared.

On his stomach, his neck cricked upward uncomfortably, he took a fix on the wall and waited in silence for the first touch. In an endless instant, he felt her tentative fingers plucking unsuccessfully at the edge of the shift, cold fingertips grazing his affrighted bottom, then up went the shift and Payne felt the horror of circulating air. He heard the sigh of some escaping pressure, smelled soapy menthol and felt a billow of soft cream smoothed onto his perineum and backside by the peerless hand of the young nurse. Perspiration poured from his face into the absorbent pillowcase.

At the first scraping, which was simultaneous with

the first involuntary little noise from the nurse, he turned over his shoulder and looked. He saw her inclined face behind a broad, heart-shaped silhouette; tears streamed down as she manipulated the razor, rinsing it when it overloaded with shaving cream in a bowl on her tray. This was an episode that appeared in no edition of Nancy Drew stories.

Her cheeks were withdrawn and her face was an altogether imploring image of loss, grief, unitemized sorrow and what not. Finally, she gave his glossy stern a wipe of towel and Payne raked down the shift. She pushed his hand away and choked, "No."

She broke out the rubber heart, swollen with liquid, and buried its nozzle in his fanny. Holding the heavy, swollen bag in both hands, she seemed to proffer it. Payne imagined the unsightly article to contain ice water. He was impaled on a frozen stalagmite and gritted down hard until she withdrew the nozzle. He looked back to see her tears but found instead that she was laughing silently. It was disturbing.

That would have been otherwise a moment for clear and immediate thought. He would have liked to see what happened to a gesture of friendship with the nurse toward who knew what. As it was, though, his feet made a furious, impatient squeaking on the waxed institutional floor. He ran through a couple of complicated maneuvers —ones that would have been illegal in an automobile: reckless U-turns, especially—just to get around the tables to the bathroom where, sitting, he had an utter cathartic letting-go as though chambers, membranes, tiny bulkheads and walls all collapsed at once in a single directional rush.

When he was finished, that careful, Byronic grandiosity that he was inclined to cultivate was completely gone. And he felt, still sitting, like a simple shriveled fly.

"How long have I been asleep?" Clovis asked.

"A long time. I don't know."

"How did I act? Did I say anything."

"You just lay there and twitched like a dog."

It wasn't long after dinner that the nurse came again. She drew Payne's curtain, herself inside, and gave him enough of her unnerving smile-play that he began to fancy trying something. Throwing up his shift behind she whispered in his ear, "You foul your linen, mister, and you're in Dutch with me!" Payne, thrilled, not hearing the words at all, not more anyway than the airy voice and smelling her fabulous dimestore jasmine, tried to twist around and kiss her.

But she deftly thrust a lubricated nozzle into his rectum, really deflating him, and delivered a column of fluid thirteen feet in length, though certainly not as the crow flies.

A moment later, catching Clovis' eyes, he cleared out, his feet squealing like wharf rats on the hard floor. This time, his easement of himself was a progressive collapse of his intestines behind their emptying contents.

From the room, he heard Clovis laughing. "Mae West! Man overboard! What are you thinking about in there?"

"Bombs."

"Bombs!" Clovis said with alarm. *What bombs?*

Then, after the third enema, he didn't have to void himself. He couldn't figure it out. Nothing happened. After twenty minutes of studying Payne, Clovis said, "You go yet?"

"No."

"What's keeping you?"

"I don't have to go anymore," Payne said with irritation.

"You didn't go after a high colonic?"

"I don't have to. Is that okay?"

"Jesus, that is something else again. Not take one after a high colonic. Not after he had one. That really takes it."

Five minutes of silence.

"Want to have a whirlpool bath?" Clovis asked. Payne focused on him.

★   ★   ★

Payne followed Jack Clovis into a large room. Clovis leaned his crutches up and hobbled and hopped along the high fluorescent-lit walls. The room was a uniform, clean, prison gray and a gutter ran in the concrete around the base of its walls. In the center of the room was a circular drain that held a metal insert like the piece that is on the burner of a gas stove.

In this room were half a dozen identical stainless-steel whirlpool baths. Deferring to possibility, Clovis adjusted the one nearest the door for Payne. They had already located the john in a military way. The bath was now filled with surging water. Payne reached in and felt the agreeable temperature throbbing powerfully against his hand. Clovis went to fill his own a few feet away. Payne got in with an inrush of breath. He felt the maniacal sensuality of the tropical water ply his flesh, reduce him to speechlessness. Clovis climbed into his, holding on, white-knuckled, with the one hand. Payne sank into seizing warmth until only his head remained above the agitated surface.

His brain sagged gently into a peaceful and celestial neutrality. His eyes moistened from the lacy steam that arose from the water as though from a druid's tarn. His mind was little more than the cipher which activates the amoeba and the paramecium.

Only then did the labyrinth of his system begin to confound him; first with bowel misgivings which, in his beatitude, he tried to ignore; then with a series of seizures that ran through his viscera like lightning. It was too late to ignore them.

He grabbed the stainless-steel sides as though it were a tossing boat and, moaning aloud, felt the sharp contractions of that most privy and yet imperious of the intestines.

Looking down in his abandonment of all hope, he saw, as though a cloud had crossed the sun, the water darken suddenly around him. And he knew that the worst had happened.

He wrenched at the controls violently until the bath shut off and he sat in the now stilled fluid. A moment later, Clovis, sensing something, carefully shut off his own and the two men sat with new silence roaring up around them.

Suddenly, Jack Clovis wrinkled his face violently.

"Good Christ, Payne! What in God's name are you cooking there!"

Payne got to his feet looking, really, as though he had just come from Miami, a city he never liked that much. And he was too far gone to be amused.

18

Doctor Proctor, manipulant-grandee of the proctoscope, an instrument which brings to the human eye vistas which are possibly forbidden (possibly not), lazed at home watching the Olympic bob-sled trials on ABC's Wide World of Sports. The lush blue carpet cuddled his pink physician's heels and when he walked across its Middle Eastern richesse, he pretended to himself that it was the guts, tripe and visceral uproar amid which his profession obliged him to live.

Here it was different. Here where the goggle-eyed street urchins of his most valuable canvases stared at one another from the soft contours of his walls, he was in-clined to dream of all the things he no longer was. Then, he would find himself a little droopy and all too inclined to pop a couple of amphetamines from his big fat doctor's stash. And then, when he overdid, as he did tonight, he would be the energetic boy of before, laughing, crying and gouging quickly at his crotch in that little athlete's ges-ture of look what we have here.

Tonight, snuffling a trifle with the upshot of his high, Proctor made his way to the darkling trophy room of his Key West home; and, once again, commenced vacuuming the hundreds of dim upright mouths of his trophies with his well-used Hoover. Standing waist-deep among the winged victories and gaping loving cups, he knew, some-how, who he was.

Often, in such a mood, his nurse would appear to his imagination, often up to something freakish which Proctor could not ordinarily have contrived. Recurrently, on the other hand, she would appear nude and aslither atop an immense conduit covered with non-fat vegetable shortening. Such a thought could not have been foreborne without eventual relief; and his little wrist-flicks at himself came to linger for the serious business at hand.

But nothing disruptive, all in all. Proctor functioned. So it was that in the morning hours when most people were asleep, Proctor, who never *had* slept, headed for the clinic in his green Aston Martin DB-4. Heel-and-toeing to keep his revs up, he brodied and drifted through the damp morning streets of the Island City.

Well, he said to himself, life is a shakedown cruise. Wanna bet? Through housework, pills and orgasms, he had lost eight pounds since nightfall. He hadn't been on a zombie run like this since the service where, with his usual athletic finesse, he had distinguished himself as a fighter pilot.

He had flown the almost legendary and sinister fire-ship, the carrier-based F4 Phantom, making night runs and day runs with the same penetrating fanaticism that vanished with very little aging and required the bolstering of pills.

For a while, all the pilot's bugaboos had haunted him: night landings on a heaving carrier deck in the fierce rocket-laden thirty-eight-thousand-pound flying piano, hoping to hell that on that blackened deck the aircraft would find one of the four arrester wires and keep him from deep-sixing off the bow.

Vertigo: One cloudless night on the South China Sea, Proctor had been practicing his sidewinder runs and barrel rolls and high-performance climbs with the afterburner pouring the last possible thrust beyond Mach II; when suddenly his brain would no longer equilibrate and he couldn't tell which end was up; somehow he flew pure instrument on the carrier landing, straight on for the Fresnel light on the ship's stern, catching the fourth wire and snatching up short of a hundred-and-eighty-degree view of the blackened South China Sea. He felt the entire rotation of his brain; all the physical perceptions which were his only moral facts gently rocked into place again; and the next day he started cinching them down with goofballs.

Soon enough, the younger pilots who had begun to resent his sheepish hand on the stick saw the old fiend was intact after all; and from then on, when he came in from a strike with leftover fuel, he sneaked in around the islands and blew up junks and sank native craft with his shock wave and really made himself felt.

Naturally, the skipper who had been watching this appealing Yankee Doodle and who was alerted to this new panache by the revived Proctor habit of picking his arrester wire on landings—traditional fighter-jock's machismo caper—called him in and, chuckling, told him to lay off because the gooks were going to load the junks with anti-aircraft equipment and start weeding out those four-million-dollar Phantoms.

Proctor quipped that he didn't care if they got the plane as long as the seat worked. But the old skipper reminded him that Charlie would find you if you ejected and make a Countess Mara with your tongue. And still Proctor didn't give a damn, really didn't give a damn! He boomed, bombed, blasted and killed and sank small craft the same as always except now he did it during bombing halts when he was supposed to have been on reconnaissance.

Into his continuous vile blue yonder, Yankee Doodle Proctor went, high as high could be on various purloinings from the flight surgeon's old kit bag; still masturbatory as all get out, he sometimes gouged at the crotch of his flight suit in the middle of combat, giggled when flak gently rocked the aircraft or snuffed one of the smaller Skyhawks that always went on strike with the dreamy, invulnerable McDonnell Phantoms.

Sometimes, in over the trees supersonically, he would get glimpses of Migs deployed on jungle runways, some of them scrambling. And once a SAM ground-to-air missile, like a white enamel tree trunk, appeared in the formation and Proctor purposely let it pick him up and follow for a thousand feet before he duped its computer brain into overshooting. Again, he giggled and gouged at his flight suit to imagine that prize gook investment on its pitiful try at killing the sun, which Proctor had substituted for himself by way of a crazy parabolic maneuver that made the pale metal wings of the Phantom lift gently with the force of God knew how many G's; that made even old giggling Yankee Doodle's face pull and flow toward his ass; that made the smooth voluptuous curves of Asia, caressed by his shock wave, clog with unimaginable scrollery of trees and detail. He climbed, sonic booms volleying over the country, after-burners pulled to the utmost and cleared out at fifty thousand feet in whorls, volutes, beautiful spirals of vapor.

Three weeks of gouging had made a shiny spot on his flight suit.

How close this all now seemed. And, really, it spoiled his driving; a sports car for God's sake with its stupid bland instruments that indicated the ridiculous landbound progress of the machine. By the time he was in the staff parking lot, he was cranky. A pharmaceutical supply truck was parked at the loading bay and Proctor, already coming down, imagined eating his way through the truck, stem to stern. Inside the first door, he spotted a gabble of creepy little interns with careful telltale stethoscopes hanging out of their pockets. Proctor told them to break it up and they did. They knew Proctor would besmirch them at staff meetings. In the involuted parlance of the world of interns, Proctor was an "asshole." But this was unfair to Proctor, an altogether harmlessly overpaid popinjay of the medical profession.

"On the table."

Payne obeyed. He could see the doctor was not in the mood for chatter. Neither, for that matter, was he. Endless nightmares of the possible violations of his body had left him rather testy.

"How do you mean, doctor?"

"I mean on the table. Right now. Crossways."

The nurse came in and the doctor looked up. Payne sat across the examining table.

"Where are we with this guy?" the doctor asked. The nurse looked at her board.

"He had the pentobarbital sodium at six this morning. Then the atropine and morphine an hour ago. I—"

"How do you feel?" the doctor asked Payne.

"Okay."

"Relaxed and ready for the operation?"

"Vaguely." Proctor looked him over, thought: tough guy with the lightest possible glazing of civilization: two years at the outside in some land-grant diploma mill. "I forget," the doctor went on to his nurse, "are these external?"

"A little of both."

"Ah, so. And thrombosed were they not?"

"I should say."

A wispy man, the dread anesthesiologist, came in wheeling a sort of portable autoclave with his ghastly instruments inside. Through the drugs he had been given that morning, Payne could feel some slow dread arise. As for Proctor, this skillful little creep—Reeves by name—with his hair parted low over his left ear and carefully deployed over his bald head, was an object of interest and admiration. He watched him lay out the materials with some delight and waited for the little man's eagerness to crest at the last possible moment before saying, "Thank you, Reeves. I think I'd rather." Reeves darkened and left the room. "Hunch your shoulders, Mister—"

"Payne. Like that?"

"Farther. There you go."

After his little moment with Reeves, Proctor had second thoughts. He knew the sacral block shouldn't be taken casually; and he didn't do them often enough to be really in practice. But what the hell. This guy was preoperatively well prepared; he'd just wind it up.

"Nurse, what kind of lumbar puncture needle did Reeves bring us?"

"A number twenty-two, doctor."

Proctor chuckled. That Reeves was a real mannerist. A little skinny needle like that; but maybe that's how they were doing it now. Used to be you had a needle like a rifle barrel and you'd get cerebrospinal fluid running down the clown's back. It made for a fast job but memorable headaches for the patient afterwards.

Proctor went at it. He pressed the needle into the fourth lumbar interspace well into the subarachnoid region and withdrew two cc's of spinal fluid which he mixed with a hundred mg's of novocaine crystals in a hyperbaric solution which he reinjected confident he had Payne's ass dead to the world for four good hours.

Just for precaution—it was really Reeve's precaution —he gave Payne fifty mg's of ephedrine sulfate in the arm. "Keep this man sitting up straight," Proctor said and went outside to the drinking fountain and popped another goofball, this one covered with lint from his pocket. He peered sadly into the middle distance and thought: *I was the darling of the fleet.*

Payne was wheeled by, on his way to the operating room. He began to review his life. Very little of it would come. He could go back—lying there numbed, the victim of purloined spinal fluid—about two weeks with any solidity; then, flashes. As: boarding school, Saturday morning, in a spectral study hall for unsatisfactory students; Payne and three other dunces watched over like meat by the master on duty, in pure Spring light, in silence. At one window of the hall, striped boy athletes rock noiselessly past for batting practice; a machine pitched hardballs out of a galvanized hopper and the base paths were still muddy. Payne shielding his eyes in apparent concentration, occasionally dozes, occasionally slips a magazine out from under the U. S. History text: *Guns And Ammo.* In his mind, he cradles a Finnish Sako rifle, sits on a ridge in the Canadian Rockies that glitters with mica and waits two hundred years for a Big Horn Ram. Something moves a few yards up the draw: The master on duty has spotted *Guns And Ammo.* Payne's heart whirls in his chest and loses traction.

"Miss?" Payne asks.

"Sir?"

"I feel like a dead Egyptian. You and Proctor are fixing to pull my brain out of my nose."

"No, sir!"

"I feel that life has handed me one in the snot locker. You see I'm the last buffalo. And I'm dying of a sucking chest wound. Isn't there something you could do in a case like mine? Some final ecstasy you could whip up?"

"Nothing that comes to mind, sir."

"Miss, if my beak falls open and cries are heard during Doctor Proctor's knifework, will that be it, as far as you're concerned? I mean, will you sign off on yours truly? As another has?"

"Possibly a leetle."

"In other circumstances I would be a simple hero to you. But maybe your life already is not unencumbered. Is there a certain someone?"

Proctor strode in. "Let's do it." Payne intoned a helpless sphincteric dirge. He was in terror. This room was filled with strange and frightful machinery which would have been the envy of any number of pirates whose names are household words.

"Will there be pain?" Payne inquired.

"I don't know what you mean."

"Surely the word rings one little bell in your medical carillon tower." Payne regretted his words instantly. He did not want to antagonize Proctor.

"It appears," said the doctor to the nurse, "that the medication has taken our friend by storm."

Proctor looked down from his end of the operating table. He had Payne on his back, in the lithotomy position; not the one Proctor was most comfortable with; but the only one a serious proctologist would consider with spinal anesthesia via the hyperbaric solutions that Reeves found so irresistible. Reeves! What a bleary little cornball.

From this perspective, Proctor saw with a tiny almost atavistic horror the ring of thrombosed hemorrhoids. And it was now a question of demonstrating the internal complications so that they could be excised without any further fiddling around.

Proctor thought helplessly of how he could have been a big, clean career aviator instead of staring up some wise guy's dirt chute.

He inserted his index finger well into Payne's rectum withdrawing and reinserting several times without, in his opinion, sufficiently extruding the internal hemorrhoids. In a moment of impatience and almost pique, he stuffed Payne's rectum with wads of dry gauze which he hauled out slowly dragging the hemorrhoids with them. Now he had a perfectly beastly little mess to clean up. The entire anal verge was clustered with indisputably pathological extrusions. Proctor sighed languorously.

With a certain annoyance, he dilated Payne's sphincter to an anal aperture of two centimeters and then, making more work space for himself, rather zealously went for, and got, three centimeters without tearing even a teensy bit of sphincteric muscle. He swiftly clipped four forceps into position to keep the site exposed. A smile broke out on his face as he remembered his Asian days.

All of the sound and movements around Payne were informed with the most sinister lack of ordinary reality. Implements passed his vision which were not unlike those with which we eat; yet, somehow, something was wrong with them. They had crooked handles or the ones you thought were spoons had trap doors or when they touched each other they rang with an unearthly clarity. And surrounding the hard if intolerable precision of all this weaponry were various loose bags, drooping neoprene tubes, cups of deep blubbery gels, fleecy, inorganic sponges in space-age colors, and the masked, make-up lacking face of the nurse, her hair yanked back in utilitarian severity.

Around himself, he could hear the doctor talking, nipping off the words as if to challenge a misunderstanding of his grandiose medical technicalities. Payne felt that something like the same smugness and expertise must attend the performance of electrocutions, the kind of officiousness that would make a condemned man hesitate before using the terms "hot seat" or "fry."

Proctor was cranky. He needn't have made this kind of a mess. And so he muttered with the usual authoritarian voice that there wasn't one thing there he couldn't clean up. Not one.

Still, he didn't know what had become of his coordination. Ordinarily, he could incise the most perfect demi-eclipse around the base of the hemorrhoid and dissect the varix from the external sphincter with a deft turn of the wrist. Truly, this was surgery that could have been performed with a rotary mower; and yet, he was barely up to it.

So, instead of a nice clean finish, he had to hunt up and down the patient's dirt chute for bleed points, stop them—in one case resorting to catgut, so nasty was the lesion—and then impatiently make a thick dressing the size of a catcher's mitt to sop up the serosanguineous ooze that was surely going to be a part of this man's postoperative period.

He had Payne wheeled away unconscious after a veritable hosing down with demerol. He indicated he would have the nurse remain. When the door was shut and Proctor looked around at the spattered operating room, the nurse stood without motion. Proctor spotted smart wads of disapprobation in her eyes.

"Nice little rectum you left him with there," she said in a brave squeak, "with your cut-and-try surgery there."

"A bleeder."

"That poor boy," she said. "I have never in my life witnessed a thing like that. It almost looked like you were trying to make some sort of meal back there."

"What meal!"

"I don't know, some, I don't know, almost like some sort of pasta fazoula or—"

"Pasta fazoula! Are you Italian? Pasta fazoula is this great Italian dish—" The nurse waved him silent with a harsh and impatient motion.

"God, Doctor, I was illustrating something oh never mind I . . ."

"Nurse, I used to sit on the starboard catapult during international emergencies, waiting to go bomb. In a forty-thousand-pound aircraft with wings that wouldn't glide a sparrow if the engines ever failed: a flying piano. And me in the driver's seat getting to feel more and more like pure crash-cargo, lady. And from my viewpoint on the steam catapult I could see, below me in the waters of the South China Sea, twenty-foot man-eating sharks that had been feeding on Oriental sea burials for a thousand years. How do you think I felt?"

"How?"

"Punk. Those sharks would break up a funeral half-way through the services and there's me on the starboard catapult: one flame-out and you're so much fish food. And you tell me pasta fazoula."

"But Doctor I—"

"Tell me cut-and-try, do you?"

"Doctor, I—"

"I've had enough. I thought that after war a man could return to a life of service with interludes of silence spent among a tasteful collection of art objects."

"Doctor, how can I make it up to you?"

Payne lay quiet as a fossil in the deep sweeping benignity of demerol, the Kuda Bux of Key West. Pale surgical lights rolled by as moons. Then it was blistering dry and hot; an expanse of macadam curled at the far edges and made twenty-nine identical mountains. Payne held a big, ice cold chronometer.

A bedside view would have shown that, if only for the time being, Proctor, Ann and Clovis had made of Nicholas Payne pure meat.

Finally, in the middle of the night, he woke up laughing in complete weakness. *Seep, seep, seep.* Clovis, in perfect health, yelled, "Shut up, can't you! I'm a dead goose as it is for crying out loud."

Payne opened his mind like the sweet dusty comic strip from a pink billet of Fleer's bubblegum and saw things as deep and appropriate as soft nudes on the noses of B29's. He saw longhorn cattle being driven over the Golden Gate Bridge, St. Teresa of Avila at the Mocambo, pale blue policemen nose-to-bung in an azure nimbus around the moon.

He had happy dreams. He could hear the punctual ringing of the first pair of steel taps on his first pair of blue suede shoes and remembered Jerry Lee Lewis climbing a piano in Miami in fiery lemon-colored underwear, assaulting the keys with hands feet head knees, two-foot platinum hair flapping the Steinway contours and howling GREAT BOWLS OF FAR!

Jerry Lee knew how to treat a piano.

He awoke early in the morning in the sharpest kind of pain and with a feeling of clarity. The principal menaces were behind. And the rather murky situation with Ann seemed to have fallen into place; though he would have been hard put to say where. He felt as if he were collecting into one shape and that he would soon make a kind of sudden expansion. He would stop feeling the little nerve headaches urge their way up from his neocortex. He would get his saliva back and his lips wouldn't stick to his teeth when he was talking.

It wasn't at all long before he remembered the dreams of Ann and saw how extremely selective they were; to the effect that she was present in the dreams and absent in reality. An insistent phrase pressed itself upon him: I couldn't have been more of a pig. He knew very well that an attempt to make something perfect—a love that would not exclude towers and romantic riskings of the neck—had turned swiftly into a regular fuck-up flambeau, staggering even in memory. No, he thought, it must be that I couldn't have been more of a pig.

Soon enough, he went on a cheerless regime of mineral oil and a soft low-residue diet. Nevertheless, early in the second day, after half a dozen Sitz baths had restored the firmer edges to his personality, he found it necessary to adjourn to the bathroom for his first postoperative bowel movement.

Why go into such a nightmare? A single enormous turd explored every surgical error Proctor had made. Somewhat to his own discredit, Payne howled like the Anti-Christ.

And when he heard Proctor and the nurse muddling around the room outside the john, he booted the door open exactly as he had booted open the door on his grandfather's disused farmstead, shamelessly revealing himself in an exhibit of fearful squattery and tragically droned, *"You bastards core me like an apple and let me have a hard stool two days later! That makes me laugh my God that makes me laugh!"*

He wouldn't shut up though he could see Ann snapping away with her Nikon. Next to his bed, wet roses soaked on a newspaper; the note was hers: *"This is it."*

Ann looking in at this ashen, pooping, howling form felt, thus early in her career, a grave seepage of idealism, an invidious pissing away of all that was good and held meaning. She found herself staring out the window past the parking lot and the blackened contours of asphalt, past the lunatic geometry of Key West roofs to the dynamo sky of America; and turned to smile inwardly; hers was one dream that wouldn't get off the ground.

It was a pleasure to sit at the wheel, the diesels not straining, and listen to the ship-to-shore. The captain found on a clear night like tonight he could pick up the other boats as far off as the Cay Sal Bank. After a month in the Tortugas and Marquesas and a week or two violating the nursery ground, he was ready to go back to Galveston. Where he was known.

"You don't figure she'd use the camera to blackmail no one?"

The mate who looked more and more like a hillbilly song star the more the running lights accentuated his face's declivities, said, "Of course not, Captain. This here is just some sort of adventurer." The captain got up happy.

"Steady as she goes," he said to the mate, who took the wheel with a gravity that was possibly not genuine.

He waited for the captain to head for the lighted companionway. "If you want yer trousers pressed, skipper, why the winch would be an awful good spot to leave them," he said, bringing down the house.

It was a starry night going to Galveston with the boom of the big trawler swaying a black metronomic line over the silver fan of wake.

And it was real life out there on the Gulf of Mexico; because down in the hold of a Key West shrimper, a person of culture was committing experience.

The tower went up with embarrassing speed and now it was Saturday on Mente Chica Key. The bats had all been dyed day-glo orange so that their bug scavenging circulation would be plain to all. Confined by a single polyethylene sheet, every last one of them was sealed in the tower.

There was a blue satin ribbon tied about the base of the tower. The tower itself stood stern and mighty and impervious to termites against the Seminole sky. Around its base, the Mid-Keys Boosters stirred by the hundreds in anticipation. There were many military personnel in Polynesian mufti. There were many retired persons of legendary mediocrity known locally as "just people." There were many snapping camera pests from the newspapers.

All around the area, the mangroves released their primitive smell and made expanses of standing water where billions upon billions of the little dark awful saltwater mosquitoes would be born *in perpetuum*, bats or no bats, quite honestly.

Nicholas Payne and C. J. Clovis flanked Dexter Fibb, aging Grand Master of the Mid-Keys Boosters, and explained how he must yank the manila rope, how he must bring down the polyethylene sheet to release the bats so that they might begin devouring the mosquitoes that this minute were making every spectator's head lumpy. Payne, unable to accustom himself to a sanitary napkin, shifted about irritably.

Dexter Fibb crushed his worn blue-and-gold yachtsman's hat about his ears, preparing himself for action, should it come his way.

As anyone could have seen by looking into their eyes, Clovis and Payne were flush with the seventeen thousand.

The dedication of the bat tower was seen as a great chance to cement the U. S. Navy's relationships with the Downtown Merchants' Association. So there were any number of Mister Fix-It types of formidable rank, often chief petty officer, on loan from the base. These helpers, enclouded by mosquitoes, gathered around bits of electronic gear, loudspeakers, strobes and emergency gadgets, sonic shark repellants and smoke bombs for attracting helicopters. One group, ordinarily employed maintaining the kind of fighter planes Doctor Proctor himself had flown, had erected a banner over their project that read:

PHANTOM PHIXERS

Some of the wives had laid out tables of country fixings, jams and jellies and whatnot, in a sentimental materialization of the kind of quasi-rural bonhomie that seemed a millimeter from actual goose-stepping and brown-shirt uproars of bumpkin fascism.

Payne moved through, scared to death. He saw the tower and the old wagon beneath, the bats whirring, vortical. The mosquitoes were definitely a problem. One reason the bats were whirring, vortical, and not sleeping was that the mosquitoes were biting them all the time and the bats couldn't do a thing about it.

To show that their husbands had gotten priority tours, some of the Navy wives wore grass skirts and red bandana tops. Beyond their muscular shoulders you could see the tower, the crowd, the whirring bat wagon, the mangroves and the hot glistening sky. Kids pegged rocks at the bat wagon and everyone swatted and dervished in clouds of mosquitoes.

One of the husbands, a chief petty officer, darkened his crew cut with an oily hand and said to mid-air: "This oscillator is givin me a fit." The chief's wife was reading the newspaper.

"Listen ta this what Pola Negri has to say: 'I was the star who introduced sex to the screen but I don't like nudity and obscenity in today's films. Movies *and* men were more romantic in my day.' I buy that."

"I do too, honey," said the chief, "but I haven't got time to think about it. Do you read me? I've got this oscillator and that rectifier back at the hangar I was mentioning which is causing me to throw a fit."

Payne was all ears. The wife saw and addressed her remarks to him.

"Don is trying to make E9 before he retires," the wife informed Payne, "then he is going to open a TV repair on Big Coppitt Key."

"What I don't have time to think about," said Don, the chief petty officer, "that is, if I am ever gonna operate a TV repair on Big Coppitt, is Pola Negri's sex life."

"Although Don would agree, wouldn't you Hon, that things in movies has got way out of line."

"I haven't got time for a bunch of beaver shows," Don told simply everybody, "Pola Negri's or anybody else's. I got this oscillator on the blink, frankly."

"What's it for?" Payne asked politely.

"Well, it's not for nothing if it's on the blink," said Don. "You follow that, don't you?"

"Yes . . ."

"And the rest I can't explain unless you got a U.S. of America Navy rate in electronics which you don't."

Payne wandered away without reply. He felt, somehow, that he was in no position to start skirmishes around here. But that wasn't enough; the chief followed him. "Me'n the wife," he said brazenly, "think you're takin this outfit to the cleaners."

"The cleaners?"

"That's right. I have had a look at the tab. There's quite the margin of profit."

"How much would you say?"

"Two-thirds."

"Way off."

"Am I?"

"I'm afraid you have no head for economics. *Econ* as we used to say."

"Uh huh. You know, us ordinree citizens has about had it with being milked all the time."

"You're not being milked."

"We're being milked. Don't contradict me."

"You're being taken to the cleaners," Payne corrected. "And if you had something going on in your head besides a few gummy notions of how to work less and keep the old lady in Monkey Ward's pedal-pushers and plastic bath clogs, you'd *never* get taken. Now, unless you want to come out and play with the grown-ups, I suggest you quit whining and go back to fixing wires for the U.S. of America Navy before you spoil your credit with them. Isn't all that many outfits have room for you time-servers."

The chief came very close, squinting. He waved a whole handful of fingers slowly in Payne's face. He tilted his head. "Amo tell you one thing sumbitch; if I see a way to come in on you, amo take it." The not quite pitiable swab was worked up to the point that, with any more goading, he would have had a philosophical outburst with references to the nation and its perpetrating enemies. There seemed to be no cure for pests like Payne but automotive decals and secret handshakes. The freaks were coming out of the woodwork.

Payne joined Clovis at the tower where the two of them greeted the faithful. Payne stood beside him with an easy winning grin and waited for the group to clear. "Do you get the feeling they're on to us?" he asked with a smile for a small lady gorged with potato salad who yoo-hooed from the mangroves, flapping at a cloud of insects with a red plastic picnic fork.

"Sure do," Clovis smiled to them all. "Let's just hope we can keep it glued together until the ceremony is over. I notice you're limping."

Some moments later, the chief petty officer of various electrical pursuits came toward the tower, only to set up the loudspeakers that would amplify Clovis' singular voice. Nevertheless, he made Payne nervous. Payne had begun to regret his speech about taking people to the cleaners; and, in fact, had lost what little interest he had had in the money; so that he was in a very bleak frame of mind about their prospects.

He had too a tremor of agony that some child would come up and tell him he hoped these bats would do the job because his baby sister was dying of encephalitis. Here, son, here's all the grimy loot we chiseled out of your dad and his neighbors and here are the keys to my Hudson Hornet and that Dodge Motor Home over there. Wire me collect, Leavenworth, if you have motor trouble. I'm cashing in. My soul is all shot to shit and I don't know where I get off next. *I am penitent,* Payne thought, *I have brought this upon myself.*

Dexter Fibb, at fifty-three, had never had a moving violation. He had never declined a luncheon speech at the Lions and he had never hesitated to dry the dishes or take out the garbage when he was asked to do so by his wife, Bambi.

Dexter Fibb loved symmetry. He loved the bat tower because it was symmetrical and he loved Bambi because her whopping bust was the same size as her gibbous backside. Dexter Fibb often grew upset with himself when he tried to cut his sideburns to the same length, and would advance them millimeter by millimeter until they were small indentations above his ears. He could never get his sleeves right when he rolled them up either; one would always be somewhat farther down on his elbow than the other and on those unfortunate mornings that he would button his shirt out of line, he would rip it from his body with a shriek and fish another heavily starched white-on-white see-thru from his top drawer.

Fibb believed in many things that verged upon superstition but which helped him through a world in which he seemed to lack some essential spiritual coordination. He read *Consumer's Digest* and evaluated his friends' cars by looking at the color of the exhaust pipe. His favorite automobile was that old model Studebaker that seemed to go backward and forward all at once.

The pilot committee of the Mid-Keys Boosters bought the bat tower mainly because Fibb made so much of its looking the same from any angle. And it is to his love of symmetry that we must ascribe his instantaneous horror at the sight of C. J. Clovis.

On the sound truck next to the door, leaking wires into the hands of the electric petty officer, this sign:

OUR GOD IS NOT DEAD.

SORRY ABOUT YOURS.

"How's she goin, Don?" Fibb asked the CPO.

"Real good, Dexter. I had this oscillator givin me a fit but I isolated the sumbitch with a circuit tester."

Fibb went inconspicuously to the microphone, still disconnected and, half-preoccupied, tried to warm it up. He did a couple of licks from old Arthur Godfrey and Paul Harvey shows. He did a quick Lipton Noodle Soup take and smiled to remember the old applause-meter. A couple of the muscular hula ladies wandered by and Fibb got randy.

He sat on the platform, waving mosquitoes away with the want-ads from the *Key West Citizen*, and tried to think what he would say. Another hula lady went by and Fibb thought how he would like to slip it to her, right in the old flange, where it counted, by God.

The chief pulled a plastic ukulele out of his truck and strummed at her wildly without effect. "You're a damn lightnin fingers," Fibb told him.

"I own every record Les Paul and Mary Ford ever cut. My wife's got all the Hugo Winterhalters. And have I got the Hi-fi. Crackerjack little sumbitch I grabbed cheap on my last tour. Diamond needle, sumbitchin speakers waist-high, AM, FM, the whole shootin match."

Dexter Fibb spotted C. J. Clovis looking just especially grotesque, all by himself, with that aluminum understructure sticking out of everywhere. He winced.

"Kind of pathetic, ain't he?" inquired the chief.

"Some people just don't draw lucky," said Dexter Fibb with some strain, watching Clovis hitch across the field.

"I don't know, Dexter. I think he come up with a handful on this go-round."

"Oh, God, who's to say, who's to say," said Fibb, eyes askew.

The chief said with craft, "Would you just want me to estimate the rake-off for you? I have a little background in econ, Dex. I could show you . . ."

The generosity of the Navy was considerable. A parking problem which had begun to look acute was quickly alleviated by the arrival of four MPs whose training showed immediately. The incoming mass of automobiles magically became rows of parked cars with walking lanes in-between that permitted people to move directly to the stage and tower.

Clovis met Payne at the bat wagon. Payne talked to a booster who was handing out ice-cream parlor fans. He limped over to Clovis, gesturing to him with his head.

"They want you to speak," said Clovis. "I told them you were a lawyer."

"Why?"

"Because I didn't want any loose legal questioning. I wanted them to figure you as an expert."

"Oh, God, I don't think I can make a speech."

"You plain have to. You make one before they open the tower and I'll do the wind-up. Hell, that'll give you a chance to get to your car before I do."

"No," said Payne the sport, "I'd wait for you." He couldn't think of a thing he could tell these people, except possibly that they'd been had.

But when the time came for him to speak, he climbed up on the platform not only ready but with a sense of mission. At his very appearance, a shimmer of antagonism passed through the crowd; and when, in his introductory remarks, he referred to beer as "the nectar of the gobs," he was actually booed, if only a little. He began to wonder exactly how he would handle himself if the crowd decided to work him over. "Beer then," he said after his joke was badly received. "Have some beer." Silence. You bastards, he thought: very well. I will win them over.

"Let me be quite frank with you," he lied. "I'd like to say that even though I don't recognize a face out here except that of my partner, I feel as if I've known you all. Everything here has reminded me of you folks. Not so much the tower as the potato salad you folks been eatin out chere." He thought he'd try a little Delta gumbo-mouth on them. "Do you know what I mean? Last night I listened to a nigra militant on TV, talking about what he called blapp people and gee as I look around I see this community is entirely short of blapp people. Not only blapp people but weirdos." The sympathetic chuckle that ensued put him entirely out of reach of hecklers. "Why God, you're the secret honky underground network of America!" Applause. "And I don't see any backs up against any walls!" More applause. "Why it's solid potato salad out there!" The applause this time was uncertain.

"Well, now. Next time you're recollecting this day, *as you will*, just remember that you bought yourselves a bat tower and all the freaks and weirdos and agitators and blapp people didn't!" Wild, bewildered applause.

"I'm just awful afraid the aforementioned citizens didn't buy a bat tower at all!"

"*NO!*" from the crowd.

"But you doozies with your prickly heads and hush-puppy shoes sure bought one!"

"*Hurray!*"

"I was just telling this chief petty officer a few minutes ago. You people have been taken to the cleaners!" A good-natured, superior murmur passed over the potato salad. "*You've been fleeced!*"

"HURRAY! HURRAY! HURRAY!"

Clovis, ashen, passed Payne on his way to the microphone. "You've got moxie," he offered, "I'll say that." Then he added: "In another hour, A1A will be a fugitive's bottleneck." Payne limped off, patting his pocket. The wad of money was as big as a pistol.

Dexter Fibb received Clovis on the podium, unable to touch him or shake his hand or really take in with his eyes Clovis' implausible lack of symmetry. Moreover,

Fibb was miffed that he had not himself been asked to speak.

The crowd, too, was sobered by the sight of the multiple amputee. "My partner's slighting remarks," he began, "about *minority groups* are not necessarily the opinion of the management. Ahaha. Ahmm." As far as the crowd was concerned, Clovis was a dead man. "You're ah you're a um a really great audience folks!" Then simply, humbly, "And a much appreciated customer." He smiled, head bowed, awaiting the kind of response Payne had gotten. It never came. Better speed things up. Better speed them right the fuck up before this dude comes down like a bomb.

The potato salad had begun to stir. Dexter Fibb nervously crushed his worn blue-and-gold yachtsman's cap about his ears, preparing himself for action, and cried, "Let's put these bats to work!"

Clovis suddenly and almost spasmodically went into his speech about encephalitis and about how bats were like little angels and how mosquitoes were like flying pus-filled syringes. But he ran down like a child's gyroscope. His face, at last, revealed his defeat.

Only Payne was able to start the applause—a strange noise like breaking waves. The vacant faces were intent with the motion of their hands beneath them. It surged through the mangroves in a gesture of confidence and of more than that: of faith.

Ultimately, though, looking into all those hopeful vacant faces gathered at this tower from every corner of the U.S.A., his own flush with the purloined funds and a special joy that went beyond that, Clovis snipped as he must with heavy shears the blue satin ribbon. Dexter Fibb gave a self-conscious rebel yell, got a red face and pulled the rope. The polyethylene came down the sides of the tower, caressing it as it went, lofting and flowing in wind-borne plastic beauty. Bright orange bats poured into the sky.

They were scattered at first, just as they ought to have been, circulating in the immediate area. But then they began to form up. A single shape, more demonstrative than an arrow, in a color derived from every neon monstrosity in the land, formed on the soaring sky at the edge of America. All the hopes of all those empty faces were pinned to that shape that held brilliant overhead a moment more then headed for the interior of the continent and disappeared.

Quite rightly, the wail went up: *"They're gone! They're gone forever! They won't ever come back!"* and so on.

And when the anguish had passed, the potato salad began to advance upon the podium. Dexter Fibb, seeing slippery-looking Payne and the horrifically malformed Clovis, cued the crowd with outraged glances at the two. A serious question with its roots deep in Econ had arisen.

With the first movement of the crowd toward him, Clovis fell to the boards, dragging the Telefunken microphone after himself, convenient to his lips. The great portable speakers transmitted his gasps and howls: "MY HEART IS ON THE FRITZ!" It was amplified over the sea of bat fans, bug loathers and mangroves. "THE FRITZ I SAID!"

Croaking even more impressively than Clovis, Dexter Fibb cried, "Look at him, he's dying!" and stared pale and mute at this crooked item on the stage. Payne listened to Clovis perform extravagantly at the microphone, bleating a ravaged play-by-play as to the condition of his ticker. Payne knelt consolingly beside him. Clovis glanced at him, simulated a grisly death rattle, looked at Payne once again in surprise, looked all around himself and said, "No." Then, without further notice, he died quite blankly.

Payne was the solitary customer at the burial. Though, because of some logistical miscalculation, row upon row of empty folding chairs faced the oblong black hole in the sod. Overhead, a green and white canopy—a pavilion— was turn-buckled tautly on a galvanized pipe frame. Four men took the coffin, a piece of mildly pretentious metal furniture containing the jury-rigged mortal remains of C. J. Clovis, and lowered away. Payne sat on a folding chair, his legs crossed tight on themselves, leaned his face heavily into his hands and thought, "Oh, gee. Oh, fuck."

Payne stayed, after the four men left, in the big open cemetery. The skeletal Poinciana trees stood upon an enormous ocean sky with tenuous, high-altitude horse-tail clouds. Key West, a clapboard town accreted upon a marine hummock at the end of the continental shelf, seemed a peculiar place to have buried Clovis, who had entrusted himself to Payne. Overhead, a pair of frigate birds circled in perfect synchronization as though fixed to the ends of a glass fulcrum.

Payne was tapped gently upon the shoulder by a recent graduate of the police academy who said, "You are under arrest."

"What is the charge?"

"Fraud."

In the police cruiser, Payne quietly began to slip a little. They drove past the cryptic gestures of docks, careened trawlers and crawfishing boats of Garrison Bight. They passed the breaking Atlantic at the foot of Simonton Street. "Take me to the Burger King," he told the cop without getting an answer. "Officer, what you see before you is a futuristic print-out of a thousand years of bog-trotting and one boat ride to an experimental republic: a fiasco." *Silence.* It was dizzying to Payne. From the inside of a police sedan, Payne believed he could see a vast and unplowed interior ridge, buried beneath flags, gum wrappers and diplomas. "I have found my swerve, officer. It makes a gentle glowing contour on the history of the New World." This hero, Nicholas Payne, began smiling. He had the oceanic feeling a thousand yards from sea. The lowering of one defunct sensorium into the sod still filled his head with the martial music of winds and supermarkets, a fugue of singing trees and internal combustion engines, of Miss America contestants past and present doing night things with sturdy flutes, an international autoharmonium of homocidal giddiness manipulated by played-out bobby soxers and sharp dressers in security councils and command modules; it was all out there, the unplowed ridge where energetic riders on winded ponies were impeded by hairdressers with bull-whips, tigerish insurance adjusters, rodents in command formation and other servants of the commonwealth. The last thing Payne said to the perplexed young policeman was, *"To me he was illustrious."*

By returning most of the money, the small discrepancy justified by the touristic utility of the empty tower, Payne avoided the brunt of sentencing. And finally, it was agreed that if he would re-enact his trial for the TV program *Night Court*, he would be let free altogether.

Payne walked into the studio. Two or three technicians wandered around trailing rubber cables and, finally, rolling a camera forward on its dolly to face a plywood judge's bench. The "Judge" himself came in a few moments later and prated in a resonating actor's voice that if Equity found out what he was getting for this bit they'd have him in the slammer so fast his head would swim. Once seated, his judicial mien returned and he was given a "policeman" who declared court was in session. Payne felt as if he were in a dream. He watched a man tried for manslaughter do some wonderful Karl Malden stuff, his upper lip whitening with the tension of vigorous speeches, slobbering with Actor's Studio reality an ad-lib monologue that had the technicians winking at each other.

Then Payne, dreaming, was called, and subsequently so were the witnesses against him. The charge was fraud. The witnesses were Dexter Fibb and five Mid-Keys Boosters, including the chief petty officer, all on TV for the first time.

When they got to the death of Clovis, Payne burst into his only tears since the actuality, a weeping sleepwalker. He looked around himself, saw the trial as though through glass. The judge tried not to beam. The director crowded behind the cameramen to see this. *Night Court*, rich with corrective lessons, was a hit.

★　★　★

Let's have this quickly now: At Galveston, Ann wired for money, a lot of it, waited three hours, got it, flew to Dallas, took a room, called George and gave him the *yes* he had waited for so many years. Hearing his tears, his gratitude, she made reservations on Delta to fly up the next day; then, headed for Neiman-Marcus.

So that: She ran across the tarmac at Detroit-Metropolitan Airport, adorable in a little mini-caftan by Oscar de la Renta made of pink linen. Over that she wore a delicate Moroccan leather coat. The sandals were Dior; and their blocky little heels looked like ivory. Anyone who says she wasn't darling has another think coming.

And George ran to her perfectly attired in an impeccably tailored glen plaid from J. Press. What seemed almost risky in his livery was the wild, yellow Pucci cravat that precisely counterpointed his sedate, seamless cordovans from Church of London.

See them, then, running thus toward one another: perfect monads of nullity.

They whirled in one another's arms.

"Darling," Ann said, "I've been through much." She had caught a little cold aboard ship and George was very, very concerned. After gathering her luggage, they went directly to a hotel where George greedily massaged her chest with Vick's Vap-O-Rub.

It is quite true that George hired the gallery. Nevertheless, Ann's first show was reviewed legitimately; and was a success. Probably the quarterly critic, Allan Lier, of *Lens* magazine, represents the consensus:

. . . Miss Fitzgerald's striking available-light photographs of commercial fishermen turning in for the night are the best sequence of the show. Frame after frame, we see these tired men backlit against the hatchway, heading for a long-earned rest. In their impatience and exhaustion, they are already in various stages of undress.

By way of contrast, the group of pictures called "Nicholas" introduces us to a private yet utterly communicated vision of what is lost in the conventional life. We see time and time again the same weary face of Nicholas: the 'shy suitor,' the spurious rodeo cowboy, the motorist. In one superb shot, in a claustrophobic laundry room, Nicholas is drubbed over the head with a toilet plunger by an attractive older woman: It is left to the viewer to speculate as to what he has done to deserve this! In another picture, he stares directly into the camera, apparently about to speak but unable to think of a single thing to say. In the most terrifying picture of them all, he rises from a toilet seeming to spring at the camera. He wears a short institutional shift and we see where his mediocrity leads. Nothing that is said here can communicate the banality which Miss Fitzgerald captures with polish and control. Thanks to her craft, humanity and attention, she has delivered a cautionary monument to the failed life.

See this show at once.

Payne headed North, making two stops in the State of Florida. One was to see Junior Place and inspect the bat cave with him; the tower bats had not been rejected by their friends and hung upside down from the roof of the cave like thousands of Indian River oranges.

He stopped on the Georgia border and bought an M. Hohner Marine Band harmonica and spent the better part of an evening failing to play Hank Williams' "I'll Never Get Out Of This World Alive."

A truck drove by with a sign: HOLD UP YOUR PACK OF AMERICAN SPACE. The question was whether he had actually seen that. That was getting to be the real question all right.

On a lonely beach in the Sea Islands, Nicholas Payne unfolded his camp stove and began to prepare his supper. He could smell the sea and the sandy groves of loblolly pine that throbbed with uncommon birds. Turned at an angle to the homemade trailer whose floor smelled balefully of departed bats, the Hudson Hornet pointed to the interior of the continent.

Payne poised a jacknife spread with peanut butter over a rigid piece of bread and lifted his face to the sea. He felt as if he had been made an example of; and that, even now, he was part of a demonstration, an exhibit. He held the knife and peanut butter steady. The sky rose over him, round and vitreous, a glass enclosure. He smiled, at one with things. He knew the great blenders hummed in state centers and benign institutions; while he, far away, put it all together at a time when life was cheap.

But then the abrasions, all the incredible abrasions, had *rendered* him. The pale, final shape of Payne, like the yolk of an egg held to the light, had come to be seen.

I am at large.

ABOUT THE AUTHOR

Thomas McGuane is the author of several highly acclaimed novels, including *The Sporting Club; The Bushwhacked Piano*, which won the Hilda Rosenthal Award of the American Academy and Institute of Arts and Letters; *Ninety-two in the Shade*, which was nominated for the National Book Award; *Panama; Nobody's Angel; Something to Be Desired; Keep the Change; To Skin a Cat*, a collection of short stories; and *An Outside Chance*, a collection of essays on sport. His books have been published in ten languages. He was born in Michigan and educated at Michigan State University, earned a Master of Fine Arts degree at the Yale School of Drama and was a Wallace Stegner Fellow at Stanford. An ardent conservationist, he is director of American Rivers and of the Craighead Wildlife-Wildlands Institute. He lives with his family in McLeod, Montana.